THE NUTCRACKER
THE SANDMAN
AND OTHER DARK FAIRY TALES

The Best Weird Tales and Fantasies of
E. T. A. HOFFMANN

— SECOND EDITION —

Edited, Annotated, and Illustrated By
M. GRANT KELLERMEYER, M.A.

Translated from the German By
ALEXANDER EWING, J. T. BEALBY, THOMAS CARLYLE,
& OTHER ANONYMOUS TRANSLATORS

— OLDSTYLE TALES PRESS —
Fort Wayne, Indiana

This edition published 2018 by
OLDSTYLE TALES PRESS
2424 N. Anthony Blvd
Fort Wayne, Indiana
46805-3604

For more information, or to request permission to reprint selections or illustrations from this book, write to the Editor at
oldstyletales@gmail.com

Readers who are interested in further titles from Oldstyle Tales Press are invited to visit our website at

— WWW.OLDSTYLETALES.COM —

— TABLE *of* CONTENTS —

Concerning What You Are About To Read

"I felt as a child feels when some fairy tale has been told it to conceal the truth it suspects..."
— E. T. A. Hoffmann

He was the godfather of modern horror, weird fiction, and fantasy – an inestimable influence on Poe, Dickens, and Hawthorne, de Maupassant, Stevenson, and James – left his fingerprints on *Frankenstein, Dr Jekyll and Mr Hyde, Dracula,* and *The Turn of the Screw,* and inspired filmmakers from Tim Burton and Christopher Nolan to David Lynch and Fritz Lang – and films from *Dr. Caligari* and *The Stepford Wives* to *The Matrix* and *Carnival of Souls*. Yet few horror fans have ever read even one of his works. Many have never even heard his name. Today he is most famous for writing the dark fantasy which Tchaikovsky frosted and fluffed up into his *Nutcracker* ballet, and for his proto-Freudian masterpiece of existential terror, "The Sandman." But his titanic influence demands that we give E. T. A. Hoffmann a much closer look, well beyond these two stories – masterpieces though they are. An expert at blending the ordinary and the uncanny, his stories were some of the first to feature supernatural invaders in a contemporary setting. Unlike Perrault or the Grimms, his macabre fairy tales aren't in a land "far, far away" or "once upon a time" – they take place in the sooty, bourgeois streets of his own time, and involve grotesque and often malformed agents of chaos piercing through the veil of the invisible world to introduce moral mayhem into the bland existence of bored daydreamers.

In Hoffmann's worlds, the "real" world is the fake one – as in *The Matrix* – a superficial façade distracting us from recognizing the wonders and horrors of true reality. Tremendously complex and literary, his gothic stories, dark fairy tales, and diabolical parables explore the relationships between reason and imagination, submission and inspiration, groundedness and sublimity, spirituality and materiality. His stories include tales of castles haunted by family curses, toys brought to life, erotic robots, sinister salesmen with malevolent motives, demonic Doppelgängers, cannibalistic pregnant women, lustful gnomes, hypnotic seducers, sleepwalking ghosts, men without shadows or reflections, and expansive worlds hidden behind the drab exterior of the ordinary prefiguring Hogwarts, Narnia, Wonderland, and Oz. His tales are famous for their blend of horror and allure, of ugliness and beauty, of reality and imagination. The swirl with the vertigo of a rich grasp of fantasy, darkened with inappropriate lusts, repressed urges, and unconscious motives. Deeply psychological and profoundly philosophical, they will shock and offend, but they will also soothe and inspire. These are the Tales of Hoffmann.

HOFFMANN THE VISIONARY: REIMAGINING MODERN HORROR AMIDST AN AGE OF CHANGE

Before the rise of Edgar Allan Poe, H. G. Wells, and H. P. Lovecraft, there was only *one* name in literary horror: Hoffmann. His influence is felt in nearly every short story writer of the 19thcentury, and while he takes a decidedly permanent back burner to his later disciples, his role as the originator of speculative fiction is difficult to deny. Hoffmann certainly had his own influences: "The Entail" makes references to Friedrich Schiller's "The Ghost Seer" and "The Robbers," while "A Ghost Story" (excerpted from *Die Serapionsbrüder*) is mostly constructed off of a major subplot in M. G. Lewis' Gothic masterpiece, "The Monk." The works of Goethe (especially "The Sorrows of Young Werther," "Faust," and "The Sorcerer's Apprentice") also factor into his imaginative universe of wild emotions, secret allegiances, and violent impulses, as do those of Shakespeare, Ludwig Tieck, and – most notably – the fairy tales of Perrault, the Brothers Grimm, and Jacques Callot. But Hoffmann broke with all of these writers in his realism. While Goethe set "Faust" and "The Sorcerer's Apprentice" in Medieval Times, Schiller went for the Gothic conventions of the 17th century, and the fairy tale writers distant lands in vague timelines, Hoffmann had no patience for such distance and romance. His monsters roam the snowy streets of newly-industrialized Berlin and Dresden, wearing the same fashions as his contemporaries, and piercing the normalcy of relatable, middle-class settings. Even today, with the distance of two centuries, his stories seem unnervingly personal. We sense that even if these antagonists sport powdered periwigs and buckled shoes, there is something immediate and tactile about them. Although writers of horror would always find it attractive to set a story in the romantic past, most would adopt Hoffmann's manner of making their lurking creatures a part of the contemporary scenery. Hawthorne, Poe, de Maupassant, Dickens, O'Brien, James, Stevenson, Shelley, and Stoker would all avoid the tradition of planting horror stories in a moldy Italian castle during the Renaissance, with unrelatable stock-characters like Udolpho, Manfred, or Ambrosio.

Another development that Hoffmann added to the modern horror story was a profound psychological and philosophical subtext. Radcliffe and Walpole certainly crafted intriguing backstories, rife with sexual misdeeds and repressed emotions (to say nothing of Shakespeare, Schiller, and Goethe), but Hoffmann's approach to horror took on a rich complexity which almost singlehandedly steered the short story as a genre into the 19th century. He was one of the very first writers to work heavily in this medium, and as the century began to embrace the cheaper, more commercial format of tales (which could be serialized or printed in cheap magazines for middle-class readers at fractions of the cost of a hardback book), Hoffmann's legacy couldn't be missed in the style and themes of his descendants. One reason for his popularity (although Goethe considered him "sick" and Walter Scott recommended psychiatric attention) was the profound *authenticity* of his stories. He speaks of gruelingly awkward experiences, cringe-worthy humiliations, and scandalously inappropriate attractions. Instead of writing protagonists with good hearts and good deeds, he created characters like the incestuous Councillor Krespel who envies his daughter's lover, the manic-depressive Nathanael, who falls in love with a sex doll, the bumbling Student Anselmus, whose ham-fisted incompetence makes him a figure of public ridicule, and even the eccentric Godpapa Drosselmeier, whose passive-aggressive attentions towards his goddaughter smack of sadism and latent pedophilia. Humiliation was key to all of Hoffmann's works, and an ever-present element in his own life.

Writing about his musical philosophy, Hoffmann once said that artistic creativity:

> "reveals an unknown kingdom to mankind: a world that has nothing in common with the outward, material world that surrounds it, and in which we leave behind all predetermined conceptual feelings in order to give ourselves up to the inexpressible."

Every story he would ever pen would follow this dictum, using the power of the imagination to exceed the limitations of the body, physics, and society itself. His stories' bizarre – even nightmarish – sense of psychological vertigo and often confusing lack of restrictions stem from a life which often shocked his friends and family, stymied his career, and hampered his success. Throughout his fiction, Hoffmann extols the virtues of the *authentic* life (even if it be lonely or eccentric), which was best expressed through "poetry" (i.e. the arts), and was the only defense against the soulless drudgery and robotic servitude which he so dreaded as a public servant. Most who read Hoffmann immediately sense the deep level of personality which is infused in his writing: it is raw and personal, smoldering with scathing insecurities, ludicrous embarrassments, boiling lusts, and uncontrollable frenzies – as if written from the personal experiences of a highly emotional, socially frustrated individual. Such is indeed the case.

HOFFMANN THE MAN:
SLEEPWALKING THROUGH THE NIGHTMARES OF WAKING LIFE

Psychologists have suggested that Hoffmann may have suffered everything from manic-depression and autism to psychosis and ADHD. His mind was imaginative and uncontrollable, causing him to flit from passion to passion, from crush to crush, and from profession to profession with little concern for the future. He was given to emotional outbursts, highly uncensored opinions, and wild rhapsodies in public. He was by education a lawyer, by profession a government functionary, but also moonlighted as a composer (he wrote a successful opera and a symphony), a music critic (having only read the score to Beethoven's Fifth Symphony – without hearing it – he wrote a famous review which had a heavy hand in making it a global sensation), draftsman, caricaturist, toymaker, mechanic, tinkerer, musician, novelist, poet, and short story writer. His career finally ended – along with his life – when he wrote a galling satire which offended several important Prussian officials and landed him in court for libel. In danger of losing everything, he managed his defense from his sickbed (stricken with paralyzing syphilis), while dictating the last of his stories. Hoffmann was convicted, but the King of Prussia pitied the moribund author and softened the sentence (so long as a few offensive passages be deleted). His career and health were wrecked, however, and he died at forty-six.

Like Poe – his greatest protégé – Hoffmann has been slandered by history. He has been caricatured (even as he himself had caricatured so many others) as a drunken, lecherous creep given over to drug-fueled hallucinations, and crippled by the self-loathing which should be expected from a sexual deviant's conscience. It should be noted that these intense critiques oversimplify a very complex man – but just *barely*. Hoffmann's proclivity to public displays of emotion truly haunted him wherever he went. Early in his life – in an episode that inspired "The Entail," while he was running high off of Goethe's "Young Werther" (TLDR: a manic-depressive poet commits suicide after falling in love with his best friend's wife and humiliating himself after a violent declaration of his unrequited love), he was fired from a job as a music instructor to a married woman when his obvious lust for the woman began to shock her family. This would not be the last time such an event would take place, nor the most seminal. In the midst of the Napoleonic Wars – an era of political chaos, rabid nationalism, and collective misery in Europe – Hoffmann married a Polish-Prussian woman and was delighted by the birth of a girl, his only child. When the war reached Prussia, political turmoil caused the family to separate, and when the French overtook Warsaw, Hoffmann lost his job as a government official. Around this time Hoffmann learned that his two year old daughter had died – a shocking loss which would haunt him throughout his life and work.

When the Hoffmanns reunited in Bamberg, they took in his wife's young niece, who lived with them for several years, leaving at the age of twelve – another deprivation which, he felt, reenacted the death of his daughter. But the worst romantic experience of his life – one which would relentlessly be depicted in his fiction – was on its way. In the midst of his sorrow he began to tutor a girl about the same age as he niece, the bright and impressionable Julia Marc. Like so many of his future characters, he became enamored by the girl's singing voice and fostered a profoundly inappropriate attachment to the girl. Her parents were concerned about his fawning obsession, but things truly boiled over when he publicly upbraided her young fiancé. Hoffmann had grown deeply devoted to Julia, now sixteen and shapely, and he was disgusted when she was set up for an arranged marriage with another teenager, Johann Graepel – a fat, lazy, drunken, aristocrat whom Hoffmann considered vulgar and gnome-like. While on a picnic with the family, Hoffmann humiliated her inebriated beau after he fell over with drink, declaring the marriage doomed and the groom a shame. It was too much for the Marcs, who immediately fired the smitten tutor – but he *was* right: the pair would marry that year and divorce before she was twenty (a far more unusual, scandalous, and serious step then than today). Even Hoffmann's prophecy that the unnaturally old-looking youth – somehow obsese but emaciated – was not long for this world proved true, and Graepel died soon after the divorce. But it was too late: Julia would be sullied and corrupted by her revolting husband, and Hoffmann had become the object of public scandal yet again. Depressed, miserable, and uninspired, Hoffmann fought through what biographers agree to be the worst years of his life, culminating in a mystical epiphany in 1814: he would turn from the highly academic, structured world of music to the more liberated genre of literature. Spiritually resurrected by the change, he penned what many consider to be his masterpiece, the farcical fantasy "The Golden Pot" which follows the mounting humiliations of the Student Anselmus as he searches the streets of modern Germany for his love, Serpentina (a metaphysical being who transforms into the form of a snake), while dodging the machinations of an evil apple monger (whose secret identity is that of a powerful witch).

HOFFMANN THE PHILOSOPHER: TRANSCENDING MALAISE THROUGH AUTHENTICITY & SUFFERING

Hoffmann's first novella was a crowning achievement, and the start of a successful – if not controversial – literary career. He seemed to relive the humiliation of his preposterous romances in his stories, which frequently feature either a scandalously inappropriate attraction (e.g., between father and daughter, a grown man and a life-size robot, or an impulsive bachelor and faithful housewife) or an unrequited May-December obsession. In most of his stories (e.g., "The Lost Reflection," "Nutcracker and the King of Mice," "The Entail," "Automatons," "The Cremona Violin," "The King's Betrothed," "The Mines of Falun," "The Vampire," "The Deserted House," "The Sandman," "The Fermata," "Doppelgängers," and "Magnetism") enthusiastic, artsy-types prone to extreme emotions and impulsive outbursts are humiliated by their disastrous attachment to an unavailable girl (a seductive demon, eight year old goddaughter, married baroness, engaged stranger, bastard daughter, sexually awakening daughter, female spirit of the mines, vampiric pregnant wife, geriatric madwoman, mechanical sex-doll, two heartless coquettes, friend's wife, and engaged patient – respectively). Sometimes it is the woman who suffers the more crushing fate ("Magnetism," "Doppelgängers," "Automatons," etc.), but usually it is the wildly inappropriate male whose ill-advised fantasy leads to a psychological breakdown, spiritual trauma, or physical death. Adultery, incest, pedophilia, and sexual fetishes factor prominently in Hoffmann's tales (ergo, Goethe and Scott's shocked rejection of his art) but never as programs for a life-well-lived: unlike the proudly deviant Marquis de Sade, Hoffmann was nothing if not self-critical, and his unconsummated romances – which almost always end in either death or madness – became hallmarks of his style. He did not praise or exemplify lifestyles of lust and abuse, but played them out to what he saw the natural conclusion: self-destruction by way of the unnatural worship of a deeply flawed, obviously misguided attraction.

Another prominent theme in Hoffmann's fiction is the existence of parallel universes which actualize the truth hidden by hypocrisy and modesty. His protagonists are relatable – poor students, bored children, and alienated outsiders – who experience psychedelic adventures and hallucinogenic terrors all from the comfort of the regular world. Cheap toys lead children to easily accessible realms of wonder, bumbling salesmen take the form of demonic mesmerists, and sensible girls find their future husbands growing in their gardens. He saw no need to tell about fairy tales set in "a land far, far away" or "once upon a time" because he saw the fantastical in the ordinary and recognized the bizarre and macabre in the bourgeois and mundane. His settings are relatable, but his plots probe the psychological in visionary ways that imply an expansive interpretation of the everyday – suggesting that profound, metaphysical currents are churning just beneath our feet, unnoticed by those who have become too distracted by the minutiae of the material world. It is hardly necessary to point out the way in which this motif revolutionized Western literature (especially children's and Young Adult fiction), but a short discussion of this may help explore the way in which Hoffmann's legacy is undervalued in today's academy. In stories like "The Golden Pot," "The Sandman," "Nutcracker," "The King's Betrothed," "The Stranger Child," and "Councillor Krespel," Hoffmann invests his characters with hidden identities, secret affiliations, and supernatural doubles – often exiles from an entire alternate universe which satirizes the mortal realm's hypocrisies and folly. This genre of story has since been dubbed "Down the Rabbit Hole," an allusion to one of Hoffmann's earliest disciples (Lewis Carrol's *Through the Looking Glass* and *Alice in Wonderland* have undeniable roots in "The Nutcracker," "The Golden Pot," and "The King's Betrothed").

The motif of a young person discovering and exploring a satirical parallel universe (one which teaches them to see beyond superficiality, and which trains them for an independent and critical-thinking adulthood) don't stop there, of course: the entire canon of *The Wizard of Oz*, Neil Gaiman's *Coraline, The Neverending Story, The Tenth Kingdom, The Chronicles of Narnia* series, *The Phantom of the Opera, Peter Pan,* the *Harry Potter* series, *Charlie and the Chocolate Factory, James and the Giant Peach, Flatland, Pan's Labyrinth,* Jim Henson's *Labyrinth,* the *TRON* and *Matrix* films, and a whole host of Studio Ghibli films (*Spirited Away, Totoro, Ponyo, The Cat Returns,* etc.) are all *directly* and undeniably descended from Hoffmann. While fairy tales (Perrault, Callot, Grimm, Andersen) often used this motif, it was almost always in the already magical world of a land far, far away and during the innately magical once upon a time. Along with a few predecessors like Dante (*Inferno*), Swift (*Gulliver's Travels*), and Shakespeare (*Tempest, Midsummer Night's Dream*) Hoffmann among the very first introduced the concept of slipping off from the regular, unmagical, modern world into a Doppelgänger universe where you encounter doubles of the people in your waking life – doubles who train you to see through artifice and hypocrisy. Alice, Dorothy, Harry Potter, Charlie, James, and Neo (just like Hoffmann's Marie, Anselmus, and Ännchen) all return to their waking worlds armed with new insights and the confidence necessary to unmask the world's falsehoods, navigate society's pitfalls, and avoid mankind's illusions. Hoffmann's virtually unprecedented blend of realism and fantasy was among the very first examples of this now ubiquitous trope.

HOFFMANN THE MYSTIC: LIBERATING THE IMAGINATION FROM SOCIETAL OPPRESSION

Related to this idea is a third prominent theme in Hoffmann's writing: the balance between imagination and reality, and the perils of personal duplicity. Like his Doppelgänger universes, Hoffmann peoples his stories with literal Doppelgängers: physical duplications of his characters. Sometimes we are unsure if the Doppelgänger is real or imagined; sometimes the Other-Self is an actual human being – a sort of evil twin – and other times it is an implied similarity in an innocent bystander, or a figure in a dream, or a character in a story-within-a-story. Evil doubles have haunted literature since ancient mythology, but Hoffmann's dark twins left a larger impression on the Western canon than any previous writer. In stories like "The Sandman," "The King's Betrothed," "The Entail," "Nutcracker," "The Golden Pot," "The Vampire," "Mines of Falun," "The Lost Reflection," "The Stranger Child," and more, Hoffmann juxtaposes mortal beings with seemingly (or overtly) supernatural personifications which magnify the mortals' innate traits and character. Among the first writers to duplicate this trope were Edgar Allan Poe ("House of Usher," "William Wilson," "Metzengerstein," "Black Cat," etc.) and Nathaniel Hawthorne ("House of Seven Gables"), while the Late Victorians, like Stevenson ("Dr. Jekyll and Mr. Hyde," "Markheim"),

Conan Doyle ("A Pastoral Horror"), Stoker ("Crooken Sands"), James ("The Jolly Corner"), Wells ("The Stolen Body"), Noyes ("The Midnight Express"), and Dickens ("To Be Read at Dusk") reveled in Hoffmann's archetype, using the idea of a metaphysical double to point out inconsistencies in their characters' lives.

Whether battling an evil twin or a supernatural villain, Hoffmann's protagonists are regularly traumatized by a failing grip on reality. Usually, this is the sharp double edge of the sword with which they have decoded the hypocrisies of the mortal world: while they are now empowered to identify fakeness and to celebrate the life of the imagination, they are often rocked by vertigo when forced to maintain their precarious balance between the soul-feeding life of the Mind and the life-preserving realm of the Body. Both, Hoffmann insists, must be nurtured to maintain a healthy existence: a life lived purely in the Body is soulless and robotic (hence his frequent use of automatons as a motif; Olimpia in "The Sandman" and the clockwork castle in "Nutcracker" are examples of this fate), but one lived entirely in the imagination is violently rootless and prone to insanity (the fates of Nathanael in "The Sandman" and Elis in "The Mines of Falun" illustrate the manic self-destruction that can result from an over-indulgence of imagination and a lack of physical connection).

While Hoffmann's protagonists rarely avoid these pitfalls or orchestrate a successful harmony between the two realms, it is not at all unheard of. In "The King's Betrothed," a father who dresses up as a wizard and is clueless to his daughter's sexual maturation almost loses her to an anthropomorphic (and notably phallic) carrot who attempts to lure her to his subterranean kingdom with erotic sublimations. Her human suitor is also lost in the clouds: a ludicrous poet consumed with writing self-important verses and utterly unthreatened by the gnome's appearance. Suddenly shocked by his barely contained lust for his nubile daughter, the father wakes up from his dress-up illusions, and unites with the wannabe poet to expose the carrot-gnome's kingdom for what it is: a fungal land of decay, rot, and darkness. Shaken from her naïve attraction, the girl returns to her suitor, whose horrible poetry ends up vanquishing the gnome, alerting him to his lack of skill and turning him from a daydreamer into a lover. The father – awakened from his delusions by his incestuous impulses – hands his daughter over to the young man and prepares for his natural role as a grounded grandfather.

Hoffmann's masterpiece, "The Golden Pot" also follows the airheaded daydreamer, Anselmus, as he recognizes the reality of the hidden world, while maintaining a grip on his physical needs. Nearly drowned, driven to suicide, and threatened with madness, Anselmus ultimately chooses the supernatural world of Atlantis over the sludgy streets of Napoleonic Germany, but brings bits of his middle-class background with him: he and his salamander lover, Serpentina, live in a humble cottage, raise a bustling family, and eschew pretentions in favor of a simple life.

Ensconced in the world of imagination where anything is possible, he chooses a balanced existence which successfully acknowledges the reality of the parallel universe, while accepting only the indulgences which he needs to survive and thrive. This is also found in "The Stranger Child" and "Nutcracker" where the young protagonists successfully see behind adults' hypocritical facades, challenging the social narratives which push them towards an unimaginative life of social climbing and sycophancy. Instead, both the siblings in "Child" and Marie in "Nutcracker" embrace their new-found insight without allowing it to blow them off into self-indulgent insanity (unlike poor, doomed Nathanael), and successfully manage a balance between personal authenticity and physical reality. They learn to love their imaginations and trust their instincts, without neglecting the social and physical demands of the living world.

HOFFMANN THE WRITER:
DARK FAIRY TALES EXPOSING THE NIGHT-SIDE OF MODERNITY

In total, Hoffmann penned some fifty tales which could be classified as speculative fiction: dark fantasies, weird fictions, horror stories, modern fairy tales, and science fiction. Of these I have selected thirteen to represent his best efforts, although some longer pieces ("The Devil's Elixir") and some repetitive stories ("Mesmerism," "Doppelgängers") are highly recommended but weren't included here. Among the thirteen there developed three different classes of stories – classes which most of Hoffmann's tales tend to fall into. The first, and the most delightfully indulgent, are the Gothic Tales. Influenced as he was by the British Gothic Novel and the Gothicism of Germany's "Storm and Stress" writers (Goethe, Schiller, Tieck), it is hardly surprising that Hoffmann would indulge in the macabre and ghoulish. The best of these is "The Entail" ("Das Majorat"), also published as "The Walled-Up Door." A haunted house story, it was a major influence on Poe's "House of Usher," and manages to remain hypnotic and chilling even today. The story follows a family curse started when the eccentric patriarch placed a legal requirement that the whole of his estate should pass to the eldest male heirs of the family. What ensues is a complex and wildly tangled history of murder, guilt, sleepwalking, scratching ghosts, wolves in the snow, adulterous attractions, and doomed love. It requires two or three good reads.

"The Vampire" ("Vampirismus") is shockingly ghoulish even for Hoffmann: a man impulsively marries a strange young woman regardless of his hateful distaste for her grotesque, insane mother. He is willing to overlook her repulsive family, but when she turns up pregnant, Hoffmann takes pregnancy cravings to a whole new level when she is found sleepwalking to the graveyard with a healthy appetite. "A Ghost Story" – the preface to "Automatons" – is modelled off of "Monk" Lewis' "The

Monk" (wherein a girl dressed up as the baleful "Bloody Nun" has the misfortune to encounter the original), and tells of a plucky girl's life-changing decision to pose as the infamous White Lady (a ghost associated with her family manor) and how the encounter with the real White Lady (or at least her perception of the ghost) causes her to rapidly mature, preparing her for a heartbreaking tragedy which will require the sympathy and patience of a grown woman. Lastly, "The Mines of Falun" ("Die Bergwerke zu Falun") is a haunting ghost story about a sailor's sudden decision to become a miner after his mother's death. A classic momma's boy, he initially makes the Oedipal choice to treat a local prostitute to the gifts he usually gave his mother before leaving town for the (notably vaginal) mineshafts of Falun. There he falls in love with a maternal spirit presiding over the caves and is guided by the ghost of an old miner who was said to meet the spirit before he disappeared years ago. The ending – based on a true story of a Falun miner who disappeared on his wedding day, only to be discovered decades later – is chilling, dark, and ponderous.

The second category of story is the one which indebted L. Frank Baum, Lewis Carrol, J. K. Rowling, Hayao Miyazaki, C. S. Lewis, and Roald Dahl to him: dark fantasies and weird fairy tales. The prince of them all – as far as the court of public opinion is concerned – is "Nutcracker and the King of Mice" ("Nußknacker und Mause-König"). Far darker, stranger, and even sadder than Tchaikovsky's cheery libretto, it follows young Marie's gradual induction into the hidden world of imagination, where the falsehoods and hypocrisies of the waking world are challenged. While Tchaikovsky's Clara needs only to chuck a slipper at the rat-king before spending over half of the story indulging in Candyland, Hoffmann's heroine endures a near-fatal injury, the sacrifice of all her toys, sweets, and fine clothes, and a steady rift between her and her family before Nutcracker can finally slay the Mouse-King and bring her to Candyland (which takes up less than 15% of the plot). A story about sincerity's battle against corruption, the coming-of-age of a girl (leaving her sadder but wiser), and the necessary sacrifices required to be pure, it may lack Tchaikovsky's charm and beauty, but packs a heavy philosophical wallop leaving us with much to ponder when the transformed nutcracker comes back for Marie ("...or so they say").

A similar plot is found in "The Stranger Child" ("Das Fremde Kind"): at Christmastime, two children are visited by the androgynous spirit of child who has been exiled from his supernatural kingdom by an evil fly-like entity (who, like the King of Mice, symbolizes bureaucracy and corruption). When the children realize that their new, grotesque tutor is the very same villain in human shape, they must fight back to restore the Stranger Child to his throne and prevent Tutor Ink from claiming the mortal world as well. "The King's Betrothed" ("Die Königsbraut"), earlier described, is like "Nutcracker" in that it also depicts a girl's maturation after being courted by a grotesque gnome, but in this case the suitor is more Mouse-King than Nutcracker, representing the corruption of bureaucracy and the perils of sycophancy. Hoffmann's greatest literary achievement is probably also his first major work, also discussed earlier: "The Golden Pot" ("Der Goldene Topf") which follows the bumbling Student Anselmus' elevation from social incompetent and impoverished intellectual to the self-actualized resident of Atlantis, wed to a fiery elemental.

The third class of story is difficult to describe, but typically involves Hoffmann's darkest works: tales of devilry, deception, and Doppelgängers. These stories feature sinister father figures, seductive femme fatales, and wandering exiles shunned by society for their self-indulgent eccentricities. Chief among these, of course, is Hoffmann's horror masterpiece: "The Sandman" ("Der Sandmann"). Adored by Freud as a parable of Oedipal rage and anxiety, it follows the virtually psychotic Nathanael as he tries to avoid a fate to which he has long resigned himself: as a victim of his father's killer, the pseudo-mythological Sandman who has taken the human form of Coppelius, a murderous alchemist who robs people of their eyes (read: sanity, objectivity, reason – or, if Freud, read: testicles, virility). Encouraged by his Enlightenment-symbolizing girlfriend, Clara (literally: clarity), our doomed hero is instead drawn by the indulgence and emotion of Romanticism, ultimately cheating on Clara with the submissive Stepford Wife, Olimpia, who orgasmically agrees to all his inane banter. The ending is cataclysmic, and the legacy is impossible to overstate.

"The Lost Reflection" ("Die Abenteuer der Silvester-Nacht") follows three men who have a similar problem: all have fallen in love with a strange woman and all are in danger of losing their grip on sanity among other things (one has lost his hat and coat, one his shadow, and one his reflection). A parable on the perils of unrequited love and romantic discontent, it implies that the woman – a beautiful seductress modelled on the recently divorced Julia Marc – who has unhinged the narrator is also responsible for the other two's distress, and that she is being pimped out by her Sandman-like husband, a grotesque, impotent Italian. Inaccessible women also feature in "Automatons" ("Die Automate") where a fortune telling machine predicts that a young man will fall in love with the stranger in the picture he carries only when it is too late, and that he may have her soul, but will never enjoy her body, and in "The Deserted House" ("Das Öde Haus") wherein a similarly smitten youth falls in love with a pale hand resting on the window ledge of a decrepit house (obsessed, he finally breaks into the house and finds that his beloved is far from what he expected). One of the saddest and most lingering of Hoffmann's tales is that of "The Cremona Violin" ("Rath Krespel") and his daughter, Antonia. Krespel is a typical Hoffmann eccentric: wild, impulsive, and visionary. He tears apart beautiful violins to try to learn the secret of their beauty (ironically stifling their voices in the act). Threatened (like the father in "Gnome-King") by his budding daughter's sexual attraction to a young man, who loves to hear her virtuoso singing (which, like Christine Daae's voice in "Phantom of the Opera," has obvious, orgasmic undertones). When he learns that she suffers a heart condition which could be fatal, he forbids her from singing with her lover. We know how that usually works out, and when Krespel dreams of her wailing over a piano with a flushed face while her boyfriend fawns over each note, he is not surprised by what he finds in the morning.

HOFFMAN THE ICON:
AN INDELIBLE CULTURAL LEGACY OF SURREAL CREEPINESS

Throughout his life Hoffmann was haunted by his perceived ability to look past the masks and posturing of a society which felt was as robotic and lifeless as a clockwork castle. Depression, mania, and humiliation hounded him as he struggled to maintain the harmony with the world he was forced to interface with, and the one which he considered to be genuine: in the false, automaton world he – like Anselmus and Nutcracker – was a grotesque, awkward outsider who failed to keep in step with the other robots, but he felt that in another world where the facades were stripped away and the truth was enacted, he would be elevated and celebrated as a man of character and vision. In his writings he played this out – sometimes humiliating his stand-in (like the lecherous Councillor Krespel, who loses his daughter, or the ludicrous Nathanael whose psychosis overwhelms his future happiness), and sometimes throwing it a bone (e.g., "Golden Pot," "King's Betrothed," "Stranger Child," "Nutcracker") – though never without first wringing the Hoffmann-look-alike through the excruciating process of public shame and humiliation required for spiritual purification. He truly believed in the deeper meaning of materiality – that knights, ogres, ghouls, and princesses daydream in cubicles, grumble in traffic jams, and sigh in lonely apartments. If only they were willing to free themselves from their emptiness by realizing the falseness of daily life and achieving self-actualization. But this process was always perilous – insanity and suicide were dangers that Hoffmann felt were always near at hand if he indulged his imagination too much – and the rewards might not warrant the risks. His solution was to seek balance – between imagination and reality, desire and restraint; between Self and Other, Truth and Illusion – without either becoming a robot bound to a clockwork routine, or being blown away by the insane winds of untethered imagination.

His vision has continued with us for two centuries, manifesting in modern literature, cinema, and art. Something is "Hoffmannesque" if it flirts with the Uncanny Valley, if it barely maintains a harmony between wonder and horror, if it can neither be definitively described as realistic or dreamlike. The angular, vertigo-inducing cinema and art of German Expressionism have been inextricably linked to the Hoffmannesque aesthetic, as have the eccentric, reality-challenging films of Tim Burton, David Lynch, and Christopher Nolan. We see Hoffmann in the robotic weirdness of Agent Smith in *The Matrix*, the predatory creepiness of Count Olof in *Series of Unfortunate Events*, and in the repulsive eroticism of *The Stepford Wives*. We recognize his creative moral genius in *The Twilight Zone* and feel his complex, systemic paranoia in *The X-Files*. We see his imaginative whimsy in *Harry Potter* and his unsettling horror in *Coraline*, his tantalizing mirage of reality in *Inception* and *Fight Club*, and his obsessiveness and psychological vertigo in – well – *Psycho* and *Vertigo*. Although he may barely remain in the public consciousness (mostly for his role as the originator of Tchaikovsky's *Nutcracker* – a libretto which, for all its undeniable loveliness and magic, loses the substance and poignancy of Hoffmann's darker coming-of-age allegory), E. T. A. Hoffmann is an indelible part of modern culture and Western art. Schubert, Offenbach, and Tchaikovsky may have made tributes to him in the 19thcentury, but today – whether consciously or not – modern writers, directors, musicians, and artists are expanding his influence every day. You can almost be certain that Hoffmann is near if you watch a movie or see an artwork which blends realism and fantasy in a way that catches your breath – there's something otherworldly about it, yet it is relatable, almost as if you are sensing your own connection to a reality which you yourself cannot see. When you sense the movements behind the masks and the mind behind the machinery, when you feel the consciousness of the clockwork or experience the fear behind the familiar, you are in his uncanny domain. You are in the World of Hoffmann.

M. Grant Kellermeyer
Fort Wayne, Christmas, 2018
Revised Second Edition, New Year's Day 2025

THE SANDMAN, THE NUTCRACKER, & OTHERS

The Best Weird Fiction & Fantasies of

E. T. A. HOFFMANN

THE Automaton Chess Player, otherwise simply known as "The Turk," was a marvel of the late 18th century that stunned and perplexed the world. It was said to be a robot which could best any living chess player – or at least hold its own – in the shape of a life-sized, turbaned, silk robed Turkish sorcerer who moved his chess pieces with a mechanical arm. It was seated at a great cabinet on which stood a chess board and in which the gears and machinery were said to be stored. Since its debut at the Austro-Hungarian court in 1770, until its loss in an 1854 fire, The Turk was a futuristic vision that would become commonplace nearly two centuries later: the computer, the robot, and A.I. It defeated Napoleon, who had bested the armies of Europe, and Benjamin Franklin, who had grabbed lightning from the heavens. A delight to some and a horror to others, regardless of its secret, it was an omen of brilliant things to come. It was widely said to be a kind of hoax – Edgar Allan Poe famously recorded his own theory as to how it was operated – and that is *exactly* what it was. The cabinet did not house a mechanical program, but a *human* one: although the arm was mechanical it was operated by a chess player hidden inside the cabinet, using a peg-board computer to battle his opponents. While the wonder may have hidden a fraud, The Turk was one of the earliest archetypal robots, and its eerie ability to mime human intelligence and mannerisms (even smoking a pipe and having a voice box with the ability to cry out "Check!") disturbed its viewers with its uncanniness even as it charmed them with its genius.

II.

What was so off-putting – so unsettling – about a humanlike entity that could fake its way into human society but was never quite… "*right*"? Hoffmann was fascinated and horrified by the idea of robots – mechanical dolls, clockwork doll-houses, and life-sized mannequins liter his fiction – and found in them what Freud would call the Uncanny Valley: anthropomorphic figures not human enough to pass emotional exchanges, but not fake enough to be an obvious caricature. Inhuman things which are just realistic enough to hold their own against human beings are threats to our ability to trust and bond, and have remained an insidious archetype in world literature from the Jewish Golem to the famously creepy *Polar Express* to *The Stepford Wives*. In the following story – featuring a goateed "Fortune Teller" robot done up in a turban and Ottoman dress, a trope later made ubiquitous in carnivals and arcades – Hoffmann delves into his ideas of the uncanny with exceptionally Hoffmannesque results: a study of the difference between body and soul, the boundaries between the physical and the psychical, and the question of whether love can truly be satisfying if either the beloved's soul or her body are not included in the bargain.

The Automatons

— Excerpted from 'The Serapion Brethren,' Volume One, Section One —

{1814}

"""THE talking Turk"[1] was attracting universal attention, and setting the town in commotion. The hall where this automaton[2] was exhibited was thronged by a continual stream of visitors, of all sorts and conditions, from morning till night, all eager to listen to the oracular utterances which were whispered to them by the motionless lips of that wonderful quasi-human figure. The manner of the construction and arrangement of this automaton distinguished it in a marked degree from all puppets of the sort usually exhibited. It was, in fact, a very remarkable automaton. About the centre of a room of moderate size, containing only a few indispensable articles of furniture, at this figure, about the size of a human being, handsomely formed, dressed in a rich and tasteful Turkish costume[3], on a low seat shaped as a tripod, which the exhibitor would move if desired, to show that there was no means of communication between it and the ground. Its left hand was placed in an easy position on its knee, and its right rested on a small movable table. Its appearance, as has been said, was that of a well-proportioned, handsome man, but the most remarkable part of it was its head. A face expressing a genuine Oriental astuteness gave it an appearance of life rarely seen in wax figures, even when they represent the characteristic countenances of talented men. A light railing surrounded the figure, to prevent the spectators from crowding too closely about it; and only those who wished to inspect the construction of it (so far as the Exhibitor could allow this to be seen without divulging his secret), and the person whose turn it was to put a question to it, were allowed to go inside this railing, and close up to it. The usual mode of procedure was to whisper the question you wished to ask into the Turk's right ear; on which he would turn, first his eyes, and then his whole head, towards you; and as you were sensible of a gentle stream of air, like breath coming from his lips, you could not but suppose that the low reply which was given to you did really proceed from the interior of the figure. From time to time, after a few answers had been given, the Exhibitor would apply a key to the Turk's left side, and wind up some clockwork with a good deal of noise. Here, also, he would, if desired, open a species of lid, so that you could see inside the

---

[1] This concept blends two of 18th century inventor Wolfgang von Kempelen's two most famous creations: The Turk (a chess playing automaton, which was famously proven to be a fraud) and the Speaking Machine, a series of designs for a manually operated speech synthesizer that used a bellows to make speech-like sounds

[2] A robot in the form of a human person, typically manipulated by clockwork

[3] That is to say, wearing an Ottoman-style robe and a turbaned fez

figure a complicated piece of mechanism consisting of a number of wheels; and although you might not think it probable that this had anything to do with the speaking of the automaton, still it was evident that it occupied so much space that no human being could possibly be concealed inside, were he no bigger than Augustus's dwarf[1] who was served up in a pasty. Besides the movement of the head, which always took place before an answer was given, the Turk would sometimes also raise his right hand, and either make a warning gesture with the finger, or, as it were, motion the question away with the whole hand. When this happened, nothing but repeated urging by the questioner could extract an answer, which was then generally ambiguous or angry. It might have been that the wheel work was connected with, or answerable for, those motions of the head and hands, although even in this the agency of a sentient being seemed essential. People wearied themselves with conjectures concerning the source and agent of this marvellous Intelligence. The walls, the adjoining room, the furniture, everything connected with the exhibition, were carefully examined and scrutinised, all completely in vain. The figure and its Exhibitor were watched and scanned most closely by the eyes of the most expert in mechanical science; but the more close and minute the scrutiny, the more easy and unconstrained were the actions and proceedings of both. The Exhibitor laughed and joked in the furthest corner of the room with the spectators, leaving the figure to make its gestures and give its replies as a wholly independent thing, having no need of any connection with him. Indeed he could not wholly restrain a slightly ironical smile when the table and the figure and tripod were being overhauled and peered at in every direction, taken as close to the light as possible, and inspected by powerful magnifying glasses. The upshot of it all was, that the mechanical geniuses said the devil himself could make neither head nor tail of the confounded mechanism. And a hypothesis that the Exhibitor was a clever ventriloquist, and gave the answers himself (the breath being conveyed to the figure's mouth through hidden valves) fell to the ground, for the Exhibitor was to be heard talking loudly and distinctly to people among the audience at the very time when the Turk was making his replies.

"'Notwithstanding the enigmatical, and apparently mysterious, character of this exhibition, perhaps the interest of the public might soon have grown fainter, had it not been kept alive by the nature of the answers which the Turk gave. These were sometimes cold and severe, while occasionally they were sparkling and jocular—even broadly so at times; at others they evinced strong sense and deep astuteness, and in some instances they were in a high degree painful and tragical. But they were always strikingly apposite to the character and affairs of the questioner, who would frequently be startled by a mystical reference to futurity in the

[1] Possibly an allusion to a court dwarf named Conopas, who belonged to the niece, Julia, of Caesar Augustus. He stood 2'4"

answer given, only possible, as it would seem, in one cognizant of the hidden thoughts and feelings which dictated the question. And it happened not seldom that the Turk, questioned in German, would reply in some other language known to the questioner, in which case it would be found that the answer could not have been expressed with equal point, force, and conciseness in any other language than that selected. In short, no day passed without some fresh instance of a striking and ingenious answer of the wise Turk becoming the subject of general remark.

"'It chanced, one evening, that Lewis and Ferdinand, two college friends, were in a company where the talking Turk was the subject of conversation. People were discussing whether the strangest feature of the matter was the mysterious and unexplained human influence which seemed to endow the figure with life, or the wonderful insight into the individuality of the questioner, or the remarkable talent of the answers. They were both rather ashamed to confess that they had not seen the Turk as yet, for it was *de rigueur*[1] to see him, and every one had some tale to tell of a wonderful answer to some skilfully devised question.

""'All figures of that description," said Lewis, "which can scarcely be said to counterfeit humanity so much as to travesty it—mere images of living death or inanimate life are in the highest degree hateful to me[2]. When I was a little boy, I ran away crying from a waxwork exhibition I was taken to, and even to this day I never can enter a place of the sort without a horrible, eerie, shuddery feeling. When I see the staring, lifeless, glassy eyes of all the potentates, celebrated heroes, thieves, murderers, and so on, fixed upon me, I feel disposed to cry with Macbeth

""'Thou hast no speculation in those eyes / Which thou dost glare with[3].'

And I feel certain that most people experience the same feeling, though perhaps not to the same extent. For you may notice that scarcely any one talks, except in a whisper, in those waxwork places. You hardly ever hear a loud word. But it is not reverence for the Crowned Heads and other great people that produces this universal pianissimo[4]; it is the oppressive sense of being in the presence of something unnatural and gruesome; and what I most of all detest is anything in the shape of imitation of the motions of Human Beings by machinery. I feel sure this wonderful, ingenious Turk will haunt me with his rolling eyes, his turning head, and his waving arm, like

---

[1] Required by etiquette or custom

[2] An early and very apt description of what Freud would later term the Uncanny Valley – a concept, in his illustrations of which he would site Hoffmann's Tales

[3] From *Macbeth* Act 3, scene 4, wherein the horrified king is addressing the unblinking ghost of a friend whom he had murdered

[4] Speaking in extremely low, soft voices

some necromantic[1] goblin, when I lie awake of nights; so that the truth is I should very much prefer not going to see him. I should be quite satisfied with other people's accounts of his wit and wisdom."

"'"You know," said Ferdinand, "that I fully agree with you as to the disagreeable feeling produced by the sight of those imitations of Human Beings. But they are not all alike as regards that. Much depends on the workmanship of them, and on what they do. Now there was Ensler's rope dancer[2], one of the most perfect automatons I have ever seen. There was a vigour about his movements which was most effective, and when he suddenly sat down on his rope, and bowed in an affable manner, he was utterly delightful. I do not suppose any one ever experienced the gruesome feeling you speak of in looking at him. As for the Turk, I consider his case different altogether. The figure (which every one says is a handsome-looking one, with nothing ludicrous or repulsive about it) the figure really plays a very subordinate part in the business, and I think there can be little doubt that the turning of the head and eyes, and so forth, go on merely that our notice may be directed to them, for the very reason that it is elsewhere that the key to the mystery is to be found. That the breath comes out of the figure's mouth is very likely, perhaps certain; those who have been there say it does. It by no means follows that this breath is set in motion by the words which are spoken. There cannot be the smallest doubt that some human being is so placed as to be able, by means of acoustical and optical contrivances which we do not trace, to see and hear the persons who ask questions, and whisper answers back to them; that not a soul, even amongst our most ingenious mechanicians, has the slightest inkling, as yet, of the process by which this is done, shows that it is a remarkably ingenious one; and that, of course, is one thing which renders the exhibition very interesting. But much the most wonderful part of it, in my opinion, is the spiritual power of this unknown human being, who seems to read the very depths of the questioner's soul; the answers often display an acuteness and sagacity, and, at the same time, a species of dread half-light, half-darkness, which do really entitle them to be styled 'oracular'[3] in the highest sense of the term. Several of my friends have told me instances of the sort which have fairly astounded me, and I can no longer refrain from putting the wonderful seer-gift of this unknown person to the test, so that I intend to go there to-morrow forenoon; and you must lay aside your repugnance to 'living puppets,' and come with me."

"'Although Lewis did his best to get off, he was obliged to yield, on pain of being considered eccentric, so many were the entreaties to him not to

[1] Created through wizardry or the dark arts

[2] Either a fictitious reference or one which I have been unable to unearth

[3] Prophetic

spoil a pleasant party by his absence, for a party had been made up to go the next forenoon, and, so to speak, take the miraculous Turk by the very beard. They went accordingly, and although there was no denying that the Turk had an unmistakable air of Oriental *grandezza*[1], and that his head was handsome and effective, yet, as soon as Lewis entered the room, he was struck with a sense of the ludicrous about the whole affair, and when the Exhibitor put the key to the figure's side, and the wheels began their whirring, he made some rather silly joke to his friends about "the Turkish gentleman's having a roasting-jack[2] inside him." Every one laughed; and the Exhibitor—who did not seem to appreciate the joke very much—stopped winding up the machinery. Whether it was that the hilarious mood of the company displeased the wise Turk, or that he chanced not to be "in the vein"[3] on that particular day, his replies—though some were to very witty and ingenious questions—seemed empty and poor; and Lewis, in particular, had the misfortune to find that he was scarcely ever properly understood by the oracle, so that he received for the most part crooked answers. The Exhibitor was clearly out of temper, and the audience were on the point of going away, ill-pleased and disappointed, when Ferdinand said—

""'Gentlemen, we none of us seem to be much satisfied with the wise Turk, but perhaps we may be partly to blame ourselves, probably our questions may not have been altogether to his taste; the fact that he is turning his head round at this moment, and raising his arm" (the figure was really doing so), "seems to indicate that I am not mistaken. A question has occurred to me to put to him; and if he gives one of his apposite[4] answers to it, I think he will have quite redeemed his character."

"'Ferdinand went up to the Turk, and whispered a word or two in his ear. The Turk raised his arm as unwilling to answer. Ferdinand persisted, and then the Turk turned his head towards him.

"'Lewis saw that Ferdinand instantly turned pale; but after a few seconds he asked another question, to which he got an answer at once. It was with a most constrained smile that Ferdinand, turning to the audience, said—

""'I can assure you, gentlemen, that as far as I am concerned at any rate, the Turk has redeemed his character. I must beg you to pardon me if I conceal the question and the answer from you; of course the secrets of the Oracle may not be divulged."

"'Though Ferdinand strove hard to hide what he felt, it was but too evident from his efforts to be at ease that he was very deeply moved, and the cleverest answer could not have produced in the spectators the strange

---

[1] Grandeur, panache, style

[2] A machine that roasts meat by turning it on a spit

[3] To be in the mood, to be in the right frame of mind

[4] Apt, well-formulated, relevant

sensation, amounting to a species of awe, which his unmistakable emotion gave rise to in them. The fun and the jests were at an end; hardly another word was spoken, and the audience dispersed in uneasy silence.

""Dear Lewis," said Ferdinand, as soon as they were alone together, "I must tell you all about this. The Turk has broken my heart; for I believe I shall never get over the blow he has given me until I do really die of the fulfilment of his terrible prophecy."

"'Lewis gazed at him in the profoundest amazement; and Ferdinand continued:

""I see, now, that the mysterious being who communicates with us by the medium of the Turk, has powers at his command which compel our most secret thoughts with magic might; it may be that this strange intelligence clearly and distinctly beholds that germ of the future which fructifies[1] within us in mysterious connection with the outer world, and is thus cognizant of all that is to come upon us in distant days, like those persons who are endowed with that unhappy seer-gift which enables them to predict the hour of death."

""You must have put an extraordinary question," Lewis answered; "but I should think you are tacking on some unduly important meaning to the Oracle's ambiguous reply. Mere chance, I should imagine, has educed something which is, by accident, appropriate to your question; and you are attributing this to the mystic power of the person (most probably quite an every-day sort of creature) who speaks to us through the Turk."

""What you say," answered Ferdinand, "is quite at variance with all the conclusions you and I have come to on the subject of what is ordinarily termed 'chance.' However, you cannot be expected to comprehend the precise condition in which I am, without my telling you all about an affair which happened to me some time ago, as to which I have never breathed a syllable to any one living till now. Several years ago I was on my way back to B——, from a place a long way off in East Prussia[2], belonging to my father. In K——, I met with some young Courland[3] fellows who were going back to B—— too. We travelled together in three post carriages; and, as we had plenty of money, and were all about the time of life when people's spirits are pretty high, you may imagine the manner of our journey. We were continually playing the maddest pranks of every kind. I remember that we got to M—— about noon, and set to work to plunder the landlady's wardrobe. A crowd collected in front of the inn, and we marched up and

---

[1] Instills

[2] The far-eastern end of Prussia, on the Baltic coast, which is now divided up amongst modern Poland, Lithuania, and the Russian oblast of Kaliningrad

[3] Western Latvia

down, dressed in some of her clothes, smoking, till the postilion's[1] horn sounded, and off we set again. We reached D—— in the highest possible spirits, and were so delighted with the place and scenery, that we determined to stay there several days. We made a number of excursions in the neighbourhood, and so once, when we had been out all day at the Karlsberg[2], finding a grand bowl of punch waiting for us on our return, we dipped into it pretty freely. Although I had not taken more of it than was good for me, still, I had been in the grand sea-breeze all day, and I felt all my pulses throbbing, and my blood seemed to rush through my veins in a stream of fire. When we went to our rooms at last, I threw myself down on my bed; but, tired as I was, my sleep was scarcely more than a kind of dreamy, half-conscious condition, in which I was cognizant of all that was going on about me. I fancied I could hear soft conversation in the next room, and at last I plainly made out a male voice saying—

""'Well, good night, now; mind and be ready in good time.'

""A door opened and closed again, and then came a deep silence; but this was soon broken by one or two chords of a pianoforte[3].

""You know the magical effect of music sounding in that way in the stillness of night. I felt as though some beautiful spirit voice was speaking to me in these chords. I lay listening, expecting something in the shape of a fantasia—or some such piece of music—to follow; but fancy what it was when a most gloriously, exquisitely beautiful lady's voice sang, to a melody that went to one's very heart, the words I am going to repeat to you—

""*Mio ben ricordati / S' avvien ch' io mora / Quanto quest' anima / Fedel t' amo; Lo se pur amano / Le fredde ceneri, / Nel urna ancora / T' adorero'.*"[4]

""How can I ever hope to give you the faintest idea of the effect of those long-drawn swelling and dying notes upon me. I had never imagined anything approaching it. The melody was marvellous—quite unlike any other. It was, itself, the deep, tender sorrow of the most fervent love. As it rose in simple phrases, the clear upper notes like crystal bells, and sank till the rich low tunes died away like the sighs of a despairing plaint, a rapture which words cannot describe took possession of me—the pain of a boundless longing seized my heart like a spasm; I could scarcely breathe, my whole being was merged in an inexpressible, super-earthly delight. I did not dare to move; could only listen; soul and body were merged in ear.

---

[1] A coach employee who rides on one of the foremost horse's backs and keeps the team together. He also blows a horn to clear the road and to signal changes

[2] A local castle, museum, and fortress

[3] Viz., a piano

[4] "My dear, remember / If it happens that I die / How faithfully this soul / loves you; If they still love / The cold ashes, / In the urn / I will still adore you." From a poem by 18th century Italian man of letters, Pietro Metastasio

It was not until the tones had been for some time silent that tears, coming to my eyes, broke the spell, and restored me to myself. I suppose that sleep then came upon me, for when I was roused by the shrill notes of a posthorn, the bright morning sun was shining into my room, and I found that it had been only in my dreams that I had been enjoying a bliss more deep, a happiness more ineffable, than the world could otherwise have afforded me. For a beautiful lady came to me—it was the lady who had sung the song—and said to me, very fondly and tenderly—

"""Then you *did* recognize me, my own dear Ferdinand! I knew that I had only to sing, and I should live again in you wholly, for every note was sleeping in your heart.'

""Then I recognized, with rapture unspeakable, that she was the beloved of my soul, whose image had been enshrined in my heart since childhood. Though an adverse fate had torn her from me for a time, I had found her again now; but my deep and fervent love for her melted into that wonderful melody of sorrow, and our words and our looks grew into exquisite swelling tones of music, flowing together into a river of fire. Now, however, that I had awakened from this beautiful dream, I was obliged to confess to myself that I could trace no association of former days connected with it. I never had seen the beautiful lady before.

""I heard some one talking loudly and angrily in front of the house, and rising mechanically, I went to the window. An elderly gentleman, well dressed, was rating[1] the postilion, who had damaged something about an elegant travelling carriage; at last this was put to rights, and the gentleman called upstairs to some one, 'We're all ready now; come along, it's time to be off.' I found that there had been a young lady looking out of the window next to mine; but as she drew quickly back, and had on a broad travelling hat, I did not see her face; when she went out, she turned round and looked up at me. Heavens! she was the singer! she was the lady of my dream! For a moment her beautiful eyes rested upon me, and the beam of a crystal tone seemed to pierce my heart like the point of a burning dagger, so that I felt an actual physical smart: all my members trembled, and I was transfixed with an indescribable bliss. She got quickly into the carriage, the postilion blew a cheerful tune as if in jubilant defiance, and in a moment they had disappeared round the corner of the street. I remained at the window like a man in a dream. My Courland friends came in to fetch me for an excursion which had been arranged: I never spoke; they thought I was ill. How could I have uttered a single word connected with what had occurred? I abstained from making any inquiries in the hotel about the occupants of the room next to mine; I felt that every word relating to her uttered by any lips but mine would be a desecration of my tender secret. I resolved to keep it always faithfully from thenceforth, to bear it about with me always, and to be for ever true to her—my only love for evermore—

[1] Upbraiding, chewing out

although I might never see her again. You can quite understand my feelings. I know you will not blame me for having immediately given up everybody and everything but the most eager search for the very slightest trace of my unknown love. My jovial Courland friends were now perfectly unendurable to me; I slipped away from them quietly in the night, and was off as fast as I could travel to B——, to go on with my work there. You know I was always pretty good at drawing. Well, in B—— I took lessons in miniature painting from good masters, and got on so well that in a short time I was able to carry out the idea which had set me on this tack—to paint a portrait of her, as like as it could be made. I worked at it secretly, with locked doors. No human eye has ever seen it; for I had another picture the exact size of it framed, and put her portrait into the frame instead of it, myself. Ever since, I have worn it next my heart.

"""I have never mentioned this affair—much the most important event in my life—until to-day; and you are the only creature in the world, Lewis, to whom I have breathed a word of my secret. Yet this very day a hostile influence—I know not whence or what—comes piercing into my heart and life! When I went up to the Turk, I asked—thinking of my beloved—

""""Will there ever be a time again for me like that which was the happiest in my life?'

"""The Turk was most unwilling to answer me, as I daresay you observed; but at last, as I persisted, he said—

""""I am looking into your breast; but the glitter of the gold, which is towards me, distracts me. Turn the picture round.'

"""Have I words for the feeling which went shuddering through me? I am sure you must have seen how I was startled. The picture was really placed on my breast in the way the Turk had said; I turned it round, unobserved, and repeated my question. Then the figure said, in a sorrowful tone—

""""Unhappy man! At the very moment when next you see her, she will be lost to you for ever!'"

"'Lewis was about to try to cheer his friend, who had fallen into a deep reverie, but some mutual acquaintances came in, and they were interrupted.

"'The story of this fresh instance of a mysterious answer by the Turk spread in the town, and people busied themselves in conjectures as to the unfavourable prophecy which had so upset the unprejudiced Ferdinand. His friends were besieged with questions, and Lewis had to invent a marvellous tale, which had all the more universal a success that it was remote from the truth. The coterie of people with whom Ferdinand had been induced to go and see the Turk was in the habit of meeting once a week, and at their next meeting the Turk was necessarily the topic of conversation, as efforts were continually being made to obtain, from Ferdinand himself, full particulars of an adventure which had thrown him into such an evident despondency. Lewis felt most deeply how bitter a blow it was to Ferdinand to find the secret of his romantic love, preserved so long and faithfully, penetrated by a fearful, unknown power; and he, like Ferdinand, was almost convinced that the mysterious link which attaches the present to the future must be clear to the vision of that power to which the most hidden secrets were thus manifest. Lewis could not help believing the Oracle; but the malevolence, the relentlessness with which the misfortune impending over his friend had been announced, made him indignant with the undiscovered Being which spoke by the mouth of the Turk, so that he placed himself in persistent opposition to the Automaton's many admirers; and whilst they considered that there was much impressiveness about its most natural movements, enhancing the effect of its oracular sayings, he maintained that it was those very turnings of the head and rollings of the eyes which he considered so absurd, and that this was the reason why he could not help making a joke on the subject; a joke which had put the Exhibitor out of temper, and probably the invisible agent as well. Indeed the latter had shown that this was so by giving a number of stupid and unmeaning answers.

""I must tell you," said Lewis, "that the moment I went into the room the figure reminded me of a most delightful Nutcracker which a cousin of mine once gave me at Christmas time when I was a little boy. The little fellow had the gravest and most comical face ever seen, and when he had a hard nut to crack there was some arrangement inside him which made him roll his great eyes, which projected far out of his head, and this gave him such an absurdly life-like effect that I could play with him for hours; in fact, in my secret soul, I almost thought he was real. All the marionettes I have seen since then, however perfect, I have thought stiff and lifeless compared to my glorious Nutcracker. I had heard much of some wonderful automatons in the Arsenal at Dantzig[1], and I took care to go and see them when I was there some years ago. Soon after I got into the place where they were, an old-fashioned German soldier came marching up to me, and fired off his musket with such a bang that the great vaulted hall rang again. There were other similar tricks which I forget about now; but at length I was taken into a room where I found the God of War—the terrible Mars himself—with all his suite. He was seated, in a rather grotesque dress, on a throne ornamented with arms of all sorts; heralds and warriors were standing round him. As soon as we came before the throne, a set of drummers began to roll their drums, and fifers blew on their fifes in the most horrible way—all out of tune—so that one had to put one's fingers in one's ears. My remark was that the God of War was very badly off for a band, and every one agreed with me. The drums and fifes stopped; the

[1] Modern Gdansk, Poland, once part of East Prussia

heralds began to turn their heads about, and stamp with their halberds[1], and finally the God of War, after rolling his eyes for a time, started up from his seat, and seemed to be coming straight at us. However, he soon sank back on his throne again, and after a little more drumming and fifing, everything reverted to its state of wooden repose. As I came away from seeing these automatons, I said to myself, 'Nothing like my Nutcracker!' And now that I have seen the sage Turk, I say again, 'Give me my Nutcracker.'

"'"People laughed at this, of course; though it was believed to be 'more jest than earnest,' for, to say nothing of the remarkable cleverness of many of the Turk's answers, the indiscoverable connection between him and the hidden Being who, besides speaking through him, must produce the movements which accompanied his answers, was unquestionably very wonderful, at all events a masterpiece of mechanical and acoustical skill."

"'Lewis was himself obliged to admit this; and every one was extolling the inventor of the automaton, when an elderly gentleman who, as a general rule, spoke very little, and had been taking no part in the conversation on the present occasion, rose from his chair (as he was in the habit of doing when he did finally say a few words, always greatly to the point) and began, in his usual polite manner, as follows:

"'"Will you be good enough to allow me, gentlemen—I beg you to pardon me. You have reason to admire the curious work of art which has been interesting us all for so long; but you are wrong in supposing the commonplace person who exhibits it to be the inventor of it. The truth is that he really has no hand at all in what are the truly remarkable features of it. The originator of them is a gentleman highly skilled in matters of the kind—one who lives amongst us, and has done so for many years—whom we all know very well, and greatly respect and esteem."

"'Universal surprise was created by this, and the elderly gentleman was besieged with questions, on which he continued;

"'"The gentleman to whom I allude is none other than Professor X——. The Turk had been here a couple of days, and nobody had taken any particular notice of him, though Professor X—- took care to go and see him at once, because everything in the shape of an Automaton interests him in the highest degree. When he had heard one or two of the Turk's answers, he took the Exhibitor apart and whispered a word or two in his ear. The man turned pale, and shut up his exhibition as soon as the two or three people who were then in the room had gone away. The bills[2] disappeared from the walls, and nothing more was heard of the Talking Turk for a fortnight. Then new bills came out, and the Turk was found with the fine

[1] Poleaxes (ornamental staffs topped with an axe head and a long, thin, spearhead) – the symbolic weapon of a sergeant during the 16th – 18th centuries

[2] Event posters, advertisements

new head, and all the other arrangements as they are at present—an unsolvable riddle. It is since that time that his answers have been so clever and so interesting. But that all this is the work of Professor X—— admits of no question. The Exhibitor, in the interval, when the figure was not being exhibited, spent all his time with him. Also it is well known that the Professor passed several days in succession in the room where the figure is. Besides, gentlemen, you are no doubt aware that the Professor himself possesses a number of most extraordinary automatons, chiefly musical, which he has long vied with Hofrath B—— in producing, keeping up with him a correspondence concerning all sorts of mechanical, and, people say, even *magical* arts and pursuits, and that, did he but choose, he could astonish the world with them. But he works in complete privacy, although he is always ready to show his extraordinary inventions to all who take a real interest in such matters."

"'It was, in fact, matter of notoriety that this Professor X——, whose principal pursuits were natural philosophy and chemistry, delighted, next to them, in occupying himself with mechanical research; but no one in the assemblage had had the slightest idea that he had had any connection with the "Talking Turk," and it was from the merest hearsay that people knew anything concerning the curiosities which the old gentleman had referred to. Ferdinand and Lewis felt strangely and vividly impressed by the old gentleman's account of Professor X——, and the influence which he had brought to bear on that strange automaton.

"'"I cannot hide from you," said Ferdinand, "that a hope is dawning upon me that, if I get nearer to this Professor X——, I may, perhaps, come upon a clue to the mystery which is weighing so terribly upon me at present. And it is possible that the true significance and import of the relations which exist between the Turk (or rather the hidden entity which employs him as the organ of its oracular utterances) and myself might, could I get to comprehend it, perhaps comfort me, and weaken the impression of those words, for me so terrible. I have made up my mind to make the acquaintance of this mysterious man, on the pretext of seeing his automatons; and as they are musical ones, it will not be devoid of interest for you to come with me."

"'"As if it were not sufficient for me," said Lewis, "to be able to aid you, in your necessity, with counsel and help! But I cannot deny that even to-day, when the old gentleman was mentioning Professor X——'s connection with the Turk, strange ideas came into my mind; although perhaps I am going a long way about in search of what lies close at hand, could one but see it. For instance, to look as close at hand as possible for the solution of the mystery, may it not be the case that the invisible being knew that you wore the picture next your heart, so that a mere lucky guess might account for the rest? Perhaps it was taking its revenge upon you for the rather uncourteous style in which we were joking about the Turk's wisdom."

""Not one human soul," Ferdinand answered, "has ever set eyes on the picture; this I told you before. And I have never told any creature but yourself of the adventure which has had such an immensely important influence on my whole life. It is an utter impossibility that the Turk can have got to know of this in any ordinary manner. Much more probably, what you say you are 'going a long roundabout way' in search of may be much nearer the truth."

""Well then," said Lewis, "what I mean is this; that this automaton, strongly as I appeared to-day to assert the contrary, is really one of the most extraordinary phenomena ever beheld, and that everything goes to prove that whoever controls and directs it has at his command higher powers than is supposed by those who go there simply to gape at things, and do no more than wonder at what is wonderful. The figure is nothing more than the outward form of the communication; but that form has been cleverly selected, as such, since the shape, appearance, and movements of it are well adapted to occupy the attention in a manner favourable for the preservation of the secret, and, particularly, to work upon the questioners favourably as regards the intelligence, whatsoever it is, which gives the answers. There cannot be any human being concealed inside the figure; that is as good as proved, so that it is clearly the result of some acoustic deception that we think the answers come from the Turk's mouth. But how this is accomplished—how the Being who gives the answers is placed in a position to hear the questions and see the questioners, and at the same time to be audible by them—certainly remains a complete mystery to me. Of course all this merely implies great acoustic and mechanical skill on the part of the inventor, and remarkable acuteness, or, I might say, systematic craftiness, in leaving no stone unturned in the process of deceiving us. And I admit that this part of the riddle interests me the less, inasmuch as it falls completely into the shade in comparison with the circumstance (which, is the only part of the affair which is so extraordinarily remarkable) that the Turk often reads the very soul of the questioner. How, if it were possible to this Being which gives the answers, to acquire by some process unknown to us, a psychic influence over us, and to place itself in a spiritual *rapport*[1] with us, so that it can comprehend and read our minds and thoughts, and more than that, have cognizance of our whole inner being; so that, if it does not clearly speak out the secrets which are lying dormant within us, it does yet evoke and call forth, in a species of *extasis*[2] induced by its *rapport* with the exterior spiritual principle, the suggestions, the outlines, the shadowings of all which is reposing within our breasts, clearly seen by the eye of the spirit, in brightest illumination! On this assumption the psychical power would strike the strings within us, so as to make them give forth a clear and vibrating chord, audible to us,

---

[1] He is describing telepathy

[2] Rapture, extasy

and intelligible by us, instead of merely murmuring, as they do at other times; so that it is we who answer our own selves; the voice which we hear is produced from within ourselves by the operation of this unknown spiritual power, and vague presentiments and anticipations of the future brighten into spoken prognostications—just as, in dreams, we often find that a voice, unfamiliar to us, tells us of things which we do not know, or as to which we are in doubt, being, in reality, a voice proceeding from ourselves, although it seems to convey to us knowledge which previously we did not possess. No doubt the Turk (that is to say, the hidden power which is connected with him) seldom finds it necessary to place himself *en rapport* with people in this way. Hundreds of them can be dealt with in the cursory, superficial manner adapted to their queries and characters, and it is seldom that a question is put which calls for the exercise of anything besides ready wit. But by any strained or exalted condition of the questioner the Turk would be affected in quite a different way, and he would then employ those means which render possible the production of a psychic *rapport*, giving him the power to answer from out of the inner depths of the questioner. His hesitation in replying to deep questions of this kind may be due to the delay which he grants himself to gain a few moments for the bringing into play of the power in question. This is my true and genuine opinion; and you see that I have not that contemptuous notion of this work of art (or whatever may be the proper term to apply to it) that I would have had you believe I had. But I do not wish to conceal anything from you; though I see that if you adopt my idea, I shall not have given you any real comfort at all."

""You are wrong there, dear friend," said Ferdinand. "The very fact that your opinion does chime in with a vague notion which I felt, dimly, in my own mind, comforts me very much. It is only myself that I have to take into account; my precious secret is not discovered, for I know that you will guard it as a sacred treasure. And, by-the-bye, I must tell you of a most extraordinary feature of the matter, which I had forgotten till now. Just as the Turk was speaking his latter words, I fancied that I heard one or two broken phrases of the sorrowful melody, '*mio ben ricordati*,' and then it seemed to me that one single, long-drawn note of the glorious voice which I heard on that eventful night went floating by."

""Well," said Lewis, "and I remember, too, that, just as your answer was being given to you, I happened to place my hand on the railing which surrounds the figure. I felt it thrill and vibrate in my hand, and I fancied also that I could hear a kind of musical sound, for I cannot say it was a vocal note, passing across the room. I paid no attention to it, because, as you know, my head is always full of music, and I have several times been wonderfully deceived in a similar way; but I was very much astonished, in my own mind, when I traced the mysterious connection between that sound and your adventure in D——."

"'The fact that Lewis had heard the sound as well as himself, was to Ferdinand a proof of the psychic *rapport* which existed between them; and as they further diseased the marvels of the affair, he began to feel the heavy burden which had weighed upon him since he heard the fatal answer lifted away, and was ready to go forward bravely to meet whatsoever the future might have in store.

""'It is impossible that I can lose her," he said. "She is my heart's queen, and will always be there, as long as my own life endures."

"'They went and called on Professor X——, in high hope that he would be able to throw light on many questions relating to occult sympathies[1] and the like, in which they were deeply interested. They found him to be an old man, dressed in old-fashioned French style, exceedingly keen and lively, with small grey eyes which had an unpleasant way of fixing themselves on one, and a sarcastic simile, not very attractive, playing about his mouth.

"'When they had expressed their wish to see some of his automatons, he said, "Ah! and you really take an interest in mechanical matters, do you? Perhaps you have done something in that direction yourselves? Well, I can show you, in this house here, what you will look for in vain in the rest of Europe: I may say, in the known world."

"'There was something most unpleasant about the Professor's voice; it was a high-pitched, screaming sort of discordant tenor, exactly suited to the mountebank[2] tone in which he proclaimed his treasures. He fetched his keys with a great clatter, and opened the door of a tastefully and elegantly furnished hall, where the automatons were. There was a piano in the middle of the loom, on a raised platform; beside it, on the right, a life-sized figure of a man, with a flute in his hand; on the left, a female figure, seated at an instrument somewhat resembling a piano; behind her were two boys, with a drum and a triangle. In the background our two friends noticed an orchestrion[3] (which was an instrument already known to them), and all round the walls were a number of musical clocks. The Professor passed, in a cursory manner, close by the orchestrion and the clocks, and just touched the automatons, almost imperceptibly; then he sat down at the piano, and began to play, *pianissimo*, an *andante*[4] in the style of a march. He played it once through by himself; and as he commenced it for the second time the flute-player put his instrument to his lips, and took up the melody; then one of the boys drummed softly on his drum in the most accurate time, and the other just touched his triangle, so that you could hear it and no more. Presently the lady came in with full chords, of a sound something

[1] Viz., telepathy

[2] Huckster, quack, side-show shill

[3] A complex mechanical instrument meant to sound like an orchestra

[4] A classical piece performed in a stately, walking pace ("andante" is Italian for "going/walking")

like those of a harmonica, which she produced by pressing down the keys of her instrument; and now the whole room kept growing more and more alive; the musical clocks came in one by one, with the utmost rhythmical precision; the boy drummed louder; the triangle rang through the room, and lastly the orchestrion set to work, and drummed and trumpeted *fortissimo*[1], so that the whole place shook again; and this went on till the Professor wound up the whole business with one final chord, all the machines finishing also, with the utmost precision. Our friends bestowed the applause which the Professor's complacent smile (with its undercurrent of sarcasm) seemed to demand of them. He went up to the figures to set about exhibiting some further similar musical feats; but Lewis and Ferdinand, as if by a preconcerted arrangement, declared that they had pressing business which prevented their making a longer stay, and took their leave of the inventor and his machines.

""Most interesting and ingenious, wasn't it?" said Ferdinand; but Lewis's anger, long restrained, broke out.

""Oh! confusion on that wretched Professor!" he cried. "What a terrible, terrible disappointment! Where are all the revelations we expected? What became of the learned, instructive discourse which we thought he would deliver to us, as to disciples at Sais[2]?"

""At the same time," said Ferdinand, "we have seen some very ingenious mechanical inventions, curious and interesting from a musical point of view. Clearly, the flute-player is the same as Vaucanson's[3] well-known machine; and a similar mechanism applied to the fingers of the female figure is, I suppose, what enables her to bring out those really beautiful tones from her instrument. The way in which all the machines work together is really astonishing."

""It is exactly that which drives me so wild," said Lewis. "All that machine-music (in which I include the Professor's own playing) makes every bone in my body ache. I am sure I do not know when I shall get over it! The fact of any human being's doing anything in association with those lifeless figures which counterfeit the appearance and movements of humanity has always, to me, something fearful, unnatural, I may say terrible, about it. I suppose it would be possible, by means of certain mechanical arrangements inside them, to construct automatons which should dance, and then to set them to dance with human beings, and twist and turn about in all sorts of figures; so that we should have a living man putting his arms about a lifeless partner of wood, and whirling round and

---

[1] Extremely loudly

[2] *The Disciples at Sais* is a fragment of a philosophical novel by the 18th century German Romantic poet, Novalis, and is made up of a series of fictitious Socratic dialogues had at the Egyptian temple in Sais

[3] Jacques de Vaucanson was an 18th century French engineer and inventor. He designed two famous automata, one of which played a tambourine

round with her, or rather it. Could you look at such a sight, for an instant, without horror? At all events, all machine-music is to me a thing altogether monstrous and abominable; and a good stocking-loom[1] is, in my opinion, worth all the most perfect and ingenious musical clocks in the universe put together. For is it the breath, merely, of the performer on a wind-instrument, or the skilful, supple fingers of the performer on a stringed instrument, which evoke those tones which lay upon us a spell of such power, and awaken that inexpressible feeling, akin to nothing else on earth, the sense of a distant spirit world, and of our own higher life therein? Is it not, rather, the mind, the soul, the heart, which merely employ those bodily organs to give forth into our external life that which is felt in our inner depths? so that it can be communicated to others, and awaken kindred chords in them, opening, in harmonious echoes, that marvellous kingdom from whence those tones come darting, like beams of light? To set to work to make music by means of valves, springs, levers, cylinders, or whatever other apparatus you choose to employ, is a senseless attempt to make the means to an end accomplish what can result only when those means are animated and, in their minutest movements, controlled by the mind, the soul, and the heart. The gravest reproach you can make to a musician is that he plays without expression; because, by so doing, he is marring the whole essence of the matter. Yet the coldest and most unfeeling executant will always be far in advance of the most perfect of machines. For it is impossible that no impulse whatever, from the inner man shall ever, even for a moment, animate his rendering; whereas, in the case of a machine, no such impulse can ever do so. The attempts of mechanicians to imitate, with more or less approximation to accuracy, the human organs in the production of musical sounds, or to substitute mechanical appliances for those organs, I consider tantamount to a declaration of war against the spiritual element in music; but the greater the forces they array against it, the more victorious it is. For this very reason, the more perfect that this sort of machinery is, the more I disapprove of it; and I infinitely prefer the commonest barrel-organ, in which the mechanism attempts nothing but to be mechanical, to Vaucauson's flute-player, or the harmonica girl.

""I entirely agree with you," said Ferdinand, "and indeed you have merely put into words what I have always thought; and I was much struck with it to-day at the Professor's. Although I do not so wholly live and move and have my being in music as you do, and consequently am not so sensitively alive to imperfections in it, I, too, have always felt a repugnance to the stiffness and lifelessness of machine-music; and, I can remember, when I was a child at home, how I detested a large, ordinary musical clock, which played its little tune every hour. It is a pity that those skilful

[1] A mechanical knitting machine that loomed socks among other garments

mechanicians do not try to apply their knowledge to the improvement of musical instruments, rather than to puerilities of this sort."

""Exactly," said Lewis. "Now, in the case of instruments of the keyboard class a great deal might be done. There is a wide field open in that direction to clever mechanical people, much as has been accomplished already; particularly in instruments of the pianoforte genus. But it would be the task of a really advanced system of the 'mechanics of music' to closely observe, minutely study, and carefully discover that class of sounds which belong, most purely and strictly, to Nature herself, to obtain a knowledge of the tones which dwell in substances of every description, and then to take this mysterious music and enclose it in some description of instrument, where it should be subject to man's will, and give itself forth at his touch. All the attempts to bring music out of metal or glass cylinders, glass threads, slips of glass, or pieces of marble; or to cause strings to vibrate or sound, in ways unlike the ordinary ways, seem to me to be interesting in the highest degree: and what stands in the way of our real progress in the discovery of the marvellous acoustical secrets which lie hidden all around us in nature is, that every imperfect attempt at an experiment is at once held up to laudation as being a new and utterly perfect invention, either for vanity's sake, or for money's. This is why so many new instruments have started into existence—most of them with grand or ridiculous names—and have disappeared and been forgotten just as quickly."

""Your 'higher mechanics of music' seems to be a most interesting subject," said Ferdinand, "although, for my part, I do not as yet quite perceive the object at which it aims."

""The object at which it aims," said Lewis, "is the discovery of the most absolutely perfect kind of musical sound; and according to my theory, musical sound would be the nearer to perfection the more closely it approximated to such of the mysterious tones of nature as are not wholly dissociated from this earth."

""I presume," said Ferdinand, "that it is because I have not penetrated so deeply into this subject as you have, but you must allow me to say that I do not quite understand you."

""Then," said Lewis, "let me give you some sort of an idea how it is that all this question exhibits itself to my mind.

""In the primeval condition of the human race, while (to make use of almost the very words of a talented writer—Schubert[1]—in his 'Glimpses at the Night Side of Natural Science') mankind as yet was dwelling in its pristine holy harmony with nature, richly endowed with a heavenly instinct of prophecy and poetry; while, as yet, Mother Nature continued to nourish from the fount of her own life, the wondrous being to whom she had given birth, she encompassed him with a holy music, like the afflatus of a

---

[1] Gotthilf Heinrich Schubert was an 18th – 19th century German physician, scientist, and psychologist

continual inspiration; and wondrous tones spake of the mysteries of her unceasing activity. There has come down to us an echo from the mysterious depths of those primeval days—that beautiful notion of the music of the spheres, which, when as a boy, I first read of it in 'The Dream of Scipio[1],' filled me with the deepest and most devout reverence. I often used to listen, on quiet moonlight nights, to hear if those wondrous tones would come to me, borne on the wings of the whispering airs. However, as I said to you already, those nature-tones have not yet all departed from this world, fur we have an instance of their survival, and occurrence in that 'Music of the Air' or 'Voice of the Demon,' mentioned by a writer on Ceylon[2]—a sound which so powerfully affects the human system, that even the least impressionable persons, when they hear those tones of nature imitating, in such a terrible manner, the expression of human sorrow and suffering, are struck with painful compassion and profound terror! Indeed, I once met with an instance of a phenomenon of a similar kind myself, at a place in East Prussia. I had been living there for some time; it was about the end of autumn, when, on quiet nights, with a moderate breeze blowing, I used distinctly to hear tones, sometimes resembling the deep, stopped, pedal pipe of an organ, and sometimes like the vibrations from a deep, soft-toned bell. I often distinguished, quite clearly, the low F, and the fifth above it (the C), and not seldom the minor third above, E flat, was perceptible as well; and then this tremendous chord of the seventh, so woeful and so solemn, produced on one the effect of the most intense sorrow, and even of terror!

"""There is, about the imperceptible commencement, the swelling and the gradual dying of those nature-tones a something which has a most powerful and indescribable effect upon us; and any instrument which should be capable of producing this would, no doubt, affect us in a similar way. So that I think the harmonica comes the nearest, as regards its tone, to that perfection, which is to be measured by its influence on our minds. And it is fortunate that this instrument (which chances to be the very one which imitates those nature-tones with such exactitude) happens to be just the very one which is incapable of lending itself to frivolity or ostentation, but exhibits its characteristic qualities in the purest of simplicity. The recently invented 'harmonichord[3]' will doubtless accomplish much in this direction. This instrument, as you no doubt know, sets strings a-vibrating and a-toning (not bells, as in the harmonica) by means of mechanism,

---

[1] A surreal fantasy, said to describe a prophetic dream had by the Roman general Scipio, written by the Roman statesman, philosopher, and man of letters, Cicero. It promotes Stoic ideals of metaphysics and a mystical cosmology

[2] Obscure travel treatises

[3] A very curious kind of upright piano in which the strings are set in vibration not by the blow of the hammer but by indirectly transmitted friction

which is set in motion by the pressing down of keys, and the rotation of a cylinder. The performer has, under his control, the commencement, the swelling out, and the diminishing, of the tones much more than is the case with the harmonica, though as yet the harmonichord has not the tone of the harmonica, which sounds as if it came straight from another world."

""I have heard that instrument," said Ferdinand, "and certainly the tone of it went to the very depths of my being, although I thought the performer was doing it scant justice. As regards the rest, I think I quite understand you, although I do not, as yet, quite see into the closeness of the connection between those 'nature-tones' and music."

"'Lewis answered—"Can the music which dwells within us be any other than that which lies buried in nature as a profound mystery, comprehensible only by the inner, higher sense, uttered by instruments, as the organs of it, merely in obedience to a mighty spell, of which we are the masters? But, in the purely psychical action and operation of the spirit—that is to say, in dreams—this spell is broken; and then, in the tones of familiar instruments, we are enabled to recognise those nature-tones as wondrously engendered in the air, they come floating down to us, and swell and die away."

""I think of the Æolian harp[1]," said Ferdinand. "What is your opinion about that ingenious invention?"

""Every attempt," said Lewis, "to tempt Nature to give forth her tones is glorious, and highly worthy of attention. Only, it seems to me that, as yet, we have only offered her trifling toys, which she has often shattered to pieces in her indignation. Much grander idea than all those playthings (like Æolian harps) was the 'storm harp' which I have read of. It was made of thick chords of wire, which were stretched out at considerable distances apart, in the open country, and gave forth great, powerful chords when the wind smote upon them.

""Altogether, there is still a wide field open to thoughtful inventors in this direction, and I quite believe that the impulse recently given to natural science in general will be perceptible in this branch of it, and bring into practical existence much which is, as yet, nothing but speculation."

"Just at this moment there came suddenly floating through the air an extraordinary sound, which, as it swelled and became more distinguishable, seemed to resemble the tone of a harmonica. Lewis and Ferdinand stood rooted to the spot in amazement, not unmixed with awe; the tones took the form of a profoundly sorrowful melody sung by a female voice. Ferdinand grasped Lewis by the hand, whilst the latter whisperingly repeated the words,

""*Mio ben, ricordati, s' avvien ch' io mora*."

---

[1] Also called a "wind harp" – a type of box zither on which sounds are produced by the movement of wind over its strings

"'At the time when this occurred they were outside of the town, and before the entrance to a garden which was surrounded by lofty trees and tall hedges. There was a pretty little girl—whom they had not observed before—sitting playing in the grass near them, and she sprang up crying, "Oh, how beautifully my sister is singing again! I must take her some flowers, for she always sings sweeter and longer when she sees a beautiful carnation." And with that she gathered a bunch of flowers, and went skipping into the garden with it, leaving the gate ajar, so that our friends could see through it. What was their astonishment to see Professor X—— standing in the middle of the garden, beneath a lofty ash-tree! Instead of the repellant grin of irony with which he had received them at his house, his face wore an expression of deep melancholy earnestness, and his gaze was fixed upon the heavens, as if he were contemplating that world beyond the skies, whereof those marvellous tones, floating in the air like the breath of a zephyr[1], were telling. He walked up and down the central alley, with slow and measured steps; and, as he passed along, everything around him seemed to waken into life and movement. In every direction crystal tones came scintillating out of the dark bushes and trees, and, streaming through the air like flame, united in a wondrous concert, penetrating the inmost heart, and waking in the soul the most rapturous emotions of a higher world. Twilight was falling fast; the Professor disappeared among the hedges, and the tones died away in *pianissimo*. At length our friends went back to the town in profound silence; but, as Lewis was about to quit[2] Ferdinand, the latter clasped him firmly, saying—

""'Be true to me! Do not abandon me! I feel, too clearly, some hostile foreign influence at work upon my whole existence, smiting upon all its hidden strings, and making them resound at its pleasure. I am helpless to resist it, though it should drive me to my destruction! Can that diabolical, sneering irony, with which the Professor received us at his house, have been anything other than the expression of this hostile principle? Was it with any other intention than that of getting his hands washed of me for ever, that he fobbed us off[3] with those automatons of his?"

""'You are very probably right," said Lewis; "for I have a strong suspicion myself that, in some manner which is as yet an utter riddle to me, the Professor does exercise some sort of power or influence over your fate, or, I should rather say, over that mysterious psychical relationship, or affinity, which exists between you and this lady. It may be that, being mixed up in some way with this affinity, in his character of an element hostile to it, he strengthens it by the very fact that he opposes it: and it may also be that that which renders you so extremely unacceptable to him is the circumstance that your presence awakens, and sets into lively movement

---

[1] A wind spirit

[2] Part ways from

[3] Tricked us, sent us on this wild goose chase

all the strings and chords of this mutually sympathetic condition, and this contrary to his desire, and, very probably, in opposition to some conventional family arrangement."

"'Our friends determined to leave no stone unturned in their efforts to make a closer approach to the Professor, with the hope that they might succeed, sooner or later, in clearing up this mystery which so affected Ferdinand's destiny and fate, and they were to have paid him a visit on the following morning as a preliminary step. However, a letter, which Ferdinand unexpectedly received from his father, summoned him to B——; it was impossible for him to permit himself the smallest delay, and in a few hours he was off, as fast as post-horses could convey him, assuring Lewis, as he started, that nothing should prevent his return in a fortnight, at the very furthest.

"'It struck Lewis as a singular circumstance that, soon after Ferdinand's departure, the same old gentleman who had at first spoken of the Professor's connection with "the Talking Turk," took an opportunity of enlarging to him on the fact that X——'s mechanical inventions were simply the result of an extreme enthusiasm for mechanical pursuits, and of deep and searching investigations in natural science; he also more particularly lauded the Professor's wonderful discoveries in music, which, he said, he had not as yet communicated to any one, adding that his mysterious laboratory was a pretty garden outside the town, and that passers by had often heard wondrous tones and melodies there, just as if the whole place were peopled by fays[1] and spirits.

"'The fortnight elapsed, but Ferdinand did not come back. At length, when two months had gone by, a letter came from him to the following effect—

"'"Read and marvel; though you will learn only that which, perhaps, you strongly suspected would be the case, when you got to know more of the Professor—as I hope you did. As the horses were being changed in the village of P——, I was standing, gazing into the distance, not thinking specially of anything in particular. A carriage drove by, and stopped at the church, which was open. A young lady, simply dressed, stepped out of the carriage, followed by a young gentleman in a Russian Jaeger[2] uniform, wearing several decorations[3]; two gentlemen got down from a second carriage. The innkeeper said, 'Oh, this is the stranger couple our clergyman is marrying to-day.' Mechanically I went into the church, just as the clergyman was concluding the service with the blessing. I looked at the couple—the bride was my sweet singer. She looked at me, turned pale, and fainted. The gentleman who was behind her caught her in his arms. It was

---

[1] Fairies

[2] A light infantryman or ranger skilled in scouting, especially in forested areas. Regardless of their nationality, they invariably wore dark green uniforms

[3] That is, medals

Professor X——. What happened further I do not know, nor have I any recollection as to how I got here; probably Professor X—— can tell you all about it. But a peace and a happiness, such as I have never known before, have now taken possession of my soul. The mysterious prophecy of the Turk was a cursed falsehood, a mere result of blind groping with unskilful antennæ. Have I lost her? Is she not mine for ever in the glowing inner life?

""It will be long ere you hear of me, for I am going on to K——, and perhaps to the extreme north, as far as P——."

"'Lewis gathered the distracted condition of his friend's mind, only too plainly, from his language, and the whole affair became the greater a riddle to him when he ascertained that it was matter of certainty that Professor X—— had not quitted the town.

""How," thought he, "if all this be but a result of the conflict of mysterious psychical relations (existing, perhaps, between several people) making their way out into everyday life, and involving in their circle even outward events, independent of them, so that the deluded inner sense looks upon them as phenomena proceeding unconditionally from itself, and believes in them accordingly? It may be that the hopeful anticipation which I feel within me will be realised—for my friend's consolation. For the Turk's mysterious prophecy is fulfilled, and perhaps, through that very fulfilment, the mortal blow which menaced my friend is averted."""

LIKE Poe, Hoffmann's obsession with automatons seems tied to a metaphysical fascination with the body-spirit continuum. Where does one begin and the other end? Could they be cut loose from one another? What would a soulless body be like? Where would a bodiless soul reside? A body without a soul would be purely carnal, without hope of transcendence or spiritual connection, while a soul without a body would be impossible to form physical bonds with – all intellect and no substance. Hoffmann's own ability to recede into his mind – to dwell more comfortably in his surreal imagination than in the walls of his parlor or law office – must have caused a subconscious fear that he would one day retreat so far that he would never want to return. Indeed, his fiction is filled with characters who ultimately spurn the living world and the company of living people for fairy realms, candy lands, dream worlds, and infernal caverns. James M. McGlathery notes that the preceding story has two potential interpretations: in one, we take Ferdinand's tale at face value as a supernatural escapade; but in the other we are forced "to ponder whether the character's experiences are real or only imaginary." This possibility poses another question: why would a person choose to believe such a bizarre fantasy? What solace would it bring to a deluded mind? The most likely answer is that Ferdinand *invented* the scenario – either willfully or through unconscious self-delusion – in order to save himself from the pain of losing his beloved. At the end of the story he walks away from the church completely smug and satisfied with his ability to win and woo: she is his in spirit, and although the Russian may have her body, her spirit is far more valuable. The ending is suggestive but otherwise merely circumstantial, for a faint does not a spiritual union make. Ultimately, even if Professor X's machinations are genuine, Ferdinand seems to have found a hollow victory in the delusion that he has taken possession of his beloved's spiritual self. As Poe's tales - especially "The Oval Portrait," "Berenice," "Morella," and "Ligeia" - demonstrate, the obsessive intellectual in love may consider the spirit the purest part of his beloved, and he may idealize and idolize it as much as he chooses - worship it from the corner of his room as she quietly passes the door - but once death has taken the physical vessel from his company, nothing can replicate the union of body and soul. Even in "Morella" and "Ligeia," where a willful spirit possesses the body of another woman, a physical vessel is needed to form a bond with the doting lover. In short, Ferdinand may feel that he has robbed his beloved of her spirit, leaving the Russian with a soulless automaton, but even if he has her essence wrapped up in his pocket, it is worthless to him until it can find a fleshy form, and his one source of solace - imagined or real - is a mere delusion.

NONE of Hoffmann's tales excels in literary merit, psychological scope, or popular influence quite as sensationally as "The Sandman." While "Nutcracker and the King of Mice" has secured more attention in the genres of fantasy and children's literature, "The Sandman" reigns in the hearts of horror aficionados as his unparalleled masterpiece. Dark, swirling, and dizzy, it is a brilliant parable of predestination and freewill. Adored and analyzed by Freud, and mimicked by filmmakers from Robert Wiene and Fritz Lang to Tim Burton and Christopher Nolan, its use of unreliable narrators, psychological suspense, and philosophical subtext curry a masterful allegory of the struggle between rationality and madness –objectivity and subjectivity. Founded, like so many of Hoffmann's tales, on the perversion of a nursery story, it uses the lore of the Sandman to probe human nature's night-side. Everything the Sandman touches is spoiled; everyone he has influence over is ruined; his only desire is to sow suffering and hopelessness. While the original Sandman – a Nordic fairy who sprinkles magic sand into the eyes of wakeful children, causing them to drift off to Slumberland – was a benign creature intended to encourage children to be quiet and still, Hoffmann characteristically views this agent of order as a threat to individualism and imagination. *His* Sandman not only brings a bag of sand (in this case it is burning hot), but has another bag to collect the eyes of youngsters whom he has blinded as punishment for their attentiveness (read: nonconformist, critical thinking – of seeing things as they are, against the establishment advice). However, this icon of conformity eventually morphs into a symbol of the dangers of unchecked individualism, increasingly unhinged by egotistic paranoia and delusions. While Freud famously interpreted the eyes as symbolic testicles, others have seen them as symbols of reason and objectivity – of connecting with the Truth. Nathanael, our manic protagonist, is incessantly blinded to reality by his own all-consuming imagination. He is repeatedly deceived and misled because of his inability to separate the objective reality from the subjective experience. This treatment is somewhat unusual for Hoffmann, who typically encourages readers to embark from the inanity of everyday life to the fulfilling realms of imagination and poetry. But even in tales like "Nutcracker" and "Golden Pot," he keeps his daydreamers rooted to some semblance of reality and order (both stories end with the protagonist settling into bourgeois stability in their new supernatural homes).

II.

Indeed, "The Sandman" operates as something of a ballast to these other tales – like "The King's Betrothed" and "The Mines of Falun" it warns that pitching head-over-heels into the kingdoms of subjectivity will usually result in utter self-destruction. This is the same in "The Entail" and "Councillor Krespel," which advise their readers to be in touch with their emotions but not overwhelmed – lest they end up wrung dry and tossed aside like Antonia or Seraphina. The ultimate battle in "The Sandman" is waged between two characters representing the warring factions of German intellectualism: the rational Enlightenment (represented by the wise but unfeeling Clara) and the expressive Romantics (represented by the impulsive but sincere Nathanael). The two lovers regularly quarrel over their different interpretations of free will: Clara considers it a critical belief necessary to live a responsible and fulfilling life, while Nathanael seems to find freedom in the notion of predestination – that his life's journey is caught in the inescapable currents of Fate, and that he cannot be held responsible for his affinities. At first these seem like the heady squabbles of an A-type personality and a free spirit, but then enters a third combatant with nothing to lose. The Sandman – manifested in the grotesque figures of the alchemist Coppelius and the glass salesman Coppola – represents the ultimate fate of free spirits and daydreamers who refuse to grip the world with both hands and claim a stake in their own lives. While Freud views Coppelius as the "bad father" – an evil Doppelgänger of Nathanael's own, dominated parent – there are many other symbols absorbed by his larger-than-life persona: the power of obsession, the brute strength of the ego, and the dark, Shadow-side of human nature. Whenever the Sandman walks into Nathanael's life, only one thing is for certain: chaos, heartbreak, and loss. Whoever the Sandman is or whatever he represents, it is diametrically opposed to human community and hope – he is the embodiment of selfishness and the pustular soul of the Shadow.

The Sandman

— Excerpted from 'Night-Pieces,' Volume One —

{1816}

NATHANAEL TO LOTHAIR.

I know you are all very uneasy because I have not written for such a long, long time. Mother, to be sure, is angry, and Clara[1], I dare say, believes I am living here in riot and revelry, and quite forgetting my sweet angel, whose image is so deeply engraved upon my heart and mind. But that is not so; daily and hourly do I think of you all, and my lovely Clara's form comes to gladden me in my dreams, and smiles upon me with her bright

[1] Meaning "Light" – many critics have interpreted Clara as the embodiment of 18th century Enlightenment thinking, based in logic, reason, and order. Nathanael on the other hand represents the sentiments of the Romantics, who based their philosophies in emotion, subjectivity, and awe of the Unknown

eyes[1], as graciously as she used to do in the days when I went in and out amongst you. Oh! how could I write to you in the distracted state of mind in which I have been, and which, until now, has quite bewildered me! A terrible thing has happened to me. Dark forebodings of some awful fate threatening me are spreading themselves out over my head like black clouds, impenetrable to every friendly ray of sunlight. I must now tell you what has taken place; I must, that I see well enough, but only to think upon it makes the wild laughter[2] burst from my lips. Oh! my dear, dear Lothair, what shall I say to make you feel, if only in an inadequate way, that that which happened to me a few days ago could thus really exercise such a hostile and disturbing influence upon my life? Oh that you were here to see for yourself! but now you will, I suppose, take me for a superstitious ghost-seer. In a word, the terrible thing which I have experienced, the fatal effect of which I in vain exert every effort to shake off, is simply that some days ago, namely, on the 30th October, at twelve o'clock at noon, a dealer in weather-glasses[3] came into my room and wanted to sell me one of his wares. I bought nothing, and threatened to kick him downstairs, whereupon he went away of his own accord.

You will conclude that it can only be very peculiar relations — relations intimately intertwined with my life — that can give significance to this event, and that it must be the person of this unfortunate hawker which has had such a very inimical effect upon me. And so it really is. I will summon up all my faculties in order to narrate to you calmly and patiently as much of the early days of my youth as will suffice to put matters before you in such a way that your keen sharp intellect may grasp everything clearly and distinctly, in bright and living pictures. Just as I am beginning, I hear you laugh[4] and Clara say, "What's all this childish nonsense about!" Well, laugh at me, laugh heartily at me, pray do. But, good God! my hair is standing on end, and I seem to be entreating you to laugh at me in the same sort of frantic despair in which Franz Moor entreated Daniel to laugh him to scorn[5]. But to my story.

---

[1] Eyes immediately begin to factor into this story as a symbol of clarity, reason, and truth. While Clara's bright eyes stand to illuminate and clarify the universe, the Sandman's habit of blinding his victims brings confusion, chaos, and existential terror

[2] Another motif in this story – one representing the giddy loss of control associated with insanity

[3] Glass barometer that use the water inside a teapot-shaped device to forecast the weather

[4] Symbolically accusing him of insanity (by confronting him with wild laughter – the symptom of a lunatic)

[5] From Friedrich Schiller's magnum opus, "The Robbers." At one point the scheming Franz Moor realizes that his evil plans are untangling and that

Except at dinner we, i.e., I and my brothers and sisters, saw but little of our father all day long. His business no doubt took up most of his time. After our evening meal, which, in accordance with an old custom, was served at seven o'clock, we all went, mother with us, into father's room, and took our places around a round table. My father smoked his pipe, drinking a large glass of beer to it. Often he told us many wonderful stories, and got so excited over them that his pipe always went out; I used then to light it for him with a spill[1], and this formed my chief amusement. Often, again, he would give us picture-books to look at, whilst he sat silent and motionless in his easy-chair, puffing out such dense clouds of smoke that we were all as it were enveloped in mist. On such evenings mother was very sad; and directly it struck nine she said, "Come, children! off to bed! Come! The 'Sand-man[2]' is come I see." And I always did seem to hear something trampling upstairs with slow heavy steps; that must be the Sand-man. Once in particular I was very much frightened at this dull trampling and knocking; as mother was leading us out of the room I asked her, "O mamma! but who is this nasty Sand-man who always sends us away from papa? What does he look like?" "There is no Sand-man, my dear child," mother answered; "when I say the Sand-man is come, I only mean that you are sleepy and can't keep your eyes open, as if somebody had put sand in them." This answer of mother's did not satisfy me; nay, in my childish mind the thought clearly unfolded itself that mother denied there was a Sand-man only to prevent us being afraid — why, I always heard him come upstairs. Full of curiosity to learn something more about this Sand-man and what he had to do with us children, I at length asked the old woman who acted as my youngest sister's attendant, what sort of a man he was — the Sand-man? "Why, 'thanael, darling, don't you know?" she replied. "Oh! he's a wicked man, who comes to little children when they won't go to bed and throws handfuls of sand in their eyes, so that they jump out of their heads all bloody; and he puts them into a bag

---

exposure is inevitable, and when confronted with cataclysmic failure, he begs his servant Daniel to laugh at him as a means of relieving his repressed agony

[1] Scrap of paper twisted tightly into a cord, used to light fires

[2] In Northern European tradition, the Sandman is the mythic bringer of sleep, and is almost always seen as a benign, Santa Claus-like figure (usually a kind old man with a long white beard). He is used to explain the presence of rheum or eye madder (colloquially, "eye crusties") in the eye lashes and corners of the eye in the morning. These sand-like encrustations were said to be caused by the Sandman sprinkling magic sand over restless children, causing them to fall asleep. Although I have no doubt that 18th centuries Germans would be capable of turning this benign sleep-bringer into a figure of horror and violence (cf. the Grimm Fairy Tales, or the Christmas figure of Krampus), Nathanael's peculiarly terrifying version of the Sandman appears to be of Hoffmann's invention

and takes them to the half-moon as food for his little ones; and they sit there in the nest and have hooked beaks like owls, and they pick naughty little boys' and girls' eyes out with them." After this I formed in my own mind a horrible picture of the cruel Sand-man. When anything came blundering upstairs at night I trembled with fear and dismay; and all that my mother could get out of me were the stammered words "The Sand-man! the Sand-man!" whilst the tears coursed down my cheeks. Then I ran into my bedroom, and the whole night through tormented myself with the terrible apparition of the Sand-man. I was quite old enough to perceive that the old woman's tale about the Sand-man and his little ones' nest in the half-moon couldn't be altogether true; nevertheless the Sand-man continued to be for me a fearful incubus[1], and I was always seized with terror — my blood always ran cold, not only when I heard anybody come up the stairs, but when I heard anybody noisily open my father's room door and go in. Often he stayed away for a long season altogether; then he would come several times in close succession.

This went on for years, without my being able to accustom myself to this fearful apparition, without the image of the horrible Sand-man growing any fainter in my imagination. His intercourse with my father began to occupy my fancy ever more and more; I was restrained from asking my father about him by an unconquerable shyness; but as the years went on the desire waxed stronger and stronger within me to fathom the mystery myself and to see the fabulous Sand-man. He had been the means of disclosing to me the path of the wonderful and the adventurous, which so easily find lodgment in the mind of the child[2]. I liked nothing better than to hear or read horrible stories of goblins, witches, Tom Thumbs[3], and so on; but always at the head of them all stood the Sand-man, whose picture I scribbled in the most extraordinary and repulsive forms with both chalk and coal everywhere, on the tables, and cupboard doors, and walls. When I was ten years old my mother removed me from the nursery into a little chamber off the corridor not far from my father's room. We still had to withdraw hastily whenever, on the stroke of nine, the mysterious unknown was heard in the house. As I lay in my little chamber I could hear him go into father's room, and soon afterwards I fancied there was a fine and peculiar smelling steam spreading itself through the house. As my curiosity waxed stronger, my resolve to make somehow or other the Sand-man's acquaintance took deeper root. Often when my mother had gone past, I slipped quickly out of my room into the corridor, but I could never see anything, for always before I could reach the place where I could get sight of him, the Sand-

---

[1] Demon responsible for nightmares

[2] The Sandman comes to represent the awe and dangers of an overactive imagination – the threat of madness and loss of control

[3] Dwarves

man was well inside the door. At last, unable to resist the impulse any longer, I determined to conceal myself in father's room and there wait for the Sand-man.

One evening I perceived from my father's silence and mother's sadness that the Sand-man would come; accordingly, pleading that I was excessively tired, I left the room before nine o'clock and concealed myself in a hiding-place close beside the door. The street door creaked, and slow, heavy, echoing steps crossed the passage towards the stairs. Mother hurried past me with my brothers and sisters. Softly — softly — I opened father's room door. He sat as usual, silent and motionless, with his back towards it; he did not hear me; and in a moment I was in and behind a curtain drawn before my father's open wardrobe, which stood just inside the room. Nearer and nearer and nearer came the echoing footsteps. There was a strange coughing and shuffling and mumbling outside. My heart beat with expectation and fear. A quick step now close, close beside the door, a noisy rattle of the handle, and the door flies open with a bang. Recovering my courage with an effort, I take a cautious peep out. In the middle of the room in front of my father stands the Sand-man, the bright light of the lamp falling full upon his face. The Sand-man, the terrible Sand-man, is the old advocate[1] Coppelius[2] who often comes to dine with us.

But the most hideous figure could not have awakened greater trepidation in my heart than this Coppelius did. Picture to yourself a large broad-shouldered man, with an immensely big head, a face the colour of yellow-ochre, grey bushy eyebrows, from beneath which two piercing, greenish, cat-like eyes glittered, and a prominent Roman nose hanging over his upper lip. His distorted mouth was often screwed up into a malicious smile; then two dark-red spots appeared on his cheeks, and a strange hissing noise proceeded from between his tightly clenched teeth[3]. He always wore an ash-grey coat of an old-fashioned cut[4], a waistcoat of the same, and nether extremities to match, but black stockings and buckles set with stones on his shoes. His little wig scarcely extended beyond the crown of his head, his hair was curled round high up above his big red ears, and plastered to his temples with cosmetic, and a broad

---

[1] Lawyer

[2] The name is a Latinization of the Italian name Coppola, which means "head" in Sicilian. In one since this may suggest that Coppelius is "all in his head," or it may hint at his relationship to insanity – a condition which overtakes the functions of the head and mind

[3] Between his eyes and his hiss, Coppelius is very snake-like – a quality that aligns him with temptation, evil, and the demonic

[4] At this point in history, it would probably look like something from the mid-1700s: huge cuffs, wide lapels, long skirts, no collar, massive pockets and pocket-flaps

closed hair-bag[1] stood out prominently from his neck, so that you could see the silver buckle that fastened his folded neck-cloth. Altogether he was a most disagreeable and horribly ugly figure; but what we children detested most of all was his big coarse hairy hands; we could never fancy anything that he had once touched. This he had noticed; and so, whenever our good mother quietly placed a piece of cake or sweet fruit on our plates, he delighted to touch it under some pretext or other, until the bright tears stood in our eyes, and from disgust and loathing we lost the enjoyment of the tit-bit that was intended to please us. And he did just the same thing when father gave us a glass of sweet wine on holidays. Then he would quickly pass his hand over it, or even sometimes raise the glass to his blue lips, and he laughed quite sardonically when all we dared do was to express our vexation in stifled sobs. He habitually called us the "little brutes;" and when he was present we might not utter a sound; and we cursed the ugly spiteful man who deliberately and intentionally spoilt all our little pleasures. Mother seemed to dislike this hateful Coppelius as much as we did; for as soon as he appeared her cheerfulness and bright and natural manner were transformed into sad, gloomy seriousness. Father treated him as if he were a being of some higher race, whose ill-manners were to be tolerated, whilst no efforts ought to be spared to keep him in good-humour. He had only to give a slight hint, and his favourite dishes were cooked for him and rare wine uncorked.

As soon as I saw this Coppelius, therefore, the fearful and hideous thought arose in my mind that he, and he alone, must be the Sand-man; but I no longer conceived of the Sand-man as the bugbear[2] in the old nurse's fable, who fetched children's eyes and took them to the half-moon as food for his little ones — no! but as an ugly spectre-like fiend bringing trouble and misery and ruin, both temporal and everlasting, everywhere wherever he appeared.

I was spell-bound on the spot. At the risk of being discovered, and, as I well enough knew, of being severely punished, I remained as I was, with my head thrust through the curtains listening. My father received

[1] A black silk bag at the base of a wig, which went over the pigtail (or queue) and was tightened with a black ribbon

[2] Boogeyman, monster, spook

Coppelius in a ceremonious manner. "Come, to work!" cried the latter, in a hoarse snarling voice, throwing off his coat. Gloomily and silently my father took off his dressing-gown, and both put on long black smock-frocks[1]. Where they took them from I forgot to notice. Father opened the folding-doors of a cupboard in the wall; but I saw that what I had so long taken to be a cupboard was really a dark recess, in which was a little hearth. Coppelius approached it, and a blue flame[2] crackled upwards from it. Round about were all kinds of strange utensils. Good God! as my old father bent down over the fire how different he looked! His gentle and venerable features seemed to be drawn up by some dreadful convulsive pain into an ugly, repulsive Satanic mask. He looked like Coppelius[3]. Coppelius plied the red- hot tongs and drew bright glowing masses out of the thick smoke and began assiduously to hammer them. I fancied that there were men's faces visible round about, but without eyes, having ghastly deep black holes where the eyes should have been. "Eyes here! Eyes here!" cried Coppelius, in a hollow sepulchral voice. My blood ran cold with horror; I screamed and tumbled out of my hiding-place into the floor. Coppelius immediately seized upon me. "You little brute! You little brute!" he bleated, grinding his teeth. Then, snatching me up, he threw me on the hearth, so that the flames began to singe my hair. "Now we've got eyes — eyes — a beautiful pair of children's eyes," he whispered, and, thrusting his hands into the flames he took out some red-hot grains and was about to strew them into my eyes. Then my father clasped his hands and entreated him, saying, "Master, master[4], let my Nathanael keep his eyes — oh! do let him keep them." Coppelius laughed shrilly and replied, "Well then, the boy may keep his eyes and whine and pule his way through the world; but we will now at any rate observe the mechanism of the hand and the foot." And therewith he roughly laid hold upon me, so that my joints cracked, and twisted my hands and my feet, pulling them now this way, and now that, "That's not quite right altogether! It's better as it was! — the old fellow knew what he was about." Thus lisped and hissed Coppelius; but all around me grew black and dark; a sudden convulsive pain shot through all my nerves and bones; I knew nothing more.

I felt a soft warm breath fanning my cheek; I awakened as if out of the sleep of death; my mother was bending over me. "Is the Sand-man

---

[1] Long shirts used by rural laborers like shepherds and farmers to cover their regular clothes – an 18th century version of overalls

[2] Traditionally associated with the supernatural – a sure sign that ghosts, spirits, or demons are present

[3] Coppelius, like Mephistopheles, is not just an evil unto himself – he is also capable of corrupting good men through his influence

[4] Once again resembling Mephistopheles, it becomes clear that Coppelius is Nathanael's father's master – possibly through some Satanic pact

still there?" I stammered. "No, my dear child; he's been gone a long, long time; he'll not hurt you." Thus spoke my mother, as she kissed her recovered darling and pressed him to her heart. But why should I tire you, my dear Lothair? why do I dwell at such length on these details, when there's so much remains to be said? Enough — I was detected in my eavesdropping, and roughly handled by Coppelius. Fear and terror had brought on a violent fever, of which I lay ill several weeks. "Is the Sand-man still there?" these were the first words I uttered on coming to myself again, the first sign of my recovery, of my safety. Thus, you see, I have only to relate to you the most terrible moment of my youth for you to thoroughly understand that it must not be ascribed to the weakness of my eyesight if all that I see is colourless, but to the fact that a mysterious destiny has hung a dark veil of clouds about my life, which I shall perhaps only break through when I die.

Coppelius did not show himself again; it was reported he had left the town.

It was about a year later when, in pursuance of the old unchanged custom, we sat around the round table in the evening. Father was in very good spirits, and was telling us amusing tales about his youthful travels. As it was striking nine we all at once heard the street door creak on its hinges, and slow ponderous steps echoed across the passage and up the stairs. "That is Coppelius," said my mother, turning pale. "Yes, it is Coppelius," replied my father in a faint broken voice. The tears started from my mother's eyes. "But, father, father," she cried, "must it be so?" "This is the last time," he replied; "this is the last time he will come to me, I promise you. Go now, go and take the children. Go, go to bed — good-night."

As for me, I felt as if I were converted into cold, heavy stone; I could not get my breath. As I stood there immovable my mother seized me by the arm. "Come, Nathanael! do come along!" I suffered myself to be led away; I went into my room. "Be a good boy and keep quiet," mother called after me; "get into bed and go to sleep." But, tortured by indescribable fear and uneasiness, I could not close my eyes[1]. That hateful, hideous Coppelius stood before me with his glittering eyes, smiling maliciously down upon me; in vain did I strive to banish the image. Somewhere about midnight there was a terrific crack, as if a cannon were being fired off. The whole house shook; something went rustling and clattering past my door; the house-door was pulled to with a bang. "That is Coppelius," I cried, terror-struck, and leapt out of bed. Then I heard a wild heartrending scream; I rushed into my father's room; the door stood open, and clouds of suffocating smoke came rolling towards me. The

---

[1] The eyes continue to symbolize understanding, reason, and truth – Nathanael is incapable of avoiding the truth of Coppelius' evil nature and his father's dangerous situation

servant-maid shouted, "Oh! my master! my master!" On the floor in front of the smoking hearth lay my father, dead, his face burned black and fearfully distorted, my sisters weeping and moaning around him, and my mother lying near them in a swoon. "Coppelius, you atrocious fiend, you've killed my father," I shouted. My senses left me. Two days later, when my father was placed in his coffin, his features were mild and gentle again as they had been when he was alive. I found great consolation in the thought that his association with the diabolical Coppelius could not have ended in his everlasting ruin[1].

Our neighbours had been awakened by the explosion; the affair got talked about, and came before the magisterial authorities, who wished to cite Coppelius to clear himself. But he had disappeared from the place, leaving no traces behind him.

Now when I tell you, my dear friend, that the weather-glass hawker I spoke of was the villain Coppelius, you will not blame me for seeing impending mischief in his inauspicious reappearance. He was differently dressed; but Coppelius's figure and features are too deeply impressed upon my mind for me to be capable of making a mistake in the matter. Moreover, he has not even changed his name. He proclaims himself here, I learn, to be a Piedmontese[2] mechanician[3], and styles himself Giuseppe Coppola.

I am resolved to enter the lists against him and revenge my father's death, let the consequences be what they may.

Don't say a word to mother about the reappearance of this odious monster. Give my love to my darling Clara; I will write to her when I am in a somewhat calmer frame of mind. Adieu, &c.

CLARA TO NATHANAEL.

You are right, you have not written to me for a very long time, but nevertheless I believe that I still retain a place in your mind and thoughts. It is a proof that you were thinking a good deal about me when you were sending off your last letter to brother Lothair, for instead of directing it to him you directed it to me[4]. With joy I tore open the envelope, and did not perceive the mistake until I read the words, "Oh! my dear, dear Lothair."

---

[1] The peace on his face assures Nathanael that his father is not in hell

[2] Piedmont is a province in northwest Italy, and shares its borders with Switzerland to the north and France to the west. The name means "foot of the mountains," as the foothills of the Alps roll through its northern territory

[3] A scientist and engineer whose field of study is mechanics – a builder and designer of machines

[4] Psychologists might call this an intentional, unconscious act: Nathanael may have either unconsciously or consciously mailed the letter to Clara, intending for her to read it. The more colloquial term for this behavior would be "a cry for help"

Now I know I ought not to have read any more of the letter, but ought to have given it to my brother. But as you have so often in innocent raillery made it a sort of reproach against me that I possessed such a calm, and, for a woman, cool-headed temperament that I should be like the woman we read of — if the house was threatening to tumble down, I should, before hastily fleeing, stop to smooth down a crumple in the window-curtains — I need hardly tell you that the beginning of your letter quite upset me. I could scarcely breathe; there was a bright mist before my eyes. Oh! my darling Nathanael! what could this terrible thing be that had happened? Separation from you — never to see you again, the thought was like a sharp knife in my heart. I read on and on. Your description of that horrid Coppelius made my flesh creep. I now learnt for the first time what a terrible and violent death your good old father died. Brother Lothair, to whom I handed over his property, sought to comfort me, but with little success. That horrid weather-glass hawker Giuseppe Coppola followed me everywhere; and I am almost ashamed to confess it, but he was able to disturb my sound and in general calm sleep with all sorts of wonderful dream-shapes. But soon — the next day — I saw everything in a different light. Oh! do not be angry with me, my best-beloved, if, despite your strange presentiment that Coppelius will do you some mischief, Lothair tells you I am in quite as good spirits, and just the same as ever.

I will frankly confess, it seems to me that all that was fearsome and terrible of which you speak, existed only in your own self[1], and that the real true outer world had but little to do with it. I can quite admit that old Coppelius may have been highly obnoxious to you children, but your real detestation of him arose from the fact that he hated children.

Naturally enough the gruesome Sand-man of the old nurse's story was associated in your childish mind with old Coppelius, who, even though you had not believed in the Sand-man, would have been to you a ghostly bugbear, especially dangerous to children. His mysterious labours along with your father at night-time were, I daresay, nothing more than secret experiments in alchemy[2], with which your mother could not be over well pleased, owing to the large sums of money that most likely were thrown away upon them; and besides, your father, his mind full of the deceptive striving after higher knowledge, may probably have become rather indifferent to his family, as so often happens in the case of such experimentalists. So also it is equally probable that your father brought about his death by his own imprudence, and that Coppelius is not to

---

[1] Many critics interpret Coppelius as Nathanael's Shadow Self or Id: he represents Nathanael's repressed, dark nature and his appearances serve as reminders of Nathanael's hidden evil side – the Hyde to his Jekyll

[2] A pseudoscientific blend of chemistry and the occult which attempted to use early modern science to give mankind access to the supernatural world

blame for it. I must tell you that yesterday I asked our experienced neighbour, the chemist, whether in experiments of this kind an explosion could take place which would have a momentarily fatal effect. He said, "Oh, certainly!" and described to me in his prolix[1] and circumstantial way how it could be occasioned, mentioning at the same time so many strange and funny words that I could not remember them at all. Now I know you will be angry at your Clara, and will say, "Of the Mysterious which often clasps man in its invisible arms there's not a ray can find its way into this cold heart. She sees only the varied surface of the things of the world, and, like the little child, is pleased with the golden glittering fruit; at the kernel of which lies the fatal poison[2]."

Oh! my beloved Nathanael, do you believe then that the intuitive prescience of a dark power working within us to our own ruin cannot exist also in minds which are cheerful, natural, free from care? But please forgive me that I, a simple girl, presume in any way to indicate to you what I really think of such an inward strife. After all, I should not find the proper words, and you would only laugh at me, not because my thoughts were stupid, but because I was so foolish as to attempt to tell them to you.

If there is a dark and hostile power which traitorously fixes a thread in our hearts in order that, laying hold of it and drawing us by means of it along a dangerous road to ruin, which otherwise we should not have trod — if, I say, there is such a power, it must assume within us a form like ourselves, nay, it must be ourselves; for only in that way can we believe in it, and only so understood do we yield to it so far that it is able to accomplish its secret purpose. So long as we have sufficient firmness, fortified by cheerfulness, to always acknowledge foreign hostile influences for what they really are, whilst we quietly pursue the path pointed out to us by both inclination and calling, then this mysterious power perishes in its futile struggles to attain the form which is to be the reflected image of ourselves. It is also certain, Lothair adds, that if we have once voluntarily given ourselves up to this dark physical power, it often reproduces within us the strange forms which the outer world throws in our way, so that thus it is we ourselves who engender within ourselves the spirit which by some remarkable delusion we imagine to speak in that outer form[3]. It is the phantom of our own self whose intimate relationship with, and whose powerful influence upon our soul either plunges us into hell or elevates us

---

[1] Wordy, chatty

[2] Indeed, Clara – symbolizing the rationalism of the Enlightenment – challenges the thesis of Hoffmann's entire corpus of work: that the world of physical reality is merely a mask worn over the supernatural reality – that essence is more important than matter, that our reality serves as a distraction from truth, and that truth can only be experienced by un-anchoring ourselves from the mundane distractions of the material world

[3] She is referring to the defense mechanisms of projection and sublimation

to heaven. Thus you will see, my beloved Nathanael, that I and brother Lothair have well talked over the subject of dark powers and forces; and now, after I have with some difficulty written down the principal results of our discussion, they seem to me to contain many really profound thoughts. Lothair's last words, however, I don't quite understand altogether; I only dimly guess what he means; and yet I cannot help thinking it is all very true, I beg you, dear, strive to forget the ugly advocate Coppelius as well as the weather-glass hawker Giuseppe Coppola. Try and convince yourself that these foreign influences can have no power over you, that it is only the belief in their hostile power which can in reality make them dangerous to you. If every line of your letter did not betray the violent excitement of your mind, and if I did not sympathise with your condition from the bottom of my heart, I could in truth jest about the advocate Sand-man and weather-glass hawker Coppelius. Pluck up your spirits! Be cheerful! I have resolved to appear to you as your guardian-angel if that ugly man Coppola should dare take it into his head to bother you in your dreams, and drive him away with a good hearty laugh. I'm not afraid of him and his nasty hands, not the least little bit; I won't let him either as advocate spoil any dainty tit-bit I've taken, or as Sand-man rob me of my eyes[1].

My Darling, Darling Nathanael,
Eternally Your, &C. &C.

NATHANAEL TO LOTHAIR.

I am very sorry that Clara opened and read my last letter to you; of course the mistake is to be attributed to my own absence of mind[2]. She has written me a very deep philosophical letter, proving conclusively that Coppelius and Coppola only exist in my own mind and are phantoms of my own self, which will at once be dissipated, as soon as I look upon them in that light. In very truth one can hardly believe that the mind which so often sparkles in those bright, beautifully smiling, childlike eyes of hers like a sweet lovely dream could draw such subtle and scholastic distinctions. She also mentions your name. You have been talking about me. I suppose you have been giving her lectures, since she sifts and refines everything so acutely. But enough of this! I must now tell you it is

[1] A tremendously important observation: Clara speaks from a psychological attitude called the "Inner Locus of Control" which views the world as malleable to the efforts of the ego – in other words, you see yourself as capable of controlling your own destiny. Nathanael, on the other hand, has an "Outer Locus of Control," viewing himself as the helpless victim of a conspiratorial universe. Clara urges him to take charge of his life and not let the idea of the Sandman rob him of his reason (eyes) or of his enjoyment of life (tit-bits)

[2] Again, this could be interpreted as an unconscious choice – a cry for help – which raises the old syllogism: "there are no mistakes"

most certain that the weather-glass hawker Giuseppe Coppola is not the advocate Coppelius. I am attending the lectures of our recently appointed Professor of Physics, who, like the distinguished naturalist, is called Spalanzani[1], and is of Italian origin. He has known Coppola for many years; and it is also easy to tell from his accent that he really is a Piedmontese. Coppelius was a German, though no honest German, I fancy. Nevertheless I am not quite satisfied. You and Clara will perhaps take me for a gloomy dreamer, but nohow can I get rid of the impression which Coppelius's cursed face made upon me. I am glad to learn from Spalanzani that he has left the town. This Professor Spalanzani is a very queer fish. He is a little fat man, with prominent cheek-bones, thin nose, projecting lips, and small piercing eyes. You cannot get a better picture of him than by turning over one of the Berlin pocket-almanacs[2] and looking at Cagliostro's portrait engraved by Chodowiecki[3]; Spalanzani looks just like him.

Once lately, as I went up the steps to his house, I perceived that beside the curtain which generally covered a glass door there was a small chink. What it was that excited my curiosity I cannot explain; but I looked through. In the room I saw a female, tall, very slender, but of perfect proportions, and splendidly dressed, sitting at a little table, on which she had placed both her arms, her hands being folded together. She sat opposite the door, so that I could easily see her angelically beautiful face. She did not appear to notice me, and there was moreover a strangely fixed look about her eyes, I might almost say they appeared as if they had no power of vision[4]; I thought she was sleeping with her eyes open. I felt quite uncomfortable, and so I slipped away quietly into the Professor's lecture-room, which was close at hand. Afterwards I learnt that the figure which I had seen was Spalanzani's daughter, Olimpia[5], whom he keeps locked in a most wicked and unaccountable way, and no man is ever allowed to come near her. Perhaps, however, there is after all,

---

[1] Lazaro Spalanzani was an 18th century anatomist famous for his global travels in pursuit of scientific knowledge. He is best remembered today for inventing the process of artificial insemination in livestock

[2] Also called "Almanacs of the Muses" – literary periodicals popularized by the German Romantics and filled with works by poets, essayists, and philosopers

[3] Count Cagliostro was a famous impersonator whose adventures pretending to be a noble made him one of the great anti-heroes of the 18th century, along with Casanova, Count St. Germain, and the Fox Sisters. Chodowiecki was a Polish engraver who was very popular in Prussian society

[4] The painted eyes of an automaton have no power to perceive, analyze, or see the truth: she is as blind as if she had had her eyes plucked by the Sandman

[5] A name which recalls Mount Olympus and suggests that she is a gift of the gods

something peculiar about her; perhaps she's an idiot[1] or something of that sort. But why am I telling you all this? I could have told you it all better and more in detail when I see you. For in a fortnight I shall be amongst you. I must see my dear sweet angel, my Clara, again. Then the little bit of ill-temper, which, I must confess, took possession of me after her fearfully sensible letter, will be blown away. And that is the reason why I am not writing to her as well today. With all best wishes, &c.

ↂ

Nothing more strange and extraordinary can be imagined, gracious reader, than what happened to my poor friend, the young student Nathanael, and which I have undertaken to relate to you. Have you ever lived to experience anything that completely took possession of your heart and mind and thoughts to the utter exclusion of everything else? All was seething and boiling within you; your blood, heated to fever pitch, leapt through your veins and inflamed your cheeks. Your gaze was so peculiar, as if seeking to grasp in empty space forms not seen of any other eye, and all your words ended in sighs betokening some mystery. Then your friends asked you, "What is the matter with you, my dear friend? What do you see?" And, wishing to describe the inner pictures in all their vivid colours, with their lights and their shades, you in vain struggled to find words with which to express yourself. But you felt as if you must gather up all the events that had happened, wonderful, splendid, terrible, jocose, and awful, in the very first word, so that the whole might be revealed by a single electric discharge, so to speak. Yet every word and all that partook of the nature of communication by intelligible sounds seemed to be colourless, cold, and dead. Then you try and try again, and stutter and stammer, whilst your friends' prosy questions strike like icy winds upon your heart's hot fire until they extinguish it. But if, like a bold painter, you had first sketched in a few audacious strokes the outline of the picture you had in your soul, you would then easily have been able to deepen and intensify the colours one after the other, until the varied throng of living figures carried your friends away, and they, like you, saw themselves in the midst of the scene that had proceeded out of your own soul.

Strictly speaking, indulgent reader, I must indeed confess to you, nobody has asked me for the history of young Nathanael; but you are very well aware that I belong to that remarkable class of authors who, when they are bearing anything about in their minds in the manner I have just described, feel as if everybody who comes near them, and also the whole world to boot, were asking, "Oh! what is it? Oh! do tell us, my good sir?" Hence I was most powerfully impelled to narrate to you Nathanael's ominous life. My soul was full of the elements of wonder and

---

[1] Person with an intellectual disability

extraordinary peculiarity in it; but, for this very reason, and because it was necessary in the very beginning to dispose you, indulgent reader, to bear with what is fantastic — and that is not a little thing — I racked my brain to find a way of commencing the story in a significant and original manner, calculated to arrest your attention. To begin with "Once upon a time," the best beginning for a story, seemed to me too tame; with "In the small country town S—— lived," rather better, at any rate allowing plenty of room to work up to the climax; or to plunge at once in medias res[1], "'Go to the devil!' cried the student Nathanael, his eyes blazing wildly with rage and fear, when the weather-glass hawker Giuseppe Coppola"— well, that is what I really had written, when I thought I detected something of the ridiculous in Nathanael's wild glance; and the history is anything but laughable. I could not find any words which seemed fitted to reflect in even the feeblest degree the brightness of the colours of my mental vision. I determined not to begin at all. So I pray you, gracious reader, accept the three letters which my friend Lothair has been so kind as to communicate to me as the outline of the picture, into which I will endeavour to introduce more and more colour as I proceed with my narrative. Perhaps, like a good portrait-painter, I may succeed in depicting more than one figure in such wise that you will recognise it as a good likeness without being acquainted with the original, and feel as if you had very often seen the original with your own bodily eyes. Perhaps, too, you will then believe that nothing is more wonderful, nothing more fantastic than real life[2], and that all that a writer can do is to present it as a dark reflection from a dim cut mirror.

In order to make the very commencement more intelligible, it is necessary to add to the letters that, soon after the death of Nathanael's father, Clara and Lothair, the children of a distant relative, who had likewise died, leaving them orphans, were taken by Nathanael's mother into her own house. Clara and Nathanael conceived a warm affection for each other, against which not the slightest objection in the world could be urged. When therefore Nathanael left home to prosecute his studies in G——[3] they were betrothed. It is from G—— that his last letter is written,

---

[1] A literary term meaning "in the middle of the action," referring to a story which starts in the middle before flashing back in time to the beginning

[2] One of Hoffmann's artistic philosophies: he saw no need to tell about fairy tales set in "a land far, far away" or "once upon a time" because he saw the fantastical in the ordinary and recognized the bizarre and macabre in the bourgeois and mundane. His settings are relatable, but his plots probe the psychological in visionary ways that imply an expansive interpretation of the everyday – suggesting that profound, metaphysical currents are churning just beneath our feet, unnoticed by those who have become too distracted by the minutiae of the material world

[3] Probably Göttingen – a university town in northwest Germany

where he is attending the lectures of Spalanzani, the distinguished Professor of Physics.

I might now proceed comfortably with my narration, did not at this moment Clara's image rise up so vividly before my eyes that I cannot turn them away from it, just as I never could when she looked upon me and smiled so sweetly. Nowhere would she have passed for beautiful; that was the unanimous opinion of all who professed to have any technical knowledge of beauty. But whilst architects praised the pure proportions of her figure and form, painters averred that her neck, shoulders, and bosom were almost too chastely modelled, and yet, on the other hand, one and all were in love with her glorious Magdalene hair[1], and talked a good deal of nonsense about Battoni-like[2] colouring. One of them, a veritable romanticist, strangely enough likened her eyes to a lake by Ruisdael[3], in which is reflected the pure azure of the cloudless sky, the beauty of woods and flowers, and all the bright and varied life of a living landscape. Poets and musicians went still further and said, "What's all this talk about seas and reflections? How can we look upon the girl without feeling that wonderful heavenly songs and melodies beam upon us from her eyes, penetrating deep down into our hearts, till all becomes awake and throbbing with emotion? And if we cannot sing anything at all passable then, why, we are not worth much; and this we can also plainly read in the rare smile which flits around her lips when we have the hardihood to squeak out something in her presence which we pretend to call singing, in spite of the fact that it is nothing more than a few single notes confusedly linked together." And it really was so. Clara had the powerful fancy of a bright, innocent, unaffected child, a woman's deep and sympathetic heart, and an understanding clear, sharp, and discriminating. Dreamers and visionaries had but a bad time of it with her; for without saying very much — she was not by nature of a talkative disposition — she plainly asked, by her calm steady look, and rare ironical smile, "How can you imagine, my dear friends, that I can take these fleeting shadowy images for true living and breathing forms?" For this reason many found fault with her as being cold, prosaic, and devoid of

---

[1] In Western art, Mary Magdalene – one of Jesus' followers – is traditionally depicted with copious red hair (she is traditionally said to have cleaned Jesus' feet with perfume and dried it off with her hair)

[2] An 18th century Italian portrait painter whose female subjects often have what we might call summer complexions: rosy, pale skin, golden-brown hair, and enticing red lips

[3] Jakob Ruisdael was a Dutch landscape painter whose lakes could be called a deep, greenish-blue. One romantic commentator noted that "his favourite subjects were remote farms, lonely stagnant water, deep-shaded woods with marshy paths, the sea-coast — subjects of a dark melancholy kind. His sea-pieces are greatly admired"

feeling; others, however, who had reached a clearer and deeper conception of life, were extremely fond of the intelligent, childlike, large-hearted girl But none had such an affection for her as Nathanael, who was a zealous and cheerful cultivator of the fields of science and art. Clara clung to her lover with all her heart; the first clouds she encountered in life were when he had to separate from her. With what delight did she fly into his arms when, as he had promised in his last letter to Lothair, he really came back to his native town and entered his mother's room! And as Nathanael had foreseen, the moment he saw Clara again he no longer thought about either the advocate Coppelius or her sensible letter; his ill-humour had quite disappeared.

Nevertheless Nathanael was right when he told his friend Lothair that the repulsive vendor of weather-glasses, Coppola, had exercised a fatal and disturbing influence upon his life. It was quite patent to all; for even during the first few days he showed that he was completely and entirely changed. He gave himself up to gloomy reveries, and moreover acted so strangely; they had never observed anything at all like it in him before. Everything, even his own life, was to him but dreams and presentiments. His constant theme was that every man who delusively imagined himself to be free was merely the plaything of the cruel sport of mysterious powers[1], and it was vain for man to resist them; he must humbly submit to whatever destiny had decreed for him. He went so far as to maintain that it was foolish to believe that a man could do anything in art or science of his own accord; for the inspiration in which alone any true artistic work could be done did not proceed from the spirit within outwards, but was the result of the operation directed inwards of some Higher Principle existing without and beyond ourselves.

This mystic extravagance was in the highest degree repugnant to Clara's clear intelligent mind, but it seemed vain to enter upon any attempt at refutation. Yet when Nathanael went on to prove that Coppelius was the Evil Principle which had entered into him and taken possession of him at the time he was listening behind the curtain, and that this hateful demon would in some terrible way ruin their happiness, then Clara grew grave and said, "Yes, Nathanael. You are right; Coppelius is an Evil Principle; he can do dreadful things, as bad as could a Satanic power which should assume a living physical form, but only — only if you do not banish him from your mind and thoughts. So long as you believe

---

[1] Nathanael, unsurprisingly, is a proponent of predestination. While the story does prove his point in the end, we are forced to wonder if his fate was the result of a predetermined destiny, or if it was the result of his own self-fulfilling prophecy

in him he exists and is at work; your belief in him is his only power[1]." Whereupon Nathanael, quite angry because Clara would only grant the existence of the demon in his own mind, began to dilate at large upon the whole mystic doctrine of devils and awful powers, but Clara abruptly broke off the theme by making, to Nathanael's very great disgust, some quite commonplace remark. Such deep mysteries are sealed books to cold, unsusceptible characters, he thought, without being clearly conscious to himself that he counted Clara amongst these inferior natures, and accordingly he did not remit his efforts to initiate her into these mysteries. In the morning, when she was helping to prepare breakfast, he would take his stand beside her, and read all sorts of mystic books to her, until she begged him —"But, my dear Nathanael, I shall have to scold you as the Evil Principle which exercises a fatal influence upon my coffee. For if I do as you wish, and let things go their own way, and look into your eyes whilst you read, the coffee will all boil over into the fire, and you will none of you get any breakfast[2]." Then Nathanael hastily banged the book to and ran away in great displeasure to his own room.

Formerly he had possessed a peculiar talent for writing pleasing, sparkling tales, which Clara took the greatest delight in listening to; but now his productions were gloomy, unintelligible, and wanting in form[3], so that, although Clara out of forbearance towards him did not say so, he nevertheless felt how very little interest she took in them. There was nothing that Clara disliked so much as what was tedious; at such times her intellectual sleepiness was not to be overcome; it was betrayed both in her glances and in her words. Nathanael's effusions were, in truth, exceedingly tedious. His ill-humour at Clara's cold prosaic temperament continued to increase; Clara could not conceal her distaste of his dark, gloomy, wearying mysticism; and thus both began to be more and more estranged from each other without exactly being aware of it themselves. The image of the ugly Coppelius had, as Nathanael was obliged to confess to himself, faded considerably in his fancy, and it often cost him great

---

[1] With typical rationality, Clara bridges the gap between predestination and free will, making a compromise that acknowledges the power of external evil – but only if you empower it with submission

[2] Her analogy holds water: she could claim helplessness under the spell of Nathanael's reading and surrender the coffee to ruin, or she could tell him "enough," stop listening to his words, get the coffee, and return of her own free will

[3] Likewise, Hoffmann began his career with wide-eyed fantasies and satires like "Ritter Gluck" and "The Golden Pot," but by 1816 – after the Napoleonic Wars and a series of personal and professional catastrophes – he had begun penning tales like "The Lost Reflection," "Nutcracker," and "Automatons" which are particularly bizarre and swirl with existential vertigo

pains to present him in vivid colours in his literary efforts, in which he played the part of the ghoul of Destiny. At length it entered into his head to make his dismal presentiment that Coppelius would ruin his happiness the subject of a poem. He made himself and Clara, united by true love, the central figures, but represented a black hand as being from time to time thrust into their life and plucking out a joy[1] that had blossomed for them. At length, as they were standing at the altar, the terrible Coppelius appeared and touched Clara's lovely eyes, which leapt into Nathanael's own bosom, burning and hissing[2] like bloody sparks. Then Coppelius laid hold upon him, and hurled him into a blazing circle of fire, which spun round with the speed of a whirlwind, and, storming and blustering, dashed away with him. The fearful noise it made was like a furious hurricane lashing the foaming sea-waves until they rise up like black, white-headed giants in the midst of the raging struggle. But through the midst of the savage fury of the tempest he heard Clara's voice calling, "Can you not see me, dear? Coppelius has deceived you; they were not my eyes which burned so in your bosom; they were fiery drops of your own heart's blood. Look at me, I have got my own eyes still." Nathanael thought, "Yes, that is Clara, and I am hers for ever." Then this thought laid a powerful grasp upon the fiery circle so that it stood still, and the riotous turmoil died away rumbling down a dark abyss. Nathanael looked into Clara's eyes; but it was death whose gaze rested so kindly upon him.

Whilst Nathanael was writing this work he was very quiet and sober-minded; he filed and polished every line, and as he had chosen to submit himself to the limitations of metre, he did not rest until all was pure and musical. When, however, he had at length finished it and read it aloud to himself he was seized with horror and awful dread, and he screamed, "Whose hideous voice is this?" But he soon came to see in it again nothing beyond a very successful poem, and he confidently believed it would enkindle Clara's cold temperament, though to what end she should be thus aroused was not quite clear to his own mind, nor yet what would be the real purpose served by tormenting her with these dreadful pictures, which prophesied a terrible and ruinous end to her affection.

Nathanael and Clara sat in his mother's little garden. Clara was bright and cheerful, since for three entire days her lover, who had been busy writing his poem, had not teased her with his dreams or forebodings. Nathanael, too, spoke in a gay and vivacious way of things of merry import, as he formerly used to do, so that Clara said, "Ah! now I have you again. We have driven away that ugly Coppelius, you see." Then it suddenly occurred to him that he had got the poem in his pocket which he wished to read to her. He at once took out the manuscript and began

---

[1] Just as the Sandman plucks out eyes...

[2] Recalling the image of Coppelius drawing burning hot metal eyes from the fireplace

to read. Clara, anticipating something tedious as usual, prepared to submit to the infliction, and calmly resumed her knitting. But as the sombre clouds rose up darker and darker she let her knitting fall on her lap and sat with her eyes fixed in a set stare upon Nathanael's face[1]. He was quite carried away by his own work, the fire of enthusiasm coloured his cheeks a deep red, and tears started from his eyes. At length he concluded, groaning and showing great lassitude; grasping Clara's hand, he sighed as if he were being utterly melted in inconsolable grief, "Oh! Clara! Clara!" She drew him softly to her heart and said in a low but very grave and impressive tone, "Nathanael, my darling Nathanael, throw that foolish, senseless, stupid thing into the fire." Then Nathanael leapt indignantly to his feet, crying, as he pushed Clara from him, "You damned lifeless automaton[2]!" and rushed away. Clara was cut to the heart, and wept bitterly. "Oh! he has never loved me, for he does not understand me," she sobbed.

Lothair entered the arbour. Clara was obliged to tell him all that had taken place. He was passionately fond of his sister; and every word of her complaint fell like a spark upon his heart, so that the displeasure which he had long entertained against his dreamy friend Nathanael was kindled into furious anger. He hastened to find Nathanael, and upbraided him in harsh words for his irrational behaviour towards his beloved sister. The fiery Nathanael answered him in the same style. "A fantastic, crack-brained fool," was retaliated with, "A miserable, common, everyday sort of fellow." A meeting[3] was the inevitable consequence. They agreed to meet on the following morning behind the garden-wall, and fight, according to the custom of the students of the place, with sharp rapiers[4]. They went about silent and gloomy; Clara had both heard and seen the violent quarrel, and also observed the fencing-master bring the rapiers in the dusk of the evening. She had a presentiment of what was to happen. They both appeared at the appointed place wrapped up in the same gloomy silence, and threw off their coats. Their eyes flaming with the bloodthirsty light of pugnacity, they were about to begin their contest when Clara burst through the garden door[5]. Sobbing, she screamed, "You savage, terrible men! Cut me down before you attack each other; for how can I

---

[1] Her eyes – which detect truth and peg reality – are fixed on his face (the mode of expression), putting his descent into madness under the scrutiny of her observation

[2] As we shall see, Clara's cold logic and rationality hardly make her a robot – robots don't disagree or challenge others; they are programed to do only what we desire

[3] Euphemism for a duel

[4] Long swords with pointed blades

[5] Metaphorically, Reason bursts in on the scene, bringing clear thought to the two, overly emotional men

live when my lover has slain my brother, or my brother slain my lover?" Lothair let his weapon fall and gazed silently upon the ground, whilst Nathanael's heart was rent with sorrow, and all the affection which he had felt for his lovely Clara in the happiest days of her golden youth was awakened within him. His murderous weapon, too, fell from his hand; he threw himself at Clara's feet. "Oh! can you ever forgive me, my only, my dearly loved Clara? Can you, my dear brother Lothair, also forgive me?" Lothair was touched by his friend's great distress; the three young people embraced each other amidst endless tears, and swore never again to break their bond of love and fidelity.

Nathanael felt as if a heavy burden that had been weighing him down to the earth was now rolled from off him, nay, as if by offering resistance to the dark power which had possessed him, he had rescued his own self from the ruin which had threatened him. Three happy days he now spent amidst the loved ones, and then returned to G—— where he had still a year to stay before settling down in his native town for life.

Everything having reference to Coppelius had been concealed from the mother, for they knew she could not think of him without horror, since she as well as Nathanael believed him to be guilty of causing her husband's death.

When Nathanael came to the house where he lived he was greatly astonished to find it burnt down to the ground, so that nothing but the bare outer walls were left standing amidst a heap of ruins. Although the fire had broken out in the laboratory of the chemist who lived on the ground-floor, and had therefore spread upwards, some of Nathanael's bold, active friends had succeeded in time in forcing a way into his room in the upper storey and saving his books and manuscripts and instruments. They had carried them all uninjured into another house, where they engaged a room for him; this he now at once took possession of. That he lived opposite Professor Spalanzani did not strike him particularly, nor did it occur to him as anything more singular that he could, as he observed, by looking out of his window, see straight into the room where Olimpia often sat alone. Her figure he could plainly distinguish, although her features were uncertain and confused. It did at length occur to him, however, that she remained for hours together in the same position in which he had first discovered her through the glass door, sitting at a little table without any occupation whatever, and it was evident that she was constantly gazing across in his direction. He could not but confess to himself that he had never seen a finer figure. However, with Clara mistress of his heart, he remained perfectly unaffected by Olimpia's stiffness and apathy; and it was only occasionally that he sent a fugitive glance over his compendium across to her — that was all.

He was writing to Clara; a light tap came at the door. At his summons to "Come in," Coppola's repulsive face appeared peeping in. Nathanael felt his heart beat with trepidation; but, recollecting what

Spalanzani had told him about his fellow-countryman Coppola, and what he had himself so faithfully promised his beloved in respect to the Sandman Coppelius, he was ashamed at himself for this childish fear of spectres. Accordingly, he controlled himself with an effort, and said, as quietly and as calmly as he possibly could, "I don't want to buy any weather-glasses, my good friend; you had better go elsewhere." Then Coppola came right into the room, and said in a hoarse voice, screwing up his wide mouth into a hideous smile, whilst his little eyes flashed keenly from beneath his long grey eyelashes, "What! Nee weather-gless? Nee weather-gless? 've got foine oyes as well — foine oyes[1]!" Affrighted, Nathanael cried, "You stupid man, how can you have eyes? — eyes — eyes?" But Coppola, laying aside his weather-glasses, thrust his hands into his big coat-pockets and brought out several spy-glasses and spectacles, and put them on the table. "Theer! Theer! Spect'cles! Spect'cles to put 'n nose! Them's my oyes — foine oyes." And he continued to produce more and more spectacles from his pockets until the table began to gleam and flash all over. Thousands of eyes were looking and blinking convulsively, and staring up at Nathanael; he could not avert his gaze from the table. Coppola went on heaping up his spectacles, whilst wilder and ever wilder burning flashes crossed through and through each other and darted their blood-red rays into Nathanael's breast. Quite overcome, and frantic with terror, he shouted, "Stop! stop! you terrible man!" and he seized Coppola by the arm, which he had again thrust into his pocket in order to bring out still more spectacles, although the whole table was covered all over with them. With a harsh disagreeable laugh Coppola gently freed himself; and with the words "So! went none! Well, here foine gless!" he swept all his spectacles together, and put them back into his coat-pockets, whilst from a breast-pocket he produced a great number of larger and smaller perspectives. As soon as the spectacles were gone Nathanael recovered his equanimity again; and, bending his thoughts upon Clara, he clearly discerned that the gruesome incubus had proceeded only from himself, as also that Coppola was a right honest mechanician and optician, and far from being Coppelius's dreaded double and ghost. And then, besides, none of the glasses which Coppola now placed on the table had anything at all singular about them, at least nothing so weird as the spectacles; so, in order to square accounts with himself, Nathanael now really determined to buy something of the man. He took up a small, very beautifully cut pocket perspective[2], and by way of proving it[3] looked through the window. Never before in his life had he had a glass in his hands that brought out things so clearly and sharply and distinctly.

---

[1] "Fine eyes." In the original German, Coppola is meant to have an obnoxious Italian brogue

[2] Small telescope, usually some five or six inches long when extended

[3] Testing its quality

Involuntarily he directed the glass upon Spalanzani's room; Olimpia sat at the little table as usual, her arms laid upon it and her hands folded. Now he saw for the first time the regular and exquisite beauty of her features. The eyes, however, seemed to him to have a singular look of fixity and lifelesness. But as he continued to look closer and more carefully through the glass he fancied a light like humid moonbeams[1] came into them. It seemed as if their power of vision was now being enkindled; their glances shone with ever-increasing vivacity. Nathanael remained standing at the window as if glued to the spot by a wizard's spell, his gaze rivetted unchangeably upon the divinely beautiful Olimpia. A coughing and shuffling of the feet awakened him out of his enchaining dream, as it were. Coppola stood behind him, "Tre zechini" (three ducats[2]). Nathanael had completely forgotten the optician; he hastily paid the sum demanded. "Ain't 't? Foine gless? foine gless?" asked Coppola in his harsh unpleasant voice, smiling sardonically. "Yes, yes, yes," rejoined Nathanael impatiently; "adieu, my good friend." But Coppola did not leave the room without casting many peculiar side-glances upon Nathanael; and the young student heard him laughing loudly on the stairs. "Ah well!" thought he, "he's laughing at me because I've paid him too much for this little perspective — because I've given him too much money — that's it." As he softly murmured these words he fancied he detected a gasping sigh as of a dying man stealing awfully through the room; his heart stopped beating with fear. But to be sure he had heaved a deep sigh himself; it was quite plain. "Clara is quite right," said he to himself, "in holding me to be an incurable ghost-seer; and yet it's very ridiculous — ay, more than ridiculous, that the stupid thought of having paid Coppola too much for his glass should cause me this strange anxiety; I can't see any reason for it."

Now he sat down to finish his letter to Clara; but a glance through the window showed him Olimpia still in her former posture. Urged by an irresistible impulse he jumped up and seized Coppola's perspective; nor could he tear himself away from the fascinating Olimpia until his friend and brother Siegmund called for him to go to Professor Spalanzani's lecture. The curtains before the door of the all-important room were closely drawn, so that he could not see Olimpia. Nor could he even see her from his own room during the two following days, notwithstanding that he scarcely ever left his window, and maintained a scarce interrupted watch through Coppola's perspective upon her room. On the third day curtains even were drawn across the window. Plunged into the depths of

---

[1] To 19th century readers this would immediately signal something unhealthy and insidious: humidity was associated with fevers, miasma, and sickness, and the moon was associated with strong emotion and lunacy

[2] A gold coin common in many European countries. Around the time of this story, one ducat was worth about $30

despair — goaded by longing and ardent desire, he hurried outside the walls of the town. Olimpia's image hovered about his path in the air and stepped forth out of the bushes, and peeped up at him with large and lustrous eyes from the bright surface of the brook. Clara's image was completely faded from his mind; he had no thoughts except for Olimpia. He uttered his love-plaints aloud and in a lachrymose[1] tone, "Oh! my glorious, noble star of love, have you only risen to vanish again, and leave me in the darkness and hopelessness of night?"

Returning home, he became aware that there was a good deal of noisy bustle going on in Spalanzani's house. All the doors stood wide open; men were taking in all kinds of gear and furniture; the windows of the first floor were all lifted off their hinges; busy maid-servants with immense hair-brooms were driving backwards and forwards dusting and sweeping, whilst within could be heard the knocking and hammering of carpenters and upholsterers. Utterly astonished, Nathanael stood still in the street; then Siegmund joined him, laughing, and said, "Well, what do you say to our old Spalanzani?" Nathanael assured him that he could not say anything, since he knew not what it all meant; to his great astonishment, he could hear, however, that they were turning the quiet gloomy house almost inside out with their dusting and cleaning and making of alterations. Then he learned from Siegmund that Spalanzani intended giving a great concert and ball on the following day, and that half the university was invited. It was generally reported that Spalanzani was going to let his daughter Olimpia, whom he had so long so jealously guarded from every eye, make her first appearance.

Nathanael received an invitation. At the appointed hour, when the carriages were rolling up and the lights were gleaming brightly in the decorated halls, he went across to the Professor's, his heart beating high with expectation. The company was both numerous and brilliant. Olimpia was richly and tastefully dressed. One could not but admire her figure and the regular beauty of her features. The striking inward curve of her back, as well as the wasp-like smallness of her waist, appeared to be the result of too-tight lacing. There was something stiff and measured in her gait and bearing that made an unfavourable impression[2] upon many; it was ascribed to the constraint imposed upon her by the company. The concert began. Olimpia played on the piano with great skill; and sang as

---

[1] Sorrowful

[2] As Freud would later theorize, this is the effect of the Uncanny Valley: watching something cartoonish go through a series of mechanical motions can be cute (like a baby doll or wind-up toy), but the closer the imitation comes to resembling the human figure, the more terrifying it becomes, replacing cuteness with creepiness

skilfully an aria di bravura[1], in a voice which was, if anything, almost too sharp[2], but clear as glass bells. Nathanael was transported with delight; he stood in the background farthest from her, and owing to the blinding lights could not quite distinguish her features. So, without being observed, he took Coppola's glass out of his pocket, and directed it upon the beautiful Olimpia. Oh! then he perceived how her yearning eyes sought him, how every note only reached its full purity in the loving glance which penetrated to and inflamed his heart. Her artificial roulades[3] seemed to him to be the exultant cry towards heaven of the soul refined by love; and when at last, after the cadenza[4], the long trill rang shrilly and loudly through the hall, he felt as if he were suddenly grasped by burning arms and could no longer control himself — he could not help shouting aloud in his mingled pain and delight, "Olimpia!" All eyes were turned upon him; many people laughed. The face of the cathedral organist wore a still more gloomy look than it had done before, but all he said was, "Very well!"

The concert came to an end, and the ball began. Oh! to dance with her — with her — that was now the aim of all Nathanael's wishes, of all his desires. But how should he have courage to request her, the queen of the ball, to grant him the honour of a dance? And yet he couldn't tell how it came about, just as the dance began, he found himself standing close beside her, nobody having as yet asked her to be his partner; so, with some difficulty stammering out a few words, he grasped her hand. It was cold as ice; he shook with an awful, frosty shiver. But, fixing his eyes upon her face, he saw that her glance was beaming upon him with love and longing, and at the same moment he thought that the pulse began to beat in her cold hand, and the warm life-blood to course through her veins. And passion burned more intensely in his own heart also; he threw his arm round her beautiful waist and whirled her round the hall. He had always thought that he kept good and accurate time in dancing, but from the perfectly rhythmical evenness with which Olimpia danced, and which frequently put him quite out, he perceived how very faulty his own time really was. Notwithstanding, he would not dance with any other lady; and

---

[1] A difficult song meant to show off the singer's flexibility and expressiveness. Examples would include Mozart's "Der Holle Rache..." from "The Magic Flute," and "Let the Bright Seraphim" from Handel's "Samson"

[2] People tend to sing flatly (the opposite of sharp), so Olimpia's sharpness may point to too much perfection

[3] Extended embellishments of a single note. This is famously (or infamously) done by singers of the American National Anthem (throughout the song, but most notably on the following bolded words: "**Oh** say can you see..." "**Gave** proof through the night..." "O'er the land of the **free**...")

[4] A difficult passage near the end of a song used to demonstrate the singer's skill

everybody else who approached Olimpia to call upon her for a dance, he would have liked to kill on the spot. This, however, only happened twice; to his astonishment Olimpia remained after this without a partner, and he failed not on each occasion to take her out again. If Nathanael had been able to see anything else except the beautiful Olimpia, there would inevitably have been a good deal of unpleasant quarrelling and strife; for it was evident that Olimpia was the object of the smothered laughter only with difficulty suppressed, which was heard in various corners amongst the young people; and they followed her with very curious looks, but nobody knew for what reason. Nathanael, excited by dancing and the plentiful supply of wine he had consumed, had laid aside the shyness which at other times characterised him. He sat beside Olimpia, her hand in his own, and declared his love enthusiastically and passionately in words which neither of them understood, neither he nor Olimpia. And yet she perhaps did, for she sat with her eyes fixed unchangeably upon his, sighing repeatedly, "Ach! Ach! Ach[1]!" Upon this Nathanael would answer, "Oh, you glorious heavenly lady! You ray from the promised paradise of love! Oh! what a profound soul you have! my whole being is mirrored in it!" and a good deal more in the same strain. But Olimpia only continued to sigh "Ach! Ach!" again and again.

Professor Spalanzani passed by the two happy lovers once or twice, and smiled with a look of peculiar satisfaction. All at once it seemed to Nathanael, albeit he was far away in a different world, as if it were growing perceptibly darker down below at Professor Spalanzani's. He looked about him, and to his very great alarm became aware that there were only two lights left burning in the hall, and they were on the point of going out. The music and dancing had long ago ceased. "We must part — part!" he cried, wildly and despairingly; he kissed Olimpia's hand; he bent down to her mouth, but ice-cold lips met his burning ones. As he touched her cold hand, he felt his heart thrilled with awe; the legend of "The Dead Bride[2]" shot suddenly through his mind. But Olimpia had drawn him

---

[1] A poor translation: in German "Ach" is the word for "Oh." Most modern translations either put this as "Oh! Oh!" or "Ah! Ah!" Either way, the erotic significance of this orgasmic utterance comes through: Olimipia is essentially a sex toy – an object designed to express only approval and delight, a Stepford Wife

[2] Goethe's macabre ghost story "The Bride of Corinth" (based, in turn, on a Greek legend) tells of a visitor sleeping in the guest room of a respectable Corinthian family. In the middle of the night he finds a beautiful woman seeking her way into his bed; enticed, he has sex with her but learns in the morning that she was the ghost of his hosts' daughter who had died during her engagement to another man. The guest has been doomed to die a withering death by their intercourse, and the daughter's corpse is burned to prevent her

closer to her, and the kiss appeared to warm her lips into vitality[1]. Professor Spalanzani strode slowly through the empty apartment, his footsteps giving a hollow echo; and his figure had, as the flickering shadows played about him, a ghostly, awful appearance. "Do you love me? Do you love me, Olimpia? Only one little word — Do you love me?" whispered Nathanael, but she only sighed, "Ach! Ach!" as she rose to her feet. "Yes, you are my lovely, glorious star of love," said Nathanael, "and will shine for ever, purifying and ennobling my heart" "Ach! Ach!" replied Olimpia, as she moved along. Nathanael followed her; they stood before the Professor. "You have had an extraordinarily animated conversation with my daughter," said he, smiling; "well, well, my dear Mr. Nathanael, if you find pleasure in talking to the stupid girl, I am sure I shall be glad for you to come and do so." Nathanael took his leave, his heart singing and leaping in a perfect delirium of happiness.

During the next few days Spalanzani's ball was the general topic of conversation. Although the Professor had done everything to make the thing a splendid success, yet certain gay spirits related more than one thing that had occurred which was quite irregular and out of order. They were especially keen in pulling Olimpia to pieces for her taciturnity and rigid stiffness; in spite of her beautiful form they alleged that she was hopelessly stupid[2], and in this fact they discerned the reason why Spalanzani had so long kept her concealed from publicity. Nathanael heard all this with inward wrath, but nevertheless he held his tongue; for, thought he, would it indeed be worth while to prove to these fellows that it is their own stupidity which prevents them from appreciating Olimpia's profound and brilliant parts? One day Siegmund said to him, "Pray, brother, have the kindness to tell me how you, a sensible fellow, came to lose your head over that Miss Wax-face — that wooden doll across there?" Nathanael was about to fly into a rage, but he recollected himself and replied, "Tell me, Siegmund, how came it that Olimpia's divine charms could escape your eye, so keenly alive as it always is to beauty, and your acute perception as well? But Heaven be thanked for it, otherwise I should have had you for a rival, and then the blood of one of us would have had to be spilled." Siegmund, perceiving how matters stood with his friend, skilfully interposed and said, after remarking that all argument with one in love about the object of his affections was out of place, "Yet it's very strange that several of us have formed pretty much the

---

from killing any more young men. It is considered one of the earliest vampire tales and has modern descendants in movies like "The Corpse Bride," "Ghost," and "The Lost Boys"

[1] This entire episode is a parable about projection: she warms up because of his warmth, she dances because he dances with her, she looks at him with love only because he projects love into her dead gaze

[2] The word here is meant to imply a learning disability

same opinion about Olimpia. We think she is — you won't take it ill, brother? — that she is singularly statuesque and soulless. Her figure is regular, and so are her features, that can't be gainsaid; and if her eyes were not so utterly devoid of life, I may say, of the power of vision[1], she might pass for a beauty. She is strangely measured in her movements, they all seem as if they were dependent upon some wound-up clock-work. Her playing and singing has the disagreeably perfect, but insensitive time of a singing machine, and her dancing is the same. We felt quite afraid of this Olimpia, and did not like to have anything to do with her; she seemed to us to be only acting like a living creature, and as if there was some secret at the bottom of it all." Nathanael did not give way to the bitter feelings which threatened to master him at these words of Siegmund's; he fought down and got the better of his displeasure, and merely said, very earnestly, "You cold prosaic fellows may very well be afraid of her. It is only to its like[2] that the poetically organised spirit unfolds itself. Upon me alone did her loving glances fall, and through my mind and thoughts alone did they radiate; and only in her love can I find my own self again. Perhaps, however, she doesn't do quite right not to jabber a lot of nonsense and stupid talk like other shallow people. It is true, she speaks but few words; but the few words she does speak are genuine hieroglyphs of the inner world of Love and of the higher cognition of the intellectual life revealed in the intuition of the Eternal beyond the grave. But you have no understanding for all these things, and I am only wasting words." "God be with you, brother," said Siegmund very gently, almost sadly, "but it seems to me that you are in a very bad way. You may rely upon me, if all — No, I can't say any more." It all at once dawned upon Nathanael that his cold prosaic friend Siegmund really and sincerely wished him well, and so he warmly shook his proffered hand.

Nathanael had completely forgotten that there was a Clara in the world, whom he had once loved — and his mother and Lothair. They had all vanished from his mind; he lived for Olimpia alone. He sat beside her every day for hours together, rhapsodising about his love and sympathy enkindled into life, and about psychic elective affinity[3] — all of which Olimpia listened to with great reverence. He fished up from the very bottom of his desk all the things that he had ever written — poems, fancy

---

[1] Unlike Clara (whom Nathanael ironically accuses of being a robot), Olimpia lacks the ability to reason, understand, consider, rationalize, and voice opinions

[2] "Poetically minded spirits only reveal themselves to like-minded individuals"

[3] An allusion to Goethe's erotic novel about a disastrous ménage a trois, "Elective Affinities." The concept behind the phrase is that some people are almost magnetically drawn to be attracted to similar minded individuals – even if the match is immoral, improper, or bizarre

sketches, visions, romances[1], tales, and the heap was increased daily with all kinds of aimless sonnets, stanzas, canzonets. All these he read to Olimpia hour after hour without growing tired; but then he had never had such an exemplary listener. She neither embroidered, nor knitted; she did not look out of the window, or feed a bird, or play with a little pet dog or a favourite cat, neither did she twist a piece of paper or anything of that kind round her finger; she did not forcibly convert a yawn into a low affected cough — in short, she sat hour after hour with her eyes bent unchangeably upon her lover's face, without moving or altering her position, and her gaze grew more ardent and more ardent still. And it was only when at last Nathanael rose and kissed her lips or her hand that she said, "Ach! Ach!" and then "Good-night, dear." Arrived in his own room, Nathanael would break out with, "Oh! what a brilliant — what a profound mind! Only you — you alone understand me." And his heart trembled with rapture when he reflected upon the wondrous harmony which daily revealed itself between his own and his Olimpia's character; for he fancied that she had expressed in respect to his works and his poetic genius the identical sentiments which he himself cherished deep down in his own heart in respect to the same, and even as if it was his own heart's voice speaking to him. And it must indeed have been so; for Olimpia never uttered any other words than those already mentioned. And when Nathanael himself in his clear and sober moments, as, for instance, directly after waking in a morning, thought about her utter passivity and taciturnity, he only said, "What are words — but words? The glance of her heavenly eyes says more than any tongue of earth. And how can, anyway, a child of heaven accustom herself to the narrow circle which the exigencies of a wretched mundane life demand?"

Professor Spalanzani appeared to be greatly pleased at the intimacy that had sprung up between his daughter Olimpia and Nathanael, and showed the young man many unmistakable proofs of his good feeling towards him; and when Nathanael ventured at length to hint very delicately at an alliance with Olimpia, the Professor smiled all over his face at once, and said he should allow his daughter to make a perfectly free choice. Encouraged by these words, and with the fire of desire burning in his heart, Nathanael resolved the very next day to implore Olimpia to tell him frankly, in plain words, what he had long read in her sweet loving glances — that she would be his for ever. He looked for the ring which his mother had given him at parting; he would present it to Olimpia as a symbol of his devotion, and of the happy life he was to lead with her from that time onwards. Whilst looking for it he came across his letters from Clara and Lothair; he threw them carelessly aside, found the ring, put it in his pocket, and ran across to Olimpia. Whilst still on the stairs, in the entrance-passage, he heard an extraordinary hubbub; the

---

[1] Novels with elements of fantasy or the supernatural

noise seemed to proceed from Spalanzani's study. There was a stamping — a rattling — pushing — knocking against the door, with curses and oaths intermingled. "Leave hold — leave hold — you monster — you rascal — staked your life and honour upon it? — Ha! ha! ha! ha! — That was not our wager — I, I made the eyes — I the clock-work. — Go to the devil with your clock-work — you damned dog of a watch-maker — be off — Satan — stop — you paltry turner[1] — you infernal beast! — stop — begone — let me go." The voices which were thus making all this racket and rumpus were those of Spalanzani and the fearsome Coppelius. Nathanael rushed in, impelled by some nameless dread. The Professor was grasping a female figure by the shoulders, the Italian Coppola held her by the feet; and they were pulling and dragging each other backwards and forwards, fighting furiously to get possession of her. Nathanael recoiled with horror on recognising that the figure was Olimpia. Boiling with rage, he was about to tear his beloved from the grasp of the madmen, when Coppola by an extraordinary exertion of strength twisted the figure out of the Professor's hands and gave him such a terrible blow with her, that he reeled backwards and fell over the table all amongst the phials and retorts, the bottles and glass cylinders, which covered it: all these things were smashed into a thousand pieces. But Coppola threw the figure across his shoulder, and, laughing shrilly and horribly, ran hastily down the stairs, the figure's ugly feet hanging down and banging and rattling like wood against the steps. Nathanael was stupefied; — he had seen only too distinctly that in Olimpia's pallid waxed face there were no eyes, merely black holes in their stead; she was an inanimate puppet. Spalanzani was rolling on the floor; the pieces of glass had cut his head and breast and arm; the blood was escaping from him in streams. But he gathered his strength together by an effort.

"After him — after him! What do you stand staring there for? Coppelius — Coppelius — he's stolen my best automaton — at which I've worked for twenty years — staked my life upon it — the clock-work — speech — movement — mine — your eyes — stolen your eyes[2] — damn him — curse him — after him — fetch me back Olimpia — there are the eyes." And now Nathanael saw a pair of bloody eyes lying on the floor staring at him; Spalanzani seized them with his uninjured hand and threw them at him, so that they hit his breast Then madness dug her burning talons into him and swept down into his heart, rending his mind and thoughts to shreds. "Aha! aha! aha! Fire-wheel[3] — fire-wheel! Spin

---

[1] "Worthless wood-worker"

[2] Fascinatingly, Spalanzani doesn't say "her eyes" – instead, he quite correctly charges that Coppola has taken over Nathanael's ability to perceive correctly – he has taken his vision from him

[3] A firework which spins around in rapid circles, making the illusion of a fiery circle

round, fire-wheel! merrily, merrily! Aha! wooden doll! spin round, pretty wooden doll!" and he threw himself upon the Professor, clutching him fast by the throat. He would certainly have strangled him had not several people, attracted by the noise, rushed in and torn away the madman; and so they saved the Professor, whose wounds were immediately dressed. Siegmund, with all his strength, was not able to subdue the frantic lunatic, who continued to scream in a dreadful way, "Spin round, wooden doll!" and to strike out right and left with his doubled fists. At length the united strength of several succeeded in overpowering him by throwing him on the floor and binding him. His cries passed into a brutish bellow that was awful to hear; and thus raging with the harrowing violence of madness, he was taken away to the madhouse.

Before continuing my narration of what happened further to the unfortunate Nathanael, I will tell you, indulgent reader, in case you take any interest in that skilful mechanician and fabricator of automata, Spalanzani, that he recovered completely from his wounds. He had, however, to leave the university, for Nathanael's fate had created a great sensation; and the opinion was pretty generally expressed that it was an imposture altogether unpardonable to have smuggled a wooden puppet instead of a living person into intelligent tea-circles — for Olimpia had been present at several with success. Lawyers called it a cunning piece of knavery, and all the harder to punish since it was directed against the public; and it had been so craftily contrived that it had escaped unobserved by all except a few preternaturally acute students, although everybody was very wise now and remembered to have thought of several facts which occurred to them as suspicious. But these latter could not succeed in making out any sort of a consistent tale. For was it, for instance, a thing likely to occur to any one as suspicious that, according to the declaration of an elegant beau of these tea-parties, Olimpia had, contrary to all good manners, sneezed oftener than she had yawned? The former must have been, in the opinion of this elegant gentleman, the winding up of the concealed clock-work; it had always been accompanied by an observable creaking, and so on. The Professor of Poetry and Eloquence took a pinch of snuff, and, slapping the lid to and clearing his throat, said solemnly, "My most honourable ladies and gentlemen, don't you see then where the rub[1] is? The whole thing is an allegory[2], a continuous metaphor. You understand me? Sapienti sat. " But several most honourable gentlemen did not rest satisfied with this explanation;

---

[1] Problem

[2] Indeed, Olimpia's successful ruse proves the pettiness and fakeness of the society that accepted her as one of their own, implying that the entire city is overrun with sycophantic automatons with beating hearts and working minds – automatons who fake their way into others' graces by fawning, posturing, and performing

the history of this automaton had sunk deeply into their souls, and an absurd mistrust of human figures began to prevail. Several lovers, in order to be fully convinced that they were not paying court to a wooden puppet[1], required that their mistress should sing and dance a little out of time, should embroider or knit or play with her little pug, &c., when being read to, but above all things else that she should do something more than merely listen — that she should frequently speak in such a way as to really show that her words presupposed as a condition some thinking and feeling. The bonds of love were in many cases drawn closer in consequence, and so of course became more engaging; in other instances they gradually relaxed and fell away. "I cannot really be made responsible for it," was the remark of more than one young gallant. At the tea-gatherings everybody, in order to ward off suspicion, yawned to an incredible extent and never sneezed. Spalanzani was obliged, as has been said, to leave the place in order to escape a criminal charge of having fraudulently imposed an automaton upon human society. Coppola, too, had also disappeared.

When Nathanael awoke he felt as if he had been oppressed by a terrible nightmare; he opened his eyes[2] and experienced an indescribable sensation of mental comfort, whilst a soft and most beautiful sensation of warmth pervaded his body. He lay on his own bed in his own room at home; Clara was bending over him, and at a little distance stood his mother and Lothair. "At last, at last, O my darling Nathanael; now we have you again; now you are cured of your grievous illness, now you are mine again." And Clara's words came from the depths of her heart; and she clasped him in her arms. The bright scalding tears streamed from his eyes, he was so overcome with mingled feelings of sorrow and delight; and he gasped forth, "My Clara, my Clara!" Siegmund, who had staunchly stood by his friend in his hour of need, now came into the room. Nathanael gave him his hand —"My faithful brother, you have not deserted me." Every trace of insanity had left him, and in the tender hands of his mother and his beloved, and his friends, he quickly recovered his strength again. Good fortune had in the meantime visited the house; a niggardly[3] old uncle, from whom they had never expected to get anything, had died, and left Nathanael's mother not only a considerable fortune, but also a small estate, pleasantly situated not far from the town. There they resolved to go and live, Nathanael and his mother, and Clara, to whom he was now to be married, and Lothair. Nathanael was become gentler and more childlike than he had ever been

---

[1] Suddenly unnerved by Olimpia's successful illusion, the people of the town begin appreciating imperfections in one another, to the point of demanding them as proof of their lovers' humanity

[2] His vision has been restored: he sees life for what it is

[3] Cheapskate

before, and now began really to understand Clara's supremely pure and noble character. None of them ever reminded him, even in the remotest degree, of the past. But when Siegmund took leave of him, he said, "By heaven, brother! I was in a bad way, but an angel came just at the right moment and led me back upon the path of light. Yes, it was Clara." Siegmund would not let him speak further, fearing lest the painful recollections of the past might arise too vividly and too intensely in his mind.

The time came for the four happy people to move to their little property. At noon they were going through the streets. After making several purchases they found that the lofty tower of the town-house was throwing its giant shadows across the market-place. "Come," said Clara, "let us go up to the top once more and have a look at the distant hills[1]." No sooner said than done. Both of them, Nathanael and Clara, went up the tower; their mother, however, went on with the servant-girl to her new home, and Lothair, not feeling inclined to climb up all the many steps, waited below. There the two lovers stood arm-in-arm on the topmost gallery of the tower, and gazed out into the sweet-scented wooded landscape, beyond which the blue hills rose up like a giant's city.

"Oh! do look at that strange little grey bush, it looks as if it were actually walking towards us," said Clara. Mechanically[2] he put his hand into his sidepocket; he found Coppola's perspective and looked for the bush; Clara stood in front of the glass. Then a convulsive thrill shot through his pulse and veins; pale as a corpse, he fixed his staring eyes upon her; but soon they began to roll, and a fiery current flashed and sparkled in them, and he yelled fearfully, like a hunted animal. Leaping up high in the air and laughing horribly at the same time, he began to shout, in a piercing voice, "Spin round, wooden doll! Spin round, wooden doll!" With the strength of a giant he laid hold upon Clara and tried to hurl her over, but in an agony of despair she clutched fast hold of the railing that went round the gallery. Lothair heard the madman raging and Clara's scream of terror: a fearful presentiment flashed across his mind. He ran up the steps; the door of the second flight was locked[3]. Clara's scream for help rang out more loudly. Mad with rage and fear, he threw himself against the door, which at length gave way. Clara's cries were growing fainter and fainter — "Help! save me! save me!" and her voice died away in the air. "She is killed — murdered by that madman,"

---

[1] Read: speculate about our future together

[2] The symptoms of predestination? Hoffmann leaves it to us to choose whether this "mechanical" motion is mechanical because it is preordained, or because it is an unbroken habit: Nathanael can't help but overanalyze his life and instinctively reaches for Coppola's telescope

[3] Implying that Nathanael either consciously or unconsciously locked it – probably with a mind to kill Clara

shouted Lothair. The door to the gallery was also locked. Despair gave him the strength of a giant; he burst the door off its hinges. Good God! there was Clara in the grasp of the madman Nathanael, hanging over the gallery in the air; she only held to the iron bar with one hand. Quick as lightning, Lothair seized his sister and pulled her back, at the same time dealing the madman a blow in the face with his doubled fist, which sent him reeling backwards, forcing him to let go his victim.

Lothair ran down with his insensible sister in his arms. She was saved. But Nathanael ran round and round the gallery, leaping up in the air and shouting, "Spin round, fire-wheel! Spin round, fire-wheel!" The people heard the wild shouting, and a crowd began to gather. In the midst of them towered the advocate Coppelius[1], like a giant; he had only just arrived in the town, and had gone straight to the market-place. Some were going up to overpower and take charge of the madman, but Coppelius laughed and said, "Ha! ha! wait a bit; he'll come down of his own accord[2]"; and he stood gazing upwards along with the rest. All at once Nathanael stopped as if spell-bound; he bent down over the railing, and perceived Coppelius. With a piercing scream, "Ha! foine oyes! foine oyes!" he leapt over.

When Nathanael lay on the stone pavement with a broken head, Coppelius had disappeared in the crush and confusion.

Several years afterwards it was reported that, outside the door of a pretty country house in a remote district, Clara had been seen sitting hand in hand with a pleasant gentleman[3], whilst two bright boys were playing at her feet. From this it may be concluded that she eventually found that quiet domestic happiness which her cheerful, blithesome character required, and which Nathanael, with his tempest-tossed soul, could never have been able to give her.

ULTIMATELY, "The Sandman" is a story about psychological defense mechanisms run amuck – denial and projection chief amongst them – and the dangers of straying too far into a subjective worldview cut free from the perspectives and advice of others. Hoffmann experienced this sort of estrangement frequently throughout his life, finding himself at odds with his friends and family, who often shamed him for his outlandish behavior and irresponsible impulses. Inappropriate obsessions with underage students, emotional upheavals swinging from suicidal depressions to manic moods of invincibility, and self-destructive attacks against the political establishment often overtook Hoffmann's life, leaving him burdened with humiliating self-loathing and frustration. In one

[1] We are lead to question whether Coppelius has really appeared, or whether this is all in Nathanael's mind

[2] Words which prove to be prophetic and darkly ironic

[3] Very probably Siegmund

moment he seemed to have no doubts that he should leave his devoted wife for a music student barely in the first stages of puberty – almost oblivious to the catastrophic results this would have on his life and reputations – while in another he viewed himself as a pathetic lothario – a cringe-worthy embarrassment. Swinging back and forth between manic and depressive episodes taught Hoffmann to rely on others for perspective, and to be suspicious of his momentary feelings. Years after the Julia Marc affair, he would be grateful that he hadn't followed his repeated suicidal impulses, and while he never turned his back on a life rich in whimsy, imagination, and spontaneity, as he aged he began to recognize the toll that his unmoored will had exerted on his happiness. Balance was critical to keep him grounded and secure, and while a life without mirth and indulgence was unimaginable, one entirely lost to the shifting winds of impulse was every bit as terrifying as "The Sandman" suggests. Nathanael rejects Clara's offer to provide him with her vision – a clear perspective sharpened by reason – and as a result, unknowingly hands his eyes over to Coppelius, trading them for the salesman's three ducat telescope. Whenever Nathanael peers through this prejudiced perspective, he sees only that which he expects to see: Olimpia is a beautiful if strange girl, and the grey figure approaching the tower is the Sandman himself, coming for his eyes.

II.

The motif of vision which haunts this story is naturally a symbolic one – one which studies our ability to be fooled and to have our objectivity compromised. Nathanael grows up terrified by the idea of having his vision hijacked by the Sandman – a mythic figure whom he blames for compromising his father's judgment and luring him into a series of fatal alchemical experiments. Of course we have every reason to doubt this narrator as unreliable, and Clara makes a strong case for this: the Sandman was a folkloric archetype who came to represent the loss of self-control and objectivity, and this symbol was conflated with the bizarre Coppelius, who seemed to take control away from their servile father. After the latter's death, Nathanael became neurotically obsessed with suffering the same fate – having a nefarious influence strip him of self-control and self-possession, effectively robbing him of his psychological vision – and when the Italian salesman came to town, Nathanael mistakenly projected his internal anxieties onto a harmless hawker. But Clara's warning doesn't take root in her lover's heart: she is barely able to bring clarity and understanding to him in time to save him from dueling her brother. Instead, he finds solace in the arms of a 19th century Stepford Wife – the pleasantly agreeable Olimpia. Unlike Clara, who frustrates Nathanael by challenging his manias, Olimpia agrees with monosyllabic vigor, crying out *"Oh! Oh! Oh!"* to all of his comments and questions. Her orgasmic affirmation soothes his insecurities and builds up his ego to perilous heights. Essentially a sex doll (and frequently interpreted as such by productions of Offenbach's opera, "Tales of Hoffmann," and Delibes' ballet, "Coppelia"), Olimpia overwhelms Nathanael's imagination – robbing him of his eyes – soothing his bruised self-doubts with her nymphic adulation. Completely compromised, he does what any Hoffmann protagonist would do, and makes a public spectacle of himself, shocking strangers and embarrassing friends by making love to a robot. By the time Nathanael realizes that he has traded Clara's clarity for the mindless approval of a puppet, he has lost all faith in his judgment, and is barely able to beg his jilted lover for forgiveness. When the sort-of-happy couple go to the church to marry, the Sandman seems to reappear in the crowd below the steeple, leading Nathanael to anticipate further delusions and deceptions. Conflating Clara with Olimpia in that moment, he projects his sexual frustration onto the living woman and attempts to destroy her as surely and easily as Olimpia was destroyed by her creators. After Siegmund (whose name tellingly means "defender" or "protector") saves Clara, Nathanael's humiliation is complete: he sees Coppola in the crowd below, where he predicts (or so Nathanael seems to hear) that there is no need to strong arm him: "he will come down of his own accord." As if responding to a command, Nathanael screams out to the apparition that he now has the same "foine oyes" that the foreigner had been hawking earlier, and after making this sinister comparison, consigns himself to suicide. The transformation has been realized: Nathanael has lost his eyes to his new master just as hopelessly as his father lost his willpower and life. Freud was mesmerized by the story and considered it a parable of sexual impotence, and the reading is not without validity. Anxious about the prospect of having to consummate his love with Clara (an anxiety that stems from his Oedipal rage towards his own impotent father – a rage which manifests itself in the father-killing Doppelgänger Coppelius), Nathanael easily transfers his affections to an inanimate sex doll designed to affirm and confirm. This union, however, only leads to more humiliation and reinforces the idea that he is incapable of making love to a living woman. His death from the top of the phallic tower is the apotheosis of his latent performance anxieties – the ultimate case of pre-wedding cold feet.

III.

The idea of choosing between the challenges of a living, willful partner, and the allure of a self-soothing, affirming sex toy have been rehashed in dozens of books, movies, and musicals. Early German films like Fritz Lang's "Metropolis" (wherein an evil robot stirs up havoc by impersonating a popular social activist) and "The Cabinet of Dr. Caligari" (wherein a hypnotized sleepwalker is programmed to murder) are excessively Hoffmann-esque, delving into the Uncanny Valley and the tensions between reality and imagination. Modern films like "The Stepford Wives" (suburban housewives are turned into mindless robots), "Vertigo" (a man tries to fashion his girlfriend into a replicate of the dead stranger he became obsessed with), "Coraline" (a little girl finds a "Nutcracker"-like parallel universe where her parents are perfect versions of themselves, save that they have had their eyes replaced with buttons, and she is threatened with the same "Sandman"-like treatment), and "The Matrix" (a man learns that the world is a vast illusion, and is tasked with choosing between the lethargy of remaining deluded and the challenging work of fighting against the deception) build on Hoffmann's "Sandman." It remains his most psychologically powerful and literarily fertile work, forcing readers to wonder how much of the story was real, how much was imagined, and – most importantly – to what extent it matters at all. In most of Hoffmann's works, he comes to a similar conclusion: even if this is all fake, it doesn't change its reality if Experience is Truth. And in this sense, "The Sandman" – like most of Hoffmann's works – is almost postmodern in its vertigo-inducing philosophy. If reality is subjective (as the proto-postmodernist Nathanael argues with the staunch modernist Clara) then the possibilities of life are endless. Nathanael is consumed both by a belief in the limitlessness of life and in the inescapability of destiny. In a sense, he views life as a funhouse with a closing time: you can do or be anything you want (and you can make *others* do or be anything you want), but when the Manager turns the lights out and drags you into the dark, there is nothing you can do to resist. While Clara may be arguably a tad unimaginative and lacking in passion, she sees herself as the master of her life choices: she can choose to interrupt Nathanael's windy speeches to save her coffee from burning, and she can choose to break up his fight with her brother, and she can choose to reject or marry him. Her universe is far more libertarian and self-possessed, founded on free will rather than predestination. Disgusted by her willpower and lack of self-indulgence, Nathanael momentarily saturates himself in Olimpia's mindless servitude, before he recognizes himself in her: just like Olimpia, he has allowed himself to be the mindless puppet of malevolent external forces. By the time he returns to Clara – seeking counsel and education in the arts of self-control – it is far too late: like Olimpia he has resigned his destiny to impulses – willingly handing over his eyes (read: perspective, mindset, and will) to deceivers – and like her he is torn apart by the warring forces that he has allowed to control him.

THE Swedish city of Falun was once world-famous for its copper mines. During the 1600s Falun produced upwards of two-thirds of the copper used worldwide. However, it had a dark side: its history was marred by a slew of disasters – cave-ins, fires, gas pollution, industrial accidents, and more – which caused it to be synonymous with the human toll of greed. The most famous of these disasters – bloodless though it was – took place on June 24, 1687. This historical event was an economic catastrophe, though no lives were lost due to the celebration of the Midsummer holiday. As the Falun Mines' website explains:

> "The great collapse of 1687 is one of the most known events in Falun Mines's history. The mine workers had started to sound strange and disturbing in the rock. And sure enough, during the Midsummer weekend of 1687 the biggest slide ever occurred. Below ground, rubble masses were found as far down as 350 meters underground. The Great Pit, with a circumference of 1,6 kilometers and a depth of 95 metres, was what appeared afterwards. The incident became known all over Sweden, and also in Europe, because not a single miner lost their life – they had been given time off to celebrate midsummer."

To many Northern European artists and intellectuals the mines of Falun represented the allures and perils of greed and nature alike: they were stunning to behold with their towering, stone walls, sublimely illuminated by smelting fires at night (a scene which became the subject of many Romantic paintings), and the wealth which they generated was staggering to consider, but – as with all ambitious projects of the nascent Industrial Revolution, the crushing toll on human life was impossible to deny. Death seemed to be an inconvenient collateral cost to the mining company, and it was often noted how the men descending into its hellish bowels – some of whom were never seen again – where filling the company coffers with gold purchased with their life's blood. For a countercultural prophet like Hoffmann – a man fundamentally disgusted with the toll taken by corporatism, consumerism, and bureaucracy on the human soul – the metaphor was impossible to avoid exploring.

II.

One of Hoffmann's most overtly proto-Freudian tales – and historically considered one of his best and most popular, though it is not well-known today – "The Mines of Falun" is a study of the soul-crushing power which motherly devotion can wield over a devoted son, and of the perils of entertaining a strict Madonna/Whore interpretation of womankind. Miners and references to mining feature liberally in Hoffmann's works: even the Nutcracker is depicted wearing a leather miner's cap instead of the soldier's shako popularized by the ballet. Part of this is due to Hoffmann's fascination with elementals (gnomes, sylphs, salamanders, and undines – the spirits which embody the earth, air, fire, and water, respectively) and his apparent, *personal* identification with the lusty, grotesque gnomes. Vulgar, simplistic, materialistic, and oafish, gnomes represented what Hoffmann feared himself to be: like them he felt that he was ludicrous, silly, and the subject of public ridicule. Also like them, he felt that he longed to absent himself from the world of the living – to plunge into the secretive bowels of escapism. But stories like this – and many others, like "The Lost Reflection" and "The King's Betrothed" – suggest that he was well aware of the perils posed by following such a retreat. The main character of "The Mines of Falun" seeks an impossible reunion with his dead mother in the maternal embrace of the eponymous caverns of a Swedish mining town. If the Freudian symbolism of this desire to burrow into these cavernous tunnels hasn't yet popped out to, read on – it is certain to.

The Mines of Falun

— Excerpted from 'The Serapion Brethren,' Volume One, Section Two —

{1819}

"ONE bright, sunny day in July the whole population of Goethaborg[1] was assembled at the harbour. A fine East-Indiaman[2], happily returned from her long voyage, was lying at anchor, with her long, homeward-bound pennant[3], and the Swedish flag fluttering gaily in the azure sky. Hundreds of boats, skiffs, and other small craft, thronged with rejoicing seafolk, were going to and fro on the mirroring waters of the Goethaelf[4], and the cannon of Masthuggetorg[5] thundered their far-echoing greeting out to sea. The gentlemen of the East-India Company were walking up and down on the quay, reckoning up, with smiling faces, the plentiful profits they had netted, and rejoicing their hearts at the yearly increasing success of their hazardous enterprise, and at the growing commercial importance of their good town of Goethaborg. For the same reasons everybody looked at these brave adventurers with pleasure and pride, and shared their rejoicing; for their success brought sap and vigour into the whole life of the place.

"The crew of the East-Indiaman, about a hundred strong, landed in a number of boats (gaily dressed with flags for the occasion) and prepared to hold their 'Hoensning.' That is the name of the feast which the sailors hold on such occasions; it often goes on for several days. Musicians went before them, in strange, gay dresses, playing lustily on violins, oboes, fifes and

---

[1] That is, Gothenburg, Sweden's second-largest city and a major European port

[2] A merchant ship of Sweden's wildly profitable East India Company

[3] A flag flown during the final leg of a ship's journey to indicate that they are homeward bound

[4] The harbor

[5] The city fort, which would fire a gun salute to returning naval or company ships

drums, whilst others sung merry songs; after them came the crew, walking two and two; some, with gay ribbons on their hats and jackets, waved fluttering streamers; others danced and skipped; and all of them shouted and cheered at the tops of their voices, till the sounds of merriment rang far and wide.

"Thus the gay procession passed through the streets, and on to the Haga suburb, where a feast of eating and drinking was ready for them in a tavern.

"Here the best of 'Oel[1]' flowed in rivers and bumper after bumper was quaffed. Numbers of women joined them, as is always the case when sailors come home from a long voyage; dancing began, and wilder and wilder grew the revel, and louder and louder the din.

"One sailor only—a slender, handsome lad of about twenty, or scarcely so much—had slipped away from the revel, and was sitting alone outside, on the bench at the door of the tavern.

"Two or three of his shipmates came out to him, and cried, laughing loudly:

"'Now then, Elis Froebom! are you going to be a donkey, as usual, and sit out here in the sulks, instead of joining the sport like a man? Why, you might as well part company from the old ship altogether, and set sail on your own hook, as fight shy of the "Hoensning." One would think you were a regular long-shore land-lubber, and had never been afloat on blue water[2]. All the same, you've got as good pluck as any sailor that walks a deck—ay, and as cool and steady a head in a gale of wind as ever I came athwart; but, you see, you can't take your liquor! You'd sooner keep the ducats in your pocket than serve them out to the land-sharks ashore here. There, lad! take a drink of that; or Naecken[3], the sea-devil, and all the Troll will be foul of your hawse[4] before you know where you are!'

"Elis Froebom jumped up quickly from the bench; glared angrily at his shipmates; took the tumbler—which was filled to the brim with brandy—and emptied it at a draught; then he said:

"'You see I can take my glass with any man of you, Ivens; and you can ask the captain if I'm a good sailor-man, or not; so stow away that long tongue of yours, and sheer off! I don't care about all this drink and row[5] here; and what I'm doing out here by myself is no business of yours; you have nothing to do with it.'

---

[1] Beer, ale

[2] The term for the open ocean (as opposed to the coastal green waters)

[3] A dangerous, shapeshifting water spirit

[4] The channel in the bow through which the anchor cable descends

[5] Carousing, loud talk

"'All right, my hearty!' answered Ivens. 'I know all about it. You're one of these Nerica[1] men—and a moony lot the whole cargo of them are too. They're the sort of chaps that would rather sit and pipe their eye about nothing particular, than take a good glass, and see what the pretty lasses at home are made of, after a twelve-month's cruize! But just you belay there a bit. Steer full and bye, and stand off and on, and I'll send somebody out to you that'll cut you adrift, in a pig's whisper, from that old bench where you've cast your anchor[2].'

"They went; and presently a very pretty, rather refined-looking girl came out of the tavern, and sat down beside the melancholy Elis, who was still sitting, silent and thoughtful, on the bench. From her dress and general appearance there could be no doubt as to her terrible calling[3]. But the life she was leading had not yet quite marred the delicacy of the wonderfully tender features of her beautiful face; there was no trace of repulsive boldness about the expression of her dark eyes—rather a quiet, melancholy longing.

"'Aren't you coming to join your shipmates, Elis?' she said. 'Now that you're back safe and sound, after all you've gone through on your long voyage, aren't you glad to be home in the old country again?'

"The girl spoke in a soft, gentle voice, putting her arms about him. Elis Froebom looked into her eyes, as if roused from a dream. He took her hand; he pressed her to his breast. It was evident that what she had said had made its way to his heart.

"'Ah!' he said, as if collecting his thoughts, 'it's no use talking about my enjoying myself. I can't join in all that riot and uproar; there's no pleasure in it, for me. You go away, my dear child! Sing and shout like the rest of them, if you can, and let the gloomy, melancholy Elis stay out here by himself; he would only spoil your pleasure. Wait a minute, though! I like you, and I should wish you to think of me sometimes, when I'm away on the sea again.'

"With that he took two shining ducats[4] out of his pocket, and a beautiful Indian handkerchief from his breast, and gave them to the girl. But her eyes streamed with tears; she rose, laid the money on the bench, and said:

---

[1] That is, Närke, a province in south-central Sweden, known for its mining. Its principle city is Örebro

[2] "But just you stop what you're doing for a moment. Stick around and keep drinking awhile and I'll send somebody out to you who'll get you out of this funk."

[3] Viz., a prostitute

[4] The value of these coins is difficult to calculate, but they would be worth somewhere in the neighborhood of $300 today

"'Oh, keep your ducats; they only make me miserable; but I'll wear the handkerchief in dear remembrance of you. You're not likely to find me next year when you hold your Hoensning in the Haga[1].'

"And she crept slowly away down the street, with her hands pressed to her face.

"Elis fell back into his gloomy reveries. At length, as the uproar in the tavern grew loud and wild, he cried:

"'Oh, that I were lying deep, deep beneath the sea! for there's nobody left in the wide, wide world that I can be happy with now!'

"A deep, harsh voice spoke, close behind him: 'You must have been most unfortunate, youngster, to wish to die, just when life should be opening before you.'

"Elis looked round, and saw an old miner standing leaning against the boarded wall of the tavern, with folded arms, looking down at him with a grave, penetrating glance.

"As Elis looked at him, a feeling came to him as if some familiar figure had suddenly come into the deep, wild solitude in which he had thought himself lost. He pulled himself together, and told the old miner that his father had been a stout sailor, but had perished in the storm from which he himself had been saved as by a miracle; that his two soldier brothers had died in battle, and he had supported his mother with the liberal pay he drew for sailing to the East Indies. He said he had been obliged to follow the life of a sailor, having been brought up to it from childhood, and it had been a great piece of good fortune that he got into the service of the East-India Company. This voyage, the profits had been greater than usual, and each of the crew had been given a sum of money over and above his pay; so that he had hastened, in the highest spirits, with his pockets full of ducats, to the little cottage where his mother lived. But strange faces looked at him from the windows, and a young woman who opened the door to him at last told him, in a cold, harsh tone, that his mother had died three months before, and that he would find the few bits of things that were left, after paying the funeral expenses, waiting for him at the Town Hall. The death of his mother broke his heart. He felt alone in the world—as much so as if he had been wrecked on some lonely reef, helpless and miserable. All his life at sea seemed to him to have been a mistaken, purposeless driving. And when he thought of his mother, perhaps badly looked after by strangers, he thought it a wrong and horrible thing that he should have gone to sea at all, instead of staying at home and taking proper care of her. His comrades had dragged him to the Hoensning in spite of himself, and he had thought, too, that the uproar, and even the drink, might have deadened his pain; but instead of that, all the veins in his breast seemed to be bursting, and he felt as if he must bleed to death.

---

[1] One of Gothenburg's picturesque, historical city districts

"'Well,' said the old miner, 'you'll soon be off to sea again, Elis, and then your sorrow will soon be over. Old folks must die; there's no help for that: she has only gone from this miserable world to a better.'

"Ah!' said Elis, 'it is just because nobody believes in my sorrow, and that they all think me a fool to feel it—I say it's that which is driving me out of the world! I shan't go to sea any more; I'm sick of existence altogether. When the ship used to go flying along through the water, with all sail set, spreading like glorious wings, the waves playing and dashing in exquisite music, and the wind singing in the rigging, my heart used to bound. Then I could hurrah and shout on deck like the best of them. And when I was on look-out duty of dark, quiet nights, I used to think about getting home, and how glad my dear old mother would be to have me back. I could enjoy a Hoensning like the rest of them, then. And when I had shaken the ducats into mother's lap, and given her the handkerchiefs and all the other pretty things I had brought home, her eyes would sparkle with pleasure, and she would clap her hands for joy, and run out and in, and fetch me the "Aehl"[1] which she had kept for my homecoming. And when I sat with her of an evening, I would tell her of all the strange folks I had seen, and their ways and customs, and about the wonderful things I had come across in my long voyages. This delighted her; and she would tell me of my father's wonderful cruizes in the far North, and serve me up lots of strange, sailor's yarns, which I had heard a hundred times, but never could hear too often. Ah! who will give me that happiness back again? No, no! never more on land!—never more at sea! What should I do among my shipmates? They would only laugh at me. Where should I find any heart for my work? It would be nothing but an objectless striving.'

"It gives me real satisfaction to listen to you, youngster,' said the old miner. 'I have been observing you, without your knowledge, for the last hour or two, and have had my own enjoyment in so doing. All that you have said and done has shown me that you possess a profoundly thoughtful mind, and a character and nature pious, simple, and sincere. Heaven could have given you no more precious gifts; but you were never in all your born days in the least cut out for a sailor. How should the wild, unsettled sailor's life suit a meditative, melancholy Neriker like you?—for I can see that you come from Nerica by your features, and whole appearance. You are right to say good-bye to that life for ever. But you're not going to walk about idle, with your hands in your pockets? Take my advice, Elis Froebom. Go to Falun[2], and be a miner. You are young and strong. You'll soon be a first-

---

[1] Ale

[2] A city (today of some 37,000 inhabitants) in south-central Sweden which has been renowned for its copper mines since at least 1000 AD. During the 1600s Falun produced upwards of 2/3 of the copper used worldwide. However, it had a dark side: its history was marred by a slew of disasters – cave-ins, fires,

class pick-hand; then a hewer; presently a surveyor[1], and so get higher and higher. You have a lot of ducats in your pocket. Take care of them; invest them; add more to them. Very likely you'll soon get a "Hemmans[2]" of your own, and then a share in the works[3]. Take my advice, Elis Froebom; be a miner.'

"The old man's words caused him a sort of fear.

"'What?' he cried. 'Would you have me leave the bright, sunny sky that revives and refreshes me, and go down into that dreadful, hell-like abyss, and dig and tunnel like a mole for metals and ores, merely to gain a few wretched ducats? Oh, never!'

"'The usual thing,' said the old man. 'People despise what they have had no chance of knowing anything about! As if all the constant wearing, petty anxieties inseparable from business up here on the surface, were nobler than the miner's work. To his skill, knowledge, and untiring industry Nature lays bare her most secret treasures. You speak of gain with contempt, Elis Froebom. Well, there's something infinitely higher in question here, perhaps: the mole tunnels the ground from blind instinct; but, it may be, in the deepest depths, by the pale glimmer of the mine candle, men's eyes get to see clearer, and at length, growing stronger and stronger, acquire the power of reading in the stones, the gems, and the minerals, the mirroring of secrets which are hidden above the clouds. You know nothing about mining, Elis. Let me tell you a little.'

"He sat down on the bench beside Elis, and began to describe the various processes minutely, placing all the details before him in the clearest and brightest colours. He talked of the Mines of Falun, in which he said he had worked since he was a boy; he described the great main-shaft, with its dark brown sides; he told how incalculably rich the mine was in gems of the finest water. More and more vivid grew his words, more and more glowing his face. He went, in his description, through the different shafts as if they had been the alleys of some enchanted garden. The jewels came to life, the fossils began to move; the wondrous Pyrosmalite[4] and the

---

gas pollution, industrial accidents, and more – which caused it to be synonymous with the human toll of greed. What's more, it became closely associated with the eerie tale of Fet Mats Israelsson – a miner who disappeared on the eve of his wedding, and whose mummified corpse was identified by his now elderly bride decades later when it was discovered preserved in toxic mine waste – who became the inspiration for Elis

[1] Pick-hands dig out mines; hewers cut out the coal; surveyors manage safety and direct the direction of the tunnels

[2] Homestead

[3] That is, and "you'll become a shareholder in the mining company"

[4] A pearly, crystalline mineral which often appears either greyish green or pale brown

Almandine[1] flashed in the light of the miner's candles; the Rock-Crystals glittered, and darted their rays.

"Elis listened intently. The old man's strange way of speaking of all these subterranean marvels as if he were standing in the midst of them, impressed him deeply. His breast felt stifled; it seemed to him as if he were already down in these depths with the old man, and would never more look upon the friendly light of day. And yet it seemed as though the old man were opening to him a new and unknown world, to which he really properly belonged, and that he had somehow felt all the magic of that world, in mystic forebodings, since his boyhood.

"Elis Froebom,' said the old man at length, 'I have laid before you all the glories of a calling for which Nature really destined you. Think the subject well over with yourself, and then act as your better judgment counsels you.'

"He rose quickly from the bench, and strode away without any good-bye to Elis, without looking at him even. Soon he disappeared from his sight.

"Meanwhile quietness had set in in the tavern. The strong 'Aehl' and brandy had got the upper hand. Many of the sailors had gone away with the girls; others were lying snoring in corners. Elis—who could go no more to his old home—asked for, and was given, a little room to sleep in.

"Scarcely had he thrown himself, worn and weary as he was, upon his bed, when dreams began to wave their pinions over him. He thought he was sailing in a beautiful vessel on a sea calm and clear as a mirror, with a dark, cloudy sky vaulted overhead. But when he looked down into the sea he presently saw that what he had thought was water was a firm, transparent, sparkling substance, in the shimmer of which the ship, in a wonderful manner, melted away, so that he found himself standing upon this floor of crystal, with a vault of black rock above him, for that was rock which he had taken at first for clouds. Impelled by some power unknown to him he stepped onwards, but, at that moment, every thing around him began to move, and wonderful plants and flowers, of glittering metal, came shooting up out of the crystal mass he was standing on, and entwined their leaves and blossoms in the loveliest manner. The crystal floor was so transparent that Elis could distinctly see the roots of these plants. But soon, as his glance penetrated deeper and deeper, he saw, far, far down in the depths, innumerable beautiful maidens, holding each other embraced with white, gleaming arms; and it was from their hearts that the roots, plants, and flowers were growing. And when these maidens smiled, a sweet sound rang all through the vault above, and the wonderful metal-flowers shot up higher, and waved their leaves and branches in joy. An indescribable sense of rapture came upon the lad; a world of love and passionate longing awoke in his heart.

---

[1] A violet-colored garnet

"'Down, down to you!' he cried, and threw himself with outstretched arras down upon the crystal ground. But it gave way under him, and he seemed to be floating in shimmering æther[1].

"'Ha! Elis Froebom; what think you of this world of glory?' a strong voice cried. It was the old miner. But as Elis looked at him, he seemed to expand into gigantic size, and to be made of glowing metal. Elis was beginning to be terrified; but a brilliant light came darting, like a sudden lightning-flash, out of the depths of the abyss, and the earnest face of a grand, majestic woman appeared. Elis felt the rapture of his heart swelling and swelling into destroying pain. The old man had hold of him, and cried:

"'Take care, Elis Froebom! That is the queen. You may look up now.'

"He turned his head involuntarily, and saw the stars of the night sky shining through a cleft in the vault overhead. A gentle voice called his name as if in inconsolable sorrow. It was his mother's. He thought he saw her form up at the cleft. But it was a young and beautiful woman who was calling him, and stretching her hands down into the vault.

"'Take me up!' he cried to the old man. I tell you I belong to the upper world, and its familiar, friendly sky.'

"'Take care, Froebom,' said the old man solemnly; 'be faithful to the queen, whom you have devoted yourself to.'

"But now, when he looked down again into the immobile face of the majestic woman, he felt that his personality dissolved away into glowing molten stone. He screamed aloud, in nameless fear, and awoke from this dream of wonder, whose rapture and terror echoed deep within his being.

"'I suppose I could scarcely help dreaming all this extraordinary stuff,' he said to himself, as he collected his senses with difficulty; 'the old miner told me so much about the glories of the subterranean world that of course my head's quite full of it. But I never in my life felt as I do now. Perhaps I'm dreaming still. No, no; I suppose I must be a little out of sorts. Let's get into the open air. The fresh sea-breeze'll soon set me all right.'

"He pulled himself together, and ran to the Klippa Haven, where the uproar of the Hoensning was breaking out again. But he soon found that all enjoyment passed him by, that he couldn't hold any thought fast in his mind, that presages and wishes, to which he could give no name, went crossing each other in his mind. He thought of his dead mother with the bitterest sorrow; but then, again, it seemed to him that what he most longed for was to see that girl again—the one whom he gave the handkerchief to—who had spoken so nicely to him the evening before. And yet he was afraid that if she were to come meeting him out of some street she would turn out to be the old miner in the end. And he was afraid of *him*; though, at the same time, he would have liked to hear more from him of the wonders of the mine.

[1] Skies, atmospheres

"Driven hither and thither by all these fancies, he looked down into the water, and then he thought he saw the silver ripples hardening into the sparkling glimmer in which the grand ships melted away, while the dark clouds, which were beginning to gather and obscure the blue sky, seemed to sink down and thicken into a vault of rock. He was in his dream again, gazing into the immobile face of the majestic woman, and the devouring pain of passionate longing took possession of him as before.

"His shipmates roused him from his reverie to go and join one of their processions, but an unknown voice seemed to whisper in his ear:

"'What are you doing here? Away, away! Your home is in the Mines of Falun. There all the glories which you saw in your dream are waiting for you. Away, away to Falun!'

"For three days Elis hung and loitered about the streets of Goethaborg, constantly haunted by the wonderful imagery of his dream, continually urged by the unknown voice. On the fourth day he was standing at the gate through which the road to Gefle[1] goes, when a tall man walked through it, passing him. Elis fancied he recognized in this man the old miner, and he hastened on after him, but could not overtake him.

"He followed him on and on, without stopping.

"He knew he was on the road to Falun, and this circumstance quieted him in a curious way; for he felt certain that the voice of destiny had spoken to him through the old miner, and that it was he who was now leading him on to his appointed place and fate.

"And, in fact, he many times—particularly if there was any uncertainty about the road—saw the old man suddenly appear out of some ravine, or from thick bushes, or gloomy rocks, stalk away before him, without looking round, and then disappear again.

"At last, after journeying for many weary days, Elis saw, in the distance, two great lakes[2], with a thick vapour rising between them. As he mounted the hill to westward, he saw some towers and black roofs rising through the smoke. The old man appeared before him, grown to gigantic size, pointed with outstretched hand towards the vapour, and disappeared again amongst the rocks.

"'There lies Falun,' said Elis, 'the end of my journey.'

"He was right; for people, coming up from behind him, said the town of Falun lay between the lakes Runn and Warpann, and that the hill he was ascending was the Guffrisberg, where the main-shaft of the mine was.

"He went bravely on. But when he came to the enormous gulf, like the jaws of hell itself, the blood curdled in his veins, and he stood as if turned to stone at the sight of this colossal work of destruction.

---

[1] That is, the Swedish port city of Gävle

[2] Varpan and Runn Lakes, which lie on Falun's north and south sides, respectively

"The main-shaft of the Falun mines is some twelve hundred feet long, six hundred feet broad, and a hundred and eighty feet deep. Its dark brown sides go, at first for the most part, perpendicularly down, till about half way they are sloped inwards towards the centre by enormous accumulations of stones and refuse. In these, and on the sides, there peeped out here and there timberings of old shafts, formed of strong shores set close together and strongly rabbeted[1] at the ends, in the way that blockhouses[2] are built. Not a tree, not a blade of grass to be seen in all the bare, blank, crumbling congeries of stony chasms; the pointed, jagged, indented masses of rock tower aloft all round in wonderful forms, often like monstrous animals turned to stone, often like colossal human beings. In the abyss itself lie, in wild confusion—pell-mell stones, slag, and scoria, and an eternal, stupefying sulphury vapour rises from the depths, as if the hell-broth, whose reek poisons and kills all the green gladsomeness of nature, were being brewed down below. One would think this was where Dante went down and saw the Inferno, with all its horror and immitigable pain.

"As Elis looked down into this monstrous abyss, he remembered what an old sailor, one of his shipmates, had told him once. This shipmate of his, at a time when he was down with fever, thought the sea had suddenly all gone dry, and the boundless depths of the abyss had opened under him, so that he saw all the horrible creatures of the deep twining and writhing about amongst thousands of extraordinary shells, and groves of coral, in dreadful contortions, till they died, and lay dead, with their mouths all gaping. The old sailor said that to see such a vision meant death, ere long, in the waves; and in fact he did very soon after fall overboard, no one knew exactly how, and was drowned without possibility of rescue. Elis thought of that: for indeed the abyss seemed to him to be a good deal like the bottom of the sea run dry; and the black rocks, and the blue and red slag and scoria[3], were like horrible monsters shooting out polype-arms[4] at him. Two or three miners happened, just then, to be coming up from work in the mine, and in their dark mining clothes, with their black, grimy faces, they were much like ugly, diabolical creatures of some sort, slowly and painfully crawling, and forcing their way up to the surface.

"Elis felt a shudder of dread go through him, and—what he had never experienced in all his career as a sailor—his head got giddy. Unseen hands seemed to be dragging him down into the abyss.

"He closed his eyes and ran a few steps away from it; and it was not till he began climbing up the Guffrisberg again, far from the shaft, and could

---

[1] Jointed together by creating interfacing stairstep groves on two pieces of wood

[2] The main building made of logs in stereotypical American frontier fortifications

[3] Volcanic rocks

[4] Tentacles

look up at the bright, sunny sky, that he quite lost the feeling of terror which had taken possession of him. He breathed freely once more, and cried, from the depths of his heart:

"'Lord of my Life! what are the dangers of the sea compared with the horror which dwells in that awful abyss of rock? The storm may rage, the black clouds may come whirling down upon the breaking billows, but the beautiful, glorious sun soon gets the mastery again, and the storm is past. But never does the sun penetrate into these black, gloomy caverns; never a freshening breeze of spring can revive the heart down there. No! I shall not join you, black earthworms that you are! Never could I bring myself to lead that terrible life.'

"He resolved to spend that night in Falun, and set off back to Goethaborg the first thing in the morning.

"When he got to the market-place, he found a crowd of people there. A train of miners with their mine-candles in their hands, and musicians before them, was halted before a handsome house. A tall, slightly-built man, of middle age, came out, looking round him with kindly smiles. It was easy to see, by his frank manner, his open brow, and his bright, dark-blue eyes, that he was a genuine Dalkarl[1]. The miners formed a circle round him, and he shook them each cordially by the hand, saying kindly words to them all.

"Elis learned that this was Pehrson Dahlsjoe, Alderman[2], and owner of a fine 'Fraelse' at Stora-Kopparberg[3]. 'Fraelse' is the name given in Sweden to landed property leased out for the working of the lodes of copper and silver contained in it. The owners of these lands have shares in the mines and are responsible for their management.

"Elis was told, further, that the Assizes[4] were just over that day, and that then the miners went round in procession to the houses of the aldermen, the chief engineers and the minemasters, and were hospitably entertained.

"When he looked at these fine, handsome fellows, with their kindly, frank faces, he forgot all about the earthworms he had seen coming up the shaft. The healthy gladsomeness which broke out afresh in the whole circle, as if new-fanned by a spring breeze, when Pehrson Dahlsjoe came out, was of a different kidney[5] to the senseless noise and uproar of the sailors' Hoensning. The manner in which these miners enjoyed themselves went straight to the serious Elis's heart. He felt indescribably happy; but he could

---

[1] A resident of Dalarna County, in central Sweden, some sixty miles northwest of Falun

[2] An elected city official who represents a district

[3] The now-700 year old mining company – based in Kopparberg, Dalarna – which managed the Falun mines

[4] Local court sessions

[5] Temperament, disposition, attitude

scarce restrain his tears when some of the young pickmen sang an ancient ditty in praise of the miner's calling, and of the happiness of his lot, to a simple melody which touched his heart and soul.

"When this song was ended, Pehrson Dahlsjoe opened his door, and the miners all went into his house one after another. Elis followed involuntarily, and stood at the threshold, so that he overlooked the spacious floor, where the miners took their places on benches. Then the doors at the side opposite to him opened, and a beautiful young lady, in evening dress, came in. She was in the full glory of the freshest bloom of youth, tall and slight, with dark hair in many curls, and a bodice fastened with rich clasps. The miners all stood up, and a low murmur of pleasure ran through their ranks. "Ulla Dahlsjoe!" they said. "What a blessing Heaven has bestowed on our hearty alderman in her!" Even the oldest miners' eyes sparkled when she gave them her hand in kindly greeting, as she did to them all. Then she brought beautiful silver tankards, filled them with splendid Aehl (such as Falun is famous for), and handed them to the guests with a face beaming with kindness and hospitality.

"When Elis saw her a lightning flash seemed to go through his heart, kindling all the heavenly bliss, the love-longings, the passionate ardour lying hidden and imprisoned there. For it was Ulla Dahlsjoe who had held out the hand of rescue to him in his mysterious dream. He thought he understood, now, the deep significance of that dream, and, forgetting the old miner, praised the stroke of fortune which had brought him to Falun.

"Alas! he felt he was but an unknown, unnoticed stranger, standing there on the doorstep miserable, comfortless, alone—and he wished he had died before he saw Ulla, as he now must perish for love and longing. He could not move his eyes from the beautiful creature, and, as she passed close to him, he pronounced her name in a low, trembling voice. She turned, and saw him standing there with a face as red as fire, unable to utter a syllable. So she went up to him, and said, with a sweet smile:

"'I suppose you are a stranger, friend, as you are dressed as a sailor. Well! why are you standing at the door? Come in and join us."

"Elis felt as if in the blissful paradise of some happy dream, from which he would presently waken to inexpressible wretchedness. He emptied the tankard which she had given him; and Pehrson Dahlsjoe came up, and, after kindly shaking hands with him, asked him where he came from, and what had brought him to Falun.

"Elis felt the warming power of the noble liquor in his veins, and, looking the hearty Dahlsjoe in the eyes, he felt happy and courageous. He told him he was a sailor's son and had been at sea since his childhood, had just come home from the East Indies and found his mother dead; that he was now alone in the world; that the wild sea life had become altogether distasteful to him; that his keenest inclination led him to a miner's calling, and that he wished to get employment as a miner here in Falun. The latter statement, quite the reverse of his recent determination, escaped him involuntarily; it was as if he could not have said anything else to the alderman, nay as if it were the most ardent desire of his soul, although he had not known it till now, himself.

"Pehrson Dahlsjoe looked at him long and carefully, as if he would read his heart; then he said:

"'I cannot suppose, Elis Froebom, that it is mere thoughtless fickleness and the love of change that lead you to give up the calling you have followed hitherto, nor that you have omitted to maturely weigh and consider all the difficulties and hardships of the miner's life before making up your mind to take to it. It is an old belief with us that the mighty elements with which the miner has to deal, and which he controls so bravely, destroy him unless he strains all his being to keep command of them—if he gives place to other thoughts which weaken that vigour which he has to reserve wholly for his constant conflict with Earth and Fire. But if you have properly tested the sincerity of your inward call, and it has withstood the trial, you are come in a good hour. Workmen are wanted in my part of the mine. If you like, you can stay here with me, from now, and to-morrow the Captain will take you down with him, and show you what to set about.'

"Elis's heart swelled with gladness at this. He thought no more of the terror of the awful, hell-like abyss into which he had looked. The thought that he was going to see Ulla every day, and live under the same roof with her, filled him with rapture and delight. He gave way to the sweetest hopes.

"Pehrson Dahlsjoe told the miners that a young hand had applied for employment, and presented him to them then and there. They all looked approvingly at the well-knit lad, and thought he was quite cut out for a miner, as regarded his light, powerful figure, having no doubt that he would not fail in industry and straightforwardness, either.

"One of the men, well advanced in years, came and shook hands with him cordially, saying he was Head-Captain[1] in Pehrson Dahlsjoe's part of the mine, and would be very glad to give him any help and instruction in his power. Elis had to sit down beside this man, who at once began, over his tankard of Aehl, to describe with much minuteness the sort of work which Elis would have to commence with.

"Elis remembered the old miner whom he had seen at Goethaborg, and, strangely enough, found he was able to repeat nearly all that he had told him.

"'Ay,' cried the Head-Captain. 'Where can you have learned all that? It's most surprising! There can't be a doubt that you will be the finest pickman in the mine in a very short time.'

"Ulla—going backwards and forwards amongst the guests and attending to them—often nodded kindly to Elis, and told him to be sure and enjoy himself. 'You're not a stranger now, you know,' she said, 'but one

[1] Foreman

of the household. You have nothing more to do with the treacherous sea the rich mines of Falun are your home.'

"A heaven of bliss and rapture dawned upon Elis at these words of Ulla's. It was evident that she liked to be near him; and Pehrson Dahlsjoe watched his quiet earnestness of character with manifest approval.

"But Elis's heart beat violently when he stood again by the reeking hell-mouth, and went down the mine with the Captain, in his miner's clothes, with the heavy, iron-shod Dalkarl shoes on his feet. Hot vapours soon threatened to suffocate him; and then, presently, the candles flickered in the cutting draughts of cold air that blew in the lower levels. They went down deeper and deeper, on iron ladders at last scarcely a foot wide; and Elis found that his sailor's adroitness at climbing was not of the slightest service to him there.

"They got to the lowest depths of the mine at last, and the Captain showed him what work he was to set about.

"Elis thought of Ulla. Like some bright angel he saw her hovering over him, and he forgot all the terror of the abyss, and the hardness of the toilsome labour.

"It was clear in all his thoughts that it was only if he devoted himself with all the power of his mind, and with all the exertion which his body would endure, to mining work here with Pehrson Dahlsjoe, that there was any possibility of his fondest hopes being some day realized. Wherefore it came about that he was as good at his work as the most practised hand, in an incredibly short space of time.

"Staunch Pehrson Dahlsjoe got to like this good, industrious lad better and better every day, and often told him plainly that he had found in him one whom he regarded as a dear son, as well as a first-class mine-hand. Also Ulla's regard for him became more and more unmistakeable. Often, when he was going to his work, and there was any prospect of danger, she would enjoin him to be sure to take care of himself, with tears in her eyes. And she would come running to meet him when he came back, and always had the finest of Aehl, or some other refreshment, ready for him. His heart danced for joy one day when Pehrson said to him that as he had brought a good sum of money with him, there could be no doubt that—with his habits of economy and industry—he would soon have a 'Hemmans,' or perhaps even a 'Fraelse'; and then not a mineowner in all Falun would say him nay if he asked for his daughter. Fain would Elis have told him at once how unspeakably he loved Ulla, and how all his hopes of happiness were based upon her. But unconquerable shyness, and the doubt whether Ulla really liked him—though he often thought she did—sealed his lips.

"One day it chanced that Elis was at work in the lowest depths of the mine, shrouded in thick, sulphurous vapour, so that his candle only shed a feeble glimmer, and he could scarcely distinguish the run of the lode[1].

---

[1] Traceable profile of the copper deposits

Suddenly he heard—as if coming from some still deeper cutting—a knocking resounding, as if somebody was at work with a pick-hammer. As that sort of work was scarcely possible at such a depth, and as he knew nobody was down there that day but himself—because the Captain had got all the men employed in another part of the mine—this knocking and hammering struck him as strange and uncanny. He stopped working, and listened to the hollow sounds, which seemed to come nearer and nearer. All at once he saw, close by him, a black shadow and—as a keen draught of air blew away the sulphur vapour—the old miner whom he had seen in Goethaborg.

"'Good luck,' he cried, 'good luck to Elis Froebom, down here among the stones! What think you of the life, comrade?'

"Elis would fain have asked in what wonderful[1] way the old man had got into the mine; but he kept striking his hammer on the rocks with such force

that the fire-sparks went whirling all round, and the mine rang as if with distant thunder. Then he cried, in a terrible voice:

"'There's a grand run of trap[2] just here; but a scurvy, ignorant scoundrel like you sees nothing in it but a narrow streak of 'Trumm'[3] not worth a beanstalk. Down here you're a sightless mole, and you'll always be a mere abomination to the Metal Prince. You're of no use up above either—trying to get hold of the pure Regulus[4]; which you never will—hey! You want to marry Pehrson Dahlsjoe's daughter; that's what you've taken to mine work for, not from any love of your own for the thing. Mind what you're after, double-face; take care that the Metal Prince, whom you are trying to deceive, doesn't take you and dash you down so that the sharp rocks tear you limb from limb. And Ulla will never be your wife; that much I tell you.'

"Elis's anger was kindled at the old man's insulting words.

"'What are you about,' he cried, 'here in my master, Herr Pehrson Dahlsjoe's shaft, where I am doing my duty, and working as hard at it as I can? Be off out of this the way you came, or we'll see which of us two will dash the other's brains out down here.'

"With which he placed himself in a threatening attitude, and swung his hammer about the old man's ears; who only gave a sneering laugh, and Elis saw with terror how he swarmed up the narrow ladder rungs like a squirrel, and disappeared amongst the black labyrinths of the chasms.

"The young man felt paralyzed in all his limbs; he could not go on with his work, but went up. When the old Head-Captain—who had been busy in another part of the mine—saw him, he cried:

---

[1] Unimaginable, fantastical, paranormal

[2] A particularly fruitful, easy-to-mine vein of minerals

[3] A vein that starts strong, but branches out into many, insignificant threads before petering out

[4] One of the brightest stars in the sky, part of the constellation Leo

"'For God's sake, Elis, what has happened to you? You're as pale as death. I suppose it's the sulphur gas; you're not accustomed to it yet. Here, take a drink, my lad; that'll do you good.'

"Elis took a good mouthful of brandy out of the flask which the Head-Captain handed to him; and then, feeling better, told him what had happened
down in the mine, as also how he had made the uncanny old miner's acquaintance in Goethaborg.

"The Head-Captain listened silently; then dubiously shook his head and said:

"'That must have been old Torbern[1] that you met with, Elis; and I see, now, that there really is something in the tales that people tell about him. More than one hundred years ago, there was a miner here of the name of Torbern. He seems to have been one of the first to bring mining into a flourishing condition at Falun here, and in his time the profits far exceeded anything that we know of now. Nobody at that time knew so much about mining as Torbern, who had great scientific skill, and thoroughly understood all the ins and outs of the business. The richest lodes seemed to disclose themselves to him, as if he had been endowed with higher powers peculiar to himself; and as he was a gloomy, meditative man, without wife or child—with no regular home, indeed—and very seldom came up to the surface, it couldn't fail that a story soon went about that he was in compact with the mysterious power which dwells in the bowels of the earth, and fuses the metals. Disregarding Torbern's solemn warnings—for he always prophesied that some calamity would happen as soon as the miners' impulse to work ceased to be sincere love for the marvellous metals and ores—people went on enlarging the excavations more and more for the sake of mere profit, till, on St. John's Day of the year 1687[2], came the terrible landslip and subsidence which formed our present enormous

---

[1] Although a fictional character, he is almost certainly named after the 18th century Swedish minerologist and chemist, Torbern Bergman, who revolutionized the science of chemical affinities, He did *not* disappear into any mines, however

[2] June 24, also commonly called Midsummer. Indeed, this historical event was an economic catastrophe, though no lives were lost due to the celebration of Midsummer. As the Falun Mines' website puts it: "The great collapse of 1687 is one of the most known events in Falun Mines's history. The mine workers had started to sound strange and disturbing in the rock. And sure enough, during the Midsummer weekend of 1687 the biggest slide ever occurred. Below ground, rubble masses were found as far down as 350 meters underground. The Great Pit, with a circumference of 1,6 kilometers and a depth of 95 metres, was what appeared afterwards. The incident became known all over Sweden, and also in Europe, because not a single miner lost their life – they had been given time off to celebrate midsummer."

main-shaft, laying waste the whole of the works, as they were then, in the process. It was only after many months' labour that several of the shafts were, with much difficulty, got into workable order again. Nothing was seen or heard of Torbern. There seemed to be no doubt that he had been at work down below at the time of the catastrophe, so that there could be no question what his fate had been. But not long after, and particularly when the work was beginning to go on better again, the miners said they had seen old Torbern in the mine, and that he had given them valuable advice, and pointed out rich lodes to them. Others had come across him at the top of the main-shaft, walking round it, sometimes lamenting, sometimes shouting in wild anger. Other young fellows have come here in the way you yourself did, saying that an old miner had advised them to take to mining, and shewn them the way to Falun. This always happened when there was a scarcity of hands; very likely it was Torbern's way of helping on the cause. But if it really was he whom you had those words with in the mine, and if he spoke of a fine run of trap, there isn't a doubt that there must be a grand vein of ore thereabouts, and we must see, to-morrow, if we can come across it. Of course you remember that we call rich veins of the kind "trap-runs," and that a "Trumm" is a vein which goes sub-dividing into several smaller ones, and probably gets lost altogether.'

"When Elis, tossed hither and thither by various thoughts, went into Pehrson Dahlsjoe's, Ulla did not come meeting him as usual. She was sitting with downcast looks, and—as he thought—eyes which had been weeping; and beside her was a handsome young fellow, holding her hand, and trying to say all sorts of kind and amusing things, to which she seemed to pay little attention. Pehrson Dahlsjoe took Elis—who, seized by gloomy presentiments, was keeping a darksome glance riveted on the pair—into another room, and said:

"'Well, Elis, you will soon have it in your power to give me a proof of your regard and sincerity. I have always looked upon you as a son, but you will soon take the place of one altogether. The man whom you see in there is a well-to-do merchant, Eric Olavsen by name, from Goethaborg. I am giving him my daughter for his wife, at his desire. He will take her to Goethaborg, and then you will be left alone with me, my only support in my declining years. Well, you say nothing? You turn pale? I trust this step doesn't displease you, and that now that I'm going to lose my daughter you are not going to leave me too? But I hear Olavsen mentioning my name; I must go in.'

"With which he went back to the room.

"Elis felt a thousand red-hot irons tearing at his heart. He could find no words, no tears. In wild despair he ran out, out of the house, away to the great mine-shrift.

"That monstrous chasm had a terrible appearance by day; but now, when night had fallen, and the moon was just peeping down into it, the desolate crags looked like a numberless horde of horrible monsters, the direful brood of hell, rolling and writhing, in wildest confusion, all about its reeking sides and clefts, and flashing up fiery eyes, and shooting forth glowing claws to clutch the race of mortals.

"Torbern, Torbern,' Elis cried, in a terrible voice, which made the rocks re-echo. 'Torbern, I am here; you were not wrong I was a wretched fool to fix my hopes on any earthly love, up on the surface here. My treasure, and my life, my all-in-all, are down below. Torbern! take me down with you! Show me the richest veins, the lodes of ore, the glowing metal! I will dig and bore, and toil and labour. Never, never more will I come back to see the light of day. Torbern! Torbern! take me down to you!'

"He took his flint and steel from his pocket, lighted his candle, and went quickly down the shaft, into the deep cutting where he had been on the previous day, without seeing anything of the old man. But what was his amazement when, at the deepest point, he saw the vein of metal with the utmost clearness and distinctness, so that he could trace every one of its ramifications, and its risings and fallings. But as he kept his gaze fixed more and more firmly on this wonderful vein, a dazzling light seemed to come shining through the shaft, and the walls of rock grew transparent as crystal. That mysterious dream which he had had in Goethaborg came back upon him. He was looking upon those Elysian Fields[1] of glorious metallic trees and plants, on which, by way of fruits, buds, and blossoms, hung jewels streaming with fire. He saw the maidens, and he looked upon the face of the mighty queen. She put out her arms, drew him to her, and pressed him to her breast. Then a burning ray darted through his heart, and all his consciousness was merged in a feeling of floating in waves of some blue, transparent, glittering mist.

"'Elis Froebom! Elis Froebom!' a powerful voice from above cried out, and the reflection of torches began shining in the shaft. It was Pehrson Dahlsjoe come down with the Captain to search for the lad, who had been seen running in the direction of the main-shaft like a mad creature.

"They found him standing as if turned to stone, with his face pressed against the cold, hard rock.

"'What are you doing down here in the night-time, you foolish fellow?' cried Pehrson. 'Pull yourself together, and come up with us. Who knows what good news you may hear.'

"Elis went up in profound silence after Dahlsjoe, who did not cease to rate him soundly for exposing himself to such danger. It was broad daylight in the morning when they got to the house.

"Ulla threw herself into Elis's arms with a great cry, and called him by the fondest names, and Pehrson said to him:

"'You foolish fellow! How could I help seeing, long ago, that you were in love with Ulla, and that it was on her account, in all probability, that you were working so hard in the mine? Neither could I help seeing that she was

---

[1] A heavenly paradise

just as fond of you. Could I wish for a better son-in-law than a fine, hearty, hard-working, honest miner—than just yourself, Elis? What vexed me was that you never would speak.'

"'We scarcely knew ourselves,' said Ulla, 'how fond we were of each other.'

"'However that may be,' said Pehrson, 'I was annoyed that Elis didn't tell me openly and candidly of his love for you, and that was why I made up the story about Eric Olavsen, which was so nearly being the death of you, you silly fellow. Not but what I wished to try you, Ulla, into the bargain. Eric Olavsen has been married for many a day, and I give my daughter to you, Elis Froebom, for, I say it again, I couldn't wish for a better son-in-law.'

"Tears of joy and happiness ran down Elis's cheeks. The highest bliss which his imagination had pictured had come to pass so suddenly and unexpectedly that he could scarce believe it was anything but another blissful dream. The workpeople came to dinner, by Dahlsjoe's invitation, in honour of the event. Ulla had dressed in her prettiest attire, and looked more charming than ever, so that they all cried, over and over again, 'Ey! what a sweet and charming creature Elis has got for a betrothed! May God bless them and make them happy!'

"Yet the terror of the past night still lay upon Elis's pale face, and he often stared about him as if he were far away from all that was going on round him. 'Elis, darling, what is the matter?' Ulla asked anxiously. He pressed her to his heart and said, 'Yes, yes, you are my own, and all is well.' But in the midst of all his happiness he often felt as though an icy hand clutched at his heart, and a dismal voice asked him,

"Is it your highest ideal, then, to be betrothed to Ulla? Wretched fool! Have you not looked upon the face of the queen?'

"He felt himself overpowered by an indescribable, anxious alarm. He was haunted and tortured by the thought that one of the workmen would suddenly assume gigantic proportions, and to his horror he would recognize in him Torbern, come to remind him, in a terrible manner, of the subterranean realm of gems and metals to which he had devoted himself.

"And yet he could see no reason why the spectral old man should be hostile to him, or what connection there was between his mining work and his love.

"Pehrson, seeing Elis's disordered condition, attributed it to the trouble he had gone through, and his nocturnal visit to the mine. Not so, Ulla, who, seized by a secret presentiment, implored her lover to tell her what terrible thing had happened to him to tear him away from her so entirely. This almost broke his heart. It was in vain that he tried to tell her of the wonderful face which had revealed itself to him in the depths of the mine. Some unknown power seemed to seal his lips forcibly; he felt as though the terrible face of the queen were looking out from his heart, so that if he mentioned her everything about him would turn to stone, to dark, black rock, as at the sight of the Medusa's frightful head. All the glory and magnificence which had filled him with rapture in the abyss appeared to him now as a pandemonium of immitigable torture, deceptively decked out to allure him to his ruin.

"Dahlsjoe told him he must stay at home for a few days, so as to shake off the sickness which he seemed to have fallen into. And during this time Ulla's affection, which now streamed bright and clear from her candid, child-like heart, drove away the memory of his fateful adventure in the mine-depths. Joy and happiness brought him back to life, and to belief in his good fortune, and in the impossibility of its being ever interfered with by any evil power.

"When he went down the pit again, everything appeared quite different to what it used to be. The most glorious veins lay clear and distinct before his eyes. He worked twice as zealously as before; he forgot everything else. When he got to the surface again, it cost him an effort of thought to remember about Pehrson Dahlsjoe, about his Ulla, even. He felt as if divided into two halves, as if his better self, his real personality, went down to the central point of the earth, and there rested in bliss in the queen's arms, whilst *he* went to his darksome[1] dwelling in Falun. When Ulla spoke of their love, and the happiness of their future life together, he would begin to talk of the splendours of the depths, and the inestimably precious treasures that lay hidden there, and in so doing would get entangled in such wonderful, incomprehensible sayings, that alarm and terrible anxiety took possession of the poor child, who could not divine why Elis should be so completely altered from his former self. He kept telling the Captain, and Dahlsjoe himself, with the greatest delight, that he had discovered the richest veins and the most magnificent trap-runs, and when these turned out to be nothing but unproductive rock, he would laugh contemptuously and say that none but he understood the secret signs, the significant writing, fraught with hidden meaning, which the queen's own hand had inscribed on the rocks, and that it was sufficient to understand those signs without bringing to light what they indicated.

"The old Captain looked sorrowfully at Elis, who spoke, with wild gleaming eyes, of the glorious paradise which glowed down in the depths of the earth. 'That terrible old Torbern has been at him,' he whispered in Dahlsjoe's ear.

"'Pshaw! don't believe these miners' yarns,' cried Dahlsjoe. 'He's a deep-thinking serious fellow, and love has turned his head, that's all. Wait till the marriage is over, then we'll hear no more of the trap-runs, the treasures, and the subterranean paradise.'

"The wedding-day, fixed by Dahlsjoe, came at last. For a few days previously Elis had been more tranquil, more serious, more sunk in deep reflection than ever. But, on the other hand, never had he shown such

---

[1] Gloomy, depressing

affection for Ulla as at this time. He could not leave her for a moment, and never went down the mine at all. He seemed to have forgotten his restless excitement about mining work, and never a word of the subterranean kingdom crossed his lips. Ulla was all rapture. Her fear lest the dangerous powers of the subterranean world, of which she had heard old miners speak, had been luring him to his destruction, had left her; and Dahlsjoe, too, said, laughing to the Captain, 'You see, Elis was only a little light-headed for love of my Ulla.'

"Early on the morning of the wedding-day, which was St. John's Day as it chanced, Elis knocked at the door of Ulla's room. She opened it, and started back terrified at the sight of Elis, dressed in his wedding clothes already, deadly pale, with dark gloomy fire sparkling in his eyes.

"'I only want to tell you, my beloved Ulla,' he said, in a faint, trembling voice, 'that we are just arrived at the summit of the highest good fortune which it is possible for mortals to attain. Everything has been revealed to me in the night which is just over. Down in the depths below, hidden in chlorite and mica[1], lies the cherry-coloured sparkling almandine, on which the tablet of our lives is graven. I have to give it to you as a wedding present. It is more splendid than the most glorious blood-red carbuncle, and when, united in truest affection, we look into its streaming splendour together, we shall see and understand the peculiar manner in which our hearts and souls have grown together into the wonderful branch which shoots from the queen's heart, at the central point of the globe. All that is necessary is that I go and bring this stone to the surface, and that I will do now, as fast as I can. Take care of yourself meanwhile, beloved darling. I will be back to you directly.'

"Ulla implored him, with bitter tears, to give up all idea of such a dream-like undertaking, for she felt a strong presentiment of disaster; but Elis declared that without this stone he should never know a moment's peace or happiness, and that there was not the slightest danger of any kind. He pressed her fondly to his heart, and was gone.

"The guests were all assembled to accompany the bridal pair to the church of Copparberg, where they were to be married, and a crowd of girls, who were to be the bridesmaids and walk in procession before the bride (as is the custom of the place), were laughing and playing round Ulla. The musicians were tuning their instruments to begin a wedding march. It was almost noon, but Elis had not made his appearance. Suddenly some miners came running up, horror in their pale faces, with the news that there had been a terrible catastrophe, a subsidence of the earth[2], which had destroyed the whole of Pehrson Dahlsjoe's part of the mine.

---

[1] A dark, green, crystalline mineral and a shiny, metallic, silicate mineral, respectively

[2] A cave-in

"'Elis! oh, Elis! you are gone!' screamed Ulla, wildly, and fell as if dead. Then only, for the first time, Dahlsjoe learned from the Captain that Elis had gone down the main-shaft in the morning. Nobody else had been in the mine, the rest of the men having been invited to the wedding. Dahlsjoe and all the others hurried off to search, at the imminent danger of their own lives. In vain! Elis Froebom was not to be found. There could be no question that the earth-fall had buried him in the rock. And thus came desolation and mourning upon the house of brave Pehrson Dahlsjoe, at the moment when he thought he was assured of peace and happiness for the remainder of his days.

ꟹ

"Long had stout Pehrson Dahlsjoe been dead, his daughter Ulla long lost sight of and forgotten. Nobody in Falun remembered them. More than fifty years had gone by since Froebom's luckless wedding-day, when it chanced that some miners who were making a connection-passage between two shafts, found, at a depth of three hundred yards, buried in vitriolated water[1], the body of a young miner, which seemed, when they brought it to the daylight, to be turned to stone.

"The young man looked as if he were lying in a deep sleep, so perfectly preserved were the features of his lace, so wholly without trace of decay his new suit of miner's clothes, and even the flowers in his breast. The people of the neighbourhood all collected round the young man, but no one recognized him or could say who he had been, and none of the workmen missed any comrade.

"The body was going to be taken to Falun, when out of the distance an old, old woman came creeping slowly and painfully up on crutches.

"Here's the old St. John's Day grandmother!' the miners said. They had given her this name because they had noticed that she came always every year on St. John's Day up to the main shaft, and looked down into its depths, weeping, lamenting, and wringing her hands as she crept round it, then going away again.

"The moment she saw the body she threw away her crutches, lifted her arms to Heaven, and cried, in the most heartrending accents of the deepest lamentation:

"'Oh! Elis Froebom! Oh, my sweet, sweet bridegroom!'

"And she cowered down beside the body, took the stony hands and pressed them to her heart, chilled with age, but throbbing still with the fondest love, like some naphtha[2] flame under the surface ice.

"'Ah!' she said, looking round at the spectators, 'nobody, nobody among you all, remembers poor Ulla Dahlsjoe, this poor boy's happy bride

---

[1] Water which has chemically reacted to the copper and minerals in the mines, becoming a strong acid called copper sulfate

[2] A highly combustible, liquid byproduct of crude oil, used as a cheap fuel

fifty long years ago. When I went away, in my terrible sorrow and despair, to Ornaes[1], old Torbern comforted me, and told me I should see my poor Elis, who was buried in the rock upon our wedding-day, yet once more here upon earth. And I have come every year and looked for him, all longing and faithful love. And now this blessed meeting has been granted me this day. Oh, Elis! Elis! my beloved husband!'

"She wound her arms about him as if she would never part from him more, and the people all stood round in the deepest emotion.

"Fainter and fainter grew her sobs and sighs, till they ceased to be audible.

"The miners closed round. They would have raised poor Ulla, but she had breathed out her life upon her bridegroom's body. The spectators noticed now that it was beginning to crumble into dust. The appearance of petrifaction had been deceptive.

"In the church of Copparberg, where they were to have been married fifty years before, they laid in the earth the ashes of Elis Froebom, and with them the body of her who had been thus 'Faithful unto death.'"

HOFFMANN'S story builds off of several historical events and contexts. As previously mentioned, the Midsummer mine-collapse was a real catastrophe. The name Torbern is also significant: although the Torbern in Hoffmann's tale is a fictional character, he was named after the 18th century Swedish minerologist and chemist, Torbern Bergman, who revolutionized the science of chemical affinities. He did *not* disappear into any mines, however. But there *was* a famous figure in the history of Falun who did vanish. Another historical reference which Hoffmann used for inspiration – the veracity of which might surprise the reader – is the story of a Falun miner mysteriously disappearing before his wedding, and not being found until decades later, when his perfectly preserved body is identified by his aged but still-heartbroken fiancée. This incredible story took place in 1719 when the eerily-mummified corpse of "Fat" Mats Israelsson was discovered in a pool of caustic water forty-two years after he vanished. The body was missing its legs, but its clothes and skin were preserved without any sign of decay. After being brought to the surface, the corpse became as hard as wood, but retained its youthful looks. Concerned that it was a recent casualty, the authorities displayed the body to the community, and were shocked when Margaret Olsdotter identified it as the nearly-half-century-missing miner, Mats Israelsson. Scientists explained that the surrounding copper had turned the water to

[1] That is, Ornäs, a village in Dalarna

vitriol (copper sulfate) which protected the body from bacteria. His story became a cause célèbre, and the body was put on display for a third of a century before he was buried. During renovations of the local church during the 1860s, Fat Mats made a second return after a century when his body was discovered – still incorrupt – and once again put on display, this time for seventy years before being buried for good in 1930. The tale – which seemed to be a "Rip Van Winkle"-like parable of the woes of time, the allure of nature, the heartbreak of loss, and the siren-song of wild places inspired many German Romantics other than Hoffmann: G. H. von Schubert, Achim von Arnim, Johann Hebel, and Friedrich Ruckert each found literary inspiration in his sorrowful story and sublime resurrection. For Hoffmann, the symbolism behind Mats' story was three-fold: a sociological critique of industrial dehumanization, a meditation on the dangerous allure of nature, and a very personal analysis on the dangers of obsession.

II.

Well aware of his psychological blocks and his own self-sabotaging behavior (see: "The Lost Reflection"), Hoffmann wrote almost obsessively about well-intended romances ruined by the neurotic hang-ups of one party (usually the male) which prevent a successful, healthy union. Such is the case in "The Sandman," "The Vampire," and "Automatons," just to name a few. If his fiction didn't take itself so seriously (or if its plots weren't so tragic), Hoffmann could have been a literary precursor to the films of Woody Allen or the comedy of Billy Crystal. In "The Mines of Falun," it is a hopelessly obsessive love for the protagonist's mother (and an oppressive guilt for having been at sea at the time of her death) which prevents Elis from having a successful union with Ulla. Returning to shore with presents for his loving mother, Elis experiences Oedipal shame when he gifts the valuables to a prostitute (hoping, no doubt, to experience the same devotion and gratitude he experienced from his mother, but repelled by the sexual connotation of the transaction), an interaction which drives him into a deep melancholy. In typical Hoffmann style, the solution to his sorrow is elemental in nature: leaving the ephemeral realm of the winds and waves for the deeply physical world of earth and fire. And in another typically Hoffmannesque move, the symbolism of his shift is engorged with Freudian symbolism: cut adrift by the loss of his mother, he seeks to return to her protective womb by crawling through the vaginal mines of Falun in search of a uterine homecoming. When he hears his mother's voice blessing this career change in a dream, he also senses a prophetic conflict between two kinds of femininity: the stable, reliable (but possessive and critical) love of a Mother figure, and the fickle, deciduous (but empowering and inspiring) affection of a Lover. One propels man forward into the unknown heights above (in his dream, the symbolic Lover calls to him from a mineshaft high overhead) while the other preserves him in perpetual childhood and eternal dependency.

Like the spectral ghost of Torbern, another ill-fated Oedipus, Elis finds himself drawn to the mines for their own sake – not for profit or employment – and is lost to them through his childish dependency of them as a source of identity and approval. His very death occurs when he flees his wedding to first ask the blessing of the maternal Queen of the Mines – since this results in a smothering cave-in, we can guess what her response was. When Elis' corpse is found preserved in sulfuric acid fifty years later, the metaphor is completed: lost in his love for his mother, Elis appears unchanged on the outside, but the first touch of his long-lost Ulla exposes the truth, and his rotten insides dissolve into ash. Hoffmann's Freudian parable is a warning that unhealthy allegiance to the past, dependence on the approval of authority figures, and dichotomization of humanity into unrealistic gender roles will only result in arrested development and ludicrous delusions.

IN 1810 Hoffmann began teaching music to Julia Marc, the teenaged cousin of one of his close friends. Hoffmann met her when she was twelve – about a year after the death of his infant daughter, and not long after his twelve-year-old niece – who had lived with he and his wife for years – moved out of their house. James McGlathery notes that after these two losses, Julia filled a daughterly hole in Hoffmann's raw heart, filling "an emotional need for a substitute object of paternal affection." At first Hoffmann's affection for Julia was purely paternal, but as she grew into sexual maturity, a deep attraction developed within him – one which was so powerful that her family would summarily fire him due to his scandalous pining. Hoffmann's obsession with his nubile student became so all-encompassing that he feared that he was losing his sanity and dreaded that he would impulsively commit suicide in a moment of irrational mania. Initially he hoped, rather oddly, that his love for Julia would be revealed to her in a dream – relieving him of the awkward prospect of exposing himself to a humiliating rejection. But neither would ever happen: he was finally banished by Julia's mother after an emotional outburst in which Hoffmann verbally berated her fiancé for being unfit to marry her (the young banker's son had collapsed in public while inebriated). Three months later the two were married, but Hoffmann's impressions weren't merely jealous – they were prophetic, and Julia would divorce her husband a few years later. This was the end for Hoffmann, however, and he would never see Julia again. But her influence on him was irrevocable, infecting his imagination for years to come. To him she represented the childlike innocence he idealized in most of his fictional heroines: impressionable ingénues under the sway of eccentric and possessive paternal figures. It was an innocence which – though tangled up in his sexual fantasies – ultimately expressed his *own* inner idealism, an unsullied innocence of the soul to which he desired to return. In the following story Hoffmann worked to exorcise his suicidal anxieties following the Julia Marc scandal: it tells of how a family man's adulterous fascination with a prostitute named Julia results in the loss of his reflection, an existential disfigurement for which there is only one cure: the murder of his wife and young son.

The Lost Reflection

— Excerpted from 'Fantasy-Pieces in Callot's Manner,' Volume Four —

{1815}

THE BELOVED

I had a feeling of death in my heart—ice-cold death—and the sensation branched out like sharp, growing icicles into nerves that were already boiling with heat. I ran like a madman-no hat, no coat-out into the lightless stormy winter night. The weather vanes were grinding and creaking in the wind, as if Time's eternal gearwork were audibly rotating and the old year were being rolled away like a heavy weight, and ponderously pushed into a gloom-filled abyss.

You must surely know that on this season, Christmas and New Year's, even though it's so fine and pleasant for all of you, I am always driven out of my peaceful cell onto a raging, lashing sea.

Christmas! Holidays that have a rosy glow for me. I can hardly wait for it, I look forward to it so much. I am a better, finer man than the rest of the year, and there isn't a single gloomy, misanthropic thought in my mind. Once again I am a boy, shouting with joy. The faces of the angels laugh to me from the gilded fretwork decorations in the shops decorated for Christmas, and the awesome tones of the church organ penetrate the noisy bustle of the streets, as if coming from afar, with "Unto us a child is born[1]." But after the holidays everything becomes colorless again, and the glow dies away and disappears into drab darkness.

Every year more and more flowers drop away withered, their buds eternally sealed; there is no spring sun that can bring the warmth of new life into old dried-out branches. I know this well enough, but the Enemy[2] never stops maliciously rubbing it in as the year draws to an end. I hear a mocking whisper: "Look what you have lost this year; so many worthwhile things that you'll never see again. But all this makes you wiser, less tied to trivial pleasures, more serious and solid-even though you don't enjoy yourself very much."

Every New Year's Eve the Devil keeps a special treat for me. He knows just the right moment to jam his claw into my heart, keeping up a fine mockery while he licks the blood that wells out.

And there is always someone around to help him, just as yesterday the Justizrat[3] came to his aid.

He (the Justizrat) holds a big celebration every New Year's Eve, and likes to give everyone something special as a New Year's present. Only he is so clumsy and bumbling about it, for all his pains, that what was meant to give pleasure usually turns into a mess that is half slapstick and half torture.

I walked into his front hall, and the Justizrat came running to meet me, holding me back for a moment from the Holy of Holies out of which the odors of tea and expensive perfumes were pouring. He looked especially pleased with himself. He smirked at me in a very strange way and

---

[1] Isaiah 9:6 – excerpted from an Old Testament prophecy which is taken by Christians to refer to Jesus. The verse is used in several Christmas carols and, famously, in one of the choruses of Handel's "Messiah"

[2] Satan

[3] Counseller of Justice – an honorary title for distinguished lawyers

said, "My dear friend, there's something nice waiting for you in the next room. Nothing like it for a New Year's surprise. But don't be afraid!"

I felt that sinking feeling in my heart. Something was wrong, I knew, and I suddenly began to feel depressed and edgy. Then the doors were opened. I took up my courage and stepped forward, marched in, and among the women sitting on the sofa I saw her.

Yes, it was she. She herself. I hadn't seen her for years, and yet in one lightning flash the happiest moments of my life came bad to me, and gone was the pain that had resulted from being separated from her.

What marvellous chance brought her here? What miracle introduced her into the Justizrat's circle—I didn't even know that he knew her. But I didn't think of any of these questions; all I knew was that she was mine again.

I must have stood there as if halted magically in midmotion. The Justizrat kept nudging me and muttering, "Mmmm? Mmmm? How about it?"

I started to walk again, mechanically, but I saw only her, and it was all that I could do to force out, "My God, my God, it's Julia!" I was practically at the tea table before she even noticed me, but then she stood up and said coldly, "I'm so delighted to see you here. You are looking well."

And with that she sat down again and asked the woman sitting next to her on the sofa, "Is there going to be anything interesting at the theatre the next few weeks?"

You see a miraculously beautiful flower, glowing with beauty, filling the air with scent, hinting at even more hidden beauty. You hurry over to it, but the moment that you bend down to look into its chalice, the glistening petals are pushed aside and out pops a smooth, cold, slimy, little lizard that tries to cut you down with its glare.

That's just what happened to me. Like a perfect oaf I made a bow to the ladies, and since spite and idiocy often go together, as I stepped back I knocked a cup of hot tea out of the Justizrat's hand-he was standing right behind me-and all over his beautifully pleated jacket. The company roared at the Justizrat's mishap, and even more at me. In short, everything was going along smoothly enough for a madhouse, but I just gave up.

Julia, however, hadn't laughed, and as I looked at her again I thought for a moment that a gleam of our wonderful past came through to me, a fragment of our former life of love and poetry. At this point someone in the next room began to improvise on the piano, and the company began to show signs of life. I heard that this was someone I did not know, a great pianist named Berger, who played divinely, and that you had to listen to him.

"Will you stop making that noise with the teaspoons, Minchen," bawled the Justizrat, and with a coyly contorted hand and a languorous "Eh bien!" he beckoned the ladies to the door, to approach the virtuoso. Julia arose too and walked slowly into the next room.

There was something strange about her whole figure, I thought. Somehow she seemed larger, more developed, almost lush. Her blouse was cut low, only half covering her breasts, shoulders and neck; her sleeves were puffed, and reached only to her elbows; and her hair was parted at the forehead and pulled back into plaits-all of which gave her an antique look, much like one of the young women in Mieris's[1] paintings. Somehow it seemed to me as if I had seen her like this before. She had taken off her gloves, and ornate bracelets on her wrist helped carry through the complete identity of her dress with the past and awaken more vividly dark memories.

She turned toward me before she went into the music room, and for an instant her angel-like, normally pleasant face seemed strained into a sneer. An uncomfortable, unpleasant feeling arose in me, like a cramp running through my nervous system.

"Oh, he plays divinely," lisped a girl, apparently inspired by the sweet tea, and I don't know how it happened, but Julia's arm was in mine, and I led her, or rather she led me, into the next room. Berger was raising the wildest hurricanes, and like a roaring surf his mighty chords rose and fell. It did me good.

Then Julia was standing beside me, and said more softly and more sweetly than before, "I wish you were sitting at the piano, singing softly about pleasures and hopes that have been lost." The Enemy had left me, and in just the name, "Julia!" I wanted to proclaim the bliss that filled me.

But the crowd pushed between us and we were separated. Now she was obviously avoiding me, but I was lucky enough to touch her clothing and close enough to breathe in her perfume, and the springtime of the past arose in a hundred shining colors.

Berger let the hurricane blow itself out, the skies became clear, and pretty little melodies, like the golden clouds of dawn, hovered in pianissimo[2]. Well-earned applause broke out when he finished, and the guests began to move around the room. It came about that I found myself facing Julia again. The spirit rose more mightily in me. I wanted to seize her and embrace her, but a bustling servant crowded between us with a platter of drinks, calling in a very offensive way, "Help yourself, please, help yourself."

The tray was filled with cups of steaming punch, but in the very middle was a huge cut-crystal goblet, also apparently filled with punch. How did that get there, among all the ordinary punch cups? He knows—the Enemy that I'm gradually coming to understand. Like Clemens in Tieck's

---

[1] Franz van Mieris the Elder was a 17th century Dutch painter who specialized in domestic scenes, often populated by alluring, middleclass women

[2] Very soft, faint music

"Oktavian"[1] he walks about making a pleasant squiggle with one foot, and is very fond of red capes and feathers. Julia picked up this sparkling, beautifully cui goblet and offered it to me, saying, "Are you still willing to take a glass from my hand?" "Julia, Julia," I sighed.

As I took the glass, my fingers brushed against hers, and electric sensations ran through me. I drank and drank, and it seemed to me that little flickering blue flames licked around the goblet and my lip. Then the goblet was empty, and I really don't know myself how it happened, but I was now sitting on an ottoman in a small room lit only by an alabaster lamp, and Julia was sitting beside me, demure and innocent-looking as ever. Berger had started to play again, the andante from Mozart's sublime E-flat Symphony, and on the swan's wings of song my sunlike love soared high. Yes, it was Julia, Julia herself, as pretty as an angel and as demure; our talk a longing lament of love, more looks than words, her hand resting in mine.

"I will never let you go," I was saying. "Your love is the spark that glows in me, kindling a higher life in art and poetry. Without you, without your love, everything is dead and lifeless. Didn't you come here so that you could be mine forever?"

At this very moment there tottered into the room a spindle-shanked[2] cretin, eyes a-pop like a frog's, who said, in a mixture of croak and cackle, "Where the Devil is my wife?"

Julia stood up and said to me in a distant, cold voice, "Shall we go back to the party? My husband is looking for me. You've been very amusing again, darling, as overemotional as ever; but you should watch how much you drink."

The spindle-legged monkey reached for her hand and she followed him into the living room with a laugh.

"Lost forever," I screamed aloud..."Oh, yes; codille, darling," bleated an animal playing ombre[3].

I ran out into the stormy night.

IN THE BEER CELLAR

Promenading up and down under the linden trees can be a fine thing, but not on a New Year's Eve when it is bitter cold and snow is falling. Bareheaded and without a coat I finally felt the cold when icy shivers began to interrupt my feverishness. I trudged over the Opern Bridge, past the Castle, over the Schleusen Bridge, past the Mint. I was on Jaegerstrasse

---

[1] The Romantic German poet, Johann Ludwig Tieck, wrote the comic play, “Caesar Octavius,” in 1804, featuring the fey character, Clemens

[2] That is, bony-legged

[3] Ombre is a fast-paced, trick-taking card game, and – like “checkmate” – “codille” is the expression used to denote a winning move

close to Thiermann's shop[1]. Friendly lights were burning inside. I was about to go in, since I was freezing and I needed a good drink of something strong, when a merry group came bursting out, babbling loudly about fine oysters and good Eilfer wine. One of them—I could see by the lantern light that he was a very impressive-looking officer in the uhlans[2]—was shouting, "You know, he was right, that fellow who cursed them out in Mainz last year for not bringing out the Eilfer, he was right!"

They all laughed uproariously.

Without thinking, I continued a little farther, then stopped in front of a beer cellar[3] out of which a single light was shining. Wasn't it Shakespeare's Henry V who once felt so tired and discouraged that he "remembered the poor creature, small beer?"[4] Indeed, the same thing was happening to me. My tongue was practically cracking with thirst for a bottle of good English beer. I hastened down into the cellar.

"Yes, sir?" said the owner of the beer cellar, touching his cap amiably as he came toward me.

I asked for a bottle of good English beer and a pipe of good tobacco, and soon found myself sublimely immersed in fleshly comforts which even the Devil had to respect enough to leave me alone. Ah, Justizrat! If you had seen me descend from your bright living room to a gloomy beer cellar, you would have turned away from me in contempt and muttered, "It's not surprising that a fellow like that can ruin a first-class jacket."

I must have looked very odd to the others in the beer cellar, since I had no hat or coat. The waiter was just about to say something about it when there was a bang on the window, and a voice shouted down, "Open up! Open up! It's me!"

The tavern keeper went outside and came right back carrying two torches high; following him came a very tall, slender stranger who forgot to lower his head as he came through the low doorway and received a good knock. A black beretlike cap, though, kept him from serious injury.

The stranger sidled along the wall in a very peculiar manner, and sat down opposite me, while lights were placed upon the table. You could characterize him briefly as pleasant but unhappy.

He called for beer and a pipe somewhat grumpily, and then with a few puffs, created such a fog bank that we seemed to be swimming in a cloud. His face had something so individual and attractive about it that I liked him despite his dark moroseness. He had a full head of black hair, parted in the middle and hanging down in small locks on both sides of his head,

---

[1] Landmarks in the western Berlin Mitte neighborhood

[2] A unit of light cavalry

[3] A bar located in the basement of a building – often with a seedy character

[4] Actually, it was from Henry IV, part 2, act 2, scene 2. Small beer is a cheap lager with a low alcohol rate (between .5 and 3% ABV)

so that he looked like someone out of a Rubens[1] picture. When he threw off his heavy cloak, I could see that he was wearing a black tunic with lots of lacing, and it struck me as very odd that he had slippers pulled on over his boots. I became aware of this when he knocked out his pipe on his foot after about five minutes of smoking.

We didn't converse right away, for the stranger was preoccupied with some strange plants which he took out of a little botanical case and started to examine closely. I indicated my astonishment at the plants and asked him, since they seemed freshly gathered, whether he had been at the botanical garden or Boucher the florist's. He smiled in a strange way, and replied slowly, "Botany does not seem to be your speciality, or else you would not have asked such a..." he hesitated and I supplied in a low voice, "foolish..." "...question," he finished, waving aside my assertion. "If you were a botanist, you would have seen at a glance that these are alpine flora and that they are from Chimborazo[2]." He said the last part very softly, and you can guess that I felt a little strange. This reply prevented further questions, but I kept having the feeling more and more strongly that I knew him-perhaps not "physically" but "mentally."

At this point there came another rapping at the window. The tavern keeper opened the door and a voice called in, "Be so good as to cover your mirrors."

"Aha!" said the host, "General Suvarov[3] is late tonight," and he threw a cloth covering over the mirror. A short, dried-up-looking fellow came tumbling in with frantic, clumsy haste. He was engulfed in a cloak of peculiar brownish color, which bubbled and flapped around him as he bounced across the room toward us, so that in the dim light it looked as if a series of forms were dissolving and emerging from one another, as in Ensler's magic lantern show[4]. He rubbed his hands together inside his overlong sleeves and cried, "Cold! Cold! It's so cold! Altogether different in

---

[1] Peter Paul Rubens was a late-16, early-17th century Flemish painter – one of the greatest of his era – known for his expressive, dramatic, Baroque portraits

[2] The highest mountain in Ecuador

[3] Alexander Suvarov was an 18th century Russian general, who is still considered one of the greatest field marshals and tacticians in world history – frequently compared to Napoleon, to whom he is often regarded a close second – and still rated as Russia's foremost military commander of all time. Suvarov – who, like many military geniuses, was a notorious eccentric – was said to harbor a phobia of mirrors

[4] An early type of projector that used a light source behind transparent slides to display fantastical designs and images on a screen, while careful manipulation of the slides and lenses done in a showmanship way could create the impression that the images are moving or transforming in a kaleidoscopic way

Italy." Finally he took a seat between me and the tall man and said, "Horrible smoke.., tobacco on tobacco... I wish I had a pipeful."

In my pocket I had a small steel tobacco box, polished like a mirror; I reached it out to the little man. He took one look at it, and thrust out both hands, shoving it away, crying, "Take that damned mirror away." His voice was filled with horror, and as I stared at him with amazement I saw that he had become a different person. He had burst into the beer cellar with a pleasant, youthful face, but now a deathly pale, shrivelled, terrified old man's face glared at me with hollow eyes. I turned in horror to the tall man. I was almost ready to shout, "For God's sake, look at him!" when I saw that the tall stranger was not paying any attention, but was completely engrossed in his plants from Chimborazo. At that moment the little man called, "Northern wine[1]!" in a very affected manner.

After a time the conversation became more lively again. I wasn't quite at ease with the little man, but the tall man had the ability of offering deep and fascinating insights upon seemingly insignificant things, although at times he seemed to struggle to express himself and groped for words, and at times used words improperly, which often gave his statements an air of droll originality. In this way, by appealing to me more and more, he offset the bad impression created by the little man.

The little man seemed to be driven by springs, for he slid back and forth on his chair and waved his hands about in perpetual gesticulations, and a shudder, like icewater down my back, ran through me when I saw very clearly that he had two different faces, the pleasant young man's and the unlovely demonic old man's. For the most part he turned his old man's face upon the tall man, who sat impervious and quiet, in contrast to the perpetual motion of the small man in brown, although it was not as unpleasant as when it had looked at me for the first time. In the masquerade of life our true inner essence often shines out beyond our mask when we meet a similar person, and it so happened that we three strange beings in a beer cellar looked at one another and knew what we were. Our conversation ran along morbid lines, in the sardonic humor that emerges only when you are wounded, almost to the point of death.

"There are hidden hooks and snares there, too," said the tall man.

"Oh, God," I joined in, "the Devil has set so many hooks for us everywhere, walls, arbors, hedge roses, and so on, and as we brush past them we leave something of our true self caught there. It seems to me, gentlemen, that all of us lose something this way, just as right now I have no hat or coat. They are both hanging on a hook at the Justizrat's, as you may know."

Both the tall and the short man visibly winced, as if they had been unexpectedly struck. The little man looked at me with hatred from his old man's face, leaped up on his chair and fussily adjusted the cloth that hung

---

[1] That is, German (often, specifically, white Rhenish) wine

over the mirror, while the tall man made a point of pinching the candle wicks. The conversation limped along, and in its course a fine young artist named Philipp was mentioned, together with a portrait of a princess painted with intense love and longing, which she must have inspired in him. "More than just a likeness, a true image," said the tall man.

"So completely true," I said, "that you could almost say it was stolen from a mirror."

The little man leaped up in a frenzy, and transfixing me with his flaming eyes, showing his old man's face, he screamed, "That's idiotic, crazy-who can steal your reflection? Who? Perhaps you think the Devil can? He would break the glass with his clumsy claws and the girl's fine white hands would be slashed and bloody. Erkhhhh. Show me a reflection, a stolen reflection, and I'll leap a thousand yards for you, you stupid fool!"

The tall man got up, strode over to the little man, and said in a contemptuous voice, "Don't make such a nuisance of yourself, my friend, or I'll throw you out and you'll be as miserable as your own reflection."

"Ha, ha, ha," laughed the little man with furious scorn. "You think so? Do you think so? You miserable dog, I at least still have my shadow, I still have my shadow!" And he leaped out of his chair and rushed out of the cellar. I could hear his nasty neighing laughter outside, and his shouts of "I still have my shadow!"

The tall man, as if completely crushed, sank back into his chair as pale as death. He took his head in both his hands and sighed deeply and groaned. "What's wrong?" I asked sympathetically. "Sir," he replied somewhat incoherently, "that nasty little fellow-followed me here, even in this tavern, where I used to be alone-nobody around, except once in a while an earth-elemental[1] would dive under the table for bread crumbs—he's made me miserable—there's no getting it back-I've lost ... I've lost ... my...oh, I can't go on..." and he leaped up and dashed out into the street.

He happened to pass the lights, and I saw that—he cast no shadow! I was delighted, for I recognized him and knew all about him. I ran out after him. "Peter Schlemihl, Peter Schlemihl[2]. "

I shouted. But he had kicked off his slippers, and I saw him striding away beyond the police tower, disappearing into the night.

I was about to return to the cellar, but the owner slammed the door in my face, proclaiming loudly, "From guests like these the Good Lord deliver me!"

---

[1] That is, a gnome

[2] A fictional character from Adelbert von Chamisso's 1814 fantasy novella, *Peter Schlemihl's Miraculous Story.* He sells his shadow to the devil for a bottomless wallet, but realizes that he has damned himself to a miserable, lonely existence (as his condition horrifies people and leaves him friendless), rendering his wealth useless

Herr Mathieu is a good friend of mine and his porter[1] keeps his eyes open. He opened the door for me right away when I came to the Golden Eagle and pulled at the bell. I explained matters: that I had been to a party, had left my hat and coat behind, that my house key was in my coat pocket, and that I had no chance of waking my deaf landlady. He was a goodhearted fellow (the porter) and found a room for me, set lights about in it, and wished me a good night. A beautiful wide mirror, however, was covered, and though I don't know why I did it, I pulled off the cloth and set both my candles on the table in front of the mirror. When I looked in, I was so pale and tired-looking that I could hardly recognize myself. Then it seemed to me that from the remote background of the reflection there came floating a dark form, which as I focused my attention upon it, took on the features of a beautiful woman—Julia—shining with a magic radiance. I said very softly, "Julia, Julia!"

At this I heard a groaning and moaning which seemed to come from behind the drawn curtains of a canopy bed which stood in the farthest corner of the room. I listened closely. The groaning grew louder, seemingly more painful. The image of Julia had disappeared, and resolutely I seized a candle, ripped the curtains of the bed apart, and looked in. How can I describe my feelings to you when I saw before me the little man whom I had met at the beer cellar, asleep on the bed, youthful features dominant (though contorted with pain), muttering in his sleep, "Giuletta, Giuletta[2]!" The name enraged me. I was no longer fearful, but seized the little man and gave him a good shake, shouting, "Heigh[3], my friend! What are you doing in my room? Wake up and get the Devil out of here!"

The little man blinked his eyes open and looked at me darkly. "That was really a bad dream," he said. "I must thank you for waking me." He spoke softly, almost murmured. I don't know why but he looked different to me; the pain which he obviously felt aroused my sympathy, and instead of being angry I felt very sorry for him. It didn't take much conversation to learn that the porter had inadvertently given me the room which had already been assigned to the little man, and that it was I who had intruded, disturbing his sleep.

"Sir," said the little man. "I must have seemed like an utter lunatic to you in the beer cellar. Blame my behavior on this: every now and then, I must confess, a mad spirit seizes control of me and makes me lose all concept of what is right and proper. Perhaps the same thing has happened to you at times?"

---

[1] Doorman

[2] Italian for Julia (often Anglicized as Juliet), which – in Latin – means "youthful"

[3] "Get up!," "Up and at 'em!"

"Oh, God, yes," I replied dejectedly. "Just this evening, when I saw Julia again."

"Julia!" crackled the little man in an unpleasant tone. His face suddenly aged and his features twitched. "Let me alone. And please be good enough to cover the mirror again," he said, looking sadly at his pillow.

"Sir," I said. "The name of my eternally lost love seems to awaken strange memories in you; so much so that your face has changed from its usual pleasant appearance. Still, I have hopes of spending the night here quietly with you, so I am going to cover the mirror and go to bed."

He raised himself to a sitting position, looked at me with his pleasant young face, and seized my hand, saying, while pressing it gently, "Sleep well, my friend. I see that we are companions in misery. Julia...Giuletta...Well, if it must be, it must be. I cannot help it; I must tell you my deepest secret, and then you will hate and despise me."

He slowly climbed out of bed, wrapped himself in a generous white robe, and crept slowly, almost like a ghost, to the great mirror and stood in front of it. Ah— Brightly and clearly the mirror reflected the two lighted candles, the furniture, me—but the little man was not there! He stood, head bowed toward it, in front of the mirror, but he cast no reflection! Turning to me, deep despair on his face, he pressed my hands and said, "Now you know the depths of my misery. Schlemihl, a goodhearted fellow, is to be envied, compared to me. He was irresponsible for a moment and sold his shadow. But—I—I gave my reflection to her...to her!"

Sobbing deeply, hands pressed over his eyes, the little man turned to the bed and threw himself on it. I simply stood in astonishment, with suspicion, contempt, disgust, sympathy and pity all intermingled, for and against the little man. But while I was standing there, he began to snore so melodiously that it was contagious, and I couldn't resist the narcotic power of his tones. I quickly covered the mirror again, put out the candles, threw myself upon the bed like the little man, and immediately fell asleep... It must have been early morning when a light awakened me, and I opened my eyes to see the little man, still in his white dressing gown, nightcap on his head, back turned to me, sitting at the table busily writing by the light of the two candles. There was a weird[1] look about him, and I felt the chill of the supernatural. I fell into a waking-dream then, and was back at the Justizrat's again, sitting beside Julia on the ottoman. But the whole party seemed to be only a comic candy display in the window of Fuchs, Weide and Schoch (or somewhere similar) for Christmas, and the Justizrat was a splendid gumdrop with a coat made of pleated notepaper. Trees and rosebushes rose higher and higher about us, and Julia stood up, handing me the crystal goblet, out of which blue flames licked. Someone tugged at my arm and there was the little brown man, his old man's face on, whispering loudly to me, "Don't drink it, don't drink it. Look at her closely.

---

[1] In this instance, unnervingly uncanny with suggestions of the otherworldly

Haven't you seen her and been warned against her in Brueghel and Callot and Rembrandt[1]?"

I looked at Julia with horror, and indeed, with her pleated dress and ruffled sleeves and strange coiffure[2], she did look like one of the alluring young women, surrounded by demonic monsters, from the work of those masters.

"What are you afraid of?" said Julia. "I have you and your reflection, once and for all." I seized the goblet, but the little man leaped to my shoulder in the form of a squirrel, and waved his tail through the blue flames, chattering, "Don't drink it, don't drink it." At this point the sugar figures in the display came alive and moved their hands and feet ludicrously. The Justizrat ran up to me and called out in a thin little voice, "Why all the uproar, my friend? Why all the commotion? All you have to do is get to your feet; for quite a while I've been watching you stride away over tables and chairs."

The little man had completely disappeared. Julia no longer held the goblet in her hand. "Why wouldn't you drink?" she asked. "Wasn't the flame streaming out of the goblet simply the kisses you once got from me?"

I wanted to take her in my arms, but Schlemihl stepped between us and said, "This is Mina, who married my servant, Rascal[3]." He stepped on a couple of the candy figures, who made groaning noises. They started to multiply enormously, hundreds and thousands of them, and they swarmed all over me, buzzing like a hive of bees. The gumdrop Justizrat, who had continued to climb, had swung up as far as my neckcloth, which he kept pulling tighter and tighter. "Justizrat, you confounded gumdrop," I screamed out loud, and startled myself out of sleep. It was bright day, already eleven o'clock.

I was just thinking to myself that the whole adventure with the little brown man had only been an exceptionally vivid dream, when the waiter who brought in my breakfast told me that the stranger who had shared his room with me had left early, and presented his compliments[4]. Upon the table where I had seen the weird little man sitting and writing I found a fresh manuscript, whose content I am sharing with you, since it is unquestionably the remarkable story of the little man in brown. It is as follows.

---

[1] Three famous artists – a German, Frenchman, and Dutchman, respectively – who thrived between the 16th and 17th centuries, and were known for their emotionally complex portraits which often had moral overtones warning against the vanities of greed and lust. Brueghel and Callot, in particular, featured dark, paranormal, and fantastical elements

[2] Hairdo

[3] In *Peter Schlemihl's Miraculous Story,* Peter falls in love with the coquettish Mina, but she proves false, abandoning him for his treacherous servant, Rascal

[4] "and shared with me his [Peter's] best regards"

Things finally worked out so that Erasmus Spikher was able to fulfill the wish that he had cherished all his life. He climbed into the coach with high spirits and a well-filled knapsack. He was leaving his home in the North and journeying to the beautiful land of Italy[1]. His devoted wife was weeping copiously, and she lifted little Rasmus (after carefully wiping his mouth and nose) into the coach to kiss his father goodbye..."Farewell, Erasmus Spikher," said his wife, sobbing. "I will keep your house well for you.

Think of me often, remain true to me, and do not lose your hat if you fall asleep near the window, as you always do." Spikher promised.

In the beautiful city of Florence Spikher found some fellow Germans, young men filled with high spirits and joie de vivre, who spent their time revelling in the sensual delights which Italy so well affords. He impressed them as a good fellow and he was often invited to social occasions since he had the talent of supplying soberness to the mad abandon about him, and gave the party a highly individual touch.

One evening in the grove of a splendid fragrant public garden, the young men (Erasmus could be included here, since he was only twenty-seven) gathered for an exceptionally merry feast.

Each of the men, except Spikher, brought along a girl. The men were dressed in the picturesque old Germanic costume, and the women wore bright dresses, each styled differently, often fantastically, so that they seemed like wonderful mobile flowers. Every now and then one of the girls would sing an Italian love song, accompanied by the plaintive notes of mandolins, and the men would respond with a lusty German chorus or round, as glasses filled with fine Syracuse wine clinked. Yes, indeed, Italy is the land of love.

The evening breezes sighed with passion, oranges and jasmine breathed out perfume through the grove, and it all formed a part in the banter and play which the girls (delightfully merry as only Italian women can be) began. Wilder and noisier grew the fun. Friedrich, the most excited of all, leaped to his feet, one arm around his mistress, waving high a glass of sparkling Syracuse wine with the other, and shouted, "You wonderful women of Italy! Where can true, blissful love be found except with you? You are love incarnate! But you, Erasmus," he continued, turning to Spikher, "You don't seem to understand this. You've violated your promise, propriety and the custom. You didn't bring a girl with you, and you have been sitting here moodily, so quiet and self-concerned that if you hadn't

---

[1] Germans were (and still are) well-known for their love of vacationing in Italy (comparable to the Japanese affection for Paris), a tradition which is featured in many literary classics such as Thomas Mann's *Death in Venice* and J. W. von Goethe's *Italian Journey*

been drinking and singing with us I'd believe you were suffering an attack of melancholy."

"Friedrich," replied Erasmus, "I have to confess that I cannot enjoy myself like that. You know that I have a wife at home, and I love her. If I took up with a girl for even one night it would be betraying my wife. For you young bachelors it's different, but I have a family."

The young men laughed uproariously, for when Erasmus announced his family obligations his pleasant young face became very grave, and he really looked very strange. Friedrich's mistress, when Spikher's words had been translated for her (for the two men had spoken German), turned very seriously to Erasmus, and said, half-threateningly, finger raised, "Cold-blooded, heartless German watch out—you haven't seen Giuletta yet."

At that very instant a rustling noise indicated that someone was approaching, and out of the dark night into the area lighted by the candles strode a remarkably beautiful girl. Her white dress, which only half-hid her bosom, shoulders and neck, fell in rich broad folds; her sleeves, puffed and full, came only to her elbows; her thick hair, parted in the front, fell in braids at the back.

Golden chains around her throat, rich bracelets upon her wrists, completed her antique costume.

She looked exactly if she were a woman from Miens[1] or Rembrandt walking about. "Giuletta," shrieked the girls in astonishment and delight.

Giuletta, who was by far the most beautiful of all the women present, asked in a sweet, pleasant voice, "Good Germans, may I join you? I'll sit with that gentleman over there. He doesn't have a girl, and he doesn't seem to be having a very good time, either." She turned very graciously to Erasmus, and sat down upon the empty seat beside him-empty because everyone thought Erasmus would bring a girl along, too. The girls whispered to each other, "Isn't Giuletta beautiful tonight," and the young men said, "How about Erasmus? Was he joking with us? He's got the best-looking girl of all!"

As for Erasmus, at the first glance he cast at Giuletta, he was so aroused that he didn't even know what powerful passions were working in him. As she came close to him, a strange force seized him and crushed his breast so that he couldn't even breathe. Eyes fixed in a rigid stare at her, mouth agape, he sat there not able to utter a syllable, while all the others were commenting upon Giuletta's charm and beauty.

Giuletta took a full goblet, and standing up, handed it with a friendly smile to Erasmus. He seized the goblet, touching her soft fingers, and as he drank, fire seemed to stream through his veins. Then Giuletta asked him in a bantering way, "Am I to be your girl friend?" Erasmus threw himself wildly upon the ground in front of her, pressed her hands to his breast, and

---

[1] Jan Miense Molenaer, another 17th century Dutch master known for his appealing domestic scenes of music, women, and wealth

cried in maudlin tones, "Yes, yes, yes! You goddess! I've always been in love with you. I've seen you in my dreams, you are my fortune, my happiness, my higher life!"

The others all thought the wine had gone to Erasmus's head, since they had never seen him like this before; he seemed to be a different man.

"You are my life! I don't care if I am destroyed, as long as it's with you," Erasmus shouted.

"You set me on fire!" But Giuletta just took him gently in her arms. He became quieter again, and took his seat beside her. And once again the gaiety which had been interrupted by Erasmus and Giuletta began with songs and laughter. Giuletta sang, and it was as if the tones of her beautiful voice aroused in everyone sensations of pleasure never felt before but only suspected to exist. Her full but clear voice conveyed a secret ardor which inflamed them all. The young men clasped their mistresses more closely, and passion leaped from eye to eye.

Dawn was breaking with a rosy shimmer when Giuletta said that she had to leave. Erasmus got ready to accompany her home, but she refused but gave him the address at which he could find her in the future. During the chorus which the men sang to end the party, Giuletta disappeared from the grove and was seen walking through a distant allée[1], preceded by two linkmen[2]. Erasmus did not dare follow her.

The young men left arm in arm with their mistresses, full of high spirits, and Erasmus, greatly disturbed and internally shattered by the torments of love, followed, preceded by his boy with a torch. After leaving his friends, he was passing down the distant street which led to his dwelling, and his servant had just knocked out the torch against the stucco of the house, when a strange figure mysteriously appeared in the spraying sparks in front of Erasmus. It was a tall, thin, dried-out-looking man with a Roman nose that came to a sharp point, glowing eyes, mouth contorted into a sneer, wrapped in a flame-red cloak with brightly polished steel buttons. He laughed and called out in an unpleasant yelping voice, "Ho, ho, you look as if you came out of a picture book with that cloak, slit doublet[3] and plumed hat. You show a real sense of humor, Signor Erasmus Spikher, but aren't you afraid of being laughed at on the streets? Signor, signor, crawl quietly back into your parchment binding."

"What the Devil is my clothing to you?" said Erasmus with anger, and shoving the red-clad stranger aside, he was about to pass by when the

---

[1] A narrow walkway in a garden or park lined by decorative trees or bushes

[2] Men hired to carry torches or lanterns (links) ahead of a coach or pedestrian traveling at night to provide them with light

[3] A short-skirted jacket with slits in the sleeves and torso to reveal the lining beneath, which is commonly associated with 16th century and early 17th century fashion

stranger called after him, "Don't be in such a hurry. You won't get to Giuletta that way."

"What are you saying about Giuletta?" cried Erasmus wildly. He tried to seize the red-clad man by the breast, but he turned and disappeared so rapidly that Erasmus couldn't even see where he went, and Erasmus was left standing in astonishment, in his hand a steel button that had been ripped from the stranger's cloak..."That's the Miracle Doctor Dapertutto[1]. What did he want?" asked Erasmus's servant. But Erasmus was seized with horror, and without replying, hastened home.

When, some time later, Erasmus called on Giuletta, she received him in a very gracious and friendly manner, yet to Erasmus's fiery passion she opposed a mild indifference. Only once in a while did her eyes flash, whereupon Erasmus would feel shudders pass through him, from his innermost being, when she regarded him with an enigmatic stare. She never told him that she loved him, but her whole attitude and behaviour led him to think so, and he found himself more and more deeply entangled with her. He seldom saw his old friends, however, for Giuletta took him into other circles.

Once Erasmus met Friedrich at a time when Erasmus was depressed, thinking about his native land and his home. Friedrich said, "Don't you know, Spikher, that you are moving in a very dangerous circle of acquaintances? You must realize by now that the beautiful Giuletta is one of the craftiest courtesans on earth. There are all sorts of strange stories going around about her, and they put her in a very peculiar light. I can see from you that she can exercise an irresistible power over men when she wants to. You have changed completely and are totally under her spell. You don't think of your wife and family any more."

Erasmus covered his face with his hands and sobbed, crying out his wife's name[2]. Friedrich saw that a difficult internal battle had begun in Spikher. "Erasmus," he said, "let us get out of here immediately."

"Yes, Friedrich," said Erasmus heavily. "You are right. I don't know why I am suddenly overcome by such dark horrible foreboding—I must leave right away, today."

The two friends hastened along the street, but directly across from them came Signor Dapertutto, who laughed in Erasmus's face, and cried nasally, "Hurry, hurry; a little faster. Giuletta waiting; her heart is full of longing, and her eyes are full of tears. Make haste. Make haste."

Erasmus stood as if struck by lightning.

---

[1] Based on the Italian word (though this *is* the spelling in Corsican) "dappertutto," which means "everywhere" or "omnipresent"

[2] Note, however, that his wife isn't even given a name (she is as anonymous to the text as she is forgettable to her husband), whereas Giuletta/Julia has two names or more, and her name is repeated like a chant throughout the story

"This scoundrel," said Friedrich, "this charlatan—I cannot stand him. He is always in and out of Giuletta's, and he sells her his magical potions."

"What!" cried Erasmus. "That disgusting creature visits Giuletta, Giuletta?"

"Where have you been so long? Everything is waiting for you. Didn't you think of me at all. "

breathed a soft voice from the balcony. It was Giuletta, in front of whose house the two friends, without noticing it, had stopped. With a leap Erasmus was in the house.

"He is gone, and cannot be saved," said Friedrich to himself, and walked slowly away.

Never before had Giuletta been more amiable. She wore the same clothing that she had worn when she first met Erasmus, and beauty, charm and youth shone from her. Erasmus completely forgot his conversation with Friedrich, and now more than ever his irresistible passion seized him. This was the first time that Giuletta showed without reservation her deepest love for him.

She seemed to see only him, and to live for him only. At a villa which Giuletta had rented for the summer, a festival was being celebrated, and they went there. Among the company was a young Italian with a brutal ugly face and even worse manners, who kept paying court to Giuletta and arousing Erasmus's jealousy. Fuming with rage, Erasmus left the company and paced up and down in a side path of the garden. Giuletta came looking for him. "What is wrong with you?"

"Aren't you mine alone?" she asked. She embraced him and planted a kiss upon his lips. Sparks of passion flew through Erasmus, and in a passion he crushed her to himself, crying, "No, I will not leave you, no matter how low I fall." Giuletta smiled strangely at these words, and cast at him that peculiar oblique glance which never failed to arouse a chilly feeling in him.

They returned to the company, and the unpleasant young Italian now took over Erasmus's role.

Obviously enraged with jealousy, he made all sorts of pointed insults against Germans, particularly Spikher. Finally Spikher could bear it no longer, and he strode up to the Italian and said, "That's enough of your insults, unless you'd like to get thrown into the pond and try your hand at swimming." In an instant a dagger gleamed in the Italian's hand, but Erasmus dodged, seized him by the throat, threw him to the ground, and shattered his neck with a kick. The Italian gasped out his life on the spot.

Pandemonium broke loose around Erasmus. He lost consciousness, but felt himself being lifted and carried away. When he awoke later, as if from a deep enchantment, he lay at Giuletta's feet in a small room, while she, head bowed over him, held him in both her arms.

"You bad, bad German," she finally said, softly and mildly. "If you knew how frightened you've made me! You've come very close to disaster, but I've managed to save you. You are no longer safe in Florence, though, or even Italy. You must leave, and you must leave me, and I love you so much."

The thought of leaving Giuletta threw Erasmus into pain and sorrow. "Let me stay here," he cried. "I'm willing to die. Dying is better than living without you."

But suddenly it seemed to him as if a soft, distant voice was calling his name painfully. It was the voice of his wife at home. Erasmus was stricken dumb. Strangely enough, Giuletta asked him, "Are you thinking of your wife? Ah, Erasmus, you will forget me only too soon!"

"If I could only remain yours forever and ever," said Erasmus. They were standing directly in front of the beautiful wide mirror, which was set in the wall, and on the sides of it tapers were burning brightly. More firmly, more closely, Giuletta pressed Erasmus to her, while she murmured softly in his ear, "Leave me your reflection, my beloved; it will be mine and will remain with me forever."

"Giuletta," cried Erasmus in amazement. "What do you mean? My reflection?" He looked in the mirror, which showed him himself and Giuletta in sweet, close embrace. "How can you keep my reflection? It is part of me. It springs out to meet me from every clear body of water or polished surface."

"Aren't you willing to give me even this dream of your ego[1]? Even though you say you want to be mine, body and soul? Won't you even give me this trivial thing, so that after you leave, it can accompany me in the loveless, pleasureless life that is left to me?"

Hot tears started from Giuletta's beautiful dark eyes.

At this point Erasmus, mad with pain and passion, cried, "Do I have to leave? If I have to, my reflection will be yours forever and a day. No power—not even the Devil—can take it away from you until you own me, body and soul."

Giuletta's kisses burned like fire on his mouth as he said this, and then she released him and stretched out her arms longingly to the mirror. Erasmus saw his image step forward independent of his movements, glide into Giuletta's arms, and disappear with her in a strange vapor. Then Erasmus heard all sorts of hideous voices bleating and laughing in demoniac scorn, and, seized with a spasm of terror, he sank to the floor. But his horror and fear aroused him, and in thick dense darkness he stumbled out the door and down the steps. In front of the house he was seized and lifted into a carriage, which rolled away with him rapidly.

"Things have changed somewhat, it seems," said a man in German, who had taken a seat beside him. "Nevertheless, everything will be all right if you give yourself over to me, completely. Dear Giuletta has done her share, and has recommended you to me. You are a fine, pleasant young man and you have a strong inclination to pleasant pranks and jokes—

---

[1] "This mere shade of your soul?"

which please Giuletta and me nicely. That was a real nice German kick in the neck. Did you see how Amoroso's tongue protruded—purple and swollen—it was a fine sight and the strangling noises and groans—ha, ha, ha." The man's voice was so repellent in its mockery, his chatter so gruesomely unpleasant, that his words felt like dagger blows in Erasmus's chest.

"Whoever you are," he said, "don't say any more about it. I regret it bitterly."

"Regret? Regret?" replied the unknown man. "I'll be bound that you probably regret knowing Giuletta and winning her love."

"Ah, Giuletta, Giuletta!" sighed Spikher.

"Now," said the man, "you are being childish. Everything will run smoothly. It is horrible that you have to leave her, I know, but if you were to remain here, I could keep your enemies daggers away from you, and even the authorities."

The thought of being able to stay with Giuletta appealed strongly to Erasmus. "How, how can that be?"

"I know a magical way to strike your enemies with blindness, in short, that you will always appear to them with a different face, and they will never recognize you again. Since it is getting on toward daylight, perhaps you will be good enough to look long and attentively into any mirror. I shall then perform certain operations upon your reflection, without damaging it in the least, and you will be hidden and can live forever with Giuletta. As happy as can be; no danger at all."

"Oh, God," screamed Erasmus.

"Why call upon God, my most worthy friend," asked the stranger with a sneer.

"I—I have..." began Erasmus.

"Left your reflection behind—with Giuletta—" interrupted the other. "Fine. Bravissimo, my dear sir. And now you course through floods and forests, cities and towns, until you find your wife and little Rasmus, and become a paterfamilias[1] again. No reflection, of course—though this really shouldn't bother your wife since she has you physically. Even though Giuletta will eternally own your dream-ego."

A torch procession of singers drew near at this moment, and the light the torches cast into the carriage revealed to Erasmus the sneering visage of Dr. Dapertutto. Erasmus leaped out of the carriage and ran toward the procession, for he had recognized Friedrich's resounding bass voice among the singers. It was his friends returning from a party in the countryside. Erasmus breathlessly told Friedrich everything that had happened, only withholding mention of the loss of his reflection. Friedrich hurried with him into the city, and arrangements were made so rapidly that when dawn

---

[1] Family man (Latin: father of the family)

broke, Erasmus, mounted on a fast horse, had already left Florence far behind.

Spikher set down in his manuscript the many adventures that befell him upon his journey.

Among the most remarkable is the incident which first caused him to appreciate the loss of his reflection. He had stopped over in a large town, since his tired horse needed a rest, and he had sat down without thinking at a well-filled inn table, not noticing that a fine clear mirror hung before him. A devil of a waiter, who stood behind his chair, noticed that the chair seemed to be empty in the reflection and did not show the person who was sitting in it. He shared his observation with Erasmus's neighbor, who in turn called it to the attention of his. A murmuring and whispering thereupon ran all around the table, and the guests first stared at Erasmus, then at the mirror.

Erasmus, however, was unaware that the disturbance concerned him, until a grave gentleman stood up, took Erasmus to the mirror, looked in, and then turning to the company, cried out loudly, "'Struth[1]. He's not there. He doesn't reflect."

"What? No reflection? He's not in the mirror?" everyone cried in confusion. "He's a mauvais sujet[2], a homo nefas[3]. Kick him out the door!"

Raging and filled with shame, Erasmus fled to his room, but he had hardly gotten there when he was informed by the police that he must either appear with full, complete, impeccably accurate reflection before the magistrate within one hour or leave the town. He rushed away, followed by the idle mob, tormented by street urchins, who called after him, "There he goes. He sold his reflection to the Devil. There he goes!" Finally he escaped. And from then on, under the pretext of having a phobia against mirrors, he insisted on having them covered. For this reason he was nicknamed General Suvarov, since Suvarov acted the same way.

When he finally reached his home city and his house, his wife and child received him with joy, and he began to think that calm, peaceful domesticity would heal the pain of his lost reflection.

One day, however, it happened that Spikher, who had now put Giuletta completely out of his mind, was playing with little Rasmus. Rasmus's little hands were covered with soot from the stove, and he dragged his fingers across his father's face. "Daddy! I've turned you black. Look, look!" cried the child, and before Spikher could prevent it or avoid it, the little boy held a mirror in front of him, looking into it at the same time. The child dropped the mirror with a scream of terror and ran away to his room.

---

[1] "[God]'s truth" is an oath of surprise or declaration comparable to "by God!" or the French "Ma foi!"

[2] French: "a bad subject" (a scoundrel, a villain)

[3] Latin: "an evil man"

Spikher's wife soon came to him, astonishment and terror plainly on her face. "What has Rasmus told me—" she began. "Perhaps that I don't have a reflection, dear," interrupted Spikher with a forced smile, and he feverishly tried to prove that the story was too foolish to believe, that one could not lose a reflection, but if one did, since a mirror image was only an illusion, it didn't matter much, that staring into a mirror led to vanity, and pseudo-philosophical nonsense about the reflection dividing the ego into truth and dream. While he was declaiming[1], his wife removed the covering from a mirror that hung in the room and looked into it. She fell to the floor as if struck by lightning. Spikher lifted her up, but when she regained consciousness, she pushed him away with horror. "Leave me, get away from me, you demon! You are not my husband. No! You are a demon from Hell, who wants to destroy my chance of heaven, who wants to corrupt me. Away! Leave me alone! You have no power over me, damned spirit!"

Her voice screamed through the room, through the halls; the domestics[2] fled the house in terror, and in rage and despair Erasmus rushed out of the house. Madly he ran through the empty walks of the town park. Giuletta's form seemed to arise in front of him, angelic in beauty, and he cried aloud, "Is this your revenge, Giuletta, because I abandoned you and left you nothing but my reflection in a mirror? Giuletta, I will be yours, body and soul. I sacrificed you for her, Giuletta, and now she has rejected me. Giuletta, let me be yours—body, life, and soul!"

"That can be done quite easily, caro signore[3]," said Dr. Dapertutto, who was suddenly standing beside him, clad in scarlet cloak with polished steel buttons. These were words of comfort to Erasmus, and he paid no heed to Dapertutto's sneering, unpleasant face. Erasmus stopped and asked in despair, "How can I find her again? She is eternally lost to me."

"On the contrary," answered Dapertutto, "she is not far from here, and she longs for your true self, honored sir; you yourself have had the insight to see that a reflection is nothing but a worthless illusion. And as soon as she has the real you—body, life, and soul—she will return your reflection, smooth and undamaged with the utmost gratitude."

"Take me to her, take me to her," cried Erasmus. "Where is she?" "A certain trivial matter must come first," replied Dapertutto, "before you can see her and redeem your reflection. You are not entirely free to dispose of your worthy self, since you are tied by certain bonds which have to be dissolved first. Your worthy wife. Your promising little son."

"What do you mean?" cried Erasmus wildly.

"This bond," continued Dapertutto, "can be dissolved incontrovertibly, easily and humanely. You may remember from your Florentine days that I have the knack of preparing wonder-working

---

[1] Lecturing

[2] Servants

[3] Italian: “my dear sir”

medications. I have a splendid household aid here at hand. Those who stand in the way of you and your beloved Giuletta—let them have the benefit of a couple of drops, and they will sink down quietly, no pain, no embarrassment. It is what they call dying, and death is said to be bitter; but don't bitter almonds[1] taste very nice? The death in this little bottle has only that kind of bitterness. Immediately after the happy collapse, your worthy family will exude a pleasant odor of almonds. Take it, honored sir."

He handed a small phial to Erasmus. "I should poison my wife and child?" shrieked Erasmus.

"Who spoke of poison?" continued the red-clad man, very calmly. "It's just a delicious household remedy. It's true that I have other ways of regaining your freedom for you, but for you I would like the process to be natural, humane, if you know what I mean. I really feel strongly about it. Take it and have courage, my friend."

Erasmus found the phial in his hand, he knew not how.

Without thinking, he ran home, to his room. His wife had spent the whole night amid a thousand fears and torments, asserting continually that the person who had returned was not her husband but a spirit from Hell who had assumed her husband's form. As a result, the moment Erasmus set foot in the house, everyone ran. Only little Rasmus had the courage to approach him and ask in childish fashion why he had not brought his reflection back with him, since Mother was dying of grief because of it. Erasmus stared wildly at the little boy, Dapertutto's phial in his hand. His son's pet dove was on his shoulder, and it so happened that the dove pecked at the stopper of the phial, dropped its head, and toppled over, dead. Erasmus was overcome with horror.

"Betrayer," he shouted. "You cannot make me do it!"

He threw the phial out through the open window, and it shattered upon the concrete pavement of the court. A luscious odor of almonds rose in the air and spread into the room, while little Rasmus ran away in terror.

Erasmus spent the whole day in torment until midnight. More and more vividly each moment the image of Giuletta rose in his mind. On one occasion, in the past, her necklace of red berries (which Italian women wear like pearls) had broken, and while Erasmus was picking up the berries he concealed one and kept it faithfully, because it had been on Giuletta's neck. At this point he took out the berry and fixed his gaze upon it, focusing his thought on his lost love. It seemed to him that a magical aroma emerged from the berry, the scent which used to surround Giuletta.

"Ah, Giuletta, if I could only see you one more time, and then go down in shame and disgrace..."

He had hardly spoken, when a soft rustling came along the walk outside. He heard footsteps—there was a knock on the door. Fear and hope

[1] The flavor and smell associated with cyanide, which shares a chemical compound – amygdalin – with bitter almonds

stopped his breath. He opened the door, and in walked Giuletta, as remarkably beautiful and charming as ever. Mad with desire, Erasmus seized her in his arms.

"I am here, beloved," she whispered softly, gently. "See how well I have preserved your reflection?"

She took the cloth down from the mirror on the wall, and Erasmus saw his image nestled in embrace with Giuletta, independent of him, not following his movements. He shook with terror.

"Giuletta," he cried, "must you drive me mad? Give me my reflection and take me—body, life, soul!"

"There is still something between us, dear Erasmus," said Giuletta. "You know what it is. Hasn't Dapertutto told you?"

"For God's sake, Giuletta," cried Erasmus. "If that is the only way I can become yours, I would rather die."

"You don't have to do it the way Dapertutto suggested," said Giuletta. "It is really a shame that a vow and a priest's blessing can do so much, but you must loose the bond that ties you or else you can never be entirely mine. There is a better way than the one that Dapertutto proposed."

"What is it?" asked Spikher eagerly. Giuletta placed her arm around his neck, and leaning her head upon his breast whispered up softly, "You just write your name, Erasmus Spikher, upon a little slip of paper, under only a few words: 'I give to my good friend Dr. Dapertutto power over my wife and over my child, so that he can govern and dispose of them according to his will, and dissolve the bond which ties me, because I, from this day, with body and immortal soul, wish to belong to Giuletta, whom I have chosen as wife, and to whom I will bind myself eternally with a special vow.'"

Erasmus shivered and twitched with pain. Fiery kisses burned upon his lips, and he found the little piece of paper which Giuletta had given to him in his hand. Gigantic, Dapertutto suddenly stood behind Giuletta and handed Erasmus a steel pen. A vein on Erasmus's left hand burst open and blood spurted out.

"Dip it, dip it, write, write," said the red-clad figure harshly.

"Write, write, my eternal, my only lover," whispered Giuletta.

He had filled the pen with his blood and started to write when the door suddenly opened and a white figure entered. With staring eyes fixed on Erasmus, it called painfully and leadenly, "Erasmus, Erasmus! What are you doing? For the sake of our Saviour, don't do this horrible deed."

Erasmus recognized his wife in the warning figure, and threw the pen and paper far from him.

Sparks and flashes shot out of Giuletta's eyes; her face was horribly distorted; her body seemed to glow with rage.

"Away from me, demon; you can have no part of my soul. In the name of the Saviour, begone. Snake—Hell glows through you," cried Erasmus, and with a violent blow he knocked back Giuletta, who was trying to embrace him again. A screaming and howling broke loose, and a rustling, as of raven feathers. Giuletta and Dapertutto disappeared in a thick stinking smoke, which as it poured out of the walls put out the lights.

Dawn finally came, and Erasmus went to his wife. He found her calm and restrained. Little Rasmus sat very cheerfully upon her bed. She held out her hand to her exhausted husband and said, "I now know everything that happened to you in Italy, and I pity you with all my heart. The power of the Enemy is great. He is given to ill-doing and he could not resist the desire to make away with your reflection and use it to his own purposes. Look into the mirror again, husband."

Erasmus, trembling, looked into the mirror, completely dejected. It remained blank and clear; no other Erasmus Spikher looked back at him.

"It is just as well that the mirror does not reflect you," said his wife, "for you look very foolish, Erasmus. But you must recognize that if you do not have a reflection, you will be laughed at, and you cannot be the proper father for a family; your wife and children cannot respect you. Rasmus is already laughing at you and next will paint a mustache on you with soot, since you cannot see it.

"Go out into the world again, and see if you can track down your reflection, away from the Devil. When you have it back, you will be very welcome here. Kiss me" (Erasmus did) "and now—goodbye. Send little Rasmus new stockings every once in a while, for he keeps sliding on his knees and needs quite a few pairs. If you get to Nuremberg, you can also send him a painted soldier and a spice cake, like a devoted father. Farewell, dear Erasmus."

His wife turned upon her other side and went back to sleep. Spikher lifted up little Rasmus and hugged him to his breast. But since Rasmus cried quite a bit, Spikher set him down again, and went into the wide world. He struck upon a certain Peter Schlemihl, who had sold his shadow; they planned to travel together, so that Erasmus Spikher could provide the necessary shadow and Peter Schlemihl could reflect properly in a mirror. But nothing came of it.

"THE Lost Reflection" borrows tropes from Goethe's *Faust*, the "Wandering Jew" mythology, Coleridge's "The Rime of the Ancient Mariner," and – most notably – Adelbert von Chamisso's 1814 fantasy novella, *Peter Schlemihl's Miraculous Story.* His cameo in Hoffmann's tale would be comparable to writing a story today where Jack Sparrow, Marty McFly, or George Bailey make an appearance – telegraphing to the readers that the tale they are reading is set in a similar universe (with similar perils, virtues, and lessons) to the iconic guest's source material. In Chamisso's story, Schlemihl is a luckless everyman who meets the devil in the gardens of a rich merchant he recently befriended. Satan quickly sizes his vices up and offers to sell him a bottomless wallet for the price of his seemingly cheap price of his shadow. At first buoyed by his limitless wealth, Peter quickly realizes that he has damned himself to a miserable, lonely existence (as his condition horrifies people and leaves him friendless), rendering his wealth useless. Worse still, he falls in love with a beautiful girl whose father refuses to give his consent to their marriage unless he can get control of his life and prove himself worthy by retrieving his shadow. The devil is willing to barter, but the next trade will be even steeper: it will cost him his soul. Once bitten, twice shy, Peter refuses to play the devil's game, tosses away his wallet, and abandons his hopes of marriage, dedicating himself to science while having further adventures (including a memorable acquisition of the mythological seven-league boots, which allow the wearer to travel twenty miles with each step). He ends the novel sadder and wiser, wary of get-rich-quick-schemes, and resigned to a lonely life, stigmatized by his unnatural missing shadow (read: lost innocence foolishly surrendered in pursuit of vanities) and heartbroken by his disappointed romance. The shared themes of "The Lost Reflection" are obvious, and the early appearance of Schlemihl (whose name popularized the Yiddish word "*schlemiel,*" meaning a "hopelessly incompetent ... bungler") alerted Hoffmann's contemporaries to its mood and underlying messages.

II.

The bumbling, lovelorn characters of "The Lost Reflection" are not the only schlemiels being humiliated by his story. Hoffmann's tortured odyssey served as a literary self-flagellation: simultaneously cursing and redeeming himself for his fanatical obsession with the teenaged Julia Marc. Lust, like an intoxicant, pollutes and distorts the minds and souls of his characters (the sexually unnerved protagonist, the pathetic Schlemihl, and the tragic Erasmus). All three men seem to be victims of the same woman (or same *type* of woman): a seductive, bare shouldered prostitute being pimped out by the Devil. While a merely biographical interpretation of this story might unfairly characterize it as a chauvinistic character assassination of the harmless Julia (whose misshapen, lecherous fiancé physically resembled the nefarious Dapertutto), a psychological survey of its symbolism and motifs reveals a more complex portrait of shame, self-loathing, and duplicity. All three men are tormented by the power that their respective women (or shared woman) wield over their flimsy willpower, toppling their convictions, and endangering their places in society. The narrator is in jeopardy of earning a reputation (flirting with a married woman at a civil function, becoming drunk in public, and roaming around the snowy streets without a coat or hat like a lunatic), while Erasmus has been completely banished from his family, forced to associate with fellow fools, forever adrift in a lonely world. The insidious force of this story is not *women*, but the human *will*. All three men have had their wills toppled and dominated – incapable of shaking off their overpowering obsessions, all three roam through the night bereft of a part of their physical-spiritual identity: the narrator his keys and coat (which tie him to security and place), Peter his shadow (which ties him to reality and society), and Erasmus his reflection (which ties him to his soul and self-awareness). All three meet on New Year's Eve, a time of year that is traditionally meant for self-reflection (pun rather intended) and community, but all three meet in a dingy beer cellar, hiding their respective deficits, nursing their respective wounds. Julia – or Giulietta – doesn't represent the entirety of womankind, but rather serves as a manifestation of Obsession itself. Beautiful, appealing, impossibly perfect, she seems to step out the paintings of the Great Masters (who, no doubt, saw her as their artistic muse, too) and offers a goblet of habit forming narcotic to the passionate (or merely impressionable) men whom she encounters. Lead around by the Mephistophelean Dr. Dapertutto (a leering, sneering, possessive archetype common to Hoffmann's fiction) who may either be her cuckold husband or her diabolical pimp, she ruins homes, upsets brilliant minds, and destroys careers.

III.

Julia's appealing form and sinister nature are virtually vampiric, sharing a likeness with Keats' dominating "La Belle Dame Sans Merci," Coleridge's insidious Geraldine and Life-in-Death, the biblical Whore of Babylon, and Shakespeare's Lady Macbeth. More than a personification of womankind, Julia seems to symbolize the power of an *idée fixe* – whether it be sex, drugs, art, vanity, power, money, imagination, or fame – to consume and possess a soul to its absolute detriment. Erasmus barely escapes committing the murder of his family (*Faust's* Gretchen – condemned to the chopping block for strangling her child – is not so lucky) – the price his Obsession demanded for his release – but could not recover his shattered relationship with them. In typical Hoffmann fashion, the rift between husband and family is centered around humiliation and shame: his wife affirms his love but announces that both she and their son have lost their respect for a man who can't keep his own reflection. Sexually and socially shamed, burning with humiliation and despair, Erasmus is sent forth into a cold and inhospitable world, incapable of enjoying the warm community of a New Year's celebration. When Hoffmann wrote this story, Julia was probably going through her own humiliating experience: the details of her loveless marriage and inevitable divorce were leaking into the public, and while his adoration of her had been spoiled by her marriage to a man he considered "a bastard... a common, prosaic putz," he must have felt like a fairy tale had ended: the virtuous virgin was now the defamed divorcee, and in spite of his efforts, both his and her happiness had been irreparably crushed. It was likely a New Year's spent in somber reflection about what he had lost to her, and what could never be recovered...

MUSIC has almost always been seen as a sublime expression of the unconscious: singers, players, and composers allow humanity to express and vicariously experience the most complex emotions of our hearts. Amongst these emotions are the spiritual and the aspirational, but close beside them are the carnal and the passionate. Operatic singing, especially, has frequently been interpreted as a sublimation of sexual furor, and prima donnas have stunned the world into a stupor of awe with their rapturous singing. Like many Catholic saints (e.g. Teresa of Avilla) whose ecstatic trances and visions seemed to unite the spiritual and the sexual, 19th century opera singers such as Jenny Lind, Adelina Patti, and Christina Nilsson won the adoration of millions of libidinous fanboys with their titillating blend of the artistic and erotic. In an age when well-polished women were likely to be soft-spoken and mild-mannered, there was something electrifying about hearing one of these divas sustain a quavering, high E6 note: saturated with sensuality and produced with sweaty, face-flushing physical expression. Indeed, it was common for strangers to propose to these performers, or commit suicide in despair of a hopeless adoration. The motif worked its way into world literature as well: in George du Maurier's *Trilby* (inspired by the following story and others by Hoffmann), the title character – a raucous, Irish bohemian – is entranced by the hypnotic Svengali, who uses magnetism to turn the lovable tomboy into an international singing sensation. Steeped in male anxieties about seductive foreigners (Svengali would in turn be a huge influence on *Dracula*), *Trilby* describes the mingled arousal and horror that her friends experience upon realizing that Svengali is capable of inspiring such passionate singing in her (suggestive of the passionate cries of orgasm). Also inspired by *Trilby*, Gaston Leroux created the trope's *most* famous iteration with his Gothic masterpiece *The Phantom of the Opera*. Like *Trilby*, his heroine – the chaste Christine Daae – appears to be sublimating her intense sexual imagination into shockingly expressive, orgasmic singing. Christine herself openly recognizes the erotic nature of her inspiration, as does her jealous suitor, Raoul de Chagny, who loathes her anonymous teacher for bringing such passion out of her. The eponymous anti-hero is ultimately unveiled to be – like Svengali – a social outcast with a genius for hypnosis and slight of hand, and there is no question as to the carnal nature of *his* feelings for Christine, whom he ultimately kidnaps and threatens to rape.

II.

In the following story – one of Hoffmann's most famous – we have a reiteration of his most common trope: an inappropriate love between an eccentric, older male and a young, virginal girl. These stories always end in the sexual humiliation of the spastic suitor, and (frequently) the death or departure of the girl. As in "The Lost Reflection," the primary inspiration for this motif was Hoffmann's miscarried suit of his teenaged music pupil, Julia Marc. He blended into this imprudent attraction his strong feelings of loss for his daughter (who died as a toddler) and his niece (who moved in shortly after the death and left the Hoffmann's shortly before he met Julia). Hoffmann recognized the impropriety of his attraction, and the shame of it nearly drove him to – in his own words – insanity and suicide. In "The Cremona Violin" the indelicacy exists between a peculiar polymath (like Hoffmann he appears to be part musician, part engineer, part civil servant, part tinker, part composer, and part mystic) and his once estranged daughter. Like the Phantom, he is intensely jealous of his pupil's rapturous singing voice, which he considers his property, and like Svengali, he wields an almost supernatural control over her, and like Hoffmann he spoils the promise of their artistic relationship through the violence of his possessive infatuation. Krespel is nothing if not a flawed and complicated figure, and the *most* complicated element of his life is the tangled nature of his relationship with his daughter – one where he simultaneously takes on the roles of a hopeless suitor, devoted parent, and inspiring teacher.

The Cremona Violin

— *Excerpted from 'The Serapion Brethren,' Volume One, Section One* —

{1818}

COUNCILLOR[1] Krespel was one of the strangest, oddest men I ever met with in my life. When I went to live in H—— for a time the whole town was full of talk about him, as he happened to be just then in the midst of one of the very craziest of his schemes. Krespel had the reputation of being both a clever, learn lawyer and a skilful diplomatist. One of the reigning princes of Germany — not, however, one of the most powerful[2] — had appealed to him for assistance in drawing up a memorial, which he was desirous of presenting at the Imperial Court[3] with the view of furthering his legitimate claims upon a certain strip of territory. The project was crowned with the happiest success; and as Krespel had once complained that he could never find a dwelling sufficiently comfortable to suit him, the prince, to reward him for the memorial, undertook to defray the cost of building a house which Krespel might erect just as he pleased. Moreover, the prince was willing to purchase any site that he should fancy. This offer, however, the Councillor would not accept; he

---

[1] A government administrator, functionary, or advisor

[2] Before the unification of Germany in 1871, Germany consisted of dozens of micro-states and city-states, and some half-dozen major principalities like Bavaria, Saxony, and Prussia

[3] To the Holy Roman Emperor – sanctioned ruler of most of central Europe until the dissolution of the Holy Roman Empire in 1806

insisted that the house should be built in his garden, situated in a very beautiful neighbourhood outside the town-walls. So he bought all kinds of materials and had them carted out. Then he might have been seen day after day, attired in his curious garments (which he had made himself according to certain fixed rules of his own), slacking the lime, riddling the sand, packing up the bricks and stones in regular heaps, and so on. All this he did without once consulting an architect or thinking about a plan[1]. One fine day, however, he went to an experienced builder of the town and requested him to be in his garden at daybreak the next morning, with all his journeymen and apprentices, and a large body of labourers, &c., to build him his house. Naturally the builder asked for the architect's plan, and was not a little astonished when Krespel replied that none was needed, and that things would turn out all right in the end, just as he wanted them. Next morning, when the builder and his men came to the place, they found a trench drawn out in the shape of an exact square; and Krespel said, "Here's where you must lay the foundations; then carry up the walls until I say they are high enough." "Without windows and doors, and without partition walls?" broke in the builder, as if alarmed at Krespel's mad folly. "Do what I tell you, my dear sir," replied the Councillor quite calmly; "leave the rest to me; it will be all right." It was only the promise of high pay that could induce the builder to proceed with the ridiculous building; but none has ever been erected under merrier circumstances. As there was an abundant supply of food and drink, the workmen never left their work; and amidst their continuous laughter the four walls were run up with incredible quickness, until one day Krespel cried, "Stop!" Then the workmen, laying down trowel and hammer, came down from the scaffoldings and gathered round Krespel in a circle, whilst every laughing face was asking, "Well, and what now?" "Make way!" cried Krespel; and then running to one end of the garden, he strode slowly towards the square of brick-work. When he came close to the wall he shook his head in a dissatisfied manner, ran to the other end of the garden, again strode slowly towards the brick-work square, and proceeded to act as before. These tactics he pursued several times, until at length, running his sharp nose hard against the wall, he cried, "Come here, come here, men! break me a door in here! Here's where I want a door made!" He gave the exact dimensions in feet and inches, and they did as he bid them. Then he stepped inside the structure, and smiled with satisfaction as the builder remarked that the walls were just the height of a good two-storeyed house. Krespel walked thoughtfully backwards and forwards across the space within, the bricklayers behind him with hammers and picks, and wherever he cried, "Make a window here, six feet

---

[1] Hoffmann's recurring motif of the unrestricted-yet-unpractical imagination: stunningly unique, yet ominously disorganized

high by four feet broad!" "There a little window, three feet by two!" a hole was made in a trice.

It was at this stage of the proceedings that I came to H——; and it was highly amusing to see how hundreds of people stood round about the garden and raised a loud shout whenever the stones flew out and a new window appeared where nobody had for a moment expected it. And in the same manner Krespel proceeded with the buildings and fittings of the rest of the house, and with all the work necessary to that end; everything had to be done on the spot in accordance with the instructions which the Councillor gave from time to time. However, the absurdity of the whole business, the growing conviction that things would in the end turn out better than might have been expected, but above all, Krespel's generosity — which indeed cost him nothing — kept them all in good-humour. Thus were the difficulties overcome which necessarily arose out of this eccentric way of building, and in a short time there was a completely finished house, its outside, indeed, presenting a most extraordinary appearance, no two windows, &c., being alike, but on the other hand the interior arrangements suggested a peculiar feeling of comfort. All who entered the house bore witness to the truth of this; and I too experienced it myself when I was taken in by Krespel after I had become more intimate with him. For hitherto I had not exchanged a word with this eccentric man; his building had occupied him so much that he had not even once been to Professor M——'s to dinner, as he was in the habit of going on Tuesdays. Indeed, in reply to a special invitation, he sent word that he should not set foot over the threshold before the house-warming of his new building took place. All his friends and acquaintances, therefore, confidently looked forward to a great banquet; but Krespel invited nobody except the masters, journeymen, apprentices, and labourers who had built the house. He entertained them with the choicest viands: bricklayer's apprentices devoured partridge pies regardless of consequences; young joiners polished off roast pheasants with the greatest success; whilst hungry labourers helped themselves for once to the choicest morsels of truffes fricassées . In the evening their wives and daughters came, and there was a great ball. After waltzing a short while with the wives of the masters, Krespel sat down amongst the town-musicians, took a violin in his hand, and directed the orchestra until daylight.

On the Tuesday after this festival, which exhibited Councillor Krespel in the character of a friend of the people, I at length saw him appear, to my no little joy, at Professor M——'s. Anything more strange and fantastic than Krespel's behaviour it would be impossible to find. He was so stiff and awkward in his movements, that he looked every moment as if he would run up against something or do some damage. But he did not; and the lady of the house seemed to be well aware that he would not, for she did not grow a shade paler when he rushed with heavy steps round a table crowded with beautiful cups, or when he manœuvred near a large mirror that reached down to the floor, or even when he seized a flower-pot of beautifully painted porcelain and swung it round in the air as if desirous of making its colours play. Moreover, before dinner he subjected everything in the Professor's room to a most minute examination; he also took down a picture from the wall and hung it up again, standing on one of the cushioned chairs to do so. At the same time he talked a good deal and vehemently; at one time his thoughts kept leaping, as it were, from one subject to another (this was most conspicuous during dinner); at another, he was unable to have done with an idea; seizing upon it again and again, he gave it all sorts of wonderful twists and turns, and couldn't get back into the ordinary track until something else took hold of his fancy. Sometimes his voice was rough and harsh and screeching, and sometimes it was low and drawling and singing; but at no time did it harmonize with what he was talking about. Music was the subject of conversation; the praises of a new composer were being sung, when Krespel, smiling, said in his low singing tones, "I wish the devil with his pitchfork would hurl that atrocious garbler of music millions of fathoms down to the bottomless pit of hell!" Then he burst out passionately and wildly, "She is an angel of heaven, nothing but pure God-given music! — the paragon and queen of song!"— and tears stood in his eyes[1]. To understand this, we had to go back to a celebrated artiste, who had been the subject of conversation an hour before.

Just at this time a roast hare was on the table; I noticed that Krespel carefully removed every particle of meat from the bones on his plate, and was most particular in his inquiries after the hare's feet; these the Professor's little five-year-old daughter now brought to him with a very pretty smile. Besides, the children had cast many friendly glances towards Krespel during dinner; now they rose and drew nearer to him, but not without signs of timorous awe. What's the meaning of that? thought I to myself. Dessert was brought in; then the Councillor took a little box from his pocket, in which he had a miniature lathe of steel. This he immediately screwed fast to the table, and turning the bones with incredible skill and rapidity, he made all sorts of little fancy boxes and balls, which the children received with cries of delight. Just as we were rising from table, the Professor's niece asked, "And what is our Antonia doing?" Krespel's face was like that of one who has bitten of a sour orange and wants to look as if it were a sweet one; but this expression soon changed into the likeness of a hideous mask, whilst he laughed behind it with downright bitter, fierce, and as it seemed to me, satanic scorn. "Our

[1] A highly intense depiction of a person with strong mood swings, and probably manic-depression

Antonia[1]? our dear Antonia?" he asked in his drawling, disagreeable singing way. The Professor hastened to intervene; in the reproving glance which he gave his niece I read that she had touched a point likely to stir up unpleasant memories in Krespel's heart. "How are you getting on with your violins?" interposed the Professor in a jovial manner, taking the Councillor by both hands. Then Krespel's countenance cleared up, and with a firm voice he replied, "Capitally, Professor; you recollect my telling you of the lucky chance which threw that splendid Amati[2] into my hands. Well, I've only cut it open today — not before today. I hope Antonia has carefully taken the rest of it to pieces." "Antonia is a good child," remarked the Professor. "Yes, indeed, that she is," cried the Councillor, whisking himself round; then, seizing his hat and stick, he hastily rushed out of the room. I saw in the mirror how that tears were standing in his eyes.

As soon as the Councillor was gone, I at once urged the Professor to explain to me what Krespel had to do with violins, and particularly with Antonia. "Well," replied the Professor, "not only is the Councillor a remarkably eccentric fellow altogether, but he practises violin-making in his own crack-brained way." "Violin-making!" I exclaimed, perfectly astonished. "Yes," continued the Professor, "according to the judgment of men who understand the thing, Krespel makes the very best violins that can be found nowadays; formerly he would frequently let other people play on those in which he had been especially successful, but that's been all over and done with now for a long time. As soon as he has finished a violin he plays on it himself for one or two hours, with very remarkable power and with the most exquisite expression, then he hangs it up beside the rest, and never touches it again or suffers anybody else to touch it. If a violin by any of the eminent old masters is hunted up anywhere, the Councillor buys it immediately, no matter what the price put upon it. But he plays it as he does his own violins, only once; then he takes it to pieces in order to examine closely its inner structure, and should he fancy he hasn't found exactly what he sought for, he in a pet throws the pieces into a big chest, which is already full of the remains of broken violins." "But who and what[3] is Antonia?" I inquired, hastily and impetuously. "Well, now, that," continued the Professor, "that is a thing which might very well

---

[1] Pronounced AN-toe-NEE-uh, the meaningful name means "beautiful," and "priceless"

[2] Like the famous Stradivarius, Amati violins – made by the Amati family of Cremona, Italy – were widely regarded for their luscious, warm sound and detailed craftsmanship

[3] The narrator appears to sense that Antonia is more than a person – she represents an ideal. This feeling is also reflected in Krespel's objectification and dehumanization of her – transforming her into a "what" rather than a "who"

make me conceive an unconquerable aversion to the Councillor, were I not convinced that there is some peculiar secret behind it, for he is such a good-natured fellow at bottom as to be sometimes guilty of weakness. When he came to H—— several years ago, he led the life of an anchorite, along with an old housekeeper, in —— Street. Soon, by his oddities, he excited the curiosity of his neighbours; and immediately he became aware of this, he sought and made acquaintances. Not only in my house but everywhere we became so accustomed to him that he grew to be indispensable. In spite of his rude exterior, even the children liked him, without ever proving a nuisance to him; for notwithstanding all their friendly passages together, they always retained a certain timorous awe of him, which secured him against all over-familiarity. You have today had an example of the way in which he wins their hearts by his ready skill in various things[1]. We all took him at first for a crusty old bachelor, and he never contradicted us. After he had been living here some time, he went away, nobody knew where, and returned at the end of some months. The evening following his return his windows were lit up to an unusual extent! this alone was sufficient to arouse his neighbours' attention, and they soon heard the surpassingly beautiful voice of a female singing to the accompaniment of a piano. Then the music of a violin was heard chiming in and entering upon a keen ardent contest with the voice. They knew at once that the player was the Councillor. I myself mixed in the large crowd which had gathered in front of his house to listen to this extraordinary concert; and I must confess that, beside this voice and the peculiar, deep, soul-stirring impression which the execution made upon me, the singing of the most celebrated artistes whom I had ever heard seemed to me feeble and void of expression. Until then I had had no conception of such long-sustained notes, of such nightingale trills, of such undulations of musical sound, of such swelling up to the strength of organ-notes, of such dying away to the faintest whisper. There was not one whom the sweet witchery did not enthral; and when the singer ceased, nothing but soft sighs broke the impressive silence. Somewhere about midnight the Councillor was heard talking violently, and another male voice seemed, to judge from the tones, to be reproaching him, whilst at intervals the broken words of a sobbing girl could be detected. The Councillor continued to shout with increasing violence, until he fell into that drawling, singing way that you know. He was interrupted by a loud scream from the girl, and then all was as still as death. Suddenly a loud racket was heard on the stairs; a young man rushed out sobbing, threw himself into a post-chaise[2] which stood below, and drove rapidly away. The next day the Councillor was very cheerful, and nobody had the

---

[1] A common trait in Hoffmann's eccentric characters: like Drosselmeier, they stun and delight children with their imaginative tinkering

[2] A four-wheeled coach used to transport travelers and the regional mail

courage to question him about the events of the previous night. But on inquiring of the housekeeper, we gathered that the Councillor had brought home with him an extraordinarily pretty young lady whom he called Antonia, and she it was who had sung so beautifully. A young man also had come along with them; he had treated Antonia very tenderly, and must evidently have been her betrothed. But he, since the Councillor peremptorily insisted on it, had had to go away again in a hurry. What the relations between Antonia and the Councillor are has remained until now a secret, but this much is certain, that he tyrannises over the poor girl in the most hateful fashion. He watches her as Doctor Bartholo watches his ward in the Barber of Seville[1]; she hardly dare show herself at the window; and if, yielding now and again to her earnest entreaties, he takes her into society, he follows her with Argus[2]' eyes, and will on no account suffer a musical note to be sounded, far less let Antonia sing — indeed, she is not permitted to sing in his own house. Antonia's singing on that memorable night, has, therefore, come to be regarded by the townspeople in the light of a tradition of some marvellous wonder that suffices to stir the heart and the fancy; and even those who did not hear it often exclaim, whenever any other singer attempts to display her powers in the place, 'What sort of a wretched squeaking do you call that? Nobody but Antonia knows how to sing.'"

Having a singular weakness for such like fantastic histories, I found it necessary, as may easily be imagined, to make Antonia's acquaintance. I had myself often enough heard the popular sayings about her singing, but had never imagined that that exquisite artiste was living in the place, held a captive in the bonds of this eccentric Krespel like the victim of a tyrannous sorcerer. Naturally enough I heard in my dreams on the following night Antonia's marvellous voice, and as she besought me in the most touching manner in a glorious adagio[3] movement (very ridiculously it seemed to me, as if I had composed it myself) to save her, I soon resolved, like a second Astolpho[4], to penetrate into Krespel's house, as if into another Alcina's magic castle, and deliver the queen of song from her ignominious fetters.

It all came about in a different way from what I had expected; I had seen the Councillor scarcely more than two or three times, and eagerly

---

[1] In Rossini's opera, Doctor Bartolo is the tyrannical, possessive guardian of the beautiful Rosina. An ugly, miserable curmudgeon, he plans to marry her once she is of age, in order to collect her large dowry

[2] A fearsome giant in Greek mythology whose surname Panoptes means "all-seeing one"

[3] One with a slow, expressive tempo (the word "adagio" means "easy-going")

[4] A character in the medieval "Matter of France" who is remarkable for his wit, manners, beauty, and charm, and who uses stealth and luck to seduce reclusive women

discussed with him the best method of constructing violins, when he invited me to call and see him. I did so; and he showed me his treasures of violins. There were fully thirty of them hanging up in a closet; one amongst them bore conspicuously all the marks of great antiquity (a carved lion's head, &c.), and, hung up higher than the rest and surmounted by a crown of flowers, it seemed to exercise a queenly supremacy over them. "This violin," said Krespel, on my making some inquiry relative to it, "this violin is a very remarkable and curious specimen of the work of some unknown master, probably of Tartini's[1] age. I am perfectly convinced that there is something especially exceptional in its inner construction, and that, if I took it to pieces, a secret would be revealed to me which I have long been seeking to discover, but — laugh at me if you like — this senseless thing which only gives signs of life and sound as I make it, often speaks to me in a strange way of itself. The first time I played upon it I somehow fancied that I was only the magnetiser[2] who has the power of moving his subject to reveal of his own accord in words the visions of his inner nature. Don't go away with the belief that I am such a fool as to attach even the slightest importance to such fantastic notions, and yet it's certainly strange that I could never prevail upon myself to cut open that dumb lifeless thing there. I am very pleased now that I have not cut it open, for since Antonia has been with me I sometimes play to her upon this violin. For Antonia is fond of it — very fond of it." As the Councillor uttered these words with visible signs of emotion, I felt encouraged to hazard the question, "Will you not play it to me, Councillor." Krespel made a wry face, and falling into his drawling, singing way, said, "No, my good sir!" and that was an end of the matter. Then I had to look at all sorts of rare curiosities, the greater part of them childish trifles; at last thrusting his arm into a chest, he brought out a folded piece of paper, which he pressed into my hand, adding solemnly, "You are a lover of art; take this present as a priceless memento, which you must value at all times above everything else." Therewith he took me by the shoulders and gently pushed me towards the door, embracing me on the threshold. That is to say, I was in a symbolical manner virtually kicked out of doors. Unfolding the paper, I found a piece of a first string of a violin about an eighth of an inch in length, with the words, "A piece of the treble string with which the

---

[1] Giuseppe Tartini (1692 – 1770) was a famous composer and violinist, most remembered for his macabre "Devil's Trill" Sonata in G minor, which was said to have been played to him in a dream by Satan

[2] One who uses the principles of animal magnetism to influence others, like a hypnotist

deceased Staraitz[1] strung his violin for the last concert at which he ever played."

This summary dismissal at mention of Antonia's name led me to infer that I should never see her; but I was mistaken, for on my second visit to the Councillor's I found her in his room, assisting him to put a violin together. At first sight Antonia did not make a strong impression; but soon I found it impossible to tear myself away from her blue eyes, her sweet rosy lips, her uncommonly graceful, lovely form. She was very pale; but a shrewd remark or a merry sally would call up a winning smile on her face and suffuse her cheeks with a deep burning flush, which, however, soon faded away to a faint rosy glow. My conversation with her was quite unconstrained, and yet I saw nothing whatever of the Argus-like watchings on Krespel's part which the Professor had imputed to him; on the contrary, his behaviour moved along the customary lines, nay, he even seemed to approve of my conversation with Antonia. So I often stepped in to see the Councillor; and as we became accustomed to each other's society, a singular feeling of homeliness, taking possession of our little circle of three, filled our hearts with inward happiness. I still continued to derive exquisite enjoyment from the Councillor's strange crotchets and oddities; but it was of course Antonia's irresistible charms alone which attracted me, and led me to put up with a good deal which I should otherwise, in the frame of mind in which I then was, have impatiently shunned. For it only too often happened that in the Councillor's characteristic extravagance there was mingled much that was dull and tiresome; and it was in a special degree irritating to me that, as often as I turned the conversation upon music, and particularly upon singing, he was sure to interrupt me, with that sardonic smile upon his face and those repulsive singing tones of his, by some remark of a quite opposite tendency, very often of a commonplace character. From the great distress which at such times Antonia's glances betrayed, I perceived that he only did it to deprive me of a pretext for calling upon her for a song. But I didn't relinquish my design. The hindrances which the Councillor threw in my way only strengthened my resolution to overcome them; I must hear Antonia sing if I was not to pine away in reveries and dim aspirations for want of hearing her.

One evening Krespel was in an uncommonly good humour; he had been taking an old Cremona[2] violin to pieces, and had discovered that the sound-post was fixed half a line more obliquely than usual — an important discovery! one of incalculable advantage in the practical work of making violins! I succeeded in setting him off at full speed on his hobby of the true art of violin-playing. Mention of the way in which the

---

[1] Possibly an allusion to the violinist Karl Stamitz, who died twenty-some years before the story was written

[2] That is, and Amati from Cremona, Italy

old masters picked up their dexterity in execution from really great singers (which was what Krespel happened just then to be expatiating upon), naturally paved the way for the remark that now the practice was the exact opposite of this, the vocal score erroneously following the affected and abrupt transitions and rapid scaling of the instrumentalists. "What is more nonsensical," I cried, leaping from my chair, running to the piano, and opening it quickly, "what is more nonsensical than such an execrable style as this, which, far from being music, is much more like the noise of peas rolling across the floor?" At the same time I sang several of the modern fermatas[1], which rush up and down and hum like a well-spun peg-top, striking a few villanous chords by way of accompaniment Krespel laughed outrageously and screamed, "Ha! ha! methinks I hear our German–Italians or our Italian–Germans struggling with an aria from Pucitta, or Portogallo, or some other Maestro di capella, or rather schiavo d'un primo uomo[2]." Now, thought I, now's the time; so turning to Antonia, I remarked, "Antonia knows nothing of such singing as that, I believe?" At the same time I struck up one of old Leonardo Leo's beautiful soul-stirring songs. Then Antonia's cheeks glowed; heavenly radiance sparkled in her eyes, which grew full of reawakened inspiration; she hastened to the piano; she opened her lips; but at that very moment Krespel pushed her away, grasped me by the shoulders, and with a shriek that rose up to a tenor pitch, cried, "My son — my son — my son!" And then he immediately went on, singing very softly, and grasping my hand with a bow that was the pink of politeness, "In very truth, my esteemed and honourable student-friend, in very truth it would be a violation of the codes of social intercourse, as well as of all good manners, were I to express aloud and in a stirring way my wish that here, on this very spot, the devil from hell would softly break your neck with his burning claws, and so in a sense make short work of you; but, setting that aside, you must acknowledge, my dearest friend, that it is rapidly growing dark, and there are no lamps burning to-night so that, even though I did not kick you downstairs at once, your darling limbs might still run a risk of suffering damage. Go home by all means; and cherish a kind

---

[1] Presumably songs rife with fermatas – the music symbol which denotes a long, sustained note. Such a song – like Schubert's "Ave Maria" – would be slow, expressive, and emotionally powerful

[2] German-Italians: Until the rise of Wagner – even during the hey-day of Mozart – German vocalists and opera writers looked to Italy and the Italian language for inspiration, often coming across as weak imitators; Vincenzo Pucitta: an Italian composer of operas little remembered today; Portogallo: the nickname of Portuguese composer Mark Anthony Simao – also little remembered today; Maestro di capella: Chapel Master, or choir director; "schiavo d'un...": literally "the slave of a primo uomo" (primo uomo is the male version of a prima donna – think the Three Tenors)

remembrance of your faithful friend, if it should happen that you never — pray, understand me — if you should never see him in his own house again." Therewith he embraced me, and, still keeping fast hold of me, turned with me slowly towards the door, so that I could not get another single look at Antonia. Of course it is plain enough that in my position I couldn't thrash the Councillor, though that is what he really deserved. The Professor enjoyed a good laugh at my expense, and assured me that I had ruined for ever all hopes of retaining the Councillor's friendship. Antonia was too dear to me, I might say too holy, for me to go and play the part of the languishing lover and stand gazing up at her window, or to fill the rôle of the lovesick adventurer. Completely upset, I went away from H——; but, as is usual in such cases, the brilliant colours of the picture of my fancy faded, and the recollection of Antonia, as well as of Antonia's singing (which I had never heard), often fell upon my heart like a soft faint trembling light, comforting me.

Two years afterwards I received an appointment in B—— and set out on a journey to the south of Germany. The towers of M——[1] rose before me in the red vaporous glow of the evening; the nearer I came the more was I oppressed by an indescribable feeling of the most agonising distress; it lay upon me like a heavy burden; I could not breathe; I was obliged to get out of my carriage into the open air. But my anguish continued to increase until it became actual physical pain. Soon I seemed to hear the strains of a solemn chorale floating in the air; the sounds continued to grow more distinct; I realised the fact that they were men's voices chanting a church chorale. "What's that? what's that?" I cried, a burning stab darting as it were through my breast "Don't you see?" replied the coachman, who was driving along beside me, "why, don't you see? they're burying somebody up yonder in yon churchyard." And indeed we were near the churchyard; I saw a circle of men clothed in black standing round a grave, which was on the point of being closed. Tears started to my eyes; I somehow fancied they were burying there all the joy and all the happiness of life. Moving on rapidly down the hill, I was no longer able to see into the churchyard; the chorale came to an end, and I perceived not far distant from the gate some of the mourners returning from the funeral. The Professor, with his niece on his arm, both in deep mourning, went close past me without noticing me. The young lady had her handkerchief pressed close to her eyes, and was weeping bitterly. In the frame of mind in which I then was I could not possibly go into the town, so I sent on my servant with the carriage to the hotel where I usually put up, whilst I took a turn in the familiar neighbourhood, to get rid of a mood that was possibly only due to physical causes, such as heating on the journey, &c. On arriving at a well-known avenue, which leads to a

---

[1] Almost certainly these oddly veiled geographies correlate to Bavaria and Munich, respectively

pleasure resort, I came upon a most extraordinary spectacle. Councillor Krespel was being conducted by two mourners, from whom he appeared to be endeavouring to make his escape by all sorts of strange twists and turns. As usual, he was dressed in his own curious home-made grey coat; but from his little cocked-hat[1], which he wore perched over one ear in military fashion, a long narrow ribbon of black crape fluttered backwards and forwards in the wind. Around his waist he had buckled a black sword-belt; but instead of a sword he had stuck a long fiddle-bow into it. A creepy shudder ran through my limbs: "He's insane," thought I, as I slowly followed them. The Councillor's companions led him as far as his house, where he embraced them, laughing loudly. They left him; and then his glance fell upon me, for I now stood near him. He stared at me fixedly for some time; then he cried in a hollow voice, "Welcome, my student-friend! you also understand it!" Therewith he took me by the arm and pulled me into the house, up the steps, into the room where the violins hung. They were all draped in black crape; the violin of the old master was missing; in its place was a cypress wreath[2]. I knew what had happened. "Antonia! Antonia!" I cried in inconsolable grief. The Councillor, with his arms crossed on his breast, stood beside me, as if turned into stone. I pointed to the cypress wreath. "When she died," said he in a very hoarse solemn voice, "when she died, the soundpost of that violin broke into pieces with a ringing crack, and the sound-board was split from end to end. The faithful instrument could only live with her and in her; it lies beside her in the coffin, it has been buried with her." Deeply agitated, I sank down upon a chair, whilst the Councillor began to sing a gay song in a husky voice; it was truly horrible to see him hopping about on one foot, and the crape strings[3] (he still had his hat on) flying about the room and up to the violins hanging on the walls. Indeed, I could not repress a loud cry that rose to my lips when, on the Councillor making an abrupt turn, the crape came all over me; I fancied he wanted to envelop me in it and drag me down into the horrible dark depths of insanity. Suddenly he stood still and addressed me in his singing way, "My son! my son! why do you call out? Have you espied the angel of death? That always precedes the ceremony." Stepping into the middle of the room, he took the violin-bow out of his sword-belt and, holding it over his head with both hands, broke it into a thousand pieces. Then, with a loud laugh, he cried, "Now you imagine my sentence is pronounced, don't you, my son? but it's nothing of the kind — not at all! not at all! Now I'm free — free — free — hurrah! I'm free! Now I shall make no more violins — no more violins — Hurrah! no more violins!"

---

[1] A military-style three-cornered hat

[2] Cypress – a narrow conifer native to the Mediterranean – is traditionally associated with graveyards and all things funerary

[3] In traditional mourning dress, men's hats are bound in black crape material

This he sang to a horrible mirthful tune, again spinning round on one foot. Perfectly aghast, I was making the best of my way to the door, when he held me fast, saying quite calmly, "Stay, my student friend, pray don't think from this outbreak of grief, which is torturing me as if with the agonies of death, that I am insane; I only do it because a short time ago I made myself a dressing-gown in which I wanted to look like Fate or like God!" The Councillor then went on with a medley of silly and awful rubbish, until he fell down utterly exhausted; I called up the old housekeeper, and was very pleased to find myself in the open air again.

I never doubted for a moment that Krespel had become insane; the Professor, however, asserted the contrary. "There are men," he remarked, "from whom nature or a special destiny has taken away the cover behind which the mad folly of the rest of us runs its course unobserved. They are like thin-skinned insects, which, as we watch the restless play of their muscles, seem to be misshapen, while nevertheless everything soon comes back into its proper form again. All that with us remains thought, passes over with Krespel into action. That bitter scorn which the spirit that is wrapped up in the doings and dealings of the earth often has at hand, Krespel gives vent to in outrageous gestures and agile caprioles[1]. But these are his lightning conductor. What comes up out of the earth he gives again to the earth, but what is divine, that he keeps; and so I believe that his inner consciousness, in spite of the apparent madness which springs from it to the surface, is as right as a trivet. To be sure, Antonia's sudden death grieves him sore, but I warrant that tomorrow will see him going along in his old jog-trot way as usual." And the Professor's prediction was almost literally filled. Next day the Councillor appeared to be just as he formerly was, only he averred that he would never make another violin, nor yet ever play on another. And, as I learned later, he kept his word.

Hints which the Professor let fall confirmed my own private conviction that the so carefully guarded secret of the Councillor's relations to Antonia, nay, that even her death, was a crime which must weigh heavily upon him, a crime that could not be atoned for. I determined that I would not leave H—— without taxing him with the offence which I conceived him to be guilty of; I determined to shake his heart down to its very roots, and so compel him to make open confession of the terrible deed. The more I reflected upon the matter the clearer it grew in my own mind that Krespel must be a villain, and in the same proportion did my intended reproach, which assumed of itself the form of a real rhetorical masterpiece, wax more fiery and more impressive. Thus equipped and mightily incensed, I hurried to his house. I found him with a calm smiling countenance making playthings. "How can peace," I burst out, "how can peace find lodgment even for a single moment in your

[1] A playful leap or bound – as of a prancing horse

breast, so long as the memory of your horrible deed preys like a serpent upon you?" He gazed at me in amazement, and laid his chisel aside. "What do you mean, my dear sir?" he asked; "pray take a seat." But my indignation chafing me more and more, I went on to accuse him directly of having murdered Antonia, and to threaten him with the vengeance of the Eternal[1].

Further, as a newly full-fledged lawyer, full of my profession, I went so far as to give him to understand that I would leave no stone unturned to get a clue to the business, and so deliver him here in this world into the hands of an earthly judge. I must confess that I was considerably disconcerted when, at the conclusion of my violent and pompous harangue, the Councillor, without answering so much as a single word, calmly fixed his eyes upon me as though expecting me to go on again. And this I did indeed attempt to do, but it sounded so ill-founded and so stupid as well that I soon grew silent again. Krespel gloated over my embarrassment, whilst a malicious ironical smile flitted across his face. Then he grew very grave, and addressed me in solemn tones. "Young man, no doubt you think I am foolish, insane; that I can pardon you, since we are both confined in the same madhouse; and you only blame me for deluding myself with the idea that I am God the Father because you imagine yourself to be God the Son[2]. But how do you dare desire to insinuate yourself into the secrets and lay bare the hidden motives of a life that is strange to you and that must continue so? She has gone and the mystery is solved." He ceased speaking, rose, and traversed the room backwards and forwards several times. I ventured to ask for an explanation; he fixed his eyes upon me, grasped me by the hand, and led me to the window, which he threw wide open. Propping himself upon his arms, he leaned out, and, looking down into the garden, told me the history of his life. When he finished I left him, touched and ashamed.

In a few words, his relations with Antonia rose in the following way. Twenty years before, the Councillor had been led into Italy by his favourite engrossing passion of hunting up and buying the best violins of the old masters. At that time he had not yet begun to make them himself, and so of course he had not begun to take to pieces those which he bought. In Venice he heard the celebrated singer Angela —— i, who at that time was playing with splendid success as prima donna at St. Benedict's Theatre. His enthusiasm was awakened, not only in her art — which Signora Angela had indeed brought to a high pitch of perfection — but in her angelic beauty as well. He sought her acquaintance; and in spite of all his rugged manners he succeeded in winning her heart,

---

[1] That is, with Hell, with damnation

[2] In other words, he accuses the narrator of having a Messiah Complex – becoming delusionally convinced that he is destined to bring an almost supernatural level of justice to the world

principally through his bold and yet at the same time masterly violin-playing. Close intimacy led in a few weeks to marriage, which, however, was kept a secret, because Angela was unwilling to sever her connection with the theatre, neither did she wish to part with her professional name, that by which she was celebrated, nor to add to it the cacophonous "Krespel[1]." With the most extravagant irony he described to me what a strange life of worry and torture Angela led him as soon as she became his wife. Krespel was of opinion that more capriciousness and waywardness were concentrated in Angela's little person than in all the rest of the prima donnas in the world put together. If he now and again presumed to stand up in his own defence, she let loose a whole army of abbots, musical composers, and students upon him, who, ignorant of his true connection with Angela, soundly rated him as a most intolerable, ungallant lover for not submitting to all the Signora's caprices. It was just after one of these stormy scenes that Krespel fled to Angela's country seat to try and forget in playing fantasias on his Cremona, violin the annoyances of the day. But he had not been there long before the Signora, who had followed hard after him, stepped into the room. She was in an affectionate humour; she embraced her husband, overwhelmed him with sweet and languishing glances, and rested her pretty head on his shoulder. But Krespel, carried away into the world of music, continued to play on until the walls echoed again; thus he chanced to touch the Signora somewhat ungently with his arm and the fiddle-bow. She leapt back full of fury, shrieking that he was a "German brute," snatched the violin from his hands, and dashed it on the marble table into a thousand pieces. Krespel stood like a statue of stone before her; but then, as if awakening out of a dream, he seized her with the strength of a giant and threw her out of the window of her own house, and, without troubling himself about anything more, fled back to Venice — to Germany. It was not, however, until some time had elapsed that he had a clear recollection of what he had done; although he knew that the window was scarcely five feet from the ground, and although he was fully cognisant of the necessity, under the above-mentioned circumstances, of throwing the Signora out of the window, he yet felt troubled by a sense of painful uneasiness, and the more so since she had imparted to him in no ambiguous terms an interesting secret as to her condition. He hardly dared to make inquiries; and he was not a little surprised about eight months afterwards at receiving a tender letter from his beloved wife, in which she made not the slightest allusion to what had

[1] Although many married women performed on the stages of Europe as actresses, singers, and musicians, it was not tremendously common and was viewed as slightly inappropriate for a woman with a family to divide her time between her career and her household. Furthermore, the truly guttural name "Cremona Violin" would certainly be a change from her undoubtedly melodic-sounding Italian surname (all of which we know is that it ends in "I")

taken place in her country house, only adding to the intelligence that she had been safely delivered of a sweet little daughter the heartfelt prayer that her dear husband and now a happy father would come at once to Venice. That however Krespel did not do; rather he appealed to a confidential friend for a more circumstantial account of the details, and learned that the Signora had alighted upon the soft grass as lightly as a bird, and that the sole consequences of the fall or shock had been psychic. That is to say, after Krespel's heroic deed she had become completely altered; she never showed a trace of caprice, of her former freaks, or of her teasing habits; and the composer who wrote for the next carnival was the happiest fellow under the sun, since the Signora was willing to sing his music without the scores and hundreds of changes which she at other times had insisted upon. "To be sure," added his friend, "there was every reason for preserving the secret of Angela's cure, else every day would see lady singers flying through windows." The Councillor was not a little excited at this news; he engaged horses; he took his seat in the carriage. "Stop!" he cried suddenly. "Why, there's not a shadow of doubt," he murmured to himself, "that as soon as Angela sets eyes upon me again the evil spirit will recover his power and once more take possession of her. And since I have already thrown her out of the window, what could I do if a similar case were to occur again? What would there be left for me to do?" He got out of the carriage, and wrote an affectionate letter to his wife, making graceful allusion to her tenderness in especially dwelling upon the fact that his tiny daughter had like him a little mole behind the ear, and — remained in Germany. Now ensued an active correspondence between them. Assurances of unchanged affection — invitations — laments over the absence of the beloved one — thwarted wishes — hopes, &c. — flew backwards and forwards from Venice to H—— from H—— to Venice. At length Angela came to Germany, and, as is well known, sang with brilliant success as prima donna at the great theatre in F——. Despite the fact that she was no longer young, she won all hearts by the irresistible charm of her wonderfully splendid singing. At that time she had not lost her voice in the least degree. Meanwhile, Antonia had been growing up; and her mother never tired of writing to tell her father how that a singer of the first rank was developing in her. Krespel's friends in F—— also confirmed this intelligence, and urged him to come for once to F—— to see and admire this uncommon sight of two such glorious singers. They had not the slightest suspicion of the close relations in which Krespel stood to the pair. Willingly would he have seen with his own eyes the daughter who occupied so large a place in his heart, and who moreover often appeared to him in his dreams; but as often as he thought upon his wife he felt very uncomfortable, and so he remained at home amongst his broken violins. There was a certain promising young composer, B—— of F—— who was found to have suddenly disappeared, nobody knew where. This young man fell so deeply in love with Antonia that, as she returned his love, he earnestly besought her mother to consent to an immediate union, sanctified as it would further be by art. Angela had nothing to urge against his suit; and the Councillor the more readily gave his consent that the young composer's productions had found favour before his rigorous critical judgment. Krespel was expecting to hear of the consummation of the marriage, when he received instead a black-sealed[1] envelope addressed in a strange hand. Doctor R—— conveyed to the Councillor the sad intelligence that Angela had fallen seriously ill in consequence of a cold caught at the theatre, and that during the night immediately preceding what was to have been Antonia's wedding-day, she had died. To him, the Doctor, Angela had disclosed the fact that she was Krespel's wife, and that Antonia was his daughter; he, Krespel, had better hasten therefore to take charge of the orphan. Notwithstanding that the Councillor was a good deal upset by this news of Angela's death, he soon began to feel that an antipathetic, disturbing influence had departed out of his life, and that now for the first time he could begin to breathe freely. The very same day he set out for F——. You could not credit how heartrending was the Councillor's description of the moment when he first saw Antonia. Even in the fantastic oddities of his expression there was such a marvellous power of description that I am unable to give even so much as a faint indication of it. Antonia inherited all her mother's amiability and all her mother's charms, but not the repellent reverse of the medal. There was no chronic moral ulcer, which might break out from time to time. Antonia's betrothed put in an appearance, whilst Antonia herself, fathoming with happy instinct the deeper-lying character of her wonderful father, sang one of old Padre Martini's[2] motets[3], which, she knew, Krespel in the heyday of his courtship had never grown tired of hearing her mother sing. The tears ran in streams down Krespel's cheeks; even Angela he had never heard sing like that. Antonia's voice was of a very remarkable and altogether peculiar timbre, at one time it was like the sighing of an Æolian

---

[1] Letters with bad news – usually of a death – were traditionally sealed in black wax to warn the recipient of eminent sorrow

[2] Giambattista Martini was an 18th century composer of choral and church music, perhaps best remembered for recognizing and encouraging the young Mozart's nascent talent

[3] Short *a cappella* choral work

harp[1], at another like the warbled gush of the nightingale. It seemed as if there was not room for such notes in the human breast. Antonia, blushing with joy and happiness, sang on and on — all her most beautiful songs, B—— playing between whiles as only enthusiasm that is intoxicated with delight can play. Krespel was at first transported with rapture, then he grew thoughtful — still — absorbed in reflection. At length he leapt to his feet, pressed Antonia to his heart, and begged her in a low husky voice, "Sing no more if you love me — my heart is bursting — I fear — I fear — don't sing again."

"No!" remarked the Councillor next day to Doctor R—— "when, as she sang, her blushes gathered into two dark red spots on her pale cheeks, I knew it had nothing to do with your nonsensical family likenesses, I knew it was what I dreaded[2]." The Doctor, whose countenance had shown signs of deep distress from the very beginning of the conversation, replied, "Whether it arises from a too early taxing of her powers of song, or whether
the fault is Nature's — enough, Antonia labours under an organic failure in the chest, while it is from it too that her voice derives its wonderful power and its singular timbre, which I might almost say transcend the limits of human capabilities of song. But it bears the announcement of her early death; for, if she continues to sing, I wouldn't give her at the most more than six months longer to live." Krespel's heart was lacerated as if by the stabs of hundreds of stinging knives. It was as though his life had been for the first time overshadowed by a beautiful tree full of the most magnificent blossoms, and now it was to be sawn to pieces at the roots, so that it could not grow green and blossom any more. His resolution was taken. He told Antonia all; he put the alternatives before her — whether she would follow her betrothed and yield to his and the world's seductions, but with the certainty of dying early, or whether she would spread round her father in his old days that joy and peace which had hitherto been unknown to him, and so secure a long life. She threw herself sobbing into his arms, and he, knowing the heartrending trial that was before her, did not press for a more explicit declaration. He talked the matter over with her betrothed; but, notwithstanding that the latter averred that no note should ever cross Antonia's lips, the Councillor was only too well aware that even B—— could not resist the temptation of hearing her sing, at any rate arias of his own composition. And the world,

[1] A delicate stringed instrument rather like a wind chime: played by the wind (a by necessity, usually set up in an open space where wind is common), its ethereal, otherworldly tones are always unique to the wind that stirs it

[2] Armchair Freudians will immediately perk up at what certainly appears to be the sublimation of incestuous desires: using the metaphor of music to hide his otherwise loathsome urges, Krespel is becoming increasingly conscious that his lust is becoming too overt to conceal and restrain

the musical public, even though acquainted with the nature of the singer's affliction, would certainly not relinquish its claims to hear her, for in cases where pleasure is concerned people of this class are very selfish and cruel. The Councillor disappeared from F—— along with Antonia, and came to H——. B—— was in despair when he learnt that they had gone. He set out on their track, overtook them, and arrived at H—— at the same time that they did. "Let me see him only once, and then die!" entreated Antonia "Die! die!" cried Krespel, wild with anger, an icy shudder running through him. His daughter, the only creature in the wide world who had awakened in him the springs of unknown joy, who alone had reconciled him to life, tore herself away from his heart, and he — he suffered the terrible trial to take place. B—— sat down to the piano; Antonia sang; Krespel fiddled away merrily, until the two red spots[1] showed themselves on Antonia's cheeks. Then he bade her stop; and as B was taking leave of his betrothed, she suddenly fell to the floor with a loud scream. "I thought," continued Krespel in his narration, "I thought that she was, as I had anticipated, really dead; but as I had prepared myself for the worst, my calmness did not leave me, nor my self-command desert me. I grasped B—— who stood like a silly sheep in his dismay, by the shoulders, and said (here the Councillor fell into his singing tone), 'Now that you, my estimable pianoforte-player, have, as you wished and desired, really murdered your betrothed, you may quietly take your departure; at least have the goodness to make yourself scarce before I run my bright hanger[2] through your heart. My daughter, who, as you see, is rather pale, could very well do with some colour from your precious blood. Make haste and run, for I might also hurl a nimble knife or two after you.' I must, I suppose, have looked rather formidable as I uttered these words, for, with a cry of the greatest terror, B—— tore himself loose from my grasp, rushed out of the room, and down the steps." Directly after B—— was gone, when the Councillor tried to lift up his daughter, who lay unconscious on the floor, she opened her eyes with a deep sigh, but soon closed them again as if about to die. Then Krespel's grief found vent aloud, and would not be comforted. The Doctor, whom the old housekeeper had called in, pronounced Antonia's case a somewhat serious but by no means dangerous attack; and she did indeed recover more quickly than her father had dared to hope. She now clung to him with the most confiding childlike affection; she entered into his favourite hobbies — into his mad schemes and whims. She helped him

---

[1] Without being overly crass, this repeated visual might easily be viewed as a symptom of sexual arousal, or even as an allusion to erect, engorged nipples

[2] Alternatively described as a long knife or a short sword, this razor-sharp weapon was used by hunters, foot soldiers, and sailors

take old violins to pieces and glue new ones together. "I won't sing again any more, but live for you," she often said, sweetly smiling upon him, after she had been asked to sing and had refused. Such appeals however the Councillor was anxious to spare her as much as possible; therefore it was that he was unwilling to take her into society, and solicitously shunned all music. He well understood how painful it must be for her to forego altogether the exercise of that art which she had brought to such a pitch of perfection. When the Councillor bought the wonderful violin that he had buried with Antonia, and was about to take it to pieces, she met him with such sadness in her face and softly breathed the petition, "What! this as well?" By some power, which he could not explain, he felt impelled to leave this particular instrument unbroken, and to play upon it. Scarcely had he drawn the first few notes from it than Antonia cried aloud with joy, "Why, that's me! — now I shall sing again." And, in truth, there was something remarkably striking about the clear, silvery, bell-like tones of the violin; they seemed to have been engendered in the human soul. Krespel's heart was deeply moved; he played, too, better than ever. As he ran up and down the scale, playing bold passages with consummate power and expression, she clapped her hands together and cried with delight, "I did that well! I did that well!"

From this time onwards her life was filled with peace and cheerfulness. She often said to the Councillor, "I should like to sing something, father." Then Krespel would take his violin down from the wall and play her most beautiful songs, and her heart was right glad and happy. Shortly before my arrival in H—— the Councillor fancied one night that he heard somebody playing the piano in the adjoining room, and he soon made out distinctly that B—— was flourishing on the instrument in his usual style. He wished to get up, but felt himself held down as if by a dead weight, and lying as if fettered in iron bonds[1]; he was utterly unable to move an inch. Then Antonia's voice was heard singing low and soft; soon, however, it began to rise and rise in volume until it became an ear-splitting fortissimo[2]; and at length she passed over into a powerfully impressive song which B—— had once composed for her in the devotional style of the old masters. Krespel described his condition as being incomprehensible, for terrible anguish was mingled with a delight he had never experienced before. All at once he was surrounded by a dazzling brightness, in which he beheld B—— and Antonia locked in a close embrace, and gazing at each other in a rapture of ecstasy. The music of the song and of the pianoforte accompanying it went on without any visible signs that Antonia sang or that B—— touched the instrument.

---

[1] An early description of sleep paralysis

[2] A musical annotation which means to play (or sing) as loud as possible. Again, we might feel driven to interpret this moment as sexually charged, as it seems to describe the vocals of a sexual climax

Then the Councillor fell into a sort of dead faint, whilst the images vanished away. On awakening he still felt the terrible anguish of his dream. He rushed into Antonia's room. She lay on the sofa, her eyes closed, a sweet angelic smile on her face, her hands devoutly folded, and looking as if asleep and dreaming of the joys and raptures of heaven. But she was — dead.

ONE of Hoffmann's most enduring and enigmatic characters, Krespel was inspired by a pair of German eccentrics whose idiosyncratic behavior - like Hoffmann's own - made them the subject of popular curiosity and ridicule. One of these men was Councillor Johann Bernhard Crespel - an archivist, lawyer, and writer living in Frankfurt - whose quirky, self-designed house, odd clothing, mannerisms, and name are represented in Krespel. The other, Councilor Carl Philipp Heinrich Pistor - a Berlin lawyer, scientist, and engineer - was remembered for his strange hobby of dismantling valuable Amati violins "for research purposes." However, the complex, psychological core of Krespel is all Hoffmann; as Benno von Wiese remarks, while these more comic details are borrowed from Crespel and Pistor, the character's "life story, which is as funny as it is heartbreakingly sad" was entirely original. Hoffmann "made his councillor into a completely original characer, on the whole much more sinister than the original [viz., Crespel]." The rest of the story is largely knit together from

> "some autobiographical elements, such as Hoffmann's own grimacing... What appears to the world on the surface to be a harmless quirk is in truth, in its bizarreness, the expression of Hoffmann's dualism, for which man is a stranger and prisoner on earth and, thus harnessed to the yoke of earthly things, must always buck against the thorns."

On the whole, like "The Lost Reflection" (written three years prior) "The Cremona Violin" provided a literary catharsis for his humiliating experience with the too-young Julia Marc, and was written shortly after her embarrassing divorce from the lethargic playboy her parents had arranged her to marry at the time of Hoffmann's severance. While "The Lost Reflection" - which depicted Julia as an insidious temptress, prostituted by her vulgar husband - was written *during* Marc's first marriage, "Cremona Violin" - which restores her to her innocence and ends with her death - was likely penned after the ignominy of her failed marriage. For Hoffmann, her misery is enough to make him wonder what part his *own* selfishness played in her destruction. The willful Krespel - part parent, part teacher, and part suitor - demands that Antonia reserve her singing for him, in arrogant defiance of the fact that she will eventually want to share her music (a metaphor for love in both its sublime and carnal forms) with an eligible male closer to her in age and temperament. Like Hoffmann, Krespel's repression of his student's natural desire to range the world and find a suitable companion drives her into the arms of an opportunistic lover, with tragic results.

II.

Outside of its biographical parallels, "The Cremona Violin" is a grim philosophical treatise on the consequences of jealousy, the boundlessness of art, the dangers of repression, and the holiness of inspiration. As to the first theme, Hoffmann lays out the way that covetousness almost universally rots the soul with ingratitude and shortsightedness: Krespel is a ruined man after he drives his daughter to her grave – a musician without a song – and learns to repent of his jealousy far too late. His discomfort at the idea of the virginal Antonia sharing her orgasmic singing with a single man of marriageable age failed to recognize the pop culture maxim that "nature will find a way," which leads us to the second theme: the boundlessness of art. Like Pistor, who shocked his friends by deconstructing priceless Amatis in a selfish bid to understand their secrets – robbing the world of their songs – Krespel does not at first realize that neither Antonia nor the Amati violins were made to be understood, analyzed, or possessed – the beauty of their respective songs is not a logical puzzle but a spiritual reality. Art is not made to be kept, but shared, and beauty is not made to be hidden but to be exhibited. Like many overly analytical critics, he boils spiritual expression down to a physical matter of engineering withhold considering the incomprehensible influence of the human soul – a component which cannot be channeled once the physical vessel (be it an fragile violin or Antonia's beating heart) has been destroyed. His desperate mission to understand the secret behind the Amatis is comparable to his desire to hold onto and restrict Antonia, preventing her from sharing her gift with others. With her preventable death he learns that – as with the destroyed fiddles – to deconstruct is to destroy, and in his attempt to possess Antonia's song, he stifles it forever, as surely as he shatters his bow into a thousand pieces.

III.

This leads to the third theme: the dangers of repression. A common motif in Hoffmann, this concept plays out in stories like "The Sandman," "The King's Betrothed," and "The Lost Reflection." In "Cremona Violin" the danger comes from suppressing expression – denying the "boundlessness of art" – and denying it its natural outlets. While Antonia's death may have been inevitable in either case, perhaps it would not be shrouded in so much shame and secrecy if Krespel had allowed her to flourish without his domineering oversight. Indeed, he is left to wonder if his dream was disconnected from her death, a metaphysical expression of a spiritual reality, or exactly what it appears to be. One way or another, by holding his daughter back from her true nature, he forces the unconscious Self to the surface, where it expresses itself in such a powerful way – whether literally or in a dream – that she dies through the force of its orgasmic resurrection. Finally, Krespel learns all too late that he should respect the holiness of inspiration: to understand the beauty of music, he resorts to symbolic defilement of the violins he should cherish, metaphorically raping them by forcing his way into their hidden regions and guarded mysteries. Likewise, he fails to respect the awe and wonder of Antonia's artfulness, and rather than allow it to flourish with a blessing, he tries to restrain her spirit by confining her body, without realizing that to crush one is to crush the other. Rather than viewing Antonia's gorgeous singing voice as a holy mystery worth sharing and celebrating, he fears the power it will give her over *him*, fears what its discovery will mean for their relationship, and fears what lusty young men will do to procure its possession. Ultimately "Krespel," one of Hoffmann's finest and most popular tales, is a story that – like Poe's "The Oval Portrait" – bemoans the fate of the man foolish enough to think that the spiritual can be captured and preserved indefinitely like a trinket on a shelf. Only too late do they learn that failing to appreciate what is here in the present may mean an eternal future of shame and regret.

BEFORE psychiatry even had a name – before Adler or Freud or even William James – Hoffmann was a student of human behavior and psychological influences. He befriended several of Germany's most renowned proto-psychiatrists, and as a result of his conversations with them, infused his writing with up-to-date psychological theory. The following story is a fascinating bridge between the late 18th and early 20th centuries – between Radcliffe and Freud, between Monk Lewis and Jung. The story is patterned off of a common Gothic trope: the Lady in White. Sometimes this figure is in Grey, other times in Yellow, Black, or Brown, but she is always identified by her telltale garments – usually in one of these funeral shades. The ghost of a wronged woman, a murdered wife, an insane child murderer, or a fallen mistress, this female archetype lingers in the hoary hallways that she roamed in life as a visual reminder that the glory of the past is almost always speckled with unsavory events and regrettable injustices. They appear to remind contemporary residents and guests that they are standing on tainted soil – to shame the descendants of their wrong doers and to warn or frighten off young women from following her life story. Specifically, Hoffmann seems to be modelling the girl in his story on an episode in "Monk" Lewis' "The Monk," wherein a playful girl decides to masquerade as the resident ghost, the Bleeding Nun, only to encounter the spirit itself. Rather than staying with Gothic conventions, however, Hoffmann puts on his psychiatrist's hat and tries to solve the problem with a Pavlovian experiment. It doesn't go well.

A Ghost Story

— Excerpted from 'The Serapion Brethren,' Volume Two, Section Three —

{1819}

"YOU may remember that some little time ago, just before the last campaign, I was paying a visit to Colonel Von P—— at his country house. The colonel was a good-tempered, jovial man, and his wife quietness and simpleness personified. At the time I speak of the son was away with the army, so that the family circle consisted, besides the colonel and his lady, of two daughters, and an elderly French lady, who was trying to persuade herself that she was fulfilling the duties of a species of governess though the young ladies appeared to be beyond the period of being "governessed." The elder of the two was a most lively and cheerful creature, vivacious even to ungovernability; not without plenty of brains, but so constituted that she could not go five yards without cutting at least three "entrechats[1]." She sprung, in the same fashion, in her conversation, and in all that she did, restlessly from one thing to another. I myself have seen her, within the space of five minutes, work at needlework, read, draw, sing, and dance, or cry about her poor cousin who was killed in battle, one moment, and while the bitter tears were still in her eyes, burst into a splendid, infectious burst of laughter when the French-woman spilt the contents of her snuff-box over the pug, who at once began to sneeze frightfully, and the old lady cried, "Ah, che fatalita! Ah carino! Poverino[2]!"

"'For she always spoke to the dog in Italian because he was born in Padua. Moreover, this young lady was the loveliest blonde ever seen, and, in all her odd caprices, full of the utmost charm, goodness, kindliness and attractiveness, so that, whether she would or no, she exerted the most irresistible charm over every one.

"The younger sister was the greatest possible contrast to her (her name was Adelgunda[3]). I strive in vain to find words in which to express to you the extraordinary impression which this girl produced upon me when first I saw her. Picture to yourselves the most exquisite figure, and the most marvellously beautiful face; but the cheeks and lips wear a deathly pallor, and the figure moves gently, softly, slowly, with measured steps; and then, when a low-toned word is heard from the scarce opened lips and dies away in the spacious chamber, one feels a sort of shudder of spectral awe; of course I soon got over this eery feeling, and, when I managed to get her to emerge from her deep self-absorbed condition and converse, I was obliged to admit that the strangeness, the eeriness, was only external, and by no means came from within. In the little she said there displayed themselves a delicate womanliness, a clear head, and a kindly disposition. There was not a trace of over-excitability, though her melancholy smile, and her glance, heavy as with tears, seemed to speak of some morbid bodily condition producing a hostile influence on her mental state. It struck me as very strange that the whole family, not excepting the French lady, seemed to get into a state of much anxiety as soon as any one began to talk to this girl, and tried to interrupt the conversation, often breaking into it in a very forced manner. But the most extraordinary thing of all was that, as soon as it was eight o'clock in the evening, the young lady was reminded, first by the French lady and then by her mother, sister, and father, that it was time to go to her room, just as little children are sent to bed that they may not overtire themselves. The French lady went with her, so that they neither of them ever appeared at supper, which was at nine o'clock. The lady of the house, probably remarking my surprise at those proceedings, threw out (by way

---

[1] A ballet jump where a dancer crosses their legs in the air, sometimes beating them together

[2] "Oh what a fate! Oh dear! Poor thing!"

[3] A Germanic name meaning, a worthy struggle, or a noble warrior

of preventing indiscreet inquiries) a sort of sketchy statement to the effect that Adelgunda was in very poor health, that, particularly about nine in the evening, she was liable to feverish attacks, and that the doctors had ordered her to have complete rest at that time. I saw there must be more in the affair than this, though I could not imagine what it might be; and it was only this very day that I ascertained the terrible truth, and discovered what the events were which have wrecked the peace of that happy circle in the most frightful manner.

"'Adelgunda was at one time the most blooming, vigorous, cheerful creature to be seen. Her fourteenth birthday came, and a number of her friends and companions had been invited to spend it with her. They were all sitting in a circle in the shrubbery, laughing and amusing themselves, taking little heed that the evening was getting darker and darker, for the soft July breeze was blowing refreshingly, and they were just beginning thoroughly to enjoy themselves. In the magic twilight they set about all sorts of dances, pretending to be elves and woodland sprites. Adelgunda cried, "Listen, children! I shall go and appear to you as the White Lady[1] whom our gardener used to tell us about so often while he was alive. But you must come to the bottom of the garden, where the old ruins are." She wrapped her white shawl round her, and went lightly dancing down the leafy alley, the girls following her, in full tide of laughter and fun. But Adelgunda had scarcely reached the old crumbling arches, when she suddenly stopped, and stood as if paralyzed in every limb. The castle clock struck nine.

""'Look, look!" cried she, in a hollow voice of the deepest terror. "Don't you see it? the figure—close before me—stretching her hand out at me. Don't you see her?"

"The children saw nothing whatever; but terror came upon them, and they all ran away, except one, more courageous than the rest, who hastened up to Adelgunda, and was going to take her in her arms. But Adelgunda, turning pale as death, fell to the ground. At the screams of the other girl every body came hastening from the castle, and Adelgunda was carried in. At last she recovered from her faint, and, trembling all over, told them that as soon as she reached the ruins she saw an airy form, as if shrouded in mist, stretching its hand out towards her. Of course every one ascribed this vision

---

[1] Long-observed family ghosts associated with a particular property are often given names in accord with their clothing and sometimes their apparent life station, era of origin, or behavior (e.g., the Green Cavalier, the Weeping Lady, the Laughing Soldier, the Black Nun, or the Blue Lady). They typically have vague, sketchy histories which are filled in by rumor and speculation, and – like banshees – are often said to herald bad news, and impending death, or a family disaster

to some deceptiveness of the twilight; and Adelgunda recovered from her alarm so completely that night that no further evil consequences were anticipated, and the whole affair was supposed to be at an end. However, it turned out altogether otherwise. The next evening, when the clock struck nine, Adelgunda sprung up, in the midst of the people about her, and cried—

""'There she is! there she is. Don't you see her—just before me?"

"'Since that unlucky evening, Adelgunda declared that, as soon as the clock struck nine, the figure stood before her, remaining visible for several seconds, although no one but herself could see anything of it, or trace by any psychic sensation the proximity of an unknown spiritual principle. So that poor Adelgunda was thought to be out of her mind; and, in strange perversion of feeling, the family were ashamed of this condition of hers. I have told you already how she was dealt with in consequence. There was, of course, no lack of doctors, or of plans of treatment for ridding the poor soul of the "fixed idea[1]," as people were pleased to term the apparition which she said she saw. But nothing had any effect; and she implored, with tears, that she might be left in peace, inasmuch as the form which, in its vague,
uncertain traits, had nothing terrible or alarming about it, no longer caused her any fear; although, for a time after seeing it she felt as if her inner being and all her thoughts and ideas were turned out from her, and were hovering, bodiless, about, outside of her. At last the colonel made the acquaintance of a celebrated doctor, who had the reputation of being specially clever in the treatment of the mentally afflicted. When this doctor heard Adelgunda's story he laughed aloud, and said nothing could be easier than to cure a condition of the kind, which resulted solely from an over-excited imagination. The idea of the appearing of the spectre was so intimately associated with the striking of nine o'clock, that the mind could not dissociate them. So that all that was necessary was to effect this separation by external means; as to which there was no difficulty, as it was only necessary to deceive the patient as to the time, and let nine o'clock pass without her being aware of it. If the apparition did not then appear, she would be convinced, herself, that it was an illusion; and measures to give tone to the general system would be all that would then be necessary to complete the cure. This unfortunate advice was taken. One night all the clocks at the castle were put back an hour—the hollow, booming tower clock included—so that, when Adelgunda awoke in the morning, she found herself an hour wrong in her time. When evening came, the family were assembled, as usual, in a cheerful corner room; no stranger was present, and the mother constrained herself to talk about all

---

[1] An obsession bordering on mania

sorts of cheerful subjects. The colonel began (as was his habit, when in specially good humour) to carry on an encounter of wit with the old French lady, in which Augusta, the elder of the daughters, aided and abetted him. Everybody was laughing, and more full of enjoyment than ever. The clock on the wall struck eight (so that it was really nine o'clock) and Adelgunda fell back in her chair, pale as death; her work dropped from her hands; she rose, with a face of horror, stared before her into the empty part of the room, and murmured, in a hollow voice—

"'"What! an hour earlier! Don't you see it? Don't you see it? Right before me!"

"'Every one rose up in alarm. But as none of them saw the smallest vestige of anything, the colonel cried—

"'"Calm yourself, Adelgunda, there is nothing there! It is a vision of your brain, a deception of your fancy. We see nothing, nothing whatever; and if there really were a figure close to you we should see it as well as you! Calm yourself."

"'"Oh God!" cried Adelgunda, "they think I am out of my mind. See! it is stretching out its long arm, it is making signs to me!"

"'And, as though she were acting under the influence of another, without exercise of her own will, with eyes fixed and staring, she put her hand back behind her, took up a plate which chanced to be on the table, held it out before her into vacancy, and let it go, and it went hovering about amongst the lookers on, and then deposited itself gently on the table. The mother and Augusta fainted; and these fainting fits were succeeded by violent nervous fever. The colonel forced himself to retain his self-control, but the profound impression which this extraordinary occurrence made on him was evident in his agitated and disturbed condition.

"'The French lady had fallen on her knees and prayed in silence with her face turned to the floor, and both she and Adelgunda remained free from evil consequences. The mother very soon died. Augusta survived the fever; but it would have been better had she died. She who, when I first saw her, was an embodiment of vigorous, magnificent youthful happiness, is now hopelessly insane, and that in a form which seems to me the most terrible and gruesome of all the forms of fixed idea ever heard of. For she thinks she is the invisible phantom which haunts Adelgunda; and therefore she avoids every one, or, at all events, refrains from speaking, or moving if anybody is present. She scarce dares to breathe, because she firmly believes that if she betrays her presence in any way every one will die. Doors are opened for her, and her food is set down, she slinks in and out, eats in secret, and so forth. Can a more painful condition be imagined?

"'The colonel, in his pain and despair, followed the colours[1] to the next campaign, and fell in the victorious engagement at W——. It is remarkable, most remarkable that, since then, Adelgunda has never seen the phantom. She nurses her sister with the utmost care, and the French lady helps her. Only this very day Sylvester told me that the uncle of these poor girls is here, taking the advice of our celebrated R——, as to the means of cure to be tried in Augusta's case. God grant that the cure may succeed, improbable as it seems.'"

A frequent trope in Hoffmann's fiction is the innocent girl fortified into becoming a virtuous woman through acts of mercy and self-sacrifice. This is the case with Adelgung in "A Ghost Story." We are led to believe that she is not long for this world, marked for death (as she appears to have been) by the Lady in White. Gothic stereotypes lead us to expect a recurring haunting that mounts up to a climactic death, and Hoffmann doesn't disappoint – but he *does* fool us. It is not Adelgung whose death is heralded, but her mother's and that of her sister's sanity. The psychological experiment of changing the clock – a prototype of Ivan Pavlov's famous dog-and-bell experiment – had deftly sought to test the doctor's materialist hypothesis: there *is* no ghost; it is merely a visually hallucination brought on by audial conditioning caused by the clock's tolling "nine." The hypothesis is ahead of its time and clever enough, but Hoffmann uses it as a foil to prove the ghost's reality and to get one step ahead of skeptical readers. Adelgung *still* sees the ghost, but unlike her female relatives, she finds herself drawn to it in this final confrontation: like Marie who forgives Nutcracker his ugliness and reaches out to him in pity, Adelgung extends a hand to the enigmatic specter – handing it a plate (which it takes and moves through thin air) and offering it a connection with reality. By sacrificing her comfort, pride, and skepticism, Adelgung spares herself the death that we anticipated and is trained to care for the *real* Lady in White: her mentally-compromised sister. Indeed, if we read Hoffmann looking for Doppelgängers, there is little doubt that the appearance of the spectral Lady in White is meant to presage the sister's loss of her sanity and her adoption of the Lady in White persona. As she handed the plate to the invisible apparition on that fateful night, she spends the following years leaving plates of food out for her sister to "secretly" eat in private. Essentially, her experience with the ghost was an initiation into her future as guardian to her insane sister. Once a wilting fourteen year old whose imminent death was widely anticipated, Adelgung has matured into a competent, if sadder, adult woman whose affection for the invisible – ghosts and madwomen alike – earns our pathos.

[1] Accompanied the army

THE modern concept of a vampire is only about two centuries old and some change. Aristocratic, posh, and stylish, we picture a vampire as a vision of seductive, masculine power bent over a sleeping woman, and greedily drinking blood from her ivory neck. During Hoffmann's prime the vampire was considered more of a ghoul or cannibal: eating the flesh of the recently dead. What's more, it was hardly well-dressed or suave, but wild and zombie-like: a stinking, fetid corpse with skeletal features, glowing eyes, and putrid flesh. Bram Stoker, J. Sheridan Le Fanu, and Lord Byron largely led to the change in visualization during the course of the 19th century, from repulsive to seductive. Stoker, naturally, introduced us to his courtly Count, influenced by the deep eroticism found in Le Fanu's lesbian vampire novella *Carmilla*. Byron, however, was the first major influence in what we view as a vampire today – and it had nothing to do with his *writing* and everything to do with his reputation. Byron was infamously considered "mad, bad, and dangerous to know," was notorious as a very successful and prolific seducer of women (and men) and was responsible for at least one woman's suicide (Mary Shelley's heart-broken half-sister). His reputation as a lady killer and sex fiend was blurred into a convincing caricature by his personal doctor – a narcotic-addicted sycophant who despised Byron as much as he adored him – John Polidori. His *The Vampyre* was written during the same brainstorming session that caused Shelley to write *Frankenstein*, but his blood sucker looked far more like *Byron* – a suave, masculine, tall-dark-and-handsome type – than the rotting ghouls of Eastern European legend. Byron himself had been heavily influenced by Balkan folklore, using it to inspire his own vampire narrative in the Gothic epic "The Giaour," wherein the vampire is described as a loathsome monster. Partially influenced by Byron, partially by "The Giaour," Polidori shifted the collective image of a vampire from a necrophilic cannibal to an erotic seducer living on the blood of the young and beautiful. His vampire, Lord Ruthven, was widely recognized as a caricature of Byron, so much so that – to both men's chagrin – it was widely believed that Byron wrote the novel himself. Hoffmann's own contribution to vampiric literature is interesting because it takes place on the verge of the shift – just after *The Vampyre* though prior to *Carmilla* (upon which it had a tremendous influence) – and contains both the Gothic gore and Victorian eroticism that contributed to the vampire mythos. Added to this is an especially Hoffmannesque bugbear: a neurotically nightmarish treatment of pregnancy cravings...

The Vampire

— Excerpted from 'The Serapion Brethren,' Volume Four, Section Eight —

{1821}

"THIS discussion about vampirism," said Cyprian, "reminds me of a ghastly story which I either heard or read a very long time ago. But I think I heard it, because I seem to remember that the person who told it said that the circumstances had actually happened, and mentioned the name of the family and of their country seat where it took place. But if this story is known to you as being in print, please to stop me and prevent my going on with it, because there's nothing more wearisome than to tell people things which they have known for ever so long."

"I foresee," said Ottmar, "that you are going to give us something unusually awful and terrible. But remember Saint Serapion[1] and be as concise as you can, so that Vincenz may have his turn; for I see that he is waiting impatiently to read us that long-promised story of his."

"Hush! hush!" said Vincenz. "I could not wish anything better than that Cyprian should hang up a fine dark canvas by way of a background so as to throw out the figures of my tale, which I think are brightly and variedly coloured, and certainly excessively active. So begin, my Cyprianus, and be as gloomy, as frightful, as terrible as the vampirish Lord Byron[2] himself, though I know nothing about him, as I have never read a word of his writings."

ↀ

Count Hyppolitus[3] (began Cyprian) had just returned from a long time spent in travelling to take possession of the rich inheritance which his

---

[1] He is referring to the so-called "Serapiontic Principle" espoused both by the fictional characters in *The Serapion Brethren* and by Hoffmann's own literary set. The "Serapion Principle" was an agreement not to allow one's creativity and imagination to be dampened or held back by reality – not to censor or filter or limit the gush of artistry produced by the often fantastical muses of inspiration. St. Seraphin of Montenegro was a 16th century Italian monk and mystic whose October 12 feast day happened to be the date of the first meeting of Hoffmann's own "Serapion Brethren" literary club. They named their group after the saint and his fictionalized version of that gathering does the same. The principle became connected with Seraphin because – they claimed – he was also a mystical visionary who did not allow his surreal, often bizarre impressions of the metaphysical world to be dampened or restrained to appeal to the "rational" sensibilities of others: the Serpion Brethren must not limit their creativity in an inauthentic to be accepted by the disapproving, unimaginative bourgeoisie

[2] The famously "mad, bad, and dangerous to know" English Romantic poet whose seductive good looks, sexual dynamism, and reputation for ruining his mistresses' lives made him the obvious model for the first, English-language vampire novel – "The Vampyre" – written by his own friend and doctor, John Polidori

[3] A name meaning "stampeding horses" or "a horse let loose"

father, recently dead, had left to him. The ancestral home was situated in the most beautiful and charming country imaginable, and the income from the property was amply sufficient to defray the cost of most extensive improvements. Whatever in the way of architecture and landscape gardening had struck the Count during his travels—particularly in England—as specially delightful and apposite, he was going to reproduce in his own demesne[1]. Architects, landscape gardeners, and labourers of all sorts arrived on the scene as they were wanted, and there commenced at once a complete reconstruction of the place, whilst an extensive park was laid out on the grandest scale, which involved the including within its boundaries of the church, the parsonage, and the burial ground. All those improvements the Count, who possessed the necessary knowledge, superintended himself, devoting himself to this occupation body and soul; so that a year slipped away without its ever having occurred to him to take an old uncle's advice and let the light of his countenance shine in the Residenz[2] before the eyes of the young ladies, so that the most beautiful, the best, and the most nobly born amongst them might fall to his share as wife. One morning, as he was sitting at his drawing table sketching the ground-plan of a new building, a certain elderly Baroness—distantly related to his father—was announced as having come to call. When Hyppolitus heard her name he remembered that his father had always spoken of her with the greatest indignation—nay, with absolute abhorrence, and had often warned people who were going to approach
her to keep aloof, without explaining what the danger connected with her was. If he was questioned more closely, he said there were certain matters as to which it was better to keep silence. Thus much was certain, that there were rumours current in the Residenz of some most remarkable and unprecedented criminal trial in which the Baroness had been involved, which had led to her separation from her husband, driven her from her home—which was at some considerable distance—and for the suppression of the consequences of which she was indebted to the prince's forbearance. Hyppolitus felt a very painful and disagreeable impression at the coming of a person whom his father had so detested, although the reasons for this detestation were not known to him. But the laws of hospitality, more binding in the country than in town, obliged him to receive this visit.

Never had any one, without being at all ill-favoured in the usual acceptation of that term, made by her exterior such a disagreeable impression upon the Count as did this Baroness. When she came in she looked him through and through with a glance of fire, and then she cast her eyes down and apologized for her coming in terms which were almost

[1] Estate grounds

[2] A noble family's official place of residence

over humble. She expressed her sorrow that his father, influenced by prejudices against her with which her enemies had impregnated his mind, had formed a mortal hatred to her, and though she was almost starving, in the depths of her poverty he had never given her the smallest help or support. As she had now, unexpectedly as she said, come into possession of a small sum of money she had found it possible to leave the Residenz and go to a small country town a short distance off. However, as she was engaged in this journey she had not found it possible to resist the desire to see the son of the man whom, notwithstanding his irreconcilable hatred, she had never ceased to regard with feelings of the highest esteem. The tone in which all this was spoken had the moving accents of sincerity, and the Count was all the more affected by it that, having turned his eyes away from her repulsive face, he had fixed them upon a marvellously charming and beautiful creature who was with her. The Baroness finished her speech. The Count did not seem to be aware that she had done so. He remained silent. She begged him to pardon—and attribute to her embarrassment at being where she was—her having neglected to explain that her companion was her daughter Aurelia[1]. On this the Count found words, and blushing up to the eyes implored the Baroness, with the agitation of a young man overpowered by love, to let him atone in some degree for his lather's shortcomings—the result of misunderstandings—and to favour him by paying him a long visit. In warmly enforcing this request he took her hand. But the words and the breath died away on his lips and his blood ran cold. For he felt his hand grasped as if in a vice by fingers cold and stiff as death, and the tall bony form of the Baroness, who was staring at him with eyes evidently deprived of the faculty of sight[2], seemed to him in its gay many tinted attire like some bedizened corpse.

"Oh, good heavens! how unfortunate just at this moment," Aurelia cried out, and went on to lament in a gentle heart-penetrating voice that her mother was now and then suddenly seized by a tetanic spasm[3], but that it generally passed off very quickly without its being necessary to take any measures with regard to it.

Hyppolitus disengaged himself with some difficulty from the Baroness, and all the glowing life of sweetest love delight came back to him as he took Aurelia's hand and pressed it warmly to his lips. Although he had almost come to man's estate[4] it was the first time that he felt the full force of passion, so that it was impossible for him to hide what he felt,

---

[1] A name meaning "golden"

[2] That is, they are clouded over – like those of a blind person *or* a corpse

[3] Sudden, involuntary, violent muscle contractions, which can range from those caused by leg cramps and shivers to those inflicted by tetanus and childbirth

[4] The prime of adult manhood

and the manner in which Aurelia received his avowal in a noble, simple, child-like delight, kindled the fairest of hopes within him. The Baroness recovered in a few minutes, and, seemingly quite unaware of what had been happening, expressed her gratitude to the Count for his invitation to pay a visit of some duration at the Castle, saying she would be but too happy to forget the injustice with which his father had treated her.

Thus the Count's household arrangements and domestic position were completely changed, and he could not but believe that some special favour of fortune had brought to him the only woman in all the world who, as a warmly beloved and deeply adored wife, was capable of bestowing upon him the highest conceivable happiness.

The Baroness's manner of conduct underwent little alteration. She continued to be silent, grave, much wrapped up in herself, and when opportunity offered, evinced a gentle disposition, and a heart disposed towards any innocent enjoyment. The Count had become accustomed to the death-like whiteness of her face, to the very remarkable network of wrinkles which covered it, and to the generally spectral appearance which she displayed; but all this he set down to the invalid condition of her health, and also, in some measure, to a disposition which she evinced to gloomy romanticism[1]. The servants told him that she often went out for walks in the night-time, through the park to the churchyard. He was much annoyed that his father's prejudices had influenced him to the extent that they had; and the most earnest recommendations of his uncle that he should conquer the feeling which had taken possession of him, and give up a relationship which must sooner or later drive him to his ruin, had no effect upon him.

In complete certainty of Aurelia's sincere affection, he asked for her hand; and it may be imagined with what joy the Baroness received this proposal, which transferred her into the lap of luxury from a position of the deepest poverty. The pallor and the strange expression, which spoke of some invincible inward pain or trouble, had disappeared from Aurelia's face. The blissfulness of love beamed in her eyes, and shimmered in roses on her cheeks.

On the morning of the wedding-day a terrible event shattered the Count's hopes. The Baroness was found lying on her face dead, not far from the churchyard: and when the Count was looking out of his window on getting up, full of the bliss of the happiness which he had attained, her body was being brought back to the Castle. He supposed she was only in one of her usual attacks; but all efforts to bring her back to life were ineffectual. She was dead. Aurelia, instead of giving way to violent grief, seemed rather to be struck dumb and tearless by this blow, which appeared to have a paralyzing effect on her.

---

[1] A tendency to indulge in flights of imagination and grandiose, morbid thoughts

The Count was much distressed for her, and only ventured—most cautiously and most gently—to remind her that her orphaned condition rendered it necessary that conventionalities should be disregarded, and that the most essential matter in the circumstances was to hasten on the marriage as much as possible, notwithstanding the loss of her mother. At this Aurelia fell into the Count's arms, and, whilst a flood of tears ran down her cheeks, cried in a most eager manner, and in a voice which was shrill with urgency:

"Yes, yes! For the love of all the saints. For the sake of my soul's salvation—yes!"

The Count ascribed this burst of emotion to the bitter sense that, in her orphaned condition, she did not know whither to betake herself, seeing that she could not go on staying in the Castle[1]. He took pains to procure a worthy matron as a companion for her[2], till in a few weeks, the wedding-day again came round. And this time no mischance interfered with it, and it crowned the bliss of Aurelia and Hyppolitus. But Aurelia had all this while been in a curiously strained and excited condition. It was not grief for her mother, but she seemed to be unceasingly, and without cessation, tortured by some inward anxiety. In the midst of the most delicious love-passage she would suddenly clasp the Count in her arms, pale as death, and like a person suddenly seized by some terror—just as if she were trying her very utmost to resist some extraneous power which was threatening to force her to destruction—and would cry, "Oh, no—no! Never, never!" Now that she was married, however, it seemed that this strange, overstrained, excited condition in which she had been, abated and left her, and the terrible inward anxiety and disturbance under which she had been labouring seemed to disappear.

The Count could not but suspect the existence of some secret evil mystery by which Aurelia's inner being was tormented, but he very properly thought it would be unkind and unfeeling to ask her about it whilst her excitement lasted, and she herself avoided any explanation on the subject. However, a time came when he thought he might venture to hint gently, that perhaps it would lie well if she indicated to him the cause of the strange condition of her mind. She herself at once said it would be a satisfaction to her to open her mind to him, her beloved husband. And great was his amazement to learn that what was at the bottom of the mystery, was the atrociously wicked life which her mother had led, that was so perturbing her mind.

---

[1] That is, he is aware that – without her mother or some other chaperone – it would be socially unacceptable for her, a single woman, to keep staying at his mansion, and he ascribes her anxiety to her worry about where she would go and what would become of her until they are married

[2] He went to great trouble to find a suitable chaperone for her – a respected, elderly woman

"Can there be anything more terrible," she said, "than to have to hate, detest, and abhor one's own mother?"

Thus the prejudices (as they were called) of his father and uncle had not been unfounded, and the Baroness had deceived him in the most deliberate manner. He was obliged to confess to himself—and he made no secret of it—that it was a fortunate circumstance that the Baroness had died on the morning of his wedding-day. But Aurelia declared that as soon as her mother was dead she had been seized by dark and terrible terrors, and could not help thinking that her mother would rise from her grave, and drag her from her husband's arms into perdition[1].

She said she dimly remembered, one morning when she was a mere child, being awakened by a frightful commotion in the house. Doors opened and shut; strangers' voices cried out in confusion. At last, things becoming quieter, her nurse[2] took her in her arms, and carried her into a large room where there were many people, and the man who had often played with her, and given her sweetmeats, lying stretched on a long table. This man she had always called "Papa," and she stretched her hands out to him, and wanted to kiss him. But his lips, always warm before, were cold as ice, and Aurelia broke into violent weeping, without knowing why. The nurse took her to a strange house, where she remained a long while, till at last a lady came and took her away in a carriage. This was her mother, who soon after took her to the Residenz.

When Aurelia got to be about sixteen, a man came to the house whom her mother welcomed joyfully, and treated with much confidentiality, receiving him with much intimacy of friendship, as being a dear old friend. He came more and more frequently, and the Baroness's style of existence was soon greatly altered for the better. Instead of living in an attic, and subsisting on the poorest of fare, and wearing the most wretched old clothes, she took a fine lodging in the most fashionable quarter, wore fine dresses, ate and drank with this stranger of the best and most expensive food and drink daily (he was her daily guest), and took her part in all the public pleasurings which the Residenz had to offer.

Aurelia was the person upon whom this bettering of her mother's circumstances (evidently attributable solely to the stranger) exercised no influence whatever. She remained shut up in her room when her mother went out to enjoy herself in the stranger's company, and was obliged to live just as miserably as before. This man, though about forty, had a very fresh and youthful appearance, a tall, handsome person, and a face by no means devoid of a certain amount of manly good looks. Notwithstanding this, he was repugnant to Aurelia on account of his style of behaviour. He seemed to try to constrain himself, to conduct himself like a gentleman

[1] Damnation, hell

[2] A young child's servant-caregiver

and person of some cultivation, but there was constantly, and most evidently, piercing through this exterior veneer the unmistakable evidence of his really being a totally uncultured person, whose manners and habits were those of the very lowest ranks of the people. And the way in which he began to look at Aurelia filled her with terror—nay, with an abhorrence of which she could not explain the reason to herself.

Up to this point the Baroness had never taken the trouble to say a single word to Aurelia about this stranger. But now she told her his name, adding that this Baron was a man of great wealth, and a distant relation. She lauded his good looks, and his various delightful qualities, and ended by asking Aurelia if she thought she could bring herself to take a liking to him. Aurelia made no secret of the inward detestation which she felt for him. The Baroness darted a glance of lightning at her, which terrified her excessively, and told her she was a foolish, ignorant creature. After this she was kinder to her than she had ever been before. She was provided with grand dresses in the height of the fashion, and taken to share in all the public pleasures. The man now strove to gain her favour in a manner which rendered him more and more abhorrent to her. But her delicate, maidenly instincts were wounded in the most mortal manner, when an unfortunate accident rendered her an unwilling, secret witness of an abominable atrocity between her abandoned and depraved mother and him. When, a few days after this, this man, after having taken a good deal of wine, clasped Aurelia in his arms in a way which left no doubt as to his intention, her desperation gave her strength, and she pushed him from her so that he fell down on his back. She rushed away and bolted herself in her own room. The Baroness told her, very calmly and deliberately, that, inasmuch as the Baron paid all the household expenses, and she had not the slightest intention of going back to the old poverty of their previous life, this was a case in which any absurd coyness would be both ludicrous and inconvenient, and that she would really have to make up her mind to comply with the Baron's wishes, because, if not, he had threatened to part company at once. Instead of being affected by Aurelia's bitter tears and agonized intreaties, the old woman, breaking into the most brazen and shameless laughter, talked in the most depraved manner of a state of matters which would cause Aurelia to bid, for ever, farewell to every feeling of enjoyment of life in such unrestrained and detestable depravity, defying and insulting all sense of ordinary propriety, so that her shame and terror were undescribable at what she was obliged to hear. In fact she gave herself up for lost, and her only means of salvation appeared to her
to be immediate flight.

She had managed to possess herself of the key of the hall door, had got together the few little necessaries which she absolutely required, and, just after midnight, was moving softly through the dimly-lighted front hall, at a time when she thought her mother was sure to be last asleep.

She was on the point of stepping quietly out into the street, when the door opened with a clang, and heavy footsteps came noisily up the steps. The Baroness came staggering and stumbling into the hall, right up to Aurelia's feet, nothing upon her but a kind of miserable wrapper[1] all covered with dirt, her breast and her arms naked, her grey hair all hanging down and dishevelled. And close after her came the stranger, who seized her by the hair, and dragged her into the middle of the hall, crying out in a yelling voice—

"Wait, you old devil, you witch of hell! I'll serve you up a wedding breakfast!" And with a good thick cudgel which he had in his hand he set to and belaboured and maltreated her in the most shameful manner. She made a terrible screaming and outcry, whilst Aurelia, scarcely knowing what she was about, screamed aloud out of the window for help.

It chanced that there was a patrol of armed police just passing. The men came at once into the house.

"Seize him!" cried the Baroness, writhing in convulsions of rage and pain. "Seize him—hold him fast! Look at his bare back. He's——"

When the police sergeant heard the Baroness speak the name he shouted out in the greatest delight—

"Hoho! We've got you at last, Devil Alias, have we?" And in spite of his violent resistance, they marched him off.

But notwithstanding all this which had been happening, the Baroness had understood well enough what Aurelia's idea had been. She contented herself with taking her somewhat roughly by the arm, pushing her into her room, and locking her up in it, without saying a word. She went out early the next morning, and did not come back till late in the evening. And during this time Aurelia remained a prisoner in her room, never seeing nor hearing a creature, and having nothing to eat or drink. This went on for several days. The Baroness often glared at her with eyes flashing with anger, and seemed to be wrestling with some decision, until, one evening, letters came which seemed to cause her satisfaction.

"Silly creature! all this is your fault. However, it seems to be all coming right now, and all I hope is that the terrible punishment which the Evil Spirit was threatening you with may not come upon you." This was what the Baroness said to Aurelia, and then she became more kind and friendly, and Aurelia, no longer distressed by the presence of the horrible man, and having given up the idea of escaping, was allowed a little more freedom.

Some time had elapsed, when one day, as Aurelia was sitting alone in her room, she heard a great clamour approaching in the street. The maid came running in, and said that they were taking the hangman's son of — — to prison, that he had been branded on the back there for robbery and murder, and had escaped, and was now retaken.

---

[1] A loose robe

Aurelia, full of anxious presentiment, tottered to the window. Her presentiment was not fallacious. It was the stranger (as we have styled him), and he was being brought along, firmly bound upon a tumbril[1], surrounded by a strong guard. He was being taken back to undergo his sentence. Aurelia, nearly fainting, sank back into her chair, as his frightfully wild look fell upon her, while he shook his clenched fist up at the window with the most threatening gestures.

After this the Baroness was still a great deal away from the house; but she never took Aurelia with her, so that the latter led a sorrowful, miserable existence—occupied in thinking many thoughts as to destiny, and the threatening future which might unexpectedly come upon her.

From the maidservant (who had only come into the house subsequently to the nocturnal adventure which has been described, and who had probably only quite recently heard about the intimacy of the terms in which the Baroness had been living with this criminal), Aurelia learned that the folks in the Residenz were very much grieved at the Baroness's having been so deceived and imposed upon by a scoundrel of this description. But Aurelia knew only too well how differently the matter had really stood; and it seemed to her impossible that, at all events, the men of the police, who had apprehended the fellow in the Baroness's very house, should not have known all about the intimacy of the relations between them, inasmuch as she herself had told them his name, and directed their attention to the brand-marks on his back, as proofs of his identity. Moreover, this loquacious maid sometimes talked in a very ambiguous way about that which people were, here and there, thinking and saying; and, for that matter, would like very much to know better about—as to the courts having been making careful investigations, and having gone so far as to threaten the Baroness with arrest, on account of strange disclosures which the hangman's son had made concerning her.

Aurelia was obliged to admit, in her own mind, that it was another proof of her mother's depraved way of looking at things that, even after this terrible affair, she should have found it possible to go on living in the Residenz. But at last she felt herself constrained to leave the place where she knew she was the object of but too well-founded, shameful suspicion, and fly to a more distant spot. On this journey she came to the Count's Castle, and there ensued what has been related.

Aurelia could not but consider herself marvellously fortunate to have got clear of all these troubles. But how profound was her horror when, speaking to her mother in this blessed sense of the merciful intervention of Heaven in her regard, the latter, with fires of hell in her eyes, cried out in a yelling voice—

---

[1] A rough, open cart (like a haycart) used to convey condemned prisoners to their deaths, most famously in the French Revolution

"You are my misfortune, horrible creature that you are! But in the midst of your imagined happiness vengeance will overtake you, if I should be carried away by a sudden death. In those tetanic spasms, which your birth cost me[1], the subtle craft of the devil——"

Here Aurelia suddenly stopped. She threw herself upon her husband's breast, and implored him to spare her the complete recital of what the Baroness had said to her in the delirium of her insanity. She said she felt her inmost heart and soul crushed to pieces at the bare idea of the frightful threatenings—far beyond the wildest imagination's conception of the terrible—uttered to her by her mother, possessed, as she was at the time, by the most diabolical powers.

The Count comforted his bride to the best of his ability, although he felt himself permeated by the coldest and most deathly shuddering horror. Even when he had regained some calmness, he could not but confess to himself that the profound horribleness of the Baroness, even now that she was dead, cast a deep shadow over his life, sun-bright as it otherwise seemed to be.

In a very short time Aurelia began to alter very perceptibly. Whilst the deathly paleness of her face, and the fatigued appearance of her eyes, seemed to point to some bodily ailment, her mental state—confused, variable, restless, as if she were constantly frightened at something—led to the conclusion that there was some fresh mystery perturbing her system. She shunned her husband. She shut herself up in her rooms, sought the most solitary walks in the park. And when she then allowed herself to be seen, her eyes, red with weeping, her contorted features, gave unmistakable evidence of some terrible suffering which she had been undergoing. It was in vain that the Count took every possible pains to discover the cause of this condition of hers, and the only thing which had any effect in bringing him out of the hopeless state into which those remarkable symptoms of his wife's had plunged him, was the deliberate opinion of a celebrated doctor, that this strangely excited condition of the Countess was nothing other than the natural result of a bodily state which indicated the happy result of a fortunate marriage[2]. This doctor, on one occasion when he was at table with the Count and Countess, permitted himself sundry allusions to this presumed state of what the German nation calls "good hope[3]." The Countess seemed to listen to all this with indifference for some time. But suddenly her attention became

---

[1] Here the Countess compares her neurological convulsions with those she suffered in childbirth, suggesting that there is a connection – at least in their family – between intercourse/childbearing and moral/physical degeneration

[2] Viz., she is pregnant

[3] "Guter Hoffnung sein" (to be of good hope) is a old German idiom for being pregnant

vividly awakened when the doctor spoke of the wonderful longings[1] which women in that condition become possessed by, and which they cannot resist without the most injurious effects supervening upon their own health, and even upon that of the child. The Countess overwhelmed the doctor with questions, and the latter did not weary of quoting the strangest and most entertaining cases of this description from his own practice and experience.

"Moreover," he said, "there are cases on record in which women have been led, by these strange, abnormal longings, to commit most terrible crimes. There was a certain blacksmith's wife, who had such an irresistible longing for her husband's flesh that, one night, when he came home the worse for liquor, she set upon him with a large knife, and cut him about so frightfully that he died in a few hours' time."

Scarcely had the doctor said these words, when the Countess fell back in her chair fainting, and was with much difficulty recovered from the succession of hysterical attacks which supervened. The doctor then saw that he had acted very thoughtlessly in alluding to such a frightful occurrence in the presence of a lady whose nervous system was in such a delicate condition.

However, this crisis seemed to have a beneficial effect upon her, for she became calmer; although, soon afterwards there came upon her a very remarkable condition of rigidity, as of benumbedness. There was a darksome[2] fire in her eyes, and her deathlike pallor increased to such an extent, that the Count was driven into new and most tormenting doubts as to her condition. The most inexplicable thing was that she never took the smallest morsel of anything to eat, evincing the utmost repugnance at the sight of all food, particularly meat. This repugnance was so invincible that she was constantly obliged to get up and leave the table, with the most marked indications of loathing. The doctor's skill was in vain, and the Count's most urgent and affectionate entreaties were powerless to induce her to take even a single drop of medicine of any kind. And, inasmuch as weeks, nay, months, had passed without her having taken so much as a morsel of food, and it had become an unfathomable mystery how she managed to keep alive, the doctor came to the conclusion that there was something in the case which lay beyond the domain of ordinary human science. He made some pretext for leaving the Castle, but the Count saw clearly enough that this doctor, whose skilfulness was well approved, and who had a high reputation to maintain, felt that the

---

[1] Viz., pregnancy cravings

[2] Gloomy, sinister

Countess's condition was too unintelligible, and, in fact, too strangely mysterious, for him to stay on there, witness of an illness impossible to be understood—as to which he felt he had no power to render assistance.

It may be readily imagined into what a state of mind all this put the Count. But there was more to come. Just at this juncture an old, privileged servant took an opportunity, when he found the Count alone, of telling him that the Countess went out every night, and did not come home till daybreak.

The Count's blood ran cold. It struck him, as a matter which he had not quite realized before, that, for a short time back, there had fallen upon him, regularly about midnight, a curiously unnatural sleepiness, which he now believed to be caused by some narcotic[1] administered to him by the Countess, to enable her to get away unobserved. The darkest suspicions and forebodings came into his mind. He thought of the diabolical mother, and that, perhaps, her instincts had begun to awake in her daughter. He thought of some possibility of a conjugal infidelity. He remembered the terrible hangman's son.

It was so ordained that the very next night was to explain this terrible mystery to him—that which alone could be the key to the Countess's strange condition.

She herself used, every evening, to make the tea which the Count always took before going to bed. This evening he did not take a drop of it, and when he went to bed he had not the slightest symptom of the sleepiness which generally came upon him as it got towards midnight. However, he lay back on his pillows, and had all the appearance of being fast asleep as usual.

And then the Countess rose up very quietly, with the utmost precautions, came up to his bedside, held a lamp to his eyes, and then, convinced that he was sound asleep, went softly out of the room.

His heart throbbed fast. He got up, put on a cloak, and went after the Countess. It was a fine moonlight night, so that, though Aurelia had got a considerable start of him, he could see her distinctly going along in the
distance in her white dress. She went through the park, right on to the burying-ground, and there she disappeared at the wall. The Count ran quickly after her in through the gate of the burying-ground, which he found open. There, in the bright moonlight, he saw a circle of frightful, spectral-looking creatures. Old women, half naked, were cowering down upon the ground, and in the midst of them lay the corpse of a man, which they were tearing at with wolfish appetite.

Aurelia was amongst them.

---

[1] He is suspicious that she is drugging him with opiates (most likely laudanum) to make him sleep through her nocturnal infidelities

The Count took flight in the wildest horror, and ran, without any idea where he was going or what he was doing, impelled by the deadliest terror, all about the walks in the park, till he found himself at the door of his own Castle as the day was breaking, bathed in cold perspiration. Involuntarily, without the capability of taking hold of a thought, he dashed up the steps, and went bursting through the passages and into his own bedroom. There lay the Countess, to all appearance in the deepest and sweetest of sleeps. And the Count would fain have persuaded himself that some deceptive dream-image, or (inasmuch as his cloak, wet with dew, was a proof, if any had been needed, that he had really been to the burying-ground in the night) some soul-deceiving phantom had been the cause of his deathly horror. He did not wait for Aurelia's waking, but left the room, dressed, and got on to a horse. His ride, in the exquisite morning, amid sweet-scented trees and shrubs, whence the happy songs of the newly-awakened birds greeted him, drove from his memory for a time the terrible images of the night. He went back to the Castle comforted and gladdened in heart.

But when he and the Countess sate down alone together at table, and, the dishes being brought and handed, she rose to hurry away, with loathing, at the sight of the food as usual[1], the terrible conviction that what he had seen was true, was reality, impressed itself irresistibly on his mind. In the wildest fury he rose from his seat, crying—

"Accursed misbirth of hell! I understand your hatred of the food of mankind. You get your sustenance out of the burying-ground, damnable creature that you are!"

As soon as those words had passed his lips, the Countess flew at him, uttering a sound between a snarl and a howl, and bit him on the breast with the fury of a hyena. He dashed her from him on to the ground, raving fiercely as she was, and she gave up the ghost[2] in the most terrible convulsions.

The Count became a maniac.

HOFFMANN'S influence on the modern vampire story is surprisingly strong. While Polidori holds the title of first major vampire story in the English language, and while Germans, Slavs, and Poles had been writing about vampires for some five centuries or more, his nuanced treatment – the beautiful vampire winning its way into the trust of an aristocratic circle – was something rather new. Samuel Taylor Coleridge had written about a similar set-up in his 1797 poem "Christabel" (although the malevolent Geraldine is more monster than vampire), but Hoffmann's

[1] Cf. morning sickness

[2] Died

hallmark dedication to realism (setting the tale in the near past rather than – as Coleridge – in a nondescript medieval time) would have ramifications for Le Fanu's design of *Carmilla* (also about a female vampire who is introduced to a respectable family by a witch-like mother who almost immediately then disappears), which would be the pattern upon which Stoker developed *Dracula* (with bits and pieces borrowed from *The Vampyre* and *Trilby*). Hoffmann's own unique take on the vampire myth, however, has never been replicated and bears unpacking. Like so many of his horror motifs, the idea of pregnancy cravings leading to necrophagia seems to have its roots in the unconscious. Freud, of course, would have had much to say about the obvious anxieties of fatherhood. Hoffmann represents his pregnant antagonist completing a transformation complained of by husbands for centuries: she "turns into her mother." And, in a Freudian sense, she goes from desired sexual partner to used-up nag – from Madonna to Whore, or – more accurately – from innocent child to worldly woman.

II.

Hoffmann certainly seemed to have a thing for young, unspoiled girls. His experience living with his overbearing, independent mother certainly made him wary of critical, unnurturing women, and he found himself perpetually drawn to imaginative, impressionable ingénues who would not trespass on his creativity with lectures about practical life. A basic Freudian interpretation of the story points to Aurelia's climactic exposure (being taught by a coven of matronly, saggy-breasted women how to consume the body of a man) as a common masculine anxiety of watching your pretty, young wife become her mother and – with the introduction of children – gradually eat away at your time, resources, peace of mind, and creativity. The demands of fatherhood and marriage were challenging for an independent, imaginative loner like Hoffmann, and as a result of his uncharitable depiction of a young mother's natural shift of attention from her needy husband to her infant child, the story is unquestionably troubled by a roiling misogynistic subtext – one which expresses resentment toward a whole host of incel bogeymen: women who become mothers, jealousy of children, distrust of mothers-in-law, fear of infidelity, and tremendous anxiety about being "used" – like the man's corpse being fed on by the Count's new bride, as she is coached and encouraged the coven of old women, seemingly passing on the age-old wisdom of how wives use and deceive their husbands. However, as with nearly all of Hoffmann's work, "The Vampire" speaks with conviction and sincerity not of a politically correct, postmodern parable of gender roles, but as a viscerally honest expression of his personal anxieties and crippling interpersonal insecurities.

ONE of Hoffmann's most ambitious attempts at Gothic fiction is also one of his more complex: involving multiple plots layered one over the other, jumping back and forth in time, with entire casts of characters existing in each timeline. Biographically, the framing narrative about an emotionally flustered young man's aborted dalliance with a married woman borrows from Hoffmann's own scandalous attentions toward Dora Hatt. As with the young Julia Marc, Dora was one of Hoffmann's music students, but unlike Marc, she was an older, married woman with children. Their lessons began in 1794, but within two years her family – outraged at Hoffmann's barely restrained lust – fired him just as the Marc family would do years later. "The Entail" was written after both humiliating experiences, and in many ways Hoffmann blends the married woman Hatt and the affianced ingénue Marc into the mysterious Baroness Seraphina. Like so many of his masterworks, the story is founded in deep, social humiliation, the orgasmic metaphor of making music, and the frustrations caused by a society burdened with rampant bureaucracy, shameless nepotism, and inflexible traditions.

One of the story's most memorable scenes involves a sleep-walker – a man whose dreams are so haunted by his conscience that they overtake his body, sending him into a liminal state of reality, one mirroring Hoffmann's own adulterous fantasies. As translator and critic J. M. Cohen remarks in his commentary on "The Entail":

> "The most important events in Hoffmann's life were fantasies; his early love of Dora Hatt and his later love for Julia Marc had no basis in reality—the ladies were not as he imagined them; on the other hand the Napoleonic wars, which he affected to disregard, were the very real background to a great deal of his life. Dream and reality had changed places for him."

II.

An early example of the haunted house genre, "The Entail" has been cited as a strong influence on Edgar Allan Poe's "The Fall of the House of Usher," and offers a brilliantly subtle ghost story built around a family curse, crossed-star lovers, repressed emotions, concealed crimes, and an intricate web of psychological symbolism. While the story is admittedly long and often confusing, its visionary embrace of the haunted house story drags the genre out of the melodramas of Radcliffe, Lewis, and Walpole, transporting it into a contemporary setting with understated rather than excessive Gothic touches. Set in the coastal stronghold of a Prussian nobleman, alchemist, and wizard, "The Entail" follows the trans-generational secrets and tragedies of his progeny as they scuffle over his estate, dragging family friends and servants into their vortex of disillusionment. Unlike "Nutcracker," "The Sandman," or "The Stranger Child," this story avoids Hoffmann's preferred blend of fantasy, fairy tale, and weird fiction, and presents a straight-forward ghost story (in the manner of "The Vampire," "Mines of Falun," and – well – "A Ghost Story").

It foreshadows many psychologically complex masterpieces of the same genre – *The Turn of the Screw, The Haunting of Hill House, We Have Always Lived in the Castle, The Shining*, and Poe's "Usher." It demonstrates Hoffmann's ability to conjure mood with restrained vigor – whipping up a believable atmosphere of doom and dread – a classic ghost story, complete with hidden rooms, crumbling towers, sleep walking servants, buried treasure, dangerous heights, and adulterous lust, it posits a good read for a long, windy winter night, and promises some surprises along the way.

The Entail

— Excerpted from 'Night-Pieces,' Volume Two —

{1817}

NOT far from the shore of the Baltic Sea is situated the ancestral castle of the noble family Von R—— called R— sitten. It is a wild and desolate neighbourhood, hardly anything more than a single blade of grass shooting up here and there from the bottomless drift-sand; and instead of the garden[1] that generally ornaments a baronial residence, the bare walls are approached on the landward side by a thin forest of firs, that with their never-changing vesture of gloom despise the bright garniture of Spring, and where, instead of the joyous carolling of little birds awakened anew to gladness, nothing is heard but the ominous croak of the raven and the whirring scream of the storm-boding[2] sea-gull. A quarter of a mile distant Nature suddenly changes[3]. As if by the wave of a magician's wand you are transported into the midst of thriving fields, fertile arable land, and meadows. You see, too, the large and prosperous village, with the land-steward's spacious dwelling-house; and at the angle of a pleasant thicket of alders you may observe the foundations of a large castle, which one of the former proprietors had intended to erect. His successors, however, living on their property in Courland[4], left the building in its unfinished state; nor would Freiherr[5] Roderick von R—— proceed with the structure when he again took up his residence on the ancestral estate,

---

[1] Landscaped grounds surrounding a house

[2] Conventional wisdom holds that when seagulls fly inland, you can expect a storm shortly thereafter

[3] This description was a probable influence on Poe's "House of Usher," which describes a haunted manor on a blighted patch of ground which seems to be infected by the house's influence

[4] A province in Latvia, on the Baltic coast, at that time a culturally Prussian governorate of the Russian Empire

[5] Baron (literally "Free Man")

since the lonely old castle was more suitable to his temperament, which was morose and averse to human society. He had its ruinous walls repaired as well as circumstances would admit, and then shut himself up within them along with a cross-grained house-steward and a slender establishment of servants.

He was seldom seen in the village, but on the other hand he often walked and rode along the sea-beach; and people claimed to have heard him from a distance, talking to the waves and listening to the rolling and hissing of the surf, as though he could hear the answering voice of the spirit of the sea[1]. Upon the topmost summit of the watch-tower he had a sort of study fitted up and supplied with telescopes — with a complete set of astronomical apparatus, in fact. Thence during the daytime he frequently watched the ships sailing past on the distant horizon like white-winged sea-gulls; and there he spent the starlight nights engaged in astronomical, or, as some professed to know, with astrological labours, in which the old house-steward assisted him. At any rate the rumour was current during his own lifetime that he was devoted to the occult sciences or the so-called Black Art, and that he had been driven out of Courland in consequence of the failure of an experiment by which an august princely house had been most seriously offended. The slightest allusion to his residence in Courland filled him with horror; but for all the troubles which had there unhinged the tenor of his life he held his predecessors entirely to blame, in that they had wickedly deserted the home of their ancestors. In order to fetter, for the future, at least the head of the family to the ancestral castle, he converted it into a property of entail[2]. The sovereign was the more willing to ratify this arrangement since by its means he would secure for his country a family distinguished for all chivalrous virtues, and which had already begun to ramify into foreign countries.

Neither Roderick's son Hubert, nor the next Roderick, who was so called after his grandfather, would live in their ancestral castle; both preferred Courland. It is conceivable, too, that, being more cheerful and fond of life than the gloomy astrologer, they were repelled by the grim loneliness of the place. Freiherr Roderick had granted shelter and subsistence on the property to two old maids, sisters of his father, who were living in indigence, having been but niggardly provided for. They, together with an aged serving-woman, occupied the small warm rooms of one of the wings; besides them and the cook, who had a large apartment

---

[1] This is a similar arrangement to Hoffmann's story "Doge and Dogaresse," wherein a murdered Venetian nobleman is revenged by the spirit of the sea – whom he loved as a wife – which sinks the ship of his escaping murderers

[2] A legal settlement which requires that the inheritance of a property be retained to a particular group (usually a family). This prevents the property from being sold outside of the family

on the ground floor adjoining the kitchen, the only other person was a worn-out chasseur[1], who tottered about through the lofty rooms and halls of the main building, and discharged the duties of castellan[2]. The rest of the servants lived in the village with the land-steward. The only time at which the desolated and deserted castle became the scene of life and activity was late in autumn, when the snow first began to fall and the season for wolf-hunting and boar-hunting arrived. Then came Freiherr Roderick with his wife, attended by relatives and friends and a numerous retinue, from Courland. The neighbouring nobility, and even amateur lovers of the chase who lived in the town hard by, came down in such numbers that the main building, together with the wings, barely sufficed to hold the crowd of guests. Well-served fires roared in all the stoves and fireplaces, while the spits were creaking from early dawn until late at night, and hundreds of light-hearted people, masters and servants, were running up and down stairs; here was heard the jingling and rattling of drinking glasses and jovial hunting choruses, there the footsteps of those dancing to the sound of the shrill music — everywhere loud mirth and jollity; so that for four or five weeks together the castle was more like a first-rate hostelry situated on a main highroad than the abode of a country gentleman. This time Freiherr Roderick devoted, as well as he was able, to serious business, for, withdrawing from the revelry of his guests, he discharged the duties attached to his position as lord of the entail. He not only had a complete statement of the revenues laid before him, but he listened to every proposal for improvement and to every the least complaint of his tenants, endeavouring to establish order in everything, and check all wrongdoing and injustice as far as lay in his power.

In these matters of business he was honestly assisted by the old advocate V—— who had been law agent of the R—— family and Justitiarius[3] of their estates in P—— from father to son for many years; accordingly, V—— was wont to set out for the estate at least a week before the day fixed for the arrival of the Freiherr. In the year 179 — the time came round again when old V—— was to start on his journey for R— sitten. However strong and healthy the old man, now seventy years of age, might feel, he was yet quite assured that a helping hand would prove beneficial to him in his business. So he said to me one day as if in jest, "Cousin!" (I was his great-nephew, but he called me "cousin," owing to the fact that his own Christian name and mine were both the same)—

---

[1] A member of a light cavalry unit designed for reconnaissance, swift movement, and shock tactics

[2] Manager of a castle

[3] Or justiciary: a regent or executor who monitors the maintenance of an estate. This particular justiciary is in charge of making sure that the R—sitten estate is kept in good shape according to the original baron's will

"Cousin, I was thinking it would not be amiss if you went along with me to R— sitten and felt the sea-breezes blow about your ears a bit. Besides giving me good help in my often laborious work, you may for once in a while see how you like the rollicking life of a hunter, and how, after drawing up a neatly-written protocol one morning, you will frame the next when you come to look in the glaring eyes of such a sturdy brute as a grim shaggy wolf or a wild boar gnashing his teeth, and whether you know how to bring him down with a well-aimed shot." Of course I could not have heard such strange accounts of the merry hunting parties at R— sitten, or entertain such a true heartfelt affection for my excellent old great-uncle as I did, without being highly delighted that he wanted to take me with him this time. As I was already pretty well skilled in the sort of business he had to transact, I promised to work with unwearied industry, so as to relieve him of all care and trouble.

Next day we sat in the carriage on our way to R— sitten, well wrapped up in good fur coats, driving through a thick snowstorm, the first harbinger of the coming winter. On the journey the old gentleman told me many remarkable stories about the Freiherr Roderick, who had established the estate-tail and appointed him (V——), in spite of his youth, to be his Justitiarius and executor. He spoke of the harsh and violent character of the old nobleman, which seemed to be inherited by all the family, since even the present master of the estate, whom he had known as a mild-tempered and almost effeminate youth, acquired more and more as the years went by the same disposition. He therefore recommended me strongly to behave with as much resolute self-reliance and as little embarrassment as possible, if I desired to possess any consideration in the Freiherr's eyes; and at length he began to describe the apartments in the castle which he had selected to be his own once for all, since they were warm and comfortable, and so conveniently retired that we could withdraw from the noisy convivialities of the hilarious company whenever we pleased. The rooms, namely, which were on every visit reserved for him, were two small ones, hung with warm tapestry, close beside the large hall of justice, in the wing opposite that in which the two old maids resided.

At last, after a rapid but wearying journey, we arrived at R— sitten, late at night. We drove through the village; it was Sunday, and from the alehouse proceeded the sounds of music, and dancing, and merrymaking; the steward's house was lit up from basement to garret, and music and song were there too. All the more striking therefore was the inhospitable desolation into which we now drove. The sea-wind howled in sharp cutting dirges as it were about us, whilst the sombre firs, as if they had been roused by the wind from a deep magic trance, groaned hoarsely in a responsive chorus. The bare black walls of the castle towered above the snow-covered ground; we drew up at the gates, which were fast locked.

But no shouting or cracking of whips, no knocking or hammering, was of any avail; the whole castle seemed to be dead; not a single light was visible at any of the windows. The old gentleman shouted in his strong stentorian voice, “Francis, Francis, where the deuce are you? In the devil’s name rouse yourself; we are all freezing here outside the gates. The snow is cutting our faces till they bleed. Why the devil don’t you stir yourself?” Then the watch-dog began to whine, and a wandering light was visible on the ground floor. There was a rattling of keys, and soon the ponderous wings of the gate creaked back on their hinges. “Ha! a hearty welcome, a hearty welcome, Herr Justitiarius. Ugh! it’s rough weather!” cried old Francis, holding the lantern above his head, so that the light fell full upon his withered face, which was drawn up into a curious grimace, that was meant for a friendly smile. The carriage drove into the court, and we got out; then I obtained a full view of the old servant’s extraordinary figure, almost hidden in his wide old-fashioned chasseur livery, with its many extraordinary lace decorations. Whilst there were only a few grey locks on his broad white forehead, the lower part of his face wore the ruddy hue of health; and, notwithstanding that the cramped muscles of his face gave it something of the appearance of a whimsical mask, yet the rather stupid good-nature which beamed from his eyes and played about his mouth compensated for all the rest.

“Now, old Francis,” began my great-uncle, knocking the snow from his fur coat in the entrance hall, “now, old man, is everything prepared? Have you had the hangings in my room well dusted, and the beds carried in? and have you had a big roaring fire both yesterday and today[1]?” “No,” replied Francis, quite calmly, “no, my worshipful Herr Justitiarius, we’ve got none of that done.” “Good Heavens!” burst out my great-uncle, “I wrote to you in proper time; you know that I always come at the time I fix. Here’s a fine piece of stupid carelessness! I shall have to sleep in rooms as cold as ice.” “But you see, worshipful Herr Justitiarius,” continued Francis, most carefully clipping a burning thief[2] from the wick of the candle with the snuffers and stamping it out with his foot, “but, you see, sir, all that would not have been of much good, especially the fires, for the wind and the snow have taken up their quarters too much in the rooms, driving in through the broken windows, and then”—— “What!” cried my uncle, interrupting him as he spread out his fur coat and placing his arms akimbo[3], “do you mean to tell me the windows are broken, and you, the castellan of the house, have done nothing to get them mended?” “But, worshipful Herr Justitiarius,” resumed the old servant calmly and

---

[1] In order to drive out the cold and damp as much as possible, old rooms were often heated up for two or three days before guests were expected

[2] My only guess about this strange phrase is that it refers to a part of the wick which has become entirely burned and is preventing the light from being clear

[3] Hands on hips, elbows bent outward

composedly, "but we can't very well get at them owing to the great masses of stones and rubbish lying all over the room." "Damn it all, how come there to be stones and rubbish in my room?" cried my uncle. "Your lasting health and good luck, young gentleman[1]!" said the old man, bowing politely to me, as I happened to sneeze; but he immediately added, "They are the stones and plaster of the partition wall which fell in at the great shock." "Have you had an earthquake?" blazed up my uncle, now fairly in a rage. "No, not an earthquake, worshipful Herr Justitiarius," replied the old man, grinning all over his face, "but three days ago the heavy wainscot ceiling of the justice-hall fell in with a tremendous crash." "Then may the"—— My uncle was about to rip out a terrific oath in his violent passionate manner, but jerking up his right arm above his head and taking off his fox-skin cap with his left, he suddenly checked himself; and turning to me, he said with a hearty laugh, "By my troth, cousin, we must hold our tongues; we mustn't ask any more questions, or else we shall hear of some still worse misfortune, or have the whole castle tumbling to pieces about our ears." "But," he continued, wheeling round again to the old servant, "but, bless me, Francis, could you not have had the common sense to get me another room cleaned and warmed? Could you not have quickly fitted up a room in the main building for the court-day?" "All that has been already done," said the old man, pointing to the staircase with a gesture that invited us to follow him, and at once beginning to ascend them.

"Now there's a most curious noodle for you!" exclaimed my uncle as we followed old Francis. The way led through long lofty vaulted corridors, in the dense darkness of which Francis's flickering light threw a strange reflection. The pillars, capitals, and vari-coloured arches seemed as if they were floating before us in the air; our own shadows stalked along beside us in gigantic shape, and the grotesque paintings on the walls over which they glided seemed all of a tremble and shake; whilst their voices, we could imagine, were whispering in the sound of our echoing footsteps, "Wake us not, oh! wake us not — us whimsical spirits who sleep here in these old stones." At last, after we had traversed a long suite of cold and gloomy apartments, Francis opened the door of a hall in which a fire blazing brightly in the grate offered us as it were a home-like welcome with its pleasant crackling. I felt quite comfortable the moment I entered, but my uncle, standing still in the middle of the hall, looked round him and said in a tone which was so very grave as to be almost solemn, "And so this is to be the justice-hall[2]!" Francis held his candle above his head, so that my eye fell upon a light spot in the wide dark wall about the size of a door; then he said in a pained and muffled voice, "Justice has been already

[1] A traditional German blessing, often shortened to "Gesundheit" (literally "healthiness!")

[2] The master bedroom where the Justiciar sleeps

dealt out here[1]." "What possesses you, old man?" asked my uncle, quickly throwing aside his fur coat and drawing near to the fire. "It slipped over my lips, I couldn't help it," said Francis; then he lit the great candles and opened the door of the adjoining room, which was very snugly fitted up for our reception. In a short time a table was spread for us before the fire, and the old man served us with several well-dressed dishes, which were followed by a brimming bowl of punch, prepared in true Northern style — a very acceptable sight to two weary travellers like my uncle and myself. My uncle then, tired with his journey, went to bed as soon as he had finished supper; but my spirits were too much excited by the novelty and strangeness of the place, as well as by the punch, for me to think of sleep. Meanwhile, Francis cleared the table, stirred up the fire, and bowing and scraping politely, left me to myself.

Now I sat alone in the lofty spacious Rittersaal or Knight's Hall. The snow-flakes had ceased to beat against the lattice, and the storm had ceased to whistle; the sky was clear, and the bright full moon shone in through the wide oriel-windows[2], illuminating with magical effect all the dark corners of the curious room into which the dim light of my candles and the fire could not penetrate. As one often finds in old castles, the walls and ceiling of the hall were ornamented in a peculiar antique fashion, the former with fantastic paintings and carvings, gilded and coloured in gorgeous tints, the latter with heavy wainscoting. Standing out conspicuously from the great pictures, which represented for the most part wild bloody scenes in bear-hunts and wolf-hunts, were the heads of men and animals carved in wood and joined on to the painted bodies, so that the whole, especially in the flickering light of the fire and the soft beams of the moon, had an effect as if all were alive and instinct with terrible reality. Between these pictures reliefs of knights had been inserted, of life size, walking along in hunting costume; probably they were the ancestors of the family who had delighted in the chase. Everything, both in the paintings and in the carved work, bore the dingy hue of extreme old age; so much the more conspicuous therefore was the bright bare place on that one of the walls through which were two doors leading into adjoining apartments. I soon concluded that there too there must have been a door, that had been bricked up later; and hence it was that this new part of the wall, which had neither been painted like the rest, nor yet ornamented with carvings, formed such a striking contrast with the others. Who does not know with what mysterious power the mind is enthralled in the midst of unusual and singularly strange circumstances? Even the dullest imagination is aroused when it comes

---

[1] Francis inadvertently makes a pun implying that the room has been the scene of some grim act

[2] A rounded bay window that projects from the walls of a house

into a valley girt[1] around by fantastic rocks, or within the gloomy walls of a church or an abbey, and it begins to have glimpses of things it has never yet experienced. When I add that I was twenty years of age, and had drunk several glasses of strong punch, it will easily be conceived that as I sat thus in the Rittersaal I was in a more exceptional frame of mind than I had ever been before. Let the reader picture to himself the stillness of the night within, and without the rumbling roar of the sea — the peculiar piping of the wind, which rang upon my ears like the tones of a mighty organ played upon by spectral hands — the passing scudding clouds which, shining bright and white, often seemed to peep in through the rattling oriel-windows like giants sailings past — in very truth, I felt, from the slight shudder which shook me, that possibly a new sphere of existences might now be revealed to me visibly and perceptibly. But this feeling was like the shivery sensations that one has on hearing a graphically narrated ghost story, such as we all like. At this moment it occurred to me that I should never be in a more seasonable mood for reading the book which, in common with every one who had the least leaning towards the romantic, I at that time carried about in my pocket — I mean Schiller's "Ghost-seer[2]." I read and read, and my imagination grew ever more and more excited. I came to the marvellously enthralling description of the wedding feast at Count Von V——'s.

Just as I was reading of the entrance of Jeronimo's bloody figure[3], the door leading from the gallery into the antechamber flew open with a tremendous bang. I started to my feet in terror; the book fell from my hands. In the very same moment, however, all was still again, and I began to be ashamed of my childish fears. The door must have been burst open by a strong gust of wind or in some other natural manner. It is nothing; my over-strained fancy converts every ordinary occurrence into the supernatural. Having thus calmed my fears, I picked up my book from the ground, and again threw myself in the arm-chair; but there came a sound of soft, slow, measured footsteps moving diagonally across the hall, whilst

[1] Belted, surrounded

[2] One of Germany's most important Romantic poets, Friedrich Schiller wrote several works of the macabre, including his unfinished Gothic masterpiece, "The Ghost-Seer." Published in 1787, it details the mysterious adventures of a German prince in Venice who is beset by scheming priests who desire to corrupt him and turn him into a mouthpiece for the Catholic Church. A story filled with intrigue, hauntings, murder, and lust, it is among Schiller's most popular works

[3] In one of the stories told to the protagonist, a man murders his brother and steals his fiancée. At the fateful wedding feast, he is accosted by a strange monk in bloody robes. Annoyed and frightened, he engages his stalker, only to have the figure of his mutilated brother reveal himself under the gory vestments

there was a sighing and moaning at intervals, and in this sighing and moaning there was expressed the deepest trouble, the most hopeless grief, that a human being can know. "Ha! it must be some sick animal locked up somewhere in the basement storey. Such acoustic deceptions at night time, making distant sounds appear close at hand, are well known to everybody. Who will suffer himself to be terrified at such a thing as that?" Thus I calmed my fears again. But now there was a scratching at the new portion of the wall, whilst louder and deeper sighs were audible, as if gasped out by some one in the last throes of mortal anguish. "Yes, yes; it is some poor animal locked up somewhere; I will shout as loudly as I can, I will stamp violently on the floor, then all will be still, or else the animal below will make itself heard more distinctly, and in its natural cries," I thought. But the blood ran cold in my veins; the cold sweat, too, stood upon my forehead, and I remained sitting in my chair as if transfixed, quite unable to rise, still less to cry out. At length the abominable scratching ceased, and I again heard the footsteps. Life and motion seemed to be awakened in me; I leapt to my feet, and went two or three steps forward. But then there came an ice-cold draught of wind through the hall, whilst at the same moment the moon cast her bright light upon the statue of a grave if not almost terrible-looking man; and then, as though his warning voice rang through the louder thunders of the waves and the shriller piping of the wind, I heard distinctly, *"No further, no further! or you will sink beneath all the fearful horrors of the world of spectres."* Then the door was slammed too with the same violent bang as before, and I plainly heard the footsteps in the anteroom, then going down the stairs. The main door of the castle was opened with a creaking noise, and afterwards closed again. Then it seemed as if a horse were brought out of the stable, and after a while taken back again, and finally all was still.

At that same moment my attention was attracted to my old uncle in the adjoining room; he was groaning and moaning painfully. This brought me fully to consciousness again; I seized the candles and hurried into the room to him. He appeared to be struggling with an ugly, unpleasant dream. "Wake up, wake up!" I cried loudly, taking him gently by the hand, and letting the full glare of the light fall upon his face. He started up with a stifled shout, and then, looking kindly at me, said, "Ay, you have done quite right — that you have, cousin, to wake me. I have had a very ugly dream, and it's all solely owing to this room and that hall, for they made me think of past times and many wonderful[1] things that have happened here. But now let us turn to and have a good sound sleep." Therewith the old gentleman rolled himself in the bed-covering and appeared to fall asleep at once. But when I had extinguished the candles and likewise crept into bed, I heard him praying in a low tone to himself.

---

[1] Awe-inspiring (as opposed to "excellent")

ଔ

Next morning we began work in earnest; the land-steward brought his account-books, and various other people came, some to get a dispute settled, some to get arrangements made about other matters. At noon my uncle took me with him to the wing where the two old Baronesses lived, that we might pay our respects to them with all due form. Francis having announced us, we had to wait some time before a little old dame, bent with the weight of her sixty years, and attired in gay-coloured silks, who styled herself the noble ladies' lady-inwaiting, appeared and led us into the sanctuary. There we were received with comical ceremony by the old ladies, whose curious style of dress had gone out of fashion years and years before. I especially was an object of astonishment to them when my uncle, with considerable humour, introduced me as a young lawyer who had come to assist him in his business. Their countenances plainly indicated their belief that, owing to my youth, the welfare of the tenants of R— sitten was placed in jeopardy. Although there was a good deal that was truly ridiculous during the whole of this interview with the old ladies, I was nevertheless still shivering from the terror of the preceding night; I felt as if I had come in contact with an unknown power, or rather as if I had grazed against the outer edge of a circle, one step across which would be enough to plunge me irretrievably into destruction, as though it were only by the exertion of all the power of my will that I should be able to guard myself against that awful dread which never slackens its hold upon you until it ends in incurable insanity. Hence it was that the old Baronesses, with their remarkable towering head-dresses, and their peculiar stuff gowns, tricked off with gay flowers and ribbons, instead of striking me as merely ridiculous, had an appearance that was both ghostly and awe-inspiring. My fancy seemed to glean from their yellow withered faces and blinking eyes, ocular proof of the fact that they had succeeded in establishing themselves on at least a good footing with the ghosts who haunted the castle, as it derived auricular confirmation of the same fact from the wretched French[1] which they croaked, partly between their tightly-closed blue lips and partly through their long thin noses, and also that they themselves possessed the power of setting trouble and dire

[1] Throughout the 18th century, French was the universal language of high society and diplomacy (hence the term "lingua franca," used to describe a common vernacular used in global business). This was, however, before the Napoleonic Wars and the rise of nationalism in Europe. After the wars, countries began taking a distinct pride in their national languages, customs, literature, music, culture, and fashion. To these old beldames the use of French is a sign of their upbringing, but to the protagonist it is a treasonous artifact of an earlier time

mischief at work. My uncle, who always had a keen eye for a bit of fun, entangled the old dames in his ironical way in such a mish-mash of nonsensical rubbish that, had I been in any other mood, I should not have known how to swallow down my immoderate laughter; but, as I have just said, the Baronesses and their twaddle were, and continued to be, in my regard, ghostly, so that my old uncle, who was aiming at affording me an especial diversion, glanced across at me time after time utterly astonished. So after dinner, when we were alone together in our room, he burst out, "But in Heaven's name, cousin, tell me what is the matter with you? You don't laugh; you don't talk; you don't eat; and you don't drink. Are you ill, or is anything else the matter with you?" I now hesitated not a moment to tell him circumstantially all my terrible, awful experiences of the previous night. I did not conceal anything, and above all I did not conceal that I had drunk a good deal of punch, and had been reading Schiller's "Ghost-seer." "This I must confess to," I add, "for only so can I credibly explain how it was that my over-strained and active imagination could create all those ghostly spirits, which only exist within the sphere of my own brain." I fully expected that my uncle would now pepper me well with the stinging pellets of his wit for this my fanciful ghost-seeing; but, on the contrary, he grew very grave, and his eyes became riveted in a set stare upon the floor, until he jerked up his head and said, fixing me with his keen fiery eyes, "Your book I am not acquainted with, cousin; but your ghostly visitants were due neither to it nor to the fumes of the punch. I must tell you that I dreamt exactly the same things that you saw and heard. Like you, I sat in the easy-chair beside the fire (at least I dreamt so); but what was only revealed to you as slight noises I saw and distinctly comprehended with the eye of my mind. Yes, I beheld that foul fiend come in, stealthily and feebly step across to the bricked-up door, and scratch at the wall in hopeless despair until the blood gushed out from beneath his torn finger-nails; then he went downstairs, took a horse out of the stable, and finally put him back again. Did you also hear the cock crowing in a distant farmyard up at the village? You came and awoke me, and I soon resisted the baneful ghost of that terrible man, who is still able to disturb in this fearful way the quiet lives of the living." The old gentleman stopped; and I did not like to ask him further questions, being well aware that he would explain everything to me when he deemed that the proper time was come for doing so. After sitting for a while, deeply absorbed in his own thoughts, he went on, "Cousin, do you think you have courage enough to encounter the ghost again now that you know all that happens — that is to say, along with me?" Of course I declared that I now felt quite strong enough, and ready for what he wished. "Then let us watch together during the coming night," the old gentleman went on to say. "There is a voice within me telling me that this evil spirit must fly, not so much before the power of my will as before my courage, which rests upon a basis of firm conviction. I feel that it is not at all presumption in me, but rather a good and pious deed, if I venture life and limb to exorcise this foul fiend that is banishing the sons from the old castle of their ancestors. But what am I thinking about? There can be no risk in the case at all, for with such a firm, honest mind and pious trust that I feel I possess, I and everybody cannot fail to be, now and always, victorious over such ghostly antagonists. And yet if, after all, it should be God's will that this evil power be enabled to work me mischief, then you must bear witness, cousin, that I fell in honest Christian fight against the spirit of hell which was here busy about its fiendish work. As for yourself, keep at a distance; no harm will happen to you then."

Our attention was busily engaged with divers kinds of business until evening came. As on the day before, Francis had cleared away the remains of the supper, and brought us our punch. The full moon shone brightly through the gleaming clouds, the sea-waves roared, and the night-wind howled and shook the oriel window till the panes rattled. Although inwardly excited, we forced ourselves to converse on indifferent topics. The old gentleman had placed his striking watch on the table; it struck twelve. Then the door flew open with a terrific bang, and, just as on the preceding night, soft slow footsteps moved stealthily across the hall in a diagonal direction, whilst there were the same sounds of sighing and moaning. My uncle turned pale, but his eyes shone with an unusual brilliance. He rose from his arm-chair, stretching his tall figure up to its full height, so that as he stood there with his left arm propped against his side and with his right stretched out towards the middle of the hall, he had the appearance of a hero issuing his commands. But the sighing and moaning were growing every moment louder and more perceptible, and then the scratching at the wall began more horribly even than on the previous night. My uncle strode forwards straight towards the walled-up door, and his steps were so firm that they echoed along the floor. He stopped immediately in front of the place, where the scratching noise continued to grow worse and worse, and said in a strong solemn voice, such as I had never before heard from his lips, "Daniel, Daniel! what are you doing here at this hour?" Then there was a horrible unearthly scream, followed by a dull thud as if a heavy weight had fallen to the ground. "Seek for pardon and mercy at the throne of the Almighty; that is your place. Away with you from the scenes of this life, in which you can nevermore have part." And as the old gentleman uttered these words in a tone still stronger than before, a feeble wail seemed to pass through the air and die away in the blustering of the storm, which was just beginning to rage. Crossing over to the door, the old gentleman slammed it to, so that the echo rang loudly through the empty anteroom. There was something so supernatural almost in both his language and his gestures that I was deeply struck with awe. On resuming his seat in his arm-chair his face was as if transfigured; he folded his hands and prayed inwardly. In this way several minutes passed, when he asked me in that gentle tone which always went right to my heart, and which he always had so completely at his command, "Well, cousin?" Agitated and shaken by awe, terror, fear, and pious respect and love, I threw myself upon my knees and rained down my warm tears upon the hand he offered me. He clasped me in his arms, and pressing me fervently to his heart said very tenderly, "Now we will go and have a good quiet sleep, good cousin;" and we did so. And as nothing of an unusual nature occurred on the following night, we soon recovered our former cheerfulness, to the prejudice of the old Baronesses; for though there did still continue to be something ghostly about them and their odd manners, yet it emanated from a diverting ghost which the old gentleman knew how to call up in a droll fashion.

At length, after the lapse of several days, the Baron put in his appearance, along with his wife and a numerous train of servants for the hunting; the guests who had been invited also arrived, and the castle, now suddenly awakened to animation, became the scene of the noisy life and revelry which have been before described. When the Baron came into our hall soon after his arrival, he seemed to be disagreeably surprised at the change in our quarters. Casting an ill-tempered glance towards the bricked-up door, he turned abruptly round and passed his hand across his forehead, as if desirous of banishing some disagreeable recollection. My great-uncle mentioned the damage done to the justice-hall and the adjoining apartments; but the Baron found fault with Francis for not accommodating us with better lodgings, and he good-naturedly requested the old gentleman to order anything he might want to make his new room comfortable; for it was much less satisfactory in this respect than that which he had usually occupied. On the whole, the Baron's bearing towards my old uncle was not merely cordial, but largely coloured by a certain deferential respect, as if the relation in which he stood towards him was that of a younger relative. But this was the sole trait that could in any way reconcile me to his harsh, imperious character, which was now developed more and more every day. As for me, he seemed to notice me but little; if he did notice me at all, he saw in me nothing more than the usual secretary or clerk. On the occasion of the very first important memorandum that I drew up, he began to point out mistakes, as he conceived, in the wording. My blood boiled, and I was about to make a caustic reply, when my uncle interposed, informing him briefly that I did my work exactly in the way he wished, and that in legal matters of this kind he alone was responsible. When we were left alone, I complained bitterly of the Baron, who would, I said, always inspire me with growing aversion. "I assure you, cousin," replied the old gentleman, "that the Baron, notwithstanding his unpleasant manner, is really one of the most excellent and kind-hearted men in the world. As I have already told you, he did not assume these manners until the time he became lord of the entail; previous to then he was a modest, gentle youth. Besides, he is not, after all, so bad as you make him out to be; and further, I should like to

know why you are so averse to him." As my uncle said these words he smiled mockingly, and the blood rushed hotly and furiously into my face. I could not pretend to hide from myself — I saw it only too clearly, and felt it too unmistakably — that my peculiar antipathy to the Baron sprang out of the fact that I loved, even to madness, a being who appeared to me to be the loveliest and most fascinating of her sex who had ever trod the earth. This lady was none other than the Baroness herself. Her appearance exercised a powerful and irresistible charm upon me at the very moment of her arrival, when I saw her traversing the apartments in her Russian sable cloak, which fitted close to the exquisite symmetry of her shape, and with a rich veil wrapped about her head. Moreover, the circumstance that the two old aunts, with still more extraordinary gowns and beribboned head-dresses than I had yet seen them wear, were sweeping along one on each side of her and cackling their welcomes in French, whilst the Baroness was looking about her in a way so gentle as to baffle all description, nodding graciously first to one and then to another, and then adding in her flute-like voice a few German words in the pure sonorous dialect of Courland — all this formed a truly remarkable and unusual picture, and my imagination involuntarily connected it with the ghostly midnight visitant — the Baroness being the angel of light who was to break the ban of the spectral powers of evil. This wondrously lovely lady stood forth in startling reality before my mind's eye. At that time she could hardly be nineteen years of age, and her face, as delicately beautiful as her form, bore the impression of the most angelic good-nature; but what I especially noticed was the indescribable fascination of her dark eyes, for a soft melancholy gleam of aspiration shone in them like dewy moonshine, whilst a perfect elysium of rapture and delight was revealed in her sweet and beautiful smile. She often seemed completely lost in her own thoughts, and at such moments her lovely face was swept by dark
and fleeting shadows. Many observers would have concluded that she was affected by some distressing pain; but it rather seemed to me that she was struggling with gloomy apprehensions of a future pregnant with dark misfortunes; and with these, strangely enough, I connected the apparition of the castle, though I could not give the least explanation of why I did so.

On the morning following the Baron's arrival, when the company assembled to breakfast, my old uncle introduced me to the Baroness; and, as usually happens with people in the frame of mind in which I then was, I behaved with indescribable absurdity[1]. In answer to the beautiful lady's simple inquiries how I liked the castle, &c., I entangled myself in the most extraordinary and nonsensical phrases, so that the old aunts ascribed my embarrassment simply and solely to my profound respect for the noble lady, and thought they were called upon condescendingly to take my part,

[1] The public humiliation which is typical of a Hoffmann protagonist

which they did by praising me in French as a very nice and clever young man, as a *garçon très joli* (handsome lad). This vexed me; so suddenly recovering my self-possession, I threw out a *bonmot*[1] in better French than the old dames were mistresses of; whereupon they opened their eyes wide in astonishment, and pampered their long thin noses with a liberal supply of snuff. From the Baroness's turning from me with a more serious air to talk to some other lady, I perceived that my *bonmot* bordered closely upon folly; this vexed me still more, and I wished the two old ladies to the devil. My old uncle's irony had long before brought me through the stage of the languishing love-sick swain[2], who in childish infatuation coddles his love-troubles; but I knew very well that the Baroness had made a deeper and more powerful impression upon my heart than any other woman had hitherto done. I saw and heard nothing but her; nevertheless I had a most explicit and unequivocal consciousness that it would be not only absurd, but even utter madness to dream of an amour, albeit I perceived no less clearly the impossibility of gazing and adoring at a distance like a love-lorn boy. Of such conduct I should have been perfectly ashamed. But what I could do, and what I resolved to do, was to become more intimate with this beautiful girl without allowing her to get any glimpse of my real feelings, to drink the sweet poison of her looks and words, and then, when far away from her, to bear her image in my heart for many, many days, perhaps for ever. I was excited by this romantic and chivalric attachment to such a degree, that, as I pondered over it during sleepless nights, I was childish enough to address myself in pathetic monologues, and even to sigh lugubriously, "Seraphina[3]! O Seraphina!" till at last my old uncle woke up and cried, "Cousin, cousin! I believe you are dreaming aloud. Do it by daytime, if you can possibly contrive it, but at night have the goodness to let me sleep." I was very much afraid that the old gentleman, who had not failed to remark my excitement on the Baroness's arrival, had heard the name, and would overwhelm me with his sarcastic wit. But next morning all he said, as we went into the justice-hall, was, "God grant every man the proper amount of common sense, and sufficient watchfulness to keep it well under hand. It's a bad look-out when a man becomes converted into a fantastic coxcomb[4] without so much as a word of warning." Then he took his seat at the great table and added, "Write neatly and distinctly, good cousin, that I may be able to read it without any trouble."

---

[1] French: literally "good word" – a witty comment or perfect comeback. We are led to assume that his bon mot took the form of profanity

[2] An admirer or suitor

[3] The Baroness's first name means "fiery one," and is an allusion to a burning angel of light, making it a fitting contrast to the icy Baltic winter that inundates the castle

[4] A vain, delusional fool

The respect, nay, the almost filial veneration which the Baron entertained towards my uncle, was manifested on all occasions. Thus, at the dinner-table he had to occupy the seat — which many envied him — beside the Baroness; as for me, chance threw me first in one place and then in another; but for the most part, two or three officers from the neighbouring capital were wont to attach me to them, in order that they might empty to their own satisfaction their budget of news and amusing anecdotes, whilst diligently passing the wine about. Thus it happened that for several days in succession I sat at the bottom of the table at a great distance from the Baroness. At length, however, chance brought me nearer to her. Just as the doors of the dining-hall were thrown open for the assembled company, I happened to be in the midst of a conversation with the Baroness's companion and confidante — a lady no longer in the bloom of youth, but by no means ill-looking, and not without intelligence — and she seemed to take some interest in my remarks. According to etiquette, it was my duty to offer her my arm, and I was not a little pleased when she took her place quite close to the Baroness, who gave her a friendly nod. It may be readily imagined that all that I now said was intended not only for my fair neighbour, but also mainly for the Baroness. Whether it was that the inward tension of my feelings imparted an especial animation to all I said, at any rate my companion's attention became more riveted with every succeeding moment; in fact, she was at last entirely absorbed in the visions of the kaleidoscopic world which I unfolded to her gaze. As remarked, she was not without intelligence, and it soon came to pass that our conversation, completely independent of the multitude of words spoken by the other guests (which rambled about first to this subject and then to that), maintained its own free course, launching an effective word now and again whither I wanted it. For I did not fail to observe that my companion shot a significant glance or two across to the Baroness, and that the latter took pains to listen to us. And this was particularly the case when the conversation turned upon music and I began to speak with enthusiasm of this glorious and sacred art; nor did I conceal that, despite the fact of my having devoted myself to the dry tedious study of the law, I possessed tolerable skill on the harpsichord, could sing, and had even set several songs to music[1].

The majority of the company had gone into another room to take coffee and liqueurs; but, unawares, without knowing how it came about, I found myself near the Baroness, who was talking with her confidante. She at once addressed me, repeating in a still more cordial manner and in the tone in which one talks to an acquaintance, her inquiries as to how I liked living in the castle, &c. I assured her that for the first few days, not only the dreary desolation of the situation, but the ancient castle itself had

---

[1] Much like Hoffmann himself – a lawyer who moonlighted as a composer and musician

affected me strangely, but even in this mood I had found much of deep interest, and that now my only wish was to be excused from the stirring scenes of the hunt, for I had not been accustomed to them. The Baroness smiled and said, "I can readily believe that this wild life in our fir forests cannot be very congenial to you. You are a musician, and, unless I am utterly mistaken, a poet as well. I am passionately fond of both arts. I can also play the harp a little, but I have to do without it here in R— sitten, for my husband does not like me to bring it with me[1]. Its soft strains would harmonize but ill with the wild shouts of the hunters and the ringing blare of their bugles, which are the only sounds that ought to be heard here. And O heaven! how I should like to hear a little music!" I protested that I would exert all the skill I had at my command to fulfil her wish, for there must surely without doubt be an instrument of some kind in the castle, even though it were only an old harpsichord. Then the Lady Adelheid (the Baroness's confidante) burst out into a silvery laugh and asked, did I not know that within the memory of man no other instrument had ever been heard in the castle except cracked trumpets, and hunting-horns which in the midst of joy would only sound lugubrious notes, and the twanging fiddles, untuned violoncellos, and braying oboes of itinerant musicians. The Baroness reiterated her wish that she should like to have some music, and especially should like to hear me; and both she and Adelheid racked their brains all to no purpose to devise some scheme by which they could get a decent pianoforte brought to the Castle. At this moment old Francis crossed the room. "Here's the man who always can give the best advice, and can procure everything, even things before unheard of and unseen." With these words the Lady Adelheid called him to her, and as she endeavoured to make him comprehend what it was that was wanted, the Baroness listened with her hands clasped and her head bent forward, looking upon the old man's face with a gentle smile. She made a most attractive picture, like some lovely, winsome child that is all eagerness to have a wished-for toy in its hands. Francis, after having adduced in his prolix[2] manner several reasons why it would be downright impossible to procure such a wonderful instrument in such a big hurry, finally stroked his beard[3] with an air of self-flattery and said, "But the land-steward's lady up at the village

---

[1] Expensive, heavy, awkwardly shaped, and very large, the harp is truly not a practical instrument to pack for a vacation

[2] Wordy, verbose

[3] Tremendously unfashionable during the 18th and early 19th century (even peasants were generally clean shaven, and only soldiers of particular armies kept mustaches), Francis' beard underscores his backwardness. At the beginning of the 18th century, Peter the Great even made it illegal for nobles to grow beards, and had them forcibly shaved if they refused to comply

performs on the manichord[1], or whatever is the outlandish name they now call it, with uncommon skill, and sings to it so fine and mournful-like that it makes your eyes red, just like onions do, and makes you feel as if you would like to dance with both legs at once." "And you say she has a pianoforte?" interposed Lady Adelheid. "Aye, to be sure," continued the old man; "it comed[2] straight from Dresden; a"—("Oh, that's fine!" interrupted the Baroness)—"a beautiful instrument," went on the old man, "but a little weakly; for not long ago, when the organist began to play on it the hymn 'In all Thy works,'[3] he broke it all to pieces, so that"—("Good gracious!" exclaimed both the Baroness and Lady Adelheid)—"so that," went on the old man again, "it had to be taken to R—— to be mended, and cost a lot of money." "But has it come back again?" asked Lady Adelheid impatiently. "Aye, to be sure, my lady, and the steward's lady will reckon it a high honour ——" At this moment the Baron chanced to pass. He looked across at our group rather astonished, and whispered with a sarcastic smile to the Baroness, "So you have to take counsel of Francis again, I see?" The Baroness cast down her eyes blushing, whilst old Francis breaking off terrified, suddenly threw himself into military posture, his head erect, and his arms close and straight down his side. The old aunts came sailing down upon us in their stuff gowns and carried off the Baroness. Lady Adelheid followed her, and I was left alone as if spell-bound. A struggle began to rage within me between my rapturous anticipations of now being able to be near her whom I adored, who completely swayed all my thoughts and feelings, and my sulky ill-humour and annoyance at the Baron, whom I regarded as a barbarous tyrant. If he were not, would the grey-haired old servant have assumed such a slavish attitude?

"Do you hear? Can you see, I say?" cried my great-uncle, tapping me on the shoulder; — we were going upstairs to our own apartments. "Don't force yourself so on the Baroness's attention," he said when we reached the room. "What good can come of it? Leave that to the young fops[4] who like to pay court to ladies; there are plenty of them to do it." I related how it had all come about, and challenged him to say if I had deserved his reproof. His only reply to this, however, was, "Humph! humph!" as he drew on his dressing-gown. Then, having lit his pipe, he took his seat in his easy-chair and began to talk about the adventures of the hunt on the preceding day, bantering me on my bad shots. All was quiet in the castle;

---

[1] A clavichord, a small keyboard instrument with a twangy, tinny sound, rather like a harpsichord

[2] In the German, Hoffmann gives Francis a rural dialect rather analogous to the British Cornish or American hillbilly accents

[3] A "pious but gloomy" hymn from the short-lived 17th century composer Paul Fleming

[4] Vain party boys given to expressive fashions and indulgent lifestyles

all the visitors, both gentlemen and ladies, were busy in their own rooms dressing for the evening. For the musicians with the twanging fiddles, untuned violoncellos, and braying oboes, of whom Lady Adelheid had spoken, were come, and a merrymaking of no less importance than a ball, to be given in the best possible style, was in anticipation. My old uncle, preferring a quiet sleep to such foolish pastimes, stayed in his chamber. I, however, had just finished dressing when there came a light tap at our door, and Francis entered. Smiling in his self-satisfied way, he announced to me that the manichord had just arrived from the land-steward's lady in a sledge, and had been carried into the Baroness's apartments. Lady Adelheid sent her compliments and would I go over at once. It may be conceived how my pulse beat, and also with what a delicious tremor at heart I opened the door of the room in which I was to find her. Lady Adelheid came to meet me with a joyful smile. The Baroness, already in full dress for the ball, was sitting in a meditative attitude beside the mysterious case or box, in which slumbered the music that I was called upon to awaken. When she rose, her beauty shone upon me with such glorious splendour that I stood staring at her unable to utter a word. "Come, Theodore"—(for, according to the kindly custom of the North, which is found again farther south[1], she addressed everybody by his or her Christian name)—"Come, Theodore," she said pleasantly, "here's the instrument come. Heaven grant it be not altogether unworthy of your skill!" As I opened the lid I was greeted by the rattling of a score of broken strings, and when I attempted to strike a chord, the effect was hideous and abominable, for all the strings which were not broken were completely out of tune. "I doubt not our friend the organist has been putting his delicate little hands upon it again," said Lady Adelheid laughing; but the Baroness was very much annoyed and said, "Oh, it really is a slice of bad luck! I am doomed, I see, never to have any pleasure here." I searched in the case of the instrument, and fortunately found some coils of strings, but no tuning-key anywhere. Hence fresh laments. "Any key will do if the ward will fit on the pegs," I explained; then both Lady Adelheid and the Baroness ran backwards and forwards in gay spirits, and before long a whole magazine[2] of bright keys lay before me on the sounding-board.

Then I set to work diligently, and both the ladies assisted me all they could, trying first one peg and then another. At length one of the tiresome keys fitted, and they exclaimed joyfully, "This will do! it will do!" But when I had drawn the first creaking string up to just proper pitch, it suddenly snapped, and the ladies recoiled in alarm. The Baroness, handling the brittle wires with her delicate little fingers, gave me the

---

[1] Namely, in Italy

[2] Stockpile, load

numbers[1] as I wanted them, and carefully held the coil whilst I unrolled it. Suddenly one of them coiled itself up again with a whirr, making the Baroness utter an impatient "Oh!" Lady Adelheid enjoyed a hearty laugh, whilst I pursued the tangled coil to the corner of the room. After we had all united our efforts to extract a perfectly straight string from it, and had tried it again, to our mortification it again broke; but at last — at last we found some good coils; the strings began to hold, and gradually the discordant jangling gave place to pure melodious chords. "Ha! it will go! it will go! The instrument is getting in tune!" exclaimed the Baroness, looking at me with her lovely smile. How quickly did this common interest banish all the strangeness and shyness which the artificial manners of social intercourse impose. A kind of confidential familiarity arose between us, which, burning through me like an electric current, consumed the timorous nervousness and constraint which had lain like ice upon my heart. That peculiar mood of diffused melting sadness which is engendered of such love as mine was had quite left me; and accordingly, when the pianoforte was brought into something like tune, instead of interpreting my deeper feelings in dreamy improvisations, as I had intended, I began with those sweet and charming canzonets which have reached us from the South[2]. During this or the other *Senza di te* (Without thee), or *Sentimi idol mio* (Hear me, my darling), or *Almen se nonpos'io* (At least if I cannot), with numberless *Morir mi sentos* (I feel I am dying), and *Addios* (Farewell), and *O dios!* (O Heaven!), a brighter and brighter brilliancy shone in Seraphina's eyes[3]. She had seated herself close beside me at the instrument; I felt her breath fanning my cheek; and as she placed her arm behind me on the chair-back, a white ribbon, getting disengaged from her beautiful ball-dress, fell across my shoulder[4], where by my singing and Seraphina's soft sighs it was kept in a continual flutter backwards and forwards, like a true love-messenger. It is a wonder how I kept from losing my head.

As I was running my fingers aimlessly over the keys, thinking of a new song, Lady Adelheid, who had been sitting in one of the corners of the room, ran across to us, and, kneeling down before the Baroness, begged her, as she took both her hands and clasped them to her bosom, "Oh, dear Baroness! darling Seraphina! now you must sing too." To this she replied, "Whatever are you thinking about, Adelheid? How could I

---

[1] The strings – of varying width depending on the required note – are catalogued by numbers

[2] Canzonetta (Italian: "little songs") are short vocal songs

[3] Note that he has specifically been tasked to play love songs exclusively, and in particular songs about deep, repressed emotion

[4] Recalling how Marie binds Nutcracker's injured shoulder with a ribbon from her dress

dream of letting our virtuoso[1] friend hear such poor singing as mine?" And she looked so lovely, as, like a shy good child, she cast down her eyes and blushed, timidly contending with the desire to sing. That I too added my entreaties can easily be imagined; nor, upon her making mention of some little Courland *Volkslieder,* or popular songs[2], did I desist from my entreaties until she stretched out her left hand towards the instrument and tried a few notes by way of introduction. I rose to make way for her at the piano, but she would not permit me to do so, asserting that she could not play a single chord, and for that reason, since she would have to sing without accompaniment, her performance would be poor and uncertain. She began in a sweet voice, pure as a bell, that came straight from her heart, and sang a song whose simple melody bore all the characteristics of those *Volkslieder* which proceed from the lips with such a lustrous brightness, so to speak, that we cannot help perceiving in the glad light which surrounds us our own higher poetic nature. There lies a mysterious charm in the insignificant words of the text which converts them into a hieroglyphic scroll representative of the unutterable emotions which throng our hearts. Who does not know that Spanish canzonet the substance of which is in words little more than, *"With my maiden I embarked on the sea; a storm came on, and my timid maiden was tossed up and down: nay, I will never again embark on the sea with my maiden?*[3]*"* And the Baroness's little song contained nothing more than, *"Lately I was dancing with my sweetheart at a wedding; a flower fell out of my hair; he picked it up and gave it me, and said, 'When, sweetheart mine, shall we go to a wedding again?'"* When, on her beginning the second verse of the song, I played an arpeggio[4] accompaniment, and further when, in the inspiration which now took possession of me, I at once stole from the Baroness's own lips the melodies of the other songs she sang, I doubtless appeared in her eyes, and in those of the Lady Adelheid, to be one of the greatest of masters in the art of music, for they overwhelmed me with enthusiastic praise. The lights and illuminations from the ball-room, situated in one of the wings of the castle, now shone across into the Baroness's chamber, whilst a discordant bleating of trumpets and French horns[5] announced that it was time to gather for the ball. "Oh, now I must go," said the Baroness. I started up from the pianoforte. "You have

---

[1] An expert musician renowned for their style and technique

[2] German folk songs (equivalent to Britain's "Greensleeves," "Loch Lomond," and "Danny Boy," or America's "Daisy, Daisy," "You Are My Sunshine," or "Shenandoah")

[3] Me, for one: I can't find any references to such a song

[4] Ascending and descending successions of notes which creating a rolling, flowing sound

[5] A large, curled brass horn with a flared bell, originally used for signaling in hunting parties

afforded me a delightful hour; these have been the pleasantest moments I have ever spent in R— sitten," she added, offering me her hand; and as in the extreme intoxication of delight I pressed it to my lips, I felt her fingers close upon my hand with a sudden convulsive tremor. I do not know how I managed to reach my uncle's chamber, and still less how I got into the ball-room. There was a certain Gascon[1] who was afraid to go into battle since he was all heart, and every wound would be fatal to him. I might be compared to him; and so might everybody else who is in the same mood that I was in; every touch was then fatal. The Baroness's hand — her tremulous fingers — had affected me like a poisoned arrow; my blood was burning in my veins.

ᨊ

On the following morning my old uncle, without asking any direct questions, had soon drawn from me a full account of the hour I had spent in the Baroness's society, and I was not a little abashed when the smile vanished from his lips and the jocular note from his words, and he grew serious all at once, saying, "Cousin, I beg you will resist this folly which is taking such a powerful hold upon you. Let me tell you that your present conduct, as harmless as it now appears, may lead to the most terrible consequences. In your thoughtless fatuity[2] you are standing on a thin crust of ice, which may break under you ere you are aware of it, and let you in with a plunge. I shall take good care not to hold you fast by the coat-tails, for I know you will scramble out again pretty quick, and then, when you are lying sick unto death, you will say, 'I got this little bit of a cold in a dream.' But I warn you that a malignant fever will gnaw at your vitals, and years will pass before you recover yourself, and are a man again. The deuce take your music if you can put it to no better use than to cozen sentimental young women out of their quiet peace of mind." "But," I began, interrupting the old gentleman, "but have I ever thought of insinuating myself as the Baroness's lover?" "You puppy!" cried the old gentleman, "if I thought so I would pitch you out of this window." At this juncture the Baron entered, and put an end to the painful conversation; and the business to which I now had to turn my attention brought me back from my love-sick reveries, in which I saw and thought of nothing but Seraphina.

---

[1] Possibly a reference to the 1614 novel, "The Adventures of Baron de Faenteste," by Agrippa d'Aubigne. Before the advent of literature's most famous Gascon, Dumas' musketeer D'Artagnan, Gascons – residents of the French province of Gascony, on the border with Spain – were caricatured as braggish, impulsive, silly, and overly emotional

[2] Stupidity, impulsivity, idiocy

In general society the Baroness only occasionally interchanged a few friendly words with me; but hardly an evening passed in which a secret message was not brought to me from Lady Adelheid, summoning me to Seraphina. It soon came to pass that our music alternated with conversations on divers topics. Whenever I and Seraphina began to get too absorbed in sentimental dreams and vague aspirations, the Lady Adelheid, though now hardly young enough to be so naïve and droll as she once was, yet intervened with all sorts of merry and somewhat chaotic nonsense. From several hints she let fall, I soon discovered that the Baroness really had something preying upon her mind, even as I thought I had read in her eyes the very first moment I saw her; and I clearly discerned the hostile influence of the apparition of the castle. Something terrible had happened or was to happen. Although I was often strongly impelled to tell Seraphina in what way I had come in contact with the invisible enemy, and how my old uncle had banished him, undoubtedly for ever, I yet felt my tongue fettered by a hesitation which was inexplicable to myself even, whenever I opened my mouth to speak.

One day the Baroness failed to appear at the dinner table; it was said that she was a little unwell, and could not leave her room. Sympathetic inquiries were addressed to the Baron as to whether her illness was of a grave nature. He smiled in a very disagreeable way, in fact, it was almost like bitter irony, and said, "Nothing more than a slight catarrh[1], which she has got from our blustering sea-breezes. They can't tolerate any sweet voices; the only sounds they will endure are the hoarse 'Halloos' of the chase." At these words the Baron hurled a keen searching look at me across the table, for I sat obliquely opposite to him. He had not spoken to his neighbour, but to me. Lady Adelheid, who sat beside me, blushed a scarlet red. Fixing her eyes upon the plate in front of her, and scribbling about on it with her fork, she whispered, "And yet you must see Seraphina today; your sweet songs shall today also bring soothing and comfort to her poor heart." Adelheid addressed these words to me; but at this moment it struck me that I was almost apparently entangled in a base and forbidden intrigue with the Baroness, which could only end in some terrible crime. My old uncle's warning fell heavily upon my heart. What should I do? Not see her again? That was impossible so long as I remained in the castle; and even if I might leave the castle and return to K— —[2] I had not the will to do it Oh! I felt only too deeply that I was not strong enough to shake myself out of this dream, which was mocking one with delusive hopes of happiness. Adelheid I almost regarded in the light of a common go-between; I would despise her, and yet, upon second

---

[1] A cold defined by lots of mucus

[2] Likely Königsberg (modern Kaliningrad). Now in Russian territory between Lithuania and Poland, this city was once the capital of Prussia and remained an important German city until its loss to Russia in World War II

thoughts, I could not help being ashamed of my folly. Had anything ever happened during those blissful evening hours which could in the least degree lead to any nearer relation with Seraphina than was permissible by propriety and morality? How dare I let the thought enter my mind that the Baroness would ever entertain any warm feeling for me? And yet I was convinced of the danger of my situation.

We broke up from dinner earlier than usual, in order to go again after some wolves which had been seen in the fir-wood close by the castle. A little hunting was just the thing I wanted in the excited frame of mind in which I then was. I expressed to my uncle my resolve to accompany the party; he gave me an approving smile and said, "That's right; I am glad you are going out with them for once. I shall stay at home, so you can take my firelock[1] with you, and buckle my whinger[2] round your waist; in case of need it is a good and trusty weapon, if you only keep your presence of mind." That part of the wood in which the wolves were supposed to lie was surrounded by the huntsmen. It was bitterly cold; the wind howled through the firs, and drove the light snow-flakes right in my face, so that when at length it came on to be dusk I could scarcely see six paces before me. Quite benumbed by the cold, I left the place that had been assigned
to me and sought shelter deeper in the wood. There, leaning against a tree, with my firelock under my arm, I forgot the wolf-hunt entirely; my thoughts had travelled back to Seraphina's cosy room. After a time shots were heard in the far distance; but at the same moment there was a rustling in the reed-bank, and I saw not ten paces from me a huge wolf about to run past me. I took aim, and fired, but missed. The brute sprang towards me with glaring eyes; I should have been lost had I not had sufficient presence of mind to draw my hunting-knife, and, just as the brute was flying at me, to drive it deep into his throat, so that the blood spurted out over my hand and arm. One of the Baron's keepers, who had stood not far from me, came running up with a loud shout, and at his repeated "Halloo!" all the rest soon gathered round us. The Baron hastened up to me, saying, "For God's sake, you are bleeding — you are bleeding. Are you wounded?" I assured him that I was not. Then he turned to the keeper[3] who had stood nearest to me, and overwhelmed him with reproaches for not having shot after me when I missed. And notwithstanding that the man maintained this to have been perfectly impossible, since in the very same moment the wolf had rushed upon me, and any shot would have been at the risk of hitting me, the Baron

---

[1] Flintlock musket

[2] A long knife

[3] Gamekeeper – a servant who helps manage an estate's hunting and fishing gear, assists hunters with loading muskets, and is expected to have a good sense of where to look for game

persisted in saying that he ought to have taken especial care of me as a less experienced hunter. Meanwhile the keepers had lifted up the dead animal; it was one of the largest that had been seen for a long time; and everybody admired my courage and resolution, although to myself what I had done appeared quite natural I had not for a moment thought of the danger I had run. The Baron in particular seemed to take very great interest in the matter; I thought he would never be done asking me whether, though I was not wounded by the brute, I did not fear the ill effects that would follow from the fright As we went back to the castle, the Baron took me by the arm like a friend, and I had to give my firelock to a keeper to carry. He still continued to talk about my heroic deed, so that eventually I came to believe in my own heroism, and lost all my constraint and embarrassment, and felt that I had established myself in the Baron's eyes as a man of courage and uncommon resolution. The schoolboy had passed his examination successfully, was now no longer a schoolboy, and all the submissive nervousness of the schoolboy had left him. I now conceived I had earned a right to try and gain Seraphina's favour. Everybody knows of course what ridiculous combinations the fancy of a love-sick youth is capable of. In the castle, over the smoking punchbowl, by the fireside, I was the hero of the hour. Besides myself the Baron was the only one of the party who had killed a wolf — also a formidable one; the rest had to be content with ascribing their bad shots to the weather and the darkness, and with relating thrilling stories of their former exploits in hunting and the dangers they had escaped. I thought, too, that I might reap an especial share of praise and admiration from my old uncle as well; and so, with a view to this end, I related to him my adventure at pretty considerable length, nor did I forget to paint the savage brute's wild and bloodthirsty appearance in very startling colours. The old gentleman, however, only laughed in my face and said, "God is powerful even in the weak[1]."

Tired of drinking and of the company, I was going quietly along the corridor towards the justice-hall when I saw a figure with a light slip in before me. On entering the hall I saw it was Lady Adelheid. "This is the way we have to wander about like ghosts or sleep-walkers in order to catch you, my brave slayer of wolves," she whispered, taking my arm. The words "ghosts" and "sleep-walkers," pronounced in the place where we were, fell like lead upon my heart; they immediately brought to my recollection the ghostly apparitions of those two awful nights. As then, so now, the wind came howling in from the sea in deep organ-like cadences, rattling the oriel windows again and again and whistling fearfully through them, whilst the moon cast her pale gleams exactly upon the mysterious part of the wall where the scratching had been heard. I fancied I

---

[1] Another way of saying "even a blind squirrel finds a nut every now and then," or "even a broken clock is right twice a day"

discerned stains of blood upon it. Doubtless Lady Adelheid, who still had hold of my hand, must have felt the cold icy shiver which ran through me. "What's the matter with you?" she whispered softly; "what's the matter with you? You are as cold as marble. Come, I will call you back into life. Do you know how very impatient the Baroness is to see you? And until she does see you she will not believe that the ugly wolf has not really bitten you. She is in a terrible state of anxiety about you. Why, my friend — oh! how have you awakened this interest in the little Seraphina? I have never seen her like this. Ah! — so now the pulse is beginning to prickle; see how quickly the dead man comes to life! Well, come along — but softly, still! Come, we must go to the little Baroness." I suffered myself to be led away in silence. The way in which Adelheid spoke of the Baroness seemed to me undignified, and the innuendo of an understanding between us[1] positively shameful. When I entered the room along with Adelheid, Seraphina, with a low-breathed "Oh!" advanced three or four paces quickly to meet me; but then, as if recollecting herself, she stood still in the middle of the room. I ventured to take her hand and press it to my lips. Allowing it to rest in mine, she asked, "But, for Heaven's sake! is it your business to meddle with wolves? Don't you know that the fabulous days of Orpheus and Amphion[2] are long past, and that wild beasts have quite lost all respect for even the most admirable of singers?" But this gleeful turn, by which the Baroness at once effectually guarded against all misinterpretation of her warm interest in me, I was put immediately into the proper key and the proper mood. Why I did not take my usual place at the pianoforte I cannot explain, even to myself, nor why I sat down beside the Baroness on the sofa. Her question, "And what were you doing then to get into danger?" was an indication of our tacit agreement that conversation, not music, was to engage our attention for that evening. After I had narrated my adventure in the wood, and mentioned the warm interest which the Baron had taken in it, delicately hinting that I had not thought him capable of so much feeling, the Baroness began in a tender and almost melancholy tone, "Oh! how violent and rude you must think the Baron; but I assure you it is only whilst we are living within these gloomy, ghostly walls, and during the time there is hunting going on in the dismal fir-forests, that his character completely changes, at least his outward behaviour does. What principally disquiets him in this unpleasant way is the thought, which constantly haunts him, that something terrible will happen here. And that undoubtedly accounts for the fact of his being so greatly agitated by your adventure, which fortunately has had no ill consequences. He won't have the meanest[3] of

---

[1] That is to say, an understood mutual attraction bent on consumation

[2] Two heroes of Greek mythology famous for their ability to lull animals into submission through their beautiful singing

[3] Least valuable

his servants exposed to danger, if he knows it, still less a new-won friend whom he has come to like; and I am perfectly certain that Gottlieb, whom he blames for having left you in the lurch, will be punished; even if he escapes being locked up in a dungeon, he will yet have to suffer the punishment, so mortifying to a hunter, of going out the next time there is a hunt with only a club in his hand instead of a rifle. The circumstance that hunts like those which are held here are always attended with danger, and the fact that the Baron, though always fearing some sad accident, is yet so fond of hunting that he cannot desist from provoking the demon of mischief[1], make his existence here a kind of conflict, the ill effects of which I also have to feel. Many queer stories are current about his ancestor who established the entail; and I know myself that there is some dark family secret locked within these walls like a horrible ghost which drives away the owners, and makes it impossible for them to bear with it longer than a few weeks at a time — and that only amid a tumult of jovial guests. But I— Oh! how lonely I am in the midst of this noisy, merry company! And how the ghostly influences which breathe upon me from the walls stir and excite my very heart! You, my dear friend, have given me, through your musical skill, the first cheerful moments I have spent here. How can I thank you sufficiently for your kindness!" I kissed the hand she offered to me, saying, that even on the very first day, or rather during the very first night, I had experienced the ghostliness of the place in all its horrors. The Baroness fixed her staring eyes upon my face, as I went on to describe the ghostly character of the building, discernible everywhere throughout the castle, particularly in the decorations of the justice-hall, and to speak of the roaring of the wind from the sea, &c. Possibly my voice and my expressions indicated that I had something more in my mind than what I said; at any rate when I concluded, the Baroness cried vehemently, "No, no; something dreadful has happened to you in that hall, which I never enter without shuddering. I beg you — pray, pray, tell me all."

Seraphina's face had grown deadly pale; and I saw plainly that it would be more advisable to give her a faithful account of all that I had experienced than to leave her excited imagination to conjure up some apparition that might perhaps, in a way I could not foresee, be far more horrible than what I had actually encountered. As she listened to me her fear and strained anxiety increased from moment to moment; and when I mentioned the scratching on the wall she screamed, "It's horrible! Yes, yes, it's in that wall that the awful secret is concealed!" But as I went on to describe with what spiritual power and superiority of will my old uncle had banished the ghost, she sighed deeply, as though she had shaken off a heavy burden that had weighed oppressively upon her. She leaned back in

---

[1] Exactly like Theodor, who cannot resist the appeal of Seraphina, in spite of the looming danger

the sofa and held her hands before her face. Now I first noticed that Adelheid had left us. A considerable pause ensued, and as Seraphina still continued silent, I softly rose, and going to the pianoforte, endeavoured in swelling chords to invoke the bright spirits of consolation to come and deliver Seraphina from the dark influence to which my narration had subjected her. Then I soon began to sing as softly as I was able one of the Abbé Steffani's[1] canzonas. The melancholy strains of the *Ochi, perchè piangete* (O eyes, why weep you?) roused Seraphina out of her reverie, and she listened to me with a gentle smile upon her face, and bright pearl-like tears in her eyes. How am I to account for it that I kneeled down before her, that she bent over towards me, that I threw my arms about her, that a long ardent kiss was imprinted on my lips? How am I to account for it that I did not lose my senses when she drew me softly towards her, how that I tore myself from her arms, and, quickly rising to my feet, hurried to the pianoforte? Turning from me, the Baroness took a few steps towards the window, then she turned round again and approached me with an air of almost proud dignity, which was not at all usual with her. Looking me straight in the face, she said, "Your uncle is the most worthy old man I know; he is the guardian-angel of our family. May he include me in his pious prayers!" I was unable to utter a word; the subtle poison that I had imbibed with her kiss burned and boiled in every pulse and nerve. Lady Adelheid came in. The violence of my inward conflict burst out at length in a passionate flood of tears, which I was unable to repress. Adelheid looked at me with wonder and smiled dubiously; — I could have murdered her. The Baroness gave me her hand, and said with inexpressible gentleness, "Farewell, my dear friend. Fare you right well; and remember that nobody perhaps has ever understood your music better than I have. Oh! these notes! they will echo long, long in my heart." I forced myself to utter a few stupid, disconnected words, and hurried up to my uncle's room. The old gentleman had already gone to bed. I stayed in the hall, and falling upon my knees, I wept aloud; I called upon my beloved by name, I gave myself up completely and regardlessly to all the absurd folly of a love-sick lunatic, until at last the extravagant noise I made awoke my uncle. But his loud call, "Cousin, I believe you have gone cranky, or else you're having another tussle with a wolf[2]. Be off to bed with you if you will be so very kind"— these words compelled me to enter his room, where I got into bed with the fixed resolve to dream only of Seraphina.

ↄ?

[1] Agostino Steffani was an Italian priest and composer who flourished in the early 18th century

[2] The wolf becomes a metaphor for an internal temptation – a monster from within

It would be somewhere past midnight when I thought I heard distant voices, a running backwards and forwards, and an opening and banging of doors — for I had not yet fallen asleep. I listened attentively; I heard footsteps approaching the corridor; the hall door was opened, and soon there came a knock at our door. "Who is there?" I cried. A voice from without answered, "Herr Justitiarius, Herr Justitiarius, wake up, wake up!" I recognised Francis's voice, and as I asked, "Is the castle on fire?" the old gentleman woke up in his turn and asked, "Where — where is there a fire? Is it that cursed apparition again? where is it?" "Oh! please get up, Herr Justitiarius," said Francis, "Please get up; the Baron wants you." "What does the Baron want me for?" inquired my uncle further; "what does he want me for at this time of night? does he not know that all law business goes to bed along with the lawyer, and sleeps as soundly as he does?" "Oh!" cried Francis, now anxiously; "please, Herr Justitiarius, good sir, please get up. My lady the Baroness is dying." I started up with a cry of dismay. "Open the door for Francis," said the old gentleman to me. I stumbled about the room almost distracted, and could find neither door nor lock; my uncle had to come and help me. Francis came in, his face pale and troubled, and lit the candles. We had scarcely thrown on our clothes when we heard the Baron calling in the hall, "Can I speak to you, good V——?" "But what have you dressed for, cousin? the Baron only wanted me," asked the old gentleman, on the point of going out. "I must go down — I must see her and then die," I replied tragically, and as if my heart were rent by hopeless grief. "Ay, just so; you are right, cousin," he said, banging the door to in my face, so that the hinges creaked, and locking it on the outside. At the first moment, deeply incensed at this restraint, I thought of bursting the door open; but quickly reflecting that this would entail the disagreeable consequences of a piece of outrageous insanity, I resolved to await the old gentleman's return; then however, let the cost be what it might, I would escape his watchfulness. I heard him talking vehemently with the Baron, and several times distinguished my own name, but could not make out anything further. Every moment my position grew more intolerable. At length I heard that some one brought a message to the Baron, who immediately hurried off. My old uncle entered the room again. "She is dead!" I cried, running towards him, "And you are a stupid fool," he interrupted coolly; then he laid hold upon me and forced me into a chair. "I must go down," I cried, "I must go down and see her, even though it cost me my life." "Do so, good cousin," said he, locking the door, taking out the key, and putting it in his pocket. I now flew into a perfectly frantic rage; stretching out my hand towards the rifle, I screamed, "If you don't instantly open the door I will send this bullet through my brains[1]." Then the old gentleman planted himself immediately in front of me, and fixing his keen piercing eyes upon me said, "Boy, do you think you can frighten me with your idle threats? Do you think I should set much value on your life if you can go and throw it away in childish folly like a broken plaything? What have you to do with the Baron's wife? who has given you the right to insinuate yourself, like a tiresome puppy, where you have no claim to be, and where you are not wanted? do you wish to go and act the love-sick swain at the solemn hour of death?" I sank back in my chair utterly confounded After a while the old gentleman went on more gently, "And now let me tell you that this pretended illness of the Baroness is in all probability nothing. Lady Adelheid always loses her head at the least little thing. If a rain-drop falls upon her nose, she screams, 'What fearful weather it is!' Unfortunately the noise penetrated to the old aunts, and they, in the midst of unseasonable floods of tears, put in an appearance armed with an entire arsenal of strengthening drops, elixirs of life, and the deuce knows what. A sharp fainting-fit"—— The old gentleman checked himself; doubtless he observed the struggle that was going on within me. He took a few turns through the room; then again planting himself in front of me, he had a good hearty laugh and said, "Cousin, cousin, what nonsensical folly have you now got in your head? Ah well! I suppose it can't be helped; the devil is to play his pretty games here in divers sorts of ways. You have tumbled very nicely into his clutches, and now he's making you dance to a sweet tune," He again took a few turns up and down, and again went on, "It's no use to think of sleep now; and it occurred to me that we might have a pipe, and so spend the few hours that are left of the darkness and the night." With these words he took a clay pipe from the cupboard, and proceeded to fill it slowly and carefully, humming a song to himself; then he rummaged about amongst a heap of papers, until he found a sheet, which he picked out and rolled into a spill and lighted. Blowing the tobacco-smoke from him in thick clouds, he said, speaking between his teeth, "Well, cousin, what was that story about the wolf?"

I know not how it was, but this calm, quiet behaviour of the old gentleman operated strangely upon me. I seemed to be no longer in R—sitten, and the Baroness was so far, far distant from me that I could only reach her on the wings of thought. The old gentleman's last question, however, annoyed me. "But do you find my hunting exploit so amusing?" I broke in — "so well fitted for banter?" "By no means," he rejoined, "by no means, cousin mine; but you've no idea what a comical face such a

---

[1] Theodor's character is largely modelled on Goethe's emotionally wild lawyer-poet Werther – protagonist of the novel "The Sorrows of Young Werther" – who shoots himself in the head the night after he finally bears his soul to his married friend Lotte, with whom he is passionately in love in spite of his friendship with her down-to-earth nobleman husband

whipper-snapper as you cuts, and how ludicrously he acts as well, when Providence for once in a while honours him by putting him in the way to meet with something out of the usual run of things. I once had a college friend who was a quiet, sober fellow, and always on good terms with himself. By accident he became entangled in an affair of honour[1] — I say by accident, because he himself was never in any way aggressive; and although most of the fellows looked upon him as a poor thing, as a poltroon[2], he yet showed so much firm and resolute courage in this affair as greatly to excite everybody's admiration. But from that time onwards he was also completely changed. The sober and industrious youth became a bragging, insufferable bully. He was always drinking and rioting, and fighting about all sorts of childish trifles, until he was run through in a duel by the Senior[3] of an exclusive corps. I merely tell you the story, cousin; you are at liberty to think what you please about it But to return to the Baroness and her illness"—— At this moment light footsteps were heard in the hall; I fancied, too, there was an unearthly moaning in the air. "She is dead!" the thought shot through me like a fatal flash of lightning. The old gentleman quickly rose to his feet and called out, "Francis, Francis!" "Yes, my good Herr Justitiarius," he replied from without. "Francis," went on my uncle, "rake the fire together a bit in the grate, and if you can manage it, you had better make us a good cup or two of tea." "It is devilish cold," and he turned to me, "and I think we had better go and sit round the fire and talk a little." He opened the door, and I followed him mechanically. "How are things going on below?" he asked. "Oh!" replied Francis; "there was not much the matter. The Lady Baroness is all right again, and ascribes her bit of a fainting-fit to a bad dream." I was going to break out into an extravagant manifestation of joy and gladness, but a stern glance from my uncle kept me quiet "And yet, after all, I think it would be better if we lay down for an hour or two. You need not mind about the tea, Francis." "As you think well, Herr Justitiarius," replied Francis, and he left the room with the wish that we might have a good night's rest, albeit the cocks were already crowing. "See here, cousin," said the old gentleman, knocking the ashes out of his pipe on the grate, "I think, cousin, that it's a very good thing no harm has happened to you either from wolves or from loaded rifles." I now saw things in the right light, and was ashamed at myself to have thus given the old gentleman good grounds for treating me like a spoiled child.

---

[1] A duel

[2] Utter coward

[3] German universities had regional clubs called Landmannschafts where students from certain areas of the country would get together and enjoy regional music, food, dancing, and traditions. They also elected officers to oversee their funds and events, the chief of whom was the "Senior"

Next morning he said to me, "Be so good as to step down, good cousin, and inquire how the Baroness is. You need only ask for Lady Adelheid; she will supply you with a full budget[1], I have no doubt" You may imagine how eagerly I hastened downstairs. But just as I was about to give a gentle knock at the door of the Baroness's anteroom, the Baron came hurriedly out of the same. He stood still in astonishment, and scrutinised me with a gloomy searching look. "What do you want here?" burst from his lips. Notwithstanding that my heart beat, I controlled myself and replied in a firm tone, "To inquire on my uncle's behalf how my lady, the Baroness, is?" "Oh! it was nothing — one of her usual nervous attacks. She is now having a quiet sleep, and will, I am sure, make her appearance at the dinner-table quite well and cheerful. Tell him that — tell him that." This the Baron said with a certain degree of passionate vehemence, which seemed to me to imply that he was more concerned about the Baroness than he was willing to show. I turned to go back to my uncle, when the Baron suddenly seized my arm and said, whilst his eyes flashed fire, "I have a word or two to say to you, young man." Here I saw the deeply injured husband before me, and feared there would be a scene which would perhaps end ignominiously for me. I was unarmed; but at that moment I remembered I had in my pocket the ingeniously-made hunting-knife which my uncle had presented to me after we got to R—sitten. I now followed the Baron, who led the way rapidly, with the determination not even to spare his life if I ran any risk of being treated dishonourably.

We entered the Baron's own room, the door of which he locked behind him. Now he began to pace restlessly backwards and forwards, with his arms folded one over the other; then he stopped in front of me and repeated, "I have a word or two to say to you, young man." I had wound myself up to a pitch of most daring courage, and I replied, raising my voice, "I hope they will be words which I may hear without resentment[2]." He stared hard at me in astonishment, as though he had failed to understand me. Then, fixing his eyes gloomily upon the floor, he threw his arms behind his back, and again began to stride up and down the room. He took down a rifle and put the ramrod down the barrel to see whether it were loaded or not[3]. My blood boiled in my veins; grasping my

[1] List of details

[2] He is implying that the Baron should be careful not to be offensive with his language if he doesn't want to be challenged to a duel

[3] The ramrod is a steel rod which is used to pack gunpowder, wadding, and a bullet tightly into the bottom of the barrel. It is also exactly the same length as the barrel, so if it is slid inside of it and appears to be flush with the muzzle, the rifle is unloaded; if the tip of it pokes out two inches or so, however, this means that a charge is sitting in the rifle's belly, preventing the ramrod from going in all the way

knife, I stepped close up to him, so as to make it impossible for him to take aim at me. "That's a handsome weapon," he said, replacing the rifle in the corner. I retired a few paces, the Baron following me. Slapping me on the shoulder, perhaps a little more violently than was necessary, he said, "I daresay I seem to you, Theodore, to be excited and irritable; and I really am so, owing to the anxieties of a sleepless night. My wife's nervous attack was not in the least dangerous; that I now see plainly. But here — here in this castle, which is haunted by an evil spirit, I always dread something terrible happening; and then it's the first time she has been ill here. And you — you alone were to blame for it." "How that can possibly be I have not the slightest conception," I replied calmly. "I wish," continued the Baron, "I wish that damned piece of mischief, my steward's wife's instrument, were chopped up into a thousand pieces, and that you — but no, no; it was to be so, it was inevitably to be so, and I alone am to blame for all. I ought to have told you, the moment you began to play music in my wife's room, of the whole state of the case, and to have informed you of my wife's temper of mind." I was about to speak; "Let me go on," said the Baron, "I must prevent your forming any rash judgment. You probably regard me as an uncultivated fellow, averse to the arts; but I am not so by any means. There is a particular consideration, however, based upon deep conviction, which constrains me to forbid the introduction here as far as possible of such music as can powerfully affect any person's mind, and to this I of course am no exception. Know that my wife suffers from a morbid excitability, which will finally destroy all the happiness of her life. Within these strange walls she is never quit of that strained over-excited condition, which at other times occurs but temporarily, and then generally as the forerunner of a serious illness. You will ask me, and quite reasonably too, why I do not spare my delicate wife the necessity of coming to live in this weird castle, and mix amongst the wild confusion of a hunting-party. Well, call it weakness — be it so; in a word, I cannot bring myself to leave her behind. I should be tortured by a thousand fears, and quite incapable of any serious business, for I am perfectly sure that I should be haunted everywhere, in the justice-hall as well as in the forest, by the most horrid ideas of all kinds of fatal mischief happening to her. And, on the other hand, I believe that the sort of life led here cannot fail to operate upon the weakly woman like strengthening chalybeate waters[1]. By my soul, the sea-breezes, sweeping keenly after their peculiar fashion through the fir-trees, and the deep baying of the hounds, and the merry ringing notes of our hunting-horns must get the better of all your sickly languishing sentimentalisings at the piano, which no man ought play in that way. I tell you, you are deliberately torturing my wife to death." These words he uttered with great emphasis, whilst his eyes flashed with a restless fire. The blood mounted to my head; I made a

[1] Mineral water

violent gesture against the Baron with my hand; I was about to speak, but he cut me short "I know what you are going to say," he began, "I know what you are going to say, and I repeat that you are going the right road to kill my wife. But that you intended this I cannot of course for a moment maintain; and yet you will understand that I must put a stop to the thing. In short, by your playing and singing you work her up to a high pitch of excitement, and then, when she drifts without anchor and rudder on the boundless sea of dreams and visions and vague aspirations which your music, like some vile charm, has summoned into existence, you plunge her down into the depths of horror with a tale about a fearful apparition which you say came and played pranks with you up in the justice-hall. Your great-uncle has told me everything; but, pray, repeat to me all you saw, or did not see, heard, felt, divined by instinct."

I braced myself up and narrated calmly how everything had happened from beginning to end, the Baron merely interposing at intervals a few words expressive of his astonishment. When I came to the part where my old uncle had met the ghost with trustful courage and had exorcised him with a few powerful words, the Baron clasped his hands, raised them folded towards Heaven, and said with deep emotion, "Yes, he is the guardian-angel of the family. His mortal remains shall rest in the vault of my ancestors." When I finished my narration, the Baron murmured to himself, "Daniel, Daniel, what are you doing here at this hour?" as he folded his arms and strode up and down the room. "And was that all, Herr Baron?" I asked, making a movement as though I would retire. Starting up as if out of a dream, the Baron took me kindly by the hand and said, "Yes, my good friend, my wife, whom you have dealt so hardly by without intending it — you must cure her again; you alone can do so." I felt I was blushing, and had I stood opposite a mirror should undoubtedly have seen in it a very blank and absurd face. The Baron seemed to exult in my embarrassment; he kept his eyes fixed intently upon my face, smiling with perfectly galling irony. "How in the world can I cure her?" I managed to stammer out at length with an effort "Well," he said, interrupting me, "you have no dangerous patient to deal with at any rate. I now make an express claim upon your skill. Since the Baroness has been drawn into the enchanted circle of your music, it would be both foolish and cruel to drag her out of it all of a sudden. Go on with your music therefore. You will always be welcome during the evening hours in my wife's apartments. But gradually select a more energetic kind of music, and effect a clever alternation of the cheerful sort with the serious; and above all things, repeat your story of the fearful ghost very very often. The Baroness will grow familiar with it; she will forget that a ghost haunts this castle; and the story will have no stronger effect upon her than any other tale of enchantment which is put before her in a romance[1] or a ghost-story book. Pray, do this, my good friend." With these words the Baron left me. I went away. I felt as if I were annihilated, to be thus humiliated to the level of a foolish and insignificant child. Fool that I was to suppose that jealousy was stirring his heart! He himself sends me to Seraphina; he sees in me only the blind instrument which, after he has made use of it, he can throw away if he thinks well. A few minutes previously I had really feared the Baron; deep down within my heart lurked the consciousness of guilt; but it was a consciousness which allowed me to feel distinctly the beauty of the higher life for which I was ripe. Now all had disappeared in the blackness of night; and I saw only the stupid boy who in childish obstinacy had persisted in taking the paper crown which he had put on his hot temples for a real golden one. I hurried away to my uncle, who was waiting for me. "Well, cousin, why have you been so long? Where have you been staying?" he cried as soon as he saw me. "I have been having some words with the Baron!" I quickly replied, carelessly and in a low voice, without being able to look at the old gentleman. "God damn it all," said he, feigning astonishment "Good gracious, boy! that's just what I thought. I suppose the Baron has challenged you[2], cousin?" The ringing peal of laughter which the old gentleman immediately afterwards broke out into taught me that this time too, as always, he had seen me through and through. I bit my lip, and durst not speak a word, for I knew very well that it would only be the signal for the old gentleman to overwhelm me beneath the torrent of teasing which was already hovering on the tip of his tongue.

The Baroness appeared at the dinner-table in an elegant morning-robe, the dazzling whiteness of which exceeded that of fresh-fallen snow. She looked worn and low-spirited; but she began to speak in her soft and melodious accents, and on raising her dark eyes there shone a sweet and yearning look full of aspiration in their voluptuous glow, and a fugitive blush flitted across her lily-white cheeks. She was more beautiful than ever. But who can fathom the follies of a young man who has got too hot blood in his head and heart? The bitter pique which the Baron had stirred up within me I transferred to the Baroness. The entire business seemed to me like a foul mystification; and I would now show that I was possessed of alarmingly good common-sense and also of extraordinary sagacity. Like a petulant child, I shunned the Baroness and escaped Adelheid when she pursued me, and found a place where I wished, right at the bottom end of the table between the two officers, with whom I began to carouse right merrily. We kept our glasses going gaily during dessert, and I was, as so frequently is the case in moods like mine, extremely noisy and loud in my

---

[1] Story of fantasy and adventure (e.g., King Arthur, Sinbad the Sailor, St. George and the Dragon)

[2] ...to a duel

joviality. A servant brought me a plate with some bonbons on it, with the words, "From Lady Adelheid." I took them; and observed on one of them, scribbled in pencil, "and Seraphina." My blood coursed tumultuously in my veins. I sent a glance in Adelheid's direction, which she met with a most sly and archly cunning look; and taking her glass in her hand, she gave me a slight nod. Almost mechanically I murmured to myself, "Seraphina!" then taking up my glass in my turn, I drained it at a single draught. My glance fell across in her direction; I perceived that she also had drunk at the very same moment and was setting down her glass. Our eyes met, and a malignant demon whispered in my ear, "Unhappy wretch, she does love you!" One of the guests now rose, and, in conformity with the custom of the North, proposed the health of the lady of the house. Our glasses rang in the midst of a tumult of joy. My heart was torn with rapture and despair; the wine burned like fire within me; everything spun round in circles; I felt as if I must hasten and throw myself at her feet and there sigh out my life. "What's the matter with you, my friend?" asked my neighbour, thus recalling me to myself; but Seraphina had left the hall. We rose from the table. I was making for the door, but Adelheid held me fast, and began to talk about divers matters; I neither heard nor understood a single word. She grasped both my hands and, laughing, shouted something in my ear. I remained dumb and motionless, as though affected by catalepsy. All I remember is that I finally took a glass of liqueur out of Adelheid's hand in a mechanical way and drank it off, and then I recollect being alone in a window, and after that I rushed out of the hall, down the stairs, and ran out into the wood. The snow was falling in thick flakes; the fir-trees were moaning as they waved to and fro in the wind. Like a maniac I ran round and round in wide circles, laughing and screaming loudly, "Look, look and see. Aha! Aha! The devil is having a fine dance with the boy who thought he would taste of strictly forbidden fruit!" Who can tell what would have been the end of my mad prank if I had not heard my name called loudly from the outside of the wood? The storm had abated; the moon shone out brightly through the broken clouds; I heard dogs barking, and perceived a dark figure approaching me. It was the old man Francis. "Why, why, my good Herr Theodore," he began, "you have quite lost your way in the rough snow-storm. The Herr Justitiarius is awaiting you with much impatience." I followed the old man in silence. I found my great-uncle working in the justice-hall. "You have done well," he cried, on seeing me, "you have done a very wise thing to go out in the open air a little and get cool. But don't drink quite so much wine; you are far too young, and it's not good for you." I did not utter a word in reply, and also took my place at the table in silence. "But now tell me, good cousin, what it was the Baron really wanted you for?" I told him all, and concluded by stating that I would not lend myself for the doubtful cure which the Baron had proposed. "And it would not be practicable," the old gentleman interrupted, "for tomorrow morning early we set off home, cousin." And so it was that I never saw Seraphina again.

As soon as we arrived in K—— my old uncle complained that he felt the effects of the wearying journey this time more than ever. His moody silence, broken only by violent outbreaks of the worst possible ill-humour, announced the return of his attacks of gout. One day I was suddenly called in; I found the old gentleman confined to his bed and unable to speak, suffering from a paralytic stroke. He held a letter in his hand, which he had crumpled up tightly in a spasmodic fit. I recognised the hand-writing of the land-steward of R— sitten; but, quite upset by my trouble, I did not venture to take the letter out of the old gentleman's hand. I did not doubt that his end was near. But his pulse began to beat again, even before the physician arrived; the old gentleman's remarkably tough constitution resisted the mortal attack, although he was in his seventieth year. That selfsame day the doctor pronounced him out of danger.

We had a more severe winter than usual; this was followed by a rough and stormy spring; and hence it was more the gout — a consequence of the inclemency of the season — than his previous accident which kept him for a long time confined to his bed. During this period he made up his mind to retire altogether from all kinds of business. He transferred his office of Justitiarius to others; and so I was cut off from all hope of ever again going to R— sitten. The old gentleman would allow no one to attend him but me; and it was to me alone that he looked for all amusement and every cheerful diversion. And though, in the hours when he was free from pain, his good spirits returned, and he had no lack of broad jests, even making mention of hunting exploits, so that I fully expected every minute to hear him make a butt of my heroic deed, when I had killed the wolf with my whinger, yet never once did he allude to our visit to R— sitten, and as may well be imagined, I was very careful, from natural shyness, not to lead him directly up to the subject. My harassing anxiety and continual attendance upon the old gentleman had thrust Seraphina's image into the background. But as soon as his sickness abated somewhat, my thoughts returned with more liveliness to that moment in the Baroness's room, which I now looked upon as a star — a bright star — that had set, for me at least, for ever. An occurrence which now happened, by making me shudder with an ice-cold thrill as at sight of a visitant from the world of spirits, revived all the pain I had formerly felt. One evening, as I was opening the pocket-book which I had carried whilst at R— sitten, there fell out of the papers I was unfolding a dark curl, wrapped about with a white ribbon; I immediately recognised it as Seraphina's hair. But, on examining the ribbon more closely, I distinctly perceived the mark of a spot of blood on it! Perhaps Adelheid had skilfully contrived to secrete it about me during the moments of conscious insanity by which I had been affected during the last days of our visit; but why was the spot of blood there? It excited forebodings of something terrible in my mind, and almost converted this too pastoral[1] love-token into an awful admonition, pointing to a passion which might entail the expenditure of precious blood. It was the same white ribbon that had fluttered about me in light wanton sportiveness as it were the first time I sat near Seraphina, and which Mysterious Night had stamped as an emblem of mortal injury. Boys ought not to play with weapons with the dangerous properties of which they are not familiar.

At last the storms of spring had ceased to bluster, and summer asserted her rights; and if the cold had formerly been unbearable, so now too was the heat when July came in. The old gentleman visibly gathered strength, and following his usual custom, went out to a garden in the suburbs. One still, warm evening, as we sat in the sweet-smelling jasmine arbour, he was in unusually good spirits, and not, as was generally the case, overflowing with sarcasm and irony, but in a gentle and almost soft and melting mood. "Cousin," he began, "I don't know how it is, but I feel so nice and warm and comfortable all over today; I have not felt like it for many years. I believe it is an augury[2] that I shall die soon." I exerted myself to drive these gloomy thoughts from his mind. "Never mind, cousin," he said, "in any case I'm not long for this world; and so I will now discharge a debt I owe you. Do you still remember our autumn in R—sitten?" This question thrilled through me like a lightning-flash, so before I was able to make any reply he continued, "It was Heaven's will that your entrance into that castle should be signalised by memorable circumstances, and that you should become involved against your own will in the deepest secrets of the house. The time has now come when you must learn all. We have often enough talked about things which you, cousin, rather dimly guessed at than really understood. In the alternation of the seasons nature represents symbolically the cycle of human life. That is a trite remark; but I interpret it differently from everybody else. The dews of spring fall, summer's vapours fade away, and it is the pure atmosphere of autumn which clearly reveals the distant landscape, and then finally earthly existence is swallowed in the night of winter. I mean that the government of the Power Inscrutable[3] is more plainly revealed in the clear-sightedness of old age. It is granted glimpses of the promised land, the pilgrimage to which begins with the death on earth. How clearly do I see at this moment the dark destiny of that house, to which I am knit by firmer ties than blood relationship can weave! Everything lies disclosed to the eyes of my spirit. And yet the things which I now see, in the form in which I see them — the essential substance of them, that is — this I

---

[1] Resembling a pleasant, romantic, rural lifestyle

[2] Omen, premonition

[3] God

cannot tell you in words; for no man's tongue is able to do so. But listen, my son, I will tell you as well as I am able, and do you think it is some remarkable story that might really happen; and lay up carefully in your soul the knowledge that the mysterious relations into which you ventured to enter, not perhaps without being summoned, might have ended in your destruction — but — that's all over now."

The history of the R—— entail, which my old uncle told me, I retain so faithfully in my memory even now that I can almost repeat it in his own words (he spoke of himself in the third person).

☙

One stormy night in the autumn of 1760 the servants of R— sitten were startled out of the midst of their sleep by a terrific crash, as if the whole of the spacious castle had tumbled into a thousand pieces. In a moment everybody was on his legs; lights were lit; the house-steward, his face deadly pale with fright and terror, came up panting with his keys; but as they proceeded through the passages and halls and rooms, suite after suite, and found all safe, and heard in the appalling silence nothing except the creaking rattle of the locks, which occasioned some difficulty in opening, and the ghost-like echo of their own footsteps, they began one and all to be utterly astounded. Nowhere was there the least trace of damage. The old house-steward was impressed by an ominous feeling of apprehension. He went up into the great Knight's Hall, which had a small cabinet[1] adjoining where Freiherr Roderick von R—— used to sleep when engaged in making his astronomical observations. Between the door of this cabinet and that of a second was a postern[2], leading through a narrow passage immediately into the astronomical tower. But directly Daniel (that was the house-steward's[3] name) opened this postern, the storm, blustering and howling terrifically, drove a heap of rubbish and broken pieces of stones all over him, which made him recoil in terror; and, dropping the candles, which went out with a hiss on the floor, he screamed, "O God! O God! The Baron! he's miserably dashed to pieces!" At the same moment he heard sounds of lamentation proceeding from the Freiherr's sleeping-cabinet[4], and on entering it he saw the servants gathered around their master's corpse. They had found him fully dressed and more magnificently than on any previous occasion, and with a calm

---

[1] A small, private room, a closet

[2] A back door

[3] Higher ranking than a butler, the house steward was the manager of the entire house staff: he paid wages, hired and fired, ordered supplies, and was kept the house accounts in order. Usually the house steward lived in a separate house on the property and was very close to the family

[4] Bedroom

earnest look upon his unchanged countenance, sitting in his large and richly decorated arm-chair as though resting after severe study. But his rest was the rest of death. When day dawned it was seen that the crowning turret of the
tower had fallen in. The huge square stones had broken through the ceiling and floor of the observatory-room, and then, carrying down in front of them a powerful beam that ran across the tower, they had dashed in with redoubled impetus the lower vaulted roof, and dragged down a portion of the castle walls and of the narrow connecting-passage. Not a single step could be taken beyond the postern threshold without risk of falling at least eighty feet into a deep chasm.

The old Freiherr had foreseen the very hour of his death, and had sent intelligence of it to his sons. Hence it happened that the very next day saw the arrival of Wolfgang, Freiherr von R—— eldest son of the deceased, and now lord of the entail. Relying confidently upon the probable truth of the old man's foreboding, he had left Vienna, which city he chanced to have reached in his travels, immediately he received the ominous letter, and hastened to R— sitten as fast as he could travel. The house-steward had draped the great hall in black, and had had the old Freiherr laid out in the clothes in which he had been found, on a magnificent state-bed, and this he had surrounded with tall silver candlesticks with burning wax-candles. Wolfgang ascended the stairs, entered the hall, and approached close to his father's corpse, without speaking a word. There he stood with his arms folded on his chest, gazing with a fixed and gloomy look and with knitted brows, into his father's pale countenance. He was like a statue; not a tear came from his eyes. At length, with an almost convulsive movement of the right arm towards the corpse, he murmured hoarsely, "Did the stars compel you to make the son whom you loved miserable?" Throwing his hands behind his back and stepping a short pace backwards, the Baron raised his eyes upwards and said in a low and well-nigh broken voice, "Poor, infatuated old man! Your carnival farce with its shallow delusions is now over. Now you no doubt see that the possessions which are so niggardly dealt out to us here on earth have nothing in common with Hereafter beyond the stars. What will — what power can reach over beyond the grave?" The Baron was silent again for some seconds, then he cried passionately, "No, your perversity shall not rob me of a grain of my earthly happiness, which you strove so hard to destroy," and therewith he took a folded paper out of his pocket and held it up between two fingers to one of the burning candles that stood close beside the corpse. The paper was caught by the flame and blazed up high; and as the reflection flickered and played upon the face of the corpse, it was as though its muscles moved and as though the old man uttered toneless words, so that the servants who stood some distance off were filled with great horror and awe. The Baron calmly finished what he was doing by carefully stamping out with his foot the last fragment of paper that fell on the floor blazing. Then, casting yet another moody glance upon his father, he hurriedly left the hall.

On the following day Daniel reported to the Freiherr the damage that had been done to the tower, and described at great length all that had taken place on the night when their dear dead master died; and he concluded by saying that it would be a very wise thing to have the tower repaired at once, for, if a further fall were to take place, there would be some danger of the whole castle — well, if not tumbling down, at any rate suffering serious damage.

"Repair the tower?" the Freiherr interrupted the old servant curtly, whilst his eyes flashed with anger, "Repair the tower? Never, never! Don't you see, old man," he went on more calmly, "don't you see that the tower could not fall in this way without some special cause? How if it was my father's own wish that the place where he carried on his unhallowed astrological labours should be destroyed — how if he had himself made certain preparations by which he was enabled to bring down the turret whenever he pleased and so occasion the ruin of the interior of the tower! But be that as it may. And if the whole castle tumbles down, I shan't care; I shall be glad. Do you imagine I am going to dwell in this weird owls' nest? No; my wise ancestor who had the foundations of a new castle laid in the beautiful valley yonder — he has begun a work which I intend to finish." Daniel said crestfallen, "Then will all your faithful old servants have to take up their bundles and go?" "That I am not going to be waited upon by helpless, weak-kneed old fellows like you is quite certain; but for all that I shall turn none away. You may all enjoy the bread of charity without working for it." "And am I," cried the old man, greatly hurt, "am I, the house-steward, to be forced to lead such a life of inactivity?" Then the Freiherr, who had turned his back upon the old man and was about to leave the room, wheeled suddenly round, his face perfectly ablaze with passion, strode up to the old man as he stretched out his doubled fist towards him, and shouted in a thundering voice, "You, you hypocritical old villain, it's you who helped my old father in his unearthly practices up yonder; you lay upon his heart like a vampire; and perhaps it was you who basely took advantage of the old man's mad folly to plant in his mind those diabolical ideas which brought me to the brink of ruin. I ought, I tell you, to kick you out like a mangy cur[1]." The old man was so terrified at these harsh terrible words that he threw himself upon his knees beside the Freiherr; but the Baron, as he spoke these last words, threw forward his right foot, perhaps quite unintentionally (as is frequently the case in anger, when the body mechanically obeys the mind, and what is in the thought is imitatively realised in action) and hit the old man so hard on the chest that he rolled over with a stifled scream. Rising painfully to his feet and uttering a most singular sound, like the howling whimper of an

---

[1] Wild dog

animal wounded to death, he looked the Freiherr through and through with a look that glared with mingled rage and despair. The purse of money which the Freiherr threw down as he went out of the room, the old man left lying on the floor where it fell.

Meanwhile all the nearest relatives of the family who lived in the neighbourhood had arrived, and the old Freiherr was interred with much pomp in the family vault in the church at R— sitten; and now, after the invited guests had departed, the new lord of the entail appeared to shake off his gloomy mood, and to be prepared to duly enjoy the property that had fallen to him. Along with V—— the old Freiherr's Justitiarius, who won his full confidence in the very first interview they had, and who was at once confirmed in his office, the Baron made an exact calculation of his sources of income, and considered how large a part he could devote to making improvements and how large a part to building a new castle. V—— was of opinion that the old Freiherr could not possibly have spent all his income every year, and that there must certainly be money concealed somewhere, since he had found nothing amongst his papers except one or two bank-notes for insignificant sums, and the ready-money in the iron safe was but very little more than a thousand thalers, or about £150[1]. Who would be so likely to know anything about it as Daniel, who in his obstinate self-willed way was perhaps only waiting to be asked about it? The Baron was now not a little concerned at the thought that Daniel, whom he had so grossly insulted, might let large sums moulder somewhere sooner than discover them to him, not so much, of course, from any motives of self-interest — for of what use could even the largest sum of money be to him, a childless old man, whose only wish was to end his days in the castle of R— sitten? — as from a desire to take vengeance for the affront put upon him. He gave V—— a circumstantial account of the entire scene with Daniel, and concluded by saying that from several items of information communicated to him he had learned that it was Daniel alone who had contrived to nourish in the old Freiherr's mind such an inexplicable aversion to ever seeing his sons in R— sitten. The Justitiarius declared that this information was perfectly false, since there was not a human creature on the face of the earth who would have been able to guide the Freiherr's thoughts in any way, far less determine them for him; and he undertook finally to draw from Daniel the secret, if he had one, as to the place in which they would be likely to find money concealed. His task proved far easier than he had anticipated, for no sooner did he begin, "But how comes it, Daniel, that your old master has left so little ready-money?" than Daniel replied, with a repulsive smile,

---

[1] A thaler was worth about a week's wages for a skilled worker, so this would be roughly 19 years' worth of income for a working class family

"Do you mean the few trifling thalers[1], Herr Justitiarius, which you found in the little strong box? Oh! the rest is lying in the vault beside our gracious master's sleeping-cabinet. But the best," he went on to say, whilst his smile passed over into an abominable grin, and his eyes flashed with malicious fire, "but the best of all — several thousand gold pieces — lies buried at the bottom of the chasm beneath the ruins." The Justitiarius at once summoned the Freiherr; they proceeded there, and then into the sleeping-cabinet, where Daniel pushed aside the wainscot in one of the corners, and a small lock became visible. Whilst the Freiherr was regarding the polished lock with covetous eyes, and making preparations to try and unlock it with the keys of the great bunch which he dragged with some difficulty out of his pocket, Daniel drew himself up to his full height, and looked down with almost malignant pride upon his master, who had now stooped down in order to see the lock better. Daniel's face was deadly pale, and he said, his voice trembling, "If I am a dog, my lord Freiherr, I have also at least a dog's fidelity." Therewith he held out a bright steel key to his master, who greedily snatched it out of his hand, and with it he easily succeeded in opening the door. They stepped into a small and low-vaulted apartment, in which stood a large iron coffer with the lid open, containing many money-bags, upon which lay a strip of parchment, written in the old Freiherr's familiar handwriting, large and old-fashioned.

One hundred and fifty thousand Imperial thalers in old Fredericks d'or[2], money saved from the revenues of the estate-tail of R— sitten; this sum has been set aside for the building of the castle. Further, the lord of the entail who succeeds me in the possession of this money shall, upon the highest hill situated eastward from the old tower of the castle (which he will find in ruins), erect a high beacon tower for the benefit of mariners, and cause a fire to be kindled on it every night. R— sitten, on Michaelmas Eve[3] of the year 1760.

— RODERICK, FREIHERR von R.

The Freiherr lifted up the bags one after the other and let them fall again into the coffer, delighted at the ringing clink of so much gold coin; then he turned round abruptly to the old house-steward, thanked him for

---

[1] The basic coin used in Prussia for essential purchases and paychecks (comparable to the British shilling, French franc, or the American dollar). It was worth about $15 in modern currency

[2] The currency of Prussia (literally: Gold Fredericks, with the image of Frederick the Great on them). A thaler was worth about three shillings (36 pence), or around $15 in modern currency, making the total worth of this discovery a stunning $2.3 million

[3] The feast day of St. Michael is September 29

the fidelity he had shown, and assured him that they were only vile tattling calumnies[1] which had induced him to treat him so harshly in the first instance. He should not only remain in the castle, but should also continue to discharge his duties, uncurtailed in any way, as house-steward, and at double the wages he was then having. "I owe you a large compensation; if you will take money, help yourself to one of these bags." As he concluded with these words, the Baron stood before the old man, with his eyes bent upon the ground, and pointed to the coffer; then, approaching it again, he once more ran his eyes over the bags. A burning flush suddenly mounted into the old house-steward's cheeks, and he uttered that awful howling whimper — a noise as of an animal wounded to death, according to the Freiherr's previous description of it to the Justitiarius. The latter shuddered, for the words which the old man murmured between his teeth sounded like, "Blood for gold." Of all this the Freiherr, absorbed in the contemplation of the treasure before him, had heard not the least. Daniel tottered in every limb, as if shaken by an ague fit; approaching the Freiherr with bowed head in a humble attitude, he kissed his hand, and drawing his handkerchief across his eyes under the pretence of wiping away his tears, said in a whining voice, "Alas! my good and gracious master, what am I, a poor childless old man, to do with money? But the doubled wages I accept with gladness, and will continue to do my duty faithfully and zealously."

The Freiherr, who had paid no particular heed to the old man's words, now let the heavy lid of the coffer fall to with a bang, so that the whole room shook and cracked, and then, locking the coffer and carefully withdrawing the key, he said carelessly, "Very well, very well, old man." But after they entered the hall he went on talking to Daniel, "But you said something about a quantity of gold pieces buried underneath the ruins of the tower?" Silently the old man stepped towards the postern, and after some difficulty unlocked it. But so soon as he threw it open the storm drove a thick mass of snow-flakes into the hall; a raven was disturbed and flew in croaking and screaming and dashed with its black wings against the window, but regaining the open postern it disappeared downwards into the chasm. The Freiherr stepped out into the corridor; but one single glance downwards, and he started back trembling. "A fearful sight! — I'm giddy!" he stammered as he sank almost fainting into the Justitiarius' arms. But quickly recovering himself by an effort, he fixed a sharp look upon the old man and asked, "Down there, you say?" Meanwhile the old man had been locking the postern, and was now leaning against it with all his bodily strength, and was gasping and grunting to get the great key out of the rusty lock. This at last accomplished, he turned round to the Baron, and, changing the huge key about backwards and forwards in his hands, replied with a peculiar smile, "Yes, there are thousands and thousands

[1] Slanders

down there — all my dear dead master's beautiful instruments — telescopes, quadrants, globes, dark mirrors, they all lie smashed to atoms underneath the ruins between the stones and the big balk." "But money — coined money," interrupted the Baron, "you spoke of gold pieces, old man?" "I only meant things which had cost several thousand gold pieces," he replied; and not another word could be got out of him.

The Baron appeared highly delighted to have all at once come into possession of all the means requisite for carrying out his favourite plan, namely, that of building a new and magnificent castle. The Justitiarius indeed stated it as his opinion that, according to the will of the deceased, the money could only be applied to the repair and complete finishing of the interior of the old castle, and further, any new erection would hardly succeed in equalling the commanding size and the severe and simple character of the old ancestral castle. The Freiherr, however, persisted in his intention, and maintained that in the disposal of property respecting which nothing was stated in the deeds of the entail the irregular will of the deceased could have no validity. He at the same time led V—— to understand that he should conceive it to be his duty to embellish R—sitten as far as the climate, soil, and environs would permit, for it was his intention to bring home shortly as his dearly loved wife a lady who was in every respect worthy of the greatest sacrifices.

The air of mystery with which the Freiherr spoke of this alliance, which possibly had been already consummated in secret, cut short all further questions from the side of the Justitiarius. Nevertheless he found in it to some extent a redeeming feature, for the Freiherr's eager grasping after riches now appeared to be due not so much to avarice strictly speaking as to the desire to make one dear to him forget the more beautiful country she was relinquishing for his sake. Otherwise he could not acquit the Baron of being avaricious, or at any rate insufferably close-fisted, seeing that, even though rolling in money and even when gloating over the old Fredericks d'or, he could not help bursting out with the peevish grumble, "I know the old rascal has concealed from us the greatest part of his wealth, but next spring I will have the ruins of the tower turned over under my own eyes."

The Freiherr had architects come, and discussed with them at great length what would be the most convenient way to proceed with his castle-building. He rejected one drawing after another; in none of them was the style of architecture sufficiently rich and grandiose. He now began to
draw plans himself, and, inspirited by this employment, which constantly placed before his eyes a sunny picture of the happiest future, brought himself into such a genial humour that it often bordered on wild exuberance of spirits, and even communicated itself to all about him. His generosity and profuse hospitality belied all imputations of avarice at any rate. Daniel also seemed to have now forgotten the insult that had been

put upon him. Towards the Freiherr, although often followed by him with mistrustful eyes on account of the treasure buried in the chasm, his bearing was both quiet and humble. But what struck everybody as extraordinary was that the old man appeared to grow younger from day to day. Possibly this might be, because he had begun to forget his grief for his old master, which had stricken him sore, and possibly also because he had not now, as he once had, to spend the cold nights in the tower without sleep, and got better food and good wine such as he liked; but whatever the cause might be, the old greybeard seemed to be growing into a vigorous man with red cheeks and well-nourished body, who could walk firmly and laugh loudly whenever he heard a jest to laugh at.

ଔ

The pleasant tenor of life at R— sitten was disturbed by the arrival of a man whom one would have judged to be quite in his element there. This was Wolfgang's younger brother Hubert, at the sight of whom Wolfgang had screamed out, with his face as pale as a corpse's, "Unhappy wretch, what do you want here?" Hubert threw himself into his brother's arms, but Wolfgang took him and led him away up to a retired room, where he locked himself in with him. They remained closeted several hours, at the end of which time Hubert came down, greatly agitated, and called for his horses. The Justitiarius intercepted him; Hubert tried to pass him; but V—— inspired by the hope that he might perhaps stifle in the bud what might else end in a bitter life-long quarrel between the brothers, besought him to stay, at least a few hours, and at the same moment the Freiherr came down calling, "Stay here, Hubert! you will think better of it." Hubert's countenance cleared up; he assumed an air of composure, and quickly pulling off his costly fur coat, and throwing it to a servant behind him, he grasped V——'s hand and went with him into the room, saying with a scornful smile, "So the lord of the entail will tolerate my presence here, it seems." V—— thought that the unfortunate misunderstanding would assuredly be smoothed away now, for it was only separation and existence apart from each other that would, he conceived, be able to foster it. Hubert took up the steel tongs which stood near the fire-grate, and as he proceeded to break up a knotty piece of wood that would only sweal, not burn, and to rake the fire together better, he said to V—— "You see what a good-natured fellow I am, Herr Justitiarius, and that I am skilful in all domestic matters. But Wolfgang is full of the most extraordinary prejudices, and — a bit of a miser." V—— did not deem it advisable to attempt to fathom further the relations between the brothers, especially as Wolfgang's face and conduct and voice plainly showed that he was shaken to the very depths of his nature by diverse violent passions.

Late in the evening V—— had occasion to go up to the Freiherr's room in order to learn his decision about some matter or other connected with the estate-tail. He found him pacing up and down the room with long strides, his arms crossed on his back, and much perturbation in his manner. On perceiving the Justitiarius he stood still, and then, taking him by both hands and looking him gloomily in the face, he said in a broken voice, "My brother is come. I know what you are going to say," he proceeded almost before V—— had opened his mouth to put a question. "Unfortunately you know nothing. You don't know that my unfortunate brother — yes, I will not call him anything worse than unfortunate — that, like a spirit of evil, he crosses my path everywhere, ruining my peace of mind. It is not his fault that I have not been made unspeakably miserable; he did his best to make me so, but Heaven willed it otherwise. Ever since he has known of the conversion of the property into an entail, he has persecuted me with deadly hatred. He envies me this property, which in his hands would only be scattered like chaff. He is the wildest spendthrift I ever heard of. His load of debt exceeds by a long way the half of the unentailed property in Courland that fell to him, and now, pursued by his creditors, who fail not to worry him for payment, he hurries here to me to beg for money." "And you, his brother, refuse to give him any?" V—— was about to interrupt him; but the Freiherr, letting V——'s hands fall, and taking a long step backwards, went on in a loud and vehement tone. "Stop! yes; I refuse. I neither can nor will give away a single thaler of the revenues of the entail. But listen, and I will tell you what was the proposal which I made the insane fellow a few hours ago, and made in vain, and then pass judgment upon the feelings of duty by which I am actuated. Our unentailed possessions in Courland are, as you are aware, considerable; the half that falls to me I am willing to renounce, but in favour of his family. For Hubert has married, in Courland, a beautiful lady, but poor. She and the children she has borne him are starving. The estates should be put under trust; sufficient should be set aside out of the revenues to support him, and his creditors be paid by arrangement. But what does he care for a quiet life — a life free of anxiety? — what does he care for wife and child? Money, ready-money, and large quantities, is what he will have, that he may squander it in infamous folly. Some demon has made him acquainted with the secret of the hundred and fifty thousand thalers, half of which he in his mad way demands, maintaining that this money is movable property and quite apart from the entailed portion. This, however, I must and will refuse him, but the feeling haunts me that he is plotting my destruction in his heart."

No matter how great the efforts which V—— made to persuade the Freiherr out of this suspicion against his brother, in which, of course, not being initiated into the more circumstantial details of the disagreement, he could only appeal to broad and somewhat superficial moral principles, he yet could not boast of the smallest success. The Freiherr commissioned him to treat with his hostile and avaricious brother Hubert. V—— proceeded to do so with all the circumspection he was master of, and was not a little gratified when Hubert at length declared, "Be it so then; I will accept my brother's proposals, but upon condition that he will now, since I am on the point of losing both my honour and my good name for ever through the severity of my creditors, make me an advance of a thousand Fredericks d'or in hard cash, and further grant that in time to come I may take up my residence, at least for a short time occasionally, in our beautiful R— sitten, along with my good brother." "Never, never!" exclaimed the Freiherr violently, when V—— laid his brother's amended counter-proposals before him. "I will never consent that Hubert stay in my house even a single minute after I have brought home my wife. Go, my good friend, tell this mar-peace[1] that he shall have two thousand Fredericks d'or, not as an advance, but as a gift — only, bid him go, bid him go." V—— now learned at one and the same time that the ground of the quarrel between the two brothers must be sought for in this marriage. Hubert listened to the Justitiarius proudly and calmly, and when he finished speaking replied in a hoarse and hollow tone, "I will think it over; but for the present I shall stay a few days in the castle." V—— exerted himself to prove to the discontented Hubert that the Freiherr, by making over his share of their unentailed property, was really doing all he possibly could do to indemnify him, and that on the whole he had no cause for complaint against his brother, although at the same time he admitted that all institutions of the nature of primogeniture[2], which vested such preponderant advantages in the eldest-born to the prejudice of the remaining children, were in many respects hateful. Hubert tore his waistcoat open from top to bottom like a man whose breast was cramped and he wanted to relieve it by fresh air. Thrusting one hand into his open shirt-frill and planting the other in his side, he spun round on one foot in a quick pirouette[3] and cried in a sharp voice, "Pshaw! What is hateful is born of hatred." Then bursting out into a shrill fit of laughter, he said, "What condescension my lord of the entail shows in being thus willing to throw his gold pieces to the poor beggar!" V—— saw plainly that all idea of a complete reconciliation between the brothers was quite out of the question.

To the Freiherr's annoyance, Hubert established himself in the rooms that had been appointed for him in one of the side wings of the castle as if with the view to a very long stay. He was observed to hold frequent and long conversations with the house-steward; nay, the latter was sometimes even seen to accompany him when he went out wolf-

---

[1] Troublemaker

[2] Laws which pass inheritances down the birth order (oldest to youngest) rather than splitting them evenly amongst all children

[3] A ballet move involving a spin while balanced on one toe

hunting. Otherwise he was very little seen, and studiously avoided meeting his brother alone, at which the latter was very glad. V—— felt how strained and unpleasant this state of things was, and was obliged to confess to himself that the peculiar uneasiness which marked all that Hubert both said and did was such as to destroy intentionally and effectually all the pleasure of the place. He now perfectly understood why the Freiherr had manifested so much alarm on seeing his brother.

One day as V—— was sitting by himself in the justice-room amongst his law-papers, Hubert came in with a grave and more composed manner than usual, and said in a voice that bordered upon melancholy, "I will accept my brother's last proposals. If you will contrive that I have the two thousand Fredericks d'or today, I will leave the castle this very night — on horseback — alone." "With the money?" asked V——. "You are right," replied Hubert; "I know what you would say — the weight! Give it me in bills on Isaac Lazarus[1] of K——. For to K—— I am going this very night. Something is driving me away from this place. The old fellow has bewitched it with evil spirits." "Do you mean your father, Herr Baron?" asked V—— sternly. Hubert's lips trembled; he had to cling to the chair to keep from falling; but then suddenly recovering himself, he cried, "To-day then, please, Herr Justitiarius," and staggered to the door, not, however, without some exertion. "He now sees that no deceptions are any longer of avail, that he can do nothing against my firm will," said the Freiherr whilst drawing up the bills on Isaac Lazarus in K——. A burden was lifted off his heart by the departure of his inimical[2] brother; and for a long time he had not been in such cheerful spirits as he was at supper. Hubert had sent his excuses; and there was not one who regretted his absence.

The room which V—— occupied was somewhat retired, and its windows looked upon the castle-yard. In the night he was suddenly startled up out of his sleep, and was under the impression that he had been awakened by a distant and pitiable moan. But listen as he would, all remained still as the grave, and so he was obliged to conclude that the sound which had fallen upon his ears was the delusion of a dream. But at the same time he was seized with such a peculiar feeling of breathless anxiety and terror that he could not stay in bed. He got up and approached the window. It was not long, however, before the castle door was opened, and a figure with a blazing torch came out of the castle and went across the court-yard. V—— recognised the figure as that of old Daniel, and saw him open the stable-door and go in, and soon afterwards bring out a saddle horse. Now a second figure came into view out of the

---

[1] The implied name of a creditor (only Jews were legally allowed to extend lines of credit (usury was outlawed in Catholic countries) and this name is cartoonishly Jewish)

[2] Hostile

darkness, well wrapped in furs, and with a fox-skin cap on his head. V—— perceived that it was Hubert; but after he had spoken excitedly with Daniel for some minutes, he returned into the castle. Daniel led back the horse into the stable and locked the door, and also that of the castle, after he had returned across the court-yard in the same way in which he crossed it before. It was evident Hubert had intended to go away on horseback, but had suddenly changed his mind; and no less evident was it that there was a dangerous understanding of some sort between Hubert and the old house-steward. V—— looked forward to the morning with burning impatience; he would acquaint the Freiherr with the occurrences of the night. Really it was now time to take precautionary measures against the attacks of Hubert's malice, which V—— was now convinced, had been betrayed in his agitated behaviour of the day before.

Next morning, at the hour when the Freiherr was in the habit of rising, V—— heard people running backwards and forwards, doors opened and slammed to, and a tumultuous confusion of voices talking and shouting. On going out of his room he met servants everywhere, who, without heeding him, ran past him with ghastly pale faces, upstairs, downstairs, in and out the rooms. At length he ascertained that the Freiherr was missing, and that they had been looking for him for hours in vain. As he had gone to bed in the presence of his personal attendant, he must have afterwards got up and gone away somewhere in his dressing-gown and slippers, taking the large candlestick with him, for these articles were also missed. V— —, his mind agitated with dark forebodings, ran up to the ill-fated hall, the cabinet adjoining which Wolfgang had chosen, like his father, for his own bedroom. The postern leading to the tower stood wide open, with a cry of horror V—— shouted, "There — he lies dashed to pieces at the bottom of the ravine." And it was so. There had been a fall of snow, so that all they could distinctly make out from above was the rigid arm of the unfortunate man protruding from between the stones. Many hours passed before the workmen succeeded, at great risk of life, in descending by means of ladders bound together, and drawing up the corpse by the aid of ropes. In the last agonies of death the Baron had kept a tight hold upon the silver candlestick; the hand in which it was clenched was the only uninjured part of his whole body, which had been shattered in the most hideous way by rebounding on the sharp stones.

Just as the corpse was drawn up and carried into the hall, and laid upon the very same spot on the large table where a few weeks before old Roderick had lain dead, Hubert burst in, his face distorted by the frenzy of despair. Quite overpowered by the fearful sight he wailed, "Brother! O my poor brother! No; this I never prayed for from the demons who had entered into me." This suspicious self-exculpation made V—— tremble; he felt impelled to proceed against Hubert as the murderer of his brother. Hubert, however, had fallen on the floor senseless; they carried him to bed; but on taking strong restoratives he soon recovered. Then he appeared in V——'s room, pale and sorrow-stricken, and with his eyes half clouded with grief; and unable to stand owing to his weakness, he slowly sank down into an easy-chair, saying, "I have wished for my brother's death, because my father had made over to him the best part of the property through the foolish conversion of it into an entail. He has now found a fearful death. I am now lord of the estate-tail, but my heart is rent with pain — I can — I shall never be happy. I confirm you in your office; you shall be invested with the most extensive powers in respect to the management of the estate, upon which I cannot bear to live." Hubert left the room, and in two or three hours was on his way to K——.

It appeared that the unfortunate Wolfgang had got up in the night, probably with the intention of going into the other cabinet where there was a library. In the stupor of sleep he had mistaken the door, and had opened the postern, taken a step out, and plunged headlong down. But after all had been said, there was nevertheless a good deal that was strained and unlikely in this explanation. If the Baron was unable to sleep and wanted to get a book out of the library, this of itself excluded all idea of sleep-stupor; but this condition alone could account for any mistaking of the postern for the door of the cabinet. Then again, the former was fast locked, and required a good deal of exertion to unlock it. These improbabilities V—— accordingly put before the domestics, who had gathered round him, and at length the Freiherr's body-servant, Francis by name, said, "Nay, nay, my good Herr Justitiarius; it couldn't have happened in that way." "Well, how then?" asked V—— abruptly and sharply. But Francis, a faithful, honest fellow, who would have followed his master into his grave, was unwilling to speak out before the rest; he stipulated that what he had to say about the event should be confided to the Justitiarius alone in private. V—— now learned that the Freiherr used often to talk to Francis about the vast treasure which he believed lay buried beneath the ruins of the tower, and also that frequently at night, as if goaded by some malicious fiend, he would open the postern, the key of which Daniel had been obliged to give him, and would gaze with longing eyes down into the chasm where the supposed riches lay. There was now no doubt about it; on that ill-omened night the Freiherr, after his servant had left him, must have taken one of his usual walks to the postern, where he had been most likely suddenly seized with dizziness, and had fallen over. Daniel, who also seemed much upset by the Freiherr's terrible end, thought it would be a good thing to have the dangerous postern walled up; and this was at once done.

☙

Freiherr Hubert von R—— who had then succeeded to the entail, went back to Courland without once showing himself at R— sitten again. V—

— was invested with full powers for the absolute management of the property. The building of the new castle was not proceeded with; but on the other hand the old structure was put in as good a state of repair as possible. Several years passed before Hubert came again to R— sitten, late in the autumn, but after he had remained shut up in his room with V—— for several days, he went back to Courland. Passing on his way through K—— he deposited his will with the government authorities there.

The Freiherr, whose character appeared to have undergone a complete revolution, spoke more than once during his stay at R— sitten of presentiments of his approaching death. And these apprehensions were really not unfounded, for he died in the very next year. His son, named, like the deceased Baron, Hubert, soon came over from Courland to take possession of the rich inheritance; and was followed by his mother and his sister. The youth seemed to unite in his own person all the bad qualities of his ancestors: he proved himself to be proud, arrogant, impetuous, avaricious, in the very first moments after his arrival at R— sitten. He wanted to have several things which did not suit his notions of what was right and proper altered there and then: the cook he kicked out of doors; and he attempted to thrash the coachman, in which, however, he did not succeed, for the big brawny fellow had the impudence not to submit to it. In fact, he was on the high road to assuming the rôle of a harsh and severe lord of the entail, when V—— interposed in his firm earnest manner, declaring most explicitly that not a single chair should be moved, that not even a cat should leave the house if she liked to stay in it, until after the will had been opened. "You have the presumption to tell me, the lord of the entail," began the Baron. V—— however, cut short the young man, who was foaming with rage, and said, whilst he measured him with a keen searching glance, "Don't be in too great a hurry, Herr Baron. At all events, you have no right to exercise authority here until after the opening of your father's will. It is I— I alone — who am now master here; and I shall know how to meet violence with violent measures. Please to recollect that by virtue of my powers as executor of your father's will, as well as by virtue of the arrangements which have been made by the court, I am empowered to forbid your remaining in R— sitten if I think fit to do so; and so, if you wish to spare me this disagreeable step, I would advise you to go away quietly to K——." The lawyer's earnestness, and the resolute tone in which he spoke, lent the proper emphasis to his words. Hence the young Baron, who was charging with far too sharp-pointed horns, felt the weakness of his weapons against the firm bulwark, and found it convenient to cover the shame of his retreat with a burst of scornful laughter.

Three months passed and the day was come on which, in accordance with the expressed wish of the deceased, his will was to be opened at K— — where it had been deposited. In the chambers there was, besides the officers of the court, the Baron, and V—— a young man of noble appearance, whom V—— had brought with him, and who was taken to be V——'s clerk, since he had a parchment deed sticking out from the breast of his buttoned-up coat. Him the Baron treated as he did nearly all the rest, with scornful contempt; and he demanded with noisy impetuosity that they should make haste and get done with all their tiresome needless ceremonies as quickly as possible and without over many words and scribblings. He couldn't for the life of him make out why any will should be wanted at all with respect to the inheritance, and especially in the case of entailed property; and no matter what provisions were made in the will, it would depend entirely upon his decision as to whether they should be observed or not. After casting a hasty and surly glance at the handwriting and the seal, the Baron acknowledged them to be those of his dead father. Upon the clerk of the court preparing to read the will aloud, the young Baron, throwing his right arm carelessly over the back of his chair and leaning his left on the table, whilst he drummed with his fingers on its green cover, sat staring with an air of indifference out of the window. After a short preamble the deceased Freiherr Hubert von R—— declared that he had never possessed the estate-tail as its lawful owner, but that he had only managed it in the name of the deceased Freiherr Wolfgang von R——'s only son, called Roderick after his grandfather; and he it was to whom, according to the rights of family priority, the estate had fallen on his father's death. Amongst Hubert's papers would be found an exact account of all revenues and expenditure, as well as of existing movable property, &c. The will went on to relate that Wolfgang von R—— had, during his travels, made the acquaintance of Mdlle.[1] Julia de St. Val in Geneva, and had fallen so deeply in love with her that he resolved never to leave her side again. She was very poor; and her family, although noble and of good repute, did not, however, rank amongst the most illustrious, for which reason Wolfgang dared not expect to receive the consent of old Roderick to a union with her, for the old Freiherr's aim and ambition was to promote by all possible means the establishment of a powerful family. Nevertheless he ventured to write from Paris to his father, acquainting him with the fact that his affections were engaged. But what he had foreseen was actually realised; the old Baron declared categorically that he had himself chosen the future mistress of the entail, and therefore there could never be any mention made of any other. Wolfgang, instead of crossing the Channel into England, as he was to have done, returned into Geneva under the assumed name of Born, and married Julia, who after the lapse of a year bore him a son, and this son became on Wolfgang's death the real lord of the entail. In explanation of the facts why Hubert, though acquainted with all this, had kept silent so long and had represented himself as lord of the entail, various reasons

[1] Mademoiselle (French: Miss)

were assigned, based upon agreements formerly made with Wolfgang, but they seemed for the most part insufficient and devoid of real foundation.

The Baron sat staring at the clerk of the court as if thunderstruck, whilst the latter went on proclaiming all this bad news in a provokingly monotonous and jarring tone. When he finished, V—— rose, and taking the young man whom he had brought with him by the hand, said, as he bowed to the assembled company, "Here I have the honour to present to you, gentlemen, Freiherr Roderick von R—— lord of the entail of R—sitten." Baron Hubert looked at the youth, who had, as it were, fallen from the clouds to deprive him of the rich inheritance together with half the unentailed Courland estates, with suppressed fury in his gleaming eyes; then, threatening him with his doubled fist, he ran out of the court without uttering a word. Baron Roderick, on being challenged by the court-officers, produced the documents by which he was to establish his identity as the person whom he represented himself to be. He handed in an attested extract from the register of the church where his father was married, which certified that on such and such a day Wolfgang Born, merchant, born in K—— had been united in marriage with the blessing of the Church to Mdlle. Julia de St. Val, in the presence of certain witnesses, who were named. Further, he produced his own baptismal certificate (he had been baptized in Geneva as the son of the merchant Born and his wife Julia, née De St. Val, begotten in lawful wedlock), and various letters from his father to his mother, who was long since dead, but they none of them had any other signature than W.

V—— looked through all these papers with a cloud upon his face; and as he put them together again, he said, somewhat troubled, "Ah well! God will help us!"

The very next morning Freiherr Hubert von R—— presented, through an advocate whose services he had succeeded in enlisting in his cause, a statement of protest to the government authorities in K—— actually calling upon them to effectuate the immediate surrender to him of the entail of R— sitten. It was incontestable, maintained the advocate, that the deceased Freiherr Hubert Von R—— had not had the power to dispose of entailed property either by testament or in any other way. The testament in question, therefore, was nothing more than an evidential statement, written down and deposited with the court, to the effect that Freiherr Wolfgang von R—— had bequeathed the estate-tail to a son who was at that time still living; and accordingly it had as evidence no greater weight than that of any other witness, and so could not by any possibility legitimately establish the claims of the person who had announced himself to be Freiherr Roderick von R——. Hence it was rather the duty of this new claimant to prove by action at law his alleged rights of inheritance, which were hereby expressly disputed and denied, and so also to take proper steps to maintain his claim to the estate-tail, which now, according to the laws of succession, fell to Baron Hubert von R——.

By the father's death the property came at once immediately into the hands of the son. There was no need for any formal declaration to be made of his entering into possession of the inheritance, since the succession could not be alienated; at any rate, the present owner of the estate was not going to be disturbed in his possession by claims which were perfectly groundless. Whatever reasons the deceased might have had for bringing forward another heir of entail were quite irrelevant. And it might be remarked that he had himself had an intrigue[1] in Switzerland, as could be proved if necessary from the papers he had left behind him; and it was quite possible that the person whom he alleged to be his brother's son was his own son, the fruit of an unlawful love, for whom in a momentary fit of remorse he had wished to secure the entail.

However great was the balance of probability in favour of the truth of the circumstances as stated in the will, and however revolted the judges were, particularly by the last clauses of the protest, in which the son felt no compunction at accusing his dead father of a crime, yet the views of the case there stated were after all the right ones; and it was only due to V——'s restless exertions, and his explicit and solemn assurance that the proofs which were necessary to establish legitimately the identity of Freiherr Roderick von R—— should be produced in a very short time, that the surrender of the estate to the young Baron was deferred, and the contrivance of the administration of it in trust agreed to, until after the case should be settled.

V—— was only too well aware how difficult it would be for him to keep his promise. He had turned over all old Roderick's papers without finding the slightest trace of a letter or any kind of a statement bearing upon Wolfgang's relation to Mdlle. de St. Val. He was sitting wrapt in thought in old Roderick's sleeping-cabinet, every hole and comer of which he had searched, and was working at a long statement of the case that he intended despatching to a certain notary in Geneva, who had been recommended to him as a shrewd and energetic man, to request him to procure and forward certain documents which would establish the young Freiherr's cause on firm ground. It was midnight; the full moon shone in through the windows of the adjoining hall, the door of which stood open. Then V—— fancied he heard a noise as of some one coming slowly and heavily up the stairs, and also at the same time a jingling and rattling of keys. His attention was arrested; he rose to his feet and went into the hall, where he plainly made out that there was some one crossing the ante-room and approaching the door of the hall where he was. Soon afterwards the door was opened and a man came slowly in, dressed in night-clothes, his face ghastly pale and distorted; in the one hand he bore a candle-stick with the candles burning, and in the other a huge bunch of keys. V—— at once recognised the house-steward, and was on the point of addressing

[1] Sexual affair

him and inquiring what he wanted so late at night, when he was arrested by an icy shiver; there was something so unearthly and ghost-like in the old man's manner and bearing as well as in his set, pallid face. He perceived that he was in presence of a somnambulist[1]. Crossing the hall obliquely with measured strides, the old man went straight to the walled-up postern that had formerly led to the tower. He came to a halt immediately in front of it, and uttered a wailing sound that seemed to come from the bottom of his heart, and was so awful and so loud that the whole apartment rang again, making V—— tremble with dread. Then, setting the candlestick down on the floor and hanging the keys on his belt, Daniel began to scratch at the wall with both hands, so that the blood soon burst out from beneath his finger-nails, and all the while he was moaning and groaning as if tortured by nameless agony. After placing his ear against the wall in a listening attitude, he waved his hand as if hushing some one, stooped down and picked up the candlestick, and finally stole back to the door with soft measured footsteps. V—— took his own candle in his hand and cautiously followed him. They both went downstairs; the old man unlocked the great main door of the castle, V—— slipped cleverly through. Then they went to the stable, where old Daniel, to V——'s perfect astonishment, placed his candlestick so skillfully that the entire interior of the building was sufficiently lighted without the least danger. Having fetched a saddle and bridle, he put them on one of the horses which he had loosed from the manger, carefully tightening the girth[2] and taking up the stirrup-straps. Pulling the tuft of hair on the horse's forehead outside the front strap, he took him by the bridle and led him out of the stable, clicking with his tongue and patting his neck with one hand. On getting outside in the courtyard he stood several seconds in the attitude of one receiving commands, which he promised by sundry nods to carry out. Then he led the horse back into the stable, unsaddled him, and tied him to the manger[3]. This done, he took his candlestick, locked the stable, and returned to the castle, finally disappearing in his own room, the door of which he carefully bolted. V—— was deeply agitated by this scene; the presentiment of some fearful deed rose up before him like a black and fiendish spectre, and refused to leave him. Being so keenly alive as he was to the precarious position of his protégé, he felt that it would at least be his duty to turn what he had seen to his account.

Next day, just as it was beginning to be dusk, Daniel came into the Justitiarius's room to receive some instructions relating to his department of the household. V—— took him by the arms, and forcing him into a chair, in a confidential way began, "See you here, my old friend Daniel, I

[1] Sleepwalker
[2] The strap of a saddle (fastened around a horse's belly) which holds it in place
[3] Long, open trough that livestock eat from

have long been wishing to ask you what you think of all this confused mess into which Hubert's peculiar will has tumbled us. Do you really think that the young man is Wolfgang's son, begotten in lawful marriage?" The old man, leaning over the arm of his chair, and avoiding V——'s eyes, for V—— was watching him most intently, replied doggedly, "Bah! Maybe he is; maybe he is not. What does it matter to me? It's all the same to me who's master here now." "But I believe," went on V—— moving nearer to the old man and placing his hand on his shoulder, "but I believed you possessed the old Freiherr's full confidence, and in that case he assuredly would not conceal from you the real state of affairs with regard to his sons. He told you, I dare say, about the marriage which Wolfgang had made against his will, did he not?" "I don't remember to have ever heard him say anything of that sort," replied the old man, yawning with the most ill-mannered loudness. "You are sleepy, old man," said V——; "perhaps you have had a restless night?" "Not that I am aware," he rejoined coldly; "but I must go and order supper." Whereupon he rose heavily from his chair and rubbed his bent back, yawning again, and that still more loudly than before. "Stay a little while, old man," cried V—— taking hold of his hand and endeavouring to force him to resume his seat; but Daniel preferred to stand in front of the study-table; propping himself upon it with both hands, and leaning across towards V—— he asked sullenly, "Well, what do you want? What have I to do with the will? What do I care about the quarrel over the estate?" "Well, well," interposed V—— "we'll say no more about that now. Let us turn to some other topic, Daniel. You are out of humour and yawning, and all that is a sign of great weariness, and I am almost inclined to believe that it really was you last night, who"—— "Well, what did I do last night?" asked the old man without changing his position. V—— went on, "Last night, when I was sitting up above in your old master's sleeping-cabinet next the great hall, you came in at the door, your face pale and rigid; and you went across to the bricked-up postern and scratched at the wall with both your hands, groaning as if in very great pain. Do you walk in your sleep, Daniel?" The old man dropped back into the chair which V—— quickly managed to place for him; but not a sound escaped his lips. His face could not be seen, owing to the gathering dusk of the evening; V—— only noticed that he took his breath short and that his teeth were rattling together. "Yes," continued V—— after a short pause, "there is one thing that is very strange about sleep-walkers. On the day after they have been in this peculiar state in which they have acted as if they were perfectly wide awake, they don't remember the least thing, that they did." Daniel did not move. "I have come across something like what your condition was yesterday once before in the course of my experience," proceeded V——. "I had a friend who regularly began to wander about at night as you do whenever it was a full moon — nay, he often sat down and wrote letters. But what was most extraordinary was that if I began to whisper softly in his ear I could soon manage to make him speak; and he would answer correctly all the questions I put to him; and even things that he would most jealously have concealed when awake now fell from his lips unbidden, as though he were unable to offer any resistance to the power that was exerting its influence over him. Deuce take it! I really believe that, if a man who's given to walking in his sleep had ever committed any crime, and hoarded it up as a secret ever so long, it could be extracted from him by questioning when he was in this peculiar state. Happy are they who have a clean conscience like you and me, Daniel! We may walk as much as we like in our sleep; there's no fear of anybody extorting the confession of a crime from us. But come now, Daniel! when you scratch so hideously at the bricked-up postern, you want, I dare say, to go up the astronomical tower, don't you? I suppose you want to go and experiment like old Roderick — eh? Well, next time you come, I shall ask you what you want to do." Whilst V—— was speaking, the old man was shaken with continually increasing agitation; but now his whole frame seemed to heave and rock convulsively past all hope of cure, and in a shrill voice he began to utter a string of unmeaning gibberish. V—— rang for the servants. They brought lights; but as the old man's fit did not abate, they lifted him up as though he had been a mere automaton, not possessed of the power of voluntary movement[1], and carried him to bed. After continuing in this frightful state for about an hour, he fell into a profound sleep resembling a dead faint When he awoke he asked for wine; and, after he had got what he wanted, he sent away the man who was going to sit with him, and locked himself in his room as usual.

V—— had indeed really resolved to make the attempt he spoke of to Daniel, although at the same time he could not forget two facts. In the first place, Daniel, having now been made aware of his propensity to walk in his sleep, would probably adopt every measure of precaution to avoid him; and on the other hand, confessions made whilst in this condition would not be exactly fitted to serve as a basis for further proceedings. In spite of this, however, he repaired to the hall on the approach of midnight, hoping that Daniel, as frequently happens to those afflicted in this way, would be constrained to act involuntarily. About midnight there arose a great noise in the courtyard. V—— plainly heard a window broken in; then he went downstairs, and as he traversed the passages he was met by rolling clouds of suffocating smoke, which, he soon perceived were pouring out of the open door of the house-steward's room. The steward himself was just being carried out, to all appearance dead, in order to be taken and put to bed in another room. The servants related

[1] Just like an automaton, Daniel realizes that he is not his own master: he is forced to walk and talk at the will of his heavy conscience, and – when he sleepwalks – is practically a robot made to retrace the steps of his crime with no more freedom to act than a clockwork doll

that about midnight one of the under-grooms[1] had been awakened by a strange hollow knocking; he thought something had befallen the old man, and was preparing to get up and go and see if he could help him, when the night watchman in the court shouted, "Fire! Fire! The Herr House-Steward's room is all of a bright blaze!" At this outcry several servants at once appeared on the scene; but all their efforts to burst open the room door were unavailing. Whereupon they hurried out into the court, but the resolute watchman had already broken in the window, for the room was low and on the basement story, had torn down the burning curtains, and by pouring a few buckets of water on them had at once extinguished the fire. The house-steward they found lying on the floor in the middle of the room in a swoon. In his hand he still held the candlestick tightly clenched[2], the burning candles of which had caught the curtains, and so occasioned the fire. Some of the blazing rags had fallen upon the old man, burning his eyebrows and a large portion of the hair of his head. If the watchman had not seen the fire the old man must have been helplessly burned to death. The servants, moreover, to their no little astonishment found the room door secured on the inside by two quite new bolts, which had been fastened on since the previous evening, for they had not been there then. V—— perceived that the old man had wished to make it impossible for him to get out of his room; for the blind impulse which urged him to wander in his sleep he could not resist. The old man became seriously ill; he did not speak; he took but little nourishment; and lay staring before him with the reflection of death in his set eyes, just as if he were clasped in the vice-like grip of some hideous thought. V—— believed he would never rise from his bed again.

V—— had done all that could be done for his client; and he could now only await the result in patience; and so he resolved to return to K——. His departure was fixed for the following morning. As he was packing his papers together late at night, he happened to lay his hand upon a little sealed packet which Freiherr Hubert von R—— had given him, bearing the inscription, *"To be read after my will has been opened,"* and which by some unaccountable means had hitherto escaped his notice. He was on the point of breaking the seal when the door opened and Daniel came in with still, ghostlike step. Placing upon the table a black portfolio which he carried under his arm, he sank upon his knees with a deep groan, and grasping V——'s hands with a convulsive clutch he said, in a voice so hollow and hoarse that it seemed to come from the bottom of a grave, "I should not like to die on the scaffold[3]! There is One above who judges!"

---

[1] Stable boy

[2] Recall that this was the way his master's body had been found – clutching a silver candlestick in rigor mortis

[3] That is, the gallows

Then, rising with some trouble and with many painful gasps, he left the room as he had come.

V—— spent the whole of the night in reading what the black portfolio and Hubert's packet contained. Both agreed in all circumstantial particulars, and suggested naturally what further steps were to be taken. On arriving at K—— V—— immediately repaired to Freiherr Hubert von R—— who received him with ill-mannered pride. But the remarkable result of the interview, which began at noon and lasted on without interruption until late at night, was that the next day the Freiherr made a declaration before the court to the effect that he acknowledged the claimant to be, agreeably to his father's will, the son of Wolfgang von R—— eldest son of Freiherr Roderick von R—— and begotten in lawful wedlock with Mdlle. Julia de St. Val, and furthermore acknowledged him as rightful and legitimate heir to the entail. On leaving the court he found his carriage, with post-horses, standing before the door; he stepped in and was driven off at a rapid rate, leaving his mother and his sister behind him. They would perhaps never see him again, he wrote, along with other perplexing statements. Roderick's astonishment at this unexpected turn which the case had taken was very great; he pressed V—— to explain to him how this wonder had been brought about, what mysterious power was at work in the matter. V—— however, evaded his questions by giving him hopes of telling him all at some future time, and when he should have come into possession of the estate. For the surrender of the entail to him could not be effected immediately, since the court, not content with Hubert's declaration, required that Roderick should also first prove his own identity to their satisfaction. V—— proposed to the Baron that he should go and live at R— sitten, adding that Hubert's mother and sister, momentarily embarrassed by his sudden departure, would prefer to go and live quietly on the ancestral property rather than stay in the dear[1] and noisy town. The glad delight with which Roderick welcomed the prospect of dwelling, at least for a time, under the same roof with the Baroness and her daughter, betrayed the deep impression which the lovely and graceful Seraphina had made upon him. In fact, the Freiherr made such good use of his time in R— sitten that, at the end of a few weeks, he had won Seraphina's love as well as her mother's cordial approval of her marriage with him. All this was for V—— rather too quick work, since Roderick's claims to be lord of the entail still continued to be rather doubtful. The life of idyllic happiness at the castle was interrupted by letters from Courland. Hubert had not shown himself at all at the estates, but had travelled direct to St Petersburg, where he had taken military service and was now in the field against the Persians, with whom

[1] Expensive (viz., due to the high cost of living)

Russia happened to be just then waging war[1]. This obliged the Baroness and her daughter to set off immediately for their Courland estates, where everything was in confusion and disorder. Roderick, who regarded himself in the light of an accepted son-inlaw, insisted upon accompanying his beloved; and hence, since V—— likewise returned to K—— the castle was left in its previous loneliness. The house-steward's malignant complaint grew worse and worse, so that he gave up all hopes of ever getting about again; and his office was conferred upon an old chasseur, Francis by name, Wolfgang's faithful servant.

At last, after long waiting, V—— received from Switzerland information of the most favourable character. The priest who had married Roderick was long since dead; but there was found in the church register a memorandum in his hand writing, to the effect that the man of the name of Born, whom he had joined in the bonds of wedlock with Mdlle. Julia de St. Val, had established completely to his satisfaction his identity as Freiherr Wolfgang von R—— eldest son of Freiherr Roderick von R—— of R— Sitten. Besides this, two witnesses of the marriage had been discovered, a merchant of Geneva and an old French captain, who had moved to Lyons; to them also Wolfgang had in confidence stated his real name; and their affidavits confirmed the priest's notice in the church register. With these memoranda in his hands, drawn up with proper legal formalities, V—— now succeeded in securing his client in the complete possession of his rights; and as there was now no longer any hindrance to the surrender to him of the entail, it was to be put into his hands in the ensuing autumn. Hubert had fallen in his very first engagement[2], thus sharing the fate of his younger brother, who had likewise been slain in battle a year before his father's death. Thus the Courland estates fell to Baroness Seraphina von R—— and made a handsome dowry for her to take to the too happy Roderick.

November had already come in when the Baroness, along with Roderick and his betrothed, arrived at R— sitten. The formal surrender of the estate-tail to the young Baron took place, and then his marriage with Seraphina was solemnised. Many weeks passed amid a continual whirl of pleasure; but at length the wearied guests began gradually to depart from the castle, to V——'s great satisfaction, for he had made up his mind not to take his leave of R— sitten until he had initiated the young lord of the entail in all the relations and duties connected with his new position down to the minutest particulars. Roderick's uncle had kept an account of all revenues and disbursements with the most detailed accuracy; hence, since Hubert had only retained a small sum annually for his own support,

---

[1] Probably a reference to the Russo-Persian Expedition of 1796 which lasted from April to November and ended in a stalemate, although this is far too late in the century to fit into the narrative timeline

[2] "had been killed in his very first duel"

the surplus revenues had all gone to swell the capital left by the old Freiherr, till the total now amounted to a considerable sum. Hubert had only employed the income of the entail for his own purposes during the first three years, but to cover this he had given a mortgage on the security of his share of the Courland property.

From the time when old Daniel had revealed himself to V—— as a somnambulist, V—— had chosen old Roderick's bed-room for his own sitting-room, in order that he might the more securely gather from the old man what he afterwards voluntarily disclosed. Hence it was in this room and in the adjoining great hall that the Freiherr transacted business with V——. Once they were both sitting at the great table by the bright blazing fire; V—— had his pen in his hand, and was noting down various totals and calculating the riches of the lord of the entail, whilst the latter, leaning his head on his hand, was blinking at the open account-books and formidable-looking documents. Neither of them heard the hollow roar of the sea, nor the anxious cries of the sea-gulls as they dashed against the windowpanes, flapping their wings and flying backwards and forwards, announcing the oncoming storm. Neither of them heeded the storm, which arose about midnight, and was now roaring and raging with wild fury round the castle walls, so that all the sounds of ill omen in the fire-grates and narrow passages awoke, and began to whistle and shriek in a weird, unearthly way. At length, after a terrific blast, which made the whole castle shake, the hall was completely lit up by the murky glare of the full moon, and V—— exclaimed, "Awful weather!" The Freiherr, quite absorbed in the consideration of the wealth which had fallen to him, replied indifferently, as he turned over a page of the receipt-book with a satisfied smile, "It is indeed; very stormy!" But, as if clutched by the icy hand of Dread, he started to his feet as the door of the hall flew open and a pale spectral figure became visible, striding in with the stamp of death upon its face. It was Daniel, who, lying helpless under the power of disease, was deemed in the opinion of V—— as of everybody else incapable of the ability to move a single limb; but, again coming under the influence of his propensity to wander in his sleep at full moon, he had, it appeared, been unable to resist it. The Freiherr stared at the old man without uttering a sound; and when Daniel began to scratch at the wall, and moan as though in the painful agonies of death, Roderick's heart was filled with horrible dread. With his face ashy pale and his hair standing straight on end, he leapt to his feet and strode towards the old man in a threatening attitude and cried in a loud firm voice, so that the hall rang again, *"Daniel, Daniel, what are you doing here at this hour?"* Then the old man uttered that same unearthly howling whimper, like the death-cry of a wounded animal, which he had uttered when Wolfgang had offered to reward his fidelity with gold; and he fell down on the floor. V—— summoned the servants; they raised the old man up; but all attempts to restore animation proved fruitless. Then the Freiherr cried, almost beside himself, "Good God! Good God! Now I remember to have heard that a sleepwalker may die on the spot if anybody calls him by his name. Oh! oh! unfortunate wretch that I am! I have killed the poor old man! I shall never more have a peaceful moment so long as I live." When the servants had carried the corpse away and the hall was again empty, V—— took the Freiherr, who was still continuing his self-reproaches, by the hand and led him in impressive silence to the walled-up postern, and said, "The man who fell down dead at your feet, Freiherr Roderick, was the atrocious murderer of your father." The Freiherr fixed his staring eyes upon V—— as though he saw the foul fiends of hell. But V—— went on, "The time has come now for me to reveal to you the hideous secret which, weighing upon the conscience of this monster and burthening him with curses, compelled him to roam abroad in his sleep. The Eternal Power has seen fit to make the son take vengeance upon the murderer of his father. The words which you thundered in the ears of that fearful night-walker were the last words which your unhappy father spoke." V—— sat down in front of the fire, and the Freiherr, trembling and unable to utter a word, took his seat beside him. V—— began to tell him the contents of the document which Hubert had left behind him, and the seal of which he (V——) was not to break until after the opening of the will Hubert lamented, in expressions testifying to the deepest remorse, the implacable hatred against his elder brother which took root in him from the moment that old Roderick established the entail. He was deprived of all weapons; for, even if he succeeded in maliciously setting the son at variance with the father, it would serve no purpose, since even Roderick himself had not the power to deprive his eldest son of his birth-right, nor would he on principle have ever done so, no matter how his affections had been alienated from him. It was only when Wolfgang formed his connection with Julia de St. Val in Geneva that Hubert saw his way to effecting his brother's ruin. And that was the time when he came to an understanding with Daniel, to provoke the old man by villainous devices to take measures which should drive his son to despair.

He was well aware of old Roderick's opinion that the only way to ensure an illustrious future for the family to all subsequent time was by means of an alliance with one of the oldest families in the country. The old man had read this alliance in the stars, and any pernicious derangement of the constellation would only entail destruction upon the family he had founded. In this way it was that Wolfgang's union with Julia seemed to the old man like a sinful crime, committed against the ordinances of the Power which had stood by him in all his worldly undertakings; and any means that might be employed for Julia's ruin he would have regarded as justified for the same reason, for Julia had, he conceived, ranged herself against him like some demoniacal principle. Hubert knew that his brother loved Julia passionately, almost to madness in fact, and that the loss of her would infallibly make him miserable,

perhaps kill him. And Hubert was all the more ready to assist the old man in his plans as he had himself conceived an unlawful affection for Julia, and hoped to win her for himself. It was, however, determined by a special dispensation of Providence that all attacks, even the most virulent, were to be thwarted by Wolfgang's resoluteness; nay, that he should contrive to deceive his brother: the fact that his marriage was actually solemnised and that of the birth of a son were kept secret from Hubert In Roderick's mind also there occurred, along with the presentiment of his approaching death, the idea that Wolfgang had really married the Julia who was so hostile to him. In the letter which commanded his son to appear at R— sitten on a given day to take possession of the entail, he cursed him if he did not sever his connection with her. This was the letter that Wolfgang burnt beside his father's corpse. To Hubert the old man wrote, saying that Wolfgang had married Julia, but that he would part from her. This Hubert took to be a fancy of his visionary father's; accordingly he was not a little dismayed when on reaching R— sitten Wolfgang with perfect frankness not only confirmed the old man's supposition, but also went on to add that Julia had borne him a son, and that he hoped in a short time to surprise her with the pleasant intelligence of his high rank and great wealth, for she had hitherto taken him for Born, a merchant from M——. He intended going to Geneva himself to fetch his beloved wife. But before he could carry out this plan he was overtaken by death. Hubert carefully concealed what he knew about the existence of a son born to Wolfgang in lawful wedlock with Julia, and so usurped the property that really belonged to his nephew. But only a few years passed before he became a prey to bitter remorse. He was reminded of his guilt in terrible wise by destiny, in the hatred which grew up and developed more and more between his two sons. "You are a poor starving beggar!" said the elder, a boy of twelve, to the younger, "but I shall be lord of R— sitten when father dies, and then you will have to be humble and kiss my hand when you want me to give you money to buy a new coat." The younger, goaded to ungovernable fury by his brother's proud and scornful words, threw the knife at him which he happened to have in his hand, and almost killed him. Hubert, for fear of some dire misfortune, sent the younger away to St. Petersburg; and he served afterwards as officer under Suwaroff, and fell fighting against the French. Hubert was prevented revealing to the world the dishonest and deceitful way in which he had acquired possession of the estate-tail by the shame and disgrace which would have come upon him; but he would not rob the rightful owner of a single penny more. He caused inquiries to be set on foot in Geneva, and learned that Madame Born had died of grief at the incomprehensible disappearance of her husband, but that young Roderick Born was being brought up by a worthy man who had adopted him. Hubert then caused himself to be introduced under an assumed name as a relative of Born the merchant, who had perished at sea, and he forwarded at given times sufficient sums of money to give the young heir of entail a good and respectable education. How he carefully treasured up the surplus revenues from the estate, and how he drew up the terms of his will, we already know. Respecting his brother's death, Hubert spoke in strangely obscure terms, but they allowed this much to be inferred, that there must be some mystery about it, and that he had taken part, indirectly, at least, in some heinous crime.

The contents of the black portfolio made everything clear. Along with Hubert's traitorous correspondence with Daniel was a sheet of paper written and signed by Daniel. V—— read a confession at which his very soul trembled, appalled. It was at Daniel's instigation that Hubert had come to R— sitten; and it was Daniel again who had written and told him about the one hundred and fifty thousand thalers that had been found. It has been already described how Hubert was received by his brother, and how, deceived in all his hopes and wishes, he was about to go off when he was prevented by V—— Daniel's heart was tortured by an insatiable thirst for vengeance, which he was determined to take on the young man who had proposed to kick him out like a mangy cur. He it was who relentlessly and incessantly fanned the flame of passion by which Hubert's desperate heart was consumed. Whilst in the fir forests hunting wolves, out in the midst of a blinding snowstorm, they agreed to effect his destruction. "Make away with him!" murmured Hubert, looking askance and taking aim with his rifle. "Yes, make away with him," snarled Daniel, "but not in that way, not in that way! " And he made the most solemn asseverations that he would murder the Freiherr and not a soul in the world should be the wiser. When,
however, Hubert had got his money, he repented of the plot; he determined to go away in order to shun all further temptation. Daniel himself saddled his horse and brought it out of the stable; but as the Baron was about to mount, Daniel said to him in a sharp, strained voice, "I thought you would stay on the entail, Freiherr Hubert, now that it has just fallen to you, for the proud lord of the entail lies dashed to pieces at the bottom of the ravine, below the tower." The steward had observed that Wolfgang, tormented by his thirst for gold, often used to rise in the night, go to the postern which formerly led to the tower, and stand gazing with longing eyes down into the chasm, where, according to his (Daniel's) testimony, vast treasures lay buried. Relying upon this habit, Daniel waited near the hall-door on that ill-omened night; and as soon as he heard the Freiherr open the postern leading to the tower, he entered the hall and proceeded to where the Freiherr was standing, close by the brink of the chasm. On becoming aware of the presence of his villainous servant, in whose eyes the gleam of murder shone, the Freiherr turned round and said with a cry of terror, *"Daniel, Daniel, what are you doing here at this hour?"* But then Daniel shrieked wildly, "Down with you, you

mangy cur!" and with a powerful push of his foot he hurled the unhappy man over into the deep chasm.

Terribly agitated by this awful deed, Freiherr Roderick found no peace in the castle where his father had been murdered. He went to his Courland estates, and only visited R— sitten once a year, in autumn. Francis — old Francis — who had strong suspicions as to Daniel's guilt, maintained that he often haunted the place at full moon, and described the nature of the
apparition much as V—— afterwards experienced it for himself when he exorcised it. It was the disclosure of these circumstances, also, which stamped his father's memory with dishonour, that had driven young Freiherr Hubert out into the world.

☙

This was my old great-uncle's story. Now he took my hand, and whilst his eyes filled with tears, he said, in a broken voice, "Cousin, cousin! And she too — the beautiful lady — has fallen a victim to the dark destiny, the grim, mysterious power which has established itself in that old ancestral castle. Two days after we left R— sitten the Freiherr arranged an excursion on sledges as the concluding event of the visit. He drove his wife himself; but as they were going down the valley the horses, for some unexplained reason, suddenly taking fright, began to snort and kick and plunge most savagely. 'The old man! The old man is after us!' screamed the Baroness in a shrill, terrified voice. At this same moment the sledge was overturned with a violent jerk, and the Baroness was hurled to a considerable distance. They picked her up lifeless — she was quite dead. The Freiherr is perfectly inconsolable, and has settled down into a state of passivity that will kill him. We shall never go to R— sitten again, cousin!"

Here my uncle paused. As I left him my heart was rent by emotion; and nothing but the all-soothing hand of Time could assuage the deep pain which I feared would cost me my life.

Years passed. V—— was resting in his grave, and I had left my native country. Then I was driven northwards, as far as St. Petersburg, by the devastating war[1] which was sweeping over all Germany. On my return journey, not far from K—— I was driving one dark summer night along the shore of the Baltic, when I perceived in the sky before me a remarkably large bright star. On coming nearer I saw by the red flickering flame that what I had taken for a star must be a large fire, but could not

[1] Probably the 1813 War of Liberation, wherein German and Prussian units fought to expel French occupiers

understand how it could be so high up in the air. "Postilion[1], what fire is that before us yonder?" I asked the man who was driving me. "Oh! why, that's not a fire; it's the beacon tower[2] of R— sitten." "R— sitten!" [As soon as] the postilion mentioned the name, all the experiences of the eventful autumn days which I had spent there recurred to my mind with lifelike reality. I saw the Baron — Seraphina — and also the remarkably eccentric old aunts — myself as well, with my bare milk-white face, my hair elegantly curled and powdered, and wearing a delicate sky-blue coat — nay, I saw myself in my love-sick folly, sighing like a furnace, and making lugubrious odes on my mistress's eyebrows. The sombre, melancholy mood into which these memories plunged me was relieved by the bright recollection of V——'s genial jokes, shooting up like flashes of coloured light, and I found them now still more entertaining than they had been so long ago. Thus agitated by pain mingled with much peculiar pleasure, I reached R— sitten early in the morning and got out of the coach in front of the post-house, where it had stopped I recognised the house as that of the land-steward; I inquired after him. "Begging your pardon," said the clerk of the post-house, taking his pipe from his mouth and giving his night-cap a tilt, "begging your pardon; there is no land-steward here; this is a Royal Government[3] office, and the Herr Administrator is still asleep." On making further inquiries I learnt that Freiherr Roderick von R—— the last lord of the entail, had died sixteen years before[4] without descendants, and that the entail in accordance with the terms of the original deeds had now escheated[5] to the state. I went up to the castle; it was a mere heap of ruins. I was informed by an old peasant, who came out of the fir-forest, and with whom I entered into conversation, that a large portion of the stones had been employed in the construction of the beacon-tower. He also could tell the story of the ghost which was said to have haunted the castle, and he affirmed that people often heard unearthly cries and lamentations amongst the stones, especially at full moon.

Poor short-sighted old Roderick! What a malignant destiny did you conjure up to destroy with the breath of poison, in the first moments of

---

[1] A person who rides on one of the horses on the left side of a team driving a coach. Their job is to guide the horses and help ensure a safe and orderly journey

[2] Lighthouse

[3] That is, the government of the Kingdom of Prussia and King Friedrich Wilhelm III

[4] If we take this to be 1813-1814, then that puts Roderick's death at around 1797, probably only a year or two after the events described in the first half of the story

[5] Been handed over to; been restored to

its growth, that race which you intended to plant with firm roots to last on till eternity!

WITH all due respect to Hoffmann, "The Entail" virtually requires two or three reads before you can be expected to understand it – so if you leave it confused, take heart. The most confusing part of the plot, however, likely generates from a very intentional effort on Hoffmann's to layer his story with overlapping leaves of time: characters who share the same names (Theodores, Huberts, and Rodericks) also tend share the same fates, adding to a complex, accruing patina of duplicating history. I do strongly recommend reading "The Entail" twice (or even three times) in order to move past the plot and character names and warm up the deeper issues lurking beneath; in case you just want to refresh the basic plot in chronological order before you continue, the footnote at the end of this sentence will do just that[1]. Now that we are all on the same page, let's

[1] Roderick Sr. – an alchemist dabbling in the dark arts – is killed when his tower collapses and discovered by his steward Daniel, who opens a door to the tower and finds himself staring into space. According to his will, the entire R—sitten estate passes on to his oldest son, Wolfgang, who mistreats and browbeats Daniel in search of his father's hidden treasures. Conspiring with Wolfgang's wastrel brother Hubert Sr., Daniel pushes Wolfgang to his death (he tends to stare out of the door into space, wondering about the treasures buried in the wreckage below), handing the estate over to Hubert Sr. When Hubert Sr. dies, the arrogant Hubert Jr. expects to be given R—sitten, but is shocked when his father's will reveals that he has been aware of the existence of Wolfgang's secret-but-legitimate son Roderick II. The castle is given to this new heir, and Hubert Jr. is killed in a duel shortly thereafter. Meanwhile, Theodore the Elder, the family lawyer, is suspicious that Daniel had a hand in Wolfgang's death, and learns that this is so when the old man catches him sleepwalking – reenacting the murder (trying to unlock the bricked up door and attempting to saddle Hubert Sr.'s horse) and is handed a confession in legal confidence. Unaware of this intrigue, Roderick II marries the beautiful Seraphina and moves to the castle. Stumbling onto Daniel's nighttime ritual, he accidentally utters his grandfather's last words, killing the old man by speaking inadvertently to his conscience. Horrified by Daniel's continued haunting of R—sitten and fearful of his wife's hysterical reaction to the ghost, Roderick II leaves the castle in the hands of Theodore the Elder, only visiting for his annual hunt. Years later, Theodore the Elder brings his great-nephew to R—sitten where both men witness Daniel's ghost, and the Elder Theodore attempts to exorcise the ghost by repeating the statement that killed him. Theodore the Younger, meanwhile, falls passionately in love with Seraphina who finds great spiritual relief from his piano playing, and from the presence of his great-uncle. Theodore the Elder views his great-nephew's increasingly irrational love for the

unpack what this story has to offer. Hoffmann was heavily influenced by early German Romanticism – the "Storm and Stress" era of Goethe and Schiller – which emphasized strong emotion and passionate impulses. This is not, however, to say that he was celebrating or encouraging this impetuous attitude: rather, the entire plot seems to critique earlier generations for their lack of flexibility, magnanimity, and compassion. Theodore the Younger is poised to become infected by the older generations' vices, but his great-uncle intervenes multiple times to keep him from making a stupid decision – unlike the greedy Wolfgang, the murderous Hubert Sr., or the cruel Hubert Jr., Theodore the Elder has maintained an open-minded, open-handed attitude, sometimes to his detriment. The younger Theo is modelled in almost every respect on Goethe's Young Werther, the suicidal manic-depressive protagonist of his first novel. In the 1770s and 1780s "Werther Fever" rocked Europe, leaving dozens of copy-cat suicides in Werther's wake, and making his trademark blue jacket and yellow breeches and waistcoat a bold fashion statement for the 18th century's Emo boys. Young Theodore, like Young Werther, finds himself consumed with a love for his best friend's wife, and consummates a kiss with her during an emotionally climactic bonding over poetry. Like his model, Theodore nearly turns a gun on himself, but his great-uncle – who has weathered nearly three generations of foolish choices, selfish impulses, and meaningless deaths (from murders, suicides, duels, and guilty consciences) – shakes him out of it by humiliating him at the height of his passion. Such clear-headed thinking could have saved Wolfgang from terrorizing Daniel, who would later kill him, could have saved Roderick II and his mother from being hidden and denied their rightful inheritance, and could have saved Hubert Sr. from suffering from a lifetime of guilt. As he narrates the story, almost two decades later, Theodore the Younger reflects on his youthful passion with wry humor, recognizing his foolish exuberance for what it was.

---

married woman with skeptical fear and attempts to shake him from her spell, well Roderick II is seemingly unthreatened and only asks his young rival to help him dispel his wife's manic obsession with Daniel's ghost, and asks that he ease off on their eroticized music sessions which have been inflaming her imagination. During his stay at the castle Theodore the Younger impresses Seraphina by killing a wolf during a hunt, frightens her with his ghost story, and is almost driven to suicide when she falls dangerously sick due to her mania. Both Theos depart abruptly one morning, leaving Theodore the Younger heartsick but alive. In the following year, Theodore the Elder suffers a stroke when he reads of Seraphina's death in a sleighing accident – a shock which is shared by Roderick II, who dies shortly after. Before his death, the Elder Theodore tells his great-nephew about the castle's strange past, and many years later the now mature Theodore travels past R—sitten which he discovers has been handed over to the state and turned into a lighthouse

II.

But there is one character – the keystone uniting the first and second parts of the story – whose brutal end lingers in the imagination long after the story has been put down. Like Antonia in "Councillor Krespel," Seraphina is opened up by music, and by opening up, she is made vulnerable – and through vulnerability she is destroyed. Seraphina holds the key to the R—sittens' salvation; she offers them the opportunity to open their reclusive family up to the wider world – bringing new blood to the old blood, transfiguring repression into expression, and silence into singing. But she is threatened by the ghosts of R—sitten, and realizes that its labyrinth of secrecy is poised to consume her. Ironically, it is in singing and making music with Theodore the Younger that she most experiences her stifled existence: the expressiveness of their singing serves to accentuate the repressiveness of their surroundings. Theodore the Elder and Roderick II both sense the danger the castle poses to Seraphina, and both understand the dangers posed by her music making – bringing out her native expressiveness and innocence into a hostile environment of despotic selfishness and brutal silence. Theodore the Elder complicates her biography by describing how the girl born in the late 1760s appears to have married Roderick II in the mid '60s, setting himself up as her friend, peer, and ally several years before her birth. Critics like James M. McGlathery point out that it is likelier that Hoffmann has intentionally muddied Old Theo's memory than that he forgot his timeline. Instead, McGlathery argues that the septuagenarian Justiciary – who fawns over Seraphina's attention (she desires his presence as a source of comfort and protection) and has a fatal stroke when he reads the news of her death – had invented a backstory with the teenage baroness.

III.

Like most Hoffmann protagonists, he is an eccentric older male harboring a barely hidden passion for a much younger woman, and like Drosselmeier in "Nutcracker," he uses his nephew's attraction to her as a vicarious means of finding the acceptance he feels to be impossible. The catastrophic results – which humiliate uncle and nephew alike – mirror a very specific, shameful episode from Hoffmann's own life. In referring to Theodore the Younger's humbling, failed affair, and Schiller's story which inspired it, Kenneth Negus pauses to note the undeniable autobiographical elements which inspired it:

> "There are deep personal matters that are involved in this rejection on Hoffmann's part: he was attempting to remove from his life the influence of some of the thing most cherished in his youth. Why? The biographical facts with which we are concerned here [involve, as described in the biography by Hans von Muller] the woesome tale of Hoffmann's late teens and early twenties when he was in love with Dora Hatt ... an older married woman. His love was requited, and reached proportions and complications which had a deep effect on the

> immediate course of Hoffmann's life, and gave rise to much contemplation and remorse in later years... a time when he was in great danger stemming from his own guilt."

By having the nephew relive the uncle's shame, Hoffmann vicariously explores his own unresolved moral guilt, reminding himself that in no parallel universe could his affair with Hatt have worked or been justifiable. The cycle of sin that rolls through families must be learned from if the misery they cause is ever to have any meaning or redemption – if, to borrow a fashionable phrase – generational traumas and family curses are to be broken. If we accept this interpretation (especially given its precedent in many of Hoffmann's tales), we then see that both Theodores, encompassing between them the span of three generations, fail to protect and save the object of their shared affection. Both men, middle class outsiders with access to the R—sitten family, fail to override the momentum of time and society, leading to Seraphina's unhappy, inevitable demise. But the true villain of the piece seems to be the society – its laws, customs, and traditions – that allowed such a tragedy to take place at all. The title, "The Entail," refers to the legal machinery that ensures sibling rivalries, promotes murder and deceit, and leads three successive generations (Roderick I and Daniel, Wolfgang and Hubert Sr, Hubert Jr, Roderick II, and Seraphina) to miserable and preventative deaths. Roderick I dies because of his self-inflicted isolation; Wolfgang is murdered because of his greed-inspired cruelty; his assassin, Daniel, dies of shock induced by his burdened conscience; the orchestrator of the murder, Hubert Sr, lives a miserable life plagued by guilt; while his son dies in a hot-headed duel, and the final baron and baroness are innocent victims of R—sitten's violent momentum. *All* this, Hoffman-by-way-of-Theodore, ensures us, could have been avoided by eschewing the entail's rigid legal apparatus, and having a more open-handed, open-hearted legacy available for all members of the family. In short, "The Entail" is a critique of Prussian society – its prejudices, classism, inflexibility, bureaucratism, nepotism, sexism, and the glacial rate of social progress.

"I felt as a child feels when some fairy tale has been told it to conceal the truth it suspects." This quote – one of the most telling products of Hoffmann's pen – comes from the following story. Blurring the ghost story, mystery, romance, and horror genres (as so many of Hoffmann's tales do), it perfectly represents this disenchanted ethos. The basic concept behind the quote is that both society-at-large and individuals fabricate necessary falsehoods as a means of dampening the crushing pain of reality. As in "The Sandman" Hoffmann illustrates this by using a childhood superstition (in this case, a fear that looking into a mirror at night will rob you of your soul) to reflect a brutal truth of reality: the power of self-absorption to distort truth and rob you of your objectivity. By looking too closely at a desired object, Hoffmann warns, we lose our ability to guard ourselves against bias, deception, and possession. The story has served as a prototype for many strange tales of haunted houses: Henry James specifically references Hoffmann three times in "The Ghostly Rental" (a masterful ghost tale about a grotesque old man who delivers his quarterly rent to the spirit of his daughter in an abandoned manor), and H. P. Lovecraft summons the spirit of this story in "The Music of Erich Zann" (in which a curious young man is drawn to a strange part of Paris and befriends a deaf-mute cellist whose room window communicates with another dimension). Both stories – which concern the uncanny or aged occupants of mysteriously neglected residences – share direct parallels with "The Deserted House," especially in their common themes of delusion, miscommunication, treachery, and unresolved trauma. James' tale, in particular, concerns family intrigue, lies, and guilt which lead to a strange kind of haunting – one suffered by a vaguely-defined, female ghost condemned by her past behavior to a repetitive, liminal existence on the boundaries of reality – boundaries which are defined by the walls of a dilapidated house, a prison kept locked by a conscience and revenge. Hoffmann's story is concerned – as so many of Hoffmann's are – with the perils of wishful thinking, the ugliness of a vengeful spirit, and the deceptiveness of desire...

The Deserted House

— Excerpted from 'Night-Pieces,' Volume Two —

{1817}

THEY were all agreed in the belief that the actual facts of life are often far more wonderful[1] than the invention of even the liveliest imagination can be.

---

[1] Unbelievable, shocking

"It seems to me," spoke Lelio, "that history gives proof sufficient of this. And that is why the so-called historical romances seem so repulsive and tasteless to us, those stories wherein the author mingles the foolish fancies of his meager brain with the deeds of the great powers of the universe."

Franz took the word. "It is the deep reality of the inscrutable secrets surrounding us that oppresses us with a might wherein we recognize the Spirit that rules, the Spirit out of which our being springs."

"Alas," said Lelio, "it is the most terrible result of the fall of man[1], that we have lost the power of recognizing the eternal verities."

"Many are called, but few are chosen[2]," broke in Franz. "Do you not believe that an understanding of the wonders of our existence is given to some of us in the form of another sense? But if you would allow me to drag the conversation up from these dark regions where we are in danger of losing our path altogether up into the brightness of light-hearted merriment, I would like to make the scurrilous suggestion that those mortals to whom this gift of seeing the Unseen has been given remind me of bats. You know the learned anatomist Spallanzani[3] has discovered a sixth sense[4] in these little animals which can do not only the entire work of the other senses, but work of its own besides."

"Oho," laughed Edward, "according to that, the bats would be the only natural-born clairvoyants. But I know one who possesses that gift of insight, of which you were speaking, in a remarkable degree. Because of it he will often follow for days some unknown person who has happened to attract his attention by an oddity in manner, appearance, or garb; he will ponder to melancholy over some trifling incident, some lightly told story; he will combine the antipodes[5] and raise up relationships in his imagination which are unknown to everyone else."

"Wait a bit," cried Lelio. "It is our Theodore of whom you are speaking now. And it looks to me as if he were having some weird vision at this very moment. See how strangely he gazes out into the distance."

Theodore had been sitting in silence up to this moment. Now he spoke: "If my glances are strange it is because they reflect the strange things

---

[1] The Christian doctrine that man was created without sin, but willingly introduced sin, death, and evil into the world when Adam and Eve disobeyed God's only rule in the Garden of Eden

[2] Matthew 22:14

[3] Lazzaro Spallanzani was an 18th century Catholic priest and scientist who contributed considerably to the understanding of animal husbandry and biology. In particularly, he introduced the concept of echolocation when studying bats

[4] That is, echolocation

[5] "Connect the dots"

that were called up before my mental vision by your conversation, the memories of a most remarkable adventure—"

"Oh, tell it to us," interrupted his friends.

"Gladly," continued Theodore. "But first, let me set right a slight confusion in your ideas on the subject of the mysterious. You appear to confound what is merely odd and unusual with what is really mysterious or marvelous, that which surpasses comprehension or belief. The odd and the unusual, it is true, spring often from the truly marvelous, and the twigs and flowers hide the parent stem from our eyes. Both the odd and the unusual and the truly marvelous are mingled in the adventure which I am about to narrate to you, mingled in a manner which is striking and even awesome." With these words Theodore drew from his pocket a notebook in which, as his friends knew, he had written down the impressions of his late journeyings. Refreshing his memory by a look at its pages now and then, he narrated the following story.

☙

You know already that I spent the greater part of last summer in X[1]. The many old friends and acquaintances I found there, the free, jovial life, the manifold artistic and intellectual interests—all these combined to keep me in that city. I was happy as never before, and found rich nourishment for my old fondness for wandering alone through the streets, stopping to enjoy every picture in the shop windows, every placard on the walls, or watching the passers-by and choosing some one or the other of them to cast his horoscope secretly to myself.

There is one broad avenue leading to the —— Gate[2] and lined with handsome buildings of all descriptions, which is the meeting place of the rich and fashionable world. The shops which occupy the ground floor of the tall palaces are devoted to the trade in articles of luxury, and the apartments above are the dwellings of people of wealth and position. The aristocratic hotels are to be found in this avenue, the palaces of the foreign ambassadors are there and you can easily imagine that such a street would be the center of the city's life and gayety.

I had wandered through the avenue several times, when one day my attention was caught by a house which contrasted strangely with the others surrounding it. Picture to yourselves a low building but four windows broad, crowded in between two tall, handsome structures. Its one upper story was little higher than the tops of the ground-floor windows of its neighbors, its roof was dilapidated, its windows patched with paper, its discolored walls spoke of years of neglect. You can imagine how strange such a house must have looked in this street of wealth and fashion. Looking at it more attentively I perceived that the windows of the upper story were tightly closed and curtained, and that a wall had been built to hide the

---

[1] Heavily implied to be Berlin

[2] Heavily implied to be the Brandenburg Gate

windows of the ground floor. The entrance gate, a little to one side, served also as a doorway for the building, but I could find no sign of latch, lock, or even a bell on this gate. I was convinced that the house must be unoccupied, for at whatever hour of the day I happened to be passing I had never seen the faintest signs of life about it. An unoccupied house in this avenue was indeed an odd sight. But I explained the phenomenon to myself by saying that the owner was doubtless absent upon a long journey, or living upon his country estates, and that he perhaps did not wish to sell or rent the property, preferring to keep it for his own use in the eventuality of a visit to the city.

You all, the good comrades of my youth, know that I have been prone to consider myself a sort of clairvoyant, claiming to have glimpses of a strange world of wonders, a world which you, with your hard common sense, would attempt to deny or laugh away. I confess that I have often lost myself in mysteries which after all turned out to be no mysteries at all. And it looked at first as if this was to happen to me in the matter of the deserted house, that strange house which drew my steps and my thoughts to itself with a power that surprised me. But the point of my story will prove to you that I am right in asserting that I know more than you do. Listen now to what I am about to tell you.

One day, at the hour in which the fashionable world is accustomed to promenade up and down the avenue, I stood as usual before the deserted house, lost in thought. Suddenly I felt, without looking up, that some one had stopped beside me, fixing his eyes on me. It was Count P., whom I had found much in sympathy with many of my imaginings, and I knew that he also must have been deeply interested in the mystery of this house. It surprised me not a little, therefore, that he should smile ironically when I spoke of the strange impression that this deserted dwelling, here in the gay heart of the town, had made upon me. But I soon discovered the reason for his irony. Count P. had gone much farther than myself in his imaginings concerning the house. He had constructed for himself a complete history of the old building, a story weird enough to have been born in the fancy of a true poet. It would give me great pleasure to relate this story to you, but the events which happened to me in this connection are so interesting that I feel I must proceed with the narration of them at once.

When the count had completed his story to his own satisfaction, imagine his feelings on learning one day that the old house contained nothing more mysterious than a cake bakery belonging to the pastry cook whose handsome shop adjoined the old structure. The windows of the ground floor were walled up to give protection to the ovens, and the heavy curtains of the upper story were to keep the sunlight from the wares laid out there. When the count informed me of this I felt as if a bucket of cold water had been suddenly thrown over me. The demon who is the enemy of all poets caught the dreamer by the nose and tweaked him painfully.

And yet, in spite of this prosaic explanation, I could not resist stopping before the deserted house whenever I passed it, and gentle tremors rippled through my veins as vague visions arose of what might be hidden there. I could not believe in this story of the cake and candy factory. Through some strange freak of the imagination I felt as a child feels when some fairy tale has been told it to conceal the truth it suspects. I scolded myself for a silly fool; the house remained unaltered in its appearance, and the visions faded in my brain, until one day a chance incident woke them to life again.

I was wandering through the avenue as usual, and as I passed the deserted house I could not resist a hasty glance at its close-curtained upper windows. But as I looked at it, the curtain on the last window near the pastry shop began to move. A hand, an arm, came out from between its folds. I took my opera glass[1] from my pocket and saw a beautifully formed woman's hand, on the little finger of which a large diamond sparkled in unusual brilliancy; a rich bracelet glittered on the white, rounded arm. The hand set a tall, oddly formed crystal bottle on the window ledge and disappeared again behind the curtain.

I stopped as if frozen to stone; a weirdly pleasurable sensation, mingled with awe, streamed through my being with the warmth of an electric current. I stared up at the mysterious window and a sigh of longing arose from the very depths of my heart. When I came to myself again, I was angered to find that I was surrounded by a crowd which stood gazing up at the window with curious faces. I stole away inconspicuously, and the demon of all things prosaic whispered to me that what I had just seen was the rich pastry cook's wife, in her Sunday adornment, placing an empty bottle, used for rose-water or the like, on the window sill. Nothing very weird about this.

Suddenly a most sensible thought came to me. I turned and entered the shining, mirror-walled shop of the pastry cook. Blowing the steaming foam from my cup of chocolate, I remarked: "You have a very useful addition to your establishment next door." The man leaned over his counter and looked at me with a questioning smile, as if he did not understand me. I repeated that in my opinion he had been very clever to set up his bakery in the neighboring house, although the deserted appearance of the building was a strange sight in its contrasting surroundings. "Why, sir," began the pastry cook, "who told you that the house next door belongs to us? Unfortunately every attempt on our part to acquire it has been in vain, and I fancy it is all the better so, for there is something queer about the place."

You can imagine, dear friends, how interested I became upon hearing these words, and that I begged the man to tell me more about the house.

"I do not know anything very definite, sir," he said. "All that we know for a certainty is that the house belongs to the Countess S., who lives on

[1] Small binoculars used to better watch the onstage action of an opera or play

her estates and has not been to the city for years. This house, so they tell me, stood in its present shape before any of the handsome buildings were raised which are now the pride of our avenue, and in all these years there has been nothing done to it except to keep it from actual decay. Two living creatures alone dwell there, an aged misanthrope of a steward[1] and his melancholy dog, which occasionally howls at the moon from the back courtyard. According to the general story the deserted house is haunted. In very truth my brother, who is the owner of this shop, and myself have often, when our business kept us awake during the silence of the night, heard strange sounds from the other side of the wall. There was a rumbling and a scraping that frightened us both And not very long ago we heard one night a strange singing which I could not describe to you. It was evidently the voice of an old woman, but the tones were so sharp and clear, and ran up to the top of the scale in cadences and long trills, the like of which I have never heard before, although I have heard many singers in many lands. It seemed to be a French song, but I am not quite sure of that, for I could not listen long to the mad, ghostly singing, it made the hair stand erect on my head. And at times, after the street noises are quiet, we can hear deep sighs, and sometimes a mad laugh, which seem to come out of the earth. But if you lay your ear to the wall in our back room, you can hear that the noises come from the house next door." He led me into the back room and pointed through the window. "And do you see that iron chimney coming out of the wall there? It smokes so heavily sometimes, even in summer when there are no fires used that my brother has often quarreled with the old steward about it, fearing danger. But the old man excuses himself by saying that he was cooking his food. Heaven knows what the queer creature may eat, for often, when the pipe is smoking heavily, a strange and queer smell can be smelled all over the house."

The glass doors of the shop creaked in opening. The pastry cook hurried into the front room, and when he had nodded to the figure now entering he threw a meaning glance at me. I understood him perfectly. Who else could this strange guest be, but the steward who had charge of the mysterious house! Imagine a thin little man with a face the color of a mummy, with a sharp nose tight-set lips, green cat's eyes, and a crazy smile; his hair dressed in the old-fashioned style with a high toupet and a bag at the back[2], and heavily powdered. He wore a faded old brown coat which was carefully brushed, gray stockings, and broad, flat-toed shoes with buckles. And imagine further, that in spite of his meagerness this little person is robustly built, with huge fists and long, strong fingers, and that he walks to the shop counter with a strong, firm step, smiling his imbecile[3] smile, and whining out: "A couple of candied oranges—a couple of

[1] A property manager

[2] A French men's wig in the style of the mid-18th century

[3] Deranged, unhinged

macaroons—a couple of sugared chestnuts—" Picture all this to yourself and judge whether I had not sufficient cause to imagine a mystery here.

The pastry cook gathered up the wares the old man had demanded. "Weigh it out, weigh it out, honored neighbor," moaned the strange man, as he drew out a little leathern bag and sought in it for his money. I noticed that he paid for his purchase in worn old coins, some of which were no longer in use. He seemed very unhappy and murmured: "Sweet—sweet—it must all be sweet! Well, let it be! The devil has pure honey for his bride—pure honey!"

The pastry cook smiled at me and then spoke to the old man. "You do not seem to be quite well. Yes, yes, old age, old age! It takes the strength from our limbs." The old man's expression did not change, but his voice went up: "Old age?—Old age?—Lose strength?—Grow weak?—Oho!" And with this he clapped his hands together until the joints cracked, and sprang high up into the air until the entire shop trembled and the glass vessels on the walls and counters rattled and shook. But in the same moment a hideous screaming was heard; the old man had stepped on his black dog, which, creeping in behind him, had laid itself at his feet on the floor. "Devilish beast—dog of hell!" groaned the old man in his former miserable tone, opening his bag and giving the dog a large macaroon. The dog, which had burst out into a cry of distress that was truly human, was quiet at once, sat down on its haunches, and gnawed at the macaroon like a squirrel. When it had finished its tidbit, the old man had also finished the packing up and putting away of his purchases. "Good night, honored neighbor," he spoke, taking the hand of the pastry cook and pressing it until the latter cried aloud in pain. "The weak old man wishes you a good night, most honorable Sir Neighbor," he repeated, and then walked from the shop, followed closely by his black dog. The old man did not seem to have noticed me at all. I was quite dumfoundered in my astonishment.

"There, you see," began the pastry cook. "This is the way he acts when he comes in here, two or three times a month, it is. But I can get nothing out of him except the fact that he was a former valet of Count S., that he is now in charge of this house here, and that every day—for many years now—he expects the arrival of his master's family. My brother spoke to him one day about the strange noises at night; but he answered calmly, 'Yes, people say the ghosts walk about in the house.' But do not believe it, for it is not true." The hour was now come when fashion demanded that the elegant world of the city should assemble in this attractive shop. The doors opened incessantly, the place was thronged, and I could ask no further questions.

This much I knew, that Count P.'s information about the ownership and the use of the house were not correct; also that the old steward, in spite of his denial, was not living alone there, and that some mystery was hidden behind its discolored walls. How could I combine the story of the strange and gruesome singing with the appearance of the beautiful arm at the window? That arm could not be part of the wrinkled body of an old woman; the singing, according to the pastry cook's story, could not come from the throat of a blooming and youthful maiden. I decided in favor of the arm, as it was easy to explain to myself that some trick of acoustics had made the voice sound sharp and old, or that it had appeared so only in the pastry cook's fear-distorted imagination. Then I thought of the smoke, the strange odors, the oddly formed crystal bottle that I had seen, and soon the vision of a beautiful creature held enthralled by fatal magic stood as if alive before my mental vision. The old man became a wizard who perhaps quite independently of the family he served, had set up his devil's kitchen in the deserted house. My imagination had begun to work, and in my dreams that night I saw clearly the hand with the sparkling diamond on its finger, the arm with the shining bracelet. From out thin, gray mists there appeared a sweet face with sadly imploring blue eyes, then the entire exquisite figure of a beautiful girl. And I saw that what I had thought was mist was the fine steam flowing out in circles from a crystal bottle held in the hands of the vision.

"Oh, fairest creature of my dreams," I cried in rapture. "Reveal to me where thou art, what it is that enthralls thee. Ah, I know it! It is black magic that holds thee captive—thou art the unhappy slave of that malicious devil who wanders about brown-clad and bewigged in pastry shops, scattering their wares with his unholy springing, and feeding his demon dog on macaroons, after they have howled out a Satanic measure in five-eight time[1]. Oh, I know it all, thou fair and charming vision. The diamond is the reflection of the fire of thy heart. But that bracelet about thine arm is a link of the chain which the brown-clad one says is a magnetic chain. Do not believe it, O glorious one! See how it shines in the blue fire from the retort[2]. One moment more and thou art free. And now, O maiden, open thy rosebud mouth and tell me—" In this moment a gnarled fist leaped over my shoulder and clutched at the crystal bottle, which sprang into a thousand pieces in the air. With a faint, sad moan, the charming vision faded into the blackness of the night.

When morning came to put an end to my dreaming I hurried to the avenue and placed myself before the deserted house. Heavy blinds were drawn before the upper windows. The street was still quite empty, and I stepped close to the windows of the ground floor and listened and listened; but I heard no sound. The house was as quiet as the grave. The business of the day began, the passers-by became more numerous, and I was obliged to go on. I will not weary you with the recital of how for many days I crept

---

[1] An unusual, rather unsettling musical time signature that is used in songs such as Dave Brubek's "Take Five," the "Mission Impossible" theme, the "Halloween" theme, and Gustav Holst's "Mars"

[2] A a glass flask with a long, downward slanted spout used for distilling in chemistry

about the house at that hour, but without discovering anything of interest. None of my questionings could reveal anything to me, and the beautiful picture of my vision began finally to pale and fade away.

At last as I passed, late one evening, I saw that the door of the deserted house was half open and the brown-clad old man was peeping out. I stepped quickly to his side with a sudden idea. "Does not Councillor Binder live in this house?" Thus I asked the old man, pushing him before me as I entered the dimly lighted vestibule. The guardian of the old house looked at me with his piercing eyes, and answered in gentle, slow tones: "No, he does not live here, he never has lived here, he never will live here, he does not live anywhere on this avenue. But people say the ghosts walk about in this house. Yet I can assure you that it is not true. It is a quiet, a pretty house, and to-morrow the gracious Countess S. will move into it. Good night, dear gentleman." With these words the old man maneuvered me out of the house and locked the gate behind me. I heard his feet drag across the floor, I heard his coughing and the rattling of his bunch of keys, and I heard him descend some steps. Then all was silent. During the short time that I had been in the house I had noticed that the corridor was hung with old tapestries and furnished like a drawing-room with large, heavy chairs in red damask.

And now, as if called into life by my entrance into the mysterious house, my adventures began. The following day, as I walked through the avenue in the noon hour, and my eyes sought the deserted house as usual, I saw something glistening in the last window of the upper story. Coming nearer I noticed that the outer blind had been quite drawn up and the inner curtain slightly opened. The sparkle of a diamond met my eye. O kind Heaven! The face of my dream looked at me, gently imploring, from above the rounded arm on which her head was resting. But how was it possible to stand still in the moving crowd without attracting attention? Suddenly I caught sight of the benches placed in the gravel walk in the center of the avenue, and I saw that one of them was directly opposite the house. I sprang over to it, and leaning over its back, I could stare up at the mysterious window undisturbed. Yes, it was she, the charming maiden of my dream! But her eye did not seem to seek me as I had at first thought; her glance was cold and unfocused, and had it not been for an occasional motion of the hand and arm, I might have thought that I was looking at a cleverly painted picture.

I was so lost in my adoration of the mysterious being in the window, so aroused and excited throughout all my nerve centers, that I did not hear the shrill voice of an Italian street hawker, who had been offering me his wares for some time. Finally he touched me on the arm, I turned hastily and commanded him to let me alone. But he did not cease his entreaties, asserting that he had earned nothing to-day, and begging me to buy some small trifle from him. Full of impatience to get rid of him I put my hand in my pocket. With the words: "I have more beautiful things here," he opened the under drawer of his box and held out to me a little, round pocket mirror. In it, as he held it up before my face, I could see the deserted house behind me, the window, and the sweet face of my vision there.

I bought the little mirror at once, for I saw that it would make it possible for me to sit comfortably and inconspicuously, and yet watch the window. The longer I looked at the reflection in the glass, the more I fell captive to a weird and quite indescribable sensation, which I might almost call a waking dream. It was as if a lethargy had lamed my eyes, holding them fastened on the glass beyond my power to loosen them. Through my mind there rushed the memory of an old nurse's[1] tale of my earliest childhood. When my nurse was taking me off to bed, and I showed an inclination to stand peering into the great mirror in my father's room, she would tell me that when children looked into mirrors in the night time they would see a strange, hideous face there, and their eyes would be frozen so that they could not move them again. The thought struck awe to my soul, but I could not resist a peep at the mirror, I was so curious to see the strange face. Once I did believe that I saw two hideous glowing eyes shining out of the mirror. I screamed and fell down in a swoon.

All these foolish memories of my early childhood came trooping back to me. My blood ran cold through my veins. I would have thrown the mirror from me, but I could not. And now at last the beautiful eyes of the fair vision looked at me, her glance sought mine and shone deep down into my heart. The terror I had felt left me, giving way to the pleasurable pain of sweetest longing.

"You have a pretty little mirror there," said a voice beside me. I awoke from my dream, and was not a little confused when I saw smiling faces looking at me from either side. Several persons had sat down upon my bench, and it was quite certain that my staring into the window, and my probably strange expression, had afforded them great cause for amusement.

"You have a pretty little mirror there," repeated the man, as I did not answer him. His glance said more, and asked without words the reason of my staring so oddly into the little glass. He was an elderly man, neatly dressed, and his voice and eyes were so full of good nature that I could not refuse him my confidence. I told him that I had been looking in the mirror at the picture of a beautiful maiden who was sitting at a window of the deserted house. I went even farther; I asked the old man if he had not seen the fair face himself. "Over there? In the old house—in the last window?" He repeated my questions in a tone of surprise.

"Yes, yes," I exclaimed.

The old man smiled and answered: "Well, well, that was a strange delusion. My old eyes—thank Heaven for my old eyes! Yes, yes, sir. I saw a

[1] A servant tasked with caring for a family's young children

pretty face in the window there, with my own eyes; but it seemed to me to be an excellently well-painted oil portrait."

I turned quickly and looked toward the window; there was no one there, and the blind had been pulled down. "Yes," continued the old man, "yes, sir. Now it is too late to make sure of the matter, for just now the servant, who, as I know, lives there alone in the house of the Countess S., took the picture away from the window after he had dusted it, and let down the blinds."

"Was it, then, surely a picture?" I asked again, in bewilderment.

"You can trust my eyes," replied the old man. "The optical delusion was strengthened by your seeing only the reflection in the mirror. And when I was in your years it was easy enough for my fancy to call up the picture of a beautiful maiden."

"But the hand and arm moved," I exclaimed. "Oh, yes, they moved, indeed they moved," said the old man smiling, as he patted me on the shoulder. Then he arose to go, and bowing politely, closed his remarks with the words, "Beware of mirrors which can lie so vividly. Your obedient servant, sir."

You can imagine how I felt when I saw that he looked upon me as a foolish fantast. I began to be convinced that the old man was right, and that it was only my absurd imagination which insisted on raising up mysteries about the deserted house.

I hurried home full of anger and disgust, and promised myself that I would not think of the mysterious house, and would not even walk through the avenue for several days. I kept my vow, spending my days working at my desk, and my evenings in the company of jovial friends, leaving myself no time to think of the mysteries which so enthralled me. And yet, it was just in these days that I would start up out of my sleep as if awakened by a touch, only to find that all that had aroused me was merely the thought of that mysterious being whom I had seen in my vision and in the window of the deserted house. Even during my work, or in the midst of a lively conversation with my friends, I felt the same thought shoot through me like an electric current. I condemned the little mirror in which I had seen the charming picture to a prosaic daily use. I placed it on my dressing-table that I might bind my cravat[1] before it, and thus it happened one day, when I was about to utilize it for this important business, that its glass seemed dull, and that I took it up and breathed on it to rub it bright again. My heart seemed to stand still, every fiber in me trembled in delightful awe. Yes, that is all the name I can find for the feeling that came over me, when, as my breath clouded the little mirror, I saw the beautiful face of my dreams arise and smile at me through blue mists. You laugh at me? You look upon me as an incorrigible dreamer? Think what you will about it—the fair face

---

[1] Neckcloth

looked at me from out of the mirror! But as soon as the clouding vanished, the face vanished in the brightened glass.

I will not weary you with a detailed recital of my sensations the next few days. I will only say that I repeated again the experiments with the mirror, sometimes with success, sometimes without. When I had not been able to call up the vision, I would run to the deserted house and stare up at the windows; but I saw no human being anywhere about the building. I lived only in thoughts of my vision; everything else seemed indifferent to me. I neglected my friends and my studies. The tortures in my soul passed over into, or rather mingled with, physical sensations which frightened me, and which at last made me fear for my reason. One day, after an unusually severe attack, I put my little mirror in my pocket and hurried to the home of Dr. K., who was noted for his treatment of those diseases of the mind out of which physical diseases so often grow. I told him my story; I did not conceal the slightest incident from him, and I implored him to save me from the terrible fate which seemed to threaten me. He listened to me quietly, but I read astonishment in his glance. Then he said: "The danger is not as near as you believe, and I think that I may say that it can be easily prevented. You are undergoing an unusual psychical disturbance, beyond a doubt. But the fact that you understand that some evil principle seems to be trying to influence you, gives you a weapon by which you can combat it. Leave your little mirror here with me, and force yourself to take up with some work which will afford scope for all your mental energy. Do not go to the avenue; work all day, from early to late, then take a long walk, and spend your evenings in the company of your friends. Eat heartily, and drink heavy, nourishing wines. You see I am endeavoring to combat your fixed idea[1] of the face in the window of the deserted house and in the mirror, by diverting your mind to other things, and by strengthening your body. You yourself must help me in this."

I was very reluctant to part with my mirror. The physician, who had already taken it, seemed to notice my hesitation. He breathed upon the glass and holding it up to me, he asked: "Do you see anything?"

"Nothing at all," I answered, for so it was.

"Now breathe on the glass yourself," said the physician, laying the mirror in my hands.

I did as he requested. There was the vision even more clearly than ever before.

"There she is!" I cried aloud.

The physician looked into the glass, and then said: "I cannot see anything. But I will confess to you that when I looked into this glass, a queer shiver overcame me, passing away almost at once. Now do it once more."

I breathed upon the glass again and the physician laid his hand upon

---

[1] Usually left untranslated from French as an idée fixe: an all-consuming manic obsession

the back of my neck. The face appeared again, and the physician, looking into the mirror over my shoulder, turned pale. Then he took the little glass from my hands, looked at it attentively, and locked it into his desk, returning to me after a few moments' silent thought.

"Follow my instructions strictly," he said. "I must confess to you that I do not yet understand those moments of your vision. But I hope to be able to tell you more about it very soon."

Difficult as it was to me, I forced myself to live absolutely according to the doctor's orders. I soon felt the benefit of the steady work and the nourishing diet, and yet I was not free from those terrible attacks, which would come either at noon, or, more intensely still, at midnight. Even in the midst of a merry company, in the enjoyment of wine and song, glowing daggers seemed to pierce my heart, and all the strength of my intellect was powerless to resist their might over me. I was obliged to retire, and could not return to my friends until I had recovered from my condition of lethargy. It was in one of these attacks, an unusually strong one, that such an irresistible, mad longing for the picture of my dreams came over me, that I hurried out into the street and ran toward the mysterious house. While still at a distance from it, I seemed to see lights shining out through the fast-closed blinds, but when I came nearer I saw that all was dark. Crazy with my desire I rushed to the door; it fell back before the pressure of my hand. I stood in the dimly lighted vestibule, enveloped in a heavy, close[1] atmosphere. My heart beat in strange fear and impatience. Then suddenly a long, sharp tone, as from a woman's throat, shrilled through the house. I know not how it happened that I found myself suddenly in a great hall brilliantly lighted and furnished in old-fashioned magnificence of golden chairs and strange Japanese ornaments. Strongly perfumed incense arose in blue clouds about me. "Welcome—welcome, sweet bridegroom! the hour has come, our bridal hour!" I heard these words in a woman's voice, and as little as I can tell, how I came into the room, just so little do I know how it happened that suddenly a tall, youthful figure, richly dressed, seemed to arise from the blue mists. With the repeated shrill cry: "Welcome, sweet bridegroom!" she came toward me with outstretched arms—and a yellow face, distorted with age and madness, stared into mine! I fell back in terror, but the fiery, piercing glance of her eyes, like the eyes of a snake, seemed to hold me spellbound. I did not seem able to turn my eyes from this terrible old woman, I could not move another step. She came still nearer, and it seemed to me suddenly as if her hideous face were only a thin mask, beneath which I saw the features of the beautiful maiden of my vision. Already I felt the touch of her hands, when suddenly she fell at my feet with a loud scream, and a voice behind me cried:

"Oho, is the devil playing his tricks with your grace again? To bed, to bed, your grace. Else there will be blows, mighty blows!"

---

[1] Musty, muggy

I turned quickly and saw the old steward in his night clothes, swinging a whip above his head. He was about to strike the screaming figure at my feet when I caught at his arm. But he shook me from him, exclaiming: "The devil, sir! That old Satan would have murdered you if I had not come to your aid. Get away from here at once!"

I rushed from the hall, and sought in vain in the darkness for the door of the house. Behind me I heard the hissing blows of the whip and the old woman's screams. I drew breath to call aloud for help, when suddenly the ground gave way under my feet; I fell down a short flight of stairs, bringing up with such force against a door at the bottom that it sprang open, and I measured my length on the floor of a small room. From the hastily vacated bed, and from the familiar brown coat hanging over a chair, I saw that I was in the bedchamber of the old steward. There was a trampling on the stair, and the old man himself entered hastily, throwing himself at my feet. "By all the saints, sir," he entreated with folded hands, "whoever you may be, and however her grace, that old Satan of a witch has managed to entice you to this house, do not speak to anyone of what has happened here. It will cost me my position. Her crazy excellency has been punished, and is bound fast in her bed. Sleep well, good sir, sleep softly and sweetly. It is a warm and beautiful July night. There is no moon, but the stars shine brightly. A quiet good night to you." While talking, the old man had taken up a lamp, had led me out of the basement, pushed me out of the house door, and locked it behind me. I hurried home quite bewildered, and you can imagine that I was too much confused by the gruesome secret to be able to form any explanation of it in my own mind for the first few days. Only this much was certain, that I was now free from the evil spell that had held me captive so long. All my longing for the magic vision in the mirror had disappeared, and the memory of the scene in the deserted house was like the recollection of an unexpected visit to a madhouse. It was evident beyond a doubt that the steward was the tyrannical guardian of a crazy woman of noble birth, whose condition was to be hidden from the world. But the mirror? and all the other magic? Listen, and I will tell you more about it.

Some few days later I came upon Count P. at an evening entertainment. He drew me to one side and said, with a smile, "Do you know that the secrets of our deserted house are beginning to be revealed?" I listened with interest; but before the count could say more the doors of the dining-room were thrown open, and the company proceeded to the table. Quite lost in thought at the words I had just heard, I had given a young lady my arm, and had taken my place mechanically in the ceremonious procession. I led my companion to the seats arranged for us, and then turned to look at her for the first time. The vision of my mirror stood before me, feature for feature, there was no deception possible! I trembled to my innermost heart, as you can imagine; but I discovered that there was not the slightest echo even, in my heart, of the mad desire which had ruled me so entirely when my breath drew out the magic picture from the glass. My astonishment, or rather my terror, must have been apparent in my eyes. The girl looked at me in such surprise that I endeavored to control myself sufficiently to remark that I must have met her somewhere before. Her short answer, to the effect that this could hardly be possible, as she had come to the city only yesterday for the first time in her life, bewildered me still more and threw me into an awkward silence. The sweet glance from her gentle eyes brought back my courage, and I began a tentative exploring of this new companion's mind. I found that I had before me a sweet and delicate being, suffering from some psychic trouble. At a particularly merry turn of the conversation, when I would throw in a daring word like a dash of pepper, she would smile, but her smile was pained, as if a wound had been touched. "You are not very merry to-night, countess. Was it the visit this morning?" An officer sitting near us had spoken these words to my companion, but before he could finish his remark his neighbor had grasped him by the arm and whispered something in his ear, while a lady at the other side of the table, with glowing cheeks and angry eyes, began to talk loudly of the opera she had heard last evening. Tears came to the eyes of the girl sitting beside me. "Am I not foolish?" She turned to me. A few moments before she had complained of headache. "Merely the usual evidences of a nervous headache," I answered in an easy tone, "and there is nothing better for it than the merry spirit which bubbles in the foam of this poet's nectar." With these words I filled her champagne glass, and she sipped at it as she threw me a look of gratitude. Her mood brightened, and all would have been well had I not touched a glass before me with unexpected strength, arousing from it a shrill, high tone. My companion grew deadly pale, and I myself felt a sudden shiver, for the sound had exactly the tone of the mad woman's voice in the deserted house.

While we were drinking coffee I made an opportunity to get to the side of Count P. He understood the reason for my movement. "Do you know that your neighbor is Countess Edwina S.? And do you know also that it is her mother's sister who lives in the deserted house, incurably mad for many years? This morning both mother and daughter went to see the unfortunate woman. The old steward, the only person who is able to control the countess in her outbreaks, is seriously ill, and they say that the sister has finally revealed the secret to Dr. K. This eminent physician will endeavor to cure the patient, or if this is not possible, at least to prevent her terrible outbreaks of mania. This is all that I know yet."

Others joined us and we were obliged to change the subject. Dr. K. was the physician to whom I had turned in my own anxiety, and you can well imagine that I hurried to him as soon as I was free, and told him all that had happened to me in the last days. I asked him to tell me as much as he could about the mad woman, for my own peace of mind; and this is what I learned from him under promise of secrecy.

"Angelica, Countess Z.," thus the doctor began," had already passed her thirtieth year, but was still in full possession of great beauty, when Count S., although much younger than she, became so fascinated by her charm that he wooed her with ardent devotion and followed her to her father's home to try his luck there. But scarcely had the count entered the house, scarcely had he caught sight of Angelica's younger sister, Gabrielle, when he awoke as from a dream. The elder sister appeared faded and colorless beside Gabrielle, whose beauty and charm so enthralled the count that he begged her hand of her father. Count Z. gave his consent easily, as there was no doubt of Gabrielle's feelings toward her suitor. Angelica did not show the slightest anger at her lover's faithlessness. 'He believes that he has forsaken me, the foolish boy! He does not perceive that he was but my toy, a toy of which I had tired.' Thus she spoke in proud scorn, and not a look or an action on her part belied her words. But after the ceremonious betrothal of Gabrielle to Count S., Angelica was seldom seen by the members of her family. She did not appear at the dinner table, and it was said that she spent most of her time walking alone in the neighboring wood.

"A strange occurrence disturbed the monotonous quiet of life in the castle. The hunters of Count Z., assisted by peasants from the village, had captured a band of gypsies who were accused of several robberies and murders which had happened recently in the neighborhood. The men were brought to the castle courtyard, fettered together on a long chain, while the women and children were packed on a cart. Noticeable among the last was a tall, haggard old woman of terrifying aspect, wrapped from head to foot in a red shawl. She stood upright in the cart, and in an imperious tone demanded that she should be allowed to descend. The guards were so awed by her manner and appearance that they obeyed her at once.

"Count Z. came down to the courtyard and commanded that the gang should be placed in the prisons under the castle. Suddenly Countess Angelica rushed out of the door, her hair all loose, fear and anxiety in her pale face Throwing herself on her knees, she cried in a piercing voice, 'Let these people go! Let these people go! They are innocent! Father, let these people go! If you shed one drop of their blood I will pierce my heart with this knife!' The countess swung a shining knife in the air and then sank swooning to the ground. 'Yes, my beautiful darling—my golden child—I knew you would not let them hurt us,' shrilled the old woman in red. She cowered beside the countess and pressed disgusting kisses to her face and breast, murmuring crazy words. She took from out the recesses of her shawl a little vial in which a tiny goldfish seemed to swim in some silver-clear liquid. She held the vial to the countess's heart. The latter regained consciousness immediately. When her eyes fell on the gypsy woman, she sprang up, clasped the old creature ardently in her arms, and hurried with her into the castle.

"Count Z., Gabrielle, and her lover, who had come out during this scene, watched it in astonished awe. The gypsies appeared quite indifferent. They were loosed from their chains and taken separately to the prisons. Next morning Count Z. called the villagers together. The gypsies were led before them and the count announced that he had found them to be innocent of the crimes of which they were accused, and that he would grant them free passage through his domains. To the astonishment of all present, their fetters were struck off and they were set at liberty. The red-shawled woman was not among them. It was whispered that the gypsy captain, recognizable from the golden chain about his neck and the red feather in his high Spanish hat[1], had paid a secret visit to the count's room the night before. But it was discovered, a short time after the release of the gypsies, that they were indeed guiltless of the robberies and murders that had disturbed the district.

"The date set for Gabrielle's wedding approached. One day, to her great astonishment, she saw several large wagons in the courtyard being packed high with furniture, clothing, linen, with everything necessary for a complete household outfit. The wagons were driven away, and the following day Count Z. explained that, for many reasons, he had thought it best to grant Angelica's odd request that she be allowed to set up her own establishment in his house in X. He had given the house to her, and had promised her that no member of the family, not even he himself, should enter it without her express permission. He added also, that, at her urgent request, he had permitted his own valet to accompany her, to take charge of her household.

"When the wedding festivities were over, Count S. and his bride departed for their home, where they spent a year in cloudless happiness. Then the count's health failed mysteriously. It was as if some secret sorrow gnawed at his vitals, robbing him of joy and strength. All efforts of his young wife to discover the source of his trouble were fruitless. At last, when the constantly recurring fainting spells threatened to endanger his very life, he yielded to the entreaties of his physicians and left his home, ostensibly for Pisa. His young wife was prevented from accompanying him by the delicate condition of her own health.

"And now," said the doctor, "the information given me by Countess S. became, from this point on, so rhapsodical[2] that a keen observer only could guess at the true coherence of the story. Her baby, a daughter, born during her husband's absence, was spirited away from the house, and all search for it was fruitless. Her grief at this loss deepened to despair, when she received a message from her father stating that her husband, whom all believed to be in Pisa, had been found dying of heart trouble in Angelica's home in X., and that Angelica herself had become a dangerous maniac. The old count

[1] A wide-brimmed, flat-crowned, "Cordovan" hat

[2] Extravagantly emotional; manic and uncontrolled

added that all this horror had so shaken his own nerves that he feared he would not long survive it.

"As soon as Gabrielle was able to leave her bed, she hurried to her father's castle. One night, prevented from sleeping by visions of the loved ones she had lost, she seemed to hear a faint crying, like that of an infant, before the door of her chamber. Lighting her candle she opened the door. Great Heaven! there cowered the old gypsy woman, wrapped in her red shawl, staring up at her with eyes that seemed already glazing in death. In her arms she held a little child, whose crying had aroused the countess. Gabrielle's heart beat high with joy—it was her child—her lost daughter! She snatched the infant from the gypsy's arms, just as the woman fell at her feet lifeless. The countess's screams awoke the house, but the gypsy was quite dead and no effort to revive her met with success.

"The old count hurried to X. to endeavor to discover something that would throw light upon the mysterious disappearance and reappearance of the child. Angelica's madness had frightened away all her female servants; the valet alone remained with her. She appeared at first to have become quite calm and sensible. But when the count told her the story of Gabrielle's child she clapped her hands and laughed aloud, crying: 'Did the little darling arrive? You buried her, you say? How the feathers of the gold pheasant shine in the sun! Have you seen the green lion with the fiery blue eyes?' Horrified the count perceived that Angelica's mind was gone beyond a doubt, and he resolved to take her back with him to his estates, in spite of the warnings of his old valet. At the mere suggestion of removing her from the house Angelica's ravings increased to such an extent as to endanger her own life and that of the others.

"When a lucid interval came again Angelica entreated her father, with many tears, to let her live and die in the house she had chosen. Touched by her terrible trouble he granted her request, although he believed the confession which slipped from her lips during this scene to be a fantasy of her madness. She told him that Count S. had returned to her arms, and that the child which the gypsy had taken to her father's house was the fruit of their love. The rumor went abroad in the city that Count Z. had taken the unfortunate woman to his home; but the truth was that she remained hidden in the deserted house under the care of the valet. Count Z. died a short time ago, and Countess Gabrielle came here with her daughter Edwina to arrange some family affairs. It was not possible for her to avoid seeing her unfortunate sister. Strange things must have happened during this visit, but the countess has not confided anything to me, saying merely that she had found it necessary to take the mad woman away from the old valet. It had been discovered that he had controlled her outbreaks by means of force and physical cruelty; and that also, allured by Angelica's assertions that she could make gold[1], he had allowed himself to assist her in her weird[2] operations.

"It would be quite unnecessary," thus the physician ended his story, "to say anything more to you about the deeper inward relationship of all these strange things. It is clear to my mind that it was you who brought about the catastrophe, a catastrophe which will mean recovery or speedy death for the sick woman. And now I will confess to you that I was not a little alarmed, horrified even, to discover that—when I had set myself in magnetic communication with you by placing my hand on your neck—I could see the picture in the mirror with my own eyes. We both know now that the reflection in the glass was the face of Countess Edwina."

I repeat Dr. K.'s words in saying that, to my mind also, there is no further comment that can be made on all these facts. I consider it equally unnecessary to discuss at any further length with you now the mysterious relationship between Angelica, Edwina, the old valet, and myself—a relationship which seemed the work of a malicious demon who was playing his tricks with us. I will add only that I left the city soon after all these events, driven from the place by an oppression I could not shake off. The uncanny sensation left me suddenly a month or so later, giving way to a feeling of intense relief that flowed through all my veins with the warmth of an electric current. I am convinced that this change within me came about in the moment when the mad woman died.

HOFFMANN could never resist the power of a Doppelgänger. One of his most pervasive motifs – whether in the form of mirror-images (as here and as in "The Lost Reflection") or the uncanny similarities between humans and dolls (as in "Nutcracker," "The Sandman," and "Automatons"), he was pervasively drawn to the symbol of the Double. What is it about the Double that hounds our collective consciousness so? It was studied by Freud, Jung, and Adler, written about by Dostoevsky, Shakespeare, and Stevenson (not to mention Poe, Twain, and Dickens), and featured prominently in films, art, and theology. From "Jekyll and Hyde" to "The Prince and the Pauper," the ideal of the Double is one which is simultaneously optimistic and pessimistic. It ponders possibilities while implying destiny: someone looking like us might find their way into a better position, and yet they will never be able to alter their similarity to us (likewise, a mirror image of us might commit atrocities, forever associating our visage with their misdeeds). Hoffmann uses the mirror as the principal motif of "The Deserted House" – a symbol

[1] Viz., she is practicing alchemy – the notorious hybrid of chemistry, witchcraft, necromancy, and counterfeiting

[2] Paranormal, mystical, magical

of duplicity, hypocrisy, and exposed truth. A fearful force of reality, the mirror frightens Theodor with its promise of Truth and Exposure – an anxiety bred in him by his nurse's bedtime stories. The superstition that gazing into a mirror at night might hand your soul over to Satan is an ancient one (closely related to our modern "Bloody Mary" urban legend) which communicates a more practical skepticism of vanity: staring into a mirror might at first be relaxing because it offers you a chance to gaze on your own face with self-absorption, but eventually it leads to a crushing realization of your flaws, defects, and mortality. Likewise, Theodor's mirror sends him the image of a lovely girl – an initially attractive offering – but ultimately forces him to confront the vulgar reality of his infatuation by coming face-to-face with a repulsive madwoman. Edgar Allan Poe utilized this plot in two of his tales, one tragic and one comic. In "The Spectacles," a vain man falls in love with the elderly relative of a beautiful woman because he is too image-conscious to wear his glasses, and is tricked into making courting the elderly woman, whereupon he is crushed by horror and embarrassment. In "William Wilson," a knavish cad is mercilessly pursued by his mirror-image – a personification of his conscience – which he ultimately murders. For Hoffmann, this story is a balanced blend of the tragic and comic – the grotesque and the burlesque. But its moral can once again be summed up in his poignant words: "I felt as a child feels when some fairy tale has been told it to conceal the truth it suspects." In Hoffmann's highly symbolic universe nearly everything has a lurking twin – a skulking Doppelgänger eager to tear up the mask and expose us to the horrifying reality of our childish self-delusions.

ONE of Hoffmann's most common motifs – a consistent hallmark of his fiction – is the theme of parallelism. His fantasies are unlike typical fairy tales in that they don't usually depict wondrous things happening in a wondrous world – one where, for instance, witches, dragons, and gnomes are treated as a matter of course; rather, they build dramatic tension by having a parallel universe of just such wonders invading its drab, realistic twin. In this sense his fiction is both tremendously surreal and at times mundane, peopled by dull but relatable characters oppressed by dull but relatable problems (imagine a movie critical of middle-class malaise, like *Office Space,* being inexplicably crossed with a hyperactive, hallucinogenic fantasy *Little Nemo's Adventures in Slumberland*). As such, they often read like a dream journal being used for self-analysis: regular peoples' virtues and vices are caricatured to grotesque dimensions, hidden natures are exposed, neglected abilities and insights are transformed into magical powers, and repressed emotions are amplified into acts of shocking violence. "The Stranger Child" is one of Hoffmann's seven fairy tales, but it is set in the dreary Prussian countryside rather than a fairy world of charms and curses. And yet he immediately alerts us that things are not what they seem: the Baron von Brakel, father to our protagonists, calls his humble farmstead a "castle," and, in fact, it seems somewhat better than a castle: instead of intimidating ramparts, gloomy royals, and clammy drafts it hosts a dreamy woods, a loving family, and snug warmth. Hoffmann encourages us to find peace and contentment in the power of imagination. What is better than a fierce, stony castle? A cozy, little cottage that you imagine to be your castle. Throughout the story the characters are confronted by evil Doppelgängers and transcendental twins: their simple, happy father is contrasted with his medal-wearing, coach driving cousin – an ambitious and arrogant court official; they encounter an androgynous child spirit – the literal Spirit of Childhood – in whom both brother and sister project themselves and see their idealized Selves; their bulbous, grotesque tutor – sent from the Baron's cousin to re-educate and civilize his imaginative children – is revealed to be a sadistic gnome king in disguise, and so on. It is a story that emphasizes the importance of imagination, condemns the cynicism of adulthood, and warns against the smother the child within us all.

The Stranger Child

— Excerpted from 'The Serapion Brethren,' Volume Two, Section Four —

{1817}

BARON VON BRAKEL OF BRAKELHEIM.

THERE was once a noble gentleman named The Baron Thaddeus von Brakel[1], who lived in the little village of Brakelheim[2], which he had inherited from his deceased father, the old Baron von Brakel, and which, consequently, was his property. The four rustics[3], who were the other inhabitants of the village, called him "your Lordship," although, like themselves, he went about with his hair badly combed, and it was only on Sundays when he went to the neighbouring country town to church, with his lady and his two children (whose names were Felix and Christlieb[4])—that he substituted for the coarse cloth jacket, which he wore at other times, a fine green coat and a scarlet waistcoat with gold braid, which became him well. The same rustic neighbours, when any one chanced to ask, "How shall I find my way to the Baron von Brakel's?" were wont to reply: "Go straight on through the village, and up the hill where those birches are; his Lordship's castle is there." Now everybody knows that a castle is a great and lofty building, with a number of windows and doors, to say nothing of towers and glittering weathercocks; but nothing of this sort could be discovered on the hill where the birches were, all that was to be seen there being a commonplace little ordinary house, with a few small windows, which you could hardly see anything of, till you were close upon it. Now it is often the case that, at the portal of a grand castle, one suddenly halts, and—being breathed upon by the icy air which streams out of it, and glared at by the lifeless eyes of the strange sculptured figures which are fixed, like fearful warders, on the walls—loses all desires to go in, preferring to turn away. But this was by no means the case, as regarded Baron von Brakel's abode. For, first of all, the beautiful graceful birches, when one came to them, would bend their leafy branches like arms stretched out, to greet him, their rustling leaves whispering a "Welcome, welcome among us!" And when one reached the house, it seemed as if charming voices were calling, in dulcet[5] tones, out of the bright, windows, and everywhere from among the thick dark leafage of the vine which covered the walls up to the roof: "Come, come, and rest, thou dear weary wanderer; here all is comfort and hospitality." This was also confirmed by the swallows, twittering merrily in and out of

---

[1] Barkel is a Saxon surname etymologically related to the word "braken," meaning ferns. It is suggestive of the soft, sunny underbrush of unspoiled woodland or a picturesque, summery countryside, which will prove important to the story's themes

[2] Literally, Home of the Brakels

[3] Countryfolk

[4] Meaning "Happy" and "Christ's Love," respectively. Christlieb (pronounced KRIST-*leeb*) is a girl

[5] Sweet

their nests; and the stately old stork looked down, gravely and wisely, from the chimney, and said: "I have passed my summers in this place now for many and many a year, and I know no better lodging in all the world; if it weren't for my inborn love of travel, which I can't control—if it weren't so very cold here in the winter, and wood so dear—I should never stir from the spot." Thus charming and delightful, although not a castle, was Baron von Brakel's house.

VISITORS OF DISTINCTION.

Madame von Brakel got up very early one morning, and baked a cake, into which she put a great many more almonds and raisins than even into her Easter cake, for which reason it had a much more delicious odour than that one itself had. While this was in progress, the Baron von Brakel thoroughly dusted and brushed his green coat and his red waistcoat, and Felix and Christlieb were dressed in the very best clothes they possessed. The Baron said to them: "You mustn't run about in the wood to-day, as you generally do, but sit still in the room, that you may look neat and nice when your distinguished uncle comes!"

The sun had emerged, bright and smiling, from the clouds, and was darting golden beams in at the window; out in the wood the morning breeze blew fresh, and the finch, the siskin, and the nightingale were all pouring out their hearts in joy, and warbling the loveliest songs in chorus. Christlieb was sitting silent, deep in thought, at the table, now and then smoothing and arranging the bow of her pink sash, now and then industriously striving to go on with her knitting, which, somehow, would by no means answer that morning. Felix, into whose hands papa had put a fine picture-book, looked away over the tops of the pages towards the beautiful Birchwood, where, every other morning but this, he might jump about for an hour or two to his heart's content. "Oh! isn't it jolly out there!" sighed he to himself; and when, in addition, the big yard-dog, Sultan by name, came barking and bounding before the window, dashing away a short distance in the direction of the wood, coming back again, and barking and growling afresh, as if he were saying to Felix, "Aren't you coming to the wood to-day? What on earth are you doing in that stuffy room?" Felix couldn't contain himself for impatience. "Oh, darling mamma, do just let me go out, only for a little!" he cried; but Madame von Brakel answered, "No, no, stay in the room, like a good boy. I know very well how it will be; if you go, Christlieb must go too, and then away you'll both scamper, helter skelter, through brush and briar, up into the trees. And then, back you'll come, all hot and smirched, and your uncle will say, 'What ugly country children are these? I am sure no Brakels, be they big or little, can ever be like that.'"

Felix clapped the book to in a rage, and said, as the tears of disappointment came into his eyes, "If our grand uncle talks of ugly country children, I'm sure he never can have seen Peter Vollrad or Annie Hentschel, or any of the children in the village here, for I know there couldn't be prettier children anywhere than they are." "I'm sure of that," said Christlieb, as if suddenly waking from a dream; "and isn't Maggy Schulz a beautiful child too, although she hasn't anything like as pretty ribbons as mine." "Do not talk such stupid nonsense," said their papa, "you don't understand what your uncle means, in so saying."

All further representations to the effect that just this day, of all others, it was so very glorious in the wood were of no avail, Felix and Christlieb had to stay in the room, and this was all the more painful because the company cake, which was on the table, gave out the most delicious odours, and yet might not be cut into until their uncle's arrival. "Oh! if he would but come! if he would but only come!" both the children cried, and almost wept with impatience. At last a vigorous trampling of horses became audible, and a carriage appeared, which was so brilliant and so richly covered with golden ornamentation, that the children were unspeakably amazed, for they had never beheld the like of it before. A tall and very thin man glided by help of the arm of the footman, who opened the carriage door, into the arms of Baron von Brakel, to whose cheek he twice gently laid his own, and whispered mincingly, "*Bon jour*, my dear cousin; now, no ceremony, I implore!" Meanwhile the footman had also aided a short stout lady, with very red cheeks, and two children, a boy and a girl, to glide down to earth from the carriage (which he performed with much dexterity), so that each of them came to their feet on the ground.

When they were all thus safely deposited, Felix and Christlieb came forward (as they had been duly prepared by mamma and papa to do), seized each a hand of the tall thin man, and said, kissing the same, "We are very glad you are come, dear noble uncle;" then they did the same with the hands of the stout lady, and said, "We are very glad you are come, dear noble aunt;" then they went up to the children, but stood before them quite dumfounded, for they had never seen children of the sort before. The boy had on long pantaloons, a little jacket of scarlet cloth covered all over with golden knots and embroidery, and a little bright sabre at his side; while on his head was a curious red cap with a white feather, from under which he peeped shyly and bashfully with his yellow face, and his bleared, heavy eyes. The girl had on a white dress—very much like Christlieb's, but with a frightful quantity of ribbons and tags—and her hair was most curiously frizzed up into knots, and twisted upon the top of her head, where there was, besides, a little shining coronet[1].

Christlieb plucked up courage, and was going to take the little girl's hand; but she snatched it away in a hurry, and put on such an angry tearful face, that Christlieb was quite frightened, and let her alone. Felix wanted to have a closer look at the boy's pretty sabre, and put out his hand to it,

---

[1] Light crown. They are dressed like a stereotypical toy soldier and princess doll, respectively

but the youngster began to cry, "My sabre, my sabre, he's going to take my sabre!" and ran to the thin man, behind whom he hid himself. Felix grew red in the face, and said, much annoyed: "*I* don't want to take your sabre—young stupid!"

The last two words were murmured between his teeth, but Baron von Brakel seemed to have heard all, and was much put out about it, for he fingered his waistcoat nervously, and said, "Oh, Felix!" The stout lady said, "Adelgunda! Herrmann![1] the children are doing you no harm; do not be so silly." The thin gentleman saying, "They will soon make acquaintance," took Madam von Brakel by the hand, and conducted her to the house. Baron von Brakel followed him with the stout lady, to whose skirts Adelgunda and Herrmann clung. Christlieb and Felix came after them.

"The cake will be cut now," Felix whispered to his sister. "Oh, yes! oh, yes! yes!" answered she delighted. "And then we'll be off into the wood," continued Felix. "And not bother more about these stupid stranger things," added Christlieb. Felix cut a caper; and then they went into the room. Adelgunda and Herrmann might not have any of the cake, because their papa and mamma said it was not good for them; so each of them had a little biscuit[2], which the footman had to produce from a bag which he had brought. Felix and Christlieb munched bravely at the substantial piece of cake which their dear mamma had given to each, and enjoyed themselves.

THE FURTHER PROGRESS OF THE VISIT OF THE DISTINGUISHED RELATIVES.

The thin gentleman, whose name was Cyprianus von Brakel, was first cousin to the Baron Thaddeus von Brakel, but a personage of far greater distinction. For, besides bearing the title of count, he wore upon every one of his coats—aye, even on his dressing-gown—a great silver star[3]. Thus it had happened that when, about a year before, he had paid a flying visit one afternoon to his cousin, Baron Thaddeus—but alone that time, without the stout lady (who was his wife) and without the children Felix had said to him, "Please tell me, uncle, have you been made *king* now?" For Felix had seen a picture of a king in his picture-book with just such a star on his breast, and naturally thought his uncle was one, since he wore this mark of royalty. His uncle had laughed much at the question on that occasion, and replied, "No, dear child, I am not the king, but I am the king's most faithful servant and minister, who rules over a great many people. If you belonged to the line of the Counts of Brakel, perhaps you might one day wear a star

---

[1] Names which both mean "warrior" or "fighter"

[2] The word in German is "rusk," a kind of twice-baked toast that is given to teething babies

[3] A royal decoration suggesting that the King of Prussia has bestowed on him some great honor for services provided the kingdom

like this one of mine. As it is, you are only a simple 'von[1]'—a baron, and cannot expect to come to very much."

Felix did not understand his uncle in the slightest, and his father thought it did not much matter whether he did or not. The uncle told his fat lady how Felix had thought he was the king; on which she ejaculated, "Sweet, delightful, *touching* innocence!"

And now Felix and Christlieb had to come forward from the window, where they had been eating their cake with much kickering[2] and laughter. Their mother wiped the cake-crumbs and raisin-remnants from their lips, and they were handed over to their gracious uncle and aunt, who kissed them, with loud ejaculations of, "Oh, sweet and darling nature! oh rural simplicity!" and placed big cornets of paper in their hands. Tears came to the eyes of Baron Thaddeus von Brakel, and to those of his wife, over this condescension of their grand kinsfolk. Meanwhile Felix had opened his paper-cornet, and found in it bonbons, at which he set to work to munch vigorously, in which Christlieb followed his example.

"My boy! my boy!" cried his gracious uncle, "that is not the way to do it; you will destroy your teeth! You must suck them gently till the sugar dissolves in your mouth." But Felix laughed, and said, "Gracious uncle! do you think I am a baby, and haven't got teeth to bite them with?" With which he put a bonbon in his mouth and gave it such a bite that everything rattled and rang. "Delicious naivety!" the fat lady cried. The uncle agreed; but drops of perspiration stood on Baron Thaddeus von Brakel's forehead. He was ashamed of Felix's lack of polish; and the mother whispered to the boy hurriedly, "Don't make such a clattering with those teeth of yours, ill-bred boy!" This put poor Felix into a state of utter consternation, for he didn't know he was doing anything wrong. He took the half-eaten bonbon out of his mouth, put it into the paper parcel again, and handed the whole thing back to his uncle, saying, "Take your sugar away with you again!—that's all I care about, if I mayn't eat it." Christlieb, accustomed to follow Felix's example in all things, did the same with *her* paper-cornet. This was too much for poor Baron Thaddeus, who cried out, "Ah! my honoured and gracious cousin! do not be annoyed with the silliness of those simple children. Really, in the country, and in our straitened circumstances, alas! who could bring up children in the style in which you have brought up yours?" Count Cyprianus smiled a gracious smile as he glanced at Herrmann and Adelgunda. They had long since finished eating their biscuit, and were now sitting as mum as mice upon their chairs, without the slightest motion of either their faces or their limbs. The fat lady smiled

---

[1] The title "von" is added to a last name to denote nobility (e.g., when the poet and polymath Johann Goethe became an international sensation, his king ennobled him, making him Johann von Goethe). However, counts outrank barons

[2] Snickering

too, and lisped out, "Really, dear cousin, the education of our children lies nearer our hearts than anything in the world." She made a sign to Count Cyprianus, who immediately turned to Herrmann and Adelgunda, and asked them all sorts of questions, which they answered with the utmost readiness. The questions were about towns, rivers, and mountains, many thousands of miles off, and having the oddest names; also they could tell what every sort of animal was like, which was to be found in the remotest quarters of the globe. Then they spoke of plants, trees, and shrubs, just as if they had seen them themselves, and eaten of the fruits. Herrmann gave a minute description of all that had happened at a great battle three hundred years ago, or more, and was able to cite the names of all the Generals who had taken part in it. At length Adelgunda even spoke of the stars, and stated that there were all sorts of beasts, and curious figures, in the sky. This made Felix quite frightened and uneasy; he got close to his mother, and whispered, "Ah, mamma! dearest mamma! what is all that nonsense that they're blabbering about?" "Hold your tongue, stupid boy!" his mother replied. "Those are the Sciences."

Felix held his peace.

"Astonishing!" cried Baron Thaddeus. "Quite unparalleled! at their time of life!" And Fran von Brakel sighed out, "Oh, Jemini![1] what little angels! What in the world is to become of *our* little ones, out in the country here!"

Baron Thaddeus now joining in his wife's lamentations, Count Cyprianus comforted their hearts, by promising to send them, shortly, a man of much erudition, and specially skilled in the education of children.

Meanwhile the beautiful carriage had driven up to the door, and the "jaeger"[2] came in with two great bandboxes, which Herrmann and Adelgunda took and handed to Felix and Christlieb. Herrmann, making a polite bow, said, "Are you fond of playthings, *mon cher*[3]?—here I have brought you some of the finest kind." Felix hung his head. He felt melancholy; he did not know why. He held the bandbox in his hands, without expressing any thanks, and said in a murmur, "I'm not '*mon cher*,' and I'm not 'you'; I'm 'thou.'"[4] And Christlieb was nearer crying than laughing, although the box which Adelgunda had handed her was giving forth the most delightful odours, as of delicious things to eat. The dog Sultan, Felix's faithful friend and darling, was dancing and barking,

[1] "Oh my goodness!"

[2] A footman dressed in the uniform of a light infantry ranger or forester

[3] French: "my dear"

[4] In the German, his uncle is addressing him with the more professional and formal – and more polite – pronoun "Sie" instead of the more familiar informal (and his preferred) pronoun "du." "Du" is used amongst friends and peers, "Sie" between strangers and persons separated by rank, such as teachers and officers

according to his wont; but Herrmann was so frightened at him that he hid himself in a corner and began to cry. "He's not touching *thee*[1]," Felix cried. "He's only a dog. What art thou howling and screaming about? You know all about the most terrible wild beasts in the world, don't you?—and even if he were going to set upon you, haven't you your sword on?"

But Felix's words were of no avail. Herrmann went on howling till the servant had to take him in his arms and bear him off to the carriage. Adelgunda, suddenly infected by her brother's terror—or heaven knows from what other cause!—also began to scream and howl, which so affected poor Christlieb that *she* began to cry too. Amid this yelling and screaming of the children, Count Cyprianus von Brakel took his departure from Brakelheim; and so terminated the visit of those distinguished relations.

THE NEW PLAYTHINGS.

When the carriage containing Count Cyprianus von Brakel and his family had rolled down the hill, Herr Thaddeus quickly threw off his green coat and his red waistcoat; and when he had, as quickly, put on his loose jacket, and passed his big comb two or three times through his hair, he drew a long breath, stretched himself, and cried, "God be thanked!" The children, too, got out of their Sunday clothes, and felt happy and light. "To the wood! to the wood!" cried Felix, executing some of his highest jumps.

"But don't you want to see what Herrmann and Adelgunda have brought you before you set off?" said their mother. And Christlieb, who had been contemplating the boxes with longing eyes even while her clothes were being changed, thought that *that would* be a good thing to do first, and that it would be plenty of time to go to the wood afterwards. Felix was very hard to convince of this. He said, "What that can be of any consequence can that stupid pump-breeked[2] creature have brought us?—and his ribbony sister into the bargain? About the 'sciences,' as you call them, he clatters away as finely as you please. He talks about bears and lions, and tells you how to take elephants, and then he's afraid of my dear dog Sultan; has a sword on, and goes and crawls under the table!—a nice sort of sportsman *he* is!'

"Ah, dear, good Felix! just let us see, for a minute or two, what's inside the boxes." Thus prayed Christlieb; and as Felix always did anything he could to please her, he at once gave up the idea of being off to the wood immediately, and patiently sat down with her at the table on which the boxes were. The mother opened them; and then!—oh! my very dear readers! you have all been so happy when, at the time of the yearly fair, or at all events at Christmas, your parents and your friends flooded you with

---

[1] In the German, Felix makes a point to refer to him with the informal “du” pronoun (specifically is conjugated form “dir”)

[2] Wide-eyed, moon-faced

presents of every delightful kind. Remember how you danced for joy when pretty soldiers, and little fellows with barrel-organs, beautifully-dressed dolls, delightful picture-books, and all the rest, lay and stood before you. Such great delight as was then yours, Felix and Christlieb now experienced. For a really splendid assortment of the loveliest toys came out of those boxes, and all sorts of charming things to eat as well; so that the children clapped their hands again and again, crying, "Oh, how nice that is!" One paper parcel of bonbons, however, Felix laid aside with contempt; and when Christlieb begged him not to throw the glassy sugar[1] out of the window, as he was going to do, he gave up that idea, and only chucked some of the bonbons to Sultan, who had come in wagging his tail. Sultan snuffed at them, and then turned his back on them disdainfully.

"Do you see, Christlieb," Felix cried, "Sultan won't have anything to do with the wretched stuff."

But, on the whole, none of the toys caused Felix such satisfaction as a certain little sportsman, who, when a little string which stuck out beneath his jacket was pulled, put his gun to his shoulder and fired at a target which was stuck up three spans[2] in front of him. Next to him in his affections stood a little fellow, who made bows and salaams, and tinkled on a little harp when you turned a handle. But what pleased him more than all those things was a gun made of wood, and a hunting hanger[3], of wood also, and silvered over; also a beautiful hussar's[4] busby[5] and a sabre tasche[6]. Christlieb was equally delighted with a finely dressed doll and a set of charming furniture. The children forgot all about the woods, and enjoyed themselves over their playthings till quite late in the evening. They then went to their beds.

WHAT HAPPENED WITH THE NEW PLAYTHINGS IN THE WOOD.

Next day the children began where they had left off the night before; that is to say, they got out the boxes, took forth the toys, and amused themselves with them in many ways. Just as had been the case the day before, the sun shone brightly and kindly in at the windows; the birches, greeted by the sighing morning breeze, whispered and rustled; the birds rejoiced in loveliest songs of joy. Felix's heart was full of his sportsman, his hanger, his gun, and sabretasche.

"I'll tell you what it is," he cried; "it's much nicer outside! Come, Christlieb, let's be off to the woods!"

---

[1] That is, sugar glass or rock candy

[2] Two feet and a few inches

[3] Short huntsman's sword rather like a machete

[4] A light cavalryman uniformed in a distinctly Hungarian fashion

[5] Tall fur hat

[6] A large, flat satchel carried by hussars alongside their sabers

Christlieb had just undressed her big doll, and was going to put its clothes on again, a matter of the greatest moment and interest to her, for which reason she would rather not have gone out just then, and said, in a tone of entreaty, "Hadn't we better stay here and play a little longer, Felix dear?"

"I'll tell you what well do, Christlieb; we'll take the best of our toys out to the woods with us. I'll put on my hanger, and sling the gun over my shoulder; and then, you see, I shall be a regular sportsman. The little hunter and the harper can come with me, and you can take your big doll and the best of your other things with you. Come along, let's be off."

Christlieb hastened to dress her doll as quickly as possible, and then they both made off to the wood with their playthings. There they established themselves in a nice, grassy place; and after they had played for a while, and Felix was making his harper tinkle his little tune, Christlieb said, "Do you know, Felix, that harper of yours doesn't play at all nicely. Just listen how wretched it sounds out here in the wood, that eternal 'ting-ting, plang-plang.' The birds peep down from the trees as though they were disgusted with that stupid musician who insists on accompanying them." Felix turned the handle more and more strenuously, and at length cried, "I think you're right, Christlieb. What the little fellow plays sounds quite horrible. I'm quite ashamed to see those thrushes there looking down at me with such wise eyes. He must make a better job of it." With which Felix screwed away at the handle with such force that crack! crack! the whole box on which the harp-man stood flew into a thousand splinters, and his arms fell down broken.

"Oh, oh!" Felix cried. "Ah! poor little harper!" sighed Christlieb. Felix looked at the broken toy for a minute or two, and then said, "Well, he was a stupid, senseless chap, after all. He played terribly poor music, and made faces, and bowed and scraped like our cousin Pump-breeks;" and he shied the harp-player as far as he could into the thicket. "What I like is my sportsman here," he went on to say. "He makes a bull's-eye every time he fires over and over again." And he kept on making him score a long succession of bull's-eyes accordingly.

When this had gone on for some time, however, Felix said, "It's stupid, all the same, that he should always make bull's-eyes; so very unsportsmanlike, you know—papa says so. A real sportsman has got to shoot deer, hares, and so forth, running. I can't have this chap going on aiming at a target; mustn't be any more of it; one gets weary of it; won't do." And Felix broke off the target which was fixed up in front of the shooting-man. "Now then," he cried, "fire away into the open."

But it was in vain that he pulled at the thread; the little man's arms hung limp and motionless; the gun rose no more to his shoulder—his shooting was at an end.

"Ha! ha!" Felix cried; "you could shoot at your target indoors; but out in the woods here, where the sportsman's home is, you can't, eh? I suppose you're afraid of dogs, too; and if one were to come you would take to your heels, gun and all, as cousin Pump-breeks did with his sword, wouldn't you? ugh! you stupid, useless dunderhead;" with which Felix shied him into the bushes after the harp-man.

"Come, let's run about a bit," he said to Christlieb. "Ah, yes, let us," said she; "this lovely doll of mine shall run with us too; that will be fun."

So Felix and Christlieb took each an arm of the doll, and off they set in full career, through the bushes, down the brae[1], and on and on till they came to a small lake, engarlanded with water-plants, which was on their father's property, and where he sometimes shot wild-duck. Here they came to a stand, and Felix said, "Suppose we wait here a little. I have a gun now, you know, and perhaps I may hit a duck among the rushes, like father."

At that moment Christlieb screamed out, "Oh! just look at my doll; what's the matter with her?"

Indeed, that poor thing was in a miserable condition enough. Neither Felix nor Christlieb had been paying any attention to her during their run, and so the bushes had torn all the clothes off her back, both her handsome legs were broken, and of the pretty waxen face there was scarcely a trace remaining, so marred and hideous did it appear.

"Oh, my poor, beautiful doll!" wept Christlieb.

"There, you see!" cried Felix; "those are the sort of trashy things those two stupid creatures brought and gave us. That doll of yours is nothing more or less than a stupid, idiotic slut[2]. Can't so much as come for a little run with us but she must get her clothes all torn off her back, and herself spoilt and destroyed. Give me hold of her!"

Christlieb sorrowfully complied, and could scarcely restrain a cry of "Oh, oh!" as he chucked the doll, without more ado, into the pond.

"Never mind, dear!" Felix said, consoling his sister. "Never mind about the wretched thing. If I can only shoot a duck, you shall have all the beautiful wing feathers."

A rustle was heard amongst the rushes, and Felix instantly took aim with his wooden gun. But he moved it away from his shoulder speedily, saying—"Am I not a tremendous idiot myself?" Looking reflectively before him for a few minutes, he continued softly—

"How can a fellow shoot without powder and shot? And have I either the one or the other? And then, could I put powder into a wooden gun? What's the use, after all, of the stupid, wooden thing? And the hunting-knife! wooden, too. Can neither cut nor stab. Of course my cousin's sword was wooden as well! That was why he couldn't draw it when he was afraid of Sultan. I see what it all comes too. Cousin Pump-breeks was making a

---

[1] Hillside

[2] The German here is "Trine" – meaning "silly-goose". The archaic version of the word slut – at the time of the translation – had no sexual connotation, but meant a sloppy, dirty woman

fool of me with his playthings, which only make-believe to be things, and are nothing but useless trumpery." With which Felix shied the gun, the hunting knife, and finally the sabretasche into the pond. But Christlieb was terribly distressed about her doll, and Felix himself couldn't help being annoyed at the way things had turned out. And in this mood of mind they crept back to the house; and when their mother asked them what had become of their playthings, Felix truthfully related how they had been deceived in the harper, the gun, the sabretasche, and the doll.

"Ah! you foolish children!" cried Frau von Brakel, half angry; "you don't know how to deal with nice toys of the kind."

But Baron Thaddeus, who had listened to Felix's tale with evident satisfaction, said, "Let the children alone; at the bottom, I am very glad they are fairly rid of those playthings. They didn't understand them, and were only bothered and vexed by them."

Neither Frau von Brakel nor the children understood what the Baron meant in so saying.

THE STRANGER CHILD.

Soon after those events, Felix and Christlieb had run off to the wood very early one morning. Their mother had impressed upon them that they were to be home very soon again, because it was necessary that they should stay in the house and read and write a great deal more than they used to do, that they might not lose countenance before[1] the tutor, who was expected very soon. Wherefore Felix said, "We must jump and run about as much as we can for the little while that we are allowed to stay out here, that's all." So they immediately began to play at hare and hounds[2].

But that game, and also every other that they tried to play at, very soon only wearied them, and failed to amuse them after a second or two. They could not understand why it was that, on that particular day, thousands of vexatious annoyances should keep continually happening to them. The wind carried Felix's cap away into the bushes; he stumbled and fell down on his nose as he was running his best. Christlieb found herself hanging by her clothes in a thorn-tree, or banged her foot against a sharp stone, so that she had to shrink with pain. They soon gave it all up, and slunk along dejectedly through the wood.

"Let's go home," said Felix; "there's nothing else for it."

But instead of doing so, he threw himself down under a shady tree; Christlieb followed his example; and there the children lay, depressed and wretched, gazing at the ground.

"Ah!" said Christlieb; "if we only had our nice playthings."

---

[1] Viz., be embarrassed in front of; shame themselves in front of

[2] Chase each other around; play catch; play tag

"Bosh!" growled Felix; "what the better should we be? We should only smash them up and destroy them again. I'll tell you what it is, Christlieb. Mother is not far wrong, I suspect. The playthings were all right enough. But we didn't know how to play with them. And that's because we don't know anything about the 'sciences,' as they call them."

"You're quite right, Felix, dear," Christlieb said; "if we knew the 'sciences' all by heart, as those dressed-up cousins of ours do, we should still have your harp-man and your sportsman; and my poor doll would not be at the bottom of the duck-pond. Poor things that we are! Ah! we know nothing about the 'sciences'!"

And therewith Christlieb began to sob and cry bitterly, and Felix joined her in so doing. And they both howled and lamented till the wood re-echoed again, crying, "Poor unfortunate children that we are! we know nothing of the 'sciences.'"

But suddenly they ceased, and asked one another in amazement—

"Do you see, Christlieb?" "Do you hear, Felix?"

From out the deepest shades of the dark thicket which lay before the children, a wonderful luminousness began to shine, playing like moonlight over the leaves, which trembled in ecstasy. And through the whispering trees there came a sweet musical tone, like that which we hear when the wind awakens the chords slumbering within a harp. The children felt a sense of awe come over them. All their vexation had passed away from them; but tears of a sweet, unknown pain rose to their eyes.

As the radiance streamed brighter through the bushes, and the marvellous music-tones grew louder and louder, the children's hearts beat high: they gazed eagerly at the brightness, and then they saw, smiling at them from the thicket, the face of the most beautiful child imaginable, with the sun beaming on it in all its splendour.

"Oh, come to us!—come to us, darling child!" cried Christlieb and Felix, as they stretched their arms with indescribable longing towards the beautiful creature. "I am coming!—I am coming!" a sweet voice cried from the bushes; and then, as if borne on the wings of the morning breeze, the Stranger Child seemed to come hovering over to Christlieb and Felix.

HOW THE STRANGER CHILD PLAYED WITH FELIX AND CHRISTLIEB.

"I thought I heard you, out of the distance, crying and lamenting," said the Stranger Child, "and then I was very sorry for you. What is the matter, you dear children?—what is it you want?"

"Ah," Felix said, "we didn't quite know what it was that we *did* want! But now, as far as I can make out, what we wanted was just you yourself."

"That is it!" Christlieb chimed in; "now that you are with us, we are happy again. Why were you so long in coming?"

In fact, both children felt as though they had known and played with the Stranger Child for a long time already, and that their unhappiness had been only because this beloved playmate was not with them.

"You see," Felix said, in continuation, "we really haven't got any playthings left; for I, like a stupid fool, went and destroyed a number of the very finest, which my cousin Pump-breeks gave me, and I shied them away. Never mind; we shall play somehow for all that."

"How can you talk so, Felix," said the Stranger Child, laughing aloud. "Certainly the stuff you threw away wasn't of much value; but you, and Christlieb too, are in the very middle of a quantity of the most exquisite play-things that were ever seen."

"Where—where are they?" Felix and Christlieb cried.

"Look round you," said the Stranger Child; and Felix and Christlieb then saw how, out of the thick grass and the wool-like moss, all sorts of glorious flowers were peeping, with bright eyes gleaming, and between them many-coloured stones and crystalline shells sparkled and shone, while little golden insects danced up and down, humming little gentle songs.

"Now we will build a palace," said the Stranger Child. "Help me to get the stones together." And the Stranger stooped down and began choosing stones of pretty colours. Felix and Christlieb helped, and the Stranger Child knew so well how to set the stones up on one another that soon there arose tall columns, shining in the sun like polished metal, while an aerial golden roof vaulted itself over them at the top. Then the Stranger Child kissed the flowers which were peeping from the ground; when, with sweet whisperings, they shot up higher, and, embracing each other lovingly, formed sweet-scented arcades and covered walks, in which the children danced about, full of delight and gladness. The Stranger Child clapped hands; and then the golden roof of the palace, which was formed of insects' golden wings vaulted together, went asunder with a hum, and the pillars melted away into a plashing silver stream, on whose banks the varied flowers took up their stations, and peered inquiringly into its ripples, or, moving their heads from side to side, listened to its baby pattering. Then the Stranger Child plucked blades of grass, and gathered little twigs from trees, strewing them down before Felix and Christlieb. But those blades of grass presently turned into the prettiest little dolls ever seen; and the twigs became delicious little huntsmen. The dolls danced round Christlieb; let her take them up in her lap, and whispered, in delicate little voices, "Be kind to us!—love us, dearest Christlieb!" The hunters shouted, "Halloa! halloa! the hunt's up!"[1] and blew their horns, and bustled about. Then hares came darting out of the bushes, with dogs after them, and the hunters banging about. This was delightful.

[1] “The game is afoot!” “The hunt is on!”

Then all disappeared again. Christlieb and Felix cried, "What has become of the dolls? where are the hunters?" The Stranger Child said, "Oh, they are all at your disposal; they are close by you at any moment when you want them. But hadn't you rather come on through the wood a little now?" "Oh, yes! yes!" cried Felix and Christlieb. The Stranger Child took hold of their hands, crying, "Come; come!"

And with that they went off. But it could not be called "running," really, for the children floated along, lightly and easily, through amongst the trees, whilst all the birds went fluttering along beside them, singing and warbling in the blithest fashion. All of a sudden up they soared, far into the sky. "Good morning, children! Good morning, Fritz, my crony!" cried the stork in the by-going.

"Don't hurt me! don't hurt me!" screamed the hawk. "I'm not going to touch your pigeons." And he swept away as hard as his long wings would carry him, alarmed at the children. Felix shouted with delight, but Christlieb was frightened. "Oh, my breath's going!" she cried; "I shall tumble!" And just at that moment the Stranger Child let them all three down to the ground again, and said: "Now I shall sing you the Forest-Song, as a good-bye for to-day. I shall come again to-morrow." Then the Child took out a little horn, of which the golden windings looked almost as if made of wreaths of flowers, and began to sound it so beautifully that the whole wood echoed wondrously with the lovely music of it, whilst the nightingales (which had come up fluttering as if in answer to the horn's summons, and were sitting on the branches, as close as they could to the children) sang their sweetest songs. But all at once the music grew fainter and fainter, till nothing of it remained but a soft whisper, which seemed to come from the thicket into which the Stranger Child had disappeared. "To-morrow!—to-morrow I come again!" the children could just hear, as if from an immense distance. They could not give themselves any explanation of their feelings, for never, never had they known such happiness and enjoyment before in their lives.

"And, oh, I wish it were to-morrow now!" they both cried, as they hastened home as hard as they could, to tell their parents all that had happened to them.

WHAT BARON VON BRAKEL AND HIS LADY SAID, AND WHAT HAPPENED FURTHER.

"I could almost fancy the children had dreamt all this," the Baron said to his wife, when Felix and Christlieb, full of the Stranger Child, could not cease from talking of all that had happened—the delightsomeness of their new friend, the exquisite music, the wonderful events generally—"but then," said the Baron, "when I remember that they could not both have dreamt just the same things at the same time, really, when all's said and done, I cannot get to the bottom of it all."

"Don't trouble your head about it, dear," said Frau von Brakel. "My idea is that this Stranger Child was nobody but the schoolmaster's boy, Gottlieb, from the village. It must have been he that ran over, and put all this nonsense in the children's heads. We must take care that he is not allowed to do it any more."

The Baron, was by no means of his wife's opinion; and, with the view of getting better at the rights and wrongs of the affair, the children were brought in and made to describe minutely what the child was like; how it was dressed, and so forth. With respect to its appearance, both Felix and Christlieb agreed that its face was fair as the lilies; that it had cheeks like roses, cherry lips, bright blue eyes, locks of golden hair, and that it was more beautiful altogether than words could tell. As regarded its dress, all they knew was that it certainly had not a blue-striped jacket and trousers, or a black leather cap, such as the schoolmaster's Gottlieb wore. On the other hand, all they said of its dress sounded utterly fabulous and absurd. For Christlieb said its dress was wondrous beautiful, shining and gleaming, as if made of the petals of roses; whilst Felix maintained that it was sparkling golden green, like spring-leaves in the sunshine. Felix further said that the child could not possibly have any connection with such a person as a school master, because it was too deeply acquainted with sportsmanship and woodcraft, and must consequently belong to some very home and head-quarters of forest lore, and was going to be the grandest sportsman ever heard of. "Oh, Felix!" Christlieb broke in, "how can you say that dear little girl could ever be a sportsman? She may, perhaps, know a good deal about that too, but I'm sure she knows a great deal more about house-management; or how should she have dressed those dolls for me so beautifully, and made such delightful dishes?" Thus Felix thought the Stranger Child was a boy, and Christlieb, a girl; and those contradictory opinions could not be reconciled.

Fran von Brakel thought it was a pity to go into nonsense of this kind with children; but the Baron thought differently, and said: "I should only have to follow the children into the woods, to find out what wondrous sort of creature this is that comes to play with them; but I can't help feeling that if I did I should spoil what is for them a great pleasure; and for that reason I don't want to do it."

Next day, when Felix and Christlieb went off to the wood at the usual time, they found the Stranger Child waiting for them; and, if their play had been glorious on the former day, this day the Stranger Child did the most miraculous things imaginable, so that Felix and Christlieb shouted for rapture over and over again. It was delicious and most enjoyable that, during their play, the Stranger Child talked so prettily and comprehendingly with the trees, the bushes, the flowers, and the brook which ran through the wood, and they all answered so understandably that Felix and Christlieb knew everything that they said.

The Stranger Child said to the alder-thicket, "What is it that you black-looking[1] folks are muttering and whispering to each other again?" and the branches took to shaking more forcibly, and they laughed and whispered "Ha, ha, ha! we are delighting ourselves over the charming things that friend Morning-breeze was saying to us when he came rustling over from the blue hills, in advance of the sunbeams. He brought us thousands of greetings and kisses from the Golden Queen; and plenty of wing-waftings, full of the sweetest perfume."

"Oh, silence!" the flowers broke in, interrupting the talk of the branches. "Hold your tongues on the score of that flatterer, who is so vain about the perfumes which his false caresses rob us of. Never mind the thickets, children; let them lisp and whisper; look at us—listen to us. We love you so, and we dress ourselves out, day by day, in the loveliest colours merely to give you pleasure."

"And do we not love *you*, you beautiful flowers?" said the Stranger Child. But Christlieb knelt down on the ground, and stretched out her arms, as if she would take all the beautiful flowers to her heart, crying, "Ah, I love you all, every one of you!" Felix cried, "I love you all, too, flowers, in your bright dresses. Still I dote upon green, and the woods, and the trees. The woods have to take care of you, and shelter you, bonny little things that you are."

Then came a sighing out of the tall, dark fir-trees; and they said, "That is very true, you clever boy; and you are not to be afraid of us, when our cousin, the storm, comes rushing at us, and we have to hold a rather strenuous bit of argument with that rough customer."

"All right," said Felix. "Groan, and sigh, and snarl as much as you like, you green giants that you are; *then* is when the real woodsman's heart begins to rejoice."

"You are quite right there," the forest brook plashed and rustled. "But what is the good of always hunting—always rushing in storm and turmoil? Come, and sit down nicely among the moss, and listen to me. I come from far-away places, out of a deep, dark, rocky cleft. I have delightful tales to tell you; and always something new, wave after wave, for ever and ever. And I will show you the loveliest pictures, if you will but look properly into this clear mirror of mine. Vaporous blue of the sky—golden clouds—bushes, flowers and trees, and your very selves, you beautiful children, I draw lovingly into the depths of my bosom."

"Felix and Christlieb," said the Stranger Child, looking round with wondrous blissfulness, "only listen how they all love us. But the redness of the evening is rising behind the hills, and the nightingale is calling me home."

---

[1] Gossipy. This is a literal translation of a figure of speech: the word "schwartzhaftes" does literally seem to mean "black-looing," but it actually means "gossipy"

"Oh, but let us just fly a little, as we did yesterday," Felix prayed.

"Yes," said Christlieb, "but not quite so high. It makes my head so giddy."

Then the Stranger Child took them by the hands again, and they went soaring up into the golden purple of the evening sky, while the birds crowded and sang round them. That was a shouting and a jubilating! In the shining clouds Felix saw, as if in wavering flame, beautiful castles all of rubies and other precious stones. "Look! look! Christlieb!" he cried, full of rapture, "look at all those splendid palaces! Let us fly along as fast as we can, and we shall get to them." Christlieb saw the castles too, and forgot her fear, as she was not looking down, this time, but up before her.

"Those are my beloved air-castles," the Stranger Child said. "But I don't think we shall get any further to-day.".

Felix and Christlieb seemed to be in a dream, and could not make out at all how they came to find themselves, presently, with their father and mother.

CONCERNING THE STRANGER CHILD'S HOME.

In the most beautiful part of the wood beside the brook, between whispering bushes, the Stranger Child had set up a most glorious tent, made of tall, slender lilies, glowing roses, and tulips of every hue; and beneath this tent Felix and Christlieb were sitting with the Stranger Child, listening to the forest-brook as it went on whispering the strangest things imaginable.

"I'll tell you, darling boy," Felix said, "I can't properly understand all that he, there, is saying; but I somehow feel that *you* could tell me, clearly and distinctly, what it is that he goes on murmuring. But most of all I should like you to tell me where it is that you come from, and where it is that you go away to, so fast, so fast, that we never can make out how you do it."

"Do you know, sweetest girl," said Christlieb, "our mother thinks you are the schoolmaster's boy, Gottlieb."

"Hold your tongue, stupid thing!" Felix cried. "Mother has never seen this darling boy, or she wouldn't have talked about the schoolmaster's Gottlieb. But come now, tell me where it is that you live, dear boy; for we want to go and see you at your home in the winter time, when it storms and snows, and nobody can trace a track in the woods."

"Yes, yes!" said Christlieb. "Tell us, like a darling, where your home is; and all about your father and mother, and more than all, what your own name is."

The Stranger Child looked very thoughtfully at the sky, almost sorrowfully, and gave a deep sigh. Then, after some moments of silence, the Stranger Child said, "Ah, my dears, why must you ask about my home? Is it not enough for you that I come every day and play with you? I might tell you that my home lies behind those distant hills, which are like dim, jagged clouds. But though you were to travel day after day, for ever and ever, till you were standing on those hills, you would always see other, and other ranges of hills, further and further away, and my home would still be beyond them; and even if you reached them, you would still see others further away, and would have to go to them, and you would never come to where my home is."

"Ah me!" sighed Christlieb. "Then you must live hundreds and hundreds of miles away from us. It is only on a sort of visit that you are here?"

"Christlieb, darling," the Stranger Child said; "whenever you long for me with all your heart, I am with you immediately, bringing you all those plays and wonders from my home with me; and is not that quite as good as if we were in my home together, playing there?"

"Not at all," Felix said; "for I believe that your home is some most glorious place, full of all sorts of delightful things which you bring—some of them—here with you. I don't care how hard you may say the road is to your home, I mean to set out upon it this minute. To work one's way through forests—by difficult tracks—to climb mountains, and wade rivers, and break through all sorts of thickets, and clamber over rugged rocks—all that is a woodsman's proper business, and I'm going to do it."

"And so you shall!" said the Stranger Child, smiling pleasantly; "for when you put it all so clearly before you, and make up your mind to it, it is as good as done. The land where I live is, in truth, so beautiful and glorious that I can give you no description of it. It is my mother who reigns over that country—all glory and loveliness—as queen."

"Ah, you are a prince!" "Ah, then, you are a princess!" the two children cried together, amazed, and almost terrified.

"I am, certainly," the Stranger Child replied.

"Then you live in a beautiful palace?" Felix cried.

"Yes," said the Stranger Child. "My mother's palace is far more beautiful than those glittering castles which you saw in the evening clouds; for the gleaming pillars of her palace are all of the purest crystal, and they soar, slender and tall, into the blue of heaven; and upon them there rests a great, wide canopy; beneath that canopy sail the shining clouds, hither and thither, on golden wings, and the red of the evening and the morning rises and falls, and the sparkling stars dance in singing circles. Dearest playmates, you have heard of the fairies, who can bring about the most glorious wonders, as mortal men cannot; now, my mother is one of the most powerful fairies of all. All that lives and moves on earth she holds embraced to her heart in the purest and truest love; although, to her inward pain, many human beings will not allow themselves to come to any knowledge of her. But my mother loves children most of all; and thence it is that the festivals which she holds in her kingdom for children are the most splendid and glorious of all. It is then that beautiful spirits belonging to my mother's kingdom, and to her royal palace, fly deftly through the sky, weaving and combining a shining rainbow, from one end of her palace to another, gleaming in the most brilliant dyes. Under those rainbows they build my mother's diamond throne, all of nothing but diamonds—diamonds which are, in appearance and in perfume, like lilies, roses, and carnations; and when my mother takes her place on her throne, the spirits play on their golden harps and their crystal cymbals, and to those instruments the court singers of her court sing with voices so marvellous, that one could die of rapture to hear them. Now, those singers are beautiful birds, bigger even than eagles, with feathers all purple-red, such as you have never seen the like of. And as soon as their music begins, everything in the palace, the woods, and the gardens moves and sings; and all around there are thousands of beautiful children in charming dresses, shouting and delighting. They chase each other amongst the bushes, and throw flowers at each other in play; they climb trees, where the winds swing them and rock them; they gather gold-glittering fruit, which tastes as nothing on earth does; and they play with tame deer and other charming creatures which come bounding up to them from among the trees; then they run up and down the rainbows, or they ride on the golden pheasants, which fly up among the gleaming clouds with them on their backs."

"How delightful that must be!" Christlieb and Felix cried with rapture. "Oh, take us with you to your home! We want to stay there always!"

But the Stranger Child said, "I cannot take you with me to my home; it is too far away. You would have to be able to fly as far and as strongly as I can myself."

Felix and Christlieb were very sorry, and cast their eyes sadly down to the ground.

THE WICKED MINISTER AT THE FAIRY QUEEN'S COURT.

"And then," the Stranger Child continued, "you might not be as happy as you expect at my mother's court. Indeed, it might be a misfortune for you to go there. There are many children who cannot bear the singing of those purple-red birds, glorious as it is: it breaks their hearts, and they are obliged to die immediately. Others, who are too pert and adventurous in running up and down the rainbows, slip, and fall; and there are many who are so stupid and awkward, that they hurt the gold pheasants when they are riding on them. Then those birds, though they are good-tempered and kind-hearted, take this amiss, and they tear those children's breasts open with their sharp beaks, so that they fall down from the clouds bleeding. My mother is very very sorry when children come to misfortune in those ways, although it is all their own fault when they do. She would be only too happy if all the children in the world could enjoy the pleasures of her court and kingdom. But, although there are plenty who can fly strongly enough and far enough, they are often either too forward, or too timid, and cause her only sorrow and pain; and that is why she allows me to fly away from my home, and take to nice children all sorts of delightful playthings, as I have done to you."

"Ah," cried Christlieb, "I am sure I could never do anything to hurt those beautiful birds! But to run up and down a rainbow, that I am certain I never could. I shouldn't like that."

"Now that would be just what I should delight in," Felix said; "and that is the very reason why I want to go and see your mother, the queen. Couldn't you bring one of those rainbows here with you?"

"No," the Stranger Child said, "I could not do that. And I must tell you that I have only been able to come to you by stealing away from home. Once on a time, I was quite safe every where, just as if I were at home, and my mother's beautiful kingdom seemed to extend all over the world; but now that a bitter enemy of hers, whom she has banished from her kingdom, is going raging about everywhere, I cannot be safe from being watched, pursued, and molested."

"Well," Felix cried, jumping up, and shieing the thorn-stick which he was cutting into the air, "I should like to come across the fellow who would do anything to harm you! He would have to do with me in the first place; and then I should send for father, and he would have him taken up and put in the tower[1]."

"Ah," the Stranger Child said, "powerless as my bitter enemy is to harm me when I am at home, he is terribly dangerous when I am not there, and neither sticks nor prisons can protect me from him!"

"What sort of a nasty creature is it, then," Christlieb inquired, "that can do you so much harm?"

"I have told you that my mother is a mighty queen," the Stranger Child said; "and you know that queens, like kings, have courts and ministers[2] belonging to them."

"Yes, yes," said Felix. "My own uncle, the count, is one of those ministers, and wears a star on his breast. Do your mother's ministers wear stars like him?"

"No," the Stranger Child said; "not exactly that; for most of them are shining stars themselves, and others of them do not wear any coats on which they could stick things of the sort. I must tell you that my mother's ministers are all powerful spirits, either hovering in the sky, or dwelling in the waters, doing, and carrying out everywhere what my mother orders them to do. Once, a long while ago, there came amongst us a stranger, who called himself Pepasilio[3], who said he was very learned, and could do more, and accomplish greater things, than all the others of us. My mother took

---

[1] Prison

[2] Advisors; cabinet members

[3] Latin: Pepper sprout ("pepa silio"). It may also be broken up to the sinister, liminal-sounding phrase "on the corridor" ("pe pasilio")

him in amongst the ranks of her other ministers; but his natural spite and wickedness very soon developed themselves and came to light, Not only did he strive to undo all that the other ministers did, but he set himself specially to spoil all the happy enjoyments of children. He had pretended to the queen that he, of all others, was the very spirit who could make children glad, and happy, and clever; but instead of that, he hung himself with a weight of lead on to the tails of the pheasants, so that they could not fly aloft any more; and when the children climbed up the rose-trees, he would drag them down by the legs, so that they knocked their noses on the ground and made them bleed; and any that were jumping and dancing he dashed down to the ground, to go crawling wretchedly about there with downcast heads. Those who were singing he crammed all sorts of nasty stuff into the mouths of, so that they had to stop; for singing he could not abide. As for the poor tame beasts, he always wanted to eat them, instead of playing with them, for he said that was what they were meant for. The worst was, that with the help of his followers, he had a way of smearing all the beautiful, sparkling precious stones of the palace, the many-tinted glowing flowers, the roses and lilies, and even the shining rainbows, with a horrible black juice, so that all the glory and the beauty of them was gone, and everything became sorrowful and dead. And when he had accomplished this, he would out with a loud ringing laugh, and say that everything was now just as he wished it to be. But when, at last, he declared that he did not consider my mother to be queen at all, and that the rule really belonged to him alone,—and when he went hovering up in the shape of an enormous fly, with flashing eyes, and a great trunk, or snout, sticking out, all about my mother's throne, buzzing and humming in an abominable manner,—then she, and all the rest of her court, saw that this malignant minister, who had come amongst us under the fine name of Pepasilio, was none other than Pepser[1], the morose and gloomy King of the Gnomes. But he had foolishly overestimated his power, as well as the bravery of his followers. The ministers of the Air department surrounded the queen, and fanned perfumed breezes towards her, whilst the ministers of the Fire department rushed up and down in billows of flame, and the singers (whose bills had been cleaned out) chanted the most full-voiced choruses, so that the queen neither saw nor heard the ugly Pepser, neither could she be aware of his evil-smelling breath. Moreover, at that moment, the pheasant prince seized him with his glittering beak, and gripped him so strenuously that he screamed with agony and rage; and then the pheasant prince let him down to the earth from a height of three thousand ells[2], so that he could not stir hand or foot till his aunt, and crony, the great blue toad, took him on her back, and so carried him home. Five hundred fine

[1] Etymologically related to "pepper" in a variety of Indo-European languages

[2] 11,000 feet, or just over 2 miles

sprightly children armed themselves with fly-flappers[1], with which they banged Pepser's horrible followers to death, when they were still swarming about intending to destroy all the beautiful flowers. Now, as soon as Pepser was gone, all the black juice which he had covered everything over with, flowed away of itself, and everything was restored, and was soon beaming and shining, and blooming as gloriously as ever. You may imagine that this horrid Pepser has no more power in my mother's kingdom. But he knows that I often venture out, and he follows me everywhere, in shapes of every kind, so that, wretched[2] child that I am, I often do not know where to hide myself in my flight; and that is why I often get away from you so quickly that you cannot see what becomes of me. Therefore things must go on just as they are; and I can assure you that if I were to try to take you with me to my home, Pepser would be sure to lie in wait for us, and kill us."

Christlieb wept bitterly over the danger to which the Stranger Child must always be exposed. But Felix said, "If that horrible Pepser is nothing but a great fly, I'll soon be at him with father's big fly-flapper; and if once I give him a good crack on the nose with it, Aunty Toad will have a job to get him home, I can tell her."

HOW THE TUTOR ARRIVED, AND HOW THE CHILDREN WERE AFRAID OF HIM.

Felix and Christlieb ran home as fast as they could, crying, as they went, "Ah! the Stranger Child is a beautiful prince!"—"Ah! the Stranger Child is a beautiful princess!" They wanted, in their delight, to tell this to their parents; but they stood at the door like marble statues when they found the baron meeting them there with a stranger at his side, an extraordinary-looking personage, who muttered to himself, half intelligibly, "Ah, a nice pair of gawkies[3] those are, it seems to me!"

The baron took him by the hand, saying, "This gentleman is the tutor whom your gracious uncle has sent. So say, 'How-do-you do, sir?' to him properly."

But the children looked askance at the man, and could move neither hand nor foot. This was because they had never seen such an extraordinary-looking creature. He was scarcely more than half a head taller than Felix; but he was stumpy and thick-set, and his little weasened[4] legs formed an astonishing contrast with his body, which was stout and powerful. His shapeless head was almost to be called four-square[5], and his face was almost too ugly altogether. For not only was his nose much too long and

---

[1] Fly swatters

[2] In this sense: poor, helpless

[3] Oafs, dolts, clodhoppers

[4] Stunted, shriveled, misshapen

[5] A cube in dimensions: equally high, wide, and deep

sharp-pointed to suit with his fat, brownish cheeks, and his wide mouth, but his little prominent eyes glittered so alarmingly that one hardly liked to look at him. Moreover, he had a black periwig[1] crammed on to his four-cornered head; he was clad in black from top to toe, and his name was "Tutor Ink."

Now, as the children stood staring like stone images, their mother got angry, and cried, "Good gracious, children, what are you thinking of? This gentleman will take you for a pair of raw country gabies[2]! Come, come; give him your hands!"

The children, taking heart of grace[3], did as their mother bade them. But as soon as the tutor took hold of their hands, they jumped back with a loud cry of "Oh! oh! It hurts!" The tutor laughed aloud, and showed a needle which he had hidden in his hand, to prick the children with. Christlieb was weeping; but Felix growled, in an aside, "Just you try that again, little Big-belly!"

"Why did you do that, dear Mr. Tutor Ink?" the baron asked, rather annoyed.

The tutor answered, "Well, it is my way; I can't alter it!" With which he stuck his hands in his sides, and went on laughing, till at length his laughter sounded as ugly as the noise of a broken rattle.

"You seem to be a person fond of your little jokes, Master Tutor Ink!" the baron said. But he, and his wife, and most particularly the children, were beginning to feel very eery and uncomfortable. "Well, well," said Tutor Ink, "what sort of a state are these little crabs here in? Pretty well grounded in the sciences? We'll see directly." With which he began to ask questions of Felix and Christlieb, of the sort that their uncle and aunt had asked of their cousins. But, as they both declared that, as yet, they did not know any of the sciences, by heart, Tutor Ink beat his hands over his head till everything rang again, and cried, like a man possessed, "A pretty story indeed! No sciences! Then we've got our work cut out for us. However, we shall soon make a job of it."

Felix and Christlieb could both write fairly well, and, from many old books which their father put in their hands, and which they were fond of reading, they had learned a good many pretty stories, and could repeat them. But Tutor Ink despised all this, and said it was stupid nonsense.

Alas! there was no more running about in the woods to be so much as thought of. Instead of that, the children had to sit within the four walls of the house all day long, and babble, after Tutor Ink, things which they did not in the least understand. It was really a heart-breaking business. With what longing eyes they looked at the woods! Often it was as if they heard,

---

[1] An 18th century men's wig

[2] "This gentleman will think you are completely uncouth, country peasant urchins"

[3] Pulled themselves together

amidst the happy songs of the birds, and the rustling of the trees, the Stranger Child's voice calling to them and saying, "Felix! Christlieb! are you not coming any more to play with me? Oh, come! I have made you a palace, all of flowers; we will sit there, and I will give you all sorts of beautiful stones, and then we'll soar into the air, and build ourselves cloud-castles. Come! oh come!"

At this, the children were drawn to the woods with all their thoughts, and neither saw nor heard their tutor any longer. But he would get very angry, thump on the table with both his fists, and hum, and growl, and snarl, "*Pim—sim—prr—srr knurr kirr*—what's all this? Wait a little! "Felix, however, did not endure this very long; he jumped up, and cried, "Don't bother me with your stupid nonsense, Mr. Ink; I must be off to the woods! Go and get hold of Cousin Pump-breeks; that's the sort of stuff for *him*. Come along, Christlieb! The Stranger Child is waiting for us;" with which they started off. But Tutor Ink sprang after them with remarkable agility, and seized hold of them just outside the door. Felix fought like a man, and Tutor Ink was on the point of getting the worst of it, as the faithful Sultan came to Felix's help. Sultan—generally a good, kindly-behaved dog took a strong dislike to Tutor Ink the moment he set eyes on him. Whenever the tutor came near him, he growled, and swept about him so forcibly with his tail that he nearly knocked the tutor down, managing deftly to hit him great thumps on his little weazened legs. So Sultan came dashing up, when Felix was holding the tutor by the shoulders, and hung on to his coat-tails. Master Ink raised a doleful yell, which brought up the baron to the rescue. The tutor let go his hold of Felix, and Sultan let go his hold on the tutor's coat-tails.

"He said we weren't to go to the woods any more," cried Christlieb, weeping and lamenting. And although the baron gave Felix a good scolding, he was very sorry that the children might not go wandering, as they used, amongst the trees and bushes, and told the tutor that he wished him to go with them into the woods for a certain time every day.

The tutor did not like the idea at all. He said, "Ah, Herr Baron, if you had but a sensible piece of garden, with nicely-clipped box, and railed-in enclosures, one might go and take the children for a little walk there of forenoons! But what in all the world is the good of going into a wild forest?"

The children did not like it either, saying, "What business has Tutor Ink in our darling wood?"

HOW TUTOR INK TOOK THE CHILDREN FOR A WALK IN THE WOODS, AND WHAT HAPPENED ON THE OCCASION.

"Well, Master Ink, isn't it delightful in our wood here?" Felix said, as they were making their way through the rustling thickets. Tutor Ink made a face, and answered, "Stupid nonsense! There's no road. All that one does is to tear one's stockings. And one can't say or hear a word of sense, for the abominable screaming noise the birds are making."

"Ha, ha! master," said Felix, "I see you don't know anything about singing! And I daresay you don't hear when the morning wind is talking with the bushes, and the old forest brook is telling all those delightful tales." "And you don't even love the flowers," Christlieb chimed in; "do you, master?"

At this the tutor's face became of even a deeper cherry-brown than it was usually; and he beat with his hands about him, crying, "What stupid, ridiculous nonsense you are talking! Who has put such trash in your heads? Who ever heard that woods and streams had got the length of engaging in rational conversation? Neither is there anything in the chirping of birds. I like flowers well enough when they are nicely arranged in a room in glasses. They smell then; and one doesn't require a scent-bottle. But there are no proper flowers in woods."

"But don't you see those dear little lilies of the valley, peeping up at you with such bright, loving eyes?" Christlieb said.

"What? what?" the tutor screamed. "Flowers—eyes? Ha, ha! Nice 'eyes' indeed! The useless things haven't even got what you would call a smell!" With which Master Ink bent down and plucked up a handful of them, roots and all, and chucked them away into the thickets. To the children it seemed, almost, as if they heard a cry of pain pass through the wood. Christlieb could not help bitter tears, and Felix gnashed his teeth in anger. Just then, a little siskin[1] went fluttering close past the tutor's nose, alighted on a branch, and began a joyous song. "That is a mockingbird, I think!" said the tutor; and, taking up a stone, he threw it at the poor bird, which it struck, and silenced into death; it fell from the green branch to the ground.

Felix could restrain himself no longer. "You horrible Tutor Ink," he cried, "what had the bird done to you that you should strike it dead? Ah, where are you, you beautiful Stranger Child? Oh come! only come! Let us fly far, far away. I cannot stay beside this horrible creature any longer. I want to go to your home with you." Christlieb chimed in, sobbing and weeping bitterly, crying, "Oh, thou darling child, come to us, come to us! Rescue us, rescue us! Tutor Ink is killing us, as he is killing the flowers and the birds."

"What do you mean by the Stranger Child?" Tutor Ink asked. But at that instant there came a louder whispering and rustling amongst the bushes, mingled with melancholy, heart-breaking tones, as if of muffled bells tolling in the far distance. In a shining cloud, which came sailing over above them, they saw the beautiful face of the Stranger Child, and presently it came wholly into view, wringing its little hands, whilst tears, like glittering pearls streamed down its rosy cheeks. "Ah, darling playmates," cried the Stranger Child, in tones of sorrow, "I cannot come to you any

---

[1] A small, yellow and black finch

more. You will never see me again. Farewell, farewell! The gnome Pepser has you in his power. Oh, you poor children, good-bye, good-bye!" and the Stranger Child soared up far into the sky. But, at the children's backs, there began a horrid, fearsome sort of buzzing and humming, and snarling and growling; and lo! Tutor Ink had taken the shape of an enormous frightful-looking fly. And the horrible part of the thing was, that he had a man's face at the same time, and even some of his clothes on still. He began to fly upwards, slowly and with difficulty, evidently with the intention of following the Stranger Child. Felix and Christlieb, overpowered with terror, ran away out of the wood as quickly as they could, and did not so much as dare to look up to the sky till they had got some distance off. When they did so, they could just perceive a shining speck in the sky, glittering amongst the clouds like a star, and apparently coming nearer, and downwards. "That's the Stranger Child," Christlieb cried. The star grew bigger and bigger, and as it did, they could hear a braying of trumpets; and presently they saw that the star was a splendid bird, with wondrous shining plumage, coming soaring down to the wood, flapping its mighty wings, and singing loud and clear. "Ha!" cried Felix, "this is the pheasant prince. He will bite Master Tutor Ink to death. The Stranger Child is saved and so are we! Come, Christlieb; let us get home as fast as we can, and tell father all about it."

HOW THE BARON TURNED TUTOR INK OUT OF DOORS.

The baron and his spouse were both sitting before the door of their simple dwelling, looking at the evening-red, which was beginning to flame up from behind the blue mountains in golden streamers. They had their supper laid out on a little table: it consisted of a noble jug of splendid milk, and a plate of bread-and-butter.

"I don't know," the baron began, "where Tutor Ink can be staying out so long with the children. At first there was no getting him to go out at all to the wood, and now there's no getting him back from it. He's really a very extraordinary fellow, this Tutor Ink, taking him all in all. I sometimes almost wish he had never entered our doors. To begin with, his pricking the children with that needle was a thing that I cannot say I liked; and I don't think his knowledge of the sciences amounts to very much, either. He plappers out a lot of stuff that nobody run make head or tail of, and can tell you what kind of spatterdashes[1] the Grand Mogul[2] puts on; but when

[1] Half-gaiters: cloth or leather coverings which cover the top of the shoe, the ankle, and lower-calf, protecting them from getting wet or muddy. They are secured to the foot by buttons up one side, and a strap that goes around the bottom of the foot

[2] A term for the ruler, or Padishah, of India's Mughal Empire (1526 – 1857)

he goes outside, he can't tell a lime-tree from a chestnut; and his behaviour has always struck me as being most remarkable."

"I feel just as you do, dearest husband," said Frau von Brakel; "and, glad as I was that your great cousin should interest himself about the children, I feel quite sure, now, that he might have done it in other and better ways than by saddling us with this Tutor Ink. As regards his knowledge of the sciences, I don't pretend to give an opinion; but I know that the little black creature, with his little weeny legs, is more and more disagreeable to me every day. He has such a nasty way of gobbling things. He can't see a drop of beer at the bottom of a glass, or the fag-end[1] of a jug of milk, but he must gulp them down his throat; and if he finds the sugar-box open, he's at it in a moment, snuffing at the sugar, and dipping his fingers in it, till one has to clap to the lid in his face; and then away he darts, humming and buzzing in a way that's most disgusting and abominable."

The baron was going to carry this conversation further, when Felix and Christlieb came running home through amongst the birches.

"Hurrah! hurrah!" Felix kept shouting, "the pheasant prince has bitten Master Tutor Ink to death!"

"Oh, mamma dear," cried Christlieb, "Master Tutor Ink is not a Tutor Ink at all! What he really is, is Pepser, king of the Gnomes; a great, monstrous fly, but a fly with a wig on, and shoes and stockings!"

The parents gazed at the children in utter amazement, as they went on excitedly telling them all about the Stranger Child, whose mother was a great fairy queen; and of the Gnome King Pepser, and his combat with the pheasant prince.

"Who on earth has been cramming all this nonsense into your heads?" the baron asked over and over again. "Have you been dreaming? or what in the name of goodness has happened to you?" However, the children declared, and stuck to it, that everything had happened just as they told it, and that the horrible Pepser, who had given himself out as being Master Ink, the tutor, must be lying killed in the wood.

Frau von Brakel struck her hands over her head and cried, in much sorrow, "Oh, children, children, I don't know what on earth is to become of you, when fearful things of this sort come into your heads, and you won't let yourselves be persuaded to the contrary!"

But the baron grew very grave and thoughtful. "Felix," he said, "you are really a very sensible boy now; and I must admit that Tutor Ink has always, from the very first, struck me as being a very strange, mysterious creature. Indeed, it often seemed to me that there was something very queer about him, which I could by no means get to the bottom of; he is not like the common run of tutors at all. Your mother and I are by no means satisfied

[1] The crevasses of the bottom where what collects there is essentially negligible

with him, particularly your mother. He has such a terribly liquorish[1] tooth of his own, there's no keeping him away from sweet things! And then he hums and buzzes in such a distressing way! Altogether, I can assure you he wouldn't have been here much longer. No! But now, my dear boy, just bethink yourself calmly; even if there were, really, any such nasty things as gnomes existing in the world, could (I ask you now to think it over calmly and rationally), *could*, I say, a tutor really be a fly?"

Felix looked his father steadily in the face with his clear blue eyes, as he repeated this question. "Well," said Felix, "I never thought very much about that; in fact, I should not have believed it myself, if the Stranger Child had not said so, and if I had not seen, with my own eyes, that he is a horrible, nasty fly, and only pretends to be Tutor Ink. And then," continued Felix, while the baron shook his head in silence, like one who does not know quite what to say, or think, "see what mother says about his fondness for sweet things. Isn't that just like a fly? Flies are always grabbing at sweet things. And then, his hummings and buzzings!"

"Silence!" cried the baron. "Whatever Tutor Ink may really be, one thing is certain; that the pheasant prince has not bitten him to death, for here he comes out of the wood!"

At this the children uttered loud screams, and fled into the house.

For, in truth, Tutor Ink was approaching out of the wood, up the path among the birches. But he was all wild-looking and bewildered, with sparkling eyes, and his wig all touzled. He was buzzing and humming, and making great springs, high off the ground, first to one side, then to another, banging his head against the birches till you heard them resound. When he got to the house, he dashed at the milk-jug and popped his face into it, so that the milk ran over the sides; and he gulped it down, making a horrible noise of swallowing.

"For the love of heaven, Master Ink," cried Fran von Brakel, "what are you about?"

"Are you out of your senses?" said the baron. "Is the foul fiend[2] after you?"

But, regardless of those interrogations, Master Ink, taking his mouth from the milk-jug, threw himself down bodily on the dish of bread-and-butter; fluttered over it with his coat-tails, and, somehow, made such play over it with his weazened legs, that he smoothed it down all over. Then, with a louder buzzing, he made for the house-door; but he couldn't manage to get into the house, but staggered hither and thither as if he was drunk, banging against the windows till they rattled and rang.

"I'll tell you what it is, my good sir!" cried the baron. "This is pretty[3] behaviour! Look out, or you'll come to grief before you know where you

---

[1] Gluttonous, eager to taste, uncontrollable

[2] Satan himself

[3] Civilized, well-bred, elegant

are!" And he tried to seize Master Ink by the coat-tails; but Master Ink always managed to elude him, deftly. Here Felix came running out, with his father's big fly-flapper in his hand; and he gave it to the baron, crying, "Here you are, father; knock the horrible Pepser to death!"

The baron took the fly-flapper, and then they all set to work at Master Ink. Felix, Christlieb, and their mother took table-napkins, and made sweeps with them in the air, driving the tutor backwards and forwards, here and there; whilst the baron kept letting drive at him with the fly-flapper, which did not hit him, unfortunately, because he took good care never to stay a moment in the same place. And wilder and wilder grew the chase. *"Summ-summ——simm-simm——trr-trr,"* went the tutor, storming hither and thither; *"huss-huss,"* went the table-napkins, pursuing the foe; *"klip-klap"* fell the baron's strokes with the flapper, thick as hail. At last the baron managed to hit the tutor's coat-tails; he fell down with a groan. But just as the baron was going to get a second stroke at him, he bounced up into the air, with renewed and redoubled strength, stormed, humming and buzzing, away through the birches, and was seen no more.

"A good job," said the baron, "that we're well rid of horrible Tutor Ink: never shall he cross my threshold again."

"No; that he shall not!" said Frau von Brakel. "Tutors with such objectionable manners can do nothing but mischief, when just the contrary ought to be the case. Brags about his 'sciences,' and then goes flop into the milk-jug. A nice sort of a tutor, upon my word!"

But the children laughed and shouted, crying, "Hip-hip, hurrah! It's all right now! Father has hit Tutor Ink a good one on the nose, and we've got rid of him for good and all."

THAT WHICH CAME TO PASS IN THE WOOD, AFTER TUTOR INK WAS GOT RID OF.

Felix and Christlieb breathed freely again now. A great weight was taken off their hearts. Above all things, there was the delicious thought that, now that the horrid Pepser was gone, the Stranger Child would be sure to come back, and play with them as of yore. They hurried into the wood, full of sweet hope and happy expectancy. But everything there was silent and desolate. Not a merry note of finch or siskin was to be heard; and in place of the gladsome rustling of the bushes and the joyous voice of the brook, sighs of sorrow seemed to be passing through the air, and the sun cast only faint and feeble glimpses through the clouded sky. Presently great dark clouds began to pile themselves up; thunder muttered in the distance; a storm-wind howled, and the tall fir-trees creaked and groaned. Christlieb clung to Felix, in alarm. But he said, "What's come to you? What are you afraid of? There's going to be a thunderstorm. We must get home as fast as we can; that's all!"

So they set off to do so; but somehow—they didn't know why—instead of getting out of the wood, they seemed to keep getting farther and farther into it. The darkness deepened: great rain-drops fell, faster and faster, thicker and thicker, and flashes of lightning darted hither and thither, hissing as they passed. The children came to a stand by the edge of an impassable thicket. "Let's duck down here for a little, Christlieb," said Felix; "the storm won't last long." Christlieb was crying from fear, but she did as Felix asked her. Scarcely had they sat down among the thick bushes, however, when nasty, snarling voices began to speak, behind them, saying:

"Stupid things! Senseless creatures! You despised us; didn't know how to treat us—what to do with us. So now you can do your best without any playthings, senseless creatures that you are!" Felix looked round, and felt very eery and uncomfortable when he saw the sportsman and the harper rise up out of the thicket into which he had thrown them, staring at him with dead eyes and struggling and fighting about them with their hands. Moreover, the harper twanged on his strings so that they gave out a horrible, nasty, eery clinkering and rattling; and the sportsman went so far as to take a deliberate aim at Felix with his gun; and both of them croaked out, "Wait a little, you boy and you girl. We are obedient pupils of Master Tutor Ink: he'll be here directly, and then we'll pay you out nicely for despising us." Terrified—regardless of the rain, which was now streaming in torrents, and of the rattling peals of thunder, and the gale which was roaring through the firs—the children ran away from thence, and came to the brink of the pond which bordered the wood. But as soon as they got there, lo and behold! Christlieb's big doll, which Felix had thrown into the water, rose out of the sedges, and squeaked out, in a horrible voice, "Wait a little, you boy and you girl! Stupid things! Senseless creatures! You despised me; didn't know what to do with me—how to treat me. So now you can get on without playthings the best way you can. I am an obedient pupil of Master Tutor Ink's: he'll be here directly, and then you'll be nicely paid out for despising me." And then the nasty thing sent great splashes of water flying at Felix and Christlieb, though they were wet through already with the rain.

Felix could not endure this terrible process of haunting. Poor Christlieb was half dead, so they ran off again, as hard as they could; but soon, in the heart of the wood, they sank down, exhausted with weariness and terror. Then they heard a humming and a buzzing behind them. "Oh, heavens!" cried Felix; "here comes Tutor Ink, now!" At that moment his consciousness left him, and so did Christlieb's too.

When they came back to their senses, they found themselves lying on a bed of soft moss. The storm was over, the sun was shining bright and kindly, and the raindrops were hanging on the glittering bushes and trees like sparkling jewels. The children were much surprised to find that their clothes were quite dry, and that they felt no trace of either cold or wet. "Ah!" cried Felix, stretching his arms to the sky; "the Stranger Child must have protected us." And then they both called out so loud that the wood re-echoed: "Ah, thou darling child, do but come to us again! We do so long for you; we cannot live without you!" And it seemed, too, as though a bright beam of light came darting through the trees, making the flowers lift up their heads as it touched them. But though the children called upon their playfellow yet more movingly, nothing made itself seen. They crept home in silence and sadness. But their parents were very glad to see them, having been exceedingly anxious about them during the storm. The baron said, "It is a good thing that you are home again; for I confess I was afraid that Tutor Ink was still hanging about somewhere in the wood, and on your track."

Felix related all that had happened in the wood. "That is all stupid nonsense," their mother said. "If you are to go dreaming all that sort of stuff in the wood, you shan't be allowed to go there any more. You'll have to stop at home." And indeed—although, when they begged that they might be allowed to go back there, their mother yielded—it so came about that they didn't care very much about doing it. Alas! the Stranger Child was never there; and whenever they got far into the wood, or reached the bank of the pond, they were jeered at by the harper, the sportsman, and the doll, who cried to them, "Stupid things! Senseless creatures! You must do without playthings. You didn't know how to treat us clever, cultivated people—stupid things, senseless creatures that you are!"

This being unendurable, the children preferred staying at home.

CONCLUSION.

"I don't know," said the baron to his lady one day, "what it is that has been the matter with me for the last few days. I feel so queer and so odd, that I could almost fancy Tutor Ink has put some spell upon me. Ever since the moment when I hit him that crack with the fly-flapper, all my limbs have felt like bits of lead."

And the baron did really grow weaker and paler, day by day. He gave up walking about his grounds; he no longer went bustling about the house, cheerily ordering matters as he used to do; he sat, hour after hour, in deep meditation, and would get Felix and Christlieb to repeat to him, over and over again, all about the Stranger Child; and when they spoke eagerly of all the marvels connected with the Stranger Child, and of the beautiful brilliant kingdom which was its home, he would give a melancholy smile, and the tears would come to his eyes.

But Felix and Christlieb could not reconcile themselves to the circumstance that the Stranger Child went on keeping aloof from them, leaving them exposed to the nasty behaviour of those troublesome puppets in the thicket and the duck pond, on account of which they did not like now to frequent the wood at all.

But one morning, when it was fine and beautiful, the baron said, "Come along, children; we'll go to the wood together, you and I. Master Ink's nasty

pupils shan't do you any harm." So he took them by the hands, and they all three went together to the wood, which that day was fuller than ever of bright sunshine, perfume, and song. When they had laid themselves down amongst the tender grass, and the sweet-scented flowers, the baron began as
follows:—

"You dear children, I have for some time had a great longing to tell you a thing, and I cannot delay doing so any longer. It is, that—once on a time—I knew the beautiful Stranger Child that used to show you such lovely things in the wood, just as well as you did yourselves. When I was about your age, that child used to come to me too, and play with me in the most wonderful way. How it was that it came to leave me, I cannot quite remember; and I don't understand how I had so completely forgotten all about it till you spoke to me about what had happened to you, and then I didn't believe you, though I often had a sort of dim consciousness that what you told me was the truth. But within the last few days, I have been remembering and thinking about the delightful days of my own boyhood, in a way that I have not been able to do for many a long year. And then that beautiful magic-child came back to my memory, bright and glorious, as you saw it yourselves; and the same longing which filled your breasts came to mine too. But it is breaking my heart! I feel, and I know quite well, that this is the last time that I shall ever sit beneath these bonnie trees and bushes. I am going to leave you very soon, and when I am dead and gone, you must cling fast to that beautiful child."

Felix and Christlieb were beside themselves with grief and sorrow. They wept and lamented, crying, "No, no, father; you are not going to die! You have many a long year to be with us still, and to play with the Stranger Child along with us."

But the next day, the baron lay sick in his bed. A tall, meagre man came and felt his pulse, and said, "You'll soon be better!" But he was not soon better. On the third day, the Baron von Brakel was no more. Ah, how Frau von Brakel mourned! How the children wrung their hands and cried, "Oh, father! our dear, dear father!"

Soon, when four peasants of Brakelheim had borne their master to his grave, there came to the house some horrible fellows, almost like Tutor Ink in appearance, and they told Frau von Brakel that they must take possession of all the piece of land, and the house, and everything in it, because the deceased baron owed all that, and more besides, to his cousin, who could wait no longer for his money. So that Frau von Brakel was a beggar, and had to go away from the pretty little village of Brakelheim, where she had spent so many happy years, and go to live with a relation not very far away. She and the children had to pack up whatever little bits of clothes and effects they had left, and with many tears take their leave, and set forth upon their way. As they crossed the bridge, and heard the loud voice of the forest stream, Frau von Brakel fell down in a swoon, and

Felix and Christlieb sank on their knees beside her, and cried, with many sobs and tears, "Oh, unfortunate creatures that we are! Will no one take any pity on us?"

At that moment the distant rushing of the forest stream seemed to turn into beautiful music. The thickets gave forth mysterious sighs, and presently all the forest streamed with wonderful, sparkling fires. And lo! the Stranger Child appeared, coming forth out of the sweet-smelling leafage, surrounded by such a brilliant light and radiance, that Felix and Christlieb had to shut their eyes at the brightness of it. Then they felt themselves gently touched, and the Stranger Child's beautiful voice said, "Oh, do not mourn so, dear playmates of mine! Do I not love you as much as ever? Can I ever leave you? No, no! Although you do not see me with your bodily eyes, I am always with you and about you, helping you with all my power to be always happy and fortunate. Only keep me in your hearts, as you have done hitherto, and neither the wicked Pepser, nor any other adversary, will have power to harm you. Only go on loving me truly and faithfully."

"Oh, that we shall—that we shall!" the children cried. "We love you with all our souls!"

When they were able to open their eyes again, the Stranger Child had vanished; but all their pain was gone from them, and they felt that a heavenly joy and gladness had arisen within their hearts. Frau von Brakel recovered slowly from her swoon, and said, "Children, I saw you in a dream. You seemed to be standing in a blaze of gleaming gold, and the sight has strengthened and refreshed me in a wonderful way."

Delight beamed in the children's eyes, and shone in their cheeks. They related how the Stranger Child had come to them and comforted them. And their mother said, "I do not know how it is that I feel compelled to believe in this story of yours to-day, nor how my believing in it seems to have taken away all my sorrow and anxiety. Let us go on our way with confidence."

They were kindly received and welcomed by their relatives, and all that the Stranger Child promised came to pass. Whatever Felix and Christlieb undertook was sure to prosper, and they and their mother became quite happy. And, as their lives went on, they still, in dreams, played with the Stranger Child, which, never ceased to bring to them the loveliest wonders from its fairy home.

WHILE "The Stranger Child" is not a particularly strong story, plot-wise – with its meandering and seeming spontaneous plot twists – it is shocking in its use of imagination. In a world before *Frankenstein*, "Rip Van Winkle," or the Tales of Poe had appeared on bookshelves, Hoffmann's seamless blend of realism with fantasy was tremendously unsettling.

Whereas the fairy tales of Perrault and the Grimms occurred in ostensibly magical universes where such things could be expected, and the Gothic novels of the previous century were set in exotic locales during remote time periods, Hoffmann's choice to intrude his grotesque caricatures into the familiar, bourgeois world of Napoleonic Europe brought a nightmarish realism to his stories. He makes certain that we understand that the Baron von Brakel lives in a rural homestead rather than a fairy tale citadel, and that his children – far from being the cherubic children who typically prance, preen, and pray in cautionary fairy tales – scarf their food down sloppily, embarrass their parents in front of guests with their non-conformist stubbornness, and angrily destroy toys that fail to please them. Hardly Hansel and Gretel – for all of their sappy "darlings," "dearests," and "lovelies" – these complex characters don't quite fit the mold of the fairy tale universe that we expect them to inhabit. They fail to live up to the expectations of the perfect children we know from the Grimms: they are spoiled, bratty, rude, and uncultured. And yet Hoffmann emphasizes the way this – their unapologetic disinterest in others' approval – has preserved them from turning into the even *more* unbearable, creepily "perfect" sycophants, Hermann and Adelgunda. Overly polished, elaborately dressed, and emotionally stunted, these two Doppelgängers of the country-bred siblings are intentionally compared to the toys being trucked in by their judgmental relatives: with his fake sword and fancy coat Hermann is more toy soldier than living boy, and with her strange features and overabundant ribbons, Adelgunda is more doll than girl. This, Hoffmann warns us, is the peril of forcing compliance in children.

II.

Enter Ink. Sent by the Baron's disapproving cousin, Tutor Ink acts as an agent of pain, unhappiness, and disappointment: his mission is to destroy the children's imaginations, deaden their Edenic lack of self-awareness, and subjugate their willfulness. It is uncanny that Tutor Ink looks so inhuman while in the human universe, yet seems to pass with adults. Children see the goblin in him – as do readers – but adults have their vision clouded by a lack – or loss – of imagination. Contrasted with the Stranger Child – a timeless spirit of youth and imagination who has manifested to their child-like father (a man who seems to die once he realizes that he has grown up and lives in a world without patience for unambitious, financially illiterate men of leisure) – Ink represents the gruesome vulgarity of adulthood. His sole task is to punish the children into forget their supernatural playmate – to drive the innocence from their hearts – and he is nearly successful. When the discarded toys – gifts from their aristocratic cousin who sponsored Ink and presumably approves of his diabolical mission – come to life and taunt the Brakel children like corpses rising from their graves, we are reminded that even something as innocent-seeming as a fancy toy can hide a darker purpose.

The children initially "shy" their toys into the brush and pond of the forest when they realize that – like Hermann and Adelgunda – they are pretty but insubstantial: they break easily, are out of tune, and prove to have thin coats of paint which barely conceal their hypocrisy. Compare this to Christ's injunction to the hypocritical Pharisees in Matthew 23:

> "You are like whitewashed tombs, which look beautiful on the outside but on the inside are full of the bones of the dead and everything unclean. In the same way, on the outside you appear to people as righteous but on the inside you are full of hypocrisy and wickedness."

Like Ink, they are emissaries of the Enemy – devilish spies sent to challenge the siblings' rural happiness by sowing discontent in their hearts. "The Stranger Child" is not Hoffmann's most horrifying tale by a long shot, but its nightmarish imagery, blurring of fantasy and reality, and themes of imperiled children make it a memorable story and a disturbing fairy tale.

III.

And what of the Stranger Child? Who or what are they? It is tempting to think that Hoffmann was influenced by Marian apparitions which often followed this formula. Many of the most famous of these events involves two or more children, usually living in rural poverty, who are approached by a luminous, supernatural personality – in this case the Virgin Mary – who encourages them to continue in their innocence, to avoid the disappointing temptations of the adult world, and to lead others to meet them and follow their Gospel of child-like love and authenticity. However, none of these events – including the apparitions of La Salette (1846), Lourdes (1858), Fatima (1917), Kibeho (1981), or Medjugorje (1981 also) – took place during Hoffmann's lifetime. The youthful sprite also presages icons of children's fantasy like Peter Pan, who introduces himself to a set of siblings just as their innocence is about to be assaulted by the machinations of cynical adults (viz., Wendy is "to grow up"), inviting them to play with him in Neverland where their innocence can be preserved. Ultimately, Pan's solution is limited in its soundness, because he wants them to be completely preserved and unchanged – never growing up and never returning to the mortal world – but the Stranger Child's wisdom is applicable to imaginative types of all ages and societies: it is not a summons to retreat into fantasy, but a call to face reality with exuberant hope and childlike joy – the undying bliss of imagination and self-acceptance. In her essay on the story, Christina Weiler writes:

> "[The story] allows for creative transgressions of societal limitations, provoking the child to use imagination to transform the natural world around her or him, establishing connections to it, and filling it with wonder... [The Stranger Child] inspires them to find dolls in the grass and soldiers among the twigs, rather than passively accepting sterile, mechanical toys from automaton-like relatives from "the city"; the more "natural" play produces a more imaginative child that

> understands what one may or may not do, and thus provides a constructive kind of transgression. 'Artificiality' and 'automation' function as impediments to such productive play."

And so, Hoffmann reminds us, something as simple as playtime can be revolutionary – a subversive act of rebellion against the oppressive forces that conspire to crush hope and convert children into slaves of commerce. The Stranger Child – like a Marian apparition or Peter Pan – comes to encourage the children to preserve their joy and light by rejecting the sour siren call of industry and income. They may be poorer, yes, and certainly less powerful or prestigious (they will wear no star-shaped medals or carry no silver sabers), but they will be free of the marionette strings that cause their relatives to dance mirthlessly to the tune of their masters. As Hoffmann urges us all, they will find liberty in the transgressive rebellion of preserving their imaginations and dismissing the regard of others for a clean conscience and a simple life.

MOST famous and proliferate of all Hoffmann's tales, "Nutcracker and the King of Mice" was *not*, however, very well received by its contemporaries. Hoffmann himself considered it a flop, and tweaked the plot considerably into "The Stranger Child" – another Christmas tale about two siblings who befriend an exiled supernatural being who is pursued by a villainous animal hybrid (in this case a fly), whom the children help to restore to his throne. While "The Stranger Child" was better reviewed during Hoffmann's lifetime, it would be his *earlier* Yuletide fairy tale that would preserve his fame in the coming centuries. And a fairy tale it most certainly is: with its plot about a disguised prince cursed with an ugly exterior and only restored to his rightful form by the unqualified love of a good woman, "Nutcracker" builds on the legacy of European folk classics like "Beauty and the Beast," "The Six Wild Swans," "The Frog Prince," and "King Thrush-beard" (or in German, "König Drosselbart" – the obvious source of Godfather Drosselmeier's surname). The moral shared by all these stories is that a broken society can be prejudiced against good people for stupid and superficial reasons, but that wise and discerning hearts will choose to protect, appreciate, and love a virtuous outcast without casting judgment on their looks or power – a choice which may ultimately lead to their own spiritual reclamation and mental liberation. For Hoffmann – who considered himself physically and psychologically ludicrous – this childlike ability to see beyond society's measures of worth and to value a person for their character rather than their external value was priceless, and he often identified it in the young girls who always seemed to feature in his life (Julia Mark being the most significant, along with his niece who briefly lived with his family, and his daughter who died as a toddler).

II.

The modern conceptions we now have of "The Nutcracker" are largely due to two important developments in its history: firstly, there was a French adaptation of Hoffmann's story written by Alexandre Dumas, which toned down Hoffmann's erotic and horror elements and humanized the largely unlikable Herr Drosselmeier (who in Hoffmann's tale is aloof, cruel, overly sensitive, and frightening); secondly, of course,was the libretto of Pytor Tchaikovsky's ballet which *wildly* overemphasized the penultimate "Candyland" chapter (in Hoffmann's tale, this occupies exactly 14.8% of the plot, while Tchaikovsky makes it over 45% of his ballet, adding new characters like the Sugar Plum Fairy and her Cavalier). Transforming Hoffmann's Kafkaesque dark fantasy into a charming Christmas fairy tale was enough to rehabilitate the story and introduce it to new generations. While the original tale is not drastically different, there is a strong atmosphere of unease and anxiety that doesn't exist in Tchaikovsky's ballet: Drosselmeier gaslights Marie (Clara in the ballet) by pretending not to know about her experiences (of which he is *clearly* the orchestrator) and frightens her multiple times with his weird stories and nonsense poems; her parents, too, threaten her with punishment if she doesn't shut up about Nutcracker, and by the end of the story she is a disillusioned daydreamer suffering from depression and a potentially fatal infection. Ultimately, Drosselmeier seems to be urging Marie through a ritualistic initiation into the world of perceiving-things-as-they-are: as in "The Golden Pot," Hoffmann uses a character's imagination to bring energizing vision to the mundane and ordinary comforts to the imagination. The fickle eccentric Drosselmeier uses Marie's open-mindedness to break a curse settled on his nephew by a gluttonous mouse (representing corruption) and a spoiled princess (representing the aristocracy): she sees things as they are, and doesn't question Drosselmeier's satirical parable (instead of assuming that the mouse and princess are symbols of a prejudiced, shallow society, she takes them at face value), causing her feelings for the ugly Nutcracker to become deeply held convictions. Today "Nutcracker" is warmly regarded as a cozy Christmas story, but Hoffmann's original – brooding with direful gloom, fearturing psychological abuse, a nearly fatal wound to the young protagonist, and a sinister mist of erotic subtext – was *hardly* cozy. It is a wild, manic indictment of bourgeois culture, presenting a revolutionary treatise on the power of imagination to free the soul and the staggering costs of releasing oneself from society's power – as Marie will find out, it may cost you your friends, your family, your health, and your home, and – as some somber theorists believe – maybe even your life.

Nutcracker and the King of Mice

— *Excerpted from 'The Serapion Brethren,' Volume One, Section Two* — {1817}

CHRISTMAS EVE

"ON the 24th of December[1] Dr. Stahlbaum's[2] children were not allowed, on any pretext whatever, at any time of all that day, to go into the small drawing-room, much less into the best drawing-room into which it opened.

---

[1] In most European cultures, Christmas Eve is considered a time when the laws of Nature are loosened or suspended (similar to Hallowe'en Night) where supernatural events – both fantastical and frightening – are likelier to occur

[2] Literally, "Steel Tree." Some commentators have noted that the barren, cold, masculine connotations with this name were meant to pre-condition readers into expected the dull, unimaginative, and spiritually sterile world of Marie's family

Fritz and Marie[1] were sitting cowered together in a corner of the back parlour when the evening twilight fell, and they began to feel terribly eerie. Seeing that no candles were brought, as was generally the case on Christmas Eve, Fritz, whispering in a mysterious fashion, confided to his young sister (who was just seven) that he had heard rattlings and rustlings going on all day, since early morning, inside the forbidden rooms[2], as well as distant hammerings[3]. Further, that a short time ago a little dark-looking man had gone slipping and creeping across the floor with a big box under his arm, though he was well aware that this little man was no other than Godpapa[4] Drosselmeier[5]. At this news Marie clapped her little hands for gladness, and cried:

"'Oh! I do wonder what pretty things Godpapa Drosselmeier has been making for us *this* time!'

"Godpapa Drosselmeier was anything but a nice-looking man. He was little and lean, with a great many wrinkles on his face, a big patch of black

---

[1] Tchaikovsky changed this to Clara ("Light"), but Hoffmann's name, which connotes the Virgin Mary (a pure girl who was entrusted with guarding and nurturing Christ in his weakened state as a small baby) is equally fitting

[2] In ghost stories these are usual haunted rooms that pose a physical danger to wayward or nosy children. In reality, these are probably the guests' rooms

[3] In German folklore, this would immediately be blamed on Poltergeists – "noisy spirits" – and be suggestive that the Supernatural is beginning its invasion of Marie's life. Already Hoffmann's "Nutcracker" sounds far more like a ghost story than Tchaikovsky's charming fairy tale

[4] Godfathers are family friends who serve as witnesses to the baptism of the family's children and pledge to guide and instruct their godchildren in the Christian faith. Drosselmeier will guide and instruct Marie in navigating the supernatural in a less orthodox fashion

[5] A reference to the Grimms' fairy tale "Koenig Drosselbart" – "King Thrush-beard." The plot – about a disguised prince's attempts to woo an indifferent girl's heart – has many similarities to this one. A self-absorbed princess rejects and humiliates any suitor whom she meets, to the embarrassment of her father. The last straw is when she mocks a well-liked king for his pointy beard (comparing it to a thrush's beak). Outraged, the king promises to marry her to the next suitor, whoever he may be. To her horror, it is a bumpkin peasant who takes her to his cottage and teaches her how to weave and sell baskets for a living. After weeks of hardship, she learns to be humble, compassionate, kind, and hardworking, and to her delight, her husband removes his disguise, revealing himself to be King Thrush-beard – beloved by his subjects as a generous and compassionate lord. Likewise, Drosselmeier appears to disguise his ego in the figure of Nutcracker, and Marie only breaks the spell by declaring her love for "Dear Drosselmeier" (meaning the nephew, but equally applying to the uncle)

plaister[1] where his right eye ought to have been, and not a hair on his head; which was why he wore a fine white wig, made of glass[2], and a very beautiful work of art. But he was a very, very clever man, who even knew and understood all about clocks and watches[3], and could make them himself. So that when one of the beautiful clocks that were in Dr. Stahlbaum's house was out of sorts, and couldn't sing, Godpapa Drosselmeier would come, take off his glass periwig and his little yellow coat[4], gird himself with a blue apron, and proceed to stick sharp-pointed instruments into the inside of the clock, in a way that made little Marie quite miserable to witness. However, this didn't really hurt the poor clock, which, on the contrary, would come to life again, and begin to whirr and sing and strike as merrily as ever; which caused everybody the greatest satisfaction. Of course, whenever he came he always brought something delightful in his pockets for the children—perhaps a little man, who would roll his eyes and make bows and scrapes, most comic to behold; or a box, out of which a little bird would jump; or something else of the kind. But for Christmas he always had some specially charming piece of ingenuity provided; something which had cost him infinite pains and labour—for which reason it was always taken away and put by with the greatest care by the children's parents.

"'Oh! what can Godpapa Drosselmeier have been making for us *this* time.' Marie cried, as we have said.

"Fritz was of opinion that, this time, it could hardly be anything but a great castle[5], a fortress, where all sorts of pretty soldiers would be drilling and marching about; and then, that other soldiers would come and try to get into the fortress, upon which the soldiers inside would fire away at them, as pluckily as you please, with cannon, till every thing banged and thundered like anything.

---

[1] In British English, this refers to a bandage – which is to say, an eyepatch

[2] Some translations indicate that, rather than a single, clunky toupee, this is meant to be depicted as being made of glass filaments: each separate hair being wrought from strands of glass. The symbolism is likely meant to indicate that – like the wig sitting on it – Drosselmeier's head is filled with complex and beautiful things. It also calls to mind monks' habit of shaving their pates as a symbol of their foreswearing worldly things, and wearing a symbolic skullcap in its place. Likewise, Drosselmeier is a priest of fantasy, having foresworn the sterile distractions of the mortal world

[3] Like Krespel, the Sandman, and so many of Hoffmann's mysterious figures, Drosselmeier is a renowned engineer and tinker

[4] Yellow – throughout the 19th century, from Goethe to Wilde – was seen as a color representing decadence and imaginative indulgence

[5] Polar opposite of the feminine, nurturing Marie, Fritz's thoughts are constantly filled with visions of war and domination – of machismo and masculine indulgence

"'No, no,' Marie said. 'Godpapa Drosselmeier once told me about a beautiful garden, with a great lake in it, and beautiful swans swimming about with great gold collars, singing lovely music. And then a lovely little girl comes down through the garden to the lake, and calls the swans and feeds them with shortbread and cake.'

"'Swans don't eat cake and shortbread,' Fritz cried, rather rudely (with masculine superiority[1]); 'and Godpapa Drosselmeier couldn't make a whole garden. After all, we have got very few of his playthings; whatever he brings is always taken away from us. So I like the things papa and mamma give us much better; we keep them, all right, ourselves, and can do what we like with them.'

"The children went on discussing as to what he might have in store for them this time. Marie called Fritz's attention to the fact that Miss Gertrude (her biggest doll) appeared to be failing a good deal as time went on, inasmuch as she was more clumsy and awkward than ever, tumbling on to the floor every two or three minutes, a thing which did not occur without leaving very ugly marks on her face, and of course a proper condition of her clothes became out of the question altogether. Scolding was of no use. Mamma too had laughed at her for being so delighted with Miss Gertrude's little new parasol. Fritz, again, remarked that a good fox was lacking to his small zoological collection, and that his army was quite without cavalry, as his papa was well aware. But the children knew that their elders had got all sorts of charming things ready for them, as also that the Child-Christ[2], at Christmas time, took special care for their wants. Marie sat in thoughtful silence, but Fritz murmured quietly to himself:

"'All the same, I should like a fox and some hussars[3]!'

"It was now quite dark; Fritz and Marie sitting close together, did not dare to utter another syllable; they felt as if there were a fluttering of gentle, invisible wings around them, whilst a very far away, but unutterably beautiful strain of music could dimly be heard. Then a bright gleam of light passed quickly athwart the wall, and the children knew that the Child-Christ had sped away, on shining wings, to other happy children. At this moment a silvery bell said, 'Kling-ling! Kling-ling!' the doors flew open, and such a brilliance of light came streaming from the drawing-room that the children stood rooted where they were with cries of 'Oh! Oh!'

---

[1] Hoffmann makes no mistakes with his characterization of Fritz as an embodiment of the insensitive, destructive male animus

[2] In Germany, Saint Nicholas (Father Christmas) visits early in December on St. Nicholas Day, bringing treats and small toys, but it is the Christ Child (Christkindl) who brings presents on Christmas Eve. Later, on Twelfth Night in January, the Three Wise Men bring even more presents

[3] Highly disciplined light cavalrymen known for their bravery and style, flamboyantly uniformed in a distinctly Hungarian fashion

"But papa and mamma came and took their hands, saying, 'Come now, darlings, and see what the blessed Child-Christ has brought for you[1].'

THE CHRISTMAS PRESENTS

"I appeal to yourself, kind reader (or listener)—Fritz, Theodore, Ernest, or whatsoever your name may chance to be—and I would beg you to bring vividly before your mind's eye your last Christmas table, all glorious with its various delightful Christmas presents; and then perhaps you will be able to form some idea of the manner in which the two children stood speechless with brilliant glances fixed on all the beautiful things; how, after a little, Marie, with a sigh, cried, 'Oh, how lovely! how lovely!' and Fritz gave several jumps of delight. The children had certainly been very, very good and well-behaved all the foregoing year to be thus rewarded; for never had so many beautiful and delightful things been provided for them as this time. The great Christmas tree on the table bore many apples of silver and gold, and all its branches were heavy with bud and blossom, consisting of sugar almonds, many-tinted bonbons, and all sorts of charming things to eat. Perhaps the prettiest thing about this wonder-tree, however, was the fact that in all the recesses of its spreading branches hundreds of little tapers glittered like stars, inviting the children to pluck its flowers and fruit. Also, all round the tree on every side everything shone and glittered in the loveliest manner. Oh, how many beautiful things there were! Who, oh who, could describe them all? Marie gazed there at the most delicious dolls, and all kinds of toys, and (what was the prettiest thing of all) a little silk dress with many-tinted ribbons was hung upon a projecting branch in such sort that she could admire it on all its sides; which she accordingly did, crying out several times, 'Oh! the lovely, the lovely, darling little dress. And I suppose, I do believe, I shall really be allowed to put it on!' Fritz, in the meantime, had had two or three trials how his new fox (which he had actually found on the table) could gallop; and now stated that he seemed a wildish sort of brute; but, no matter, he felt sure he would soon get him well in order; and he set to work to muster his new squadron of hussars, admirably equipped, in red and gold uniforms, with real silver swords, and mounted on such shining white horses that you would have thought they were of pure silver too.

"When the children had sobered down a little, and were beginning upon the beautiful picture books (which were open, so that you could see all sorts of most beautiful flowers and people of every hue, to say nothing of lovely children playing, all as naturally represented as if they were really alive and could speak), there came another tinkling of a bell, to announce the display of Godpapa Drosselmeier's Christmas present, which was on

---

[1] In much of Europe it is traditional to open presents on Christmas Eve – not Christmas morning

another table, against the wall, concealed by a curtain. When this curtain was drawn, what did the children behold?

"On a green lawn, bright with flowers, stood a lordly castle with a great many shining windows and golden towers. A chime of bells was going on inside it; doors and windows opened, and you saw very small, but beautiful, ladies and gentlemen, with plumed hats, and long robes down to their heels, walking up and down in the rooms of it. In the central hall, which seemed all in a blaze, there were quantities of little candles burning in silver chandeliers; children, in little short doublets, were dancing to the chimes of the bells. A gentleman, in an emerald green mantle, came to a window, made signs thereat, and then disappeared inside again; also, even Godpapa Drosselmeier himself (but scarcely taller than papa's thumb) came now and then, and stood at the castle door, then went in again[1].

"Fritz had been looking on with the rest at the beautiful castle and the people walking about and dancing in it, with his arms leant on the table; then he said:

"'Godpapa Drosselmeier, let me go into your castle for a little[2].'

"Drosselmeier answered that this could not possibly be done. In which he was right; for it was silly of Fritz to want to go into a castle which was not so tall as himself, golden towers and all. And Fritz saw that this was so.

"After a short time, as the ladies and gentlemen kept on walking about just in the same fashion, the children dancing, and the emerald man looking out at the same window, and God papa Drosselmeier coming to the door Fritz cried impatiently:

"'Godpapa Drosselmeier, please come out at that other door!'

"'That can't be done, dear Fritz,' answered Drosselmeier.

"'Well,' resumed Fritz, 'make that green man that looks out so often walk about with the others.'

"'And that can't be done, either,' said his godpapa, once more.

"'Make the children come down, then,' said Fritz. 'I want to see them nearer.'

---

[1] Like the story "Automatons," this displays Hoffmann's fascination with robots and the uncanny – it is an eerily realistic doll's house which invites comparisons between fantasy and reality, and like so many of Hoffmann's tales ("Automatons," "Sandman," "King's Betrothed") it lures its characters from the living comforts of reality with the perfectly satisfying illusions of a manufactured imitation

[2] The allure is almost too strong for Fritz, who longs to leave the reality of this world for the perfection of Drosselmeier's illusion

"'Nonsense, nothing of that sort can be done,' cried Drosselmeier, with impatience. 'The machinery must work as it's doing now; it can't be altered, you know[1].'

"Oh,' said Fritz, 'it can't be done, eh? Very well, then, Godpapa Drosselmeier, I'll tell you what it is. If your little creatures in the castle there can only always do the same thing, they're not much worth, and I think precious little of them! No, give me my hussars. They've got to manœuvre backwards and forwards just as I want them, and are not fastened up in a house.'

"With which he made off to the other table, and set his squadron of silver horse trotting here and there, wheeling and charging and slashing right and left to his heart's content. Marie had slipped away softly, too, for she was tired of the promenading and dancing of the puppets in the castle, though, kind and gentle as she was, she did not like to show it as her brother did. Drosselmeier, somewhat annoyed, said to the parents—'After all, an ingenious piece of mechanism like this is not a matter for children, who don't understand it; I shall put my castle back in its box again.' But the mother came to the rescue, and made him show her the clever machinery which moved the figures, Drosselmeier taking it all to pieces, putting it together again, and quite recovering his temper in the process. So that he gave the children all sorts of delightful brown men and women with golden faces, hands and legs, which were made of ginger cake, and with which they were greatly content.

MARIE'S PET AND PROTÉGEÉ

"But there was a reason wherefore Marie found it against the grain to come away from the table where the Christmas presents were laid out; and this was, that she had just noticed a something there which she had not observed at first. Fritz's hussars having taken ground to the right at some distance from the tree, in front of which they had previously been paraded, there became visible a most delicious little man, who was standing there quiet and unobtrusive, as if waiting patiently till it should be his turn to be noticed[2]. Objection, considerable objection, might, perhaps, have been taken to him on the score of his figure, for his body was rather too tall and

---

[1] Drosselmeier may be trying to instill a lesson in free will to the children: perfection can only be maintained when life is under the strict control of predestination, and while a life of free will is destined to be disappointing by its very nature, it is far more satisfying for its liberties. Later in the story, this lesson will become terrifying when Marie meets the lemming-like serfs of Candy Land

[2] Virtually an avatar of Hoffmann's own ego: he believed himself to be ludicrous, grotesque, unlovable, and yet (in spite of his often demanding and even violent personality) thought he was, at his core, shy, modest, and unassuming

stout for his legs, which were short and slight; moreover, his head was a good deal too large. But much of this was atoned for by the elegance of his costume, which showed him to be a person of taste and cultivation. He had on a very pretty violet hussar's jacket[1], all over knobs and braiding, pantaloons of the same, and the loveliest little boots ever seen even on a hussar officer—fitting his dear little legs just as if they had been painted on to them. It was funny, certainly, that, dressed in this style as he was, he had on a little, rather absurd, short cloak on his shoulders, which looked almost as if it were made of wood, and on his head a cap like a miner's[2]. But Marie remembered that Godpapa Drosselmeier often appeared in a terribly ugly morning jacket, and with a frightful looking cap on his head, and yet was a very very darling godpapa.

"As Marie kept looking at this little man, whom she had quite fallen in love with at first sight, she saw more and more clearly what a sweet nature and disposition was legible in his countenance. Those green eyes of his (which stuck, perhaps, a little more prominently out of his head than was quite desirable[3]) beamed with kindliness and benevolence. It was one of his beauties, too, that his chin was set off with a well kept beard of white cotton, as this drew attention to the sweet smile which his bright red lips always expressed.

"'Oh, papa, dear!' cried Marie at last, 'whose is that most darling little man beside the tree?'

"Well,' was the answer, 'that little fellow is going to do plenty of good service for all of you; he's going to crack nuts for you, and he is to belong to Louise just as much as to you and Fritz.' With which papa took him up from the table, and on his lifting the end of his wooden cloak, the little man opened his mouth wider and wider, displaying two rows of very white,

---

[1] Also called a dolman jacket: inspired by Turkish fashion, this was a tight-fitting uniform cut off at the waist with heavy braiding about the chest, a high collar, and usually very bold colors (greens, blues, reds, whites, and purples)

[2] Or a Fahrhaube. Rather like a leather fez, this was part of the traditional costume of Central European miners and became adopted by many military units of sappers or engineers (since they shared with miners the task of digging). Toy-making miners in Germany's Sonneberg region carved the world's most desirable and recognizable nutcrackers until the 20th century, and short, cylindrical miner caps continue to show up on many nutcrackers as an allusion to their traditional creators' day job. This cap is mentioned in several other Hoffmann tales, and lends a suggestion of the gnome, the elemental spirit of the earth, and a paragon of all that is grotesque, unassuming, and inelegant – in short, the nutcracker's spirit animal

[3] As with the Sandman, eyes are used as a motif of the soul – the organ of spirituality, which simultaneously is entrusted with interpreting reality. Nutcracker's bulging eyes imply that he is uncommonly perceptive and in tune with the spiritual world

sharp teeth. Marie, directed by her father, put a nut into his mouth, and—knack—he had bitten it in two, so that the shells fell down, and Marie got the kernel. So then it was explained to all that this charming little man belonged to the Nutcracker family[1], and was practising the profession of his ancestors. 'And,' said papa, 'as friend Nutcracker seems to have made such an impression on you, Marie, he shall be given over to your special care and charge, though, as I said, Louise and Fritz are to have the same right to his services as you.'

"Marie took him into her arms at once, and made him crack some more nuts; but she picked out all the smallest, so that he might not have to open his mouth so terribly wide, because that was not nice for him. Then sister Louise came, and he had to crack some nuts for her too,' which duty he seemed very glad to perform, as he kept on smiling most courteously.

"Meanwhile, Fritz was a little tired, after so much drill and manœuvring, so he joined his sisters, and laughed beyond measure at the funny little fellow, who (as Fritz wanted his share of the nuts) was passed from hand to hand, and was continually snapping his month open and shut. Fritz gave him all the biggest and hardest nuts he could find, but all at once there was a 'crack—crack,' and three teeth fell out of Nutcracker's mouth, and all his lower jaw was loose and wobbly.

"'Ah! my poor darling Nutcracker,' Marie cried, and took him away from Fritz.

---

[1] Carved nutcrackers have been in existence since before the Middle Ages, and wooden nutcrackers made in the shape of soldiers or kings first came into vogue during the 17th century. The first ones to resemble our modern idea of a nutcracker, however – a wooden man standing on a small platform, whose mouth breaks the nut by using a lever in the back – first became popularized shortly before Hoffmann wrote this story, during the Napoleonic Wars. Even to this day, most nutcrackers sport Napoleonic-style uniforms suggesting the fashion of the 1780s-1820s. The most desirable nutcrackers were carved by miners (during the off hours as a second source of income) from the Sonneberg region of Germany, in the heavily wooded state of Thuringia. These miners – usually short men who fit in the cramped mines – were renowned throughout Europe as toymakers (carving soldiers, horses, blocks, clocks, wagons, ships, and dollhouses) and were the source of the legend of Santa Claus's diminutive helpers. Nutcrackers of Hoffmann's time were far more Hoffmannesque than today's: with stubby legs, bulging eyes, exaggerated smiles, and hand-carved (rather than just painted) expressions, these troll-like clowns were both grotesque and comical, easily merging Hoffmann's favorite complimentary themes of vague horror and vulgar humor. Standing at about seven inches, nutcrackers were popular throughout Germany, Russia, and Eastern Europe until World War II veterans brought them back to their home countries, turning a Central European burlesque toy into a global symbol of Christmastime

"'A nice sort of chap he is!' said Fritz. 'Calls himself a nutcracker, and can't give a decent bite—doesn't seem to know much about his business. Hand him over here, Marie! I'll keep him biting nuts if he drops all the rest of his teeth, and his jaw into the bargain. What's the good of a chap like him[1]!'

"'No, no,' said Marie, in tears; 'you shan't have him, my darling Nutcracker; see how he's looking at me so mournfully, and showing me his poor sore mouth. But you're a hard-hearted creature! You beat your horses, and you've had one of your soldiers shot.'

"'Those things must be done[2],' said Fritz; 'and you don't understand anything about such matters. But Nutcracker's as much mine as yours, so hand him over!'

"Marie began to cry bitterly, and wrapped the wounded Nutcracker quickly up in her little pocket-handkerchief. Papa and mamma came with Drosselmeier, who took Fritz's part, to Marie's regret. But papa said, 'I have put Nutcracker in Marie's special charge, and as he seems to have need just now of her care, she has full power over him, and nobody else has anything to say in the matter. And I'm surprised that Fritz should expect further service from a man wounded in the execution of his duty. As a good soldier, he ought to know better than that.'

"Fritz was much ashamed, and, troubling himself no further as to nuts or nutcrackers, crept off to the other side of the table, where his hussars (having established the necessary outposts and videttes[3]) were bivouacking for the night. Marie got Nutcracker's lost teeth together, bound a pretty white ribbon, taken from her dress, about his poor chin, and then wrapped the poor little fellow, who was looking very pale and frightened, more tenderly and carefully than before in her handkerchief. Thus she held him, rocking him like a child in her arms, as she looked at the picture-books. She grew quite angry (which was not usual with her) with Godpapa Drosselmeier because he laughed so, and kept asking how she could make

---

[1] Fritz – a practical realist without a single hint of sentiment or empathy – only views Nutcracker for his capital worth. Marie, on the other hand, recognizes him for his intrinsic value as a sincere and faithful soul. This tenderness will later be Nutcracker's salvation

[2] The Napoleonic Wars had formally ended the previous year with the butchery of Waterloo. Hoffmann, dislodged and impoverished by the years of war and disheartened by the millions of deaths, saw little admirable in the spirits of the boyish men whose cynical thirst for glory and dispassionate disregard for human suffering had left Europe in tatters

[3] Mounted sentries positioned on the fringes of an encampment

such a fuss about an ugly little fellow like that[1]. That odd and peculiar likeness to Drosselmeier, which had struck her when she saw Nutcracker at first, occurred to her mind again now, and she said, with much earnestness:

"'Who knows, godpapa, if you were to be dressed the same as my darling Nutcracker, and had on the same shining boots—who knows whether you
mightn't look almost as handsome as he does[2]?'

"Marie did not understand why papa and mamma laughed so heartily, nor why Godpapa Drosselmeier's nose got so red[3], nor why he did not join so
much in the laughter as before. Probably there was some special reason for these things.

WONDERFUL EVENTS

"We must now explain that, in the sitting-room, on the left-hand as you go in, there stands, against the wall, a high, glass-fronted cupboard, where all the children's Christmas presents are yearly put away to be kept. Louise, the elder sister, was still quite little when her father had this cupboard constructed by a very skilful workman, who had put in it such transparent panes of glass, and altogether made the whole affair so splendid, that the things, when inside it, looked almost more shining and lovely than when one had them actually in one's hands. In the upper shelves, which were beyond the reach of Fritz and Marie, were stowed Godpapa Drosselmeier's works of art; immediately under them was the shelf for the picture-books. Fritz and Marie were allowed to do what they liked with the two lower shelves, but it always came about that the lower one of all was that in which Marie put away her dolls, as their place of residence, whilst Fritz utilized the shelf above this as cantonments[4] for his troops of all arms. So that, on the evening as to which we are speaking,

---

[1] Hoffmann's Drosselmeier plays far more mind games than Tchaikovsky's. It is certainly possible that he is merely testing Marie's compassion, although it may also be the manic perverseness and wild insensitivity that we see in so many of Hoffmann's eccentrics

[2] Virtually all critics agree that – whether Nutcracker is a stand-in for Hoffmann or not – he certainly represents an avatar of the grotesque, aloof Drosselmeier. Marie's ability to love this miniature Doppleganger of her aged uncle might be interpreted as his subliminal way of teaching her to feel the same compassion and appreciation for himself

[3] All of Hoffmann's literary stand-ins experience a degree of humiliation for their detachment from reality and propriety. Here, Drosselmeier blushes at the suggestion that Marie might find him handsome and lovable – although this is likely the exact intention of giving her Nutcracker

[4] Camps

Fritz had quartered his hussars in his—the upper—shelf of these two, whilst Marie had put Miss Gertrude rather in a corner, established her new doll in the well-appointed chamber there, with all its appropriate furniture, and invited herself to tea and cakes with her. This chamber was splendidly furnished, everything on a first-rate scale, and in good and admirable style, as I have already said—and I don't know if you, my observant reader, have the satisfaction of possessing an equally well-appointed room for your dolls; a little beautifully-flowered sofa, a number of the most charming little chairs, a nice little tea-table, and, above all, a beautiful little white bed, where your pretty darlings of dolls go to sleep? All this was in a corner of the shelf, the walls of which, in this part, had beautiful little pictures hanging on them; and you may well imagine that, in such a delightful chamber as this, the new doll (whose name, as Marie had discovered, was Miss Clara[1]) thought herself extremely comfortably settled, and remarkably well off.

"It was getting very late, not so very far from midnight, indeed, before the children could tear themselves away from all these Yuletide fascinations, and Godpapa Drosselmeier had been gone a considerable time. They remained riveted beside the glass cupboard, although their mother several times reminded them that it was long after bedtime. 'Yes,' said Fritz, 'I know well enough that these poor fellows (meaning his hussars) are tired enough, and awfully anxious to turn in for the night, though as long as I'm here, not a man-jack of them dares to nod his head[2].' With which he went off. But Marie earnestly begged for just a little while longer, saying she had such a number of things to see to, and promising that as soon as ever she had got them all settled she would go to bed at once. Marie was a very good and reasonable child, and therefore her mother allowed her to remain for a little longer with her toys; but lest she should be too much occupied with her new doll and the other playthings so as to forget to put out the candles which were lighted all round on the wall sconces, she herself put all of them out, leaving merely the lamp which hung from the ceiling to give a soft and pleasant light. 'Come soon to your bed, Marie, or you'll never be up in time in the morning,' cried her mother as she went away into the bedroom.

"As soon as Marie was alone, she set rapidly to work to do the thing which was chiefly at her heart to accomplish, and which, though she scarcely knew why, she somehow did not like to set about in her mother's presence. She had been holding Nutcracker, wrapped in the handkerchief, carefully in her arms all this time, and she now laid him softly down on the table, gently unrolled the handkerchief, and examined his wounds.

---

[1] Tchaikovsky borrowed this name for the protagonist of his ballet. Meaning "light," Clara may have struck his ear as more romantic and charming than the more dour, common name "Marie"

[2] Fritz continues to prove himself to be a budding and sadistic tyrant

"Nutcracker was very pale, but at the same time he was smiling with a melancholy and pathetic kindliness which went straight to Marie's heart.

"Oh, my darling little Nutcracker!' said she, very softly, 'don't you be vexed because brother Fritz has hurt you so: he didn't mean it, you know; he's only a little bit hardened with his soldiering and that, but he's a good, nice boy, I can assure you: and I'll take the greatest care of you, and nurse you, till you're quite, quite better and happy again. And your teeth shall be put in again for you, and your shoulder set right; Godpapa Drosselmeier will see to that; he knows how to do things of the kind——'

"Marie could not finish what she was going to say, because at the mention of Godpapa Drosselmeier, friend Nutcracker made a most horrible, ugly face[1]. A sort of green sparkle of much sharpness seemed to dart out of his eyes. This was only for an instant, however; and just as Marie was going to be terribly frightened, she found that she was looking at the very same nice, kindly face, with the pathetic smile which she had seen before, and she saw plainly that it was nothing but some draught of air making the lamp flicker that had seemed to produce the change.

"'Well!' she said, 'I certainly am a silly girl to be so easily frightened, and think that a wooden doll could make faces at me! But I'm too fond, really, of Nutcracker, because he's so funny, and so kind and nice; and so he must be taken the greatest care of, and properly nursed till he's quite well.'

"With which she took him in her arms again, approached the cupboard, and kneeling down beside it, said to her new doll:

"I'm going to ask a favour of you, Miss Clara—that you will give up your bed to this poor sick, wounded Nutcracker, and make yourself as comfortable as you can on the sofa here. Remember that you're quite well and strong yourself, or you wouldn't have such fat, red cheeks, and that there are very few dolls indeed who have as comfortable a sofa as this to lie upon.'

"Miss Clara, in her Christmas full dress, looked very grand and disdainful, and said not so much as 'Muck[2]!'

"Very well,' said Marie, 'why should I make such a fuss, and stand on any ceremony?'—took the bed and moved it forward; laid Nutcracker carefully and tenderly down on it; wrapped another pretty ribbon, taken from her own dress, about his hurt shoulder, and drew the bed-clothes up to his nose.

---

[1] Nutcracker's disgusted reaction to the mere mention of (as we shall learn) his uncle's name is likely to surprise fans of Tchaikovsky. Although Drosselmeier does seem to be grooming Marie to save him from his curse, it has been over a decade since the transformation, and Drosselmeier doesn't seem to be in any rush to rescue his miserable nephew

[2] "Make so much as a peep"

"But he shan't stay with that nasty Clara,' she said, and moved the bed, with Nutcracker in it, up to the upper shelf, so that it was placed near the village in which Fritz's hussars had their cantonments. She closed the cupboard, and was moving away to go to bed, when—listen, children! there begun a low soft rustling and rattling, and a sort of whispering noise, all round, in all directions, from all quarters of the room—behind the stove, under the chairs, behind the cupboards. The clock on the wall 'warned' louder and louder, but could not strike. Marie looked at it, and saw that the big gilt owl[1] which was on the top of it had drooped its wings so that they covered the whole of the clock, and had stretched its cat-like head, with the crooked beak, a long way forward. And the 'warning' kept growing louder and louder, with distinct words: 'Clocks, clockies, stop ticking. No sound, but cautious "warning." Mousey king's ears are fine. Prr-prr. Only sing "poom, poom"; sing the olden song of doom! prr-prr; poom, poom. Bells go chime! Soon rings out the fated time!' And then came 'Poom! poom!' quite hoarsely and smothered, twelve times.

"Marie grew terribly frightened, and was going to rush away as best she could, when she noticed that Godpapa Drosselmeier was up on the top of the clock instead of the owl, with his yellow coat-tails hanging down on both sides, like wings. But she manned[2] herself, and called out in a loud voice of anguish:

"Godpapa! godpapa! what are you up there for? Come down to me, and don't frighten me so terribly, you naughty, naughty Godpapa Drosselmeier!'

"But then there begun a sort of wild kickering and queaking, everywhere, all about, and presently there was a sound as of running and trotting, as of thousands of little feet behind the walls, and thousands of little lights began to glitter out between the chinks of the woodwork. But they were not lights; no, no! little glittering eyes; and Marie became aware that, everywhere, mice[3] were peeping and squeezing themselves out through every chink. Presently they were trotting and galloping in all directions over the room; orderly bodies, continually increasing, of mice, forming themselves into regular troops and squadrons, in good order, just as Fritz's soldiers did when manœuvres were going on. As Marie was not afraid of mice (as many children are), she could not help being amused by this, and her first alarm had nearly left her, when suddenly there came such

[1] An animal traditionally associated with the supernatural, with esoteric wisdom, and with the understanding of hidden meanings – all things which Marie shall soon experience

[2] Steeled, toughened, gathered...

[3] Throughout this story, mice – traditional enemy of children's treasures (they eat sweets, chew through books and clothes, nibble on toys, and terrify youngsters by their very sight) – are used as a symbol of corruption, nepotism, greed, and selfishness

a sharp and terrible piping noise that the blood ran cold in her veins. Ah! what did she see then? Well, truly, kind reader, I know that your heart is in the right place, just as much as my friend Field Marshal Fritz's is, itself, but if you had seen what now came before Marie's eyes, you would have made a clean pair of heels of it; nay, I consider that you would have plumped into your bed, and drawn the blankets further over your head than necessity demanded.

"But poor Marie hadn't it in her power to do any such thing, because, right at her feet, as if impelled by some subterranean power, sand, and lime, and broken stone came bursting up, and then seven mouse-heads, with seven shining crowns upon them, rose through the floor, hissing and piping in a most horrible way[1]. Quickly the body of the mouse which had those seven crowned heads forced its way up through the floor, and this enormous creature shouted, with its seven heads, aloud to the assembled multitude, squeaking to them with all the seven mouths in full chorus; and then the entire army set itself in motion, and went trot, trot, right up to the cupboard—and, in fact, to Marie, who was standing beside it.

"Marie's heart had been beating so with terror that she had thought it must jump out of her breast, and she must die. But now it seemed to her as if the blood in her veins stood still. Half fainting, she leant backwards, and then there was a 'klirr, klirr, prr,' and the pane of the cupboard, which she had broken with her elbow, fell in shivers to the floor. She felt, for a moment, a sharp, stinging pain in her arm, but still, this seemed to make her heart lighter; she heard no more of the queaking and piping. Everything was quiet; and though she didn't dare to look, she thought the noise of the glass breaking had frightened the mice back to their holes.

"But what came to pass then? Right behind Marie a movement seemed to commence in the cupboard, and small, faint voices began to be heard, saying:

'Come, awake, measures take;
Out to the fight, out to the fight;
Shield the right, shield the right;

---

[1] The seven-headed Mouse-King was likely inspired by reports of "rat-kings." A rat-king is a grisly phenomenon (documented mostly in Germany during the Middle Ages and Early Modern Era, but spotted in various countries and continents even as recently as 2012) wherein three or more rats become fused together by dried mud, saliva, filth, and feces. With their fur matted together and tails tangled, the cluster of rats will move on dozens of feet and consume with as many mouths, while increasing the fusion of their bodies by urinating and pooping on one another. Early accounts described the rat-king as a single mutant with multiple head, but modern observations have confirmed the entangling of multiple rats as the source of the urban legend. Hoffmann uses this hungry, demanding, multiheaded creature as the personification of bureaucracy and nepotism

Aim and away, this is the night.'
And harmonica-bells began ringing as prettily as you please.

"Oh! that's my little peal of bells!' cried Marie, and went nearer and looked in. Then she saw that there was bright light in the cupboard, and everything busily in motion there; dolls and little figures of various kinds all running about together, and struggling with their little arms. At this point, Nutcracker rose from his bed, cast off the bedclothes, and sprung with both feet on to the floor (of the shelf), crying out at the top of his voice:
'Knack, knack, knack,
Stupid mousey pack,
All their skulls we'll crack.
Mousey pack, knack, knack,
Mousey pack, crick and crack,
Cowardly lot of schnack!'

"And with this he drew his little sword, waved it in the air, and cried:

"'Ye, my trusty vassals, brethren and friends, are ye ready to stand by me in this great battle?'

"Immediately three scaramouches, one pantaloon[1], four chimney-sweeps, two zither-players, and a drummer cried, in eager accents:

"'Yes, your highness; we will stand by you in loyal duty; we will follow you to the death, the victory, and the fray!' And they precipitated themselves after Nutcracker (who, in the excitement of the moment, had dared that perilous leap) to the bottom shelf. Now *they* might well dare this perilous leap, for not only had they got plenty of clothes on, of cloth and silk, but besides, there was not much in their insides except cotton and sawdust, so that they plumped down like little wool-sacks. But as for poor Nutcracker, he would certainly have broken his anus and legs; for, bethink you, it was nearly two feet from where he had stood to the shelf below, and his body was as fragile as if he had been made of elm-wood. Yes, Nutcracker would have broken his arms and legs, had not Miss Clara started up, at the moment of his spring, from her sofa, and received the hero, drawn sword and all, in her tender arms.

"'Oh! you dear, good Clara!' cried Marie, 'how I did misunderstand you. I believe you were quite willing to let dear Nutcracker have your bed.'

"But Miss Clara now cried, as she pressed the young hero gently to her silken breast:

"'Oh, my lord! go not into this battle and danger, sick and wounded as you are. See how your trusty vassals, clowns and pantaloon, chimney-sweeps, zithermen and drummer, are already arrayed below; and the puzzle-figures, in my shelf here, are in motion, and preparing for the fray!

---

[1] Scaramouche: a type of singing clown; pantaloon: a comical old man wearing baggy trousers

Deign, then, oh my lord, to rest in these arms of mine, and contemplate your victory from a safe coign of vantage.'

"Thus spoke Clara. But Nutcracker behaved so impatiently, and kicked so with his legs, that Clara was obliged to put him down on the shelf in a hurry. However, he at once sank gracefully on one knee, and expressed himself as follows:

"'Oh, lady! the kind protection and aid which you have afforded me, will ever be present to my heart, in battle and in victory!'

"On this, Clara bowed herself so as to be able to take hold of him by his arms, raised him gently up, quickly loosed her girdle, which was ornamented with many spangles, and would have placed it about his shoulders. But the little man drew himself swiftly two steps back, laid his hand upon his heart, and said, with much solemnity:

"Oh, lady! do not bestow this mark of your favour upon me; for——' He hesitated, gave a deep sigh, took the ribbon, with which Marie had bound him, from his shoulders, pressed it to his lips, put it on as a cognizance for the fight, and, waving his glittering sword, sprang, like a bird, over the ledge of the cupboard down to the floor.

"You will observe, kind reader, that Nutcracker, even before he really came to life, had felt and understood all Marie's goodness and regard, and that it was because of his gratitude and devotion to her, that he would not take, or wear even, a ribbon of Miss Clara's, although it was exceedingly pretty and charming. This good, true-hearted Nutcracker preferred Marie's much commoner and more unpretending token[1].

"But what is going to happen, further, now? At the moment when Nutcracker sprang down, the queaking and piping commenced again worse than ever. Alas! under the big table, the hordes of the mouse army had taken up a position, densely massed, under the command of the terrible mouse with the seven heads. So what is to be the result?

THE BATTLE

"Beat the *Generale*[2], trusty vassal-drummer!' cried Nutcracker, very loud; and immediately the drummer began to roll his drum in the most splendid style, so that the windows of the glass cupboard rattled and resounded. Then there began a cracking and a clattering inside, and Marie saw all the lids of the boxes in which Fritz's army was quartered bursting open, and the soldiers all came out and jumped down to the bottom shelf, where they formed up in good order. Nutcracker hurried up and down the ranks, speaking words of encouragement.

"'There's not a dog of a trumpeter taking the trouble to sound a call!' he cried in a fury. Then he turned to the pantaloon (who was looking

---

[1] Just as she herself has preferred him – an ugly wooden novelty doll – to her many fine toys

[2] General Quarters: the drum signal that calls soldiers to battle stations

decidedly pale), and, wobbling his long chin a good deal, said, in a tone of solemnity:

"'I know how brave and experienced you are, General! What is essential here, is a rapid comprehension of the situation, and immediate utilization of the passing moment. I entrust you with the command of the cavalry and artillery. You can do without a horse; your own legs are long, and you can gallop on them as fast as is necessary. Do your duty!'

"Immediately Pantaloon put his long, lean fingers to his month, and gave such a piercing crow that it rang as if a hundred little trumpets had been sounding lustily. Then there began a tramping and a neighing in the cupboard; and Fritz's dragoons and cuirassiers[1]—but above all, the new glittering hussars—marched out, and thru came to a halt, drawn up on the floor. They then marched past Nutcracker by regiments, with *guidons*[2] flying and bands playing; after which they wheeled into line, and formed up at right angles to the line of march. Upon this, Fritz's artillery came rattling up, and formed action front in advance of the halted cavalry. Then it went 'boom-boom!' and Marie saw the sugar-plums doing terrible execution amongst the thickly-massed mouse-battalions, which were powdered quite white by them, and greatly put to shame. But a battery of heavy guns, which had taken up a strong position on mamma's footstool, was what did the greatest execution; and 'poom-poom-poom!' kept up a murderous fire of gingerbread nuts into the enemy's ranks with most destructive effect, mowing the mice down in great numbers. The enemy, however, was not materially checked in his advance, and had even possessed himself of one or two of the heavy guns, when there came 'prr-prr-prr!' and Marie could scarcely see what was happening, for smoke and dust; but this much is certain, that every corps engaged fought with the utmost bravery and determination, and it was for a long time doubtful which side would gain the day. The mice kept on developing fresh bodies of their forces, as they were advanced to the scene of action; their little silver balls—like pills in size—which they delivered with great precision (their musketry practice being specially fine) took effect even inside the glass cupboard. Clara and Gertrude ran up and down in utter despair, wringing their hands, and loudly lamenting.

"Must I—the very loveliest doll in all the world—perish miserably in the very flower of my youth?' cried Miss Clara.

"'Oh! was it for this,' wept Gertrude, 'that I have taken such pains to *conserver*[3] myself all these years? Must I be shot here in my own drawing-room after all?"

---

[1] Heavy cavalry protected by helmets and breastplates

[2] A swallow-tail flag used to represent a cavalry regiment

[3] French: preserve, conserve. This is a cheeky allusion to the doll's closely-guarded virginity

"On this, they fell into each other's arms, and howled so terribly that you could hear them above all the din of the battle. For you have no idea of the hurly-burly that went on now, dear auditor! It went prr-prr-poof, piff-schnetterdeng—schnetterdeng—boom-booroom—boom-booroom—boom all confusedly and higgledy-piggledy; and the mouse-king and the mice squeaked and screamed; and then again Nutcracker's powerful voice was heard shouting words of command, and issuing important orders, and he was seen striding along amongst his battalions in the thick of the fire.

'Pantaloon had made several most brilliant cavalry charges, and covered himself with glory. But Fritz's hussars were subjected—by the mice—to a heavy fire of very evil-smelling shot[1], which made horrid spots on their red tunics; this caused them to hesitate, and hang rather back for a time. Pantaloon made them take ground to the left, in *échelon*[2], and, in the excitement of the moment, he, with his dragoons and cuirassiers, executed a somewhat analogous movement. That is to say, they brought up the right shoulder, wheeled to the left, and marched home to their quarters. This had the effect of bringing the battery of artillery on the footstool into imminent danger, and it was not long before a large body of exceedingly ugly mice delivered such a vigorous assault on this position that the whole of the footstool, with the guns and gunners, fell into the enemy's hands. Nutcracker seemed much disconcerted, and ordered his right wing to commence a retrograde movement. A soldier of your experience, my dear Fritz, knows well that such a movement is almost tantamount to a regular retreat, and you grieve, with me, in anticipation, for the disaster which threatens the army of Marie's beloved little Nutcracker. But turn your glance in the other direction, and look at this left wing of Nutcracker's, where all is still going well, and you will see that there is yet much hope for the commander-in-chief and his cause.

"During the hottest part of the engagement masses of mouse-cavalry had been quietly debouching[3] from under the chest of drawers, and had subsequently made a most determined advance upon the left wing of Nutcracker's force, uttering loud and horrible queakings. But what a reception they met with! Very slowly, as the nature the *terrain* necessitated (for the ledge at the bottom of the cupboard had to be passed), the regiment of motto-figures, commanded by two Chinese Emperors, advanced, and formed square. These fine, brilliantly-uniformed troops, consisting of gardeners, Tyrolese[4], Tungooses[5], hairdressers, harlequins, Cupids, lions, tigers, unicorns, and monkeys, fought with the utmost

---

[1] By hurling their own feces

[2] A V-shaped military formation

[3] Charging out of hiding

[4] A mountain climber (as of Austria's Tyrol Alps)

[5] Or Tungus – a Siberian ethnic group

courage, coolness, and steady endurance. This *bataillon d'élite*[1] would have wrested the victory from the enemy had not one of his cavalry captains, pushing forward in a rash and foolhardy manner, made a charge upon one of the Chinese Emperors, and bitten off his head. This Chinese Emperor, in his fall, knocked over and smothered a couple of Tungooses and a unicorn, and this created a gap, through which the enemy effected a rush, which resulted in the whole battalion being bitten to death. But the enemy gained little advantage by this; for as soon as one of the mouse-cavalry soldiers bit one of these brave adversaries to death, he found that there was a small piece of printed paper sticking in his throat, of which he died in a moment. Still, this was of small advantage to Nutcracker's army, which, having once commenced a retrograde movement, went on retreating farther and farther, suffering greater and greater loss. So that the unfortunate Nutcracker found himself driven back close to the front of the cupboard, with a very small remnant of his army.

"'Bring up the reserves! Pantaloon! Scaramouch! Drummer! where the devil have you got to?' shouted Nutcracker, who was still reckoning on reinforcements from the cupboard. And there did, in fact, advance a small contingent of brown gingerbread men and women, with gilt faces, hats, and helmets; but they laid about them so clumsily that they never hit any of the enemy, and soon knocked off the cap of their commander-in-chief, Nutcracker, himself. And the enemy's chasseurs soon bit their legs off, so that they tumbled topsy-turvy, and killed several of Nutcracker's companions-in-arms into the bargain.

"Nutcracker was now hard pressed, and closely hemmed in by the enemy, and in a position of extreme peril, He tried to jump the bottom ledge of the cupboard, but his legs were not long enough. Clara and Gertrude had fainted; so they could give him no assistance. Hussars and heavy dragoons came charging up at him, and he shouted in wild despair:

"'A horse! a horse! My kingdom for a horse!'[2]

"At this moment two of the enemy's riflemen seized him by his wooden cloak, and the king of the mice went rushing up to him, squeaking in triumph out of all his seven throats.

"Marie could contain herself no longer. 'Oh! my poor Nutcracker!' she sobbed, took her left shoe off, without very distinctly knowing what she was about, and threw it as hard as she could into the thick of the enemy, straight at their king.

"Instantly everything vanished and disappeared. All was silence. Nothing to be seen. But Marie felt a more stinging pain than before in her left arm, and fell on the floor insensible.

---

[1] An elite fighting force

[2] A famous line from Shakespeare's Richard III, where the antagonist finds himself surrounded in battle and bemoans that his kingdom has been lost for the want of a horse

"When Marie awoke from a death-like sleep she was lying in her little bed; and the sun was shining brightly in at the window, which was all covered with frost-flowers. There was a stranger gentleman sitting beside her, whom she recognized as Dr. Wendelstern. 'She's awake,' he said softly, and her mother came and looked at her very scrutinizingly and anxiously.

"'Oh, mother!' whispered Marie, 'are all those horrid mice gone away, and is Nutcracker quite safe?'

"'Don't talk such nonsense, Marie,' answered her mother. 'What have the mice to do with Nutcracker? You're a very naughty girl, and have caused us all a great deal of anxiety. See what comes of children not doing as they're told! You were playing with your toys so late last night that you fell asleep. I don't know whether or not some mouse jumped out and frightened you, though there are no mice here, generally. But, at all events, you broke a pane of the glass cupboard with your elbow, and cut your arm so badly that Dr. Wendelstern (who has just taken a number of pieces of the glass out of your arm) thinks that if it had been only a little higher up you might have had a stiff arm for life, or even have bled to death. Thank Heaven, I awoke about twelve o'clock and missed you; and I found you lying insensible in front of the glass cupboard, bleeding frightfully, with a number of Fritz's lead soldiers scattered round you, and other toys, broken motto-figures, and gingerbread men; and Nutcracker was lying on your bleeding arm, with your left shoe not far off.'

"Oh, mother, mother,' said Marie, 'these were the remains of the tremendous battle between the toys and the mice; and what frightened me so terribly was that the mice were going to take Nutcracker (who was the commander-in-chief of the toy army) a prisoner. Then I threw my shoe in among the mice, and after that I know nothing more that happened.'

"Dr. Wendelstern gave a significant look at the mother, who said very gently to Marie:

"'Never mind, dear, keep yourself quiet. The mice are all gone away, and Nutcracker's in the cupboard, quite safe and sound.'

"Here Marie's father came in, and had a long consultation with Dr. Wendelstern. Then he felt Marie's pulse, and she heard them talking about 'wound-fever.' She had to stay in bed, and take medicine, for some days, although she didn't feel at all ill, except that her arm was rather stiff and painful. She knew Nutcracker had got safe out of the battle, and she seemed to remember, as if in a dream, that he had said, quite distinctly, in a very melancholy tone:

"'Marie! dearest lady! I am most deeply indebted to you. But it is in your power to do even more for me still.'

"She thought and thought what this could possibly be; but in vain; she couldn't make it out. She wasn't able to play on account of her arm; and when she tried to read, or look through the picture-books, everything wavered before her eyes so strangely that she was obliged to stop. So that the days seemed very long to her, and she could scarcely pass the time till evening, when her mother came and sat at her bedside, telling and reading her all sorts of nice stories. She had just finished telling her the story of Prince Fakardin[1], when the door opened and in came Godpapa Drosselmeier, saying:

"'I've come to see with my own eyes how Marie's getting on.'

"When Marie saw Godpapa Drosselmeier in his little yellow coat, the scene of the night when Nutcracker lost the battle with the mice came so vividly back to her that she couldn't help crying out:

"'Oh! Godpapa Drosselmeier, how nasty you were! I saw you quite well when you were sitting on the clock, covering it all over with your wings, to prevent it from striking and frightening the mice. I heard you quite well when you called the mouse-king. Why didn't you help Nutcracker? Why didn't you help *me*, you nasty godpapa? It's nobody's fault but yours that I'm lying here with a bad arm.'

"Her mother, in much alarm, asked what she meant. But Drosselmeier began making extraordinary faces, and said, in a snarling voice, like a sort of chant in monotone:

"'Pendulums could only rattle—couldn't tick, ne'er a click; all the clockies stopped their ticking: no more clicking; then they all struck loud "cling-clang." Dollies! Don't your heads downhang! Hink and hank, and honk and hank. Doll-girls! don't your heads downhang! Cling and ring! The battle's over—Nutcracker all safe in clover. Comes the owl, on downy wing—Scares away the mouses' king. Pak and pik and pik and pook—clocks, bim-boom—grr-grr. Pendulums must click again. Tick and tack, grr and brr, prr and purr.'

"Marie fixed wide eyes of terror upon Godpapa Drosselmeier, because he was looking quite different, and far more horrid, than usual, and was jerking his right arm backwards and forwards as if he were some puppet moved by a handle[2]. She was beginning to grow terribly frightened at him when her mother came in, and Fritz (who had arrived in the meantime) laughed heartily, crying, 'Why, godpapa, you *are* going on funnily! You're just like my old Jumping Jack[3] that I threw away last month.'

"But the mother looked very grave, and said, 'This is a most extraordinary way of going on, Mr. Drosselmeier. What can you mean by it?'

"'My goodness!' said Drosselmeier, laughing, 'did you never hear my nice Watchmaker's Song? I always sing it to little invalids like Marie.' Then he hastened to sit down beside Marie's bed, and said to her, 'Don't be vexed

---

[1] Likely Fakhr-al-Din, a Lebanese nobleman, master builder, and patriot

[2] Flirting with the Uncanny Valley and the typically Hoffmannesque horror that lurks in the boundaries between humans and automatons

[3] A wooden figure whose arms and legs leap out when a string is pulled

with me because I didn't gouge out all the mouse-king's fourteen eyes. That couldn't be managed exactly; but, to make up for it, here's something which I know will please you greatly.'

"He dived into one of his pockets, and what he slowly, slowly brought out of it was—Nutcracker! whose teeth he had put in again quite firmly, and set his broken jaw completely to rights. Marie shouted for joy, and her mother laughed and said, 'Now you see for yourself how nice Godpapa Drosselmeier is to Nutcracker.'

"'But you must admit, Marie,' said her godpapa, 'that Nutcracker is far from being what you might call a handsome fellow, and you can't say he has a pretty face[1]. If you like I'll tell you how it was that the ugliness came into his family, and has been handed down in it from one generation to another. Did ever you hear about the Princess Pirlipat, the witch Mouseyrinks, and the clever Clockmaker?'

"I say, Godpapa Drosselmeier,' interrupted Fritz at this juncture, 'you've put Nutcracker's teeth in again all right, and his jaw isn't wobbly as it was; but what's become of his sword? Why haven't you given him a sword?'

"Oh,' cried Drosselmeier, annoyed, 'you must always be bothering and finding fault with something or other, boy. What have I to do with Nutcracker's sword? I've put his mouth to rights for him; he must look out for a sword for himself[2].'

"Yes, yes,' said Fritz, 'so he must, of course, if he's a right sort of fellow.'

"'So tell me, Marie,' continued Drosselmeier, 'if you know the story of Princess Pirlipat?'

"'Oh no,' said Marie. 'Tell it me, please—do tell it me!'

"'I hope it won't be as strange and terrible as your stories generally are[3],' said her mother.

"'Oh no, nothing of the kind,' said Drosselmeier. 'On the contrary, it's quite a funny story which I'm going to have the honour of telling this time.'

"'Go on then—do tell it to us,' cried the children; and Drosselmeier commenced as follows:—

THE STORY OF THE HARD NUT

---

[1] Like Beauty and the Beast or The Frog Prince, the point of Drosselmeier's initiation of Marie into this world of magic is to teach her to look beyond physical beauty and to appreciate a man for his character in spite of his ugliness

[2] As we will later see, this loss of his sword has significance for his relationship to Marie, who must arm him herself and by so doing, empower him to fight off his demons

[3] This far darker version of Drosselmeier than most fans of the ballet are used to must tell truly nightmare-worthy stories for Marie's mother to fear them

"Pirlipat's mother was a king's wife, so that, of course, she was a queen; and Pirlipat herself was a princess by birth as soon as ever she was born. The king was quite beside himself with joy over his beautiful little daughter as she lay in her cradle, and he danced round and round upon one leg, crying again and again,

""Hurrah! hurrah! hip, hip, hurrah! Did anybody ever see anything so lovely as my little Pirlipat?"

"'And all the ministers of state, and the generals, the presidents, and the officers of the staff, danced about on one leg, as the king did, and cried as loud as they could, "No, no—never!"

"Indeed, there was no denying that a lovelier baby than Princess Pirlipat was never born since the world began. Her little face looked as if it were woven of the most delicate white and rose-coloured silk; her eyes were of sparkling azure, and her hair all in little curls like threads of gold. Moreover, she had come into the world with two rows of little pearly teeth, with which, two hours after her birth, she bit the Lord High Chancellor in the fingers, when he was making a careful examination of her features, so that he cried, "Oh! Gemini!" quite loud.

"'There are persons who assert that "Oh Lord" was the expression he employed, and opinions are still considerably divided on this point. At all events, she bit him in the fingers; and the realm learned, with much gratification, that both intelligence and discrimination[1] dwelt within her angelical little frame.

"'All was joy and gladness, as I have said, save that the queen was very anxious and uneasy, nobody could tell why. One remarkable circumstance was, that she had Pirlipat's cradle most scrupulously guarded. Not only were there lifeguardsmen[2] always at the doors of the nursery, but—over and above the two head nurses close to the cradle—there had always to be six other nurses all round the room at night. And what seemed rather a funny thing, which nobody could understand, was that each of these six nurses had always to have a cat in her lap, and to keep on stroking it all night long, so that it might never stop purring.

"'It is impossible that you, my reader, should know the reason of all these precautions; but I do, and shall proceed to tell you at once.

"'Once upon a time, many great kings and very grand princes were assembled at Pirlipat's father's court, and very great doings were toward. Tournaments, theatricals, and state balls were going on on the grandest scale, and the king, to show that he had no lack of gold and silver, made up his mind to make a good hole in the crown revenues for once, and launch out regardless of expense. Wherefore (having previously ascertained, privately, from the state head master cook that the court astronomer had

---

[1] Hoffmann's way of taking a dig at his favorite adversary: pompous, expendable government bureaucrats

[2] Body guards; secret servicemen

indicated a propitious hour for pork-butching), he resolved to give a grand pudding-and-sausage banquet. He jumped into a state carriage, and personally invited all the kings and the princes—to a basin of soup, merely—that he might enjoy their astonishment at the magnificence of the entertainment. Then he said to the queen, very graciously:

""'My darling, *you* know exactly how I like my puddings[1] and sausages!"

"The queen quite understood what this meant. It meant that she should undertake the important duty of making the puddings and the sausages herself[2], which was a thing she had done on one or two previous occasions. So the chancellor of the exchequer was ordered to issue out of store the great golden sausage-kettle, and the silver *casseroles*. A great fire of sandal-wood[3] was kindled, the queen put on her damask[4] kitchen apron, and soon the most delicious aroma of pudding-broth rose steaming out of the kettle. This sweet smell penetrated into the very council chamber. The king could not control himself.

""'Excuse me for a few minutes, my lords and gentlemen," he cried, rushed to the kitchen, embraced the queen[5], stirred in the kettle a little with his golden sceptre[6], and then went back, easier in his mind, to the council chamber.

"'The important juncture had now arrived when the fat had to be cut up into little square pieces, and browned on silver spits. The ladies-in-waiting retired, because the queen, from motives of love and duty to her royal consort, thought it proper to perform this important task in solitude[7]. But when the fat began to brown, a delicate little whispering voice made itself audible, saying, "Give me some of that, sister! I want some of it, too; I am a queen as well as yourself; give me some."

"'The queen knew well who was speaking. It was Dame Mouseyrinks, who had been established in the palace for many years. She claimed relationship to the royal family, and she was queen of the realm of Mousolia

---

[1] Savory dishes like haggis and black pudding, similar to sausage

[2] An eccentric – bordering on outrageous – task for a queen to undertake: even most middle class housewives usually employed a cook

[3] A rare and costly choice for firewood

[4] An expensive, luxurious, patterned fabric

[5] We must imagine that somehow there is a deeper, erotic subtext to this episode: the king cannot control his passion for his wife as she cooks him sausages. Perhaps the most obvious interpretation is that the phallic nature of the sausages represents her ability to pack and engorge his own "sausage" by being the woman to bear his children, i.e., to "cook" his sausage pudding, channeling his sexual energy into the production of a household

[6] It's difficult to imagine this scene being less suggestive: the king puts his golden scepter into his wife's golden pot, stirs it around and runs off, leaving her to "cook" the results of his little addition

[7] Why? Because this whole episode is about sex

herself, and lived with a considerable retinue of her own under the kitchen hearth. The queen was a kind-hearted, benevolent woman; and, although she didn't exactly care to recognize Dame Mouseyrinks as a sister and a queen, she was willing, at this festive season, to spare her the tit-bits she had a mind to. So she said, "Come out, then, Dame Mouseyrinks; of course you shall taste my browned fat."

"'So Dame Mouseyrinks came running out as fast as she could, held up her pretty little paws, and took morsel after morsel of the browned fat as the queen held them out to her. But then all Dame Mouseyrink's uncles, and her cousins, and her aunts, came jumping out too; and her seven sons (who were terrible ne'er-do-weels) into the bargain; and they all set-to at the browned fat, and the queen was too frightened to keep them at bay[1]. Most fortunately the mistress of the robes[2] came in, and drove these importunate visitors away, so that a little of the browned fat was left; and this, when the court mathematician (an ex-senior wrangler of his university) was called in (which he had to be, on purpose), it was found possible, by means of skilfully devised apparatus provided with special micrometer screws, and so forth, to apportion and distribute amongst the whole of the sausages, &c., under construction.

"'The kettledrums and the trumpets summoned all the great princes and potentates to the feast. They assembled in their robes of state; some of them on white palfreys[3], some in crystal coaches. The king received them with much gracious ceremony, and took his seat at the head of the table, with his crown on, and his sceptre in his hand. Even during the serving of the white pudding course, it was observed that he turned pale, and raised his eyes to heaven; sighs heaved his bosom; some terrible inward pain was clearly raging within him. But when the black-puddings were handed round, he fell back in his seat, loudly sobbing and groaning.

"'Every one rose from the table, and the court physician tried in vain to feel his pulse. Ultimately, after the administration of most powerful remedies—burnt feathers, and the like—his majesty seemed to recover his senses to some extent, and stammered, scarce audibly, the words: "Too little fat!"

"'The queen cast herself down at his feet in despair, and cried, in a voice broken by sobs, "Oh, my poor unfortunate royal consort! Ah, what tortures you are doomed to endure! But see the culprit here at your feet! Punish her severely! Alas! Dame Mouseyrinks, her uncles, her seven sons, her cousins and her aunts, came and ate up nearly all the fat—and——

"Here the queen fell back insensible.

---

[1] This is an obvious parody of bureaucratic nepotism

[2] One of the chief ladies in waiting in charge of the queen's wardrobe and jewelry, and often in charge of managing the entire female court

[3] A tame horse

"'But the king jumped up, all anger, and cried in a terrible voice, "Mistress of the robes, what is the meaning of this?"

"The mistress of the robes told all she knew, and the king resolved to take revenge on Dame Mouseyrinks and her family for eating up the fat which ought to have been in the sausages. The privy council was summoned, and it was resolved that Dame Mouseyrinks should be tried for her life, and all her property confiscated. But as his majesty was of opinion that she might go on consuming the fat, which was his appanage, the whole matter was referred to the court Clockmaker and Arcanist[1]—whose name was the same as mine—Christian Elias Drosselmeier, and he undertook to expel Dame Mouseyrinks and all her relations from the palace precincts forever, by means of a certain politico-diplomatic procedure. He invented certain ingenious little machines, into which pieces of browned fat were inserted; and he placed these machines down all about the dwelling of Dame Mouseyrinks. Now she herself was much too knowing not to see through Drosselmeier's artifice; but all her remonstrances and warnings to her relations were unavailing. Enticed by the fragrant odour of the browned fat, all her seven sons, and a great many of her uncles, her cousins and her aunts, walked into Drosselmeier's little machines, and were immediately taken prisoners by the fall of a small grating; after which they met with a shameful death in the kitchen.

"Dame Mouseyrinks left this scene of horror with her small following. Rage and despair filled her breast. The court rejoiced greatly; the queen was very anxious, because she knew Dame Mouseyrinks' character, and knew well that she would never allow the death of her sons and other relatives to go unavenged. And, in fact, one day when the queen was cooking a *fricassée*[2] of sheep's lights[3] for the king (a dish to which he was exceedingly partial), Dame Mouseyrinks suddenly made her appearance, and said: "My sons and my uncles, my cousins and my aunts, are now no more. Have a care, lady, lest the queen of the mice bites your little princess in two! Have a care!"

"With which she vanished, and was no more seen. But the queen was so frightened that she dropped the *fricassée* into the fire; so this was the second time Dame Mouseyrinks spoiled one of the king's favourite dishes, at which he was very irate.

"'But this is enough for to-night; we'll go on with the rest of it another time.'

"Sorely as Marie—who had ideas of her own about this story—begged Godpapa Drosselmeier to go on with it, he would not be persuaded, but

---

[1] An expert in the arcane creations of various sorts of luxuries (e.g., crystalware, porcelain, jappaning wood)

[2] A dish of stewed meat in a white sauce

[3] Lungs

jumped up, saying, 'Too much at a time wouldn't be good for you; the rest to-morrow.'

"Just as Drosselmeier was going out of the door, Fritz said: I say, Godpapa Drosselmeier, was it really you who invented mousetraps?'

"'How can you ask such silly questions?' cried his mother. But Drosselmeier laughed oddly, and said: 'Well, you know I'm a clever clockmaker. Mousetraps had to be invented some time or other[1].'

"And now you know, children,' said Godpapa Drosselmeier the next evening, 'why it was the queen took such precautions about her little Pirlipat. Had she not always the fear before her eyes of Dame Mouseyrinks coming back and carrying out her threat of biting the princess to death? Drosselmeier's ingenious machines were of no avail against the clever, crafty Dame Mouseyrinks, and nobody save the court astronomer, who was also state astrologer and reader of the stars, knew that the family of the Cat Purr had the power to keep her at bay. This was the reason why each of the lady nurses was obliged to keep one of the sons of that family (each of whom was given the honorary rank and title of "privy councillor of legation") in her lap, and render his onerous duty less irksome by gently scratching his back.

"One night, just after midnight, one of the chief nurses stationed close to the cradle, woke suddenly from a profound sleep. Everything lay buried in slumber. Not a purr to be heard—deep, deathlike silence, so that the death-watch[2] ticking in the wainscot sounded quite loud. What were the feelings of this principal nurse when she saw, close beside her, a great, hideous mouse, standing on its hind legs, with its horrid head laid on the princess's face! She sprang up with a scream of terror. Everybody awoke; but then Dame Mouseyrinks (for she was the great big mouse in Pirlipat's cradle) ran quickly away into the corner of the room. The privy councillors of legation dashed after her, but too late! She was off and away through a chink in the floor. The noise awoke Pirlipat, who cried terribly. "Heaven be thanked, she is still alive!" cried all the nurses; but what was their horror when they looked at Pirlipat, and saw what the beautiful, delicate little thing had turned into. An enormous bloated head (instead of the pretty little golden-haired one), at the top of a diminutive, crumpled-up body, and green, wooden-looking eyes staring, where the lovely azure-blue pair had been, whilst her mouth had stretched across from the one ear to the other.

---

[1] Indeed; the first reference to mousetraps come from the 1530s, and were referenced in Shakespeare in 1603. These were largely boxes with tripwires or props which the mouse was likely to knock over, locking them inside. The springloaded mousetrap we all picture, however, wasn't invented until 1884

[2] The deathwatch beetle – a wood-boring insect who makes a noise like a ticking clock and has long been associated with imminent death – was also referenced in Poe's "The Tell-Tale Heart"

"'Of course the queen nearly died of weeping and loud lamentation, and the walls of the king's study had all to be hung with padded arras, because he kept on banging his head against them, crying:

""'Oh! wretched king that I am! Oh, wretched king that I am!"

"'Of course he might have seen, then, that it would have been much better to eat his puddings with no fat in them at all, and let Dame Mouseyrinks and her folk stay on under the hearthstone. But Pirlipat's royal father thought not of that. What he did was to lay all the blame on the court Clockmaker and Arcanist, Christian Elias Drosselmeier, of Nürnberg. Wherefore he promulgated a sapient edict to the effect that said Drosselmeier should, within the space of four weeks, restore Princess Pirlipat to her pristine condition,—or, at least, indicate an unmistakable and reliable process whereby that might be accomplished,—or else suffer a shameful death by the axe of the common headsman.

"'Drosselmeier was not a little alarmed; but he soon began to place confidence in his art, and in his luck; so he proceeded to execute the first operation which seemed to him to be expedient. He took Princess Pirlipat very carefully to pieces, screwed off her hands and her feet, and examined her interior structure. Unfortunately, he found that the bigger she got the more deformed she would be, so that he didn't see what was to be done at all. He put her carefully together again, and sank down beside her cradle—which he wasn't allowed to go away from—in the deepest dejection.

"'The fourth week had come, and Wednesday of the fourth week, when the king came in, with eyes gleaming with anger, made threatening gestures with his sceptre, and cried:

""'Christian Elias Drosselmeier, restore the princess, or prepare for death!"

"'Drosselmeier began to weep bitterly. The little princess kept on cracking nuts, an occupation which seemed to afford her much quiet satisfaction. For the first time the Arcanist was struck by Pirlipat's remarkable appetite for nuts, and the circumstance that she had been born with teeth. And the fact had been that immediately after her transformation she had begun to cry, and she had gone on crying till by chance she got hold of a nut. She at once cracked it, and ate the kernel, after which she was quite quiet. From that time her nurses found that nothing would do but to go on giving her nuts.

""'Oh, holy instinct of nature—eternal, mysterious, inscrutable Interdependence of Things!'" cried Drosselmeier, "thou pointest out to me the door of the secret. I will knock, and it shall be opened unto me[1]."

"'He at once begged for an interview with the Court Astronomer, and was conducted to him closely guarded. They embraced, with many tears, for they were great friends, and then retired into a private closet, where

---

[1] A reference to the Bible verse: "Ask and it shall be given unto you; seek and ye shall find; knock and it will be opened unto you"

they referred to many books treating of sympathies, antipathies[1], and other mysterious subjects. Night came on. The Court Astronomer consulted the stars, and, with the assistance of Drosselmeier (himself an adept in astrology), drew the princess's horoscope. This was an exceedingly difficult operation, for the lines kept getting more and more entangled and confused for ever so long. But at last—oh what joy!—it lay plain before them that all the princess had to do to be delivered from the enchantment which made her so hideous, and get back her former beauty, was to eat the sweet kernel of the nut Crackatook.

"'Now this nut Crackatook had a shell so hard that you might have fired a forty-eight pounder[2] at it without producing the slightest effect on it. Moreover, it was essential that this nut should be cracked, in the princess's presence, by the teeth of a man whose beard had never known a razor, and who had never had on boots[3]. This man had to hand the kernel to her with his eyes closed, and he might not open them till he had made seven steps backwards without a stumble.

"'Drosselmeier and the astronomer had been at work on this problem uninterruptedly for three days and three nights; and on the Saturday the king was sitting at dinner, when Drosselmeier—who was to have been beheaded on the Sunday morning—burst joyfully in to announce that he had found out what had to be done to restore Princess Pirlipat to her pristine beauty. The king embraced him in a burst of rapture, and promised him a diamond sword, four decorations, and two Sunday suits.

"'"Set to work immediately after dinner," the monarch cried: adding, kindly, "Take care, dear Arcanist, that the young unshaven gentleman in shoes, with the nut Crackatook all ready in his hand, is on the spot; and be sure that he touches no liquor beforehand, so that he mayn't trip up when he makes his seven backward steps like a crab. He can get as drunk as a lord afterwards, if he likes."

"'Drosselmeier was dismayed at this utterance of the king's, and stammered out, not without trembling and hesitation, that, though the remedy was discovered, both the nut Crackatook and the young gentleman who was to crack it had still to be searched for, and that it was matter of doubt whether they ever would be got hold of at all. The king, greatly incensed, whirled his sceptre round his crowned head, and shouted, in the voice of a lion:

---

[1] An example of a sympathy would be magnetized steel and iron; an antipathy would be oil and water

[2] A cannon capable of firing a 48 pound ball. The stereotypical ship's cannon is a nine-pounder (often called a "long nine") and most field guns used on battlefields were six-pounders. Forty-eights were used exclusively in siege warfare to destroy frotifications

[3] This seemingly bizarre requirement ensures that this man is a stranger to pretensions

""'Very well, then you must be beheaded!"

"'It was exceedingly fortunate for the wretched Drosselmeier that the king had thoroughly enjoyed his dinner that day, and was consequently in an admirable temper, and disposed to listen to the sensible advice which the queen, who was very sorry for Drosselmeier, did not spare to give him. Drosselmeier took heart, and represented that he really had fulfilled the conditions, and discovered the necessary measures, and had gained his life, consequently. The king said this was all bosh and nonsense; but at length, after two or three glasses of liqueurs, decreed that Drosselmeier and the astronomer should start off immediately, and not come back without the nut Crackatook in their pockets. The man who was to crack it (by the queen's suggestion) might be heard of by means of advertisements in the local and foreign newspapers and gazettes.'

"Godpapa Drosselmeier interrupted his story at this point, and promised to finish it on the following evening.

"Next evening, as soon as the lights were brought, Godpapa Drosselmeier duly arrived, and went on with his story as follows:—

"'Drosselmeier and the court astronomer had been journeying for fifteen long years without finding the slightest trace of the nut Crackatook. I might go on for more than four weeks telling you where all they had been, and what extraordinary things they had seen. I shall not do so, however, but merely mention that Drosselmeier, in his profound discouragement, at last began to feel a most powerful longing to see his dear native town of Nürnberg once again. And he was more powerfully moved by this longing than usual one day, when he happened to be smoking a pipe of kanaster[1] with his friend in the middle of a great forest in Asia, and he cried:

""'Oh, Nürnberg, Nürnberg! dear native town—he who still knows thee not, place of renown—though far he has travelled, and great cities seen—as London, and Paris, and Peterwardeen[2]—knoweth not what it is happy to be—still must his longing heart languish for thee—for thee, O Nürnberg, exquisite town—where the houses have windows both upstairs and down!"

"'As Drosselmeier lamented thus dolefully, the astronomer, seized with compassionate sympathy, began to weep and howl so terribly that he was heard throughout the length and breadth of Asia. But he collected himself again, wiped the tears from his eyes, and said:

""'After all, dearest colleague, why should we sit and weep and howl here? Why not come to Nürnberg? Does it matter a brass farthing, after all, where and how we search for this horrible nut Crackatook?"

""'That's true, too," answered Drosselmeier, consoled. They both got up immediately, knocked the ashes out of their pipes, started off, and travelled straight on without stopping, from that forest right in the centre of Asia till they came to Nürnberg. As soon as they got there, Drosselmeier

---

[1] A Persian tobacco

[2] That is, Petrovaradin, a fortress city on the Danube in modern Serbia

went straight to his cousin the toy maker and doll-carver, and gilder and varnisher, whom he had not seen for a great many long years. To him he told all the tale of Princess Pirlipat, Dame Mouseyrinks, and the nut Crackatook, so that he clapped his hands repeatedly, and cried in amazement:

""Dear me, cousin, these things are really wonderful—very wonderful, indeed!"

"'Drosselmeier told him, further, some of the adventures he had met with on his long journey—how he had spent two years at the court of the King of Dates; how the Prince of Almonds had expelled him with ignominy from his territory; how he had applied in vain to the Natural History Society at Squirreltown—in short, how he had been everywhere utterly unsuccessful in discovering the faintest trace of the nut Crackatook. During this narrative, Christoph Zacharias had kept frequently snapping his fingers, twisting himself round on one foot, smacking with his tongue, etc.; then he cried:

""Ee—aye—oh!—that really would be the very deuce and all."

"'At last he threw his hat and wig in the air, warmly embraced his cousin, and cried:

""Cousin, cousin, you're a made man—a made man you are—for either I am much deceived, or I have got the nut Crackatook myself!"

"'He immediately produced a little cardboard box, out of which he took a gilded nut of medium size.

""Look there!" he said, showing this nut to his cousin; "the state of matters as regards this nut is this. Several years ago, at Christmas time, a stranger man came here with a sack of nuts, which he offered for sale. Just in front of my shop he got into a quarrel, and put the sack down the better to defend himself from the nut-sellers of the place, who attacked him. Just then a heavily-loaded waggon drove over the sack, and all the nuts were smashed but one. The stranger man, with an odd smile, offered to sell me this nut for a twenty-kreuzer piece[1] of the year 1796. This struck me as strange. I found just such a coin in my pocket, so I bought the nut, and I gilt it over, though I didn't know why I took the trouble quite, or should have given so much for it."

"'All question as to its being really the long-sought nut Crackatook was dispelled when the Court Astronomer carefully scraped away the gilding, and found the word "Crackatook" graven on the shell in Chinese characters.

"The joy of the exiles was great, as you may imagine; and the cousin was even happier, for Drosselmeier assured him that *he* was a made man too, as he was sure of a good pension, and all the gold leaf he would want for the rest of his life for his gilding, free, gratis, for nothing.

---

[1] Similar to the shilling (20 kreuzers made up one gulden, or gold piece), a silver kreuzer (itself worth about five pennies) was used to buy everyday items like a lunch, a book, or a pair of socks

"'The Arcanist and the Astronomer had both got on their nightcaps, and were going to turn into bed, when the astronomer said:

"'"I tell you what it is, dear colleague, one piece of good fortune never comes alone. I feel convinced that we've not only found the nut, but the young gentleman who is to crack it, and hand the beauty-restoring kernel to the princess, into the bargain. I mean none other than your cousin's son here, and I don't intend to close an eye this night till I've drawn that youngster's horoscope."

"'With which he threw away his nightcap, and at once set to work to consult the stars. The cousin's son was a nice-looking, well-grown young fellow, had never been shaved, and had never worn boots. True, he had been a Jumping Jack for a Christmas or two in his earlier days, but there was scarcely any trace of this discoverable about him, his appearance had been so altered by his father's care. He had appeared last Christmas in a beautiful red coat with gold trimmings, a sword by his side, his hat under his arm, and a fine wig with a pigtail. Thus apparelled, he stood in his father's shop exceeding lovely to behold, and from his native *galanterie* he occupied himself in cracking nuts for the young ladies, who called him "the handsome nutcracker."

"'Next morning the Astronomer fell, with much emotion, into the Arcanist's arms, crying:

"'"This is the very man!—we have got him!—he is found! Only, dearest colleague, two things we must keep carefully in view. In the first place, we must construct a most substantial pigtail for this precious nephew of yours, which shall be connected with his lower jaw in such sort that it shall be capable of communicating a very powerful pull to it. And next, when we get back to the Residenz, we must carefully conceal the fact that we have brought the young gentleman who is to shiver the nut back with us. He must not make his appearance for a considerable time after us. I read in the horoscope that if two or three others bite at the nut unsuccessfully to begin with, the king will promise the man who breaks it,—and, as a consequence, restores the princess her good looks,—the princess's hand and the succession to the crown."

"The doll-maker cousin was immensely delighted with the idea of his son's marrying Princess Pirlipat, and being a prince and king, so he gave him wholly over to the envoys to do what they liked with him. The pigtail which Drosselmeier attached to him proved to be a very powerful and efficient instrument, as he exemplified by cracking the hardest of peach-stones with the utmost ease.

"'Drosselmeier and the Astronomer, having at once sent the news to the Residenz of the discovery of the nut Crackatook, the necessary advertisements were at once put in the newspapers, and, by the time that our travellers got there, several nice young gentlemen, among whom there were princes even, had arrived, having sufficient confidence in their teeth to try to disenchant the princess. The ambassadors were horrified when they saw poor Pirlipat again. The diminutive body with tiny hands and feet was not big enough to support the great shapeless head. The hideousness of the face was enhanced by a beard like white cotton, which had grown about the mouth and chin. Everything had turned out as the court astronomer had read it in the horoscope. One milksop in shoes after another bit his teeth and his jaws into agonies over the nut, without doing the princess the slightest good in the world. And then, when he was carried out on the verge of insensibility by the dentists who were in attendance on purpose, he would sigh:

""Ah dear, that was a hard nut."

"Now when the king, in the anguish of his soul, had promised to him who should disenchant the princess his daughter and the kingdom, the charming, gentle young Drosselmeier made his appearance, and begged to be allowed to make an attempt. None of the previous ones had pleased the princess so much. She pressed her little hands to her heart and sighed:

""Ah, I hope it will be he who will crack the nut, and be my husband."

"When he had politely saluted the king, the queen, and the Princess Pirlipat, he received the nut Crackatook from the hands of the Clerk of the Closet[1], put it between his teeth, made a strong effort with his head, and—crack—crack—the shell was shattered into a number of pieces. He neatly cleared the kernel from the pieces of husk which were sticking to it, and, making a leg, presented it courteously to the princess, after which he closed his eyes and began his backward steps. The princess swallowed the kernel, and—oh marvel!—the monstrosity vanished, and in its place there stood a wonderfully beautiful lady, with a face which seemed woven of delicate lily-white and rose-red silk, eyes of sparkling azure, and hair all in little curls like threads of gold.

"Trumpets and kettledrums mingled in the loud rejoicings of the populace. The king and all his court danced about on one leg, as they had done at Pirlipat's birth, and the queen had to be treated with Eau de Cologne[2], having fallen into a fainting fit from joy and delight. All this tremendous tumult interfered not a little with young Drosselmeier's self-possession, for he still had to make his seven backward steps. But he collected himself as best he could, and was just stretching out his right foot to make his seventh step, when up came Dame Mouseyrinks through the floor, making a horrible weaking and squeaking, so that Drosselmeier, as he was putting his foot down, trod upon her, and stumbled so that he almost fell. Oh misery!—all in an instant he was transmogrified, just as the princess had been before: his body all shrivelled up, and could scarcely support the great shapeless head with enormous projecting eyes, and the wide gaping mouth. In the place where his pigtail used to be a scanty wooden cloak hung down, controlling the movements of his nether jaw.

---

[1] The king's personal manager

[2] Strong, alcohol based cologne

"'The clockmaker and the astronomer were wild with terror and consternation, but they saw that Dame Mouseyrinks was wallowing in her gore on the floor. Her wickedness had not escaped punishment, for young Drosselmeier had squashed her so in the throat with the sharp point of his shoe that she was mortally hurt.

"'But as Dame Mouseyrinks lay in her death agony she queaked and cheeped in a lamentable style, and cried:

"'"Oh, Crackatook, thou nut so hard!—Oh, fate, which none may disregard!—Hee hee, pee pee, woe's me, I cry!—since I through that hard nut must die.—But, brave young Nutcracker, I see—you soon must follow after me.—My sweet young son, with sevenfold crown—will soon bring Master Cracker down.—His mother's death he will repay—so, Nutcracker, beware that day!—Oh, life most sweet, I feebly cry,—I leave you now, for I must die. Queak!"

"'With this cry died Dame Mouseyrinks, and her body was carried out by the Court Stovelighter. Meantime nobody had been troubling themselves about young Drosselmeier. But the princess reminded the king of his promise, and he at once directed that the young hero should be conducted to his presence. But when the poor wretch came forward in his transmogrified condition the princess put both her hands to her face, and cried:

"'"Oh please take away that horrid Nutcracker!"

"'So that the Lord Chamberlain seized him immediately by his little shoulders, and shied him out at the door. The king, furious at the idea of a nutcracker being brought before him as a son-in-law, laid all the blame upon the clockmaker and the astronomer, and ordered them both to be banished for ever.

"'The horoscope which the astronomer had drawn in Nürnberg had said nothing about this; but that didn't hinder him from taking some fresh observations. And the stars told him that young Drosselmeier would conduct himself so admirably in his new condition that he would yet be a prince and a king, in spite of his transmogrification; but also that his deformity would only disappear after the son of Dame Mouseyrinks, the seven-headed king of the mice (whom she had born after the death of her original seven sons) should perish by his hand, and a lady should fall in love with him notwithstanding his deformity.

"'That is the story of the hard nut, children, and now you know why people so often use the expression "that was a hard nut," and why Nutcrackers are so ugly.'

"Thus did Godpapa Drosselmeier finish his tale. Marie thought the Princess Pirlipat was a nasty ungrateful thing[1]. Fritz, on the other hand,

---

[1] In large part, Pirlipat has been poised to be a foil to Marie: both are young and pretty girls, both rather spoiled, and both have been protected by

was of opinion that if Nutcracker had been a proper sort of fellow he would soon have settled the mouse king's hash, and got his good looks back again.

UNCLE AND NEPHEW

"Should any of my respected readers or listeners ever have happened to be cut by glass they will know what an exceedingly nasty thing it is, and how long it takes to get well. Marie was obliged to stay in bed a whole week, because she felt so terribly giddy[1] whenever she tried to stand up; but at last she was quite well again, and able to jump about as of old. Things in the glass cupboard looked very fine indeed—everything new and shiny, trees and flowers and houses—toys of every kind. Above all, Marie found her dear Nutcracker again, smiling at her in the second shelf, with his teeth all sound and right. As she looked at this pet of hers with much fondness, it suddenly struck her that all Godpapa Drosselmeier's story had been about Nutcracker, and his family feud with Dame Mouseyrinks and her people. And now she knew that her Nutcracker was none other than young Mr. Drosselmeier, of Nürnberg, Godpapa Drosselmeier's delightful nephew, unfortunately under the spells of Dame Mouseyrinks. For whilst the story was being told, Marie couldn't doubt for a moment that the clever clockmaker at Pirlipat's father's court was Godpapa Drosselmeier himself.

"But why didn't your uncle help you? Why didn't he help you?' Marie cried, sorrowfully, as she felt more and more clearly every moment that in the battle, which she had witnessed, the question in dispute had been no less a matter than Nutcracker's crown and kingdom. Wern't all the other toys his subjects? And wasn't it clear that the astronomer's prophecy that he was to be rightful King of Toyland had come true?'

"Whilst the clever Marie was weighing all these things in her mind, she kept expecting that Nutcracker and his vassals[2] would give some indications of being alive, and make some movements as she looked at them. This, however, was by no means the case. Everything in the cupboard kept quite motionless and still. Marie thought this was the effect of Dame Mouseyrinks's enchantments, and those of her seven-headed son, which still were keeping up their power.

"'But,' she said, 'though you're not able to move, or to say the least little word to me, dear Mr. Drosselmeier, I know you understand me, and see how very well I wish you. Always reckon on my assistance when you require it. At all events, I will ask your uncle to aid you with all has great skill and talents, whenever there may be an opportunity.'

Nutcracker (he transformed Pirlipat from her curse and led the toys against the mice to protect Marie). Pirlipat, however, is vain and cold-hearted. Drosselmeier uses these story to teach Marie how not to be, thus encouraging her to be warm towards Nutcracker in spite of his looks

[1] Dizzy and faint – the result of an infection from the wound

[2] Servants, subjects

"Nutcracker still kept quiet and motionless. But Marie fancied that a gentle sigh came breathing through the glass cupboard, which made its panes ring in a wonderful, though all but imperceptible, manner—whilst something like a little bell-toned voice seemed to sing:

"Marie fine, angel mine! I will be thine, if thou wilt be mine!'

"Although a sort of cold shiver ran through her at this, still it caused her the keenest pleasure.

"Twilight came on. Marie's father came in with Godpapa Drosselmeier, and presently Louise set out the tea-table, and the family took their places round it, talking in the pleasantest and merriest manner about all sorts of things. Marie had taken her little stool, and sat down at her godpapa's feet in silence. When everybody happened to cease talking at the same time, Marie looked her godpapa full in the face with her great blue eyes, and said:

"'I know now, godpapa, that my Nutcracker is your nephew, young Mr. Drosselmeier from Nürnberg. The prophecy has come true: he is a king and a prince, just as your friend the astronomer said he would be. But you know as well as I do that he is at war with Dame Mouseyrinks's son—that horrid king of the mice. Why don't you help him?'

"Marie told the whole story of the battle, as she had witnessed it, and was frequently interrupted by the loud laughter of her mother and sister; but Fritz and Drosselmeier listened quite gravely.

"'Where in the name of goodness has the child got her head filled with all that nonsense?' cried her father.

"'She has such a lively imagination, you see,' said her mother; 'she dreamt it all when she was feverish with her arm.'

"'It is all nonsense,' cried Fritz, 'and it isn't true! my red hussars are not such cowards as all that. If they were, do you suppose I should command them[1]?'

"But godpapa smiled strangely, and took little Marie on his knee, speaking more gently to her than ever he had been known to do before.

"'More is given to you, Marie dear,' he said, 'than to me, or the others. You are a born princess, like Pirlipat, and reign in a bright beautiful country. But you still have much to suffer, if you mean to befriend poor transformed Nutcracker; for the king of the mice lies in wait for him at every turn. But I cannot help him; you, and you only, can do that. So be faithful and true.'

"Neither Marie nor any of the others knew what Godpapa Drosselmeier meant by these words. But they struck Dr. Stahlbaum—the father—as being so strange that he felt Drosselmeier's pulse, and said:

"'There seems a good deal of congestion about the head, my dear sir. I'll just write you a little prescription.'

"But Marie's mother shook her head meditatively, and said:

---

[1] Note that Fritz's reaction is to disbelieve that his soldiers would be so cowardly, not that toys can't come to life

"'I have a strong idea what Mr. Drosselmeier means, though I can't exactly put it in words[1].'

VICTORY

"It was not very long before Marie was awakened one bright moonlight night by a curious noise, which came from one of the corners of her room. There was a sound as of small stones being thrown, and rolled here and there; and between whiles came a horrid cheeping and squeaking.

"'Oh, dear me! here come these abominable mice again!' cried Marie, in terror, and she would have awakened her mother. But the noise suddenly ceased; and she could not move a muscle—for she saw the king of the mice working himself out through a hole in the wall; and at last he came into the room, ran about in it, and got on to the little table at her bed-head with a great jump.

"Hee-hehee!' he cried; 'give me your sweetmeats! out with your cakes, marchpane[2] and sugar-stick, gingerbread cakes! Don't pause to argue! If yield them you won't, I'll chew up Nutcracker! See if I don't!'

"As he cried out these terrible words he gnashed and chattered his teeth most frightfully, and then made off again through the hole in the wall. This frightened Marie so that she was quite pale in the morning, and so upset that she scarcely could utter a word. A hundred times she felt impelled to tell her mother or her sister, or at all events her brother, what had happened. But she thought, 'of course none of them would believe me. They would only laugh at me.'

"But she saw well enough that to succour Nutcracker she would have to sacrifice all her sweet things[3]; so she laid out all she had of them at the bottom of the cupboard next evening.

---

[1] To Mrs. Stahlbaum, Drosselmeier's words touch on an archetypal truth because they describe the process of growing up: a catharsis of pain and humiliation are often required to develop a child into an adult, and several of the characters he describes – the ravenous Mouse King and the transfigured Nutcracker – share an archetypal relationship with genuine human experiences like corruption and selfishness, compassion and love. Like many stories coated in symbolism (e.g., Alice in Wonderland, The Wizard of Oz, The Chronicles of Narnia), something within it rings true to her, although the archetypes are prevented from being immediately understood due to their fairy tale disguises

[2] Marzipan – a confection made with honey and almond meal, similar to gingerbread

[3] Marie, still a child, learns the virtue of self-sacrifice in the name of loyalty, compassion, and love, and although the sacrifice of her candy may seem like a shallow loss, it is a significant step in her maturation from child to young adult

"'I can't make out how the mice have got into the sitting-room,' said her mother. 'This is something quite new. There never were any there before. See, Marie, they've eaten up all your sweetmeats.'

"And so it was: the epicure mouse king hadn't found the marchpane altogether to his taste, but had gnawed all round the edges of it, so that what he had left of it had to be thrown into the ash-pit. Marie never minded about her sweetmeats, being delighted to think that she had saved Nutcracker by means of them. But what were her feelings when next night there came a queaking again close by her ear. Alas! The king of the mice was there again, with his eyes glaring worse than the night before.

"Give me your sugar toys,' he cried; give them you must, or else I'll chew Nutcracker up into dust!'

"Then he was gone again.

"Marie was very sorry. She had as beautiful a collection of sugar-toys as ever a little girl could boast of. Not only had she a charming little shepherd, with his shepherd looking after a flock of milk-white sheep, with a nice dog jumping about them, but two postmen with letters in their hands, and four couples of prettily dressed young gentlemen and most beautifully dressed young ladies, swinging in a Russian swing. Then there were two or three dancers, and behind them Farmer Feldkuemmel and the Maid of Orleans[1]. Marie didn't much care about *them*; but back in the corner there was a little baby with red cheeks, and this was Marie's darling. The tears came to her eyes.

"'Ah!' she cried, turning to Nutcracker, 'I really will do all I can to help you. But it's very hard.'

"Nutcracker looked at her so piteously that she determined to sacrifice everything—for she remembered the mouse king with all his seven mouths wide open to swallow the poor young fellow; so that night she set down all her sugar figures in front of the cupboard, as she had the sweetmeats the night before. She kissed the shepherd, the shepherdess, and the lambs; and at last she brought her best beloved of all, the little red-cheeked baby from its corner, but did put it a little further back than the rest. Farmer Feldkuemmel and the Maid of Orleans had to stand in the front rank of all.

"'This is really getting too bad,' said Marie's mother the next morning; 'some nasty mouse or other must have made a hole in the glass cupboard, for poor Marie's sugar figures are all eaten and gnawed.' Marie really could not restrain her tears. But she was soon able to smile again; for she thought, 'What does it matter? Nutcracker is safe.'

"In the evening Marie's mother was telling her father and Godpapa Drosselmeier about the mischief which some mouse was doing in the children's cupboard, and her father said:

---

[1] A farcical character from a comedy by the German playwright Auguste von Kutzebue – an English equivalent would probably be Old MacDonald; the Maid of Orleans is the moniker of Joan of Arc

"'It's a regular nuisance! What a pity it is that we can't get rid of it. It's destroying all the poor child's things.'

"Fritz intervened, and remarked:

"The baker downstairs has a fine grey Councillor-of-Legation[1]; I'll go and get hold of him, and he'll soon put a stop to it, and bite the mouse's head off, even if it's Dame Mouseyrinks herself, or her son, the king of the mice.'

"'Oh, yes!' said his mother, laughing, 'and jump up on to the chairs and tables, knock down the cups and glasses, and do ever so much mischief besides.'

"'No, no!' answered Fritz; 'the baker's Councillor-of-Legation's a very clever fellow. I wish I could walk about on the edge of the roof, as he does.'

"'Don't let us have a nasty cat in the house in the night-time,' said Louise, who hated cats.

"Fritz is quite right though,' said the mother; 'unless we set a trap. Haven't we got such a thing in the house?'

"Godpapa Drosselmeier's the man to get us one,' said Fritz; 'it was he who invented them, you know.' Everybody laughed. And when the mother said they did not possess such a thing, Drosselmeier said he had plenty; and he actually sent a very fine one round that day. When the cook was browning the fat, Marie—with her head full of the marvels of her godpapa's tale—called out to her:

"Ah, take care, Queen! Remember Dame Mouseyrinks and her people.' But Fritz drew his sword, and cried, 'Let them come if they dare! I'll give an account of them.' But everything about the hearth remained quiet and undisturbed. As Drosselmeier was fixing the browned fat on a fine thread, and setting the trap gently down in the glass cupboard, Fritz cried:

"'Now, Godpapa Clockmaker, mind that the mouse king doesn't play you some trick!'

"Ah, how did it fare with Marie that night? Something as cold as ice went tripping about on her arm, and something rough and nasty laid itself on her cheek, and cheeped and queaked in her ear. The horrible mouse king came and sat on her shoulder, foamed a blood-red foam out of all his seven mouths, and chattering and grinding his teeth, he hissed into Marie's ear:

"'Hiss, hiss!—keep away—don't go in there—ware of that house—don't you be caught—death to the mouse—hand out your picture-books—none of your scornful looks!—Give me your dresses—also your laces—or, if you don't, leave you I won't—Nutcracker I'll bite—drag him out of your sight—

[1] Referring to a cat, Fritz takes this war very seriously, probably recalling the Coalition of the Allied Armies which fought Napoleon just a few years prior. Some translations put this as "taskforce advisor" – in other words, "here's someone who can help our cause"

his last hour is near—so tremble for fear!—Fee, fa, fo, fum—his last hour is come!—Hee hee, pee pee—queak—queak!'

"Marie was overwhelmed with anguish and sorrow, and was looking quite pale and upset when her mother said to her next morning:

"'This horrid mouse hasn't been caught. But never mind, dear, we'll catch the nasty thing yet, never fear. If the traps won't do, Fritz shall fetch the grey Councillor of Legation.'

"As soon as Marie was alone, she went up to the glass cupboard, and said to Nutcracker, in a voice broken by sobs:

"'Ah, my dear, good Mr. Drosselmeier, what can I do for you, poor unfortunate girl that I am! Even if I give that horrid king of the mice all my picture-books, and my new dress which the Child Christ gave me at Christmas as well, he's sure to go on asking for more; so I soon shan't have anything more left, and he'll want to eat me! Oh, poor thing that I am! What shall I do? What shall I do?'

"As she was thus crying and lamenting, she noticed that a great spot of blood had been left, since the eventful night of the battle, upon Nutcracker's neck. Since she had known that he was really young Mr. Drosselmeier, her godpapa's nephew, she had given up carrying him in her arms, and petting and kissing him; indeed, she felt a delicacy about touching him at all. But now she took him carefully out of his shelf, and began to wipe off this blood-spot with her handkerchief. What were her feelings when she found that Nutcracker was growing warmer and warmer in her hand, and beginning to move! She put him back into the cupboard as fast as she could. His mouth began to wobble backwards and forwards, and he began to whisper, with much difficulty:

"'Ah, dearest Miss Stahlbaum—most precious of friends! How deeply I am indebted to you for everything—for *everything*! But don't, don't sacrifice any of your picture-books or pretty dresses for me. Get me a sword[1]—a sword is what I want. If you get me that, I'll manage the rest—though—he may——'

"There Nutcracker's speech died away, and his eyes, which had been expressing the most sympathetic grief, grew staring and lifeless again.

"Marie felt no fear; she jumped for joy, rather, now that she knew how to help Nutcracker without further painful sacrifices. But where on earth was she to get hold of a sword for him? She resolved to take counsel with Fritz; and that evening, when their father and mother had gone out, and they two were sitting beside the glass cupboard, she told him what had

[1] In order to defeat the Mouse King, Nutcracker must be empowered – supported, encouraged, and believed in – by Marie. Without her fidelity, he is powerless, and only through her active empowerment, can he overcome the odds stacked against him and drive evil and corruption from the Stahlbaum house

passed between her and Nutcracker with the king of the mice, and what it was that was required to rescue Nutcracker.

"The thing which chiefly exercised Fritz's mind was Marie's statement as to the unexemplary conduct of his red hussars in the great battle. He asked her once more, most seriously, to assure him if it really was the truth; and when she had repeated her statement, on her word of honour, he advanced to the cupboard, and made his hussars a most affecting address; and, as a punishment for their behaviour, he solemnly took their plumes one by one out of their busbies[1], and prohibited them from sounding the march of the hussars of the guard[2] for the space of a twelvemonth. When he had performed this duty, he turned to Marie, and said:

"As far as the sword is concerned, I have it in my power to assist Nutcracker. I placed an old Colonel of Cuirassiers on retirement on a pension, no longer ago than yesterday, so that he has no further occasion for his sabre, which is sharp.'

"This Colonel was settled, on his pension, in the back corner of the third shelf. He was fetched out from thence, and his sabre—still a bright and handsome silver weapon—taken off, and girt about Nutcracker.

"Next night Marie could not close an eye for anxiety. About midnight she fancied she heard a strange stirring and noise in the sitting-room—a rustling and a clanging—and all at once came a shrill 'Queak!'

"'The king of the mice! The king of the mice!' she cried, and jumped out of bed, all terror. Everything was silent; but soon there came a gentle tapping at the door of her room, and a soft voice made itself heard, saying:

"Please to open your door, dearest Miss Stahlbaum! Don't be in the least degree alarmed; good, happy news!'

"It was Drosselmeier's voice—young Drosselmeier's, I mean. She threw on her dressing-gown, and opened the door as quickly as possible. There stood Nutcracker, with his sword, all covered with blood, in his right hand, and a little wax taper in his left. When he saw Marie he knelt down on one knee, and said:

"'It was you, and you only, dearest lady, who inspired me with knightly valour, and steeled me with strength to do battle with the insolent caitiff[3] who dared to insult you. The treacherous king of the mice lies vanquished and writhing in his gore! Deign, lady, to accept these tokens of victory from the hand of him who is, till death, your true and faithful knight.'

"With this Nutcracker took from his left arm the seven crowns of the mouse king, which he had ranged upon it, and handed them to Marie, who

---

[1] Bearskin hat, as popularized by the Buckingham Palace guard

[2] What would amount to their fight song – a common punishment for units which have displayed cowardice, since playing their march is a point of pride and honor for military units

[3] A revolting coward or villain

received them with the keenest pleasure. Nutcracker rose, and continued as follows:

"Oh! my best beloved Miss Stahlbaum, if you would only take the trouble to follow me for a few steps, what glorious and beautiful things I could show you, at this supreme moment when I have overcome my hereditary foe! Do—do come with me, dearest lady!'

TOYLAND

"I feel quite convinced, children, that none of you would have hesitated for a moment to go with good, kind Nutcracker, who had always shown himself to be such a charming person, and Marie was all the more disposed to do as he asked her, because she knew what her just claims on his gratitude were, and was sure that he would keep his word, and show her all sorts of beautiful things. So she said:

"'I will go with you, dear Mr. Drosselmeier; but it mustn't be very far, and it won't do to be very long, because, you know, I haven't had any sleep yet.'

"'Then we will go by the shortest route,' said Nutcracker, 'although it is, perhaps, rather the most difficult.'

"He went on in front, followed by Marie, till he stopped before the big old wardrobe. Marie was surprised to see that, though it was generally shut, the doors of it were now wide open, so that she could see her father's travelling cloak of fox-fur hanging in the front. Nutcracker clambered deftly up this cloak, by the edgings and trimmings of it, so as to get hold of the big tassel which was fastened at the back of it by a thick cord. He gave this tassel a tug, and a pretty little ladder of cedar-wood let itself quickly down through one of the arm-holes of the cloak[1].

"'Now, Miss Stahlbaum, step up that ladder, if you will be so kind,' said Nutcracker. Marie did so. But as soon as she had got up through the arm-hole, and begun to look out at the neck, all at once a dazzling light came streaming on to her, and she found herself standing on a lovely, sweet-scented meadow, from which millions of sparks were streaming upward, like the glitter of beautiful gems.

"This is Candy Mead[2], where we are now,' said Nutcracker. 'But we'll go in at that gate there.'

"Marie looked up and saw a beautiful gateway on the meadow, only a few steps off. It seemed to be made of white, brown, and raisin-coloured

---

[1] The portal to Toyland is, curiously enough, hidden in her father's coat. There are obvious Freudian allusions here, since it appears that she must allow Nutcracker to replace her father in her mind as male guardian (literally allowing him to put on his clothes, or, less literally, but according to the idiom, "fill his shoes")

[2] An archaic word for "meadow" or "fields"

marble[1]; but when she came close to it she saw it was all of baked sugar-almonds and raisins, which—as Nutcracker said when they were going through it—was the reason it was called 'Almond and Raisin Gate.' There was a gallery running round the upper part of it, apparently made of barley-sugar, and in this gallery six monkeys, dressed in red doublets[2], were playing on brass instruments in the most delightful manner ever heard; so that it was all that Marie could do to notice that she was walking along upon a beautiful variegated marble pavement, which, however, was really a mosaic of lozenges of all colours. Presently the sweetest of odours came breathing round her, streaming from a beautiful little wood on both sides of the way. There was such a glittering and sparkling among the dark foliage, that one could see all the gold and silver fruits hanging on the many-tinted stems, and these stems and branches were all ornamented and dressed up in ribbons and bunches of flowers, like brides and bridegrooms, and festive wedding guests. And as the orange perfume came wafted, as if on the wings of gentle zephyrs, there was a soughing[3] among the leaves and branches, and all the goldleaf and tinsel rustled and tinkled like beautiful music, to which the sparkling lights could not help dancing.

"'Oh, how charming this is!' cried Marie, enraptured.

"'This is Christmas Wood, dearest Miss Stahlbaum,' said Nutcracker,

"Ah!' said Marie, 'if I could only stay here for a little! Oh, it is so lovely!'

"Nutcracker clapped his little hands, and immediately there appeared a number of little shepherds and shepherdesses, and hunters and huntresses, so white and delicate that you would have thought they were made of pure sugar, whom Marie had not noticed before, although they had been walking about in the wood: and they brought a beautiful gold reclining chair, laid down a white satin cushion in it, and politely invited Marie to take a seat. As soon as she did so, the shepherds and shepherdesses danced a pretty ballet, to which the hunters and huntresses played the music on their horns, and then they all disappeared amongst the thickets.

"I must really apologize for the poor style in which this dance was executed, dearest Miss Stahlbaum,' said Nutcracker. 'These people all belong to our Wire Ballet Troupe, and can only do the same thing over and over again[4]. Had we not better go on a little farther?'

"'Oh, I'm sure it was all most delightful, and I enjoyed it immensely!' said Marie, as she stood up and followed Nutcracker, who was going on leading the way. They went by the side of a gently rippling brook, which seemed to be what was giving out all the perfume which filled the wood.

---

[1] Sweet bread

[2] Short jackets

[3] Moaning, rusting, as of wind

[4] Not unlike the automaton inhabitants of Drosselmeier's robotic castle who, bereft of free will, are predestined to repeat the same endless moves

"'This is Orange Brook,' said Nutcracker; 'but, except for its sweet scent, it is nothing like as fine a water as the River Lemonade, a beautiful broad stream, which falls—as this one does also—into the Almond-milk Sea.'

"And, indeed, Marie soon heard a louder plashing and rushing, and came in sight of the River Lemonade, which went rolling along in swelling waves of a yellowish colour, between banks covered with a herbage and underwood which shone like green carbuncles. A remarkable freshness and coolness, strengthening heart and breast, exhaled from this fine river. Not far from it a dark yellow stream crept sluggishly along, giving out a most delicious odour; and on its banks sat numbers of pretty children, angling for little fat fishes, which they ate as soon as they caught them. These fish were very much like filberts[1], Marie saw when she came closer. A short distance farther, on the banks of this stream, stood a nice little village. The houses of this village, and the church, the parsonage, the barns, and so forth, were all dark brown with gilt roofs, and many of the walls looked as if they were plastered over with lemon-peel and shelled almonds.

"'That is Gingerthorpe on the Honey River,' said Nutcracker. 'It is famed for the good looks of its inhabitants; but they are very short-tempered people, because they suffer so much from tooth-ache. So we won't go there at present.'

"At this moment Marie caught sight of a little town where the houses were all sorts of colours and quite transparent, exceedingly pretty to look at. Nutcracker went on towards this town, and Marie heard a noise of bustle and merriment, and saw some thousands of nice little folks unloading a number of waggons which were drawn up in the market-place. What they were unloading from the waggons looked like packages of coloured paper, and tablets of chocolate.

"'This is Bonbonville,' Nutcracker said. 'An embassy has just arrived from Paperland and the King of Chocolate. These poor Bonbonville people have been vexatiously threatened lately by the Fly-Admiral's forces, so they are covering their houses over with their presents from Paperland, and constructing fortifications with the fine pieces of workmanship which the Chocolate-King has sent them. But oh! dearest Miss Stahlbaum, we are not going to restrict ourselves to seeing the small towns and villages of this country. Let us be off to the metropolis.'

"He stepped quickly onwards, and Marie followed him, all expectation. Soon a beautiful rosy vapour began to rise, suffusing everything with a soft splendour. She saw that this was reflected from a rose-red, shining water, which went plashing and rushing away in front of them in wavelets of roseate silver. And on this delightful water, which kept broadening and broadening out wider and wider, like a great lake, the loveliest swans were floating, white as silver, with collars of gold. And, as if vieing with each

[1] Hazelnuts

other, they were singing the most beautiful songs, at which little fish, glittering like diamonds, danced up and down in the rosy ripples.

"'Oh!' cried Marie, in the greatest delight, 'this must be the lake which Godpapa Drosselmeier was once going to make for me, and I am the girl who is to play with the swans.'

"Nutcracker gave a sneering sort of laugh, such as she had never seen in him before, and said:

"'My uncle could never make a thing of this kind. You would be much more likely to do it yourself. But don't let us bother about that. Rather let us go sailing over the water, Lake Rosa here, to the metropolis.'

THE METROPOLIS

"Nutcracker clapped his little hands again, and the waves of Lake Rosa began to sound louder and to plash higher, and Marie became aware of a sort of car[1] approaching from the distance, made wholly of glittering precious stones of every colour, and drawn by two dolphins with scales of gold. Twelve of the dearest little Moor boys, with head-dresses and doublets made of humming-birds' feathers woven together, jumped to land, and carried first Marie and then Nutcracker, gently gliding above the water, into the car, which immediately began to move along over the lake of its own accord. Ah! how beautiful it was when Marie went onward thus over the waters in the shell-shaped car, with the rose-perfume breathing around her, and the rosy waves plashing. The two golden-scaled dolphins lifted their nostrils, and sent streams of crystal high in the air; and as these fell down in glittering, sparkling rainbows, there was a sound as of two delicate, silvery voices, singing, 'Who comes over the rosy sea?—Fairy is she. Bim-bim—fishes; sim-sim—swans; sfa-sfa—golden birds; tratrah, rosy waves, wake you, and sing, sparkle and ring, sprinkle and kling—this is the fairy we languish to see—coming at last to us over the sea. Rosy waves dash—bright dolphins play—merrily, merrily on!'

"But the twelve little black boys at the back of the car seemed to take some umbrage at this song of the water-jets; for they shook the sunshades they were holding so that the palm leaves they were made of clattered and rattled together; and as they shook them they stamped an odd sort of rhythm with their feet, and sang:

"'Klapp and klipp, and klipp and klapp, and up and down.'

"Moors are merry, amusing fellows,' said Nutcracker, a little put out; 'but they'll set the whole lake into a state of regular mutiny on my hands!' And in fact there did begin a confused, and confusing, noise of strange voices which seemed to be floating both in the water and in the air. However, Marie paid no attention to it, but went on looking into the perfumed rosy waves, from each of which a pretty girl's face smiled back to her.

---

[1] Chariot

"Oh! look at Princess Pirlipat,' she cried, clapping her hands with gladness, 'smiling at me so charmingly down there! Do look at her, Mr. Drosselmeier.'

"But Nutcracker sighed, almost sorrowfully, and said:

"'That is not Princess Pirlipat, dearest Miss Stahlbaum, it is only yourself; always your own lovely face smiling up from the rosy waves[1].' At this Marie drew her head quickly back, closed her eyes as tightly as she could, and was terribly ashamed. But just then the twelve Moors lifted her out of the car and set her on shore. She found herself in a small thicket or grove, almost more beautiful even than Christmas Wood, everything glittered and sparkled so in it. And the fruit on the trees was extraordinarily wonderful and beautiful, and not only of very curious colours, but with the most delicious perfume.

"'Ah!' said Nutcracker, 'here we are in Comfit[2] Grove, and yonder lies the metropolis.'

"How shall I set about describing all the wonderful and beautiful sights which Marie now saw, or give any idea of the splendour and magnificence of the city which lay stretched out before her on a flowery plain? Not only did the walls and towers of it shine in the brightest and most gorgeous colours, but the shapes and appearance of the buildings were like nothing to be seen on earth. Instead of roofs the houses had on beautiful twining crowns, and the towers were garlanded with beautiful leaf-work, sculptured and carved into exquisite, intricate designs. As they passed in at the gateway, which looked as if it was made entirely of macaroons and sugared fruits, silver soldiers presented arms, and a little man in a brocade dressing-gown threw himself upon Nutcracker's neck, crying:

"'Welcome, dearest prince! welcome to Sweetmeatburgh[3]!'

"Marie wondered not a little to see such a very grand personage recognise young Mr. Drosselmeier as a prince. But she heard such a number of small delicate voices making such a loud clamouring and talking, and such a laughing and chattering going on, and such a singing and playing, that she couldn't give her attention to anything else, but asked Drosselmeier what was the meaning of it all.

"'Oh, it is nothing out of the common, dearest Miss Stahlbaum,' he answered. 'Sweetmeatburgh is a large, populous city, full of mirth and entertainment. This is only the usual thing that is always going on here every day. Please to come on a little farther.'

"After a few paces more they were in the great marketplace, which presented the most magnificent appearance. All the houses which were

---

[1] Marie recognizes that she holds within her the potential to become vain like Pirlipat, and checks her attitude before she can bring further heartache to Nutcracker

[2] Sugared nuts

[3] Other translations employ the far more appealing “Candyland”

round it were of filagreed sugar-work, with galleries towering above galleries; and in the centre stood a lofty cake covered with sugar, by way of obelisk, with fountains round it spouting orgeade, lemonade, and other delicious beverages into the air. The runnels[1] at the sides of the footways were full of creams, which you might have ladled up with a spoon if you had chosen. But prettier than all this were the delightful little people who were crowding about everywhere by the thousand, shouting, laughing, playing, and singing, in short, producing all that jubilant uproar which Marie had heard from the distance. There were beautifully dressed ladies and gentlemen, Greeks and Armenians, Tyrolese and Jews, officers and soldiers, clergymen, shepherds, jack-puddings, in short, people of every conceivable kind to be found in the world.

"The tumult grew greater towards one of the corners; the people streamed asunder. For the Great Mogul happened to be passing along there in his palanquin[2], attended by three-and-ninety grandees of the realm, and seven hundred slaves. But it chanced that the Fishermen's Guild, about five hundred strong, were keeping a festival at the opposite corner of the place; and it was rather an unfortunate coincidence that the Grand Turk took it in his head just at this particular moment to go out for a ride, and crossed the square with three thousand Janissaries[3]. And, as if this were not enough, the grand procession of the Interrupted Sacrifice came along at the same time, marching up towards the obelisk with a full orchestra playing, and the chorus singing:

"'Hail! all hail to the glorious sun!'

"So there was a thronging and a shoving, a driving and a squeaking; and soon lamentations arose, and cries of pain, for one of the fishermen had knocked a Brahmin's[4] head off in the throng, and the Great Mogul had been very nearly run down by a jack-pudding[5]. The din grew wilder and wilder. People were beginning to shove one another, and even to come to fisticuffs; when the man in the brocade dressing-gown who had welcomed Nutcracker as prince at the gate, clambered up to the top of the obelisk, and, after a very clear-tinkling bell had rung thrice, shouted, very loudly, three several times:

"Pastrycook! pastrycook! pastrycook!'

"Instantly the tumult subsided. Everybody tried to save his bacon as quickly as he could; and, after the entangled processions had been got disentangled, the dirt properly brushed off the Great Mogul, and the Brahmin's head stuck oп again all right, the merry noise went on just the same as before.

---

[1] Gutters

[2] Litter – a covered couch supported by two poles and carried by servants

[3] Turkish infantrymen

[4] Hindi holy man

[5] Type of clown

"'Tell me why that gentleman called out "Pastrycook," Mr. Drosselmeier, please,' said Marie.

"'Ah! dearest Miss Stahlbaum,' said Nutcracker, 'in this place "Pastrycook" means a certain unknown and very terrible Power, which, it is believed, can do with people just what it chooses. It represents the Fate, or Destiny, which rules these happy little people, and they stand in such awe and terror of it that the mere mention of its name quells the wildest tumult in a moment, as the burgomaster has just shown. Nobody thinks further of earthly matters, cuffs in the ribs, broken heads, or the like. Every one retires within himself, and says:

""'What is man? and what his ultimate destiny[1]?"'

"Marie could not forbear a cry of admiration and utmost astonishment as she now found herself all of a sudden before a castle, shining in roseate radiance, with a hundred beautiful towers. Here and there at intervals upon its walls were rich bouquets of violets, narcissus, tulips, carnations, whose dark, glowing colours heightened the dazzling whiteness, inclining to rose-colour, of the walls. The great dome of the central building, as well as the pyramidal roofs of the towers, were set all over with thousands of sparkling gold and silver stars.

"'Aha!' said Nutcracker, 'here we are at Marchpane Castle at last!'

"Marie was sunk and absorbed in contemplation of this magic palace. But the fact did not escape her that the roof was wanting to one of the principal towers, and that little men, up upon a scaffold made of sticks of cinnamon, were busy putting it on again. But before she had had time to ask Nutcracker about this, he said:

"'This beautiful castle was a short time since threatened with tremendous havoc, if not with total destruction. Sweet-tooth the giant happened to be passing by, and he bit off the top of that tower there, and was beginning to gnaw at the great dome. But the Sweetmeatburgh people brought him a whole quarter of the town by way of tribute, and a considerable slice of Comfit Grove into the bargain. This stopped his mouth, and he went on his way.'

"At this moment soft, beautiful music was heard, and out came twelve little pages with lighted clove-sticks, which they held in their little hands by way of torches. Each of their heads was a pearl, their bodies were emeralds and rubies, and their feet were beautifully-worked pure gold. After them came four ladies about the size of Marie's Miss Clara, but so gloriously and brilliantly attired that Marie saw in a moment that they could be nothing but princesses of the blood royal. They embraced Nutcracker most tenderly, and shed tears of gladness, saying:

"'Oh, dearest prince! beloved brother!'

---

[1] Even the sugary citizens of Candyland have a concept of a god which fills them with existential dread and anxiety

"Nutcracker seemed deeply affected. He wiped away his tears, which flowed thick and fast, and then he took Marie by the hand and said, with much pathos and solemnity:

"This is Miss Marie Stahlbaum, the daughter of a most worthy medical man, and the preserver of my life. Had she not thrown her slipper just in the nick of time—had she not procured me the pensioned Colonel's sword—I should have been lying in my cold grave at this moment, bitten to death by the accursed king of the mice. I ask you to tell me candidly, can Princess Pirlipat, princess though she be, compare for a moment with Miss Stahlbaum here in beauty, in goodness, in virtues of every kind? My answer is, emphatically "No."'

"All the ladies cried 'No;' and they fell upon Marie's neck with sobs and tears, and cried:

"Ah! noble preserver of our beloved royal brother! Excellent Miss Stahlbaum!'

"They now conducted Marie and Nutcracker into the castle, to a hall whose walls were composed of sparkling crystal. But what delighted Marie most of all was the furniture. There were the most darling little chairs, bureaus, writing-tables, and so forth, standing about everywhere, all made of cedar or Brazil-wood, covered with golden flowers. The princesses made Marie and Nutcracker sit down, and said that they would themselves prepare a banquet. So they went and brought quantities of little cups and dishes of the finest Japanese porcelain, and spoons, knives and forks, graters and stew-pans, and other kitchen utensils of gold and silver. Then they fetched the most delightful fruits and sugar things—such as Marie had never seen the like of—and began to squeeze the fruit in the daintiest way with their little hands, and to grate the spices and rub down the sugar-almonds; in short, they set to work so skilfully that Marie could see very well how accomplished they were in kitchen matters, and what a magnificent banquet there was going to be. Knowing her own skill in this line, she wished, in her secret heart, that she might be allowed to go and help the princesses, and have a finger in all these pies herself. And the prettiest of Nutcracker's sisters, just as if she had read the wishes of Marie's heart, handed her a little gold mortar[1], saying:

"'Sweet friend, dear preserver of my brother, would you mind just pounding a little of this sugar-candy?'

"Now as Marie went on pounding in the mortar with good will and the utmost enjoyment—and the sound of it was like a lovely song—Nutcracker began to relate, with much minuteness and prolixity, all that had happened on the occasion of the terrible engagement between his forces and the army of the king of the mice; how he had had the worst of it on account of the bad behaviour of his troops; how the horrible mouse king had all but bitten

---

[1] A heavy bowl which, along with a pestle, is used to crush and grind herbs and spices

him to death, so that Marie had had to sacrifice a number of his subjects who were in her service, etc., etc.

"During all this it seemed to Marie as if what Nutcracker was saying—and even the sound of her own mortar—kept growing more and more indistinct, and going farther and farther away. Presently she saw a silver mistiness rising up all about, like clouds, in which the princesses, the pages, Nutcracker, and she herself were floating. And a curious singing and a buzzing and humming began, which seemed to die away in the distance; and then she seemed to be going up—up—up, as if on waves constantly rising and swelling higher and higher, higher and higher, higher and higher.

CONCLUSION

"And then came a 'prr-poof,' and Marie fell down from some inconceivable height.

"That was a crash and a tumble!

"However, she opened her eyes, and, lo and behold, there she was in her own bed! It was broad daylight, and her mother was standing at her bedside, saying:

"'Well, what a sleep you have had! Breakfast has been ready for ever so long.'

"Of course, dear audience, you see how it was. Marie, confounded and amazed by all the wonderful things she had seen, had fallen asleep at last in Marchpane Castle, and the Moors or the pages, or perhaps the princesses themselves, had carried her home and put her to bed.

"'Oh, mother darling,' said Marie, what a number of places young Mr. Drosselmeier has taken me to in the night, and what beautiful things I have seen!' And she gave very much the same faithful account of it all as I have done to you.

"Her mother listened, looking at her with much astonishment, and, when she had finished, said:

"'You have had a long, beautiful dream, Marie; but now you must put it all out of your head.'

"Marie firmly maintained that she had not been dreaming at all; so her mother took her to the glass cupboard, lifted out Nutcracker from his usual position on the third shelf, and said:

"'You silly girl, how can you believe that this wooden figure can have life and motion?'

"'Ah, mother,' answered Marie, 'I know perfectly well that Nutcracker is young Mr. Drosselmeier from Nürnberg, Godpapa Drosselmeier's nephew.'

"Her father and mother both burst out into ringing laughter.

"'It's all very well your laughing at poor Nutcracker, father,' cried Mary, almost weeping; 'but he spoke very highly of *you*; for when we arrived at

Marchpane Castle, and he was introducing me to his sisters, the princesses, he said you were a most worthy medical man.'

The laughter grew louder, and Louise, and even Fritz, joined in it. Marie ran into the next room, took the mouse king's seven crowns from her little box, and handed them to her mother, saying:

"Look there, then, dear mother; those are the mouse king's seven crowns which young Mr. Drosselmeier gave me last night as a proof that he had got the victory.'

"Her mother gazed in amazement at the little crowns, which were made of some very brilliant, wholly unknown metal, and worked more beautifully than any human hands could have worked them. Dr. Stahlbaum could not cease looking at them with admiration and astonishment either, and both the father and the mother enjoined Marie most earnestly to tell them where she really had got them from. But she could only repeat what she had said before; and when her father scolded her, and accused her of untruthfulness, she began to cry bitterly, and said:

"'Oh, dear me; what can I tell you except the truth, poor unfortunate girl that I am!'

"At this moment the door opened, and Godpapa Drosselmeier came in, crying:

"'Hullo! hullo! what's all this? My little Marie crying? What's all this? what's all this?'

"Dr. Stahlbaum told him all about it, and showed him the crowns. As soon as he had looked at them, however, he cried out:

"'Stuff and nonsense! stuff and nonsense! These are the crowns I used to wear on my watch-chain. I gave them as a present to Marie on her second birthday. Do you mean to tell me you don't remember?'

"None of them *did* remember anything of the kind. But Marie, seeing that her father and mother's faces were clear of clouds[1] again, ran up to her godpapa, crying:

"'You know all about the affair, Godpapa Drosselmeier; tell it to them then. Let them know from your own lips that my Nutcracker is your nephew, young Mr. Drosselmeier from Nürnberg, and that it was he who gave me the crowns.' But Drosselmeier made a very angry face, and muttered, 'Stupid stuff and nonsense!' upon which Marie's father took her in front of him, and said, with much earnestness:

"'Now just look here, Marie; let there be an end of all this foolish trash and absurd nonsense for once and for all; I'm not going to allow any more of it; and if ever I hear you say again that that idiotic, misshapen Nutcracker is your godpapa's nephew, I shall shy[2], not only Nutcracker, but all your other playthings—Miss Clara not excepted—out of the window.'

---

[1] No longer angry

[2] Throw

"Of course poor Marie dared not utter another word concerning that which her whole mind was full of, for you may well suppose that it was impossible for anyone who had seen all that she had seen to forget it. And I regret to say that even Fritz himself at once turned his back on his sister whenever she wanted to talk to him about the wondrous realm in which she had been so happy. Indeed, he is said to have frequently murmured, 'Stupid goose!' between his teeth, though I can scarcely think this compatible with his proved kindness of heart. This much, however, is matter of certainty, that, as he no longer believed what his sister said, he now, on a public parade, formally recanted what he had said to his red hussars, and, in the place of the plumes he had deprived them of, gave them much taller and finer ones of goose quills, and allowed them to sound the march of the hussars of the guard as before.

"Marie did not dare to say anything more of her adventures. But the memories of that fairy realm haunted her with a sweet intoxication, and the music of that delightful, happy country still rang sweetly in her ears. Whenever she allowed her thoughts to dwell on all those glories she saw them again, and so it came about that, instead of playing as she used to do, she sat quiet and meditative, absorbed within herself. Everybody found fault with her for being this sort of little dreamer.

"It chanced one day that Godpapa Drosselmeier was repairing one of the clocks in the house, and Marie was sitting beside the glass cupboard, sunk in her dreams and gazing at Nutcracker. All at once she said, as if involuntarily:

"Ah, dear Mr. Drosselmeier, if you really were alive, *I* shouldn't be like Princess Pirlipat, and despise you because you had had to give up being a nice handsome gentleman for my sake!'

"'Stupid stuff and nonsense!' cried Godpapa Drosselmeier.

"But, as he spoke, there came such a tremendous bang and shock that Marie fell from her chair insensible[1].

---

[1] Many critics argue that Drosselmeier's response to a comment which – using the name "Mr. Drosselmeier" – could just as easily be about him as about his nephew, causes his goddaughter to understand in a moment of clarity that she could harbor the same romantic feelings for the older man, and that he could possibly harbor similar feelings towards her. Many of Freud's case studies involve 19th century women who fainted hysterically when confronted with an psychological symbol of a repressed feeling (for instance, one woman suffered fainting spells connected to her latent sexual attraction to a family friend). The transformation of Nutcracker only comes when Marie connects her feelings for the ugly doll with her feelings for her ugly Godfather. Once she has confronted and dealt with this latent attraction – in spite of the hysterical shock it causes – she is able to move on and transfer her feelings onto his age-appropriate nephew, effectively propelling her into adulthood

"When she came back to her senses her mother was busied about her and said:

"How could you go and tumble off your chair in that way, a big girl like you? Here is Godpapa Drosselmeier's nephew come from Nürnberg. See how good you can be.'

"Marie looked up. Her godpapa had got on his yellow coat and his glass wig, and was smiling in the highest good-humour. By the hand he was holding a very small but very handsome young gentleman. His little face was red and white; he had on a beautiful red coat trimmed with gold lace, white silk stockings and shoes, with a lovely bouquet of flowers in his shirt frill. He was beautifully frizzed and powdered, and had a magnificent queue hanging down his back. The little sword at his side seemed to be made entirely of jewels, it sparkled and shone so, and the little hat under his arm was woven of flocks of silk. He gave proof of the fineness of his manners in that he had brought for Marie a quantity of the most delightful toys—above all, the very same figures as those which the mouse king had eaten up—as well as a beautiful sabre for Fritz[1]. He cracked nuts at table for the whole party; the very hardest did not withstand him. He placed them in his mouth with his left hand, tugged at his pigtail with his right, and crack! they fell in pieces.

"Marie grew red as a rose at the sight of this charming young gentleman; and she grew redder still when, after dinner, young Drosselmeier asked her to go with him to the glass cupboard in the sitting-room.

"'Play nicely together, children,' said Godpapa Drosselmeier; 'now that my clocks are all nicely in order[2], I can have no possible objection.'

"But as soon as young Drosselmeier was alone with Marie, he went down on one knee, and spake as follows:

"'Ah! my most dearly-beloved Miss Stahlbaum! 'see here at your feet the fortunate Drosselmeier, whose life you saved here on this very spot. You were kind enough to say, plainly and unmistakably, in so many words, that you would not have despised me, as Princess Pirlipat did, if I had been turned ugly for your sake. Immediately I ceased to be a contemptible Nutcracker, and resumed my former not altogether ill-looking person and form. Ah! most exquisite lady! bless me with your precious hand; share with me my crown and kingdom, and reign with me in Marchpane Castle, for there I now am king.'

---

[1] He replaces all of the casualties from the affair of the Mouse King, including Marie's dolls and Fritz's colonel's sword

[2] Literally Drosselmeier means that since his work is done there, their playtime won't get in his way, but metaphorically, he appears to be giving his consent to their blooming relationship: since things have been set back to rights – the Mouse King slain and his nephew restored – his work is done and the two can make their own decisions without his influence

"Marie raised him, and said gently:

"'Dear Mr. Drosselmeier, you are a kind, nice gentleman; and as you reign over a delightful country of charming, funny, pretty people, I accept your hand.'

"So then they were formally betrothed; and when a year and a day had come and gone, they say[1] he came and fetched her away in a golden coach, drawn by silver horses. At the marriage there danced two-and-twenty thousand of the most beautiful dolls and other figures, all glittering in pearls and diamonds; and Marie is to this day the queen of a realm where all kinds of sparkling Christmas Woods, and transparent Marchpane Castles—in short, the most wonderful and beautiful things of every kind—are to be seen—by those who have the eyes to see them[2].

ONE of the more curious elements of "Nutcracker and the King of Mice is the relationship between Marie and her eccentric godfather. As previously mentioned, the story borrows much from "don't judge a book by its cover" fairy tales like "Beauty and the Beast," "The Frog Prince," "The Wild Swans," and "King Thrush-Beard" ("König Drosselbart" – the likely source of Drosselmeier's name). Part of the story involves a sort of proxy romance between Marie and a younger version of the old tinker, and while it is overdramatic to suggest that the story is dominated by heavy

[1] This comment brings with it an unavoidably ominous tone. Some translations set it off in parentheses and word it "or so they say," causing us to wonder what is meant by this. One obvious interpretation is that Marie died and was "carried off" by the King of Candyland to a world of eternal imagination – the only respite for an openminded person in such a stodgy, bourgeois family where she is threatened by her parents and betrayed by both her siblings and the godfather who has set her on this journey. A possible explanation of the entire episode is that Marie's wound has become infected and her immune system weakened, causing her hallucinations and estranging her from her family. Within a year the infection proves fatal, and the only person who seems to understand her – her imaginary friend, Nutcracker – embodying Death, returns to take her to paradise

[2] Marie's gift – one not shared by her family – is an ability to see the mythic potential lurking behind reality: she sees things as they are, merging the fantastical with the everyday, and blending the two in such a way that they become indistinguishable. This allows her to put her faith in Nutcracker in spite of his ugliness and in spite of her skepticism. In so doing, she rescues him from the disdain and disregard of the regular world, and summons him from the realm of fantasy into the world of reality. In a sense, Marie actualizes her beliefs, establishing fantasy in the real world through faith and willpower. Like Drosselmeier, she sees the potential in the ordinary, and by believing in it, she actualizes it in her waking life

themes of pedophilia, it difficult to deny that some erotic sublimation is at work in this shadowy, suggestive text. Drosselmeier blushes shamefully when Marie provocatively comments that even the old man would present a striking figure if dressed in Nutcracker's tight uniform, and the moment of transformation (which causes Marie to faint in a fit of Freudian hysteria) comes when she utters the words "Dear Mr. Drosselmeier ... I shouldn't despise you because you had had to give up being a nice, handsome gentleman..." The vaguely addressed declaration could apply to either prepubescent nephew or geriatric uncle, and after Drosselmeier calls such a promise "stuff and nonsense," the sound of his voice (her hearing of which presumably connects the dots for her: that her aged godfather is *also* worthy of love and admiration despite his ugliness and nonconformity) is the harbinger of her fainting fit. Both characters seem to be sublimating unacceptable feelings for the other, but – like in "The King's Betrothed" – they successfully reroute their embarrassing attractions through the redeeming figure of *Young* Drosselmeier, allowing the romance to consummate itself vicariously through a socially acceptable, spiritually profitable medium.

II.

Untoward attractions aside, Hoffmann's Drosselmeier behaves much differently from Tchaikovsky's dotting protector: he frightens Marie several times, startles her with gibberish poems, makes fun of her attachment to Nutcracker, abandons her when she needs support, and has a far more villainous aspect (earning even Nutcracker's glaring disdain). But both characters serve as handlers to their goddaughters – carefully grooming them to serve as the redemptive savior of the Krakatook Saga. Marie notably spies Drosselmeier perched atop his pet grandfather clock, trying to silence the chimes and virtually overseeing (and ensuring) the following battle. He operates as a priest inducting a novice into her vows, presenting barriers to her success, pushing her towards humiliation and isolation, and testing her mettle in the crucible of self-doubt. But Marie excels at each test: she rebukes her materialistic doll Clara, detests the vain Princess Pirlipat, and refuses to exchange Nutcracker's life in return for her childish delights. After being tested three nights in a row by the devilish mouse mutant – like Christ moldering in the tomb – she is proven worthy, given the key to the Mouse-King's destruction, and inducted into the charming world of Candyland, where all of her losses are accounted for by a surplus of indulgences. Both she and Nutcracker are transformed in a redemptive apotheosis that raises them from their respective graves: Nutcracker from the fate of being chronically misunderstood by virtue of his ugliness, and Marie from a life bereft of authenticity, understanding, and belonging. In the Stahlbaum house there is no room for social nonconformity, and while the children are obviously loved and indulged, when Marie insists that her experiences were genuine (and whether they were or not,

Hoffmann wants us to understand that they are *True* – that they reflect the true nature of society whether literally or allegorically), her parents angrily upbraid her and even the once-believing Fritz becomes disgusted with her fantasies. Whether we read the story's ominous, final aside following the report that she was taken off to Candyland by her faithful suitor ("*...or so they say*") as referring to Marie's death, to her unaccountable disappearance, or to being supernaturally spirited away, Hoffmann assures us that by leaving the lifeless, fruitless Stahlbaum (lit. "Steel Tree") universe, she has been saved from a life of repressive predestination. As Jack Zipes observes, while discussing the symbolism of the Stahlbaum name, "[Marie] is imprisoned within the regulations of the family, the family follows rituals in a prescribed way, and she feels somewhat constrained by this." This is the very reality which Drosselmeier attempted to demonstrate to her with the creepy clockwork castle: modern society may *look* luscious and appealing, but behind the prancing postures is a life of mindless servitude, soulless repetition, and purposeless existence.

III.

Although Tchaikovsky's ballet is an unquestionable joy (my wife and I see it every Christmas), it tells a tale of a childish diversion – an imaginative indulgence humored in the coddled mind of a little girl – removing Hoffmann's muscle and grit. The original tale is an existential coming-of-age saga as powerful as *Harry Potter*, as complex as *Alice in Wonderland*, and as poignant as *The Wizard of Oz*. About music, Hoffmann (whom I think would have loved Tchaikovsky's romantic score, if not his pandering libretto) once said:

> "[it] reveals an unknown kingdom to mankind: a world that has nothing in common with the outward, material world that surrounds it, and in which we leave behind all predetermined conceptual feelings in order to give ourselves up to the inexpressible."

The same is true of "Nutcracker and Mouse-King," on the surface a bizarre fairy tale, but beneath which churns emotional fire and biting satire. Meditating on the difference between the story and ballet, Zipes is not quite as forgiving as I have been to Tchaikovsky (or Dumas) for what he did to Hoffmann's original, transgressive parable:

> "There is a great deal of damage done to Hoffmann's story, because at the end of his story, Marie moves off into another world, or it seems that she's going off into another world, a world of her own choosing," he says, "whereas in the ballet, it's a harmless diversion that is full of sort of dancing and merriment, but there's nothing profound in the ending of the ballet as it exists. And it's also true of Dumas' story — ends in a very fluffy, saccharine way."

On the other hand, he notes, Hoffmann's "Nutcracker" is "wild" and subversive. It allows Hoffmann to teach his readers about the importance of character and authenticity, of sacrifice and imagination, and steers them away from the thoughtless violence of Fritz (who lacks compassion), and the heartless vanity of Pirlipat (who lacks empathy). Marie learns to spurn these attitudes in pursuit of an independent, open-minded life guided by her heart and imagination rather than her material wants and vain desires. For Marie, Candyland is not a frilly fantasy of consumption and whim, but a world a creative and spiritual liberty: "a world of imagination, a world of her choice, where she can also make decisions that are more in accord with her own imagination." The process of earning that freedom is grueling, humiliating, and dangerous, and it may have cost her everything, but once she proves herself worthy of Nutcracker's love, the spells of corruption are broken, and the doors of the Living World are flung wide in grateful welcome. As Zipes concludes, she has learned the lesson that all Hoffmann stories are desperate to impart: "it's this essence is in almost all of Hoffmann's fairy tales, and essentially it's that we have to keep in touch with the child within us." The irony, of course, is that for Marie to retain her childlike wonder, she must grow up – she must outgrow her surroundings, the meager offerings of her bourgeois family and her consumerist, industrial society, she must out grow them, turn her back on them, and flee. And by fleeing and maturing, she will have a chance to preserve the childlike innocnce which Hoffmann felt himself -- and his deceased daughter and his married crushes – so cruelly robbed of. She still has a chance, but she must run for it.

WIDELY considered one of Hoffmann's greatest literary achievements, "The Golden Pot" is part mystery, part romance, part thriller, and part artistic philosophy. Biographically speaking, it was one of his first stories – proceeded by the music-inspired pieces "Don Juan" and "Ritter Gluck" – and acts as a lavish celebration of his decision to dedicate his energies towards away from composing and toward creative writing. Few people realize that Hoffmann was a substantive composer during his day – a contemporary of Beethoven and Schubert, though not on their level – whose works are still being played and recorded today (I recommend listening to *E. T. A. Hoffmann Chamber Music* by the Beethoven Trio Ravensburg and *E. T. A. Hoffmann Symphony and Overtures* by the Kölner Academie). Among his most notable pieces are his Symphony in E flat major and the supernatural opera *Undine*. To listen to them today, his music shares much with late Mozart and early Beethoven, and is rich with the passion and optimism of nascent German Romanticism: powerful, succulent, and ennobled. And yet Hoffmann was struggling to hold his head up amidst the crowd of ambitious composers eager to claim the recently-deceased Mozart's mantle for themselves. Disenchanted after years of hard work, he finally made the decision to commit himself to the literary arts and poetry – a medium which he realized would empower him to be far more indulgent and creative than either the visual or musical arts (both of which were scrutinized by the European academies which were not yet open to the experimentation that would eventually lead visionaries like Beethoven, Turner, Stravinsky, and Monet into the idols of rebellious artists everywhere). "The Golden Pot" is a bizarre and psychedelic study of the excesses of imagination: its opportunities, its perils, and its ecstasies. Adrift in a world for which he hardly seems designed, the awkward, luckless Student Anselmus bumbles his way through his bourgeois world too distracted by visions and desires to find meaningful work. When he finally does, it is only in the employment of a world-weary alchemist – like him an exile from the wonderful kingdom of Imagination – who uses his job (transcribing of old manuscripts) as an initiation rite into the indulgent universe that they both belong to. A series of hallucinogenic adventures, transcendental romances, and nightmarish perils lead Anselmus – like Hoffmann – out of the dull, grey world of the Ordinary, triumphantly into the boundless empire of the mind. But whether this story is a soaring celebration of deliverance or a cruel satire of hopeless dreams continues to be hotly debated.

The Golden Pot

— Excerpted from 'Fantasy-Pieces in Callot's Manner,' Volume Two —

{1814}

ON Ascension Day[1], about three o'clock in the afternoon in Dresden, a young man dashed through the Schwarzthor[2], or Black Gate, and ran right into a basket of apples and cookies which an old and very ugly woman had set out for sale. The crash was prodigious; what wasn't squashed or broken was scattered, and hordes of street urchins delightedly divided the booty which this quick gentleman had provided for them. At the fearful shrieking which the old hag began, her fellow vendors, leaving their cake and brandy tables, surrounded the young man, and with plebian violence[3] scolded and stormed at him. For shame and vexation he uttered no word, but merely held out his small and by no means particularly well-filled purse, which the old woman eagerly seized and stuck into her pocket.

The hostile ring of bystanders now broke; but as the young man started off, the hag called after him, "Ay, run, run your way, Devil's Bird! You'll end up in the crystal! The crystal!" The screeching harsh voice of the woman had something unearthly in it: so that the promenaders[4] paused in amazement, and the laughter, which at first had been universal, instantly died away.

The Student Anselmus[5], for the young man was no other, even though he did not in the least understand these singular phrases, felt himself seized with a certain involuntary horror; and he quickened his steps still more, until he was almost running, to escape the curious looks of the multitude, all of whom were staring at him. As he made his way through the crowd of well-dressed people, he heard them muttering on all sides: "Poor young fellow! Ha! What a vicious old witch!" The mysterious words of the old woman, oddly enough, had given this ludicrous adventure a sort of sinister turn; and the youth, previously unobserved, was now regarded with a certain sympathy. The ladies, because of his fine figure and handsome face, which the glow of inward anger rendered still more expressive, forgave him his awkwardness, as well as the dress he wore, though it was at variance with all fashion. His pike-gray frock was shaped as if the tailor had known the modern style only by hearsay; and his well-kept black satin trousers gave him a certain pedagogic[6] air, to which his gait and manner did not at all correspond.

---

[1] A moveable, Christian feast day – celebrating Christ's ascent into heaven after the resurrection – which takes place 40 days after Easter, usually in May. Although many Christian countries have different local customs, in Germany, at least, it is a sort of late-spring bookend to the late-winter Mardi Gras, closing up the eighty-day observances of Lent, Holy Week, and Eastertide – a raucous festival celebrated with great drinking, dances, and parades

[2] A city gate which once stood at Dresden's Albertplatz – on the city's northeast side – and led through the city wall until 1811

[3] Working-class candor (and implied profanity)

[4] Passing pedestrians

[5] A Latinized, German name meaning "under divine protection," which begins as a humorously out of synch name before becoming prophetic

[6] Scholarly, as of a school teacher

The Student had almost reached the end of the alley which leads out to the Linkische Bath[1]; but his breath could no longer stand such a pace. From running, he took to walking; but he still hardly dared to lift an eye from the ground, for he still saw apples and cookies dancing around him, and every kind look from this or that pretty girl seemed to him to be only a continuation of the mocking laughter at the Schwarzthor.

In this mood he reached the entrance of the Bath: groups of holiday people, one after the other, were moving in. Music of wind instruments resounded from the place, and the din of merry guests was growing louder and louder. The poor Student Anselmus was almost ready to weep; since Ascension Day had always been a family festival for him, he had hoped to participate in the felicities of the Linkische paradise; indeed, he had intended even to go to the length of a half portion of coffee with rum and a whole bottle of double beer[2], and he had put more money in his purse than was entirety convenient or advisable. And now, by accidentally kicking the apple-and—cookie basket, he had lost all the money he had with him. Of coffee, of double or single beer, of music, of looking at the pretty girls—in a word, of all his fancied enjoyments there was now nothing more to be said. He glided slowly past; and at last turned down the Elbe road, which at that time happened to be quite empty.

Beneath an elder-tree, which had grown out through the wall, he found a kind green resting place: here he sat down, and filled a pipe from the Sanitätsknaster, or health-tobacco-box[3], of which his friend the Conrector[4] Paulmann had lately made him a present. Close before him rolled and chafed the gold-dyed waves of the fair Elbe: on the other side rose lordly Dresden, stretching, bold and proud, its light towers into the airy sky; farther off, the Elbe bent itself down towards flowery meads and fresh springing woods; and in the dim distance, a range of azure peaks gave notice of remote Bohemia. But, heedless of this, the Student Anselmus, looking gloomily before him, flew forth smoky clouds into the air. His chagrin at length became audible, and he said, "In truth, I am born to losses and crosses[5] for all my life! That, as a boy, I could never guess the right way at Odds and Evens; that my bread and butter always fell on the buttered side-but I won't even mention these sorrows. But now that I've become a student, in spite of Satan, isn't it a frightful fate that I'm still as bumbling as ever? Can I put on a new coat without getting grease on it the first day, or without tearing a cursed hole in it on some nail or other? Can I ever bow to a Councillor or a lady without

---

[1] Built in 1734, just behind the Black Gate on the banks of the Elbe, the Lincke'sche Bath was a popular Dresden restaurant and entertainment center, complete with outside dining, a theater, a concert hall, and open-air spa baths. It was destroyed in World War II bombing

[2] Hoffmann's description of his intention to splurge on these basic drinks is yet another indication that he is poor

[3] It is a medicine box which he has since converted into a tobacco box

[4] Vice-principal

[5] All kinds of mishaps and misery

pitching the hat out of my hands, or even slipping on the smooth pavement, and taking an embarrassing fall? When I was in Halle[1], didn't I have to pay three or four groschen[2] every market day for broken crockery—the Devil putting it into my head to dash straight forward like a lemming[3]? Have I ever got to my college, or any other place that I had an appointment to, at the right time? Did it ever matter if I set out a half hour early, and planted myself at the door, with the knocker in my hand? Just as the clock is going to strike, souse[4]! Some devil empties a wash basin down on me, or I run into some fellow coming out, and get myself engaged in endless quarrels until the time is clean gone.

"Ah, well. Where are you fled now, you blissful dreams of coming fortune, when I proudly thought that I might even reach the height of Geheimrat[5]? And hasn't my evil star[6] estranged me from my best patrons? I had heard, for instance, that the Councillor, to whom I have a letter of introduction, cannot stand hair cut close[7]; with an immensity of trouble the barber managed to fasten a little queue[8] to the back of my head; but at my first bow his unblessed knot comes loose, and a little dog which had been snuffing around me frisks off to the Geheimrat with the queue in its mouth. I spring after it in terror, and stumble against the table, where he has been working while at breakfast; and cups, plates, ink-glass, sandbox[9] crash to the floor and a flood of chocolate and ink covers the report he has just been writing. 'Is the Devil in this man?' bellows the furious Privy Councillor, and he shoves me out of the room.

"What did it matter when Conrector Paulmann gave me hopes of copywork: will the malignant fate, which pursues me everywhere, permit it? Today even! Think of it! I intended to celebrate Ascension Day with cheerfulness of soul. I was going to stretch a point for once. I might have gone, as well as anyone else, into the Linkische Bath, and called out proudly, 'Marqueur[10], a bottle of double beer; best sort, if you please.' I might have sat till far in the evening; and moreover close by this or that fine party of well-dressed ladies. I know it, I feel it! Heart would have come into me, I should have been quite another man; nay, I might have carried it so far, that when one of them asked, 'What time is it?' or 'What is it they are playing?' I would have started up with light grace, and without overturning my glass, or stumbling over the bench, but with a graceful bow, moving a step and a half forward, I would have answered, 'Give me leave, mademoiselle! it is the

---

[1] Capital of Saxony-Anhalt in central Germany
[2] A silver coin, comparable in value to a shilling or a dollar
[3] Small, dim-witted mammals famous for following each other over cliffs
[4] "Splat!"
[5] The highest-ranking advisors of the Holy Roman Emperor
[6] Viz., bad luck
[7] A modern hairstyle at the time, suggestive of trendiness or progressive ideals
[8] The long, tied ponytail men wore in the 18th century
[9] A shaker filled with sand which was sprinkled over wet ink to instantly dry it
[10] Barman, tab-keeper

overture of the Donauweibchen[1]'; or, 'It is just going to strike six.' Could any mortal in the world have taken it ill of me? No! I say; the girls would have looked over, smiling so roguishly; as they always do when I pluck up heart to show them that I too understand the light tone of society, and know how ladies should be spoken to. And now the Devil himself leads me into that cursed apple-basket, and now I must sit moping in solitude, with nothing but a poor pipe of—"

Here the Student Anselmus was interrupted in his soliloquy by a strange rustling and whisking, which rose close by him in the grass, but soon glided up into the twigs and leaves of the elder-tree that stretched out over his head. It was as if the evening wind were shaking the leaves, as if little birds were twittering among the branches, moving their little wings in capricious flutter to and fro. Then he heard a whispering and lisping, and it seemed as if the blossoms were sounding like little crystal bells. Anselmus listened and listened. Ere long, the whispering, and lisping, and tinkling, he himself knew not how, grew to faint and half-scattered words:

"'Twixt this way, 'twixt that; 'twixt branches, 'twixt blossoms, come shoot, come twist and twirl we! Sisterkin, sisterkin! up to the shine; up, down, through and through, quick! Sunrays yellow; evening wind whispering; dewdrops pattering; blossoms all singing: sing we with branches and blossoms! Stars soon glitter; must down: 'twixt this way, 'twixt that, come shoot, come twist, come twirl we, sisterkin!"

And so it went along, in confused and confusing speech. The Student Anselmus thought:

"Well, it is only the evening wind, which tonight truly is whispering distinctly enough." But at that moment there sounded over his head, as it were, a triple harmony of clear crystal bells: he looked up, and perceived three little snakes, glittering with green and gold, twisted around the branches, and stretching out their heads to the evening sun. Then, again, began a whispering and twittering in the same words as before, and the little snakes went gliding and caressing up and down through the twigs; and while they moved so rapidly, it was as if the elder-bush were scattering a thousand glittering emeralds through the dark leaves.

"It is the evening sun sporting in the elder-bush," thought the Student Anselmus; but the bells sounded again; and Anselmus observed that one snake held out its little head to him. Through all his limbs there went a shock like electricity; he quivered in his inmost heart: he kept gazing up, and a pair of glorious dark-blue eyes were looking at him with unspeakable longing; and an unknown feeling of highest blessedness and deepest sorrow nearly rent his heart asunder. And as he looked, and still looked, full of warm desire, into those kind eyes, the crystal bells sounded louder in harmonious accord, and the glittering emeralds fell down and encircled him, flickering round him in a thousand sparkles and sporting in resplendent threads of gold. The elder-bush moved and spoke: "You lay in my shadow; my perfume flowed around you, but you understood it not. The perfume is my speech, when love kindles

[1] An 18th century musical about a seductive mermaid by Ferdinand Kauer

it." The evening wind came gliding past, and said: "I played round your temples, but you understood me not. That breath is my speech, when love kindles it." The sunbeam broke through the clouds, and the sheen of it burned, as in words: "I overflowed you, with glowing gold, but you understood me not. That glow is my speech, when love kindles it."

And, still deeper and deeper sank in the view of those glorious eyes, his longing grew keener, his desire more warm. And all rose and moved around him, as if awakening to glad life. Flowers and blossoms shed their odours round him, and their odour was like the lordly singing of a thousand softest voices, and what they sang was borne, like an echo, on the golden evening clouds, as they flitted away, into far-off lands. But as the last sunbeam abruptly sank behind the hills, and the twilight threw its veil over the scene, there came a hoarse deep voice, as from a great distance:

"Hey! hey! what chattering and jingling is that up there? Hey! hey! who catches me the ray behind the hills? Sunned enough, sung enough. Hey! hey! through bush and grass, through grass and stream. Hey! hey! Come dow-w-n, dow-w-w-n!". So the voice faded away, as in murmurs of a distant thunder; but the crystal bells broke off in sharp discords. All became mute; and the Student Anselmus observed how the three snakes, glittering and sparkling, glided through the grass towards the river; rustling and hustling, they rushed into the Elbe; and over the waves where they vanished, there crackled up a green flame, which, gleaming forward obliquely, vanished in the direction of the city.

Second Vigil

"The gentleman is ill?" said a decent burgher's[1] wife, who returning from a walk with her family, had paused here, and, with crossed arms, was looking at the mad pranks of the Student Anselmus. Anselmus had clasped the trunk of the elder-tree, and was calling incessantly up to the branches and leaves: "O glitter and shine once more, dear gold snakes: let me hear your little bell-voices once more! Look on me once more, kind eyes; O once, or I must die in pain and warm longing!" And with this, he was sighing and sobbing from the bottom of his heart most pitifully; and in his eagerness and impatience, shaking the elder-tree to and fro; which, however, instead of any reply, rustled quite stupidly and unintelligibly with its leaves; and so rather seemed, as it were, to make sport of the Student Anselmus and his sorrows.

"The gentleman is ill!" said the burgher's wife; and Anselmus felt as if someone had shaken him out of a deep dream, or poured ice-cold water on him, to awaken him without loss of time.

He now first saw clearly where he was, and recollected what a strange apparition had assaulted him, nay, so beguiled his senses, as to make him break forth into loud talk with himself. In astonishment, he gazed at the woman, and at last snatching up his hat, which had fallen to the ground in his transport[2], was about to make off in all speed. The burgher himself had come

[1] Gentleman, middle-classed townsman

[2] Ecstasy; joyous trance

toward in the meanwhile, and, setting down the child from his arm on the grass, had been leaning on his staff, and with amazement listening and looking at the Student. He now picked up the pipe and tobacco-box which the Student had let fall, and, holding them out to him, said: "Don't take on so dreadfully, my worthy sir, or alarm people in the dark, when nothing is the matter, after all, but a drop or two of Christian liquor: go home, like a good fellow, and sleep it off."

The Student Anselmus felt exceedingly ashamed; he uttered nothing but a most lamentable Ah!

"Pooh! Pooh!" said the burgher, "never mind it a jot; such a thing will happen to the best; on good old Ascension Day a man may readily enough forget himself in his joy, and gulp down a thought too much. A clergyman himself is no worse for it: I presume, my worthy sir, you are a Candidatus[1]. But, with your leave, sir, I shall fill my pipe with your tobacco; mine was used up a little while ago."

This last sentence the burgher uttered while the Student Anselmus was about to put away his pipe and box; and now the burgher slowly and deliberately cleaned his pipe, and began as slowly to fill it. Several burgher girls had come up: these were speaking secretly with the woman and each other, and tittering as they looked at Anselmus. The Student felt as if he were standing on prickly thorns, and burning needles. No sooner had he got back his pipe and tobacco-box, than he darted off as fast as he could.

All the strange things he had seen were clean gone from his memory; he simply recollected having babbled all sorts of foolish stuff beneath the elder-tree. This was the more frightful to him, as he entertained an inward horror against all soliloquists. It is Satan that chatters out of them, said his Rector; and Anselmus had honestly believed him. But to be regarded as a Candidatus Theologiae, overtaken with drink on Ascension Day! The thought was intolerable... Running on with these mad vexations, he was just about turning up Poplar Alley, by the Kosel garden, when a voice behind him called out: "Herr Anselmus! Herr Anselmus! for the love of Heaven, where are you running in such a hurry?" The Student paused, as if rooted to the ground; for he was convinced that now some new accident would befall him. The voice rose again: "Herr Anselmus, come back: we are waiting for you here at the water!" And now the Student perceived that it was his friend Conrector Paulmann's voice: he went back to the Elbe, and found the Conrector, with his two daughters, as well as Registrator[2] Heerbrand, all about to step into their gondola. Conrector Paulmann invited the Student to go with them across the Elbe, and then to pass the evening at his house in the suburb of Pirna. The Student Anselmus very gladly accepted this proposal, thinking thereby to escape the malignant destiny which had ruled over him all day.

Now, as they were crossing the river, it chanced that on the farther bank in Anton's Garden, some fireworks were just going off. Sputtering and hissing, the rockets went aloft, and their blazing stars flew to pieces in the air,

---

[1] Doctoral student studying divinity with the aim of becoming a clergyman

[2] Registrar

scattering a thousand vague shoots and flashes around them. The Student Anselmus was sitting by the steersman, sunk in deep thought, but when he noticed in the water the reflection of these darting and wavering sparks and flames, he felt as if it were the little golden snakes that were sporting in the flood. All the wonders that he had seen at the elder-tree again started forth into his heart and thoughts; and again that unspeakable longing, that glowing desire, laid hold of him here, which had agitated his bosom before in painful spasms of rapture.

"Ah! is it you again, my little golden snakes? Sing now, O sing! In your song let the kind, dear, dark-blue eyes again appear to me—Ah! are you under the waves, then?"

So cried the Student Anselmus, and at the same time made a violent movement, as if he was about to plunge into the river.

"Is the Devil in you, sir?" exclaimed the steersman, and clutched him by the lapels. The girls, who were sitting by him, shrieked in terror, and fled to the other side of the gondola. Registrator Heerbrand whispered something in Conrector Paulmann's ear, to which the latter answered at considerable length, but in so low a tone that Anselmus could distinguish nothing but the words:

"Such attacks more than once?—Never heard of it." Directly after this, Conrector Paulmann also rose, and then sat down, with a certain earnest, grave, official mien beside the Student Anselmus, taking his hand and saying: "How are you, Herr Anselmus?"

The Student Anselmus was almost losing his wits, for in his mind there was a mad contradiction, which he strove in vain to reconcile. He now saw plainly that what he had taken for the gleaming of the golden snakes was nothing but the reflection of the fireworks in Anton's Garden: but a feeling unexperienced till now, he himself did not know whether it was rapture or pain, cramped his breast together; and when the steersman struck through the water with his helm, so that the waves, curling as in anger, gurgled and chafed, he heard in their din a soft whispering: "Anselmus! Anselmus! do you see how we still skim along before you? Sisterkin looks at you again: believe, believe, believe in us!" And he thought he saw in the reflected light three green-glowing streaks: but then, when he gazed, full of fond sadness, into the water, to see whether those gentle eyes would not look up to him again, he perceived too well that the shine proceeded only from the windows in the neighbouring houses. He was sitting mute in his place, and inwardly battling with himself, when Conrector Paulmann repeated, with still greater emphasis: "How are you, Herr Anselmus?"

With the most rueful tone, Anselmus replied: "Ah! Herr Conrector, if you knew what strange things I have been dreaming, quite awake, with open eyes, just now, under an elder-tree at the wall of Linke's Garden, you would not take it amiss of me that I am a little absent, or so." "Ey, ey, Herr Anselmus!" interrupted Conrector Paulmann, "I have always taken you for a solid young man: but to dream, to dream with your eyes wide open, and then, all at once, to start up and try to jump into the water! This, begging your pardon, is what only fools or madmen would do."

The Student Anselmus was deeply affected by his friend's hard saying; then Veronica, Paulniann's eldest daughter, a most pretty blooming girl of sixteen, addressed her father: "But, dear father, something singular must have befallen Herr Anselmus; and perhaps he only thinks he was awake, while he may have really been asleep, and so all manner of wild stuff has come into his head, and is still lying in his thoughts."

"And, dearest Mademoiselle! Worthy Conrector!" cried Registrator Heerbrand, "may one not, even when awake, sometimes sink into a sort of dream state? I myself have had such fits. One afternoon, for instance, during coffee, in a sort of brown study[1] like this, in the special season of corporeal and spiritual digestion, the place where a lost Act[2] was lying occurred to me, as if by inspiration; and last night, no farther gone, there came a glorious large Latin paper[3] tripping out before my open eyes, in the very same way."

"Ah! most honoured Registrator," answered Conrector Paulmann, "you have always had a tendency to the Poetica[4]; and thus one falls into fantasies and romantic humours."

The Student Anselmus, however, was particularly gratified that in this most troublous situation, while in danger of being considered drunk or crazy, anyone should take his part; and though it was already pretty dark, he thought he noticed, for the first time, that Veronica had really very fine dark blue eyes, and this too without remembering the strange pair which he had looked at in the elder-bush. Actually, the adventure under the elder-bush had once more entirely vanished from the thoughts of the Student Anselmus; he felt himself at ease and light of heart; nay, in the capriciousness of joy, he carried it so far, that he offered a helping hand to his fair advocate Veronica, as she was stepping from the gondola; and without more ado, as she put her arm in his, escorted her home with so much dexterity and good luck that he only missed his footing once, and this being the only wet spot in the whole road, only spattered Veronica's white gown a very little by the incident.

Conrector Paulmann did not fail to observe this happy change in the Student Anselmus; he resumed his liking for him and begged forgiveness for the hard words which he had let fall before. "Yes," added he, "we have many examples to show that certain phantasms may rise before a man, and pester and plague him not a little; but this is bodily disease, and leeches are good for it, if applied to the right part, as a certain learned physician, now deceased, has directed." The Student Anselmus did not know whether he had been drunk, crazy, or sick; but in any case the leeches seemed entirely superfluous, as these supposed phantasms had utterly vanished, and the Student himself was growing happier and happier the more he prospered in serving the pretty Veronica with all sorts of dainty attentions.

As usual, after the frugal meal, there came music; the Student Anselmus had to take his seat before the harpsichord, and Veronica accompanied his

---

[1] A state of profound intellectual focus and absorption

[2] That is, a legal document

[3] An official document – most of which were written in Latin

[4] Poetic ways of expressing things

playing with her pure clear voice: "Dear Mademoiselle," said Registrator Heerbrand, "you have a voice like a crystal bell!"

"That she has not!" ejaculated the Student Anselmus, he scarcely knew how[1]. "Crystal bells in elder-trees sound strangely! strangely!" continued the Student Anselmus, murmuring half aloud.

Veronica laid her hand on his shoulder, and asked: "What are you saying now, Herr Anselmus?"

Instantly Anselmus recovered his cheerfulness, and began playing. Conrector Paulmann gave him a grim look; but Registrator Heerbrand laid a music leaf on the rack, and sang with ravishing grace one of Bandmaster Graun's bravura airs[2]. The Student Anselmus accompanied this, and much more; and a fantasy duet, which Veronica and he now fingered, and Conrector Paulmann had himself composed, again brought everyone into the gayest humour.

It was now pretty late, and Registrator Heerbrand was taking up his hat and stick, when Conrector Paulmann went up to him with a mysterious air, and said: "Hem! Would not you, honoured Registrator, mention to the good Herr Anselmus himself—Hem! what we were speaking of before?"

"With all the pleasure in the world," said Registrator Heerbrand, and having placed himself in the circle, began, without farther preamble, as follows:

"In this city is a strange remarkable man; people say he follows all manner of secret sciences."

But as there are no such sciences, I take him rather for an antiquary, and along with this for an experimental chemist. I mean no other than our Privy Archivarius Lindhorst. He lives, as you know, by himself, in his old isolated house; and when he is away from his office, he is to be found in his library or in his chemical laboratory, to which, however, he admits no stranger. Besides many curious books, he possesses a number of manuscripts, partly Arabic, Coptic, and some of them in strange characters, which do not belong to any known tongue. These he wishes to have copied properly, and for this purpose he requires a man who can draw with the pen, and so transfer these marks to parchment, in Indian ink[3], with the highest exactness and fidelity. The work is to be carried on in a separate chamber of his house, under his own supervision; and besides free board during the time of business, he will

---

[1] That is, why, for what reason

[2] A vocal piece noted for its technical difficulty (requiring daring or bravery – Italian: bravura – on the part of the singer)

[3] Known for its long-lasting nature and bold, black color

pay his copyist a speziesthaler[1], or specie-dollar, daily, and promises a handsome present when the copying is rightly finished. The hours of work are from twelve to six. From three to four, you take rest and dinner.

"Herr Archivarius Lindhorst having in vain tried one or two young people for copying these manuscripts, has at last applied to me to find him an expert calligrapher, and so I have been thinking of you, my dear Anselmus, for I know that you both write very neatly and draw with the pen to great perfection. Now, if in these bad times, and till your future establishment, you would like to earn a speziesthaler every day, and a present over and above your salary, you can go tomorrow precisely at noon, and call upon the Archivarius, whose house no doubt you know. But be on your guard against blots! If such a thing falls on your copy, you must begin it again; if it falls on the original, the Archivarius will think nothing of throwing you out the window, for he is a hot-tempered man."

The Student Anselmus was filled with joy at Registrator Heerbrand's proposal; for not only could the Student write well and draw well with the pen, but this copying with laborious calligraphic pains was a thing he delighted in more than anything else. So he thanked his patron in the most grateful terms, and promised not to fail at noon tomorrow.

All night the Student Anselmus saw nothing but clear speziesthalers, and heard nothing but their lovely clink. Who could blame the poor youth, cheated of so many hopes by capricious destiny, obliged to take counsel about every farthing, and to forego so many joys which a young heart requires! Early in the morning he brought out his black-lead pencils, his crowquills[2], his Indian ink; for better materials, thought he, the Archivarius[3] can find nowhere. Above all, he gathered together and arranged his calligraphic masterpieces and his drawings, to show them to the Archivarius, as proof of his ability to do what was desired. Everything went well with the Student; a peculiar happy star seemed to be presiding over him; his neckcloth sat right at the very first trial; no stitches burst; no loop gave way in his black silk stockings; his hat did not once fall to the dust after he had trimmed it. In a word, precisely at half-past eleven, the Student Anselmus, in his pike-gray frock and black satin lower habiliments, with a

---

[1] A "specie thaler" refers specifically to a high-quality, full-value silver coin based on the standard "Reichsthaler" weight, while a regular "thaler" (worth about $15, but with the purchasing power of a day's wages in 2025 currency) could refer to any coin issued by a particular region, which might have a lower silver content and therefore be worth less than a specie thaler; essentially, a "specie thaler" is a standardized, full-value thaler, while a "thaler" could be a lower-value variant depending on the issuer and time period, probably about $25 or $30, or almost two days' worth of wages

[2] A narrow flexible artist's pen that is usually circular in section at the holder end and that produces a very fine line which can be thickened by slight pressure

[3] Archivist

roll of calligraphic specimens and pen drawings in his pocket, was standing in the Schlossgasse, or Castle Alley, in Conradi's shop[1], and drinking one-two glasses of the best stomachic liqueur[2]; for here, thought he, slapping his pocket, which was still empty, for here speziesthalers will soon be chinking.

Notwithstanding the distance of the solitary street where the Archivarius Lindhorst's ancient residence lay, the Student Anselmus was at the front door before the stroke of twelve. He stood there, and was looking at the large fine bronze knocker; but now when, as the last stroke tingled through the air with a loud clang from the steeple clock of the Kreuzkirche[3], or Church of the Cross, he lifted his hand to grasp this same knocker, the metal visage twisted itself with a horrid rolling of its blue-gleaming eyes, into a grinning smile. Alas, it was the Applewoman of the Schwarzthor! The pointed teeth gnashed together in the loose jaws, and in their chattering through the skinny lips, there was a growl as of "You fool, fool, fool!—Wait, wait!—Why did you run!—Fool!" Horror-struck, the Student Anselmus flew back; he clutched at the door-post, but his hand caught the bell-rope, and pulled it, and in piercing discords it rang stronger and stronger, and through the whole empty house the echo repeated, as in mockery: "To the crystal, fall!" An unearthly terror seized the Student Anselmus, and quivered through all his limbs. The bell-rope lengthened downwards, and became a gigantic, transparent, white serpent, which encircled and crushed him, and girded him straiter and straiter in its coils, till his brittle paralyzed limbs went crashing in pieces and the blood spouted from his veins, penetrating into the transparent body of the serpent and dyeing it red. "Kill me! Kill me!" he wanted to cry, in his horrible agony; but the cry was only a stifled gurgle in his throat. The serpent lifted its head, and laid its long peaked tongue of glowing brass on the breast of Anselmus; then a fierce pang suddenly cut asunder the artery of life, and thought fled away from him. On returning to his senses, he was lying on his own poor truckle-bed[4]; Conrector Paulmann was standing before him, and saying: "For Heaven's sake, what mad stuff is this, dear Herr Anselmus?"

Third Vigil

"The Spirit looked upon the water, and the water moved itself and chafed in foaming billows, and plunged thundering down into the abysses, which opened their black throats and greedily swallowed it. Like triumphant conquerors, the granite rocks lifted their cleft peaky crowns, protecting the valley, till the sun took it into his paternal bosom, and clasping it with his beams as with glowing arms, cherished it and warmed it. Then a thousand germs, which had been sleeping under the desert sand, awoke from their deep slumber, and stretched out their little leaves and stalks towards the sun

---

[1] A pub

[2] Herbal liqueurs thought to aid in digestion, often spiced with such soothing additives peppermint, menthol, cinnamon, cloves, or anise

[3] A Lutheran cathedral built in 1764 in central Dresden, and still standing

[4] A rollout bed which can be stored under a larger bed when not being used

their father's face; and like smiling infants in green cradles, the flowrets rested in their buds and blossoms, till they too, awakened by their father, decked themselves in lights, which their father, to please them, tinted in a thousand varied hues.

"But in the midst of the valley was a black hill, which heaved up and down like the breast of man when warm longing swells it. From the abysses mounted steaming vapours, which rolled themselves together into huge masses, striving malignantly to hide the father's face: but he called the storm to him, which rushed there, and scattered them away; and when the pure sunbeam rested again on the bleak hill, there started from it, in the excess of its rapture, a glorious Fire-lily, opening its fair leaves like gentle lips to receive the kiss of its father.

"And now came a gleaming splendour into the valley; it was the youth Phosphorus; the Lily saw him, and begged, being seized with warm longing love: 'Be mine for ever, fair youth! For I love you, and must die if you forsake me!' Then spoke the youth Phosphorus: 'I will be yours, fair flower; but then, like a naughty child, you will leave father and mother; you will know your playmates no longer, will strive to be greater and stronger than all that now rejoices with you as your equal. The longing which now beneficently warms your whole being will be scattered into a thousand rays and torture and vex you, for sense will bring forth senses; and the highest rapture, which the spark I cast into you kindles, will be the hopeless pain wherein you shall perish, to spring up anew in foreign shape. This spark is thought!'

"'Ah!' mourned the Lily, 'can I not be yours in this glow, as it now burns in me; not still be yours? Can I love you more than now; could I look on you as now, if you were to annihilate me?' Then the youth Phosphorus kissed the Lily; and as if penetrated with light, it mounted up in flame, out of which issued a foreign being, that hastily flying from the valley, roved forth into endless space, no longer heeding its old playmates, or the youth it had loved. This youth mourned for his lost beloved; for he too loved her, it was love to the fair Lily that had brought him to the lone valley; and the granite rocks bent down their heads in participation of his grief.

"But one of these opened its bosom, and there came a black-winged dragon flying out of it, who said: 'My brethren, the Metals are sleeping in there; but I am always brisk and waking, and will help you.' Dashing forth on its black pinions, the dragon at last caught the being which had sprung from the Lily; bore it to the hill, and encircled it with his wing; then was it the Lily again; but thought, which continued with it, tore asunder its heart; and its love for the youth Phosphorus was a cutting pain, before which, as if breathed on by poisonous vapours, the flowrets which had once rejoiced in the fair Lily's presence, faded and died.

"The youth Phosphorus put on a glittering coat of mail, sporting with the light in a thousand hues, and did battle with the dragon, who struck the cuirass with his black wing, till it rung and sounded; and at this loud clang the flowrets again came to life, and like variegated[1] birds fluttered round the

---

[1] Multicolored

dragon, whose force departed; and who, thus being vanquished, hid himself in the depths of the earth. The Lily was freed; the youth Phosphorus clasped her, full of warm longing, of heavenly love; and in triumphant chorus, the flowers, the birds, nay, even the high granite rocks, did reverence to her as the Queen of the Valley."

"By your leave, worthy Herr Archivarius, this is Oriental bombast[1]," said Registrator Heerbrand: "and we beg very much you would rather, as you often do, give us something of your own most remarkable life, of your travelling adventures, for instance; above all, something true."

"What the deuce, then?" answered Archivarius Lindhorst. "True? This very thing I have been telling is the truest I could dish out for you, my friends, and belongs to my life too, in a certain sense. For I come from that very valley; and the Fire-lily, which at last ruled as queen there, was my great-great-great-great-grandmother; and so, properly speaking, I am a prince myself." All burst into a peal of laughter. "Ay, laugh your fill," continued Archivarius Lindhorst. "To you this matter, which I have related, certainly in the most brief and meagre way, may seem senseless and mad; yet, notwithstanding this, it is meant for anything but incoherent, or even allegorical, and it is, in one word, literally true. Had I known, however, that the glorious love story, to which I owe my existence, would have pleased you so little, I might have given you a little of the news my brother brought me on his visit yesterday."

"What, what is this? Have you a brother, then, Herr Archivarius? Where is he? Where does he live? In his Majesty's[2] service too? Or perhaps a private scholar?" cried the company from all quarters.

"No!" replied the Archivarius, quite cool, composedly taking a pinch of snuff, "he has joined the bad side; he has gone over to the Dragons." "What do you mean, dear Herr Archivarius?" cried Registrator Heerbrand: "Over to the Dragons?"-"Over to the Dragons?" resounded like an echo from all hands.

"Yes, over to the Dragons," continued Archivarius Lindhorst: "it was sheer desperation, I believe. You know, gentlemen, my father died a short while ago; it is but three hundred and eighty-five years ago at most, and I am still in mourning for it. He had left me, his favourite son, a fine onyx; this onyx, rightly or wrongly, my brother would have: we quarrelled about it, over my father's corpse; in such unseemly manner that the good man started up, out of all patience, and threw my wicked brother downstairs. This stuck in our brother's stomach[3], and so without loss of time he went over to the Dragons. At present, he lives in a cypress wood, not far from Tunis[4]: he has a famous magical carbuncle to watch there, which a dog of necromancer, who has set up a summerhouse in Lapland[5], has an eye to; so my poor brother only gets away for a quarter of an hour or so, when the necromancer happens to be

---

[1] "Eastern, mystical gobbledygook"

[2] Frederick Augustus I of Saxony

[3] Stuck in his craw; became a bee in his bonnet; ground his gears

[4] A port city on the North African coast, and the capital of Tunisia

[5] The northernmost – and notoriously cold – region of Finland

out looking after the salamander bed in his garden, and then he tells me in all haste what good news there is about the Springs of the Nile[1]."

For the second time, the company burst out into a peal of laughter: but the Student Anselmus began to feel quite dreary in heart; and he could scarcely look in Archivarius Lindhorst's parched countenance, and fixed earnest eyes, without shuddering internally in a way which he could not himself understand. Moreover, in the harsh and strangely metallic sound of Archivarius Lindhorst's voice there was something mysteriously piercing for the Student Anselmus, and he felt his very bones and marrow tingling as the Archivarius spoke.

The special object for which Registrator Heerbrand had taken him into the coffee house, seemed at present not attainable. After that accident at Archivarius Lindhorst's door, the Student Anselmus had withstood all inducements to risk a second visit: for, according to his own heart-felt conviction, it was only chance that had saved him, if not from death, at least from the danger of insanity. Conrector Paulmann had happened to be passing through the street at the time when Anselmus was lying quite senseless at the door, and an old woman, who had laid her cookie-and-apple basket aside, was busied about him. Conrector Paulmann had forthwith called a chair, and so had him carried home. "Think what you will of me," said the Student Anselmus, "consider me a fool or not: I say, the cursed visage of that witch at the Schwarzthor grinned on me from the doorknocker. What happened after I would rather not speak of: but if I had recovered from my faint and seen that infernal Apple-wife beside me (for the old woman whom you talk of was no other), I should that instant have been struck by apoplexy[2], or have run stark mad."

All persuasions, all sensible arguments on the part of Conrector Paulmann and Registrator Heerbrand, profited nothing; and even the blue-eyed Veronica herself could not raise him from a certain moody humour, in which he had ever since been sunk. In fact, these friends regarded him as troubled in mind, and considered ways for diverting his thoughts; to which end, Registrator Heerbrand thought, there could nothing be so serviceable as copying Archivarius Lindhorst's manuscripts. The business, therefore, was to introduce the Student in some proper way to Archivarius Lindhorst; and so Registrator Heerbrand, knowing that the Archivarius used to visit a certain coffee house almost nightly, had invited the Student Anselmus to come every evening to that same coffee house, and drink a glass of beer and smoke a pipe, at his, the Registrator's charge, till such time as Archivarius Lindhorst should in one way or another see him, and the bargain for this copying work be settled; which offer the Student Anselmus had most gratefully accepted. "God will reward you, worthy Registrator, if you bring the young man to reason!" said Conrector Paulmann. "God will reward you!" repeated Veronica,

---

[1] The source of the Nile River wasn't discovered until 1858; prior to this – because of the difficult in navigating it – the Nile's source was as synonymous with mystery and mysticism as "the dark side of the moon"

[2] A stroke

piously raising her eyes to heaven, and vividly thinking that the Student Anselmus was already a most pretty young man, even without any reason... Now accordingly, as Archivarius Lindhorst, with hat and staff, was making for the door, Registrator Heerbrand seized the Student Anselmus briskly by the hand, and stepping to meet the Herr Archivarius, he said: "Most esteemed Herr Archivarius, here is the Student Anselmus, who has an uncommon talent in calligraphy and drawing, and will undertake the copying of your rare manuscripts."

"I am most particularly glad to hear it," answered Archivarius Lindhorst sharply, then threw his three-cocked military hat[1] on his head, and shoving Registrator Heerbrand and the Student Anselmus aside, rushed downstairs with great tumult, so that both of them were left standing in great confusion, gaping at the door, which he had slammed in their faces till the bolts and hinges of it rung again.

"He is a very strange old gentleman," said Registrator Heerbrand. "Strange old gentleman. "

stammered the Student Anselmus, with a feeling as if an ice-stream were creeping over all his veins, and he were stiffening into a statue. All the guests, however, laughed, and said: "Our Archivarius is on his high horse today: tomorrow, you shall see, he will be mild as a lamb again, and won't speak a word, but will look into the smoke-vortexes of his pipe, or read the newspapers; you must not mind these freaks."

"That is true too," thought the Student Anselmus: "who would mind such a thing, after all? Did not the Archivarius tell me he was most particularly glad to hear that I would undertake the copying of his manuscripts; and why did Registrator Heerbrand step directly in his way, when he was going home? No, no, he is a good man at bottom this Privy Archivarius Lindhorst, and surprisingly liberal[2]. A little curious in his figures of speech; but what is that to me? Tomorrow at the stroke of twelve I will go to him, though fifty bronze Apple-wives should try to hinder me!"

Fourth Vigil

Gracious reader, may I venture to ask you a question? Have you ever had hours, perhaps even days or weeks, in which all your customary activities did nothing but cause you vexation and dissatisfaction; when everything that you usually consider worthy and important seemed trivial and worthless? At such a time you did not know what to do or where to turn. A dim feeling pervaded your breast that you had higher desires that must be fulfilled, desires that transcended the pleasures of this world, yet desires which your spirit, like a cowed child, did not even dare to utter. In this longing for an unknown Something, which longing hovered above you no matter where you were, like an airy dream with thin transparent forms that melted away each time you tried to examine them, you had no voice for the world about you. You passed

---

[1] A three-cornered hat, or tricorne, such as are associated with the 18th century

[2] Viz., generous

to and fro with troubled look, like a hopeless lover, and no matter what you saw being attempted or attained in the bustle of varied existence, it awakened no sorrow or joy in you. It was as if you had no share in this sublunary[1] world.

If, favourable reader, you have ever been in this mood, you know the state into which the Student Anselmus had fallen. I wish most heartily, courteous reader, that it were in my power to bring the Student Anselmus before your eyes with true vividness. For in these vigils in which I record his singular history, there is still so much more of the marvellous—which is likely to make the everyday life of ordinary mortals seem pallid—that I fear in the end you will believe in neither the Student Anselmus nor Archivarius Lindhorst; indeed, that you will even entertain doubts as to Registrator Heerbrand and Conrector Paulmann, though these two estimable persons, at least, are still walking the pavements of Dresden. Favourable reader, while you are in the faery region of glorious wonders, where both rapture and horror may be evoked; where the goddess of earnestness herself will waft her veil aside and show her countenance (though a smile often glimmers in her glance, a sportive teasing before perplexing enchantments, comparable to mothers nursing and dandling their children)—while you are in this region which the spirit lays open to us in dreams, make an effort to recognize the well-known forms which hover around you in fitful brightness even in ordinary life. You will then find that this glorious kingdom lies much closer at hand than you ever supposed; it is this kingdom which I now very heartily desire, and am striving to show you in the singular story of the Student Anselmus.

So, as was hinted, the Student Anselmus, ever since that evening when he met with Archivarius Lindhorst, had been sunk in a dreamy musing, which rendered him insensible to every outward touch from common life. He felt that an unknown Something was awakening his inmost soul, and calling forth that rapturous pain, which is even the mood of longing that announces a loftier existence to man. He delighted most when he could rove alone through meads and woods; and as if released from all that fettered him to his necessary life, could, so to speak, again find himself in the manifold images which mounted from his soul.

It happened once that in returning from a long ramble, he passed by that notable elder-tree, under which, as if taken with faery, he had formerly beheld so many marvels. He felt himself strangely attracted by the green kindly sward; but no sooner had he seated himself on it than the whole vision which he had previously seen as in a heavenly trance, and which had since as if by foreign influence been driven from his mind, again came floating before him in the liveliest colours, as if he had been looking on it a second time. Nay, it was clearer to him now than ever, that the gentle blue eyes belonged to the gold-green snake, which had wound itself through the middle of the elder-tree; and that from the turnings of its tapering body all those glorious crystal tones, which had filled him with rapture, must have broken forth. As on Ascension Day, he again clasped the elder-tree to his bosom, and cried into

---

[1] Terrestrial, earthly

the twigs and leaves: "Ah, once more shoot forth, and turn and wind yourself among the twigs, little fair green snake, that I may see you!"

"Once more look at me with your gentle eyes! Ah, I love you, and must die in pain and grief, if you do not return!" All, however, remained quite dumb and still; and as before, the elder-tree rustled quite unintelligibly with its twigs and leaves. But the Student Anselmus now felt as if he knew what it was that so moved and worked within him, nay, that so tore his bosom in the pain of an infinite longing. "What else is it," said he, "but that I love you with my whole heart and soul, and even to the death, glorious little golden snake; nay, that without you I cannot live, and must perish in hopeless woe, unless I find you again, unless I have you as the beloved of my heart. But I know it, you shall be mine; and then all that glorious dreams have promised me of another higher world shall be fulfilled."

Henceforth the Student Anselmus, every evening, when the sun was scattering its bright gold over the peaks of the trees, was to be seen under the elder-bush, calling from the depths of his heart in most lamentable tones into the branches and leaves for a sight of his beloved, of his little gold-green snake. Once as he was going on with this, there suddenly stood before him a tall lean man, wrapped up in a wide light-gray surtout[1], who, looking at him with large fiery eyes, exclaimed: "Hey, hey, what whining and whimpering is this? Hey, hey, this is Herr Anselmus that was to copy my manuscripts." The Student Anselmus felt not a little terrified at hearing this voice, for it was the very same which on Ascension Day had called: "Hey, hey, what chattering and jingling is this," and so forth. For fright and astonishment, he could not utter a word. "What ails you, Herr Anselmus," continued Archivarius Lindhorst, for the stranger was no one else; "what do you want with the elder-tree, and why did you not come to me and set about your work?"

In fact, the Student Anselmus had never yet prevailed upon himself to visit Archivarius Lindhorst's house a second time, though, that evening, he had firmly resolved on doing it. But now at this moment, when he saw his fair dreams torn asunder, and that too by the same hostile voice which had once before snatched away his beloved, a sort of desperation came over him, and he broke out fiercely into these words: "You may think me mad or not, Herr Archivarius; it is all the same to me: but here in this bush, on Ascension Day, I saw the gold-green snake—ah! the beloved of my soul; and she spoke to me in glorious crystal tones; and you, you, Herr Archivarius, cried and shouted horribly over the water."

"How is this, my dear sir?" interrupted Archivarius Lindhorst, smiling quite inexpressibly, and taking snuff.

The Student Anselmus felt his breast becoming easy, now that he had succeeded in beginning this strange story; and it seemed to him as if he were quite right in laying the whole blame upon the Archivarius, and that it was he, and no one else, who had thundered so from the distance. He courageously proceeded: "Well, then, I will tell you the whole mystery that happened to me on Ascension evening; and then you may say and do, and

---

[1] A close-fitting overcoat

think of me whatever you please." He accordingly disclosed the whole miraculous adventure, from his luckless upsetting of the apple basket, till the departure of the three gold-green snakes over the river; and how the people after that had thought him drunk or crazy. "All this," ended the Student Anselmus, "I actually saw with my eyes; and deep in my bosom those dear voices, which spoke to me, are still sounding in clear echo: it was in no way a dream; and if I am not to die of longing and desire, I must believe in these gold-green snakes, though I see by your smile, Herr Archivarius, that you hold these same snakes as nothing more than creatures of my heated and overstrained imagination."

"Not at all," replied the Archivarius, with the greatest calmness and composure; "the gold-green snakes, which you saw in the elder-bush, Herr Anselmus, were simply my three daughters; and that you have fallen over head and ears in love with the blue eyes of Serpentina the youngest, is now clear enough. Indeed, I knew it on Ascension Day myself: and as (on that occasion, sitting busied with my writing at home) I began to get annoyed with so much chattering and jingling, I called to the idle minxes that it was time to get home, for the sun was setting, and they had sung and basked enough."

The Student Anselmus felt as if he now merely heard in plain words something he had long dreamed of, and though he fancied he observed that elder-bush, wall and sward[1], and all objects about him were beginning slowly to whirl around, he took heart, and was ready to speak; but the Archivarius prevented him; for sharply pulling the glove from his left hand, and holding the stone of a ring, glittering in strange sparkles and flames before the Student's eyes, he said: "Look here, Herr Anselmus; what you see may do you good."

The Student Anselmus looked in, and O wonder! the stone emitted a cluster of rays; and the rays wove themselves together into a clear gleaming crystal mirror; in which, with many windings, now flying asunder, now twisted together, the three gold-green snakes were dancing and bounding. And when their tapering forms, glittering with a thousand sparkles, touched each other, there issued from them glorious tones, as of crystal bells; and the midmost of the three stretched forth her little head from the mirror, as if full of longing and desire, and her dark-blue eyes said: "Do you know me, then? Do you believe in me, Anselmus? In belief alone is love: can you love?" "O Serpentina! Serpentina!" cried the Student Anselmus in mad rapture; but Archivarius Lindhorst suddenly breathed on the mirror, and with an electric sputter the rays sank back into their focus; and on his hand there was now nothing but a little emerald, over which the Archivarius drew his glove.

"Did you see the golden snakes, Herr Anselmus?" said the Archivarius.

"Ah, good heaven, yes!" replied the Student, "and the fair dear Serpentina."

"Hush!" continued Archivarius Lindhorst, "enough for now: for the rest, if you decide to work with me, you may see my daughter often enough; or

---

[1] Lawn, grassy turf

rather I will grant you this real satisfaction: if you stick tightly and truly to your task, that is to say, copy every mark with the greatest clearness and correctness. But you have not come to me at all, Herr Anselmus, although Registrator Heerbrand promised I should see you immediately, and I have waited several days in vain."

Not until the mention of Registrator Heerbrand's name did the Student Anselmus again feel as if he was really standing with his two legs on the ground, and he was really the Student Anselmus, and the man talking to him really Archivarius Lindhorst. The tone of indifference, with which the latter spoke, in such rude contrast with the strange sights which like a genuine necromancer he had called forth, awakened a certain horror in the Student, which the piercing look of those fiery eyes, glowing from their bony sockets in the lean puckered visage, as from a leathern case, still farther aggravated: and the Student was again forcibly seized with the same unearthly feeling, which had before gained possession of him in the coffee house, when Archivarius Lindhorst had talked so wildly. With a great effort he retained his self-command, and as the Archivarius again asked, "Well, why did you not come?" the Student exerted his whole energies, and related to him what had happened at the street door.

"My dear Herr Anselmus," said the Archivarius, when the Student was finished; "dear Herr Anselmus, I know this Apple-wife of whom you speak; she is a vicious slut[1] that plays all sorts of vile tricks on me; but that she has turned herself to bronze and taken the shape of a doorknocker, to deter pleasant visitors from calling, is indeed very bad, and truly not to be endured. Would you please, worthy Herr Anselmus, if you come tomorrow at noon and notice any more of this grinning and growling, just be so good as to let a drop or two of this liquor fall on her nose; it will put everything to rights immediately. And now, adieu, my dear Herr Anselmus! I must make haste, therefore I would not advise you to think of returning with me. Adieu, till we meet!—Tomorrow at noon!"

The Archivarius had given the Student Anselmus a little vial, with a gold-coloured fluid in it; and he walked rapidly off; so rapidly, that in the dusk, which had now come on, he seemed to be floating down to the valley rather than walking down to it. Already he was near the Kosel garden[2]; the wind got within his wide greatcoat, and drove its breasts asunder; so that they fluttered in the air like a pair of large wings; and to the Student Anselmus, who was looking full of amazement at the course of the Archivarius, it seemed as if a large bird were spreading out its pinions for rapid flight. And now, while the Student kept gazing into the dusk, a white-gray kite with creaking cry soared up into the air; and he now saw clearly that the white flutter which he had thought to be the retiring Archivarius must have been this very kite, though he still could not understand where the Archivarius had vanished so abruptly.

---

[1] Dirty, grungy, unladylike woman (the sexual connotation didn't apply to this word until much later)

[2] A fashionable park on the banks of the Elbe

"Perhaps he may have flown away in person, this Herr Archivarius Lindhorst," said the Student Anselmus to himself; "for I now see and feel clearly, that all these foreign shapes of a distant wondrous world, which I never saw before except in peculiarly remarkable dreams, have now come into my waking life, and are making their sport of me. But be this as it will! You live and glow in my breast, lovely, gentle Serpentina; you alone can still the infinite longing which rends my soul to pieces. Ah, when shall I see your kind eyes, dear, dear Serpentina!" cried the Student Anselmus aloud.

"That is a vile unchristian name!" murmured a bass voice beside him, which belonged to some promenader returning home. The Student Anselmus, reminded where he was, hastened off at a quick pace, thinking to himself: "Wouldn't it be a real misfortune now if Conrector Paulmann or Registrator Heerbrand were to meet me?"—But neither of these gentlemen met him.

Fifth Vigil

"There is nothing in the world that can be done with this Anselmus," said Conrector Paulmann; "all my good advice, all my admonitions, are fruitless; he will apply himself to nothing; though he is a fine classical[1] scholar too, and that is the foundation of everything."

But Registrator Heerbrand, with a sly, mysterious smile, replied: "Let Anselmus take his time, my dear Conrector! he is a strange subject, this Anselmus, but there is much in him: and when I say much, I mean a Privy Secretary[2], or even a Court Councillor[3], a Hofrath."

"Hof—" began Conrector Paulmann, in the deepest amazement; the word stuck in his throat.

"Hush! hush!" continued Registrator Heerbrand, "I know what I know. These two days he has been with Archivarius Lindhorst, copying manuscripts; and last night the Archivarius meets me at the coffee house, and says: 'You have sent me a proper man, good neighbour! There is stuff in him!' And now think of Archivarius Lindhorst's influence—Hush! hush! we will talk of it this time a year from now." And with these words the Registrator, his face still wrinkled into the same sly smile, went out of the room, leaving the Conrector speechless with astonishment and curiosity, and fixed, as if by enchantment, in his chair.

But on Veronica this dialogue had made a still deeper impression. "Did I not know all along," she thought, "that Herr Anselmus was a most clever and pretty young man, to whom something great would come? Were I but certain that he really liked me! But that night when we crossed the Elbe, did he not press my hand[4] twice? Did he not look at me, in our duet, with such glances that pierced into my very heart? Yes, yes! he really likes me; and I—" Veronica

---

[1] Viz., a student of Greek and Roman literature and language

[2] A private secretary in the service of the royal family

[3] An elite member of the advisory council of high nobles and ecclesiastics, whom the prince consulted at his discretion

[4] "Take me by the hand," "hold my hand"

gave herself up, as young maidens are wont, to sweet dreams of a gay future. She was Mrs. Hofrath, Frau Hofräthinn; she occupied a fine house in the Schlossgasse, or in the Neumarkt, or in the Moritzstrasse[1]; her fashionable hat, her new Turkish shawl, became her admirably; she was breakfasting on the balcony in an elegant negligee, giving orders to her cook for the day: "And see, if you please, not to spoil that dish; it is the Hofrath's favourite." Then passing beaux[2] glanced up, and she heard distinctly: "Well, she is a heavenly woman, that Hofräthinn; how prettily the lace cap[3] suits her!" Mrs. Privy Councillor Ypsilon sends her servant to ask if it would please the Frau Hofräthinn to drive as far as the Linke Bath today? "Many compliments; extremely sorry, I am engaged to tea already with the Presidentinn Tz."[4] Then comes the Hofrath Anselmus back from his office; he is dressed in the top of the mode: "Ten, I declare," cries he, making his gold watch repeat, and giving his young lady a kiss. "How are things, little wife?"

"Guess what I have here for you?" he continues in a teasing manner, and draws from his waistcoat pocket a pair of beautiful earrings, fashioned in the newest style, and puts them on in place of the old ones. "Ah! What pretty, dainty earrings!" cried Veronica aloud; and started up from her chair, throwing aside her work, to see those fair earrings with her own eyes in the glass..."What is this?" said Conrector Paulmann, roused by the noise from his deep study of Cicero's *De Officiis*[5], and almost dropping the book from his hand; "are we taking fits, like Anselmus?" But at this moment, the Student Anselmus, who, contrary to his custom, had not been seen for several days, entered the room, to Veronica's astonishment and terror; for, in truth, he seemed altered in his whole bearing. With a certain precision, which was far from usual in him, he spoke of new tendencies of life which had become clear to his mind, of glorious prospects which were opening for him, but which many did not have the skill to discern. Conrector Paulmann, remembering Registrator Heerhrand's mysterious speech, was still more struck, and could scarcely utter a syllable, till the Student Anselmus, after letting fall some hints of urgent business at Archivarius Lindhorst's, and with elegant adroitness kissing Veronica's hand, was already down the stairs, off and away.

"This was the Hofrath," murmured Veronica to herself: "and he kissed my hand, without sliding on the floor, or treading on my foot, as he used to! He threw me the softest look too; yes, he really loves me!"

Veronica again gave way to her dreaming; yet now, it was as if a hostile shape were still coming forward among these lovely visions of her future

---

[1] Fashionable city districts popular with high-ranking civil servants

[2] Male admirers

[3] Traditionally worn by married women – comparable to saying "that wedding ring suits her!"

[4] "President Tz—." That is, president of the royal privy council. A likely possible name here could be "Tzucker"

[5] "On Duties" – a 44 BC treatise by Marcus Tullius Cicero divided into three books, in which Cicero expounds his conception of the best way to live, behave, and observe moral obligations

household life as Frau Hofräthinn, and the shape were laughing in spiteful mockery, and saying: "This is all very stupid and trashy stuff, and lies to boot; for Anselmus will never, never, be Hofrath or your husband; he does not love you in the least, though you have blue eyes, and a fine figure, and a pretty hand." Then an ice-stream poured over Veronica's soul; and a deep sorrow swept away the delight with which, a little while ago, she had seen herself in the lace cap and fashionable earrings. Tears almost rushed into her eyes, and she said aloud: "Ah! it is too true; he does not love me in the least; and I shall never, never, be Frau Hofräthinn!"

"Romantic idiocy, romantic idiocy!" cried Conrector Paulmann; then snatched his hat and stick, and hastened indignantly from the house. "This was still wanting," sighed Veronica; and felt vexed at her little sister, a girl of twelve years, because she sat so unconcerned, and kept sewing at her frame, as if nothing had happened.

Meanwhile it was almost three o'clock; and now time to tidy up the apartment, and arrange the coffee table: for the Mademoiselles Oster had announced that they were coming. But from behind every workbox which Veronica lifted aside, behind the notebooks which she took away from the harpsichord, behind every cup, behind the coffeepot which she took from the cupboard, that shape peeped forth, like a little mandrake[1], and laughed in spiteful mockery, and snapped its little spider fingers, and cried: "He will not be your husband! he will not be your husband!" And then, when she threw everything away, and fled to the middle of the room, it peered out again, with long nose, in gigantic bulk, from behind the stove, and snarled and growled: "He will not be your husband!"

"Don't you hear anything, don't you see anything?" cried Veronica, shivering with fright, and not daring to touch anything in the room. Fränzchen rose, quite grave and quiet, from her embroidering frame, and said, "What ails you today, sister? You are just making a mess. I must help you, I see."

But at this time the visitors came tripping in in a lively manner, with brisk laughter; and the same moment, Veronica perceived that it was the stove handle which she had taken for a shape, and the creaking of the ill-shut stove door for those spiteful words. Yet, overcome with horror, she did not immediately recover her composure, and her excitement, which her paleness and agitated looks betrayed, was noticed by the Mademoiselles Oster. As they at once cut short their merry talk, and pressed her to tell them what, in Heaven's name, had happened, Veronica was obliged to admit that certain strange thoughts had come into her mind; and suddenly, in open day a dread of spectres, which she did not normally feel, had got the better of her. She

---

[1] A plant whose roots (often with two appendages poking out of the top of the main trunk, which often splits into two more appendages at the bottom) have long been noted for their uncanny resemblance to a small, misshapen human figure, and is embroiled in a great deal of superstition and folklore

described in such lively colours how a little gray mannikin[1], peeping out of all the corners of the room, had mocked and plagued her, that the Mademoiselles Oster began to look around with timid glances, and began to have all sorts of unearthly notions. But Fränzchen entered at this moment with the steaming coffeepot; and the three, taking thought again, laughed outright at their folly.

Angelica, the elder of the Osters, was engaged to an officer; the young man had joined the army; but his friends had been so long without news of him that there was too little doubt of his being dead, or at least grievously wounded. This had plunged Angelica into the deepest sorrow; but today she was merry, even to extravagance, a state of things which so much surprised Veronica that she could not but speak of it, and inquire the reason.

"Darling," said Angelica, "do you fancy that my Victor is out of heart and thoughts? It is because of him I am so happy. O Heaven! so happy, so blessed in my whole soul! For my Victor is well; in a little while he will be home, advanced to Rittmeister[2], and decorated with the honours which he has won. A deep but not dangerous wound, in his right arm, which he got from a sword cut by a French hussar[3], prevents him from writing; and rapid change of quarters, for he will not consent to leave his regiment, makes it impossible for him to send me tidings. But tonight he will be ordered home, until his wound is cured. Tomorrow he will set out for home; and just as he is stepping into the coach, he will learn of his promotion to Rittmeister."

"But, my dear Angelica," interrupted Veronica. "How do you know all this?"

"Do not laugh at me, my friend," continued Angelica; "and surely you will not laugh, for the little gray mannikin, to punish you, might peep out from behind the mirror there. I cannot lay aside my belief in certain mysterious things, since often enough in life they have come before my eyes, I might say, into my very hands. For example, I cannot consider it so strange and incredible as many others do, that there should be people gifted with a certain faculty of prophecy. In the city, here, is an old woman, who possesses this gift to a high degree. She does not use cards, nor molten lead, nor coffee grounds, like ordinary fortune tellers, but after certain preparations, in which you yourself take a part, she takes a polished metallic mirror, and the strangest mixture of figures and forms, all intermingled rise up in it. She interprets these and answers your question. I was with her last night, and got those tidings of my Victor, which I have not doubted for a moment."

Angelica's narrative threw a spark into Veronica's soul, which instantly kindled with the thought of consulting this same old prophetess about Anselmus and her hopes. She learned that the crone was called Frau Rauerin[4],

---

[1] Alternative spelling of mannequin, which – in this instance – means a small human figure like a troll, imp, or fairy

[2] "Promoted to cavalry captain"

[3] Light cavalryman who is uniformed and armed in a distinctively Hungarian fashion

[4] A word meaning "rough/course woman"

and lived in a remote street near the Seethor; that she was not to be seen except on Tuesdays, Thursdays, and Fridays, from seven o'clock in the evening, but then, indeed, through the whole night till sunrise; and that she preferred her customers to come alone. It was now Thursday, and Veronica determined, under pretext of accompanying the Osters home, to visit this old woman, and lay the case before her.

Accordingly, no sooner had her friends, who lived in the Neustadt[1], parted from her at the Elbe Bridge, than she hastened towards the Seethor; and before long, she had reached the remote narrow street described to her, and at the end of it saw the little red house in which Frau Rauerin was said to live. She could not rid herself of a certain dread, nay, of a certain horror, as she approached the door. At last she summoned resolution, in spite of inward terror, and made bold to pull the bell: the door opened, and she groped through the dark passage for the stair which led to the upper story, as Angelica had directed. "Does Frau Rauerin live here?" cried she into the empty lobby as no one appeared; but instead of an answer, there rose a long clear "Mew!" and a large black cat, with its back curved up, and whisking its tail to and fro in wavy coils, stepped on before her, with much gravity, to the door of the apartment, which, on a second mew, was opened.

"Ah, see! Are you here already, daughter? Come in, love; come in!" exclaimed an advancing figure, whose appearance rooted Veronica to the floor. A long lean woman, wrapped in black rags!—while she spoke, her peaked projecting chin wagged this way and that; her toothless mouth, overshadowed by a bony hawk-nose, twisted itself into a ghastly smile, and gleaming cat's-eyes flickered in sparkles through the large spectacles. From a party-coloured clout[2] wrapped round her head, black wiry hair was sticking out; but what deformed her haggard visage to absolute horror, were two large burn marks which ran from the left cheek, over the nose.

Veronica's breathing stopped; and the scream, which was about to lighten her choked breast, became a deep sigh, as the witch's skeleton hand took hold of her, and led her into the chamber.

Here everything was awake and astir; nothing but din and tumult, and squeaking, and mewing, and croaking, and piping all at once, on every hand. The crone struck the table with her fist, and screamed: "Peace, ye vermin!" And the meer-cats[3], whimpering, clambered to the top of the high bed; and the little meer-swine[4] all ran beneath the stove, and the raven fluttered up to the round mirror; and the black cat, as if the rebuke did not apply to him,

---

[1] That is, the New Town – the expanding, fashionable districts surrounding the older, more bohemian city center

[2] Garish, Gypsy-style scarf (literally, a multi-colored cloth; parti-colored is associated with the dazzling, multi-colored clothing associated with gypsies and jesters)

[3] Vervet monkeys

[4] Guinea pigs – though now a cheap, harmless child's pet, this animal was once considered an exotic, dirty rodent

kept sitting at his ease on the cushioned chair, to which he had leapt directly after entering.

So soon as the room became quiet, Veronica took heart; she felt less frightened than she had outside in the hall; nay, the crone herself did not seem so hideous. For the first time, she now looked round the room. All sorts of odious stuffed beasts hung down from the ceiling: strange unknown household implements were lying in confusion on the floor; and in the grate was a scanty blue fire[1], which only now and then sputtered up in yellow sparkles; and at every sputter, there came a rustling from above and monstrous bats, as if with human countenances in distorted laughter, went flitting to and fro; at times, too, the flame shot up, licking the sooty wall, and then there sounded cutting howling tones of woe, which shook Veronica with fear and horror. "With your leave, Mamsell[2]!" said the crone, knitting her brows, and seizing a brush; with which, having dipped it in a copper skillet, she then besprinkled the grate. The fire went out; and as if filled with thick smoke, the room grew pitch-dark: but the crone, who had gone aside into a closet, soon returned with a lighted lamp; and now Veronica could see no beasts or implements in the apartment; it was a common meanly[3] furnished room. The crone came up to her, and said with a creaking voice: "I know what you wish, little daughter: tush, you would have me tell you whether you shall wed Anselmus, when he is Hofrath."

Veronica stiffened with amazement and terror, but the crone continued: "You told me the whole of it at home, at your father's, when the coffeepot was standing before you: I was the coffeepot; didn't you know me? Daughterkin[4], hear me! Give up, give up this Anselmus; he is a nasty creature; he trod my little sons to pieces, my dear little sons, the Apples with the red cheeks, that glide away, when people have bought them, whisk! out of their pockets, and roll back into my basket. He trades with the Old One[5]: it was but the day before yesterday, he poured that cursed Auripigment[6] on my face, and I nearly went blind with it. You can see the burn marks yet. Daughterkin, give him up, give him up! He does not love you, for he loves the gold-green snake; he will never be Hofrath, for he has joined the salamanders, and he means to wed the green snake: give him up, give him up!"

Veronica, who had a firm, steadfast spirit of her own, and could conquer girlish terror, now drew back a step, and said, with a serious resolute tone:

---

[1] Blue fire has long been associated with ghosts, witchcraft, and devilry. The sight of a yellow flame turning blue was thought to herald the arrival of a spirit. In nature it is caused when flames are exposed to stagnant, gassy air, such as might be expected in the cellar of an old, crumbling house, swampy cemetery, or damp crypt – hence the association

[2] Miss (colloquial pronunciation of "mademoiselle")

[3] Cheaply, crudely

[4] Deary, honey (literally, "little daughter")

[5] "Consorts with the Devil"

[6] Yellow arsenic sulfide – a poisonous, yellow-orange pigment used in gold paint and gold-colored ink

"Old woman! I heard of your gift of looking into the future; and wished, perhaps too curiously and thoughtlessly, to learn from you whether Anselmus, whom I love and value, could ever be mine. But if, instead of fulfilling my desire, you keep vexing me with your foolish unreasonable babble, you are doing wrong; for I have asked of you nothing but what you grant to others, as I well know. Since you are acquainted with my inmost thoughts apparently, it might perhaps have been an easy matter for you to unfold to me much that now pains and grieves my mind; but after your silly slander of the good Anselmus, I do not care to talk further with you. Goodnight!"

Veronica started to leave hastily, but the crone, with tears and lamentation, fell upon her knees; and, holding the young lady by the gown, exclaimed: "Veronica! Veronica! have you forgotten old Liese? Your nurse who has so often carried you in her arms, and dandled you?"

Veronica could scarcely believe her eyes; for here, in truth, was her old nurse, defaced only by great age and by the two burns; old Liese, who had vanished from Conrector Paulmann's house some years ago, no one knew where. The crone, too, had quite another look now: instead of the ugly many-pieced[1] clout, she had on a decent cap; instead of the black rags, a gay printed bedgown; she was neatly dressed, as of old. She rose from the floor, and taking Veronica in her arms, proceeded: "What I have just told you may seem very mad; but, unluckily, it is too true. Anselmus has done me much mischief, though it is not his own fault: he has fallen into Archivarius Lindhorst's hands, and the Old One means to marry him to his daughter. Archivarius Lindhorst is my deadliest enemy: I could tell you thousands of things about him, which, however, you would not understand, or at best be too much frightened at. He is the Wise Man, it seems; but I am the Wise Woman: let this stand for that! I see now that you love this Anselmus; and I will help you with all my strength, that so you may be happy, and wed him like a pretty bride, as you wish."

"But tell me, for Heaven's sake, Liese—" interrupted Veronica.

"Hush! child, hush!" cried the old woman, interrupting in her turn: "I know what you would say; I have become what I am, because it was to be so: I could do no other. Well, then! I know the means which will cure Anselmus of his frantic love for the green snake, and lead him, the prettiest Hofrath, into your arms; but you yourself must help."

"Tell me, Liese; I will do anything and everything, for I love Anselmus very much!" whispered Veronica, scarcely audibly.

"I know you," continued the crone, "for a courageous child: I could never frighten you to sleep with the Wauwau[2]; for that instant, your eyes were open to what the Wauwau was like. You would go without a light into the darkest

---

[1] That is, brightly spotted, many-patterned, crazily-designed

[2] Doggy (a child's onomatopoeic name for a dog, like the "bow-wow" or the "arf-arf"). Liese refers to a situation where she would try to scare Veronica into staying in her room at night by threatening that the family dog would take her for a burglar

room; and many a time, with papa's powder-mantle[1], you terrified the neighbours' children. Well, then, if you are in earnest about conquering Archivarius Lindhorst and the green snake by my art; if you are in earnest about calling Anselmus Hofrath and husband; then, at the next Equinox[2], about eleven at night, glide from your father's house, and come here: I will go with you to the crossroads, which cut the fields hard by here: we shall take what is needed, and whatever wonders you may see shall do you no whit of harm. And now, love, goodnight: Papa is waiting for you at supper."

Veronica hastened away: she had the firmest purpose not to neglect the night of the Equinox; "for," thought she, "old Liese is right; Anselmus has become entangled in strange fetters; but I will free him from them, and call him mine forever; mine he is, and shall be, the Hofrath Anselmus."

Sixth Vigil

"It may be, after all," said the Student Anselmus to himself, "that the superfine strong stomachic liqueur, which I took somewhat freely in Monsieur Conradi's, might really be the cause of all these shocking phantasms, which tortured me so at Archivarius Lindhorst's door. Therefore, I will go quite sober today, and so bid defiance to whatever farther mischief may assail me." On this occasion, as before when equipping himself for his first call on Archivarius Lindhorst, the Student Anselmus put his pen-drawings, and calligraphic masterpieces, his bars of Indian ink, and his well-pointed crow-pens, into his pockets; and was just turning to go out, when his eye lighted on the vial with the yellow liquor, which he had received from Archivarius Lindhorst. All the strange adventures he had met again rose on his mind in glowing colours; and a nameless emotion of rapture and pain thrilled through his breast. Involuntarily he exclaimed, with a most piteous voice: "Ah, am not I going to the Archivarius solely for a sight of you, gentle lovely Serpentina!" At that moment, he felt as if Serpentina's love might be the prize of some laborious perilous task which he had to undertake; and as if this task were nothing else but the copying of the Lindhorst manuscripts. That at his very entrance into the house, or more properly, before his entrance, all sorts of mysterious things might happen, as before, was no more than he anticipated.

He thought no more of Conradi's strong drink, but hastily put the vial of liquor in his waistcoat pocket, that he might act strictly by the Archivarius' directions, should the bronze Apple-woman again take it upon her to make faces at him.

---

[1] A poncho-like smock worn when a man was powdering his hair white (as was done in the 18th century) to protect his clothes from getting the white dust on them. This is not unlike a barber's cape (technically called a "chair cloth"). It would, indeed, make a good ghost costume, as Veronica is implied to have used it

[2] The fall equinox occurs in late September, around the 22nd

And the hawk-nose actually did peak itself, the cat-eyes actually did glare from the knocker, as he raised his hand to it, at the stroke of twelve. But now, without farther ceremony, he dribbled his liquor into the pestilent visage; and it folded and moulded itself, that instant, down to a glittering bowl-round knocker. The door opened, the bells sounded beautifully over all the house:

"Klingling[1], youngling, in, in, spring, spring, klingling." In good heart he mounted the fine broad stair; and feasted on the odours of some strange perfume that was floating through the house. In doubt, he paused in the hall; for he did not know at which of these many fine doors he was to knock. But Archivarius Lindhorst, in a white damask nightgown, emerged and said: "Well, it is a real pleasure to me, Herr Anselmus, that you have kept your word at last. Come this way, if you please; I must take you straight into the laboratory." And with this he stepped rapidly through the hall, and opened a little side door, which led into a long passage. Anselmus walked on in high spirits, behind the Archivarius; they passed from this corridor into a hall, or rather into a lordly greenhouse: for on both sides, up to the ceiling, grew all sorts of rare wondrous flowers, indeed, great trees with strangely formed leaves and blossoms. A magic dazzling light shone over the whole, though you could not discover where it came from, for no window whatever was to be seen. As the Student Anselmus looked in through the bushes and trees, long avenues appeared to open into remote distance. In the deep shade of thick cypress groves lay glittering marble fountains, out of which rose wondrous figures, spouting crystal jets that fell with pattering spray into the gleaming lily-cups. Strange voices cooed and rustled through the wood of curious trees; and sweetest perfumes streamed up and down.

The Archivarius had vanished: and Anselmus saw nothing but a huge bush of glowing fire-lilies before him. Intoxicated with the sight and the fine odours of this fairy-garden, Anselmus stood fixed to the spot. Then began on all sides of him a giggling and laughing; and light little voices railed at him and mocked him: "Herr Studiosus[2]! Herr Studiosus! how did you get in here?"

"Why have you dressed so bravely, Herr Anselmus? Will you chat with us for a minute and tell us how grandmamma sat down upon the egg, and young master got a stain on his Sunday waistcoat?—Can you play the new tune, now, which you learned from Daddy Cockadoodle[3], Herr Anselmus?—You look very fine in your glass periwig[4], and brown-paper[5] boots." So cried and chattered and sniggered the little voices, out of every corner, indeed, close by the Student himself, who now observed that all sorts of multicoloured birds were fluttering above him, and jeering at him. At that

---

[1] Ringing

[2] Student

[3] In the German, a more precise translation is "starling"

[4] An 18th century men's wig. This bizarre reference to a wig made out of spun glass is also used to describe Drosselmeier's appearance in "Nutcracker and Mouse-King"

[5] Literally, packing-paper – the kind of brown paper used to wrap packages

moment, the bush of fire-lilies advanced towards him; and he perceived that it was Archivarius Lindhorst, whose flowered nightgown, glittering in red and yellow, had deceived his eyes.

"I beg your pardon, worthy Herr Anselmus," said the Archivarius, "for leaving you alone: I wished, in passing, to take a peep at my fine cactus, which is to blossom tonight. But how do you like my little house-garden?"

"Ah, Heaven! It is inconceivably beautiful, Herr Archivarius," replied the Student; "but these multicoloured birds have been bantering me a little."

"What chattering is this?" cried the Archivarius angrily into the bushes. Then a huge gray Parrot came fluttering out, and perched itself beside the Archivarius on a myrtle bough, and looking at him with an uncommon earnestness and gravity through a pair of spectacles that stuck on its hooked bill, it creaked out: "Don't take it amiss, Herr Archivarius; my wild boys have been a little free or so; but the Herr Studiosus has himself to blame in the matter, for—"

"Hush! hush!" interrupted Archivarius Lindhorst; "I know the varlets[1]; but you must keep them in better discipline, my friend!—Now, come along, Herr Anselmus."

And the Archivarius again stepped forth through many a strangely decorated chamber, so that the Student Anselmus, in following him, could scarcely give a glance at all the glittering wondrous furniture and other unknown things with which all the rooms were filled. At last they entered a large apartment, where the Archivarius, casting his eyes aloft, stood still; and Anselmus got time to feast himself on the glorious sight, which the simple decoration of this hall afforded. Jutting from the azure-coloured walls rose gold-bronze trunks of high palm-trees, which wove their colossal leaves, glittering like bright emeralds, into a ceiling far up: in the middle of the chamber, and resting on three Egyptian lions, cast out of dark bronze, lay a porphyry[2] plate; and on this stood a simple flower pot made of gold, from which, as soon as he beheld it, Anselmus could not turn away his eyes. It was as if, in a thousand gleaming reflections, all sorts of shapes were sporting on the bright polished gold: often he perceived his own form, with arms stretched out in longing—ah! beneath the elder-bush-and Serpentina was winding and shooting up and down, and again looking at him with her kind eyes. Anselmus was beside himself with frantic rapture.

"Serpentina! Serpentina!" he cried aloud; and Archivarius Lindhorst whirled round abruptly, and said: "What, Herr Anselmus? If I am not wrong, you were pleased to call for my daughter; she is in the other side of the house at present, and indeed taking her lesson on the harpsichord. Let us go along."

Anselmus, scarcely knowing what he did, followed his conductor[3]; he saw or heard nothing more till Archivarius Lindhorst suddenly grasped his hand and said: "Here is the place!"

---

[1] Unmanageable, rascally servant boys

[2] A greyish-purple mineral

[3] Escort, guide

Anselmus awoke as from a dream and now perceived that he was in a high room lined on all sides with bookshelves, and nowise differing from a common library and study. In the middle stood a large writing table, with a stuffed armchair before it. "This," said Archivarius Lindhorst, "is your workroom for the present: whether you may work, some other time, in the blue library, where you so suddenly called out my daughter's name, I do not know yet. But now I would like to convince myself of your ability to execute this task appointed you, in the way I wish it and need it." The Student here gathered full courage; and not without internal self-complacence in the certainty of highly gratifying Archivarius Lindhorst, pulled out his drawings and specimens of penmanship from his pocket. But no sooner had the Archivarius cast his eye on the first leaf, a piece of writing in the finest English style, than he smiled very oddly and shook his head. These motions he repeated at every succeeding leaf, so that the Student Anselmus felt the blood mounting to his face, and at last, when the smile became quite sarcastic and contemptuous, he broke out in downright vexation: "The Herr Archivarius does not seem contented with my poor talents."

"My dear Herr Anselmus," said Archivarius Lindhorst, "you have indeed fine capacities for the art of calligraphy; but, in the meanwhile, it is clear enough, I must reckon more on your diligence and good-will, than on your attainments."

The Student Anselmus spoke at length of his often-acknowledged perfection in this art, of his fine Chinese ink, and most select crow-quills. But Archivarius Lindhorst handed him the English sheet, and said: "Be the judge yourself!" Anselmus felt as if struck by a thunderbolt, to see the way his handwriting looked: it was miserable, beyond measure. There was no rounding in the turns, no hair-stroke[1] where it should be; no proportion between the capital and single letters; indeed, villainous schoolboy pot-hooks[2] often spoiled the best lines. "And then," continued Archivarius Lindhorst, "your ink will not last." He dipped his finger in a glass of water, and as he just skimmed it over the lines, they vanished without a trace. The Student Anselmus felt as if some monster were throttling him: he could not utter a word. There stood he, with the unfortunate sheet in his hand; but Archivarius Lindhorst laughed aloud, and said: "Never mind, Herr Anselmus; what you could not do well before you will perhaps do better here. At any rate, you shall have better materials than you have been accustomed to. Begin, in Heaven's name!"

From a locked press[3], Archivarius Lindhorst now brought out a black fluid substance, which diffused a most peculiar odour; also pens, sharply pointed and of strange colour, together with a sheet of special whiteness and smoothness; then at last an Arabic manuscript: and as Anselmus sat down to work, the Archivarius left the room. The Student Anselmus had often copied

---

[1] Fine, thread-like strokes of the pen used in formal calligraphy

[2] A curving, downward-pointing flourish in formal calligraphy – characteristic of German rather than English writing

[3] Cabinet

Arabic manuscripts before; the first problem, therefore, seemed to him not so very difficult to solve.

"How those pot-hooks came into my fine English script, heaven and Archivarius Lindhorst know best," said he; "but that they are not from my hand, I will testify to the death!" At every new word that stood fair and perfect on the parchment, his courage increased, and with it his adroitness. In truth, these pens wrote exquisitely well; and the mysterious ink flowed pliantly, and black as jet, on the bright white parchment. And as he worked along so diligently, and with such strained attention, he began to feel more and more at home in the solitary room; and already he had quite fitted himself into his task, which he now hoped to finish well, when at the stroke of three the Archivarius called him into the side room to a savoury dinner. At table, Archivarius Lindhorst was in an especially good humour. He inquired about the Student Anselmus' friends, Conrector Paulmann and Registrator Heerbrand, and of the latter he had a store of merry anecdotes to tell. The good old Rhenish[1] was particularly pleasing to the Student Anselmus, and made him more talkative than he usually was. At the stroke of four, he rose to resume his labour; and this punctuality appeared to please the Archivarius.

If the copying of these Arabic manuscripts had prospered in his hands before dinner, the task now went forward much better; indeed, he could not himself comprehend the rapidity and ease with which he succeeded in transcribing the twisted strokes of this foreign character[2]. But it was as if, in his inmost soul, a voice were whispering in audible words: "Ah! could you accomplish it, if you were not thinking of her, if you did not believe in her and in her love?" Then there floated whispers, as in low, low, waving crystal tones, through the room: "I am near, near, near! I help you: be bold, be steadfast, dear Anselmus! I toil with you so that you may be mine!" And as, in the fullness of secret rapture, he caught these sounds, the unknown characters grew clearer and clearer to him; he scarcely needed to look at the original at all; nay, it was as if the letters were already standing in pale ink on the parchment, and he had nothing more to do but mark them black. So did he labour on, encompassed with dear inspiring tones as with soft sweet breath, till the clock struck six and Archivarius Lindhorst entered the apartment. He came forward to the table, with a singular smile; Anselmus rose in silence: the Archivarius still looked at him, with that mocking smile: but no sooner had he glanced over the copy, than the smile passed into deep solemn earnestness, which every feature of his face adapted itself to express. He seemed no longer the same. His eyes which usually gleamed with sparkling fire, now looked with unutterable mildness at Anselmus; a soft red tinted the pale cheeks; and instead of the irony which at other times compressed the mouth, the softly curved graceful lips now seemed to be opening for wise and soul-persuading speech. His whole form was higher, statelier; the wide nightgown spread itself like a royal mantle in broad folds

---

[1] Sweet, German white wine from the Rhein region

[2] Letters, script

over his breast and shoulders; and through the white locks, which lay on his high open brow, there wound a thin band of gold.

"Young man," began the Archivarius in solemn tone, "before you were aware of it, I knew you, and all the secret relations which bind you to the dearest and holiest of my interests!"

Serpentina loves you; a singular destiny, whose fateful threads were spun by enemies, is fulfilled, should she become yours and if you obtain, as an essential dowry, the Golden Flower Pot, which of right belongs to her. But only from effort and contest can your happiness in the higher life arise; hostile Principles assail you; and only the interior force with which you withstand these contradictions can save you from disgrace and ruin. While labouring here, you are undergoing a season of instruction: belief and full knowledge will lead you to the near goal, if you but hold fast, what you have begun well. Bear her always and truly in your thoughts, her who loves you; then you will see the marvels of the Golden Pot, and be happy forevermore.

"Farewell! Archivarius Lindhorst expects you tomorrow at noon in his cabinet[1]. Farewell!" With these words Archivarius Lindhorst softly pushed the Student Anselmus out of the door, which he then locked; and Anselmus found himself in the chamber where he had dined, the single door of which led out to the hallway.

Completely stupefied by these strange phenomena, the Student Anselmus stood lingering at the street door; he heard a window open above him, and looked up: it was Archivarius Lindhorst, quite the old man again, in his light-gray gown, as he usually appeared. The Archivarius called to him: "Hey, worthy Herr Anselmus, what are you studying over there? Tush, the Arabic is still in your head. My compliments to Herr Conrector Paulmann, if you see him; and come tomorrow precisely at noon. The fee for this day is lying in your right waistcoat pocket." The Student Anselmus actually found the speziesthaler in the pocket indicated; but he derived no pleasure from it. "What is to come of all this," said he to himself, "I do not know: but if it is some mad delusion and conjuring work that has laid hold of me, my dear Serpentina still lives and moves in my inward heart; and before I leave her, I will die; for I know that the thought in me is eternal, and no hostile Principle can take it from me: and what else is this thought but Serpentina's love?"

Seventh Vigil

At last Conrector Paulmann knocked the ashes out of his pipe, and said: "Now, then, it is time to go to bed." "Yes, indeed," replied Veronica, frightened at her father's sitting so late: for ten had struck long ago. No sooner, accordingly, had the Conrector withdrawn to his study and bedroom, and Franzchen's heavy breathing signified that she was asleep, than Veronica, who to save appearances had also gone to bed, rose softly, softly, out of it again, put on her clothes, threw her mantle round her, and glided out of doors.

Ever since the moment when Veronica had left old Liese, Anselmus had continually stood before her eyes; and it seemed as if a voice that was strange

[1] Office, study

to her kept repeating in her soul that he was reluctant because he was held prisoner by an enemy and that Veronica, by secret means of the magic art, could break these bonds. Her confidence in old Liese grew stronger every day; and even the impression of unearthliness and horror by degrees became less, so that all the mystery and strangeness of her relation to the crone appeared before her only in the colour of something singular, romantic, and so not a little attractive. Accordingly, she had a firm purpose, even at the risk of being missed from home, and encountering a thousand inconveniences, to undertake the adventure of the Equinox. And now, at last, the fateful night, in which old Liese had promised to afford comfort and help, had come; and Veronica, long used to thoughts of nightly wandering, was full of heart and hope. She sped through the solitary streets; heedless of the storm which was howling in the air and dashing thick raindrops in her face.

With a stifled droning clang, the Kreuzthurm clock struck eleven, as Veronica, quite wet, reached old Liese's house. "Are you here, dear! wait, love; wait, love—" cried a voice from above; and in a moment the crone, laden with a basket, and attended by her cat, was also standing at the door. "We will go, then, and do what is proper, and can prosper in the night, which favours the work." So speaking, the crone with her cold hand seized the shivering Veronica, to whom she gave the heavy basket to carry, while she herself produced a little cauldron, a trivet, and a spade. By the time they reached the open fields, the rain had ceased, but the storm had become louder; howlings in a thousand tones were flitting through the air. A horrible heart-piercing lamentation sounded down from the black clouds, which rolled themselves together in rapid flight and veiled all things in thickest darkness. But the crone stepped briskly forward, crying in a shrill harsh voice: "Light, light, my lad!" Then blue forky gleams went quivering and sputtering before them; and Veronica perceived that it was the cat emitting sparks, and bounding forward to light the way; while his doleful ghastly screams were heard in the momentary pauses of the storm. Her heart almost failed; it was as if ice-cold talons were clutching into her soul; but, with a strong effort, she collected herself, pressed closer to the crone, and said: "It must all be accomplished now, come of it what may!"

"Right, right, little daughter!" replied the crone; "be steady, like a good girl; you shall have something pretty, and Anselmus to boot."

At last the crone paused, and said: "Here is the place!" She dug a hole in the ground, then shook coals into it, put the trivet over them, and placed the cauldron on top of it. All this she accompanied with strange gestures, while the cat kept circling round her. From his tail there sputtered sparkles, which united into a ring of fire. The coals began to burn; and at last blue flames rose up around the cauldron. Veronica was ordered to lay off her mantle and veil, and to cower down beside the crone, who seized her hands, and pressed them hard, glaring with her fiery eyes at the maiden. Before long the strange materials (whether flowers, metals, herbs, or beasts, you could not determine), which the crone had taken from her basket and thrown into the cauldron, began to seethe and foam. The crone let go Veronica, then clutched an iron ladle, and plunged it into the glowing mass, which she began to stir, while Veronica, as she directed, was told to look steadfastly into the cauldron and fix her thoughts on Anselmus. Now the crone threw fresh ingredients, glittering pieces of metal, a lock of hair which Veronica had cut from her head, and a little ring which she had long worn, into the pot, while the old woman howled in dread, yelling tones through the gloom, and the cat, in quick, incessant motion, whimpered and whined—I wish very much, favorable reader, that on this twenty-third of September, you had been on the road to Dresden. In vain, when night sank down upon you, the people at the last stage-post tried to keep you there; the friendly host represented to you that the storm and the rain were too bitter, and moreover, for unearthly reasons, it was not safe to rush out into the dark on the night of the Equinox; but you paid no heed to him, thinking to yourself "I will give the postillion[1] a whole thaler[2] as a tip, and so, at latest, by one o'clock I shall reach Dresden. There in the Golden Angel or the Helmet or the City of Naumburg[3] a good supper and a soft bed await me."

And now as you ride toward Dresden through the dark, you suddenly observe in the distance a very strange, flickering light. As you come nearer, you can distinguish a ring of fire, and in its center, beside a pot out of which a thick vapour is mounting with quivering red flashes and sparkles, there sit two very different forms. Right through the fire your road leads, but the horses snort, and stamp, and rear; the postillion curses and prays, and does not spare his whip; the horses will not stir from the spot. Without thinking, you leap out of the stagecoach and hasten forward toward the fire.

And now you clearly see a pretty girl, obviously of gentle birth, who is kneeling by the cauldron in a thin white nightdress. The storm has loosened her braids, and her long chestnut-brown hair is floating freely in the wind. Full in the dazzling light from the flame flickering from beneath the trivet hovers her sweet face; but in the horror which has poured over it like an icy stream, it is stiff and pale as death; and by her updrawn eyebrows, by her mouth, which is vainly opened for the shriek of anguish which cannot find its way from her bosom compressed with unnamable torment-you perceive her terror, her horror. She holds her small soft hands aloft, spasmodically pressed together, as if she were calling with prayers her guardian angel to deliver her from the monsters of the Pit, which, in obedience to this potent spell are to appear at any moment! There she kneels, motionless as a figure of marble. Opposite her a long, shrivelled, copper-yellow crone with a peaked hawk-nose and glistering cat-eyes sits cowering. From the black cloak which is huddled around her protrude her skinny naked arms; as she stirs the Hell-broth, she laughs and cries with creaking voice through the raging, bellowing storm.

I can well believe that unearthly feelings might have arisen in you, too—unacquainted though you are otherwise with fear and dread—at the aspect of

---

[1] A coachman who rides on the left, foremost horse, guiding the team and managing their progress, and blew the horn that cleared the road

[2] Just under a week's worth of wages for a skilled laborer

[3] Various public houses and restaurants

this picture by Rembrandt or Breughel[1], taking place in actual life. Indeed, in horror, the hairs of your head might have stood on end. But your eye could not turn away from the gentle girl entangled in these infernal doings; and the electric stroke that quivered through all your nerves and fibres, kindled in you with the speed of lightning the courageous thought of defying the mysterious powers of the ring of fire; and at this thought your horror disappeared; nay, the thought itself came into being from your feelings of horror, as their product. Your heart felt as if you yourself were one of those guardian angels to whom the maiden, frightened almost to death, was praying; nay, as if you must instantly whip out your pocket pistol and without further ceremony blow the hag's brains out.

But while you were thinking of all of this most vividly, you cried aloud, "Holla!" or "What's the matter here?" or "What's going on there?" The postillion blew a clanging blast on his horn; the witch ladled about in her brewage, and in a trice everything vanished in thick smoke. Whether you would have found the girl, for whom you were groping in the darkness with the most heart-felt longing, I cannot say: but you surely would have destroyed the witch's spell and undone the magic circle into which Veronica had thoughtlessly entered... Alas! Neither you, favourable reader, nor any other man either drove or walked this way, on the twenty-third of September, in the tempestuous witch-favouring night; and Veronica had to abide by the cauldron, in deadly terror, till the work was near its close. She heard, indeed, the howling and raging around her; all sorts of hateful voices bellowed and bleated, and yelled and hummed; but she did not open her eyes, for she felt that the sight of the abominations and the horrors with which she was encircled might drive her into incurable destroying madness. The hag had ceased to stir the pot: its smoke grew fainter and fainter; and at last, nothing but a light spirit-flame[2] was burning in the bottom. Then she cried:

"Veronica, my child! my darling! look into the grounds there! What do you see? What do you see?"

Veronica could not answer, yet it seemed as if all sorts of perplexing shapes were dancing and whirling in the cauldron; and suddenly, with friendly look, reaching her his hand, the Student Anselmus rose from the cavity of the vessel. She cried aloud: "It is Anselmus! It is Anselmus!"

Instantly the crone turned the cock fixed at the bottom of the cauldron, and glowing metal rushed forth, hissing and bubbling, into a little mould which she had placed beside it. The hag now sprang aloft, and shrieked, capering about with wild horrific gestures: "It is done! It is done!"

"Thanks, my pretty lad; did you watch?—Pooh, pooh, he is coming! Bite him to death! Bite him to death!" But then there sounded a strong rushing through the air: it was as if a huge eagle were pouncing down, striking round him with his pinions; and there shouted a tremendous voice:

---

[1] Like Rembrandt, Pieter Bruegel the Elder was among the most significant Dutch artists from the early modern era

[2] The faint, blue flicker of burning alcohol

"Hey, hey, vermin!—It is over! It is over!—Home with you!" The crone sank down with bitter howling, and Veronica's sense and recollection forsook her.

On her returning to herself, it was broad daylight, she was lying in her bed, and Fränzchen was standing before her with a cup of steaming tea and saying to her: "Tell me, sister, what in all the world ails you? I have been standing here this hour, and you have been lying senseless, as if in a fever, and moaning and whimpering so that we were frightened to death. Father has not gone to his class this morning because of you; he will be here directly with the doctor."

Veronica took the tea in silence: and while she was drinking it, the horrid images of the night rose vividly before her eyes. "So it was all nothing but a wild dream that tortured me? Yet last night, I surely went to that old woman; it was the twenty-third of September too? Well, I must have been very sick last night, and so fancied all this; and nothing has sickened me but my perpetual thinking of Anselmus and the strange old woman who gave herself out for Liese, but was no such thing, and only made a fool of me with that story."

Fränzchen, who had left the room, again came in with Veronica's mantle, all wet, in her hand.

"Look, sister," said she, "what a sight your mantle is! The storm last night blew open the shutters and upset the chair where your mantle was hanging; and the rain has come in, and wet it for you."

This speech sank heavy on Veronica's heart, for she now saw that it was no dream which had tormented her, but that she had really been with the witch. Anguish and horror took hold of her at the thought, and a fever-frost quivered through all her frame. In spasmodic shuddering, she drew the bedclothes close over her; but with this, she felt something hard pressing on her breast, and on grasping it with her hand, it seemed like a medallion: she drew it out, as soon as Fränzchen went away with the mantle; it was a little, round, bright-polished metallic mirror. "This is a present from the woman," cried she eagerly; and it was as if fiery beams were shooting from the mirror, and penetrating into her inmost soul with benignant warmth. The fever-frost was gone, and there streamed through her whole being an unutterable feeling of contentment and cheerful delight. She could not but remember Anselmus; and as she turned her thoughts more and more intensely on him, behold, he smiled on her in friendly fashion out of the mirror, like a living miniature portrait. But before long she felt as if it were no longer the image which she saw; no! but the Student Anselmus himself alive and in person. He was sitting in a stately chamber, with the strangest furniture, and diligently writing. Veronica was about to step forward, to pat his shoulder, and say to him: "Herr Anselmus, look round; it is I!" But she could not; for it was as if a fire-stream encircled him; and yet when she looked more narrowly, this fire-stream was nothing but large books with gilt leaves. At last Veronica so far succeeded that she caught Anselmus's eye: it seemed as if he needed, in gazing at her, to bethink himself who she was; but at last he smiled and said: "Ah! Is it you, dear Mademoiselle Paulmann! But why do you like now and then to take the form of a little snake?"

At these strange words, Veronica could not help laughing aloud; and with this she awoke as from a deep dream; and hastily concealed the little mirror, for the door opened, and Conrector Paulmann with Doctor Eckstein entered the room. Dr. Eckstein stepped forward to the bedside; felt Veronica's pulse with long profound study, and then said: "Ey! Ey!" Thereupon he wrote out a prescription; again felt the pulse; a second time said: "Ey! Ey!" and then left his patient. But from these disclosures of Dr. Eckstein's, Conrector Paulmann could not clearly make out what it was that ailed Veronica.

Eighth Vigil

The Student Anselmus had now worked several days with Archivarius Lindhorst; these working hours were for him the happiest of his life; still encircled with lovely tones, with Serpentina's encouraging voice, he was filled and overflowed with a pure delight, which often rose to highest rapture. Every difficulty, every little care of his needy existence, had vanished from his thoughts; and in the new life, which had risen on him as in serene sunny splendour, he comprehended all the wonders of a higher world, which before had filled him with astonishment, nay, with dread.

His copying proceeded rapidly and lightly; for he felt more and more as if he were writing characters long known to him; and he scarcely needed to cast his eye upon the manuscript, while copying it all with the greatest exactness.

Except at the hour of dinner, Archivarius Lindhorst seldom made his appearance; and this always precisely at the moment when Anselmus had finished the last letter of some manuscript: then the Archivarius would hand him another, and immediately leave him, without uttering a word; having first stirred the ink with a little black rod, and changed the old pens for new sharp-pointed ones. One day, when Anselmus, at the stroke of twelve, had as usual mounted the stair, he found the door through which he commonly entered, standing locked and Archivarius Lindhorst came forward from the other side, dressed in his strange flower-figured dressing gown.

He called aloud: "Today come this way, good Herr Anselmus; for we must go to the chamber where the masters of Bhagavadgita[1] are waiting for us."

He stepped along the corridor, and led Anselmus through the same chambers and halls as at the first visit. The Student Anselmus again felt astonished at the marvellous beauty of the garden: but he now perceived that many of the strange flowers, hanging on the dark bushes, were in truth insects gleaming with lordly colours, hovering up and down with their little wings, as they danced and whirled in clusters, caressing one another with their antennae. On the other hand again, the rose and azure-coloured birds

---

[1] The Bhagavadgita is an episode recorded in the great Sanskrit poem of the Hindus, the Mahabharata. It occupies chapters 23 to 40 of Book VI of the Mahabharata and is composed in the form of a dialogue between Prince Arjuna and Krishna, an avatar (incarnation) of the god Vishnu

were odoriferous flowers; and the perfume which they scattered, mounted from their cups in low lovely tones, which, with the gurgling of distant fountains, and the sighing of the high groves and trees, mingled themselves into mysterious accords of a deep unutterable longing. The mock-birds, which had so jeered and flouted him before, were again fluttering to and fro over his head, and crying incessantly with their sharp small voices: "Herr Studiosus, Herr Studiosus, don't be in such a hurry! Don't peep into the clouds so! They may fall about your ears—He! He! Herr Studiosus, put your powdermantle on; cousin Screech-Owl will frizzle your toupee[1]." And so it went along, in all manner of stupid chatter, till Anselmus left the garden.

Archivarius Lindhorst at last stepped into the azure chamber: the porphyry, with the Golden Flower Pot, was gone; instead of it, in the middle of the room, stood a table overhung with violet-coloured satin, upon which lay the writing gear already known to Anselmus; and a stuffed armchair, covered with the same sort of cloth, was placed beside it.

"Dear Herr Anselmus," said Archivarius Lindhorst, "you have now copied for me a number of manuscripts, rapidly and correctly, to my no small contentment: you have gained my confidence; but the hardest is still ahead; and that is the transcribing or rather painting of certain works, written in a peculiar character; I keep them in this room, and they can only be copied on the spot."

"You will, therefore, in future, work here; but I must recommend to you the greatest foresight and attention; a false stroke, or, which may Heaven forfend[2], a blot let fall on the original, will plunge you into misfortune."

Anselmus observed that from the golden trunks of the palm-tree, little emerald leaves projected: one of these leaves the Archivarius took hold of; and Anselmus saw that the leaf was in truth a roll of parchment, which the Archivarius unfolded, and spread out before the Student on the table. Anselmus wondered not a little at these strangely intertwisted characters; and as he looked over the many points, strokes, dashes, and twirls in the manuscript, he almost lost hope of ever copying it. He fell into deep thought on the subject.

"Be of courage, young man!" cried the Archivarius; "if you have continuing belief and true love, Serpentina will help you."

His voice sounded like ringing metal; and as Anselmus looked up in utter terror, Archivarius Lindhorst was standing before him in the kingly form, which, during the first visit, he had assumed in the library. Anselmus felt as if in his deep reverence he could not but sink on his knee; but the Archivarius stepped up the trunk of a palm-tree, and vanished aloft among the emerald leaves. The Student Anselmus perceived that the Prince of the Spirits had been speaking with him, and was now gone up to his study; perhaps intending, by the beams which some of the Planets had despatched to him as envoys, to send back word what was to become of Anselmus and Serpentina.

---

[1] Periwig

[2] Avert, prevent

"It may be too," he further thought, "that he is expecting news from the springs of the Nile; or that some magician from Lapland is paying him a visit: it behooves me to set diligently about my task." And with this, he began studying the foreign characters on the roll of parchment.

The strange music of the garden sounded over him, and encircled him with sweet lovely odours; the mock-birds, too, he still heard giggling and twittering, but could not distinguish their words, a thing which greatly pleased him. At times also it was as if the leaves of the palm-trees were rustling, and as if the clear crystal tones, which Anselmus on that fateful Ascension Day had heard under the elder-bush, were beaming and flitting through the room. Wonderfully strengthened by this shining and tinkling, the Student Anselmus directed his eyes and thoughts more and more intensely on the superscription of the parchment roll; and before long he felt, as it were from his inmost soul, that the characters could denote nothing else than these words: Of the marriage of the Salamander with the green snake. Then resounded a louder triphony[1] of clear crystal bells: "Anselmus! dear Anselmus!" floated to him from the leaves; and, O wonder! on the trunk of the palm-tree the green snake came winding down.

"Serpentina! Serpentina!" cried Anselmus, in the madness of highest rapture; for as he gazed more earnestly, it was in truth a lovely glorious maiden that, looking at him with those dark blue eyes, lull of inexpressible longing, as they lived in his heart, was slowly gliding down to meet him. The leaves seemed to jut out and expand; on every hand were prickles sprouting from the trunk; but Serpentina twisted and wound herself deftly through them; and so drew her fluttering robe, glancing as if in changeful colours, along with her, that, plying round the dainty form, it nowhere caught on the projecting points and prickles of the palm-tree. She sat down by Anselmus on the same chair, clasping him with her arm, and pressing him towards her, so that he felt the breath which came from her lips, and the electric warmth of her frame.

"Dear Anselmus," began Serpentina, "you shall now be wholly mine; by your belief, by your love, you shall obtain me, and I will bring you the Golden Flower Pot, which shall make us both happy forevermore."

"O, kind, lovely Serpentina!" said Anselmus. "If I have you, what do I care for anything else! If you are but mine, I will joyfully give in to all the wonderful mysteries that have beset me since the moment when I first saw you."

"I know," continued Serpentina, "that the strange and mysterious things with which my father, often merely in the sport of his humour, has surrounded you have raised distrust and dread in your mind; but now, I hope, it shall be so no more; for I came at this moment to tell you, dear Anselmus, from the bottom of my heart and soul, everything, to the smallest detail, that you need to know for understanding my father, and so for seeing clearly what your relation to him and to me really is."

---

[1] Three-part harmony

Anselmus felt as if he were so wholly clasped and encircled by this gentle lovely form, that only with her could he move and live, and as if it were but the beating of her pulse that throbbed through his nerves and fibres; he listened to each one of her words till it sounded in his inmost heart, and, like a burning ray, kindled in him the rapture of Heaven. He had put his arm round that daintier than dainty waist; but the changeful glistering cloth of her robe was so smooth and slippery, that it seemed to him as if she could at any moment wind herself from his arms, and glide away. He trembled at the thought.

"Ah, do not leave me, gentlest Serpentina!" cried he; "you are my life."

"Not now," said Serpentina, "till I have told you everything that in your love of me you can comprehend:

"Know then, dearest, that my father is sprung from the wondrous race of the Salamanders; and that I owe my existence to his love for the green snake. In primeval times, in the Fairyland Atlantis, the potent Spirit-prince Phosphorus bore rule; and to him the Salamanders, and other spirits of the elements, were pledged by oath. Once upon a time, a Salamander, whom he loved before all others (it was my father), chanced to be walking in the stately garden, which Phosphorus' mother had decked in the lordliest fashion with her best gifts; and the Salamander heard a tall lily singing in low tones: 'Press down thy little eyelids, till my lover, the Morning-wind, awake thee.' He walked towards it: touched by his glowing breath, the lily opened her leaves: and he saw the lily's daughter, the green snake, lying asleep in the hollow of the flower."

Then was Salamander inflamed with warm love for the fair snake; and he carried her away from the lily, whose perfumes in nameless lamentation vainly called for her beloved daughter throughout all the garden. For the Salamander had borne her into the palace of Phosphorus and was there beseeching him: 'Wed me with my beloved, and she shall be mine forevermore.'—.'Madman, what do you ask?' said the Prince of the Spirits. 'Know that once the Lily was my mistress and bore rule with me; but the Spark, which I cast into her, threatened to annihilate the fair Lily; and only my victory over the black Dragon, whom now the Spirits of the Earth hold in fetters, maintains her, that her leaves continue strong enough to enclose this Spark and preserve it within them. But when you clasp the green snake, your fire will consume her frame; and a new being rapidly arising from her dust, will soar away and leave you.'

"The Salamander heeded not the warning of the Spirit-prince: full of longing ardour he folded the green snake in his arms; she crumbled into ashes; a winged being, born from her dust, soared away through the sky. Then the madness of desperation caught the Salamander; and he ran through the garden, dashing forth fire and flames; and wasted it in his wild fury, till its fairest flowers and blossoms hung down, blackened and scathed; and their lamentation filled the air."

The indignant Prince of the Spirits, in his wrath, laid hold of the Salamander, and said: 'Your fire has burnt out, your flames are extinguished, your rays darkened: sink down to the Spirits of the Earth; let them mock and jeer you, and keep you captive, till the Fire-elements shall again kindle, and beam up with you as with a new being from the Earth.' The poor Salamander sank down extinguished: but now the testy old earth-spirit, who was Phosphorus' gardener, came forth and said: 'Master! who has greater cause to complain of the Salamander than I? Had not all the fair flowers, which he has burnt, been decorated with my gayest metals; had I not stoutly nursed and tended them, and spent many a fair hue on their leaves? And yet I must pity the poor Salamander; for it was but love, in which you, O Master, have full often been entangled, that drove him to despair, and made him desolate the garden. Remit his too harsh punishment!'—'His fire is for the present extinguished,' said the Prince of the Spirits; 'but in the hapless time, when the speech of nature shall no longer be intelligible to degenerate man; when the spirits of the elements, banished into their own regions, shall speak to him only from afar, in faint, spent echoes; when, displaced from the harmonious circle, an infinite longing alone shall give him tidings of the land of marvels, which he once might inhabit while belief and love still dwelt in his soul: in this hapless time, the fire of the Salamander shall again kindle; but only to manhood shall he be permitted to rise, and entering wholly into many necessitous existence, he shall learn to endure its wants and oppressions. Yet not only shall the remembrance of his first state continue with him, but he shall again rise into the sacred harmony of all Nature; he shall understand its wonders, and the power of his fellow-spirits shall stand at his behest. Then, too, in a lily-bush, shall he find the green snake again: and the fruit of his marriage with her shall be three daughters, which, to men, shall appear in the form of their mother. In the spring season these shall disport themselves in the dark elder-bush, and sound with their lovely crystal voices.

And then if, in that needy and mean age of inward stuntedness, there shall be found a youth who understands their song; nay, if one of the little snakes look at him with her kind eyes; if the look awaken in him forecastings of the distant wondrous land, to which, having cast away the burden of the Common, he can courageously soar; if, with love to the snake, there rise in him belief in the wonders of nature, nay, in his own existence amid these wonders, then the snake shall be his.

But not till three youths of this sort have been found and wedded to the three daughters, may the Salamander cast away his heavy burden, and return to his brothers.'—'Permit me, Master,' said the earth-spirit, to make these three daughters a present, which may glorify their life with the husbands they shall find. Let each of them receive from me a flower pot, of the fairest metal which I have; I will polish it with beams borrowed from the diamond; in its glitter shall our kingdom of wonders, as it now exists in the harmony of universal nature be imaged back in glorious dazzling reflection; and from its interior, on the day of marriage, shall spring forth a fire-lily, whose eternal blossoms shall encircle the youth that is found worthy, with sweet wafting odours. Soon too shall he learn its speech, and understand the wonders of our kingdom, and dwell with his beloved in Atlantis itself.'

"Thou perceivest well, dear Anselmus, that the Salamander of whom I speak is no other than my father. In spite of his higher nature, he was forced to subject himself to the paltriest contradictions of common life; and hence, indeed, often comes the wayward humour with which he vexes many. He has told me now and then, that, for the inward make of mind, which the Spirit-prince Phosphorus required as a condition of marriage with me and my sisters, men have a name at present, which, in truth, they frequently enough misapply: they call it a childlike poetic character. This character, he says, is often found in youths, who, by reason of their high simplicity of manners, and their total want of what is called knowledge of the world, are mocked by the common mob. Ah, dear Anselmus! beneath the elder-bush, you understood my song, my look: you love the green snake, you believe in me, and will be mine for evermore! The fair lily will bloom forth from the Golden Flower Pot; and we shall dwell, happy, and united, and blessed, in Atlantis together!

"Yet I must not hide from you that in its deadly battle with the Salamanders and spirits of the earth, the black Dragon burst from their grasp, and hurried off through the air. Phosphorus, indeed, again holds him in fetters; but from the black quills, which, in the struggle, rained down on the ground, there sprang up hostile spirits, which on all hands set themselves against the Salamanders and spirits of the earth. That woman who hates you so, dear Anselmus, and who, as my father knows full well, is striving for possession of the Golden Flower Pot; that woman owes her existence to the love of such a quill (plucked in battle from the Dragon's wing) for a certain beet beside which it dropped. She knows her origin and her power; for, in the moans and convulsions of the captive Dragon, the secrets of many a mysterious constellation are revealed to her; and she uses every means and effort to work from the outward into the inward and unseen; while my father, with the beams which shoot forth from the spirit of the Salamander, withstands and subdues her. All the baneful principles which lurk in deadly herbs and poisonous beasts, she collects; and, mixing them under favourable constellations, raises therewith many a wicked spell, which overwhelms the soul of man with fear and trembling, and subjects him to the power of those demons, produced from the Dragon when it yielded in battle. Beware of that old woman, dear Anselmus! She hates you, because your childlike pious character has annihilated many of her wicked charms. Keep true, true to me; soon you will be at the goal!"

"O my Serpentina! my own Serpentina!" cried the Student Anselmus, "how could I leave you, how should I not love you forever!" A kiss was burning on his lips; he awoke as from a deep dream: Serpentina had vanished; six o'clock was striking, and it fell heavy on his heart that today he had not copied a single stroke. Full of anxiety, and dreading reproaches from the Archivarius, he looked into the sheet; and, O wonder! the copy of the mysterious manuscript was fairly concluded; and he thought, on viewing the characters more narrowly, that the writing was nothing else but Serpentina's story of her father, the favourite of the Spirit-prince Phosphorus, in Atlantis, the land of marvels. And now entered Archivarius Lindhorst, in his light-gray surtout, with hat and staff: he looked into the parchment on which Anselmus had been writing; took a large pinch of snuff, and said with a smile: "Just as I thought!—Well, Herr Anselmus, here is your speziesthaler; we will now go to the Linkische Bath: please follow me!" The Archivarius walked rapidly through the garden, in which there was such a din of singing, whistling, talking, that the Student Anselmus was quite deafened with it, and thanked Heaven when he found himself on the street... Scarcely had they walked twenty paces, when they met Registrator Heerbrand, who companionably joined them. At the Gate, they filled their pipes, which they had upon them:

Registrator Heerbrand complained that he had left his tinder-box behind, and could not strike fire. "Fire!" cried Archivarius Lindhorst, scornfully; "here is fire enough, and to spare!" And with this he snapped his fingers, out of which came streams of sparks, and directly kindled the pipes —"Observe the chemical knack of some men!" said Registrator Heerbrand; but the Student Anselmus thought, not without internal awe, of the Salamander and his history.

In the Linkische Bath, Registrator Heerbrand drank so much strong double beer, that at last, though usually a good-natured quiet man, he began singing student songs in squeaking tenor; he asked everyone sharply, whether he was his friend or not? and at last had to be taken home by the Student Anselmus, long after the Archivarius Lindhorst had gone his ways.

Ninth Vigil

The strange and mysterious things which day by day befell the Student Anselmus, had entirely withdrawn him from his customary life. He no longer visited any of his friends, and waited every morning with impatience for the hour of noon, which was to unlock his paradise. And yet while his whole soul was turned to the gentle Serpentina, and the wonders of Archivarius Lindhorst's fairy kingdom, he could not help now and then thinking of Veronica; nay, often it seemed as if she came before him and confessed with blushes how heartily she loved him; how much she longed to rescue him from the phantoms, which were mocking and befooling him. At times he felt as if a foreign power, suddenly breaking in on his mind, were drawing him with resistless force to the forgotten Veronica; as if he must needs follow her whither she pleased to lead him, nay, as if he were bound to her by ties that would not break. That very night after Serpentina had first appeared to him in the form of a lovely maiden; after the wondrous secret of the Salamander's nuptials with the green snake had been disclosed, Veronica came before him more vividly than ever. Nay, not till he awoke, was he clearly aware that he had only been dreaming; for he had felt persuaded that Veronica was actually beside him, complaining with an expression of keen sorrow, which pierced through his inmost soul, that he should sacrifice her deep true love to fantastic visions, which only the distemper of his mind called into being, and which, moreover, would at last prove his ruin. Veronica was lovelier than he had ever seen her; he could not drive her from his thoughts: and in this perplexed and contradictory mood he hastened out, hoping to get rid of it by a morning walk.

A secret magic influence led him on the Pirna gate: he was just turning into a cross street, when Conrector Paulmann, coming after him, cried out: "Ey! Ey!—Dear Herr Anselmus!—Amice! Amice! Where, in Heaven's name, have you been buried so long? We never see you at all. Do you know, Veronica is longing very much to have another song with you. So come along; you were just on the road to me, at any rate."

The Student Anselmus, constrained by this friendly violence, went along with the Conrector.

On entering the house, they were met by Veronica, attired with such neatness and attention, that Conrector Paulmann, full of amazement, asked her: "Why so decked, Mamsell? Were you expecting visitors? Well, here I bring you Herr Anselmus."

The Student Anselmus, in daintily and elegantly kissing Veronica's hand, felt a small soft pressure from it, which shot like a stream of fire over all his frame. Veronica was cheerfulness, was grace itself; and when Paulmann left them for his study, she contrived, by all manner of rogueries and waggeries, to uplift the Student Anselmus so much that he at last quite forgot his bashfulness, and jigged round the room with the playful girl. But here again the demon of awkwardness got hold of him: he jolted on a table, and Veronica's pretty little workbox fell to the floor. Anselmus lifted it; the lid had flown up; and a little round metallic mirror was glittering on him, into which he looked with peculiar delight. Veronica glided softly up to him; laid her hand on his arm, and pressing close to him, looked over his shoulder into the mirror also. And now Anselmus felt as if a battle were beginning in his soul: thoughts, images flashed out—Archivarius Lindhorst-Serpentina—the green snake—at last the tumult abated, and all this chaos arranged and shaped itself into distinct consciousness. It was now clear to him that he had always thought of Veronica alone; nay, that the form which had yesterday appeared to him in the blue chamber, had been no other than Veronica; and that the wild legend of the Salamander's marriage with the green snake had merely been written down by him from the manuscript, but nowise related in his hearing. He wondered greatly at all these dreams; and ascribed them solely to the heated state of mind into which Veronica's love had brought him, as well as to his working with Archivarius Lindhorst, in whose rooms there were, besides, so many strangely intoxicating odours. He could not help laughing heartily at the mad whim of falling in love with a little green snake; and taking a well-fed Privy Archivarius for a Salamander: "Yes, yes! It is Veronica!" cried he aloud; but on turning round his head, he looked right into Veronica's blue eyes, from which warmest love was beaming. A faint soft Ah! escaped her lips, which at that moment were burning on his.

"O happy I!" sighed the enraptured Student: "What I yesternight but dreamed, is in very deed mine today."

"But will you really marry me, then, when you are a Hofrath?" said Veronica.

"That I will," replied the Student Anselmus; and just then the door creaked, and Conrector Paulmann entered with the words:

"Now, dear Herr Anselmus, I will not let you go today. You will put up with a bad dinner; then Veronica will make us delightful coffee, which we shall drink with Registrator Heerbrand, for he promised to come here."

"Ah, Herr Conrector!" answered the Student Anselmus, "are you not aware that I must go to Archivarius Lindhorst's and copy?"

"Look, Amice!" said Conrector Paulmann, holding up his watch, which pointed to half-past twelve.

The Student Anselmus saw clearly that he was much too late for Archivarius Lindhorst; and he complied with the Conrector's wishes the more readily, as he might now hope to look at Veronica the whole day long, to obtain many a stolen glance, and little squeeze of the hand, nay, even to succeed in conquering a kiss. So high had the Student Anselmus's desires now mounted; he felt more and more contented in soul, the more fully he convinced himself that he should soon be delivered from all these fantasies, which really might have made a sheer idiot of him.

Registrator Heerbrand came, as he had promised, after dinner; and coffee being over, and the dusk come on, the Registrator, puckering his face together, and gaily rubbing his hands, signified that he had something about him, which, if mingled and reduced to form, as it were, paged and titled, by Veronica's fair hands, might be pleasant to them all, on this October evening.

"Come out, then, with this mysterious substance which you carry with you, most valued Registrator," cried Conrector Paulmann. Then Registrator Heerbrand shoved his hand into his deep pocket, and at three journeys, brought out a bottle of arrack[1], two lemons, and a quantity of sugar. Before half an hour had passed, a savoury bowl of punch was smoking on Paulmann's table. Veronica drank their health in a sip of the liquor; and before long there was plenty of gay, good-natured chat among the friends. But the Student Anselmus, as the spirit of the drink mounted into his head, felt all the images of those wondrous things, which for some time he had experienced, again coming through his mind. He saw the Archivarius in his damask dressing gown, which glittered like phosphorus; he saw the azure room, the golden palm-trees; nay, it now seemed to him as if he must still believe in Serpentina: there was a fermentation, a conflicting tumult in his soul. Veronica handed him a glass of punch; and in taking it, he gently touched her hand. "Serpentina! Veronica!" sighed he to himself. He sank into deep dreams; but Registrator Heerbrand cried quite aloud: "A strange old gentleman, whom nobody can fathom, he is and will be, this Archivarius Lindhorst. Well, long life to him! Your glass, Herr Anselmus!"

Then the Student Anselmus awoke from his dreams, and said, as he touched glasses with Registrator Heerbrand: "That proceeds, respected Herr Registrator, from the circumstance, that Archivarius Lindhorst is in reality a Salamander, who in his fury laid waste the Spirit-prince Phosphorus' garden, because the green snake had flown away from him."

"What?" inquired Conrector Paulmann.

---

[1] A rum-like spirit originating from southeast Asia, distilled from coconut sap, rice, and sugarcane

"Yes," continued the Student Anselmus; "and for this reason he is now forced to be a Royal Archivarius; and to keep house here in Dresden with his three daughters, who, after all, are nothing more than little gold-green snakes, that bask in elder-bushes, and traitorously sing, and seduce away young people, like so many sirens."

"Herr Anselmus! Herr Anselmus!" cried Conrector Paulmann, "is there a crack in your brain? In Heaven's name, what monstrous stuff is this you are babbling?"

"He is right," interrupted Registrator Heerbrand: "that fellow, that Archivarius, is a cursed Salamander, and strikes you fiery snips from his fingers, which burn holes in your surtout like red-hot tinder. Ay, ay, you are in the right, brotherkin Anselmus; and whoever says No, is saying No to me!" And at these words Registrator Heerbrand struck the table with his fist, till the glasses rung again.

"Registrator! Are you raving mad?" cried the enraged Conrector. "Herr Studiosus, Herr Studiosus! what is this you are about again?"

"Ah!" said the Student, "you too are nothing but a bird, a screech-owl, that frizzles toupees, Herr Conrector!"

"What?—I a bird?—A screech-owl, a frizzier?" cried the Conrector, full of indignation: "Sir, you are mad, born mad!"

"But the crone will get a clutch of him," cried Registrator Heerbrand.

"Yes, the crone is potent," interrupted the Student Anselmus, "though she is but of mean[1] descent; for her father was nothing but a ragged wing-feather[2], and her mother a dirty beet: but the most of her power she owes to all sorts of baneful creatures, poisonous vermin which she keeps about her."

"That is a horrid calumny[3]," cried Veronica, with eyes all glowing in anger: "old Liese is a wise woman; and the black cat is no baneful creature, but a polished young gentleman of elegant manners, and her cousin-german[4]."

"Can he eat Salamanders without singeing his whiskers, and dying like a snuffed candle?" cried Registrator Heerbrand.

"No! no!" shouted the Student Anselmus, "that he never can in this world; and the green snake loves me, and I have looked into Serpentina's eyes."

"The cat will scratch them out," cried Veronica... "Salamander, Salamander beats them all, all," hallooed Conrector Paulmann, in the highest fury: "But am I in a madhouse? Am I mad myself? What foolish nonsense am I chattering? Yes, I am mad too! mad too!" And with this, Conrector Paulmann started up; tore the peruke[5] from his head, and dashed it against the ceiling of the room; till the battered locks whizzed, and, tangled into utter disorder, it rained down powder far and wide. Then the Student Anselmus and

---

[1] Vulgar

[2] Bat

[3] Slander

[4] Archaic: first cousin, close relation

[5] A short, curled, men's wig popular during the 19th century

Registrator Heerbrand seized the punch-bowl and the glasses; and, hallooing and huzzaing, pitched them against the ceiling also, and the sherds fell jingling and tingling about their ears.

"Vivat the Salamander!—Pereat, pereat the crone!—Break the metal mirror!—Dig the cat's eyes out!—Bird, little bird, from the air-Eheu—Eheu—Evoe—Evoe, Salamander!" So shrieked, and shouted, and bellowed the three, like utter maniacs. With loud weeping, Franzchen ran out; but Veronica lay whimpering for pain and sorrow on the sofa.

At this moment the door opened: all was instantly still; and a little man, in a small gray cloak, came stepping in. His countenance had a singular air of gravity; and especially the round hooked nose, on which was a huge pair of spectacles, distinguished itself from all noses ever seen. He wore a strange peruke too; more like a feather-cap than a wig.

"Ey, many good-evenings!" grated and cackled the little comical mannikin. "Is the Student Herr Anselmus among you, gentlemen?—Best compliments from Archivarius Lindhorst; he has waited today in vain for Herr Anselmus; but tomorrow he begs most respectfully to request that Herr Anselmus does not miss the hour."

And with this, he went out again; and all of them now saw clearly that the grave little mannikin was in fact a gray parrot. Conrector Paulmann and Registrator Heerbrand raised a horselaugh, which reverberated through the room; and in the intervals, Veronica was moaning and whimpering, as if torn by nameless sorrow; but, as to the Student Anselmus, the madness of inward horror was darting through him; and unconsciously he ran through the door, along the streets. Instinctively he reached his house, his garret. Ere long Veronica came in to him, with a peaceful and friendly look, and asked him why, in the festivity, he had so vexed her; and desired him to be upon his guard against figments of the imagination while working at Archivarius Lindhorst's. "Goodnight, goodnight, my beloved friend!" whispered Veronica scarcely audibly, and breathed a kiss on his lips. He stretched out his arms to clasp her, but the dreamy shape had vanished, and he awoke cheerful and refreshed. He could not but laugh heartily at the effects of the punch; but in thinking of Veronica, he felt pervaded by a most delightful feeling. "To her alone," said he within himself, "do I owe this return from my insane whims. Indeed, I was little better than the man who believed himself to be of glass; or the one who did not dare leave his room for fear the hens should eat him, since he was a barleycorn. But so soon as I am Hofrath, I shall marry Mademoiselle Paulmann, and be happy, and there's an end to it."

At noon, as he walked through Archivarius Lindhorst's garden, he could not help wondering how all this had once appeared so strange and marvellous. He now saw nothing that was not common; earthen flowerpots, quantities of geraniums, myrtles, and the like. Instead of the glittering multi-coloured birds which used to flout him, there were nothing but a few sparrows, fluttering hither and thither, which raised an unpleasant unintelligible cry at sight of Anselmus.

The azure room also had quite a different look; and he could not understand how that glaring blue, and those unnatural golden trunks of palm-trees, with their shapeless glistening leaves, should ever have pleased him for a moment. The Archivarius looked at him with a most peculiar ironic smile, and asked: "Well, how did you like the punch last night, good Anselmus?" "Ah, doubtless you have heard from the gray parrot how—" answered the Student Anselmus, quite ashamed; but he stopped short, thinking that this appearance of the parrot was all a piece of jugglery.

"I was there myself," said Archivarius Lindhorst; "didn't you see me? But, among the mad pranks you were playing, I almost got lamed: for I was sitting in the punch bowl, at the very moment when Registrator Heerbrand laid hands on it, to dash it against the ceiling; and I had to make a quick retreat into the Conrector's pipehead[1]. Now, adieu, Herr Anselmus! Be diligent at your task; for the lost day you shall also have a speziesthaler, because you worked so well before."

"How can the Archivarius babble such mad stuff?" thought the Student Anselmus, sitting down at the table to begin the copying of the manuscript, which Archivarius Lindhorst had as usual spread out before him. But on the parchment roll, he perceived so many strange crabbed strokes and twirls all twisted together in inexplicable confusion, offering no resting point for the eye, that it seemed to him well nigh impossible to copy all this exactly. Nay, in glancing over the whole, you might have thought the parchment was nothing but a piece of thickly veined marble, or a stone sprinkled over with lichens. Nevertheless he determined to do his utmost; and boldly dipped in his pen: but the ink would not run, do what he liked; impatiently he flicked the point of his pen against his fingernail, and—Heaven and Earth!—a huge blot fell on the outspread original!

Hissing and foaming, a blue flash rose from the blot; and crackling and wavering, shot through the room to the ceiling. Then a thick vapour rolled from the walls; the leaves began to rustle, as if shaken by a tempest; and down out of them darted glaring basilisks[2] in sparkling fire; these kindled the vapour, and the bickering masses of flame rolled round Anselmus. The golden trunks of the palm-trees became gigantic snakes, which knocked their frightful heads together with piercing metallic clang; and wound their scaly bodies round Anselmus.

"Madman! suffer now the punishment of what, in capricious irreverence, thou hast done!" cried the frightful voice of the crowned Salamander, who appeared above the snakes like a glittering beam in the midst of the flame: and now the yawning jaws of the snakes poured forth cataracts of fire on Anselmus; and it was as if the fire-streams were congealing about his body, and changing into a firm ice-cold mass. But while Anselmus's limbs, more and more pressed together, and contracted, stiffened into powerlessness, his senses passed away. On returning to himself he could not stir a joint: he was as if surrounded with a glistening brightness, on which he struck if he but

[1] That is, the bowl of his smoking pipe

[2] A legendary, European reptile reputed to be a serpent king, who causes death to those who look into its eyes

tried to lift his hand— Alas! He was sitting in a well-corked crystal bottle, on a shelf in the library of Archivarius Lindhorst.

Tenth Vigil

I am probably right in doubting, gracious reader, that you were ever sealed up in a glass bottle, or even that you have ever been oppressed with such sorcery in your most vivid dreams. If you have had such dreams, you will understand the Student Anselmus's woe and will feel it keenly enough; but if you have not, then your flying imagination, for the sake of Anselmus and me, will have to be obliging enough to enclose itself for a few moments in the crystal. You are drowned in dazzling splendour; everything around you appears illuminated and begirt[1] with beaming rainbow hues: in the sheen everything seems to quiver and waver and clang and drone. You are swimming, but you are powerless and cannot move, as if you were imbedded in a firmly congealed ether which squeezes you so tightly that it is in vain that your spirit commands your dead and stiffened body. Heavier and heavier the mountainous burden lies on you; more and more every breath exhausts the tiny bit of air that still plays up and down in the tight space around you; your pulse throbs madly; and cut through with horrid anguish, every nerve is quivering and bleeding in your dead agony.

Favourable reader, have pity on the Student Anselmus! This inexpressible torture seized him in his glass prison: but he felt too well that even death could not release him, for when he had fainted with pain, he awoke again to new wretchedness when the morning sun shone into the room. He could move no limb, and his thoughts struck against the glass, stunning him with discordant clang; and instead of the words which the spirit used to speak from within him he now heard only the stifled din of madness. Then he exclaimed in his despair: "O Serpentina! Serpentina! Save me from this agony of Hell!" And it was as if faint sighs breathed around him, which spread like transparent green elder-leaves over the glass; the clanging ceased; the dazzling, perplexing glitter was gone, and he breathed more freely.

"Haven't I myself solely to blame for my misery? Ah! Haven't I sinned against you, kind, beloved Serpentina? Haven't I raised vile doubts of you? Haven't I lost my belief, and with it, all, all that was to make me so blessed? Ah! You will now never, never be mine; for me the Golden Pot is lost, and I shall not behold its wonders any more. Ah, could I but see you but once more; but once more hear your kind, sweet voice, lovely Serpentina!"

So wailed the Student Anselmus, caught with deep piercing sorrow: then a voice spoke close by him: "What the devil ails you, Herr Studiosus? What makes you lament so, out of all compass and measure?"

The Student Anselmus now perceived that on the same shelf with him were five other bottles, in which he perceived three Kreuzkirche Scholars, and two Law Clerks.

"Ah, gentlemen, my fellows in misery," cried he, "how is it possible for you to be so calm, nay, so happy, as I read in your cheerful looks? You are

---

[1] Ringed, encircled

sitting here corked up in glass bottles, as well as I, and cannot move a finger, nay, not think a reasonable thought, but there rises such a murder-tumult[1] of clanging and droning, and in your head itself a tumbling and rumbling enough to drive one mad. But of course you do not believe in the Salamander, or the green snake."

"You are pleased to jest, Mein Herr Studiosus," replied a Kreuzkirche Scholar; "we have never been better off than at present: for the speziesthalers which the mad Archivarius gave us for all kinds of pot-hook copies, are chinking in our pockets; we have now no Italian choruses to learn by heart; we go every day to Joseph's or other beer gardens, where the double-beer is sufficient, and we can look a pretty girl in the face; so we sing like real Students, *Gaudeamus igitur*[2], and are contented!"

"They of the Cross are quite right," added a Law Clerk; "I too am well furnished with speziesthalers, like my dearest colleague beside me here; and we now diligently walk about on the Weinberg[3], instead of scurvy law-copying within four walls."

"But, my best, worthiest masters!" said the Student Anselmus, "do you not observe, then, that you are all and sundry corked up in glass bottles, and cannot for your hearts walk a hairsbreadth?"

Here the Kreuzkirche Scholars and the Law Clerks set up a loud laugh, and cried: "The Student is mad; he fancies himself to be sitting in a glass bottle, and is standing on the Elbe Bridge and looking right down into the water. Let us go on our way!"

"Ah!" sighed the Student, "they have never seen the kind Serpentina; they do not know what Freedom, and life in Love, and Belief, signify; and so by reason of their folly and low-mindedness, they do not feel the oppression of the imprisonment into which the Salamander has cast them. But I, unhappy I, must perish in want and woe, if she whom I so inexpressibly love does not rescue me!"

Then, waving in faint tinkles, Serpentina's voice flitted through the room: "Anselmus! Believe, love, hope!" And every tone beamed into Anselmus's prison; and the crystal yielded to his pressure and expanded, till the breast of the captive could move and heave.

The torment of his situation became less and less, and he saw clearly that Serpentina still loved him; and that it was she alone, who had rendered his confinement tolerable. He disturbed himself no more about his inane

---

[1] A violent, tumultuous sound, as of someone frightening off an attacker while they are being murdered

[2] "Gaudeamus igitur" ("So Let Us Rejoice") is a popular German commencement song, making it comparable to "Pomp and Circumstance" in English-speaking countries. Despite its use as a formal graduation ode, it's lyrics sound like those of a drinking song: a light-hearted that makes fun of college life and celebrates the German virtues of "Wein, Weib, und Gesang": "Wine, Women, and Song"

[3] A shady lane in a posh neighborhood popular with members of high society and civil servants

companions in misfortune; but directed all his thoughts and meditations on the gentle Serpentina. Suddenly, however, there arose on the other side a dull, croaking repulsive murmur. Before long he could observe that it came from an old coffeepot, with half-broken lid, standing opposite him on a little shelf. As he looked at it more narrowly, the ugly features of a wrinkled old woman unfolded themselves gradually; and in a few moments the Apple-wife of the Schwarzthor stood before him. She grinned and laughed at him, and cried with screeching voice:

"Ey, ey, my pretty boy, must you lie in limbo now? In the crystal you ended! Didn't I tell you so long ago?"

"Mock and jeer me, you cursed witch!" said Anselmus, "you are to blame for it all; but the Salamander will catch you, you vile beet!"

"Ho, ho!" replied the crone, "not so proud, my fine copyist. You have squashed my little sons and you have scarred my nose; but I still love you, you knave, for once you were a pretty fellow, and my little daughter likes you, too. Out of the crystal you will never get unless I help you: I cannot climb up there, but my friend the rat, that lives close behind you, will eat the shelf in two; you will jingle down, and I shall catch you in my apron so that your nose doesn't get broken or your fine sleek face get injured at all. Then I will carry you to Mamsell Veronica, and you shall marry her when you become Hofrath."

"Get away, you devil's brood!" shouted the Student Anselmus in fury. "It was you alone and your hellish arts that made me commit the sin which I must now expiate[1]. But I will bear it all patiently: for only here can I be encircled with Serpentina's love and consolation. Listen to me, you hag, and despair! I defy your power: I love Serpentina and none but her forever. I will not become Hofrath, I will not look at Veronica; by your means she is enticing me to evil. If the green snake cannot be mine, I will die in sorrow and longing. Away, filthy buzzard!"

The crone laughed, till the chamber rang: "Sit and die then," cried she: "but now it is time to set to work; for I have other trade to follow here." She threw off her black cloak, and so stood in hideous nakedness; then she ran round in circles, and large folios[2] came tumbling down to her; out of these she tore parchment leaves, and rapidly patching them together in artful combination, and fixing them on her body, in a few instants she was dressed as if in strange multi-colored armor. Spitting fire, the black cat darted out of the ink-glass, which was standing on the table, and ran mewing towards the crone, who shrieked in loud triumph, and along with him vanished through the door.

Anselmus observed that she went towards the azure chamber; and directly he heard a hissing and storming in the distance; the birds in the garden were crying; the Parrot creaked out: "Help! help! Thieves! thieves!" That moment the crone returned with a bound into the room, carrying the Golden Flower Pot on her arm, and with hideous gestures, shrieking wildly

---

[1] Atone, make up for

[2] That is, large books

through the air; "Joy! joy, little son!—Kill the green snake! To her, son! To her!"

Anselmus thought he heard a deep moaning, heard Serpentina's voice. Then horror and despair took hold of him: he gathered all his force, he dashed violently, as if every nerve and artery were bursting, against the crystal; a piercing clang went through the room, and the Archivarius in his bright damask dressing gown was standing in the door.

"Hey, hey! Vermin!—Mad spell!—Witchwork!—Here, holla!" So shouted he: then the black hair of the crone started up in tufts; her red eyes glanced with infernal fire, and clenching together the peaked fangs of her abominable jaws, she hissed: "Hiss, at him! Hiss, at him! Hiss!" and laughed and neighed in scorn and mockery, and pressed the Golden Flower Pot firmly to her, and threw out of it handfuls of glittering earth on the Archivarius; but as it touched the dressing gown, the earth changed into flowers, which rained down on the ground. Then the lilies of the dressing gown flickered and flamed up; and the Archivarius caught these lilies blazing in sparky fire and dashed them on the witch; she howled with agony, but as she leaped aloft and shook her armor of parchment the lilies went out, and fell away into ashes.

"To her, my lad!" creaked the crone: then the black cat darted through the air, and bounded over the Archivarius's head towards the door; but the gray parrot fluttered out against him; caught him by the nape with his crooked bill, till red fiery blood burst down over his neck; and Serpentina's voice cried: "Saved! Saved!" Then the crone, foaming with rage and desperation, darted at the Archivarius: she threw the Golden Flower Pot behind her, and holding up the long talons of her skinny fists, tried to clutch the Archivarius by the throat: but he instantly doffed his dressing gown, and hurled it against her. Then, hissing, and sputtering, and bursting, blue flames shot from the parchment leaves, and the crone rolled around howling in agony, and strove to get fresh earth from the Flower Pot, fresh parchment leaves from the books, that she might stifle the blazing flames; and whenever any earth or leaves came down on her, the flames went out. But now, from the interior of the Archivarius issued fiery crackling beams, which darted on the crone.

"Hey, hey! To it again! Salamander! Victory!" clanged the Archivarius's voice through the chamber; and a hundred bolts whirled forth in fiery circles round the shrieking crone. Whizzing and buzzing flew cat and parrot in their furious battle; but at last the parrot, with his strong wing, dashed the cat to the ground; and with his talons transfixing and holding fast his adversary, which, in deadly agony, uttered horrid mews and howls, he, with his sharp bill, picked out his glowing eyes, and the burning froth spouted from them. Then thick vapour streamed up from the spot where the crone, hurled to the ground, was lying under the dressing gown: her howling, her terrific, piercing cry of lamentation, died away in the remote distance. The smoke, which had spread abroad with penetrating stench, cleared away; the Archivarius picked up his dressing gown; and under it lay an ugly beet.

"Honoured Herr Archivarius, here let me offer you the vanquished foe," said the parrot, holding out a black hair in his beak to Archivarius Lindhorst.

"Very right, my worthy friend," replied the Archivarius: "here lies my vanquished foe too: be so good now as manage what remains. This very day, as a small douceur[1], you shall have six coconuts, and a new pair of spectacles also, for I see the cat has villainously broken the glasses of these old ones."

"Yours forever, most honoured friend and patron!" answered the parrot, much delighted; then took the withered beet in his bill, and fluttered out with it by the window, which Archivarius Lindhorst had opened for him.

The Archivarius now lifted the Golden Flower Pot, and cried, with a strong voice, "Serpentina! Serpentina!" But as the Student Anselmus, rejoicing in the destruction of the vile witch who had hurried him into misfortune, cast his eyes on the Archivarius, behold, here stood once more the high majestic form of the Spirit-prince, looking up to him with indescribable dignity and grace..." Anselmus," said the Spirit-prince, "not you, but a hostile principle, which strove destructively to penetrate into your nature, and divide you against yourself, was to blame for your unbelief."

"You have kept your faithfulness: be free and happy." A bright flash quivered through the spirit of Anselmus: the royal triphony of the crystal bells sounded stronger and louder than he had ever heard it: his nerves and fibres thrilled; but, swelling higher and higher, the melodious tones rang through the room; the glass which enclosed Anselmus broke; and he rushed into the arms of his dear and gentle Serpentina.

Eleventh Vigil

"But tell me, best Registrator! how could the cursed punch last night mount into our heads, and drive us to all kinds of allotria[2]?" So said Conrector Paulmann, as he next morning entered his room, which still lay full of broken sherds; with his hapless peruke, dissolved into its original elements, soaked in punch among the ruin. For after the Student Anselmus ran out, Conrector Paulmann and Registrator Heerbrand had kept trotting and hobbling up and down the room, shouting like maniacs, and butting their heads together; till Franzchen, with much labour, carried her dizzy papa to bed; and Registrator Heerbrand, in the deepest exhaustion, sank on the sofa, which Veronica had left, taking refuge in her bedroom. Registrator Heerbrand had his blue handkerchief tied about his head; he looked quite pale and melancholic, and moaned out: "Ah, worthy Conrector, it was not the punch which Mamsell Veronica most admirably brewed, no! but it was simply that cursed Student who was to blame for all the mischief. Do you not observe that he has long been mente captus[3]? And are you not aware that madness is infectious? One fool makes twenty; pardon me, it is an old proverb: especially when you have drunk a glass or two, you fall into madness quite readily, and then involuntarily you manoeuvre, and go through your exercise, just as the crack-

---

[1] Bribe

[2] Wild nonsense

[3] Mentally compromised; Latin for “captured within one’s own mind”

brained fugleman[1] makes the motion. Would you believe it Conrector? I am still giddy when I think of that gray parrot!"

"Gray fiddlestick!" interrupted the Conrector: "it was nothing but Archivarius Lindhorst's little old Famulus[2], who had thrown a gray cloak over himself, and was looking for the Student Anselmus."

"It may be," answered Registrator Heerbrand; "but, I must confess, I am quite downcast in spirit; the whole night through there was such a piping and organing."

"That was I," said the Conrector, "for I snore loud."

"Well, may be," answered the Registrator: "but, Conrector, Conrector! I had reason to raise some cheerfulness among us last night—And that Anselmus spoiled it all! You do not know—O Conrector, Conrector!" And with this, Registrator Heerbrand started up; plucked the cloth from his head, embraced the Conrector, warmly pressed his hand, and again cried, in quite heart-breaking tone: "O Conrector, Conrector!" and snatching his hat and staff, rushed out of doors.

"This Anselmus will not cross my threshold again," said Conrector Paulmann; "for I see very well, that, with this moping madness of his, he robs the best gentlemen of their senses. The Registrator has now gone overboard, too: I have hitherto kept safe; but the Devil, who knocked hard last night in our carousal, may get in at last, and play his tricks with me. So Apage, Satanas[3]! Off with thee, Anselmus!" Veronica had grown quite pensive; she spoke no word; only smiled now and then very oddly, and seemed to wish to be left alone. "She, too, has Anselmus in her head," said the Conrector, full of spleen[4]: "but it is well that he does not show himself here; I know he fears me, this Anselmus, and so he will never come." These concluding words Conrector Paulmann spoke aloud; then the tears rushed into Veronica's eyes, and she said, sobbing: "Ah! how can Anselmus come? He has been corked up in the glass bottle for a long time."

"What? What?" cried Conrector Paulmann. "Ah Heaven! Ah Heaven! she is doting too, like the Registrator: the loud fit will soon come! Ah, you cursed, abominable, thrice-cursed Anselmus!" He ran forth directly to Dr. Eckstein; who smiled, and again said: "Ey! Ey!" This time, however, he prescribed nothing; but added, to the little he had uttered, the following words, as he walked away: "Nerves! Come round of itself. Take the air; walks; amusements; theatre; playing Sonntagskind, Schwestern von Prag[5]. Come around of itself."

"I have seldom seen the Doctor so eloquent," thought Conrector Paulmann; "really talkative, I declare!"

Several days and weeks and months passed. Anselmus had vanished; but Registrator Heerbrand did not make his appearance either: not till the fourth of February, when, in a fashionable new coat of the finest cloth, in shoes and

---

[1] Wingman, spokesperson, accomplice

[2] Assistant

[3] "Away with you, Satan!" "Get thee behind me, Satan!"

[4] Malice, temper, passion

[5] An operetta

silk stockings, notwithstanding the keen frost, and with a large nosegay of fresh flowers in his hand, the Registrator entered precisely at noon the parlour of Conrector Paulmann, who wondered not a little to see his friend so well dressed. With a solemn air, Registrator Heerbrand came forward to Conrector Paulmann; embraced him with the finest elegance, and then said: "Now at last, on the Saint's-day[1] of your beloved and most honoured Mamsell Veronica, I will tell you out, straightforward, what I have long had lying at my heart. That evening, that unfortunate evening, when I put the ingredients of our noxious punch in my pocket, I intended to tell to you a piece of good news, and to celebrate the happy day in convivial joys. I had learned that I was to be made Hofrath; for which promotion I have now the patent, cum nomine et sigillo Principis[2], in my pocket."

"Ah! Herr Registr—Herr Hofrath Heerbrand, I meant to say," stammered the Conrector.

"But it is you, most honoured Conrector," continued the new Hofrath; "it is you alone that can complete my happiness. For a long time, I have in secret loved your daughter, Mamsell Veronica; and I can boast of many a kind look which she has given me, evidently showing that she would not reject me. In one word, honoured Conrector! I, Hofrath Heerbrand, do now entreat of you the hand of your most amiable Mamsell Veronica, whom I, if you have nothing against it, purpose shortly to take home as my wife."

Conrector Paulmann, full of astonishment, clapped his hands repeatedly, and cried: "Ey, Ey, Ey! Herr Registr—Herr Hofrath, I meant to say-who would have thought it? Well, if Veronica does really love you, I for my share cannot object: nay, perhaps, her present melancholy is nothing but concealed love for you, most honoured Hofrath! You know what freaks[3] women have!"

At this moment Veronica entered, pale and agitated, as she now commonly was. Then Hofrath Heerbrand approached her; mentioned in a neat speech her Saint's-day, and handed her the odorous nosegay, along with a little packet; out of which, when she opened it, a pair of glittering earrings gleamed up at her. A rapid flying blush tinted her cheeks; her eyes sparkled in joy, and she cried: "O Heaven! These are the very earrings which I wore some weeks ago, and thought so much of."

"How can this be, dearest Mamsell," interrupted Hofrath Heerbrand, somewhat alarmed and hurt, "when I bought them not an hour ago, in the Schlossgasse, for cash?"

---

[1] Also called a name-day, this is the feast day of the saint a person is named after (for instance, my birthday is September 21, but my saint-day – St. Michael's Day – is September 29). Saint Veronica is celebrated on February 4th. She was the widow who was traditionally said to have benevolently dabbed Christ's blood-drenched face with her veil while he was being marched to his crucifixion

[2] "With the signature and seal of the prince"

[3] Strange tastes

But Veronica paid no attention to him; she was standing before the mirror to witness the effect of the trinkets, which she had already suspended in her pretty little ears. Conrector Paulmann disclosed to her, with grave countenance and solemn tone, his friend Heerbrand's preferment and present proposal. Veronica looked at the Hofrath with a searching look, and said: "I have long known that you wished to marry me. Well, be it so! I promise you my heart and hand; but I must now unfold to you, to both of you, I mean, my father and my bridegroom, much that is lying heavy on my heart; yes, even now, though the soup should get cold, which I see Franzchen is just putting on the table."

Without waiting for the Conrector's or the Hofrath's reply, though the words were visibly hovering on the lips of both, Veronica continued: "You may believe me, father, I loved Anselmus from my heart, and when Registrator Heerbrand, who is now become Hofrath himself, assured us that Anselmus might possibly rise that high, I resolved that he arid no other should be my husband. But then it seemed as if alien hostile beings tried snatching him away from me: I had recourse to old Liese, who was once my nurse, but is now a wise woman, and a great enchantress. She promised to help me, and give Anselmus wholly into my hands. We went at midnight on the Equinox to the crossing of the roads: she conjured certain hellish spirits, and by aid of the black cat, we manufactured a little metallic mirror, in which I, directing my thoughts on Anselmus, had but to look, in order to rule him wholly in heart and mind. But now I heartily repent having done all this; and here abjure all Satanic arts. The Salamander has conquered old Liese; I heard her shrieks; but there was no help to be given: so soon as the parrot had eaten the beet, my metallic mirror broke in two with a piercing clang." Veronica took out both the pieces of the mirror, and a lock of hair from her workbox, and handing them to Hofrath Heerbrand, she proceeded: "Here, take the fragments of the mirror, dear Hofrath; throw them down, tonight, at twelve o'clock, over the Elbe Bridge, from the place where the Cross stands; the stream is not frozen there: the lock, however, wear on your faithful breast. I here abjure all magic: and heartily wish Anselmus joy of his good fortune, seeing he is wedded with the green snake, who is much prettier and richer than I. You dear Hofrath, I will love and reverence as becomes a true honest wife."

"Alack! Alack[1]!" cried Conrector Paulmann, full of sorrow; "she is cracked, she is cracked; she can never be Frau Hofräthinn; she is cracked!"

"Not in the smallest," interrupted Hofrath Heerbrand; "I know well that Mamsell Veronica has had some kindness for the loutish Anselmus; and it may be that in some fit of passion, she has had recourse to the wise woman, who, as I perceive, can be no other than the card-caster and coffee-pourer of the Seethor; in a word, old Rauerin. Nor can it be denied that there are secret arts, which exert their influence on men but too banefully; we read of such in the ancients, and doubtless there are still such; but as to what Mamsell Veronica is pleased to say about the victory of the Salamander, and the

---

[1] "Oh no, oh no!" "Woe! Woe!"

marriage of Anselmus with the green snake, this, in reality, I take for nothing but a poetic allegory; a sort of song, wherein she sings her entire farewell to the Student."

"Take it for what you will, my dear Hofrath!" cried Veronica; "perhaps for a very stupid dream."

"That I will not do," replied Hofrath Heerbrand; "for I know well that Anselmus himself is possessed by secret powers, which vex him and drive him on to all imaginable mad escapades."

Conrector Paulmann could stand it no longer; he burst out: "Hold! For the love of Heaven, hold! Are we overtaken with that cursed punch again, or has Anselmus's madness come over us too? Herr Hofrath, what stuff is this you are talking? I will suppose, however, that it is love which haunts your brain: this soon comes to rights in marriage; otherwise, I should be apprehensive that you too had fallen into some shade of madness, most honoured Herr Hofrath; then what would become of the future branches of the family, inheriting the malum[1] of their parents? But now I give my paternal blessing to this happy union; and permit you as bride and bridegroom to take a kiss."

This immediately took place; and thus before the soup had grown cold, a formal betrothment was concluded. In a few weeks, Frau Hofräthinn Heerbrand was actually, as she had been in vision, sitting in the balcony of a fine house in the Neumarkt, and looking down with a smile at the beaux, who passing by turned their glasses up to her, and said: "She is a heavenly woman, the Hofräthinn Heerbrand."

Twelfth Vigil

How deeply did I feel, in the centre of my spirit, the blessedness of the Student Anselmus, who now, indissolubly united with his gentle Serpentina, has withdrawn to the mysterious land of wonders, recognized by him as the home towards which his bosom, filled with strange forecastings, had always longed. But in vain was all my striving to set before you, favourable reader, those glories with which Anselmus is encompassed, or even in the faintest degree to shadow them to you in words. Reluctantly I could not but acknowledge the feebleness of my every expression. I felt myself enthralled amid the paltrinesses of everyday life; I sickened in tormenting dissatisfaction; I glided about like a dreamer; in brief, I fell into that condition of the Student Anselmus, which, in the Fourth Vigil, I endeavoured to set before you. It grieved me to the heart, when I glanced over the Eleven Vigils, now happily accomplished, and thought that to insert the Twelfth, the keystone of the whole, would never be permitted me. For whenever, in the night I set myself to complete the work, it was as if mischievous spirits (they might be relations, perhaps cousins-german, of the slain witch) held a polished glittering piece of metal before me, in which I beheld my own mean self, pale, drawn, and melancholic, like Registrator Heerbrand after his bout

---

[1] Evils, vices

of punch. Then I threw down my pen, and hastened to bed, that I might behold the happy Anselmus and the fair Serpentina at least in my dreams. This had lasted for several days and nights, when at length quite unexpectedly I received a note from Archivarius Lindhorst, in which he wrote to me as follows:

Respected Sir,—It is well known to me that you have written down, in Eleven Vigils, the singular fortunes of my good son-in-law Anselmus, whilom[1] student, now poet; and are at present cudgelling your brains very sore, that in the Twelfth and Last Vigil you may tell somewhat of his happy life in Atlantis, where he now lives with my daughter, on the pleasant freehold[2], which I possess in that country. Now, notwithstanding I much regret that hereby my own peculiar nature is unfolded to the reading world; seeing it may, in my office as Privy Archivarius, expose me to a thousand inconveniences; nay, in the Collegium even give rise to the question: How far a Salamander can justly, and with binding consequences, plight himself by oath, as a Servant of the State? and how far, on the whole, important affairs may be intrusted to him, since, according to Gabalis and Swedenborg[3], the spirits of the elements are not to be trusted at all?—notwithstanding, my best friends must now avoid my embrace; fearing lest, in some sudden anger, I dart out a flash or two, and singe their hair-curls, and Sunday frocks; notwithstanding all this, I say, it is still my purpose to assist you in the completion of the work, since much good of me and of my dear married daughter (would[4] the other two were off my hands also!) has therein been said.

If you would write your Twelfth Vigil, descend your cursed five flights of stairs, leave your garret, and come over to me. In the blue palmtree-room, which you already know, you will find fit writing materials; and you can then, in few words, specify to your readers, what you have seen; a better plan for

---

[1] Previously

[2] Property

[3] The Comte de Gabalais is the protagonist of a 1670 French novel by the Abbe de Villars. As the Sacred Texts website succinctly puts it, “The book describes an encounter with a mysterious Comte de Gabalis, who is a master of the occult sciences. Gabalis initiates de Villars into the secrets of the elemental beings: the Sylphs of the Air, the Undines of the Water, the Gnomes of the Earth and the Salamanders of Fire. The Abbé is not sure whether the elementals are demons, while Gabalis encourages him to symbolically (?) marry one of the elementals.” Emanuel Swedenborg was an 18th century Swedish philosopher, scientist, theologian, and mystic, best remembered for his supernatural treatises which followed a “spiritual awakening” experienced on Easter weekend in 1744. After this, he mostly traded his scientific research for esoteric theories of the afterlife, spirits, and the spirit world, informed by his mystical visions

[4] “I wish that”

you than any long-winded description of a life which you know only by hearsay. With esteem.

Your obedient servant.
The Salamander Lindlzorst.
P. T. Royal Archivarius...

This somewhat rough, yet on the whole friendly note from Archivarius Lindhorst, gave me high pleasure. It seemed clear enough, indeed, that the singular manner in which the fortunes of his son-in-law had been revealed to me, and which I, bound to silence, must conceal even from you, gracious reader, was well known to this peculiar old gentleman; yet he had not taken it so ill as I might have apprehended. Nay, here was he offering me a helping hand in the completion of my work; and from this I might justly conclude, that at bottom he was not averse to having his marvellous existence in the world of spirits thus divulged through the press.

"It may be," thought I, "that he himself expects from this measure, perhaps, to get his two other daughters married sooner: for who knows but a spark may fall in this or that young man's breast, and kindle a longing for the green snake; whom, on Ascension Day, under the elder-bush, he will forthwith seek and find? From the misery which befell Anselmus, when he was enclosed in the glass bottle, he will take warning to be doubly and trebly on his guard against all doubt and unbelief."

Precisely at eleven o'clock, I extinguished my study lamp; and glided forth to Archivarius Lindhorst, who was already waiting for me in the lobby.

"Are you there, my worthy friend? Well, this is what I like, that you have not mistaken my good intentions: follow me!"

And with this he led the way through the garden, now filled with dazzling brightness, into the azure chamber, where I observed the same violet table, at which Anselmus had been writing.

Archivarius Lindhorst disappeared: but soon came back, carrying in his hand a fair golden goblet, out of which a high blue flame was sparkling up. "Here," said he, "I bring you the favourite drink of your friend the Bandmaster, Johannes Kreisler[1]. It is burning arrack, into which I have thrown a little sugar. Sip a little of it: I will doff my dressing gown, and to amuse myself and enjoy your worthy company while you sit looking and writing, I shall just bob up and down a little in the goblet."

"As you please, honoured Herr Archivarius," answered I: "but if I am to ply the liquor, you will get none."

"Don't fear that, my good fellow," cried the Archivarius; then hastily throwing off his dressing gown, he mounted, to my no small amazement, into the goblet, and vanished in the blaze.

---

[1] Hoffmann's fictional alter-ego, who appears in three of his novels (*Kreisleriana, The Life and Opinions of Tomcat Murr, and The Musical Sufferings of Johannes Kreisler, Musical Director*). Like all Hoffmann protagonists, he is a moody, antisocial eccentric passionately searching for meaning amidst bureaucracy

Without fear, softly blowing back the flame, I partook of the drink: it was truly precious!

Stir not the emerald leaves of the palm-trees in soft sighing and rustling, as if kissed by the breath of the morning wind? Awakened from their sleep, they move, and mysteriously whisper of the wonders, which from the far distance approach like tones of melodious harps! The azure rolls from the walls, and floats like airy vapour to and fro; but dazzling beams shoot through it; and whirling and dancing, as in jubilee of childlike sport, it mounts and mounts to immeasurable height, and vaults over the palm-trees. But brighter and brighter shoots beam upon beam, till in boundless expanse the grove opens where I behold Anselmus. Here glowing hyacinths, and tulips, and roses, lift their fair heads; and their perfumes, in loveliest sound, call to the happy youth: "Wander, wander among us, our beloved; for you understand us! Our perfume is the longing of love: we love you, and are yours for evermore!" The golden rays burn in glowing tones: "We are fire, kindled by love. Perfume is longing; but fire is desire: and do we not dwell in your bosom? We are yours!" The dark bushes, the high trees rustle and sound: "Come to us, beloved, happy one! Fire is desire; but hope is our cool shadow. Lovingly we rustle round your head: for you understand us, because love dwells in your breast!" The brooks and fountains murmur and patter: "Loved one, do not walk so quickly by: look into our crystal! Your image dwells in us, which we preserve with love, for you have understood us." In the triumphal choir, bright birds are singing: "Hear us! Hear us! We are joy, we are delight, the rapture of love!" But anxiously Anselmus turns his eyes to the glorious temple, which rises behind him in the distance.

The fair pillars seem trees; and the capitals and friezes[1] acanthus leaves, which in wondrous wreaths and figures form splendid decorations. Anselmus walks to the Temple: he views with inward delight the variegated[2] marble, the steps with their strange veins of moss. "Ah, no!" cries he, as if in the excess of rapture, "she is not far from me now; she is near!" Then Serpentina advances, in the fullness of beauty and grace, from the Temple; she bears the Golden Flower Pot, from which a bright lily has sprung. The nameless rapture of infinite longing glows in her meek eyes; she looks at Anselmus, and says: "Ah! Dearest, the Lily has opened her blossom: what we longed for is fulfilled; is there a happiness to equal ours?" Anselmus clasps her with the tenderness of warmest ardour: the lily burns in flaming beams over his head. And louder move the trees and bushes; clearer and gladder play the brooks; the birds, the shining insects dance in the waves of perfume: a gay, bright rejoicing tumult, in the air, in the water, in the earth, is holding the festival of love! Now sparkling streaks rush, gleaming over all the bushes; diamonds look from the ground like shining eyes: strange vapours are wafted hither on sounding wings: they are the spirits of the elements, who do homage to the lily, and proclaim the happiness of Anselmus. Then Anselmus raises his head, as if

---

[1] Capital: the topmost section of a pillar; frieze: the panels above the capitals but below the roof eaves, often adorned with bas relief sculptures

[2] Multicolored, dappled

encircled with a beamy glory. Is it looks? Is it words? Is it song? You hear the sound: "Serpentina! Belief in you, love of you has unfolded to my soul the inmost spirit of nature! You have brought me the lily, which sprang from gold, from the primeval force of the world, before Phosphorus[1] had kindled the spark of thought; this lily is knowledge of the sacred harmony of all beings; and in this I live in highest blessedness for evermore. Yes, I, thrice happy, have perceived what was highest: I must indeed love thee forever, O Serpentina! Never shall the golden blossoms of the lily grow pale; for, like belief and love, this knowledge is eternal."

For the vision, in which I had now beheld Anselmus bodily, in his freehold of Atlantis, I stand indebted to the arts of the Salamander; and it was fortunate that when everything had melted into air, I found a paper lying on the violet-table, with the foregoing statement of the matter, written fairly and distinctly by my own hand. But now I felt myself as if transpierced and torn in pieces by sharp sorrow. "Ah, happy Anselmus, who has cast away the burden of everyday life, who in the love of kind Serpentina flies with bold pinion, and now lives in rapture and joy on your freehold in Atlantis! while I—poor I!—must soon, nay, in few moments, leave even this fair hall, which itself is far from a Freehold in Atlantis; and again be transplanted to my garret, where, enthralled among the pettinesses of existence, my heart and my sight are so bedimmed with thousand mischiefs, as with thick fog, that the fair lily will never, never be beheld by me."

Then Archivarius Lindhorst patted me gently on the shoulder, and said: "Softly, softly, my honoured friend! Do not lament so! Were you not even now in Atlantis; and have you not at least a pretty little copyhold farm there, as the poetical possession of your inward sense? And is the blessedness of Anselmus anything else but a living in poesy? Can anything else but poesy reveal itself as the sacred harmony of all beings, as the deepest secret of nature?"

HOFFMANN'S biographers unanimously agree that "The Golden Pot" was written as an act of personal catharsis during one of the darkest periods of his life. In a sense, it was a form of creative therapy that allowed him to project his humiliations, disillusionment, and despair onto a comically romantic caricature of himself. Anselmus provided him with a ludicrous avatar to mock and redeem. In one letter written during his work on the story, he groaned:

> "Never before this dark and fateful time, in which one lives a day-to-day existence and is happy to have it, has writing so attracted me. It is as though a wondrous kingdom has opened itself to me, a kingdom that originates within me and, as it takes shape, removes me from the stress of external events."

Hoffmann's primary woes derived from the political landscape of the Napoleonic Era and the bureaucracy of German professional society that

[1] The god of the brilliantly bright morning-star (that is, the planet Venus)

dogged him throughout his life: while he suffered financially under the French occupation of Dresden, the entire continent was sagging under the blood and misery of tens of millions of recently maimed, impoverished, or displaced collateral casualties of the greatest war to darken the Europe up to that date. Throughout the story, critics have seen Anselmus' development as a cathartic journey through mourning and a transcendent resurrection from humbled degradation to aspirational apotheosis. Biographically, the novella traces Hoffmann's history of disappointments, rejections, and let-downs, allowing him to come to terms with these negative experiences, and promising the approach of a new experience: self-acceptance and creative indulgence. In order to create this feeling, Hoffmann invented a new literary genre – one which he would employ in nearly every other story he would write. The subtitle of "The Golden Pot" is "A Modern Fairy Tale" (or, "A Fairy Tale of the New Age"), and critics have used the moniker to describe his embryonic version of magic realism (a genre wherein the bizarre and fantastic comfortably invades the commonplace world). Like Borges, Marquez, Rushdie, and Toni Morrison, Hoffmann used magic realism as a means of safely criticizing the social and political realities of his society, and used the shocking juxtaposition of the mundane, contemporary world with the fantastical, supernatural world to highlight the injustices and inconsistencies that he felt had restricted his happiness and expression. Anselmus' ultimate union with Serpentina is one of the few happy endings in Hoffmann's prose and calls attention to itself for concluding with a graceful harmony rather than a rattling dissonance. Plenty of critics have challenged this ending and called it a feint: Hoffmann, they argue, is putting us on, and the entire plot is a cynical mockery of what poetic-spirited people waste their lives pathetically hoping for. Anselmus' strange experience staring into the water under the bridge has led many writers to claim that he is actually driven to suicide, and that the happy ending is not unlike Ambrose Bierce's "Occurrence at Owl Creek Bridge" – the delusional hallucinations of a dying brain. But Hoffmann himself seemed to view "The Golden Pot" as a transcendental celebration of creative liberty, and the parting words of the narrator, urging the reader to wonder if they too might have a place for them in Atlantis, encourages a less pessimistic reading.

II.

Whether cynical or sentimental, the tale is unquestionably one which radically considers the freedom which imagination can afford to sufferers. Himself miserable and burdened with self-loathing, Hoffmann found salvation in transitioning from the highly regulated world of musical composition (monitored as it was by social gatekeepers and academics), to the historically libertarian art form of literature. Even as recently as the late-20th century, many taboo subjects could find their way between the covers of a book which would be illegal to depict on a stage or screen, and one need only compare the tidy, mathematical music that Hoffmann composed (his sublime First Symphony, for instance) to the frenzied, psychedelic stories he penned to get a sense of how the transition from notes to words liberated his stagnant imagination. Ultimately, "The Golden Pot" is a story of how being true to oneself can elevate the soul from the physical drudgery of everyday life. In Hoffmann's world view, every creative person has an internal Serpentina waiting for them just beyond the vantage point of consciousness, waiting to be united to their ego, waiting to transcend their world from passive misery into creative indulgence. Anselmus fails as a citizen of his bourgeois world because he – like the protagonists of most Hermann Hesse novels – has not yet accepted his "wolf-like" side. In Hesse's 1927 novel *Steppenwolf*, Harry Haller's nonconformist, anti-social "Steppenwolf" persona nearly leads him to suicide and self-loathing, but through the assistance of his artistically- and spiritually-liberated female Doppelgänger Hermine, and the mystic matchmaker Pablo, he is invited into a realm of Jungian self-acceptance brought on by the heartfelt blessing of his inefficiencies, brought on by his newfound acceptance of his idiosyncratic, bohemian inclinations (namely, his incapacity to successfully navigate or find a home in the bourgeois world), and the spiritual union between his fractured personality: the resentful Steppenwolf who loathes conformity, and the adolescent Harry who longs for belonging. The "reconciliation of opposites," the chief theme of nearly all of Hesse's novels, and "the harmony of nature," are the twin themes of Anselmus' own metaphysical odyssey. Like Harry Haller, he must learn to embrace the bourgeois – to find wonder in the banal and commonplace – before he can find comfort and familiarity in the world of Imagination. Hesse's Haller stops rebelling against his middle-class upbringing by falling in love with its good points, and Hoffmann's Anselmus can only break the curse which anchors the sublime to the everyday by reconciling the two in his heart, transforming the grey streets of Dresden into a fantasia of adventures and the mystical land of Atlantis into a cozy, middle-class homestead. As with (the tremendously Hoffmannesque) *Steppenwolf*, "The Golden Pot" preaches a gospel of peace to outsiders, transcendence to the humiliated, and artistic vision to the despondent poet.

LIKE the fiery Salamander in "The Golden Pot," Gnomes, in alchemy, are elemental spirits connected to one of the four classical elements of nature – in this case, the bowels of the earth and its inhabitants. Capable of moving through solid earth, known for hoarding or guarding jewels, gold, and mineral deposits, Gnomes had none of the sexiness of Salamanders, intellectualism of Sylphs, or goodwill of Undines. Instead, they were uncouth, miserly tricksters consumed by thoughts of fleshly pleasure. Gnomes were noted for their lustfulness, greediness, trickiness, and ugliness, and were considered simultaneously fearful and comical. The following fairy tale can easily be described as both grotesque and ludicrous, and while it contains little of what we would commonly term "horror," it certainly exceeds the boundaries of the bizarre and the surreal. Tales of crossbreeding between humans and sinister fairy folk are as old as *The Epic of Gilgamesh* and as modern as stories of alien abductions, from the kidnap of the beautiful Persephone by the subterranean Hades, to the seduction of Christine Daae by the ghoulish Phantom of the Opera. Like in "The Nutcracker," Hoffmann retools the basic *Beauty and the Beast* plot into a bizarre love story revolving around a young girl being courted by grotesque dwarf – but there are no sugarplums here. Rather, "The King's Betrothed" is an awkwardly erotic story about deception, arrogance, corruption, and lust.

The King's Betrothed

— Excerpted from 'The Serapion Brethren,' Volume Four, Section Eight —

{1817}

CHAPTER I.

WHICH GIVES AN ACCOUNT OF THE VARIOUS CHARACTERS, AND THEIR MUTUAL RELATIONS TO EACH OTHER, AND PREPARES THE WAY, PLEASANTLY, FOR THE MANY MARVELLOUS AND MOST ENTERTAINING MATTERS OF WHICH THE SUCCEEDING CHAPTERS TREAT.

IT was a blessed year. In the fields the corn, the wheat, and the barley grew most gloriously. The boys waded in the grass, and the cattle in the clover. The trees hung so full of cherries that, with the best will in the world, the great army of the sparrows, though determined to peck everything bare, were forced to leave half the fruit for a future feast. Every creature filled itself full every day at the great guest-table of nature. Above all, however, the vegetables in Herr Dapsul[1] von Zabelthau's kitchen-garden had turned out such a splendid and beautiful crop that it

[1] Sounds like "Dapul," a name meaning "cattail": a tall, thin person

was no wonder Fräulein Aennchen[1] was unable to contain herself with joy on the subject.

We may here explain who Herr Dapsul von Zabelthau and Aennchen were.

Perhaps, dear reader, you may have at some time found yourself in that beautiful country which is watered by the pleasant, kindly river Main[2]. Soft morning breezes, breathing their perfumed breath over the plain as it shimmered in the golden splendour of the new-risen sun, you found it impossible to sit cooped up in your stuffy carriage, and you alighted and wandered into the little grove, through the trees of which, as you descended towards the valley, you came in sight of a little village. And as you were gazing, there would suddenly come towards you, through the trees, a tall, lanky man, whose strange dress and appearance riveted your attention. He had on a small grey felt hat on the top of a black periwig[3]: all his clothes were grey—coat, vest, and breeches, grey stockings—even his walking-stick coloured grey. He would come up to you with long strides, and staring at you with great sunken eyes, seemingly not aware of your existence, would cry out, almost running you down, "Good morning, sir!" And then, like one awaking from a dream, he would add in a hollow, mournful voice, "Good morning! Oh, sir, how thankful we ought to be that we have a good, fine morning. The poor people at Santa Cruz[4] just had two earthquakes, and now—at this moment—rain falling in torrents." While you have been thinking what to say to this strange creature, he, with an "Allow me, sir," has gently passed his hand across your brow, and inspected the palm of your hand. And saying, in the same hollow, melancholy accents as before, "God bless you, sir! You have a good constellation[5]," has gone striding on his way.

This odd personage was none other than Herr Dapsul Von Zabelthau, whose sole—rather miserable—possession is the village, or hamlet, of Dapsulheim[6], which lies before you in this most pleasant and smiling country into which you now enter. You are looking forward to something in the shape of breakfast, but in the little inn things have rather a gloomy aspect. Its small store of provisions was cleared out at the fair, and as you can't be expected to be content with nothing besides milk, they tell you to go to the Manor House, where the gracious Fräulein Anna[7] will entertain

---

[1] Annie – a diminutive pet name for Änna, or Anne (pronounced "EHN-*shin*")

[2] The largest tributary of the Rhein, which curls directly across Germany's midsection, flowing west to east, like a belt. Its fertile plains are home to such major cities as Frankfurt-am-Main, Offenbach, Wurzburg, and Hanau

[3] An 18th century men's wig

[4] A city in east-central Bolivia

[5] That is, a positive horoscope reading

[6] Literally, Home of the Dapsuls

[7] Miss Anna (still referring to Aennchen)

you hospitably with whatever may be forthcoming there. Accordingly, thither you betake yourself without further ceremony.

Concerning this Manor House, there is nothing further to say than that it has doors and windows, as of yore had that of Baron Tondertontonk in Westphalia[1]. But above the hall-door the family coat-of-arms makes a fine show, carved there in wood with New Zealand skilfulness. And this Manor House derives a peculiar character of its own from the circumstance that its north side leans upon the enceinte[2], or outer line of defence belonging to an old ruined castle, so that the back entrance is what was formerly the castle gate, and through it one passes at once into the courtyard of that castle, in the middle of which the tall watch-tower still stands undamaged. From the hall door, which is surmounted by the coat-of-arms, there comes meeting you a red-cheeked young lady, who, with her clear blue eyes and fair hair, is to be called very pretty indeed, although her figure may be considered just the least bit too roundly substantial. A personification of friendly kindness, she begs you to go in, and as soon as she ascertains your wants, serves you up the most delicious milk, a liberal allowance of first-rate bread and butter, uncooked ham—as good as you would find in Bayonne[3]—and a small glass of beetroot brandy. Meanwhile, this young lady (who is none other than Fräulein Anna von Zabelthau) talks to you gaily and pleasantly of rural matters, displaying anything but a limited knowledge of such subjects. Suddenly, however, there resounds a loud and terrible voice, as if from the skies, crying "Anna, Anna, Anna!" This rather startles you; but Fräulein Anna says, pleasantly, "There's papa back from his walk, calling for his breakfast from his study." "Calling from his study," you repeat, or enquire, astonished. "Yes," says Fräulein Anna, or Fräulein Aennchen, as the people call her. "Yes; papa's study is up in the tower there, and he calls down through the speaking trumpet." And you see Aennchen open the narrow door of the old lower, with a similar *déjeuner à la fourchette*[4] to that which you have had yourself, namely, a liberal helping of bread and ham, not forgetting the beetroot brandy, and go briskly in at it. But she is back directly, and taking you all over the charming kitchen-garden, has so much to say about feather-sage, rapuntika, English turnips, little greenheads, montrue, great yellow[5], and so forth, that you have no idea that all these fine names merely mean various descriptions of cabbages and salads.

I think, dear reader, that this little glimpse which you have had of Dapsulheim is sufficient to enable you to understand all the outs and ins of the establishment, concerning which I have to narrate to you all manner

---

[1] A province in west-central Germany

[2] The primary, defensive wall of a fortification

[3] A French city near the Spanish border, known for its ham

[4] Luncheon, light meal

[5] A list of common German garden-herbs

of extraordinary, barely comprehensible, matters and occurrences. Herr Dapsul von Zabelthau had, during his youth, very rarely left his parents' country place. They had been people of considerable means. His tutor, after teaching him foreign languages, particularly those of the East[1], fostered a natural inclination which he possessed towards mysticism, or rather, occupying himself with the mysterious. This tutor died, leaving as a legacy to young Dapsul a whole library of occult science, into the very depths of which he proceeded to plunge. His parents dying, he betook himself to long journeyings, and (as his tutor had impressed him with the necessity of doing) to Egypt and India. When he got home again, after many years, a cousin had looked after his affairs with such zeal that there was nothing left to him but the little hamlet of Dapsulheim. Herr Dapsul was too eagerly occupied in the pursuit of the sun-born gold of a higher sphere to trouble himself about that which was earthly. He rather felt obliged to his cousin for preserving to him the pleasant, friendly Dapsulheim, with the fine, tall tower, which might have been built expressly on purpose for astrological operations, and in the upper storey and topmost height of which he at once established his study. And indeed he thanked his said cousin from the bottom of his heart.

This careful cousin now pointed out that Herr Dapsul von Zabelthau was bound to marry. Dapsul immediately admitted the necessity, and, without more ado, married at once the lady whom his cousin had selected for him. This lady disappeared almost as quickly as she had appeared on the scene. She died, after bearing him a daughter. The cousin attended to the marriage, the baptism, and the funeral; so that Dapsul, up in his tower, paid very little attention to either. For there was a very remarkable comet visible during most of the time, and Dapsul, ever melancholy and anticipative of evil, considered that he was involved in its influence[2].

The little daughter, under the careful up-bringing of an old grand-aunt, developed a remarkable aptitude for rural affairs. She had to begin at the very beginning, and, so to speak, rise from the ranks, serving successively as goose-girl, maid-of-all-work, upper farm-maid, housekeeper, and, finally, as mistress, so that Theory was all along illustrated and impressed upon her mind by a salutary share of Practice. She was exceedingly fond of ducks and geese, hens and pigeons, and even the tender broods of well-shaped piglings she was by no means indifferent to, though she did not put a ribbon and a bell round a little white sucking-pig's neck and make it into a sort of lap-dog, as a certain young lady, in

---

[1] Likely meaning some combination of Hebrew, Persian, Arabic, Hindi, and Chinese – the only non-European languages which were commonly studied at the time, each of which is associated with an "Eastern" school of religion or mysticism: Kabbalah/Judaism, Zoroastrianism, Islam, Hinduism, and Confucianism, respectively

[2] Dapsul is a devotee of astrological mysticism

another place, was once known to do. But more than anything—more than even to the fruit trees—she was devoted to the kitchen-garden. From her grand-aunt's attainments in this line she had derived very remarkable theoretical knowledge of vegetable culture (which the reader has seen for himself), as regarded digging of the ground, sowing the seed, and setting the plants. Fräulein Aennchen not only superintended all these operations, but lent most valuable manual aid. She wielded a most vigorous spade—her bitterest enemy would have admitted this. So that while Herr Dapsul von Zabelthau was immersed in astrological observations and other important matters, Fräulein Aennchen carried on the management of the place in the ablest possible manner, Dapsul looking after the celestial part of the business, and Aennchen managing the terrestrial side of things with unceasing vigilance and care.

As above said, it was small wonder that Aennchen was almost beside herself with delight at the magnificence of the yield which this season had produced in the kitchen-garden. But the carrot-bed was what surpassed everything else in the garden in its promise.

"Oh, my dear, beautiful carrots!" cried Anna over and over again, and she clapped her hands, danced, and jumped about, and conducted herself like a child who has been given a grand Christmas present.

And indeed it seemed as though the carrot-children underground were taking part in Aennchen's gladness, for some extremely delicate laughter, which just made itself heard, was undoubtedly proceeding from the carrot-bed. Aennchen didn't, however, pay much heed to it, but ran to meet one of the farm-men who was coming, holding up a letter, and calling out to her, "For you, Fräulein Aennchen. Gottlieb brought it from the town."

Aennchen saw immediately, from the hand writing, that it was from none other than young Herr Amandus von Nebelstern[1], the son of a neighbouring proprietor, now at the university. During the time when he was living at home, and in the habit of running over to Dapsulheim every day, Amandus had arrived at the conviction that in all his life he never could love anybody except Aennchen. Similarly, Aennchen was perfectly certain that she could never really care the least bit about anybody else but this brown-locked Amandus. Thus both Aennchen and Amandus had come to the conclusion and arrangement that they were to be married as soon as ever they could—the sooner the better—and be the very happiest married couple in the wide world.

Amandus had at one time been a bright, natural sort of lad enough, but at the university he had got into the hands of God knows who, and had been induced to fancy himself a marvellous poetical genius, as also to betake himself to an extreme amount of absurd extravagance in expression

---

[1] "Amandus" is a Latin name meaning "Lovable," and "Nebelstern" means "foggy star" (an allusion to his poorly-focused, nebulous aspirations and ideals) or stellar nebula.

of ideas. He carried this so far that he soon soared far away beyond everything which prosaic idiots term Sense and Reason (maintaining at the same time, as they do, that both are perfectly co-existent with the utmost liveliness of imagination).

It was from this young Amandus that the letter came which Aennchen opened and read, as follows:—

"HEAVENLY MAIDEN,—

"Dost thou see, dost thou feel, dost thou not image and figure to thyself, thy Amandus, how, circumambiated by the orange-flower-laden breath of the dewy evening, he is lying on his back in the grass, gazing heavenward with eyes filled with the holiest love and the most longing adoration? The thyme and the lavender, the rose and the gilliflower, as also the yellow-eyed narcissus and the shamefaced violet—he weaveth into garlands. And the flowers are love-thoughts—thoughts of thee, oh, Anna! But doth feeble prose beseem inspired lips? Listen! oh, listen how I can only love, and speak of my love, sonnetically!

"Love flames aloft in thousand eager sunspheres,
Joy wooeth joy within the heart so warmly:
Down from the darkling sky soft stars are shining.
Back-mirrored from the deep, still wells of love-tears.

"Delight, alas! doth die of joy too burning—
The sweetest fruit hath aye the bitt'rest kernel—
While longing beckons from the violet distance,
In pain of love my heart to dust is turning.

"In fiery billows rage the ocean surges,
Yet the bold swimmer dares the plunge full arduous,
And soon amid the waves his strong course urges.

"And on the shore, now near, the jacinth shoots:
The faithful heart holds firm: 'twill bleed to death;
But heart's blood is the sweetest of all roots.[1]

"Oh, Anna! when thou readest this sonnet of all sonnets, may all the heavenly rapture permeate thee in which all my being was dissolved when I wrote it down, and then read it out, to kindred minds, conscious, like myself, of life's highest. Think, oh, think I sweet maiden of

"Thy faithful, enraptured,

"AMANDUS VON NEBELSTERN.

"P.S.—Don't forget, oh, sublime virgin! when answering this, to send a pound or two of that Virginia tobacco which you grow yourself. It burns

[1] TRANSLATOR'S NOTE: "The translator may point out that the original of this nonsense is, itself, intentionally nonsense, and that he has done his best to render it into English—not an easy task.—A. E."

splendidly, and has a far better flavour than the Porto Rico which the Bürschen[1] smoke when they go to the Kneipe[2]."

Fräulein Aennchen pressed the letter to her lips, and said, "Oh, how dear, how beautiful! And the darling verses, rhyming so beautifully. Oh, if I were only clever enough to understand it all; but I suppose nobody can do that but a student. I wonder what that about the 'roots' means? I suppose it must be the long red English carrots, or, who knows, it may be the rapuntica. Dear fellow!"

That very day Fräulein Aennchen made it her business to pack up the tobacco, and she took a dozen of her finest goose-quills to the schoolmaster, to get him to make them into pens. Her intention was to sit down at once and begin her answer to the precious letter. As she was going out of the kitchen-garden, she was again followed by a very faint, almost imperceptible, sound of delicate laughter; and if she had paid a little attention to what was going on, she would have been sure to hear a little delicate voice saying, "Pull me, pull me! I am ripe—ripe—ripe!" However, as we have said, she paid no attention, and did not hear this.

CHAPTER II.

WHICH CONTAINS AN ACCOUNT OF THE FIRST WONDERFUL EVENT, AND OTHER MATTERS DESERVING OF PERUSAL, WITHOUT WHICH THIS TALE COULD HAVE HAD NO EXISTENCE.

Herr Dapsul Von Zabelthau generally came down from his astronomical tower about noon, to partake of a frugal repast with his daughter, which usually lasted a very short time, and during which there was generally a great predominance of silence, for Dapsul did not like to talk. And Aennchen did not trouble him by speaking much, and this all the more for the reason that if her papa did actually begin to talk, he would come out with all sorts of curious unintelligible nonsense, which made a body's head giddy. This day, however, her head was so full, and her mind so excited and taken up with the flourishing state of the kitchen-garden, and the letter from her beloved Amandus, that she talked of both subjects incessantly, mixed up, without leaving off. At last Herr Dapsul von Zabelthau laid down his knife and fork, stopped his ears with his hands, and cried out, "Oh, the dreary higgledy-piggledy of chatter and gabble!"

Aennchen stopped, alarmed, and he went on to say, in the melancholy sustained tones which were characteristic of him, "With regard to the vegetables, my dear daughter, I have long been cognizant that the manner in which the stars have worked together this season has been eminently

[1] Lads

[2] Pub

favourable to those growths, and the earthly man will be amply supplied with cabbage, radishes, and lettuce, so that the earthly matter may duly increase and withstand the fire of the world-spirit, like a properly kneaded pot. The gnomic principle will resist the attacks of the salamander[1], and I shall have the enjoyment of eating the parsnips which you cook so well. With regard to young Amandus von Nebelstern, I have not the slightest objection to your marrying him as soon as he comes back from the university. Simply send Gottlieb up to tell me when your marriage is going to take place, so that I may go with you to the church."

Herr Dapsul kept silence for a few seconds, and then, without looking at Aennchen, whose face was glowing with delight, he went on, smiling and striking his glass with his fork (two things which he seldom did at all, though he always did them together) to say, "Your Amandus has got to be, and cannot help being, where and what he is. He is, in fact, a gerund[2]; and I shall merely tell you, my dear Aennchen, that I drew up his horoscope a long while ago. His constellation is favourable enough on the whole, for the matter of that. He has Jupiter in the ascending node, Venus regarding in the sextile. The trouble is, that the path of Sirius cuts across, and, just at the point of intersection, there is a great danger from which Amandus delivers his betrothed[3]. The danger—what it is—is indiscoverable, because some strange being, which appears to set at defiance all astrological science, seems to be concerned in it. At the same time, it is evident and certain that it is only the strange psychical condition which mankind terms craziness, or mental derangement, which will enable Amandus to accomplish this deliverance. Oh, my daughter!" (here Herr Dapsul fell again into his usual pathetic tone), "may no mysterious power, which keeps itself hidden from my seer-eyes, come suddenly across your path, so that young Amandus von Nebelstern may not have to rescue you from any other danger but that of being an old maid[4]." He sighed several times consecutively, and then continued, "But the path of Sirius breaks off abruptly after this danger, and Venus and Jupiter, divided before, come together again, reconciled."

Herr Dapsul von Zabelthau had not spoken so much for years as on this occasion. He arose exhausted, and went back up into his tower.

---

[1] Alchemical musings related to the four elements which alchemists believed to make up all matter: earth, fire, water, and air. Gnomes are earth elementals; salamanders are fire elementals. This is like rambling about zodiac signs

[2] A part of speech where a verb acts as a noun. In English these words end with the "-ing" suffix

[3] More astrology musings which suggest that fortune (Amandus), esoteric wisdom (Dapsul), and love (Anna) will all be torn apart by some approaching disaster

[4] Old woman who has never married

Aennchen had her answer to Herr von Nebelstern ready in good time next morning. It was as follows:—

"MY OWN DEAREST AMANDUS—

"You cannot believe what joy your letter has given me. I have told papa about it, and he has promised to go to church with us when we're married. Be sure to come back from the university as soon as ever you can. Oh! if I only could *quite* understand your darling verses, which rhyme so beautifully. When I read them to myself aloud they sound wonderful, and *then* I think I *do* understand them quite well. But soon everything grows confused, and seems to get away from me, and I feel as if I had been reading a lot of mere words that somehow don't belong to each other at all. The schoolmaster says this must be so, and that it's the new fashionable way of speaking. But, you see, I'm—oh, well!—I'm only a stupid, foolish creature. Please do write and tell me if I couldn't be a student for a little time, without neglecting my housework. I suppose that couldn't be, though, could it? Well, well: when once we're husband and wife, perhaps I may pick up a little of your learning, and learn a little of this new, fashionable way of speaking.

"I send you the Virginian tobacco, my dearest Amandus. I've packed my bonnet-box full of it, as much as ever I could get into it; and, in the meantime, I've put my new straw hat on to Charles the Great's[1] head—you know he stands in the spare bedroom, although he has no feet, being only a bust, as you remember.

"Please don't laugh, Amandus dear; but I have made some poetry myself, and it rhymes quite nicely, some of it. Write and tell me how a person, without learning, can know so well what rhymes to what? Just listen, now—

"I love you, dearest, as my life.
And long at once to be your wife.
The bright blue sky is full of light,
When evening comes the stars shine bright.
So you must love me always truly,
And never cause me pain unduly,
I pack up the 'baccy you asked me to send,
And I hope it will yield you enjoyment no end.

"There! you must take the will for the deed[2], and when I learn the fashionable way of speaking, I'll do some better poetry. The yellow lettuces are promising splendidly this year—never was such a crop; so are the

---

[1] That is, Charlemagne, King of the Franks during the late 8th century, who served as the first emperor of the Holy Roman Empire, whose ascent has been said to mark the recovery of Western civilization from the ravages of the so-called Dark Ages following the Fall of Rome in the 5th century, and signified the beginning of the Middle Ages

[2] That is, "it's the thought that counts"

French beans; but my little dachshund, Feldmann, gave the big gander a terrible bite in the leg yesterday. However, we can't have everything perfect in this world. A hundred kisses in imagination, my dearest Amandus, from

"Your most faithful fiancée,

"ANNA VON ZABELTHAU.

"P.S.—I've been writing in an awful hurry, and that's the reason the letters are rather crooked here and there.

"P.S.—But you mustn't mind about that. Though I may write a little crookedly, my heart is all straight, and I am

"Always your faithful

"ANNA.

"P.S.—Oh, good gracious! I had almost forgot—thoughtless thing that I am. Papa sends you his kind regards, and says you have got to be, and cannot help being, where and what you are; and that you are to rescue me from a terrible danger some day. Now, I'm very glad of this, and remain, once more,

"Your most true and loving

"ANNA VON ZABELTHAU."

It was a good weight off Fräulein Aennchen's mind when she had written this letter; it had cost her a considerable effort. So she felt light-hearted and happy when she had put it in its envelope, sealed it up without burning the paper or her own fingers, and given it, together with the bonnet-boxful of tobacco, to Gottlieb to take to the post-office in the town. When she had seen properly to the poultry in the yard, she ran as fast as she could to the place she loved best—the kitchen-garden. When she got to the carrot-bed she thought it was about time to be thinking of the sweet-toothed people in the town, and be pulling the earliest of the carrots. The servant-girl was called in to help in this process. Fräulein Aennchen walked, gravely and seriously, into the middle of the bed, and grasped a stately carrot-plant. But on her pulling at it a strange sound made itself heard. Do not, reader, think of the witches' mandrake-root[1], and the horrible whining and howling which pierces the heart of man when it is drawn from the earth. No; the tone which was heard on this occasion was like very delicate, joyous laughter. But Fräulein Aennchen let the carrot-plant go, and cried out, rather frightened, "Eh! Who's that laughing at me?" But there being nothing more to be heard she took hold of the carrot-plant again—which seemed to be finer and better grown than any of the rest—and, notwithstanding the laughing, which began again, pulled up the very finest and most splendid carrot ever beheld by mortal eye. When she looked at it more closely she gave a cry of joyful surprise, so that the maid-

[1] Superstitions hold that mandrakes – leafless roots which bear a creepy resemblance to human beings – are the spirits of executed criminals, and that they will make a screaming noise when they are pulled out – a sound which will curse those who hear it

servant came running up; and she also exclaimed aloud at the beautiful miracle which disclosed itself to her eyes. For there was a beautiful ring firmly attached to the carrot, with a shining topaz mounted in it.

"Oh," cried the maid, "that's for you! It's your wedding-ring. Put it on directly."

"Stupid nonsense!" said Fräulein Aennchen. "I must get my wedding-ring from Herr Amandus von Nebelstern, not from a carrot."

However, the longer she looked at the ring the better she was pleased with it; and, indeed, it was of such wonderfully fine workmanship that it seemed to surpass anything ever produced by human skill. On the ring part of it there were hundreds and hundreds of tiny little figures twined together in the most manifold groupings, hardly to be made out with the naked eye at first, so microscopically minute were they. But when one looked at them closely for a little while they appeared to grow bigger and more distinct, and to come to life, and dance in pretty combinations. And the fire of the gem was of such a remarkable water that the like of it could not have been found in the celebrated Dresden collection[1].

"Who knows," said the maid, "how long this beautiful ring may have been underground? And it must have got shoved up somehow, and then the carrot has grown right through it."

Fräulein Aennchen took the ring off the carrot, and it was strange how the latter suddenly slipped through her fingers and disappeared in the ground. But neither she nor the maid paid much heed to this circumstance, being lost in admiration of the beautiful ring, which the young lady immediately put on the little finger of the right hand without more ado. As she did so, she felt a stinging pain all up her finger, from the root of it[2] to the point; but this pain went away again as quickly as it had come.

Of course she told her father, at mid-day, all about this strange adventure at the carrot-bed, and showed him the beautiful ring which had been sticking upon the carrot. She was going to take it off that he might examine it the better, but felt the same stinging kind of pain as when she put it on. And this pain lasted all the time she was trying to get it off, so that she had to give up trying. Herr Dapsul scanned the ring upon her finger with the most careful attention. He made her stretch her finger out, and describe with it all sorts of circles in all directions. After which he fell into a profound meditation, and went up into his tower without uttering a

---

[1] A reference to the Green Vault, an 18th century gem museum in Dresden, in eastern Germany, which still hold the record for containing the greatest collection of rare stones in all of Europe, and may be the oldest museum in the world

[2] That is, the joint where the finger connects to the palm. Hoffmann is intentionally using the word “root” (he uses the word “Grundwurzel,” or “ground root”) to draw a parallel between the carrot-roots and Anna’s human body, which the Gnome King wishes to possess

syllable. Aennchen heard him giving vent to a very considerable amount of groaning and sighing as he went.

Next morning, when she was chasing the big cock[1] about the yard (he was bent on all manner of mischief, and was skirmishing particularly with the pigeons), Herr Dapsul began lamenting so fearfully down from the tower through the speaking trumpet[2] that she cried up to him through her closed hand, "Oh papa dear, what are you making such a terrible howling for? The fowls are all going out of their wits."

Heir Dapsul hailed down to her through the speaking trumpet, saying, "Anna, my daughter Anna, come up here to me immediately."

Fräulein Aennchen was much astonished at this command, for her papa had never in all his life asked her to go into the tower, but rather had kept the door of it carefully shut. So that she was conscious of a certain sense of anxiety as she climbed the narrow winding stair, and opened the heavy door which led into its one room. Herr Dapsul von Zabelthau was seated upon a large armchair of singular form, surrounded by curious instruments and dusty books. Before him was a kind of stand, upon which there was a paper stretched in a frame, with a number of lines drawn upon it. He had on a tall pointed cap, a wide mantle[3] of grey calimanco[4], and on his chin a long white beard, so that he had quite the appearance of a magician. On account of his false beard, Aennchen didn't know him a bit just at first, and looked curiously about to see if her father were hidden away in some corner; but when she saw that the man with the beard on was really papa, she laughed most heartily, and asked if it was Yule-time, and he was going to act Father Christmas.

Paying no heed to this enquiry, Herr Dapsul von Zabelthau took a small tool of iron in his hand, touched Aennchen's forehead with it, and then stroked it along her right arm several times, from the armpit to the tip of the little finger. While this was going on she had to sit in the armchair, which he had quitted, and to lay the finger which had the ring upon it on the paper which was in the frame, in such a position that the topaz touched the central point where all the lines came together. Yellow rays immediately shot out from the topaz all round, colouring the paper all over with deep yellow light. Then the lines went flickering and crackling up and down, and the little figures which were on the ring seemed to be jumping merrily about all over the paper. Herr Dapsul, without taking his eyes from

---

[1] This story contains a great deal of phallic imagery; big cock – "große Hahn" – in German means the same thing, colloquially, as it does in English. Indeed, "cock-dance" or "cock-chase" in German has the same meaning as "cock-tease" in English. Delayed or repressed sexual congress is a major theme in the story

[2] A bull-horn

[3] Robe

[4] A type of wool fabric with a shiny, glazed appearance

the paper, had taken hold of a thin plate of some metal, which he held up high over his head with both arms, and was proceeding to press it down upon the paper; but ere he could do so he slipped his foot on the smooth stone floor, and fell, anything but softly, upon the sitting portion of his body; whilst the metal plate, which he had dropped in an instinctive attempt to break his fall, and save damage to his *Os Coccygis*[1], went clattering down upon the stones. Fräulein Aennchen awoke, with a gentle "Ah!" from a strange dreamy condition in which she had been. Herr Dapsul with some difficulty raised himself, put the grey sugar-loaf cap[2], which had fallen off, on again, arranged the false beard, and sate himself down opposite to Aennchen upon a pile of folio volumes.

"My daughter," he said, "my daughter Anna; what were your sensations? Describe your thoughts, your feelings? What were the forms seen by the eye of the spirit within your inner being?"

"Ah!" answered Anna, "I was so happy; I never was so happy in all my life. And I thought of Amandus von Nebelstern. And I saw him quite plainly before my eyes, but he was much better looking than he used to be, and he was smoking a pipe of the Virginian tobacco that I sent him, and seemed to be enjoying it tremendously. Then all at once I felt a great appetite for young carrots with sausages[3]; and lo and behold! there the dishes were before me, and I was just going to help myself to some when I woke up from the dream in a moment, with a sort of painful start."

"Amandus von Nebelstern, Virginia canaster[4], carrots, sausages[5]," quoth Herr Dapsul von Zabelthau to his daughter very reflectively. And he signed to her to stay where she was, for she was preparing to go away.

"Happy is it for you, innocent child," he began, in a tone much more lamentable than even his usual one, "that you are as yet not initiated into the profounder mysteries of the universe, and are unaware of the threatening perils which surround you[6]. You know nothing of the supernatural science of the sacred cabbala[7]. True, you will never partake the celestial joy of those wise ones who, having attained the highest step, need never eat or drink except for their pleasure, and are exempt from human necessities. But then, you have not to endure and suffer the pain of

---

[1] His tailbone

[2] A tall, conical hat (sugar used to be sold in solid, cones called loaves)

[3] More phallic symbolism

[4] A type of course tobacco used to roll cigars

[5] An early form of the Freudian therapy called free association where speaking outloud in an uncensored manner is supposed to bring about a train of associated ideas, helping the therapist to sense a pattern. Here, the pattern is undeniably phallic: Amandus (...and his penis), cigars, carrots, sausages.

[6] He infers that, unbeknownst to her, she is awaking sexually

[7] That is, the Kabbalah – the esoteric tradition of Jewish mysticism which contains elements of alchemy, astrology, magic, and psychology

attainment to that step, like your unhappy father, who is still far more liable to attacks of mere human giddiness, to whom that which he laboriously discovers only causes terror and awe, and who is still, from purely earthly necessities, obliged to eat and drink and, in fact, submit to human requirements. Learn, my charming child, blessed as you are with absence of knowledge, that the depths of the earth, and the air, water, and fire, are filled with spiritual beings of higher and yet of more restricted nature than mankind. It seems unnecessary, my little unwise one, to explain to you the peculiar nature and characteristics of the gnomes, the salamanders, sylphides, and undines[1]; you would not be able to understand them. To give you some slight idea of the danger which you may be undergoing, it is sufficient that I should tell you that these spirits are always striving eagerly to enter into unions with human beings; and as they are well aware that human beings are strongly adverse to those unions, they employ all manner of subtle and crafty artifices to delude such of the latter as they have fixed their affections upon. Often it is a twig, a flower, a glass of water, a fire-steel[2], or something else, in appearance of no importance, which they employ as a means of compassing their intent. It is true that unions of this sort often turn out exceedingly happily, as in the case of two priests, mentioned by Prince della Mirandola[3], who spent forty years of the happiest possible wedlock with a spirit of this description. It is true, moreover, that the most renowned sages have been the offspring of such unions between human beings and elementary spirits. Thus, the great Zoroaster[4] was a son of the salamander Oromasis; the great Apollonius, the sage Merlin, the valiant Count of Cleve, and the great cabbalist, Ben-Syra[5], were the glorious fruits of marriages of this description, and according to Paracelsus the beautiful Melusina was no other than a sylphide[6]. But yet,

---

[1] Sylphides are air elementals; undines are water elementals

[2] An iron striker used to create a fire-starting spark when struck against flint

[3] An 15th century Italian nobleman, mystic, and philosopher known for his controversial theological work "Oration on the Dignity of Man," which has been considered the "Manifesto of the Renaissance." He was the founder of the tradition of Christian Kabbalah, a key tenet of early modern Western esotericism. His book was the first printed book to be universally banned by the Church

[4] An Iranian religious reformer who flourished in Persia during the 7th Century B.C., and is considered the founder of Zoroastrianism. He was said, by some Medieval commentators, to have been parented by the biblical Noah's wife and a fire elemental named Oromasis

[5] Famous mystics from the Greek, Druidic, Medeival German, and Jewish philosophic traditions

[6] Paracelsus was a 16th century Swiss scientist, alchemist, mystic, and theologian. Melusina is a figure of European folklore, a female spirit of fresh

notwithstanding, the peril of such a union is much too great, for not only do the elementary spirits require of those on whom they confer their favours that the clearest light of the profoundest wisdom shall have arisen and shall shine upon them, but besides this they are extraordinarily touchy and sensitive, and revenge offences with extreme severity. Thus, it once happened that a sylphide, who was in union with a philosopher, on an occasion when he was talking with friends about a pretty woman—and perhaps rather too warmly—suddenly allowed her white beautifully-formed limb to become visible in the air, as if to convince the friends of her beauty, and then killed the poor philosopher on the spot. But ah! why should I refer to others? Why don't I speak of myself? I am aware that for the last twelve years I have been beloved by a sylphide, but she is timorous[1] and coy, and I am tortured by the thought of the danger of fettering[2] her to me more closely by cabbalistic processes, inasmuch as I am still much too dependent on earthly necessities, and consequently lack the necessary degree of wisdom. Every morning I make up my mind to fast, and I succeed in letting breakfast pass without touching any; but when mid-day comes, oh! Anna, my daughter Anna, you know well that I eat tremendously."

These latter words Herr Dapsul uttered almost in a howl, while bitter tears rolled down his lean chop-fallen cheeks. He then went on more calmly:

"But I take the greatest of pains to behave towards the elementary spirit who is thus favourably disposed towards me with the utmost refinement of manners, the most exquisite *galanterie*[3]. I never venture to smoke a pipe of tobacco without employing the proper preliminary cabbalistic precautions, for I cannot tell whether or not my tender air-spirit may like the brand of the tobacco, and so be annoyed at the defilement of her element. And I take the same precautions when I cut a hazel twig, pluck a flower, eat a fruit, or strike fire, all my efforts being directed to avoid giving offence to any elementary spirit. And yet—there, you see that nutshell, which I slid upon, and, falling over backwards, completely nullified the whole important experiment, which would have revealed to me the whole mystery of the ring? I do not remember that I have ever eaten a nut in this chamber, completely devoted as it is to science (you know now why I have my breakfast on the stairs), and it is all the clearer that some little gnome must have been hidden away in that shell, very likely having come here to prosecute his studies, and watch some of my experiments. For the elementary spirits are fond of human science, particularly such kinds of it

---

water in a holy well or river. She is usually depicted as a woman who is a serpent or fish from the waist down

[1] Nervous, shy

[2] Spiritually bonding

[3] Politeness, chivalry

as the uninitiated vulgar[1] consider to be, if not foolish and superstitious, at all events beyond the powers of the human mind to comprehend, and for that reason style 'dangerous.' Thus, when I accidentally trod upon this little student's head, I suppose he got in a rage, and threw me down. But it is probable that he had a deeper reason for preventing me from finding out the secret of the ring. Anna, my dear Anna, listen to this. I had ascertained that there is a gnome bestowing his favour upon you, and to judge by the ring he must be a gnome of rank and distinction, as well as of superior cultivation. But, my dear Anna, my most beloved little stupid girl, how do you suppose you are going to enter into any kind of union with an elementary spirit without running the most terrible risk? If you had read Cassiodorus Remus[2] you might, of course, reply that, according to his veracious chronicle, the celebrated Magdalena de la Croix[3], abbess of a convent at Cordova, in Spain, lived for thirty years in the happiest wedlock imaginable with a little gnome, whilst a similar result followed in the case of a sylph and the young Gertrude, a nun in Kloster Nazareth, near Cologne[4]. But, then, think of the learned pursuits of those ecclesiastical[5] ladies and of your own; what a mighty difference. Instead of reading in learned books you are often employing your time in feeding hens, geese, ducks, and other creatures, which simply molest and annoy all cabbalists; instead of watching the course of the stars, the heavens, you dig in the earth; instead of deciphering the traces of the future in skilfully-constructed horoscopes you are churning milk into butter, and putting sauerkraut up to pickle for mean everyday winter use; although, really, I must say that for my own part I should be very sorry to be without such articles of food. Say, is all this likely, in the long run, to content a refined philosophic elementary spirit? And then, oh Anna! it must be through you that the Dapsulheim line must continue, which earthly demand upon your being you cannot refuse to obey in any possible case. Yet, in connection with this ring, you in your instinctive way felt a strange irreflective sense of

---

[1] Uneducated simpleton lacking intelligence, culture, or imagination

[2] Seemingly fictitious – intended to sound like a typical 16th or 17th century chronicler of alchemical phenomena, complete with a Latinized name

[3] A 16th century Spanish nun from Cordoba who faked mystical experiences, including the stigmata, which – she claimed, after repenting of her deception during a serious illness – had been given her by Satan. She made her confession to the pope, himself, claiming that "at twelve years old the Devil solicited her, and lay with her, and that he had layen with her for thirty years; yet she was made the Abbess of a Monastery, and counted a saint. [...] She died full of sorrow and deeply contrite, in 1560. It may be remarked that on her confession of imposture and guilt, seventeen years before, the demoniacal stigmata disappeared"

[4] A 16th century German nun who was said to have slept with the devil

[5] Clergy

physical enjoyment. By means of the operation in which I was engaged, I desired and intended to break the power of the ring, and free you entirely from the gnome which is pursuing you. That operation failed, in consequence of the trick played me by the little student in the nut-shell. And yet, notwithstanding, I feel inspired by a courage such as I never felt before to do battle with this elementary spirit. You are my child, whom I begot, not indeed with a sylphide, salamandress, or other elementary spirit, but of that poor country lady of a fine old family, to whom the God-forgotten neighbours gave the nickname of the 'goat-girl' on account of her idyllic nature. For she used to go out with a flock of pretty little white goats, and pasture them on the green hillocks, I meanwhile blowing a reed-pipe[1] on my tower, a love-stricken young fool, by way of accompaniment. Yes, you are my own child, my flesh and blood, and I mean to rescue you. Here, this mystic file shall befree you from the pernicious ring."

With this, Herr Dapsul von Zabelthau took up a small file and began filing away with it at the ring. But scarcely had he passed it once or twice backwards and forwards when Fräulein Aennchen cried aloud in pain, "Papa, papa, you're filing my finger off!" And actually there was dark thick blood coming oozing from under the ring. Seeing this, Herr Dapsul let the file fall upon the floor, sank half fainting into the armchair, and cried, in utter despair, "Oh—oh—oh—oh! It is all over with me! Perhaps the infuriated gnome may come this very hour and bite my head off unless the sylphide saves me. Oh, Anna, Anna, go—fly!"

As her father's extraordinary talk had long made her wish herself far enough away, she ran downstairs like the wind.

CHAPTER III.

SOME ACCOUNT IS GIVEN OF THE ARRIVAL OF A REMARKABLE PERSONAGE IN DAPSULHEIM, AND OF WHAT FOLLOWED FURTHER.

Herr Dapsul Von Zabelthau had just embraced his daughter with many tears, and was moving off to ascend his tower, where he dreaded every moment the alarming visit of the incensed gnome, when the sound of a horn, loud and clear, made itself heard, and into the courtyard came bounding and curvetting[2] a little cavalier[3] of sufficiently strange and amusing appearance. His yellow horse was not at all large, and was of delicate build, so that the little rider, in spite of his large shapeless head, did not look so dwarfish as might otherwise have been the case, as he

---

[1] An instrument associated with goatherds and the wild, half-goat god, Pan

[2] Hopping, leaping

[3] A gallant, mounted soldier; a knight

sate[1] a considerable height above the horse's head. But this was attributable to the length of his body, for what of him hung over the saddle in the nature of legs and feet was hardly worth mentioning. For the rest, the little fellow had on a very rich habit of gold-yellow atlas[2], a fine high cap with a splendid grass-green plume, and riding-boots of beautifully polished mahogany[3]. With a resounding "P-r-r-r-r-r!" he reined up before Herr von Zabelthau, and seemed to be going to dismount. But he suddenly slipped under the horse's belly as quick as lightning, and having got to the other side of him, threw himself three times in succession some twelve ells[4] up in the air, turning six somersaults in every ell, and then alighted on his head in the saddle. Standing on his head there, he galloped backwards, forwards, and sideways in all sorts of extraordinary curves and ups and downs, his feet meanwhile playing trochees, dactyls, pyrrhics[5], &c., in the air. When this accomplished gymnast and trick-act rider at length stood still, and politely saluted, there were to be seen on the ground of the courtyard the words, "My most courteous greeting to you and your lady daughter, most highly respected Herr Dapsul von Zabelthau." These words he had ridden into the ground in handsome Roman uncial[6] letters. Thereupon, he sprang from his horse, turned three Catherine wheels[7], and said that he was charged by his gracious master, the Herr Baron Porphyrio von Ockerodastes, called "Cordovanspitz," to present his compliments to Herr Dapsul von Zabelthau, and to say, that if the latter had no objection, the Herr Baron proposed to pay him a friendly visit of a day or two, as he was expecting presently to be his nearest neighbour.

Herr Dapsul looked more dead than alive, so pale and motionless did he stand, leaning un his daughter. Scarcely had a half involuntary, "It—will—give—me—much—pleasure," escaped his trembling lips, when the little horseman departed with lightning speed, and similar ceremonies to those with which he had arrived.

"Ah, my daughter!" cried Herr Dapsul, weeping and lamenting, "alas! it is but too certain that this is the gnome come to carry you off, and twist my unfortunate neck. But we will pluck up the very last scrap of courage which we can scrape together. Perhaps it may be still possible to pacify this irritated elementary spirit. We must be as careful in our conduct towards

---

[1] Archaic: sat

[2] A robe of gold-yellow satin

[3] That is, dark-brown, vegetable-dyed leather

[4] 45 feet

[5] Styles and meters of poetry – the sort which Amandus so poorly writes

[6] A simple, curvy, medieval-looking calligraphy style, fl. 4th-8th centuries

[7] Cartwheel

him as ever we can. I will at once read to you, my dear child, a chapter or two of Lactantius or Thomas Aquinas[1] concerning the mode of dealing with elementary spirits, so that you mayn't make some tremendous mistake or other."

But before he could go and get hold of Lactantius or Thomas Aquinas, a band was heard in the immediate proximity, sounding very much like the kind of performance which children who are musical enough get up about Christmas-time. And a fine long procession was coming up the street. At the head of it rode some sixty or seventy little cavaliers on little yellow horses, all dressed like the one who had arrived as avant-courier[2] at first, in yellow habits, pointed caps, and boots of polished mahogany. They were followed by a coach of purest crystal, drawn by eight yellow horses, and behind this came well on to forty other less magnificent coaches, some with six horses, some with only four. And there were swarms of pages, running footmen, and other attendants, moving up and down amongst and around those coaches in brilliant costumes, so that the whole thing formed a sight as charming as uncommon. Herr Dapsul stood sunk in gloomy amazement. Aennchen, who had never dreamt that the world could contain such lovely, delightful creatures as these little horses and people, was quite out of her senses with delight, and forgot everything, even to shut her mouth, which she had opened to emit a cry of joy.

The coach and eight drew up before Herr Dapsul. Riders jumped from their horses, pages and attendants came hurrying forward, and the personage who was now lifted down the steps of the coach on their arms was none other than the Herr Baron Porphyrio von Ockerodastes, otherwise known as Cordovanspitz. Inasmuch as regarded his figure, the Herr Baron was far from comparable to the Apollo of Belvedere, or even the Dying Gladiator[3]. For,
besides the circumstances that he was scarcely three feet high, one-third of his small body consisted of his evidently too large and broad head, which was, moreover, adorned by a tremendously long Roman nose and a pair of great round projecting eyes. And as his body was disproportionately long for his height, there was nothing left for his legs and feet to occupy but some four inches or so. This small space was made the most of, however, for the little Baron's feet were the neatest and prettiest little things ever beheld. No doubt they seemed to be scarcely strong enough to support the large, important head. For the Baron's gait was somewhat tottery and uncertain, and he even toppled over altogether pretty frequently, but got up upon his feet immediately, after the manner of a jack-in-the-box. So that this toppling over had a considerable resemblance to some rather eccentric

---

[1] Two prominent Christian theologians who wrote prolifically on the supernatural

[2] Herald, announcer

[3] Famously handsome statues of powerful men

dancing step more than to anything else one could compare it to. He had on a close-fitting suit of some shining gold fabric, and a headdress, which was almost like a crown, with an enormous plume of green feathers in it.

As soon as the Baron had alighted on the ground, he hastened up to Herr Dapsul von Zabelthau, took hold of both his hands, swung himself up to his neck, and cried out, in a voice wonderfully more powerful than his shortness of stature would have led one to expect, "Oh, my Dapsul von Zabelthau, my most beloved father!" He then lowered himself down from Herr Dapsul's neck with the same deftness of skill with which he had climbed up to it, sprang, or rather slung himself, to Fräulein Aennchen, took that hand of hers which had the ring on it, covered it with loud resounding kisses, and cried out in the same almost thundering voice as before, "Oh, my loveliest Fräulein Anna von Zabelthau, my most beloved bride-elect[1]!"

He then clapped his hands, and immediately that noisy clattering child-like band struck up, and over a hundred little fellows, who had got off their horses and out of the carriages, danced as the avant-courier had done, sometimes on their heads, sometimes on their feet, in the prettiest possible trochees, spondees, iambics, pyrrhics, anapaests, tribrachs, bacchi, antibacchi, choriambs, and dactyls[2], so that it was a joy to behold them. But as this was going on, Fräulein Aennchen recovered from the terrible fright which the little Baron's speech to her had put her in, and entered into several important and necessary economic questions and considerations. "How is it possible," she asked herself, "that these little beings can find room in this place of ours? Would it hold even their servants if they were to be put to sleep in the big barn? Then what could I do with the swell folk[3] who came in the coaches, and of course expect to be put into fine bedrooms, with soft beds, as they're accustomed to be? And even if the two plough horses were to go out of the stable, and I were to be so hard hearted as to turn the old lame chestnut[4] out into the grass field, would there be anything like room enough for all those little beasts of horses that this nasty ugly Baron has brought? And just the same with the one and forty coaches. But the worst of all comes after that. Oh, my gracious! is the whole year's provender[5] anything like enough to keep all these little creatures going for even so much as a couple of days?" This last was the climax of all. She saw in her mind's eye everything eaten up—all the new vegetables, the sheep, the poultry, the salt meat—nay, the very beetroot brandy gone. And this brought the salt tears to her eyes. She thought she caught the Baron making a sort of wicked impudent face at

---

[1] Fiancée

[2] More poetic meters

[3] Gentry and nobles

[4] A brown horse

[5] Livestock food

her, and that gave her courage to say to him (while his people were keeping up their dancing with might and main), in the plainest language possible, that however flattering his visit might be to her father, it was impossible to think of such a thing as its lasting more than a couple of hours or so, as there was neither room nor anything else for the proper reception and entertainment of such a grand gentleman and such a numerous retinue. But little Cordovanspitz immediately looked as marvellously sweet and tender as any marzipan tart, pressing with closed eyes Fräulein Aennchen's hand (which was rather rough, and not particularly white) to his lips, as he assured her that the last thing he should think of was causing the dear papa and his lovely daughter the slightest inconvenience. He said he had brought everything in the kitchen and cellar department with him, and as for the lodging, he needed nothing but a little bit of ground with the open air above it, where his people could put up his ordinary travelling palace, which would accommodate him, his whole retinue, and the animals pertaining to them.

Fräulein Aennchen was so delighted with these words of the Baron Porphyrio von Ockerodastes that, to show that she wasn't grudging a little bit of hospitality, she was going to offer him the little fritter cakes she had made for the last consecration day[1], and a small glass of the beetroot brandy, unless he would have preferred double bitters, which the maid had brought from the town and recommended as strengthening to the stomach. But at this moment Cordovanspitz announced that he had chosen the kitchen garden as the site of his palace, and Aennchen's happiness was gone. But whilst the Baron's retainers, in celebration of their lord's arrival at Dapsulheim, continued their Olympian games, sometimes butting with their big heads at each other's stomachs, knocking each other over backwards, sometimes springing up in the air again, playing at skittles[2], being themselves in turn skittles, balls, and players, and so forth, Baron Porphyrio von Ockerodastes got into a very deep and interesting conversation with Herr Dapsul von Zabelthau, which seemed to go on increasing in importance till they went away together hand in hand, and up into the astronomical tower.

Full of alarm and anxiety, Fräulein Aennchen now made haste to her kitchen garden, with the view of trying to save whatever it might still be possible to save. The maid-servant was there already, standing staring before her with open mouth, motionless as a person turned like Lot's wife into a pillar of salt[3]. Aennchen at once fell into the same condition beside

---

[1] February 2, a Christian holiday – also called Candlemass – which celebrates Christ's dedication at the temple during his infancy

[2] A bowling-like game

[3] A character in Genesis 19: Lot's wife is turned into salt for turning back to watch the destruction of Sodom and Gomorrah

her. At last they both cried out, making the welkin[1] ring, "Oh, Herr Gemini! What a terrible sort of thing!" For the whole beautiful vegetable garden was turned into a wilderness. Not the trace of a plant in it, it looked like a devastated country.

"No," cried the maid, "there's no other way of accounting for it, these cursed little creatures have done it. Coming here in their coaches, forsooth! coaches, quotha! as if they were people of quality! Ha! ha! A lot of kobolds[2], that's what *they* are, trust *me* for that, Miss. And if I had a drop of holy water here I'd soon show you what all those fine things of theirs would turn to[3]. But if they come here, the little brutes, I'll bash the heads of them with this spade here." And she flourished this threatening spade over her head, whilst Anna wept aloud.

But at this point, four members of Cordovanspitz's suite came up with such very pleasant ingratiating speeches and such courteous reverences[4], being such wonderful creatures to behold, at the same time that the maid, instead of attacking them with the spade, let it slowly sink, and Fräulein Aennchen ceased weeping.

They announced themselves as being the four friends who were the most immediately attached to their lord's person, saying that they belonged to four different nationalities (as their dress indicated, symbolically, at all events), and that their names were, respectively, Pan Kapustowicz[5], from Poland; Herr von Schwartzrettig[6], from Pomerania; Signor di Broccoli, from Italy; and Monsieur de Rocambolle[7], from France. They said, moreover, that the builders would come directly, and afford the beautiful lady the gratification of seeing them erect a lovely palace, all of silk, in the shortest possible space of time.

"What good will the silken palace be to me?" cried Fräulein Aennchen, weeping aloud in her bitter sorrow. "And what do I care about your Baron Cordovanspitz, now that you have gone and destroyed my beautiful vegetables, wretched creatures that you are. All my happy days are over."

But the polite interlocutors comforted her, and assured her that they had not by any means had the blame of desolating the kitchen-garden, and that, moreover, it would very soon be growing green and flourishing in such luxuriance as she had never seen, or anybody else in the world for that matter.

---

[1] Heavens

[2] Imps, fairies

[3] When touched by Holy Water, the fine possessions of fairies are said to ash, dust, nutshells and other worthless things – revealing their true, empty nature

[4] Bows

[5] Cabbage

[6] Black raddish (Pomerania is in Germany)

[7] Leeks

The little building-people arrived, and then there began such a confused-looking, higgledy-piggledy, and helter-skeltering on the plot of ground that Fräulein Anna and the maid ran away quite frightened, and took shelter behind some thickets, whence they could see what would be the end of it all.

But though they couldn't explain to themselves how things perfectly canny *could* come about as they did, there certainly arose and formed itself before their eyes, and in a few minutes' time, a lofty and magnificent marquee[1], made of a golden-yellow material and ornamented with many-coloured garlands and plumes, occupying the whole extent of the vegetable garden, so that the cords of it went right away over the village and into the wood beyond, where they were made fast to sturdy trees.

As soon as this marquee was ready, Baron Porphyrio came down with Herr Dapsul from the astronomical tower, after profuse embraces resumed his seat in the coach and eight, and in the same order in which they had made their entry into Dapsulheim, he and his following went into the silken palace, which, when the last of the procession was within it, instantly closed itself up.

Fräulein Aennchen had never seen her papa as he was then. The very faintest trace of the melancholy which had hitherto always so distressed him had completely disappeared from his countenance. One would really almost have said he smiled. There was a sublimity about his facial expression such as sometimes indicates that some great and unexpected happiness has come upon a person. He led his daughter by the hand in silence into the house, embraced her three times consecutively, and then broke out—

"Fortunate Anna! Thrice happy girl! Fortunate father! Oh, daughter, all sorrow and melancholy, all solicitude and misgiving are over for ever! Yours is a fate such as falls to the lot of few mortals. This Baron Porphyrio von Ockerodastes, otherwise known as Cordovanspitz, is by no means a hostile gnome, although he is descended from one of those elementary spirits who, however, was so fortunate as to purify his nature by the teaching of Oromasis the Salamander. The love of this being was bestowed upon a daughter of the human race, with whom he formed a union, and became founder of the most illustrious family whose name ever adorned a parchment. I have an impression that I told you before, beloved daughter Anna, that the pupil of the great Salamander Oromasis, the noble gnome Tsilmenech (a Chaldean[2] name, which interpreted into our language has a somewhat similar significance to our word 'Thickhead'), bestowed his affection on the celebrated Magdalena de la Croix, abbess of a convent at Cordova in Spain, and lived in happy wedlock with her for nearly thirty years. And a descendant of the sublime family of higher intelligences which

[1] A massive tent, like a circus tent

[2] Of Ancient Mesopotamia

sprung from this union is our dear Baron Porphyrio von Ockerodastes, who has adopted the sobriquet of Cordovanspitz to indicate his ancestral connection with Cordova in Spain, and to distinguish himself by it from a more haughty but less worthy collateral line of the family, which bears the title of 'Saffian[1].' That a 'spitz' has been added to the 'Cordovan' doubtless possesses its own elementary astrological causes; I have not as yet gone into that subject. Following the example of his illustrious ancestor the gnome Tsilmenech, this splendid Ockerodastes of ours fell in love with you when you were only twelve years of age (Tsilmenech had done precisely the same thing in the case of Magdalena de la Croix). He was fortunate enough at that time to get a small gold ring from you, and now you wear his, so that your betrothal is indissoluble."

"What?" cried Fräulein Aennchen, in fear and amazement. "What? I betrothed to *him*—I to marry that horrible little kobold? Haven't I been engaged for ever so long to Herr Amandus von Nebelstern? No, never will I have that hideous monster of a wizard for a husband. I don't care whether he comes from Cordova or from Saffian."

"There," said Herr Dapsul von Zabelthau more gravely, "there I perceive, to my sorrow and distress, how impossible it is for celestial wisdom to penetrate into your hardened, obdurate[2], earthly sense. You stigmatize this noble, elementary, Porphyrio von Ockerodastes as 'horrible' and 'ugly,' probably, I presume, because he is only three feet high, and, with the exception of his head, has very little worth speaking of on his body in the shape of arms, legs, and other appurtenances; and a foolish, earthly goose, such as you probably think of as to be admired, can't have legs long enough, on account of coat tails. Oh, my daughter, in what a terrible misapprehension you are involved! All beauty lies in wisdom, in the thought; and the physical symbol of thought is the head. The more head, the more beauty and wisdom. And if mankind could but cast away all the other members of the body as pernicious articles of luxury tending to evil, they would reach the condition of a perfect ideal of the highest type. Whence come all trouble and difficulty, vexation and annoyance, strife and contention—in short, all the depravities and miseries of humanity, but from the accursed luxury and voluptuousness of the members? Oh, what joy, what peace, what blessedness there would be on earth if the human race could exist without arms or legs, or the nether parts of the body—in short, if we were nothing but busts! Therefore it is a happy idea of the sculptors when they represent great statesmen, or celebrated men of science and learning as busts, symbolically indicating the higher nature within them. Wherefore, my daughter Anna, no more of such words as 'ugly and abominable' applied to the noblest of spirits, the grand Porphyrio

---

[1] A type of leather made in Safi, Morrocco (Cordoba is also renowned for its leatherwork)

[2] Resistant, stubborn

von Ockerodastes, whose bride elect you most indubitably are. I must just tell you, at the same time, that by his important aid your father will soon attain that highest step of bliss towards which he has so long been striving. Porphyrio von Ockerodastes is in possession of authentic information that I am beloved by the sylphide Nehabilah (which in Syriac[1] has very much the signification of our expression 'Peaky nose'), and he has promised to assist me to the utmost of his power to render myself worthy of a union with this higher spiritual nature. I have no doubt whatever, my dear child, that you will be well satisfied with your future stepmother. All I hope is, that a favourable destiny may so order matters that our marriages may both take place at one and the same fortunate hour."

Having thus spoken, Herr Dapsul von Zabelthau, casting a significant glance at his daughter, very pathetically left the room.

It was a great weight on Aennchen's heart that she remembered having, a great while ago, really in some unaccountable way lost a little gold ring, such as a child might wear, from her finger. So that it really seemed too certain that this abominable little wizard of a creature had indeed got her immeshed in his net, so that she couldn't see how she was ever to get out of it. And over this she fell into the utmost grief and bewilderment. She felt that her oppressed heart must obtain relief; and this took place through the medium of a goose-quill, which she seized, and at once wrote off to Herr Amandus von Nebelstern as follows:

"MY DEAREST AMANDUS—

"All is over with me completely. I am the most unfortunate creature in the whole world, and I'm sobbing and crying for sheer misery so terribly that the dear dumb animals themselves are sorry for me. And *you'll* be still sorrier than they are, because it's just as great a misfortune for you as it is for me, and you can't help being quite as much distressed about it as I am myself. You know that we love one another as fondly as any two lovers possibly can, and that I am betrothed to you, and that papa was going with us to the church. Very well. All of a sudden a nasty little creature comes here in a coach and eight, with a lot of people and servants, and says I have changed rings with him, and that he and I are engaged. And—just fancy how awful! papa says as well, that I must marry this little wretch, because he belongs to a very grand family. I suppose he very likely does, judging by his following and the splendid dresses they have on. But the creature has such a horrible name that, for that alone if it were for nothing else, I never would marry him. I can't even pronounce the heathenish[2] words of the name; but one of them is Cordovanspitz, and it seems that is the family name. Write and tell me if these Cordovanspitzes really *are* so very great and aristocratic a family—people in the town will be sure to know if they are. And the things papa takes in his head at his time of life I really can't

---

[1] A dialect of Ancient Aramaic

[2] Exotic-sounding

understand; but he wants to marry again, and this nasty Cordovanspitz is going to get him a wife that flies in the air. God protect us! Our servant girl is looking over my shoulder, and says she hasn't much of an opinion of ladies who can fly in the air and swim[1] in the water, and that she'll have to be looking out for another situation[2], and hopes, for my sake, that my stepmother may break her neck the first time she goes riding through the air to St. Walpurgis. Nice state of things, isn't it? But all my hope is in *you*. For I know you are the person who ought to be, and has got to be, just where and what you are, and has to deliver me from a great danger. The danger has come, so be quick, and rescue

"Your grieved to death, but most true and loving *fiancée*,

"ANNA VON ZABELTHAU.

"P.S.—Couldn't you call this yellow little Cordovanspitz out? I'm sure you could settle his hash[3]. He's feeble on his legs.

"What I implore you to do is to put on your things as fast as you can and hasten to

"Your most unfortunate and miserable,

"But always most faithful *fiancée*.

"ANNA VON ZABELTHAU."

CHAPTER IV.

IN WHICH THE HOUSEHOLD STATE OF A GREAT KING IS DESCRIBED; AND AFTERWARDS A BLOODY DUEL AND OTHER REMARKABLE OCCURRENCES ARE TREATED OF.

Fräulein Aennchen was so miserable and distressed that she felt paralyzed in all her members. She was sitting at the window with folded arms gazing straight before her, heedless of the cackling, crowing, and queaking[4] of the fowls, which couldn't understand why on earth she didn't come and drive them into their roosts as usual, seeing that the twilight was coming on fast. Nay, she sat there with perfect indifference and allowed the maid to carry out this duty, and to hit the big cock (who opposed himself to the state of things and evinced decided resistance to her authority) a good sharp whang with her whip. For the love-pain which was rending her own heart was making her indifferent to the troubles of the dear pupils of her happier hours—those which she devoted to their up-bringing, although she had never studied Chesterfield

[1] That is, survive without air under water like a fish

[2] Job

[3] Kick his ass

[4] Archaic: squeaking

or Knigge, or consulted Madame de Genlis[1], or any of those other authorities on the mental culture of the young, who know to a hair's-breadth exactly how they ought to be moulded. In this respect she really had laid herself open to censure on the score of lack of due seriousness.

All that day Cordovanspitz had not shown himself, but had been shut up in the tower with Herr Dapsul, no doubt assisting in the carrying on of important operations. But now Fräulein Aennchen caught sight of the little creature coming tottering across the courtyard in the glowing light of the setting sun. And it struck her that he looked more hideous in that yellow habit of his than he had ever done before. The ridiculous manner in which he went wavering about, jumping here and there, seeming to topple over every minute and then pick himself up again (at which anybody else would have died of laughing), only caused her the bitterer distress. Indeed, she at last held her hands in front of her eyes, that she mightn't so much as see the little horrid creature at all. Suddenly she felt something tugging at her dress, and cried "Down, Feldmann!" thinking it was the Dachshund. But it was not the dog; and what Fräulein Aennchen saw when she took her hands from her eyes was the Herr Baron Porphyrio von Ockerodastes, who hoisted himself into her lap with extraordinary deftness, and clasped both his arms about her. She screamed aloud with fear and disgust, and started up from her chair. But Cordovanspitz kept clinging on to her neck, and instantly became so wonderfully heavy that he seemed to weigh a ton at least, and he dragged the unfortunate Aennchen back again into her chair. Having got her there, however, he slid down out of her lap, sank on one knee as gracefully as possible, and as prettily as his weakness in the direction of equilibrium permitted, and said, in a clear voice—rather peculiar, but by no means unpleasing: "Adored Anna von Zabelthau, most glorious of ladies, most choice of brides-elect; no anger, I implore, no anger, no anger. I know you think my people laid waste your beautiful vegetable garden to put up my palace. Oh, powers of the universe, if you could but look into this little body of mine which throbs with magnanimity and love; if you could but detect all the cardinal virtues which are collected in my breast, under this yellow atlas habit. Oh, how guiltless am I of the shameful cruelty which you attribute to me! How could a beneficent prince treat in such a way his very own subjects. But hold—hold! What are words, phrases? You must see with your own eyes, my betrothed, the splendours which attend you. You must come with me at once. I will lead you to my palace, where a joyful people await the arrival of her who is beloved by their lord."

It may be imagined how terrified Fräulein Aennchen was at this proposition of Cordovanspitz's, and how hard she tried to avoid going so

---

[1] 18th century thought-leaders in the burgeoning philosophies of child and young adult development: a British earl, German baron, and French comtesse, respectively

much as a single step with the little monster. But he continued to describe the extraordinary beauty and the marvellous richness of the vegetable garden which was his palace, in such eloquent and persuasive language, that at last she thought she would just have a peep into the marquee, as that couldn't do her much harm. The little creature, in his joy and delight, turned at least twelve Catherine wheels in succession, and then took her hand with much courtesy, and led her through the garden to the silken palace.

With a loud "Ah!" Fräulein Aennchen stood riveted to the ground with delight when the curtains of the entrance drew apart, displaying a vegetable garden stretching away further than the eye could reach, of such marvellous beauty and luxuriance as was never seen in the loveliest dreams. Here there was growing and flourishing every thing in the nature of colewort, rape, lettuce, pease and beans, in such a shimmer of light, and in such luxuriance that it is impossible to describe it. A band of pipes, drums and cymbals sounded louder, and the four gentlemen whose acquaintance she had previously made, viz. Herr von Schwartzrettig, Monsieur de Rocambolle, Signor di Broccoli and Pan Kapustowicz, approached with many ceremonious reverences.

"My chamberlains," said Porphyrio von Ockerodastes, smiling; and, preceded by them, he conducted Fräulein Aennchen through between the double ranks of the bodyguard of Red English Carrots to the centre of the plain, where stood a splendid throne. And around this throne were assembled the grandees[1] of the realm; the Lettuce Princes with the Bean Princesses, the Dukes of Cucumber with the Prince of Melon at their head, the Cabbage Minister, the General Officer of Onions and Carrots, the Colewort ladies, etc., etc., all in the gala dresses of their rank and station. And amidst them moved up and down well on to a hundred of the prettiest and most delightful Lavender and Fennel pages, diffusing sweet perfume. When Ockerodastes had ascended the throne with Fräulein Aennchen, Chief Court-Marshal Turnip waved his long wand of office, and immediately the band stopped playing, and the multitude listened in reverential silence as Ockerodastes raised his voice and said, in solemn accents, "My faithful and beloved subjects, you see by my side the noble Fräulein Anna von Zabelthau, whom I have chosen to be my consort. Rich in beauty and virtues, she has long watched over you with the eye of maternal affection, preparing soft and succulent beds for you, caring for you and tending you with ceaseless ardour. She will ever be a true and befitting mother of this realm. Wherefore I call upon you to evince and give expression to the dutiful approval, and the duly regulated rejoicing at the favour and benefit which I am about to graciously confer upon you."

[1] Important nobles

At a signal given by Chief Court-Marshal Turnip there arose the shout of a thousand voices, the Bulb Artillery fired their pieces[1], and the band of the Carrot Guard played the celebrated National Anthem—

"Salad and lettuce, and parsley so green."

It was a grand, a sublime moment, which drew tears from the eyes of the grandees, particularly from those of the Colewort ladies. Fräulein Aennchen, too, nearly lost all her self-control when she noticed that little Ockerodastes had a crown on his head all sparkling with diamonds, and a golden sceptre in his hand.

"Ah!" she cried clapping her hands. "Oh, Gemini! You seem to be something much grander than we thought, my dear Herr von Cordovanspitz."

"My adored Anna," he replied, "the stars compelled me to appear before your father under an assumed name. You must be told, dearest girl, that I am one of the mightiest of kings, and rule over a realm whose boundaries are not discoverable, as it has been omitted to lay them down in the maps. Oh, sweetest Anna, he who offers you his hand and crown is Daucus Carota[2] the First, King of the Vegetables. All the vegetable princes are my vassals, save that the King of the Beans reigns for one single day in every year, in conformity to an ancient usage."

"Then I am to be a queen, am I?" cried Fräulein Aennchen, overjoyed. "And all this great splendid vegetable garden is to be mine?"

King Daucus assured her that of course it was to be so, and added that he and she would jointly rule over all the vegetables in the world. She had never dreamt of anything of the kind, and thought little Cordovanspitz wasn't anything like so nasty-looking as he used to be now that he was transformed into King Daucus Carota the First, and that the crown and sceptre were very becoming to him, and the kingly mantle as well. When she reckoned into the bargain his delightful manners, and the property this marriage would bring her, she felt certain that there wasn't a country lady in all the world who could have made a better match than she, who found herself betrothed to a king before she knew where she was. So she was delighted beyond measure, and asked her royal *fiancé* whether she could not take up her abode in the palace then and there, and be married next day. But King Daucus answered that eagerly as he longed for the time when he might call her his own, certain constellations compelled him to postpone that happiness a little longer. And that Herr Dapsul von Zabelthau, moreover, must be kept in ignorance of his son-in-law's royal station, because otherwise the operations necessary for bringing about the desired union with the sylphide Nehabilah might be unsuccessful. Besides, he said, he had promised that both the weddings should take place on the same day. So Fräulein Aennchen had to take a solemn vow not to mention

---

[1] That is, cannons

[2] The scientific name for wild carrots, also called Queen Anne's lace

one syllable to Herr Dapsul of what had been happening to her. She therefore left the silken palace amid long and loud rejoicings of the people, who were in raptures with her beauty as well as with her affability and gracious condescension of manners and behaviour.

In her dreams she once more beheld the realms of the charming King Daucus, and was lapped in Elysium.

The letter which she had sent to Herr Amandus von Nebelstern made a frightful impression on him. Ere long, Fräulein Aennchen received the following answer—

'IDOL OF MY HEART, HEAVENLY ANNA,—

"Daggers—sharp, glowing, poisoned, death-dealing daggers were to me the words of your letter, which pierced my breast through and through. Oh, Anna! *you* to be torn from me. What a thought! I cannot, even now, understand how it was that I did not go mad on the spot and commit some terrible deed[1]. But I fled the face of man, overpowered with rage at my deadly destiny, after dinner—without the game of billiards which I generally play—out into the woods, where I wrung my hands, and called on your name a thousand times. It came on a tremendously heavy rain, and I had on a new cap, red velvet, with a splendid gold tassel (everybody says I never had anything so becoming). The rain was spoiling it, and it was brand-new. But what are caps, what are velvet and gold, to a despairing lover? I strode up and down till I was wet to the skin and chilled to the bone, and had a terrible pain in my stomach. This drove me into a restaurant near, where I got them to make me some excellent mulled wine, and had a pipe of your heavenly Virginia tobacco. I soon felt myself elevated on the wings of a celestial inspiration, took out my pocket-book, and, oh!—wondrous gift of poetry—the love-despair and the stomach-ache both disappeared at once. I shall content myself with writing out for you only the last of these poems; it will inspire you with heavenly hope, as it did myself.

"Wrapped in darkest sorrow—
In my heart, extinguished,
No love-tapers burning—
Joy hath no to-morrow.
"Ha! the Muse approaches,
Words and rhymes inspiring,
Little verse inscribing,
Joy returns apace.
"New love-tapers blazing,
All the heart inspiring,
Fare thee well, my sorrow,
Joy thy place doth borrow.

[1] Common euphemism for suicide

"Ay, my sweet Anna, soon shall I, thy champion, hasten to rescue you from the miscreant who would carry you off from me. So, once more take comfort, sweetest maid. Bear me ever in thy heart. He comes; he rescues you; he clasps you to his bosom, which heaves in tumultuous emotion.

"Your ever faithful

"AMANDUS VON NEBELSTERN.

"P.S.—It would be quite impossible for me to call Herr von Cordovanspitz out. For, oh Anna! every drop of blood drawn from your Amandus by the weapon of a presumptuous adversary were glorious poet's blood—ichor of the gods—which never ought to be shed. The world very properly claims that such a spirit as mine has it imposed upon it as public duty to take care of itself for the world's benefit, and preserve itself by every possible means. The sword of the poet is the word—the song. I will attack my rival with Tyrtæan[1] battle-songs; strike him to earth with sharp-pointed epigrams; hew him down with dithyrambics full of lover's fury. Such are the weapons of a true, genuine poet, powerful to shield him from every danger. And it is so accoutred that I shall appear, and do battle—victorious battle—for your hand, oh, Anna!

"Farewell. I press you once more to my heart. Hope all things from my love, and, especially, from my heroic courage, which will shun no danger to set you free from the shameful nets of captivity in which, to all appearance, you are entangled by a demoniacal monster."

Fräulein Aennchen received this letter at a time when she was playing a game at "Catch-me-if-you-can" with her royal bridegroom elect, King Daucus Carota the First, in the meadow at the back of the garden, and immensely enjoying it when, as was often the case, she suddenly ducked down in full career[2], and the little king would go shooting right away over her head. Instead of reading the letter immediately (which she had always done before), she put it in her pocket unopened, and we shall presently see that it came too late.

Herr Dapsul could not make out at all how Fräulein Aennchen had changed her mind so suddenly, and grown quite fond of Herr Porphyrio von Ockerodastes, whom she had so cordially detested before. He consulted the stars on the subject, but as they gave him no satisfactory information, he was obliged to come to the conclusion that human hearts are more mysterious and inscrutable than all the secrets of the universe, and not to be thrown light upon by any constellation. He could not think that what had produced love for the little creature in Anna's heart was merely the highness of his nature; and personal beauty he had none. If (as the reader knows) the canon of beauty, as laid down by Herr Dapsul, is very unlike the ideas which young ladies form upon that subject, he did, after

---

[1] Relating to Tyrtaeus, a 7th century B.C. Spartan poet known for his gloomy elegies and stirring, militaristic poetry about battle

[2] Archaic: at full speed

all, possess sufficient knowledge of the world to know that, although the said young women hold that good sense, wit, cleverness and pleasant manners are very agreeable fellow-lodgers in a comfortable house, still, a man who can't call himself the possessor of a properly-made, fashionable coat—were he a Shakespeare, a Goethe, a Tieck, or a Jean Paul Richter[1]—would run a decided risk of being beaten out of the field by any sufficiently well put-together lieutenant of hussars[2] in uniform, if he took it in his head to pay his addresses to one of them. Now in Fräulein Aennchen's case it was a different matter altogether. It was neither good looks nor cleverness that were in question; but it is not exactly every day that a poor country lady becomes a queen all in a moment, and accordingly it was not very likely that Herr Dapsul should hit upon the cause which had been operating, particularly as the very stars had left him in the lurch.

As may be supposed, those three, Herr Porphyrio, Herr Dapsul and Fräulein Aennchen, were one heart and one soul. This went so far that Herr Dapsul left his tower oftener than he had ever been known to do before, to chat with his much-prized son-in-law on all sorts of agreeable subjects; and not only this, but he now regularly took his breakfast in the house. About this hour, too, Herr Porphyrio was wont to come forth from his silken palace, and eat a good share of Fräulein Aennchen's bread and butter.

"Ah, ah!" she would often whisper softly in his ear, "if papa only knew that you are a real king, dearest Cordovanspitz!"

"Be still, oh heart! Melt not away in rapture," Daucus Carota the First would say. "Near, near is the joyful day!"

It chanced that the schoolmaster had sent Fräulein Aennchen a present of some of the finest radishes from his garden. She was particularly pleased at this, as Herr Dapsul was very fond of radishes, and she could not get anything from the vegetable garden because it was covered by the silk marquee. Besides this, it now occurred to her for the first time that, among all the roots and vegetables she had seen in the palace, radishes were conspicuous by their absence.

So she speedily cleaned them and served them up for her father's breakfast. He had ruthlessly shorn several of them of their leafy crowns, dipped them in salt, and eaten them with much relish, when Cordovanspitz came in.

"Oh, my Ockerodastes," Herr Dapsul called to him, "are you fond of radishes?"

---

[1] Goethe, Tieck, and Richter are three of the most famous German writers – Enlightenment-influenced Romantic poets and polymaths – from the turn of the 19th century. Johann von Goethe, in particular, remains Germany's greatest man of letters in any era

[2] Hussars are light cavalrymen who are uniformed in a distinctly Hungarian-influenced fashion, known for their dashing style and energy

There was still a particularly fine and beautiful radish on the dish. But the moment Cordovanspitz saw it his eves gleamed with fury, and he cried in a resonant voice—

"What, unworthy duke, do you dare to appear in my presence again, and to force your way, with the coolest of audacity, into a house which is under my protection? Have I not pronounced sentence of perpetual banishment upon you as a pretender to the imperial throne? Away, treasonous vassal; begone from my sight for ever!"

Two little legs had suddenly shot out beneath the radish's large head, and with them he made a spring out of the plate, placed himself close in front of Cordovanspitz, and addressed him as follows—

"Fierce and tyrannical Daucus Carota the First, you have striven in vain to exterminate my race. Had ever any of your family a head as large as mine, or that of my king? We are all gifted with talent, common-sense, wisdom, sharpness, cultivated manners: and whilst *you* loaf about in kitchens and stables, and are of no use as soon as your early youth is gone (so that in very truth it is nothing but the *diable de la jeunesse*[1] that bestows upon you your brief, transitory, little bit of good fortune), *we* enjoy the friendship of, and the intercourse with, people of position, and are greeted with acclamation as soon as ever we lift up our green heads. But I despise you, Daucus Carota. You're nothing but a low, uncultivated, ignorant Boor, like all the lot of you. Let's see which of us two is the better man."

With this the Duke of Radish, flourishing a long whip about his head, proceeded, without more ado, to attack the person of King Daucus Carota the First. The latter quickly drew his little sword, and defended himself in the bravest manner. The two little creatures darted about in the room, fighting fiercely, and executing the most wonderful leaps and bounds, till Daucus Carota pressed the Duke of Radish so hard that the latter found himself obliged to make a tremendous jump out of the window and take to the open. But Daucus Carota—with whose remarkable agility and dexterity the reader is already acquainted—bounded out after him, and followed the Duke of Radish across country.

Herr Dapsul von Zabelthau had looked on at this terrible encounter rigid and speechless, but he now broke forth into loud and bitter lamentation, crying, "Oh, daughter Anna! oh, my poor unfortunate daughter Anna! Lost—I—you—both of us. All is over with us." With which he left the room, and ascended the astronomical tower as fast as his legs would carry him.

Fräulein Aennchen couldn't understand a bit, or form the very slightest idea what in all the world had set her father into all this boundless misery all of a sudden. The whole thing had caused her the greatest pleasure; moreover, her heart was rejoiced that she had had an opportunity of seeing

---

[1] French: "the devil of youth" – meaning a mischievous spirit which roguishly blesses the young with good fortune, only for it to painfully fade with age

that her future husband was brave, as well as rich and great; for it would be difficult to find any woman in all the world capable of loving a poltroon[1]. And now that she had proof of the bravery of King Daucus Carota the First, it struck her painfully, for the first time, that Herr Amandus von Nebelstern had cried off from fighting him. If she had for a moment hesitated about sacrificing Herr Amandus to King Daucus, she was quite decided on the point now that she had an opportunity of assuring herself of all the excellencies of her future lord. She sat down and wrote the following letter:—

"MY DEAR AMANDUS,

"Everything in this world is liable to change. Everything passes away, as the schoolmaster says, and he's quite right. I'm sure *you*, my dear Amandus, are such a learned and wise student that you will agree with the schoolmaster, and not be in the very least surprised that my heart and mind have undergone the least little bit of a change. You may quite believe me when I say that I still like you very well, and I can quite imagine how nice you look in your red velvet cap with the gold tassel. But, with regard to marriage, you know very well, Amandus dear, that, clever as you are, and beautiful as are your verses, you will never, in all your days, be a king, and (don't be frightened, dear) little Herr von Cordovanspitz isn't Herr von Cordovanspitz at all, but a great king, Daucus Carota the First, who reigns over the great vegetable kingdom, and has chosen me to be his queen. Since my dear king has thrown aside his incognito he has grown much nicer-looking, and I see now that papa was quite right when he said that the head was the beauty of the man, and therefore couldn't possibly be big enough. And then, Daucus Carota the First (you see how well I remember the beautiful name and how nicely I write it now that has got so familiar to me), I was going to say that my little royal husband, that is to be, has such charming and delightful manners that there's no describing them. And what courage, what bravery there is in him! Before my eyes he put to flight the Duke of Radish, (and a very disagreeable, unfriendly creature *he* appears to be) and hey, how he did jump after him out of the window! You should just have seen him: I only wish you had! And I don't really think that my Daucus Carota would care about those weapons of yours that you speak about one bit. He seems pretty tough, and I don't believe verses would do him any harm at all, however fine and pointed they might be. So now, dear Amandus, you must just make up your mind to be contented with your lot, like a good fellow, and not be vexed with me that I am going to be a Queen instead of marrying you. Never mind, I shall always be your affectionate friend, and if ever you would like an appointment in the Carrot bodyguard, or (as you don't care so much about fighting as about learning) in the Parsley Academy or the Pumpkin Office,

---

[1] A pathetic coward

you have but to say the word and your fortune is made. Farewell, and don't be vexed with

"Your former *fiancée*, but now friend and well-wisher, as well as future Queen,

"ANNA VON ZABELTHAU.

"(but soon to be no more Von Zabelthau, but simply ANNA[1].)

"P.S.—You shall always be kept well supplied with the very finest Virginia tobacco, of that you need have no fear. As far as I can see there won't be any smoking at my court, but I shall take care to have a bed or two of Virginia tobacco planted not far from the throne, under my own special care. This will further culture and morality, and my little Daucus will no doubt have a statute specially enacted on the subject."

CHAPTER V.

IN WHICH AN ACCOUNT IS GIVEN OF A FRIGHTFUL CATASTROPHE, AND WE PROCEED WITH THE FUTURE COURSE OF EVENTS.

Fräulein Aennchen had just finished her letter to Herr Amandus von Nebelstern, when in came Herr Dapsul von Zabelthau and began, in the bitterest grief and sorrow to say, "O, my daughter Anna, how shamefully we are both deceived and betrayed! This miscreant who made me believe he was Baron Porphyrio von Ockerodastes, known as Cordovanspitz, member of a most illustrious family descended from the mighty gnome Tsilmenech and the noble Abbess of Cordova—this miscreant, I say—learn it and fall down insensible—*is* indeed a gnome, but of that lowest of all gnomish castes which has charge of the vegetables. The gnome Tsilmenech was of the highest caste of all, that, namely, to which the care of the diamonds is committed. Next comes the caste which has care of the metals in the realms of the metal-king, and then follow the flower-gnomes, who are lower in position, as depending on the sylphs. But the lowest and most ignoble are the vegetable gnomes, and not only is this deceiver Cordovanspitz a gnome of this caste, but he is actual king of it, and his name is Daucus Carota."

Fräulein Aennchen was far from fainting away, neither was she in the smallest degree frightened, but she smiled in the kindliest way at her lamenting papa, and the Courteous reader is aware of the reason. But as Herr Dapsul was very much surprised at this, and kept imploring her for Heaven's sake to realize the terrible position in which she was, and to feel the full horror of it, she thought herself at liberty to divulge the secret

[1] Royals, of course, always go by mononyms

entrusted to her. She told Herr Dapsul how the so-called Baron von Cordovanspitz had told her his real position long ago, and that since then she had found him altogether so pleasant and delightful that she couldn't wish for a better husband. Moreover she described all the marvellous beauties of the vegetable kingdom into which King Daucus Carota the First had taken her, not forgetting to duly extol the remarkably delightful manners of the inhabitants of that realm.

Herr Dapsul struck his hands together several times, and wept bitterly over the deceiving wickedness of the Gnome-king, who had been, and still was, employing means the most artful—most dangerous for himself as well—to lure the unfortunate Anna down into his dark, demoniac kingdom. "Glorious," he explained, "glorious and advantageous as may be the union of an elementary spirit with a human being, grand as is the example of this given by the wedlock of the gnome Tsilmenech with Magdalena de la Croix (which is of course the reason why this deceiver Daucus Carota has given himself out as being a descendant of that union), yet the kings and princes of those races are very different. If the Salamander kings are only irascible, the sylph kings proud and haughty, the Undine queens affectionate and jealous, the gnome kings are fierce, cruel, and deceitful. Merely to revenge themselves on the children of earth, who deprive them of their vassals, they are constantly trying their utmost to lure one of them away, who then wholly lays aside her human nature, and, becoming as shapeless as the gnomes themselves, has to go down into the earth, and is never more seen."

Fräulein Aennchen didn't seem disposed to believe what her father was telling her to her dear Daucus's discredit, but began talking again about the marvels of the beautiful vegetable country over which she was expecting so soon to reign as queen.

"Foolish, blinded child," cried Herr Dapsul, "do you not give your father credit for possessing sufficient cabalistic science to be well aware that what the abominable Daucus Carota made you suppose you saw was all deception and falsehood? No, you don't believe me, and to save you, my only child, I must convince you, and this conviction must be arrived at by most desperate methods. Come with me."

For the second time she had to go up into the astronomical tower with her papa. From a big band-box[1] Herr Dapsul took a quantity of yellow, red, white, and green ribbon, and, with strange ceremonies, he wrapped Fräulein Aennchen up in it from head to foot. He did the same to himself, and then they both went very carefully to the silken palace of Daucus Carota the First. It was close shut, and by her papa's directions, she had to rip a small opening in one of the seams of it with a large pair of scissors, and then peep in at the opening.

---

[1] A cylindrical, lidded, cardboard box – like a hat-box – used to store cloth, clothing, or other attire

Heaven be about us! what did she see? Instead of the beautiful vegetable garden, the carrot guards, the plumed ladies, lavender pages, lettuce princes, and so forth, she found herself looking down into a deep pool which seemed to be full of a colourless, disgusting-looking slime, in which all kinds of horrible creatures from the bowels of the earth were creeping and twining about. There were fat worms slowly writhing about amongst each other, and beetle-like creatures stretching out their short legs and creeping heavily out. On their backs they bore big onions; but these onions had ugly human faces, and kept fleering and leering at each other with bleared yellow eyes, and trying, with their little claws (which were close behind their ears), to catch hold of one another by their long roman noses, and drag each other down into the slime, while long, naked slugs were rolling about in crowds, with repulsive torpidity, stretching their long horns out of their depths. Fräulein Aennchen was nearly fainting away at this horrid sight. She held both hands to her face, and ran away as hard as she could.

"You see now, do you not," said Herr Dapsul, "how this atrocious Daucus Carota has been deceiving you in showing you splendours of brief duration? He dressed his vassals up in gala dresses to delude you with dazzling displays. But now you have seen the kingdom which you want to reign over in undress uniform; and when you become the consort of the frightful Daucus Carota you will have to live for ever in the subterranean realms, and never appear on the surface any more. And if—Oh, oh, what must I see, wretched, most miserable of fathers that I am?"

He got into such a state all in a moment that she felt certain some fresh misfortune had just come to light, and asked him anxiously what he was lamenting about now. However, he could do nothing for sheer sobbing, but stammer out, "Oh—oh—dau-gh-ter. Wha-t ar—e y-ou—l—l—like?" She ran to her room, looked into the looking-glass, and started back, terrified almost to death.

And she had reason; for the matter stood thus. As Herr Dapsul was trying to open the eyes of Daucus Carota's intended queen to the danger she was in of gradually losing her pretty figure and good looks, and growing more and more into the semblance of a gnome queen, he suddenly became aware of how far the process had proceeded already. Aennchen's head had got much broader and bigger, and her skin had turned yellow, so that she was quite ugly enough already. And though vanity was not one of her failings, she was woman enough to know that to grow ugly is the greatest and most frightful misfortune which can happen here below. How often had she thought how delightful it would be when she would drive, as queen, to church in the coach and eight, with the crown on her head, in satins and velvets, with diamonds, and gold chains, and rings, seated beside her royal husband, setting all the women, the schoolmaster's wife included, into amazement of admiration, and most likely, in fact, no doubt, instilling a proper sense of respect even into the minds of the pompous lord and lady of the manor themselves. Ay, indeed, how often had she been lapt[1] in these and other such eccentric dreams, and visions of the future!—Fräulein Aennchen burst into long and bitter weeping.

"Anna, my daughter Anna," cried Herr Dapsul down through the speaking trumpet; "come up here to me immediately!"

She found him dressed very much like a miner. He spoke in a tone of decision and resolution, saying, "When need is the sorest, help is often nearest. I have ascertained that Daucus Carota will not leave his palace to day, and most probably not till noon of to-morrow. He has assembled the princes of his house, the ministers, and other people of consequence to hold a council on the subject of the next crop of winter cabbage. The sitting is important, and it may be prolonged so much that we may not have any cabbage at all next winter. I mean to take advantage of this opportunity, while he is so occupied with his official affairs that he won't be able to attend to my proceedings, to prepare a weapon with which I may perhaps attack this shameful gnome, and prevail over him, so that he will be compelled to withdraw, and set you at liberty. While I am at work, do you look uninterruptedly at the palace through this glass, and tell me instantly if anybody comes out, or even looks out of it." She did as she was directed, but the marquee remained closed, although she often heard (notwithstanding that Herr Dapsul was making a tremendous hammering on plates of metal a few paces behind her), a wild, confused crying and screaming, apparently coming from the marquee, and also distinct sounds of slapping, as if people's ears were being well boxed[2]. She told Herr Dapsul this, and he was delighted, saying that the more they quarrelled in there the less they were likely to know what was being prepared for their destruction.

Fräulein Aennchen was much surprised when she found that Herr Dapsul had hammered out and made several most lovely kitchen-pots and stew-pans of copper. As an expert in such matters, she observed that the tinning of them was done in a most superior style, so that her papa must have paid careful heed to the duties legally enjoined on coppersmiths. She begged to be allowed to take these nice pots and pans down to the kitchen, and use them there. But Herr Dapsul smiled a mysterious smile, and merely said:

"All in good time, my daughter Anna. Just you go downstairs, my beloved child, and wait quietly till you see what happens to-morrow."

He gave a melancholy smile, and that infused a little hope and confidence into his luckless daughter.

Next day, as dinner-time came on, Herr Dapsul brought down his pots and pans, and betook himself to the kitchen, telling his daughter and the maid to go away and leave him by himself, as he was going to cook the

---

[1] Archaic: lapped – absorbed by, consumed by

[2] "...as if people were being slapped full in the face"

dinner. He particularly enjoined Fräulein Aennchen to be as kind and pleasant with Cordovanspitz as ever she could, when he came in—as he was pretty sure to do.

Cordovanspitz—or rather, King Daucus Carota the First—did come in very soon, and if he had borne himself like an ardent lover on previous occasions, he far outdid himself on this. Aennchen noticed, to her terror, that she had grown so small by this time, that Daucus had no difficulty in getting up into her lap to caress and kiss her; and the wretched girl had to submit to this, notwithstanding her disgust with the horrid little monster. Presently Herr Dapsul came in, and said—

"Oh, my most egregious Porphyrio von Ockerodastes, won't you come into the kitchen with my daughter and me, and see what beautiful order your future bride has got everything in there?" [1]

Aennchen had never seen the wicked, malicious look upon her father's face before, which it wore when he took little Daucus by the arm, and almost forced him from the sitting-room to the kitchen. At a sign of her father's she went there after them.

Her heart swelled within her when she saw the fire burning so merrily, the glowing coals, the beautiful copper pots and pans. As Herr Dapsul drew Cordovanspitz closer to the fire-place, the hissing and bubbling in the pots grew louder and louder, and at last changed into whimpering and groaning. And out of one of the pots came voices, crying, "Oh Daucus Carota! Oh King, rescue your faithful vassals! Rescue us poor carrots! Cut up, thrown into despicable water; rubbed over with salt and butter to our torture, we suffer indescribable woe, whereof a number of noble young parsleys are partakers with us!"

And out of the pans came the plaint: "Oh Daucus Carota! Oh King! Rescue your faithful vassals—rescue us poor carrots. We are roasting in hell—and they put so little water with us, that our direful thirst forces us to drink our own heart's blood[2]!"

And from another of the pots came: "Oh Daucus Carota! Oh King! Rescue your faithful vassals—rescue us poor carrots. A horrible cook eviscerated us, and stuffed our insides full of egg, cream, and butter, so that all our ideas and other mental qualities are in utter confusion, and we don't know ourselves what we are thinking about!"

And out of all the pots and pans came howling at once a general chorus of "Oh Daucus Carota! Mighty King! Rescue us, thy faithful vassals—rescue us poor carrots!"

---

[1] Literally, from the German: "how beautifully and comfortably your future wife has arranged everything there"

[2] That is, they are being steamed, so that they are cooking down in their own juices

On this, Cordovanspitz gave a loud, croaking cry of—"Cursed, infernal, stupid humbug[1] and nonsense!" sprang with his usual agility on to the kitchen range, looked into one of the pots, and suddenly popped down into it bodily. Herr Dapsul sprang in the act of putting on the cover, with a triumphant cry of "a Prisoner!" But with the speed of a spiral spring Cordovanspitz came bounding up out of the pot, and gave Herr Dapsul two or three ringing slaps on the face, crying "Meddling goose of an old Cabalist, you shall pay for this! Come out, my lads, one and all!"

Then there came swarming out of all the pots and pans hundreds and hundreds of little creatures about the length of one's finger, and they attached themselves firmly all over Herr Dapsul's body, threw him down backwards into an enormous dish, and there dished him up, pouring the hot juice out of the pots and pans over him, and bestrewing him with chopped egg, mace[2], and grated breadcrumbs. Having done this, Daucus Carota darted out of the window, and his people after him.

Fräulein Aennchen sank down in terror beside the dish whereon her poor papa lay, served up in this manner as if for table. She supposed he was dead, as he gave not the faintest sign of life.

She began to lament: "Ah, poor papa—you're dead now, and there's nobody to save me from this diabolical Daucus!" But Herr Dapsul opened his eyes, sprang up from the dish with renewed energy, and cried in a terrible voice, such as she had never heard him make use of before, "Ah accursed Daucus Carota, I am not at the end of my resources yet. You shall soon see what the meddling old goose of a Cabalist can do."

Aennchen had to set to work and clean him with the kitchen besom[3] from all the chopped egg, the mace, and the grated breadcrumbs; and then he seized a copper pot, crammed it on his head by way of a helmet, took a frying-pan in his left hand, and a long iron kitchen ladle in his right, and thus armed and accoutred, he darted out into the open. Fräulein Aennchen saw him running as hard as he could towards Cordovanspitz's marquee, and yet never moving from the same spot. At this her senses left her.

When she came to herself, Herr Dapsul had disappeared, and she got terribly anxious when evening came, and night, and even the next morning, without his making his appearance. She could not but dread the very worst.

CHAPTER VI.
WHICH IS THE LAST—AND, AT THE SAME TIME, THE MOST EDIFYING OF ALL.

---

[1] Bullshit, poppycock – describing something which is a bogus sham

[2] Nutmeg

[3] Broom made from dried sticks

Fräulein Aennchen was sitting in her room in the deepest sorrow, when the door opened, and who should come in but Herr Amandus von Nebelstern. All shame and contrition, she shed a flood of tears, and in the most weeping accents addressed him as follows: "Oh, my darling Amandus, pray forgive what I wrote to you in my blinded state! I was bewitched, and I am so still, no doubt. I am yellow, and I'm hideous, may God pity me! But my heart is true to you, and I am not going to marry any king at all."

"My dear girl," said Amandus, "I really don't see what you have to complain of. I consider you one of the luckiest women in the world."

"Oh, don't mock at me," she cried. "I am punished severely enough for my absurd vanity in wishing to be a Queen."

"Really and truly, my dear girl," said Amandus, "I can't make you out one bit. To tell you the real truth, your last letter drove me stark, staring mad. I first thrashed my servant-boy, then my poodle, smashed several glasses—and you know a student who's breathing out threatenings and slaughter in that sort of way isn't to be trifled with. But when I got a little calmer I made up my mind to come on here as quickly as I could, and see with my own eyes how, why, and to whom I had lost my intended bride. Love makes no distinction of class or station, and I made up my mind that I would make this King Daucus Carota give a proper account of himself, and ask him if this tale about his marrying you was mere brag, or if he really meant it—but everything here is different to what I expected. As I was passing near the grand marquee that is put up yonder, King Daucus Carota came out of it, and I soon found that I had before me the most charming prince I ever saw—at the same time he happens to be the first I ever did see; but that's nothing. For, just fancy, my dear girl, he immediately detected the sublime poet in me, praised my poems (which he has never read) above measure, and offered to appoint me Poet Laureate[1] in his service. Now a position of that sort has long been the fairest goal of my warmest wishes, so that I accepted his offer with a thousandfold delight. Oh, my dear girl, with what an enthusiasm of inspiration will I chant your praises! A poet can love queens and princesses: or rather, it is really a part of his simple duty to choose a person of that exalted station to be the lady of his heart[2]. And if he *does* get rather cracky in the head on the subject, that circumstance of itself gives rise to that celestial delirium without which no poetry is possible, and no one ought to feel any surprise at a poet's

---

[1] A poet who is officially appointed by the government to write poems for special occasions or state events

[2] The translation here is a bit florid. He is arguing that it is both acceptable and to be expected for state poets to fall in love with their country's royals – indeed it is his duty to pick at least one royal to be his muse

perhaps somewhat extravagant proceedings[1]. Remember the great Tasso[2], who must have had a considerable bee in his bonnet when in love with the Princess Leonore d'Este. Yes, my dear girl, as you are going to be a queen so soon, you will always be the lady of my heart, and I will extol you to the stars in the sublimest and most celestial verses."

"What, you have seen him, the wicked Cobold?" Fräulein Aennchen broke out in the deepest amazement. "And he has——"

But at that moment in came the little gnomish King himself, and said, in the tenderest accents, "Oh, my sweet, darling *fiancée*! Idol of my heart! Do not suppose for a moment that I am in the least degree annoyed with the little piece of rather unseemly conduct which Herr Dapsul von Zabelthau was guilty of. Oh, no—and indeed it has led to the more rapid fulfilment of my hopes; so that the solemn ceremony of our marriage will actually be celebrated to-morrow. You will be pleased to find that I have appointed Herr Amandus von Nebelstern our Poet Laureate, and I should wish him at once to favour us with a specimen of his talents, and recite one of his poems. But let us go out under the trees, for I love the open air: and I will lie in your lap, while you, my most beloved bride elect, may scratch my head a little while he is singing—for I am fond of having my head scratched in such circumstances."

Fräulein Aennschen, turned to stone with horror and alarm, made no resistance to this proposal. Daucus Carota, out under the trees, laid himself in her lap, she scratched his head, and Herr Amandus, accompanying himself on the guitar, began the first of twelve dozen songs which he had composed and written out in a thick book.

It is a matter of regret that in the Chronicle of Dapsulheim (from which all this history is taken), these songs have not been inserted, it being merely stated that the country folk who were passing, stopped on their way, and anxiously inquired who could be in such terrible pain in Herr Dapsul's wood, that he was crying and screaming out in such a style.

Daucus Carota, in Aennschen's lap, twisted and writhed, and groaned and whined more and more lamentably, as if he had a violent pain in his stomach. Moreover, Fräulein Aennchen fancied she observed, to her great

---

[1] Again, he argues that if a state poet becomes so consumed with unrequited love for his royal muse that he becomes unhinged or obsessive, it is merely the cost which must be paid for really powerful poetry – not surprising at all

[2] Torquato Tasso was a 16th century Italian poet who was known to have gone through a slew of almost ludicrously libidinous infatuations that transcended professionalism. Among these was the daughter of his patron, Elenora D'Este. Rumors said that they were caught in a compromising situation, and – to protect the princess' honor – he feigned a fit of temporary insanity caused by a combination of love and his poetic spirit (the situation to which Amandus is referring). Incidentally, he also wooed Elenora's sister and one of her ladies in waiting

amazement, that Cordovanspitz was growing smaller and smaller as the song went on. At last Herr Amandus sung the following sublime effusion (which is preserved in the Chronicle):—

"Gladly sings the Bard, enraptured,
Breath of blossoms, bright dream-visions,
Moving thro' roseate[1] spaces in Heaven,
Blessed and beautiful, whither away?
'Whither away?' oh, question of questions—
Towards that 'Whither,' the Bard is borne onward,
Caring for nought but to love, to believe.
Moving through roseate heavenly spaces,
Towards this 'Whither,' where'er it may be,
Singeth the bard, in a tumult of rapture,
Ever becoming a radiant em——"

At this point, Daucus Carota uttered a loud croaking cry, and, now dwindled into a little, little carrot, slipped down from Aennchen's lap, and into the ground, leaving no trace behind. Upon which, the great grey fungus which had grown in the night time beside the grassy bank, shot up and up; but this fungus was nothing less than Herr Dapsul von Zabelthau's grey felt hat, and he himself was under it, and fell stormily on Amandus's breast, crying out in the utmost ecstasy, "Oh, my dearest, best, most beloved Herr Amandus von Nebelstern, with that mighty song of conjuration you have beaten all my cabalistic science out of the field? What the profoundest magical art, the utmost daring of the philosopher fighting for his very existence, could not accomplish, your verses achieved, passing into the frame of the deceitful Daucus Carota like the deadliest poison, so that he must have perished of stomach-ache, in spite of his gnomish nature, if he had not made off into his kingdom. My daughter Anna is delivered—I am delivered from the horrible charm which held me spellbound here in the shape of a nasty fungus, at the risk of being hewn to pieces by my own daughter's hands; for the good soul hacks them all down with her spade, unless their edible character is unmistakable, as in the case of the mushrooms. Thanks, my most heartfelt thanks, and I have no doubt your intentions as regards my daughter have undergone no change. I am sorry to say she has lost her good looks, through the machinations of that inimical gnome; but you are too much of a philosopher to——"

"Oh, dearest papa," cried Aennchen, overjoyed; "just look there! The silken palace is gone! The abominable monster is off and away with all his tribe of salad-princes, cucumber-ministers, and Lord knows what all!" And she ran away to the vegetable garden, delighted, Herr Dapsul following as fast as he could. Herr Amandus went behind them, muttering to himself, "I'm sure I don't know quite what to make of all this. But this I maintain,

[1] Rose-colored

that that ugly little carrot creature is a vile, prosaic lubber[1], and none of your poetical kings, or my sublime lay[2] wouldn't have given him the stomach-ache, and sent him scuttling into the ground."

As Fräulein Aennchen was standing in the vegetable garden, where there wasn't the trace of a green blade to be seen, she suddenly felt a sharp pain in the finger which had on the fateful ring. At the same time a cry of piercing sorrow sounded from the ground, and the tip of a carrot peeped out. Guided by her inspiration she quickly took the ring off (it came quite easily this time), stuck it on to the carrot, and the latter disappeared, while the cry of sorrow ceased. But, oh, wonder of wonders! all at once Fräulein Aennchen was as pretty as ever, well-proportioned, and as fair and white as a country lady can be expected to be. She and her father rejoiced greatly, while Amandus stood puzzled, and not knowing what to make of it all.

Fräulein Aennchen took the spade from the maid, who had come running up, and flourished it in the air with a joyful shout of "Now let's set to work," in doing which she was unfortunate enough to deal Herr Amandus such a thwack on the head with it (just at the place where the Sensorium Commune[3] is supposed to be situated) that he fell down as one dead.

Aennchen threw the murderous weapon far from her, cast herself down beside her beloved, and broke out into the most despairing lamentations, whilst the maid poured the contents of a watering pot over him, and Herr Dapsul quickly ascended the astronomic tower to consult the stars with as little delay as possible as to whether Herr Amandus was dead or not. But it was not long before the latter opened his eyes again, jumped to his legs, clasped Fräulein Aennchen in his arms, and cried, with all the rapture of affection, "Now, my best and dearest Anna, we are one another again."

The very remarkable, scarcely credible effect of this occurrence on the two lovers very soon made itself perceptible. Fräulein Aennchen took a dislike to touching a spade, and she did really reign like a queen over the vegetable world, inasmuch as, though taking care that her vassals were properly supervised and attended to, she set no hand to the work herself, but entrusted it to maids in whom she had confidence.

Herr Amandus, for his part, saw now that everything he had ever written in the shape of verses was wretched, miserable trash, and, burying himself in the works of the real poets, both of ancient and modern times, his being was soon so filled with a beneficent enthusiasm that no room was left for any consideration of himself. He arrived at the conviction that a real

---

[1] Rascal

[2] "my ingenious singing-verses" (a lay is a sung, lyrical poem)

[3] As the 18th century English encyclopaedist, Ephraim Chambers puts it, the Sensorium Commune is: "the Seat of the Common Sense; or that Part where the sensible Soul is supposed more immediately to reside"

poem has got to be something other than a confused jumble of words shaken together under the influence of a crude, jejune[1] delirium, and threw all his own (so-called) poetry, of which he had had such a tremendous opinion, into the fire, becoming once more quite the sensible young gentleman, clear and open in heart and mind, which he had been originally.

And one morning Herr Dapsul did actually come down from his astronomical tower to go to church with Fräulein Aennchen and Herr Amandus von Nebelstern on the occasion of their marriage.

They led an exceedingly happy wedded life. But as to whether Herr Dapsul's union with the Sylphide Nehabilah ever actually came to anything the Chronicle of Dapsulheim is silent.

AT its heart, this is a story about three people who are suffering alienation as a result of their respective manias: Dapsul, whose obsession with the occult prevents him from being a present father; Amandus, whose pretentions to be a poet distract him from being an active suitor; and Aennchen, whose constant gardening saps away from her ability to mature and grow into her adulthood. The entrance of the grotesque Gnome King is just the catalyst needed to shake these three from their respective reveries. After a lifetime of solitary study – including his ludicrous costume of wizard hat and beard – Dapsul descends from his intellectual tower (almost too late) in a desperate bid to put his knowledge to good use by rescuing his green-thumbed daughter from becoming a modern Persephone. In her case, an unnatural love of vegetables isn't shaken from her heart until she almost kills her human lover with her gardening shovel – an instantly regretted act which drives her out of the garden and into his arms. Amandus, himself, is cured by the same event: his loathsome poetry seems to be knocked out of his head (though not before it is put to use in driving away his vegetable rival.

II.

The consummate daydreamer, Hoffmann himself noted the dangers of too much isolation and introversion, using this fairy tale to emphasize the importance of family and community, the silliness of too much self-indulgence (whether it be scholarly, poetical, or botanical), and the dangers of monomania. Also lurking throughout this story is Hoffmann's hallmark eroticism – steeping the tale in bizarre subtexts and archetypal symbolism. Surrounding a father and boyfriend's anxious responses to their daughter/girlfriend's sexual awakening, the story's catalyst is starkly sensual: a ring given to her as a girl by her father has been discarded in a garden (Eden imagery) at some point in childhood (latency) only to reemerge after being penetrated and filled by an engorging carrot (phallic

[1] Childishly simplistic, naïve, or superficial

symbol) which forces her father to suddenly take concern for her future (the panicked reaction of a parent whose delusions of their child's innocence are shattered), and motivates her lazy suitor to become energized and jealous (upon realizing that others have noticed her as a sexual commodity). James M. McGlathery even makes the convincing argument that Dapsul's abrupt urge to have a double wedding with a sylph is a sublimation of his sudden realization that his daughter has bloomed into a sexually viable woman. Ashamed of his own "gnomish" attraction to her, he tries to cover up his lust by suggesting – after one facile marriage and a lifetime of consistent celibacy – that he sally forth to the altar without even knowing his future bride. By and large the story tries to work out the problems of mental isolation, the perils of sudden physical reactivation (in their hasty returns to the living world, Dapsul almost gets killed, Aennchen is almost abducted, and Amandus is almost loses his honor), and the balancing effects of open community with other human beings. As for the grotesque but comical Gnome King – a walking, talking phallus embodying the ludicrous nature of carnal urges – his outward foolishness and his inward corruption serve as a humbling reminder to *both* men of the very real threats to their neutered masculinity – and serve to initiate Anna into a broader understanding of the dark, selfish side of sexuality.

—FURTHER READING—
Critical, Literary, and Biographical Works

Bleiler, E. F., editor. *The Best Tales of Hoffmann*. Dover Publications, 1979.

Hoffmann, E. T. A., and R. J. Hollingdale. *Tales of Hoffmann*. Penguin Books, 2004.

Kent, Leonard J., and Elizabeth C. Knight. *Tales of E.T.A. Hoffmann*. University of Chicago Press, 1974.

McGlathery, James M. *E. T. A. Hoffmann*. Twayne Publ., 1997.

McGlathery, James M. *Mysticism and Sexuality: E.T.A. Hoffmann*. P. Lang, 1985.

Negus, Kenneth. *E.T.A. Hoffmann's Other World: The Romantic Author and His "New Mythology"*. University of Pennsylvania Press, 1965.

— About the Editor and Illustrator —

Michael Grant Kellermeyer (b. 1987) is a "retired" English professor and current bibliographer, illustrator, editor, critic, blogger, and author based in Fort Wayne, Indiana. He earned his Bachelor of Arts in English from Anderson University (2010) and his Master of Arts in Literature from Ball State University (2012).

He taught college writing and literature in Indiana for nine years at, variously, Ball State University, Ivy Tech Community College, and the Indiana Institute of Technology. He left higher education in 2019, and today he is a proud stay-at-home dad for his daughter, Charlotte, which has allowed him to make publishing and writing his full-time professional focus.

Michael founded Oldstyle Tales Press (www.oldstyletales.com) in the spring of 2013 after noticing that it was difficult to find literary criticism or commentary on short horror fiction. Its first title, *The Best Victorian Ghost Stories*, was published in September 2013, followed shortly by editions of *Frankenstein* and Edgar Allan Poe. Today it has 37 titles in print.

In his free time, Michael plays violin, watches old movies, and spends time walking in nature, or swinging on his front porch with his wife and daughter. Michael finds joy in sandalwood shaving cream, pipe tobacco, and air-dried sheets. He loves listening to Classical music, jazz standards, and sea shanties; watching the films of Vincent Price, Alfred Hitchcock, Hayao Miyazaki, and Stanley Kubrick; and sipping gin cocktails, stovetop coffee, and mint tea.

Made in United States
Troutdale, OR
02/13/2025